The Time Hunter Tales:

Mind Wanderer
The Lost Finders
Knight of the Wolves
Storm from the Past
New Tales of the Old World

Poetry:

Pathfinding

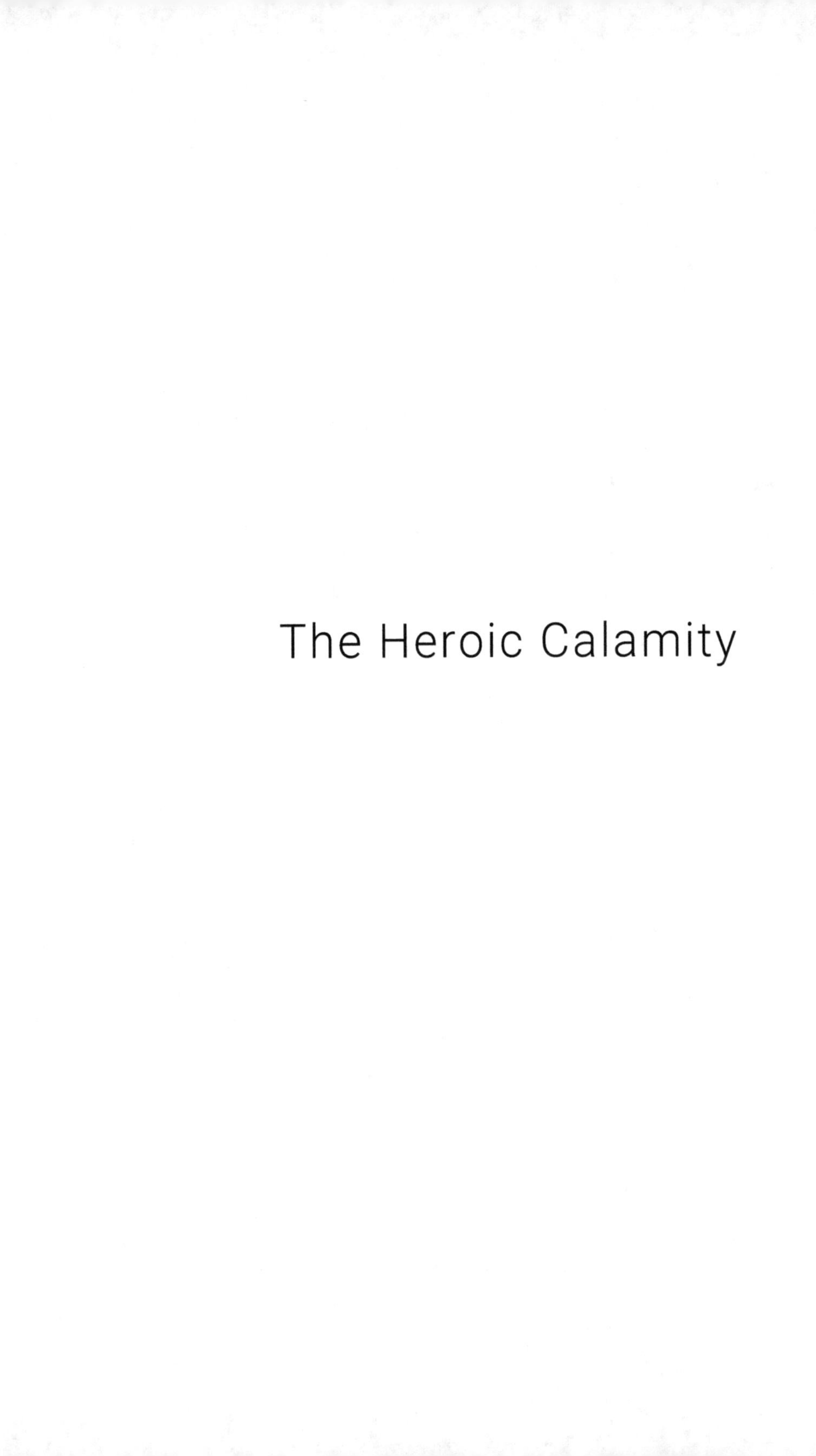

The Heroic Calamity

The Heroic Calamity

Evan A. Cushing

Primordial Albion Press

The Heroic Calamity

Published by Primordial Albion Press, 6 Albion Street, Salem, MA, USA

ISBN: 979-8-9873278-2-1 (paperback)
        979-8-9873278-3-8 (eBook)
Library of Congress Control Number: 2023918003

This cover has been designed using assets from Freepik.com

CONTENTS

CONTENTS

Part Three

Part One

Well Nuts

Manfred Endfield walked over a bridge down an ice-covered side-walk. It was the middle of winter; cars whizzed past without a second glance. "Next time bring a jacket, idiot!" Manfred derided himself, realizing too late that a sweater and thin windbreaker were not enough, especially when going over the long open bridge. He noted the zipper on his sweater was not all the way up, so Manfred stopped walking and fiddled with it. The zipper was stuck. After much fruitless struggling, Manfred slipped right off the bridge, smashing his head on one of its supports.

Manfred woke up in a dark room. "Aw hell!" he muttered. "I am so dead!"

"Yes, you are," the gray-robed skeleton towering above him rumbled.

"You are Death. I thought you would be smaller," Manfred said.

"Look, do you want to be reborn or not?" Death asked.

"No?" Manfred told the massive skeleton.

"Well tough. Now tell me your regrets," Death demanded.

"You did not challenge me to rock paper scissors, chess, or a drinking contest," Manfred said, now glad he had not died in his good coat.

"Liar!" Death snarled. Swiftly Manfred's head was held in Death's viselike grip. Soon after, Manfred was dropped back to the pitch-black floor. "You really wanted to have a drinking contest with me, but that's your only regret? Why, that's so stupid!"

"Well, how would I lose to a skeleton in a drinking contest? Plus, you guys must have some killer booze!" Manfred informed Death.

"First off, I can't get drunk." Death slumped down.

"What, so I can, but I'm dead!" Manfred shouted.

"You know the alcohol here only gets the folks that don't want a hangover or blackout dead drunk. Normally the alcohol here does not even taste like anything unless you want it to taste good; then the taste alone could kill."

"That sounds like hell!" Manfred sighed sympathetically. "By the way, where are we?"

Death groaned. A large hat appeared before him. With a small flourish Death pulled out a worn scrap of paper. "Ok, you are going to a world of magic and heroes." Then Death tossed Manfred two twenty-sided dice. "Roll them."

Manfred looked at the two dice. "Why?"

"So you can live again," Death grumbled.

"That sounds like a lot of work," Manfred complained.

"That's why it would be more of your hell than here," Death said.

Manfred shrugged and tossed the dice as hard as he could. "What did I ever do to you?" he asked.

The dice scattered far into the darkness around them. "You chose to be annoying."

"But that's how I always am," Manfred stated, now very confused.

Death ground its teeth and ignored Manfred. "You will be a hero level existence. Your abilities in your past life will be transferred over and will all be upgraded by 50%. Somehow your traits in life were all very good." A sheet of paper was tossed over to Manfred. A long list of names with numbers next to them was on it. The number five hundred was set at the top. All the numbers shown after were five hundred or less. Things like poison immunity and sword master were all listed under the five hundred category.

"So wait, it's like an RPG? How does leveling work?" Manfred asked.

"Lots of training or experience in one thing will get you more skilled; overcoming major hardships will give you talents," Death replied evenly.

Manfred swiftly chose something called translation: all for two hundred. After he did, the list shrank. Only things three hundred and under were left. The system began to make sense and Manfred started getting a bit intrigued. He looked over the bottom of the list after discounting things like soft hair, never bald, and nice teeth, each for one point. He found something called full power strike: strength for fifty mainly because it was set all around powers at forty, almost like someone misplaced it or tried to hide it. He chose that and the ability right under it, danger sense, for thirty, then a few hundred under entries that innate map for twenty. After quickly scrolling back to the top Manfred chose an ability called skill retention: past life for two hundred. "Ok all done. What now?" he asked.

"Now? I will mess with you." Death laughed.

"Why?" Manfred asked.

"Karma?" Death said.

Fire Bad

Lindy Shrew opened her eyes and yawned. A lump was on her head and she was tied to a pyre. "I was Manfred. Or did I know him? Well, he seems like a jerk, so it was likely me." Then she smelled smoke. "Now is this reality or a weird dream?"

Lindy looked up. A crowd was all around her. "Burn the monster!" they clamored. Lindy noted that when she focused on those around her a small window popped up. The man in change had on a nice set of full plate and a long sword slung at his hips. A torch was in one of his hands; his other hand seemed to be waving around widely. Words like troll and shapeshifter and abomination were thrown around more than things like I, then, and A, so Lindy ignored the man's wailing and gesturing.

As Lindy focused on the well-armored rabble-rouser, a small window appeared over his head.

Sir Ren the Just
Human male age 23
Affiliation: Hardeen Hills of Derndell kingdom, Iron Mound
    Syndicate (slavers, monster hunters, smugglers)
Job: Sheriff
Status: Knight of the realm, sworn to service of Duke
    Mondrow Master of Hardeen Hills
Abilities: strength 20, vitality 25, mind 12, agility 18

Talents: goad, alcohol tolerance: high, language: common
Derndell
Curse: swift to anger
Skills: sword: expert, armor proficiency pate/ chain/
leather: journeyman, law: adept. lie: master, strong-
arm: expert, dagger: beginner, athletics: beginner.

Lindy then looked over at a man in the crowd.

Dan
Human male age 35
Affiliation: Hardeen hills of Derndell kingdom
Job: Miller
Status: Nobody
Abilities: strength 12, vitality 13, mind 6, agility 4
Talents: forgettable, single minded, language common
Derndell
Wound: lung damage
Skills: milling: journeyman, barter: adept, athletics: adept,
intimidate basic: adept

Lindy swiftly looked at herself. The crowd was getting louder so Sir
Ren's rabble-rousing was likely getting to the point.

Lindy Shrew
Female human age 12
Affiliation: none
Job: hero to be
Status: beggar
Abilities: strength 380, vitality 500, mind 320, agility 459
Talents: translation: all. full power strike: strength. dan-
ger sense, innate map, skill retention: Manfred End-
field, photographic memory, sixth sense: intuition,

toughness, favored environment: darkness, cold resistance: high, enhanced trait: willpower, analysis: extreme, good hair, quick learner

Mutation: troll blood (extra burnable, swift regeneration)

Curse: catastrophic encounters, heavily sleeper, light
sensitivity: mild

Skills: sword: journeyman, dagger: master, unarmed:
master, bow: master, throwing: expert, athletics: expert, armor proficiency leather/ cloth: adept, literacy:
journeyman, history-other world: journeyman, intimi-
date-innate: adept, diplomacy: beginner, awareness:
expert

Sir Ren turned around. A sadistic glint shone in his eyes. "Outcasts should not hunt Outcasts," Lindy smirked.

"Nice try, monster," Sir Ren glowered.

"Well said, slaver," Lindy proclaimed agreeably.

"Your lies will not work on me or the people" Sir Ren shouted, then he threw his torch on the pyre.

Sir Ren smirked and turned to walk away. Only Lindy's arms were tied to the post, so she braced her legs and bellowed, "This has been a blast but I will be going now!" Sir Ren turned around, still smiling, until Lindy pulled the pillar of wood she had been tied to out from the ground. Before Sir Ren could react, Lindy crouched down and spun the pillar of wood resting on her back, killing Sir Ren and three other guards who had been standing on a stage nearby. The townspeople ran away. Lindy flexed her thin arms, snapping the pillar in half. "This life will take some getting used to," she sighed.

Two individuals were left in the village square. One hustled to the edge of the dirt clearing. The other, who looked slightly older, drew his sword and stepped forward.

Haldin Gasteen

Human male age 32

Affiliation: Derndell kingdom hero academy 3rd branch, Hardeen Hills explorer society

Job: hero mid-grade

Status: Professor

Abilities: strength 250, vitality 300, mind 182, agility 315.

Talents: analysis: high, pain tolerance: high, fire resistance: high, mind control: immunity, venom resistance: moderate, swift charge, sixth sense: intuition, enhanced trait: stamina, project voice, innate spell: blink, keen ears, never bald, good teeth, sense magic

Language: common Derndell/ old sineesterion, dark light school runes, code: unified explorer society

Skills: sword: expert, dagger: expert, throwing: adept, trap sense: master, navigation: expert, history: expert, law: journeyman, illusion magic: journeyman, counter spell: expert, athletics: expert, survival: expert, tracking: adept. literacy: adept, diplomacy: journeyman, commerce: adept, first aid-herbalist: adept, smithing: beginner, alchemy: beginner

Lindy whistled. "You can tell I am not a shapeshifter, right, Professor Haldin Gasteen?"

Haldin stopped and asked, "What are you?"

Lindy shrugged. "Human, hero to be, may have a distant troll ancestor."

Haldin made ready to leap at any time. "How distant?"

Lindy rustled her hair. "Old enough to be called a mutation by one of my talents."

Haldin sheathed his sword. "You have much to learn if you want to become as powerful as me."

"My abilities all exceed yours," Lindy said. She swiped up Sir Ren's sword. Haldin put his hand on his sword's hilt. After a few more steps in the professor's direction, Lindy stopped. Her danger sense was going mad.

Soon after Haldin began looking around frantically. "An adult dragon?" he howled before picking up Lindy and running out of the town with his companion close behind.

"Um, where are we going?" Lindy asked.

"I am saving your life, kid! Quiet down!" Haldin snapped. They sped out of town. From the crest of a hill the trio saw a large red dragon hovering just above the town square. It had already begun burning the village to ashes.

So that's what catastrophic encounters means, Lindy realized before easily wriggling out of the professor's grasp and snatching his sword. Haldin did not have time to look spooked before Lindy threw the sword at the hovering dragon's chest. The dragon swerved madly, forcing the sword to land on its wing instead. The dragon's right wing was blown off. No longer able to keep itself aloft, the dragon fell on the village manor's barn, impaling itself on a gaudy weather vane and dying miserably.

Lindy tried to ignore the shocked looks of her two new acquaintances. She failed dismally. "What?" Lindy asked, rolling her eyes.

"Have you been enrolled at a hero academy?" Haldin asked.

"I am a beggar, not a student," Lindy sighed.

Haldin studied Lindy for a while. "By law, all heroes must train in their class. Come with me."

"Are we going to your academy, professor?" Lindy asked.

"Yes. But before we do, where are your relatives?" Haldin inquired as he settled his emotions.

Lindy's only memories were of the time Manfred Endfield met Death. "I don't know, but the village was going to burn me to death, so the sooner we are away from here the better."

They slowed down and walked down the other slope of their vantage point. Rocks of the mountains around the village gave way to pine trees. Haldin's companion asked, "Could I analyze you?"

"That would only be fair," Lindy smirked.

"You analyzed us as well, didn't you?" Haldin's companion asked, scowling. From the companion's light plate mail, thin build, forceful aura, and ambiguous face, being able to discern its gender was a challenge.

"If I did, I would know your name and gender," Lindy chuckled. The companion's aura became harder to read.

"Relax, she is just a kid. Let me know if you find anything interesting." Haldin sighed.

"Yes sir!" Lindy cheered and the companion replied.

Caldrin Faywind

Female half-elf age 128

Affiliation: Derndell kingdom hero academy 3rd branch

Job: hero journeyman

Status: professor's aide

Abilities: strength 132, vitality 200. mind 231, agility 289

Talents: analysis: moderate. resistance mind control: high, keen senses: all, detect lies: moderate, unerring strike, true sense

Analysis resistance: moderate

Language: common Derndell/ old magic/ jungle elvish

Blessing: good luck

Skills: armor use plate/ leather/ cloth: journeyman, dagger: adept, ice magic: expert, healing magic: journeyman, spirit magic: adept, counter spell: adept, read lips: beginner, stealth: adept, survival: journeyman, tracking: beginner. literacy: adept, bluff: adept. bow: beginner, club: beginner. staff: adept

"Good luck? Some good that did you, Miss Faywind. Kind of old for a follower, hah." Lindy shrugged. Haldin seemed intrigued by his new acquaintance's words, while Caldrin became flustered.

"Sir. This child's abilities are far above ours! Her skills exceed mine," Caldrin almost shouted.

"What level of analysis does she have?" Haldin asked. Caldrin furrowed her brow then became deathly pale. Haldin looked around then closed his eyes. Seconds later his arms gripped Lindy's shoulders. "Extreme level. How did you get that?"

"How do I get analysis resistance?" Lindy asked, looking away from Haldin and up at Caldrin.

"Get enough fools to analyze you," Caldrin muttered.

"Well, I don't remember much before today, so I only know my stats," Lindy shrugged.

"That's not a lie," Caldrin said. Right as she spoke an ogre who was on fire bolted out of the woods. Lindy rushed at it but before she arrived the ogre tripped on a small rock and fell. The fires around it soon killed it off. "My luck is still good," Caldrin sighed happily.

"And mine is still terrible," Lindy groaned. By unspoken agreement, Haldin led his two companions down the mountainous woodland road. It took most of the day passing small rabbits, uncounted trees, and vine-covered boulders. Eventually the sun began to set. One of the vine-wrapped boulders unfurled nearby Lindy. A dryad showed itself. Its roots ripped outward, trying to trap her limbs and choke her to death. Lindy's danger sense had forewarned her of many phantom dangers that did not materialize throughout the day, and so had been tensed up and unhappy. However, Lindy had also sharpened her senses and mind in response to these potential dangers. Before the vines had roped her in, Lindy had dashed at the dryad and ripped off its head.

Caldrin managed to yell, "Don't!" The rest of her words did not materialize because they caught in her mind when Lindy ripped off a chunk of the rock shell the dryad had been hiding in. She bashed its corpse to mush with it by the time Caldrin had begun to respond. After a short pause, Caldrin wailed, "Why did you do that?"

Lindy looked up and tossed the hunk of rock aside. Her rags and body were covered in green goo. "That thing was trying to kill me."

Caldrin glared at the child before her. "We could have talked it into letting you go."

"No, you could not have. At least not before I was dead again." Lindy glared back with far more intensity than the half-elf was used to. The little girl seemed more like a dragon or a lich than a young child then. Lindy began to walk down the road. "We keep going down this way, right?" she asked, not bothering to turn around.

Haldin shrugged and followed after the odd but fascinating child. He motioned to his aide, choosing to let her deal with this while he observed, at least for now. Caldrin ran after the child and grabbed her thin arm. "Listen to your elders!" The child looked up, her eyes cold but with all the mischievous ill-meaning mirth seen only in deranged psychopaths, pixies, and gremlins.

"How old are you in human years, half-elf?" Lindy hissed.

Caldrin steeled her agitated mental state that screamed how bad an idea it would be to seriously anger this thin rag and gore-covered child, and ignored the child's query. "Get ready to make camp soon."

Lindy's eyes become cold and blank when Caldrin moved to turn away. Lindy kicked the woman's legs out from under her. Ripping the half-elf's dagger from her belt, Lindy pressed it to the hero's neck. "How old in human years are you?" Lindy said robotically.

"Hey, stop it, you two," Haldin pleaded. He did not move, judging that with Lindy's speed she could slit his aide's neck before either of them could react.

"Fine," Caldrin spat. "Thirty-two and three fourths. Happy?"

"Very," Lindy smiled, leaping off the half-elf and handing the stolen dagger back, handle first. Caldrin rose to her knees and tried to take back her dagger but it was held fast and even began to crack. "You are younger," Lindy said. Then she let go of the dagger, causing Caldrin to fall on the ground again.

"Can you alter how your status is seen?" Haldin asked, drawing closer.

"Nothing like that." Lindy shook her head, watching Caldrin rise. When Lindy was satisfied the half-elf was not a threat at that moment, she looked over at the professor. "Are you familiar with the concept of reincarnation, Professor Gasteen?"

"Who isn't? It's a very common belief. Sadly, not something we can prove. Why, do you know something?" Haldin asked.

"Counting my past life I should be around fifty. Not that I remember a lot of it, but my past life was not lived in this world or time." Lindy laughed. Then she turned to Caldrin. "My past life was not this dangerous. I've been on edge. I know I snapped at you. I'll try to keep that from happening again. So where are we camping, young one?" Lindy inquired.

"Down the hill at a river. You will be taking a bath," Caldrin answered, her gaze searching and hands clenched.

"Ok, will do. Maybe you can tell me about the monsters around here while we camp? It would be nice to know how to deal with them," Lindy agreed. Haldin walked off and his companions followed him.

"You don't need to know more ways to kill now," Caldrin admonished.

Lindy nodded and answered in a tone rich with meaning and a voice filled with wisdom. "You are right, but I need to know what not to kill and why."

"Fine, after your bath." Caldrin could not help but smirk agreeably.

A short walk later they were near the road in a small clearing. A line of trees hid them from direct view all around. A small clear river ran down from the mountains. A short walk away around its bank sat a few large rocks that would serve to conceal the occasional solo bather. Lindy took off her torn shoes that were more like very rough sandals than shoes. Given their damage and her thin gore-covered rag it was not even enough clothing to qualify for a plural format. She waded into the water, looking closely at her body as she did. "I really am a little girl now. Well, the more things change, the more you have to adapt to survive and overcome all the chaos in life." In the middle of washing, Lindy's danger sense went off like mad again. She had noticed she could roughly discern how dangerous and close something was by the feeling she got. Lindy had tried to zero in on detecting distance and level of danger separately but so far, she had not been able to separate those two bits of data from the vague mess of feelings she got from danger sense. Lindy could roughly work out that something small, long, and very fast was swimming right for her. Having darkness as her favored environment and intuition helped Lindy with locking onto her presumed attacker.

River Serpent Newt
River serpent age ten
Job: newt
Status: opportunistic scavenger
Abilities: strength 29, vitality 15, mind 4, agility 32
Talents: paralyzing bite, full body venom: moderate, heat sense, water breathing: only, resistance cold: moderate, resistance poison: high, resistance electricity: mild. strong bite: low, sonic speech, echolocation, low grade exoskeleton, slimly: mild
Skills: swimming: adept, athletics: journeyman, bite: adept. intimidate: journeyman, sonic magic: beginner

"Time for something stupid," Lindy grumbled ruefully. She controlled her strength and used her full power strike to snap her fingers. This caused a small localized whirlwind that plowed right into the river serpent and the water around it, blowing the monster back up the river. Lindy got dressed and fled back to camp.

When she got near camp Lindy heard Caldrin saying, "You think she is all right, master?"

Lindy hid a few trees away, willfully slowing her breathing and movement to the bare minimum she could stand. Haldin replied, "With that might, yes. Do you believe what she told us before?"

"Well, that child truly believed what she was saying. So, I did not see any lies in her words and she does seem far older than she should, but I can't bring myself to take most of what she said seriously."

Lindy let out the breath she had been holding and Caldrin perked up. Lindy was all smiles as she scampered over. "I respect your opinion," she giggled.

"That was quick," Haldin allowed.

"Well, a river serpent newt sort of chased me out," Lindy explained mildly.

"Did you kill it?" Caldrin demanded.

Lindy put her hands on her hips and puffed out her chest. "Probably not. I only blew it back up the river." Her prideful tone contrasted with the uncertainty in her wording.

"So, you know wind magic?" Caldrin smirked smugly, seeming like this proved something.

Lindy slowly raised one of her arms. Both the adults tensed. "Nope, it was like this." Lindy snapped her fingers like before into the forest but this time she did not hold back at all. A massive gust of wind rocketed into the dark. Woodland trees were ripped from the earth, rocks shattered, and the land was ground into a torn dusty mess. This single move obliterated a long line of woodland directly in line with Lindy's arm but many times wider than her spindly form. She let out an impressed whistle. "Well, it was a bit weaker than that."

"What did she say?" Caldrin shouted. She was temporarily shell shocked.

Haldin was not much better. His ears were bleeding. After shaking his head slightly he regained his shattered equilibrium and confused senses. "You punted a river serpent up river without killing it?" Lindy nodded her head, felling like this was the beginning of a scolding. "Without killing it?" Haldin clarified.

"That's right. I did not want to kill something I should not have," Lindy replied. Caldrin had swiftly finished healing herself and so began working on Haldin.

"You let something that dangerous go?" Caldrin asked, her face in her palm.

"Well yes, I did not see where it landed but it should have landed back in some water. I am sure it will only be mildly angry for a little while," Lindy explained, sitting down at the destabilized campfire.

"This is going to be a long night," Caldrin grumbled. She spent a good six hours detailing what was dangerous in the area and why, along with a list of wildlife and monsters whose fights could be avoided. All of this was very informative for Lindy, which only made the half-elf aide even more exasperated at Lindy's ignorance.

Due to the long info session, Caldrin got close to two hours of sleep. Lindy got more like two and a fourth because she managed to get to sleep leaning against a tree with her eyes half open. Caldrin only noticed what had happened when the first rays of daylight sprouted. Haldin was able to get a full six hours of rest as his companions were also on guard duty.

When Lindy was kicked awake she found a watery broth filled with wild root vegetables. Lindy felt she had seen far better food at some time, somewhere, likely in the old life she barely recalled even having. "I am no cook, but this is healthy and not poisonous," was how the professor reviewed his own work. Needless to say, this did not endear Lindy to the food but she would not say no to the only edible chow on offer, and ate all she was given. It could have been her hunger affecting her judgment but the food was not nearly as bad as she had been fearing.

"A bit of pepper or something that tastes like it and dissolved in water and this would be perfect. Some chicken broth or light meat base instead of water might be good but the cost and transport could be a problem," was Lindy's review.

"When did you learn to cook?" Caldrin asked, sounding mildly annoyed. Despite the human child's completely annoying mannerisms,

Caldrin found Lindy mysterious and intriguing, but more along the lines of a fellow living being and possible traveler from another world than a true research subject and new powerhouse for heroes like her boss. *When did I empathize this fast with anyone?* Caldrin wondered, concerned with her own emotions over this hyperactive mess of trouble called Lindy Shrew.

The rest of the day was quiet; no monsters were in sight. A few boars, wolves, foxes, and bears did poke their heads out of the underbrush along the road more than once, but they all fled when they looked into Lindy's eyes.

At some point Haldin frowned, saying, "Miss Shrew, your status and affiliation changed."

"Really?" Lindy wondered as she looked over her stats.

Lindy Shrew
Female human age 12
Affiliation: hero?
Embodiments: banished from death, living natural disas-
    ter
Job: hero to be
Status: common sense bane: moderate

All her other stats were the same.

"Well that was fast." Lindy nodded.

"But why does your status look like a talent?" Haldin fretted.

"Because that is the bane of common sense?" Lindy hazarded her guess.

Caldrin massaged her temples with her fingers. "That's the stupidest thing I have ever heard. Too bad it makes sense," she moaned.

By that time, the sun was passing the mountains behind them and igniting the sky into a dark purple and dayglow yellow. Lindy and her two acquaintances arrived in a village set into the edge of a valley that stretched as far as the eye could see. A team of ten armed teenagers and two well-armed middle-aged adults was in the center of town. Small tents and bedrolls with sickly less-well-dressed folks seemed to radiate from around the center of town. Three of the teenagers and one of the adults walked to meet them at the edge of the village. One of the teenagers, a cheery looking girl, greeted them. "Professor Haldin, good afternoon."

> **Genney the Sage**
> Female human age 14
> Affiliation: Derndell kingdom hero academy 3rd branch
> Job: hero in training
> Status: Seer
> Abilities: strength 72, vitality 117. mind 237, agility 92
> Blessing: Seer
> Embodiments: favored of fate
> Talents: luck: moderate, danger sense, toughness, fear-lessness, analysis: low, analysis defense: high. extend healing, empower magic, true effort, shadow step, language: common Derndell/star runes/ high oldlin
> Skills: mediation: adept, healing magic: journeyman, astrology: adept, staff: beginner, lighting magic: adept, light magic: beginner. athletics: beginner, cooking: adept, diplomacy: beginner, barter: beginner, literacy: adept, complex mathematics: beginner

Genney's head swiveled as if struck. Her eyes locked onto Lindy's. "You analyzed me."

Caldrin struck Lindy on the head with only enough force to get Lindy to remodel her facial expression into something less bemused and idiotic. "You know it's rude to analyze others without consent."

Lindy rubbed her head. "How would I know that? My memories of my life around here began right before that dragon!"

The man that had accompanied Genney asked, "So journeyman Faywind, this child is another refugee?"

Caldrin smirked. "No, she is a dragon slayer, and a new hero we found."

The man's brows furrowed. "But I only took off one of its wings. The fall was what killed it!" Lindy said.

The man kneeled down and looked Lindy in the eyes. "I am junior professor Kelmo. I will be analyzing your stats now, ok?"

Lindy laughed in Kelmo's face and winked. Genney correctly inferred what was meant and explained to her chaperone, "That's a yes."

Kelmo closed his eyes in a huff. Seconds after, his eyes rocketed open. "That's impossible!"

Haldin leaned in. "What did you find?"

"What I saw was absurd but I could not make out all of it." Kelmo ground his teeth.

"Even your high-level analysis did not see all of that?" Haldin seemed giddier than before. Caldrin, however, seemed totally used to Lindy's propensity to ignore what was commonly taken for granted.

"So, what's going on in this town?" Lindy asked.

"A river serpent landed in the town's reservoir and poisoned the well," a muscle-bound boy around Genney's age said.

"That does not sound normal. Should we help?" Lindy asked without any trace of irony. Only then did Caldrin deflate a little.

"So how do you know a river serpent did it?" Haldin asked amicably. Kelmo gave up thinking about Lindy and waved to the new arrivals to follow him deeper into the dusty town.

Kelmo walked slowly, looking closely at the pale villagers and checking them. Each one was deathly pale with labored breathing and vacant gazes. When he was examining a young child and elderly man who both looked worse for wear, Kelmo spoke gravely as if to distract himself. "We found the pulped remains of a very young river serpent. It must have been alive in the reservoir like that for at least a day, because the entire well source is highly venomous. We arrived this morning and most of the villagers had collapsed by then."

Lindy waved her arms as if she were a kindergartner begging to be called on in class. "So do you have antivenom for river serpents?"

"What's antivenom?" Genney asked.

"How do you know that term?" Kelmo scowled, glaring at his senior colleague.

Haldin noticed. "I did not tell her anything classified."

Lindy smiled sweetly but her eyes were cold when she looked at Kelmo. "So all you need is intact river serpent venom glands and other poisonous bits, some other things you seem to know about, and a test subject, right?"

Kelmo sighed and grudgingly answered, not meeting his students' gazes. "Why a test subject?"

"Because these folks are too weak to ensure what you whip up works. Even if this fails you will get lots of great test data." Lindy's smile became wicked.

Their now heated conversation had drawn the other adults and students who listed intently. "If nothing works, then what?" Kelmo demanded.

"Then you did all you could and only lose one more person," Lindy told him, looking around at the village, her face betraying some pain for the first time.

"No one would volunteer for that." Kelmo's tone was firm.

Lindy's vision seemed to dim. "We only need someone who has no medical skills and no idea how to properly hunt river serpents, but is very strong in body." The crowd became anxious and unsatisfied because they could think of no one that met those criteria. "Also someone who no one would miss would be great. So, use me."

Almost everyone seemed to agree with Lindy's plan very quickly after she had volunteered. Caldrin butted in. "Are you really ok with that, Lindy Shrew?"

Lindy looked around at the pained townsfolk. "Yes, this should be fine. Worst case, I can annoy Death himself again until he kicks me out." Then she whispered, "After all, this was probably my fault." Lindy's near apology was low enough that only Caldrin with her keen hearing and Genney who was leaning over to look closely at Lindy's face managed to hear it. Genney looked around, her gaze looking onto Caldrin's. The half-elf nodded simply and walked out of the crowd. This was enough for the young sage to confirm Lindy's mistake.

Kelmo looked over at Genney and told her, "Look after your new underclassman." Lindy began to sulk at being treated the age she looked.

Genney gripped Lindy's hand firmly and led her off to a small tent slightly removed from the rest of the area. A small plank hung from a spear jammed forcefully in the ground. The plank read *Girls' Changing Room: Heroines Only.* Lindy's feet froze causing Genney to trip. The seer looked up from the dirt seeming to expect a castle wall in place of the slightly younger and far shorter child she had been holding hands with. "Death really has an awful sense of humor," Lindy sighed.

Sensing her companion's unease, Genney pointed over to a small log. "How about we sit over there and talk for a bit. Just us girls." Lindy smirked self-deprecatingly and allowed herself to be walked over. Half an hour of silence later, Genney could not stand it and asked kindly, certain the younger child had a lot troubling her. "So tell me a little about yourself."

Lindy looked up at the darkening night sky. Her words came spilling out in a way that could only be seen as her mocking herself. "I know I am reincarnated, as in I remember a few things from my past life. Most of my skills from that life are still with me even if the memories are hazy. The thing is, my first memory of this life is being burned at the stake. This world is not even the one from my past life." Lindy glared at the night sky and hollered, "Oh and Death is such an asshole!"

Genney looked shocked then she begin to laugh wildly. "So you are a priestess like me?" Lindy did not look amused that her soul-wrenching confession about her reincarnation was being laughed at. Genney got herself under control. Small tears of joy hung at the corners of her eyes. "Sorry, I do not remember when I met Fate, but I do know she gave me power in this life. This is the first time I've met anyone empowered by Death. Let alone one who remembers meeting a high-ranking world spirit."

Lindy sighed. "Empowered by Death. Right. But it's more like what does not kill you makes you stronger if it does not smash you to pieces first, kind of like a bone. I have not gotten to the best part of this. I was a forty-year-old man in my past life and my past world had no magic. Not only that but like I said, I have no memories of this life until a few days ago, so I am still getting used to, well..." She spread her arms all around her. "This."

"That's lot to take in." Genney nodded blankly. She knew all of this would take her time to process but she knew right then she wanted to get to know the young girl emanating a far more forceful and strong presence than anyone she had seen. In Genney's eyes the child named Lindy was destined to shake this world and Genney wanted to see every second of it as her friend and confidant.

Lindy grinned savagely. "Life is indeed chaotic. The least I can do is live or die trying to do well. All while laughing in the face of my eventual demise." Only then did Lindy seem to calm down.

"That's rather bleak. Shouldn't we live for today?" Genney asked, fearing her new friend would do something crazy and disappear like so many others who had given up on the path of combat. As someone who had lived in the hero academy for longer than she knew, Genney had seen more than a few of her classmates and teachers die in the wilderness. More than a few seemed to welcome it. After all, in a world this dangerous there was no such thing as truly safe.

"You are not wrong but I'd argue that's not all there is to life." Lindy nodded in a way unfit for the age she looked, and patted Genney on the shoulder. "All we can do is do the best we can, accept that, and move on. Life is not forgiving, so giving up or getting bogged down in what could be or what was will not help. The only thing we can do in this life is live and therefore we should try to live well. It's a lot of work but it's worth it," Lindy explained.

Genney felt a light in her heart. She felt at peace even in a town in as dire straits as this one. The fear and trepidation were gone. She felt that she had to work so the town could recover because that would help her live with herself, and so it was worth it. Now all she needed was to get Lindy to be her friend. When Genney looked down at the child next to her she found Lindy was fast asleep. Genney placed the smaller girl's head on her lap and let her new friend nap.

When Lindy opened her eyes, she was in a dark void and Death's empty eyes were looking directly into hers. "Having fun yet?" Lindy asked acidly.

"Very much. Thanks for that. What about you?" Death seemed to sneer.

"Better than I expected and it should get better. So, what's going on in that empty head of yours?" Lindy laughed, her face inches from Death's.

"Are you able to take this seriously now?" Death asked, sounding miffed.

Lindy shrugged, now serious. "Yup, that's off my bucket list. What's up?"

"Work for me," Death stated firmly.

"What's in it for me?" Lindy asked.

Death slouched. "What do you want?"

"To live. Why do you care?" Lindy replied.

"I am overworked and you are interesting." Cold mist rushed from Death's ribs, its voice riding on that wind.

"So, what should I do?" Lindy asked, mildly annoyed at how few details she was getting.

A long arm reached out and a bone hand the size of Lindy stuck out one finger that pressed gently on her forehead. "The same as now causes havoc by being you," Death explained.

Lindy was unhappy with what Death seemed to be insinuating so she demanded it elaborate. "You want me to kill and spread pain. That's how you see me?"

"That's how your life will go. I can always end you if you don't," Death told her.

Lindy sighed angrily. "Don't screw with me. That's no choice. Can I say no?"

"Die now or work for me." Death's ultimatum stung. Lindy still had to help the town she had accidentally poisoned or at the very least see them well again.

"I hate you, but fine, on one condition," Lindy firmly stated, not bothering to hide her rage.

"What is it?" Death asked.

"No one else in my new world can have this role and I will be alive and able until either I fail badly enough at it or quit." Lindy glared at the very image of the grim reaper.

"Fine," Death wheezed, "but be prepared to be overworked. I may have a few side jobs for you as well."

"You are a huge pain. Thanks again for my life," Lindy grimaced.

"Your potential is far higher than I first thought. Your life should have been a quite painful one, but it looks like I was very wrong. For that at least you have my condolences." Death frowned slightly.

Lindy looked up at the towering skeleton draped in darkness. "That's not very fitting for something that harvests the dead to say."

"I could say the same. For someone I outsource some of the harvesting to, a sense of humor is disconcerting," Death shot back.

Darkness swerved around Lindy before Death's visage faded completely. Lindy yelled back, "I plan to live for a very long time so I might as well enjoy it!" Inwardly Lindy finished *so I can fix what I break with my own hands.* She felt a jolt and opened her eyes. Caldrin was looking at her and Genney was a little red in the face. "How much did you hear?" Lindy asked.

"She's like a little griffin, so cute, and might as well enjoy it," Caldrin smirked. Before Genney could compose herself the half-elf added, "Ok you two, we are ready. Come on."

"A griffin?" Lindy mused.

"It's nothing. Come on!" Genney practically picked the younger girl off her feet and led to where the antivenom tests were planned to take place. By the height of the moon Lindy felt she must have slept until midnight.

Caldrin led them past clusters of townsfolk huddled in mounds of blankets, through newly cleared alleyways. The few glances that followed them would be the sickly locals or those who had been caring for them; after a hard day, both were nearly lifeless. At a large tent next to the town's main well, Kelmo, his aide, and some of the more medically adept students were gathered. Caldrin nodded to them. "Zender, she can't die, ok?"

Zender shrugged. "She might."

Lindy spoke at the same time as the aides. "This is life or death." The crowd zeroed in on the child in their midst but she ignored them and instead locked eyes with Caldrin. "You are becoming predicable."

Kelmo clapped his hands and waved Lindy over to a clump of bedding. "Lie down. We start now," he told her. A small glass of well water was handed to her and Lindy chugged it instantly.

Looking around from her new perch, Lindy gave a thumbs up to Genney. The gesture seemed unfamiliar to her. Before anything more could be communicated, Zender walked in front of Lindy. "This may sting," he told her as he stabbed a thin glass pipe into her arm. After adding a funnel to the top of the pipe some goo was poured in from one of eight full test tubes hanging from Zender's belt. Lindy died again.

Upon seeing Death lounging around reading a book labeled *How to Win at Chess and Life,* Lindy face-palmed. "Well shit!" she almost yelled.

Death looked up. His book faded from existence. "That was fast. What happened?"

"Death by messed-up antivenom," Lindy shrugged. A long pause followed. "Send me back," she demanded.

"Why? You failed," Death told her.

"That was not our agreement," Lindy smiled.

Death thought for a while. "It could be read like that. Ok fine, but don't make a habit of this, otherwise I will say you failed at your job."

"If I was not relying on others then I'd live forever, present company excluded, of course," Lindy agreed.

"Well, I am keeping you alive," Death warned.

"I know. Well, see you." Lindy waved. The next thing she knew, the sound of a scuffle filled her ears. Opening her eyes she spied Kelmo and Zender in a fist fight with Caldrin. Genney was dodging around trying to stop the fight. The other students and Haldin were staying away from the combat. Lindy raised her head. She felt great. "Ok, what did I miss?" she yelled over. Everyone stopped. If not for their breathing, slack jaws, and the local crickets having what sounded like a bug rendition of a jazz fest, it would have seemed like time had stopped completely.

Caldrin was the first to speak, her voice shaking. "You died."

"I got better. So can we continue?" Lindy asked.

Genney ran over ahead of the professors and Zender. She hugged Lindy tight. "What took you so long?"

"I had to say hi to Death," Lindy smirked. Then she cleared her throat and looked up at Zender. "That last one was a bit strong. How about a lighter one this time?" Zender shrugged and checked her pulse, then wordlessly handed Lindy a new cup of well water which she swiftly scarfed down. Genney backed up but remained at Lindy's side. "Ok, third time's the charm. Let's go," Lindy cheered.

"This is the second round," Zender replied, as he repeated the last process.

"Oh, I know," Lindy laughed. Soon after she vomited up a lot of bile. "Ok, I still feel like crap, so I am going to say that's not it."

Zender shook his head. "Language, young lady. We wait for half an hour. If you are not free from the venom, then we try again." Lindy rolled her eyes. The square was silent. A bit over half an hour later Lindy still felt slightly ill — same as before, but with less vomiting. The failed antivenom was no longer making her feel vile, so she took that as a win.

After she was certain half an hour had passed, Lindy spoke up. "Ok, I am ready for the next one. Do your worst."

"That's not what a doctor does," Zender told her, his bedside manner now fraying.

"Do you use bloodletting and mercury in treatments?" Lindy asked.

Zender looked surprised and seemed somewhat mollified. "Of course I do."

Lindy sighed and changed the subject abruptly. "Fine, I am ready for the next one."

Following the now familiar process, Zender tried again. Twenty minutes later Lindy began to feel better. "Ok, this may work," she told him.

An hour passed and Lindy felt like herself again. "Ok, that worked. Although keep in mind, my vitality more than likely far surpasses the townsfolk's, so recovery time and dosages may vary."

Zender looked over from a desk covered in bottles and papers, all surrounding a small portable alchemy lab. "Who do you think I am?" he asked.

"A doctor that plays around with heavy metals?" Lindy asked.

Zender paused to steady his annoyance at the young test subject before him. Before he could scold her Caldrin commented, "She is technically not wrong."

Zender got back to work while Lindy left the tent. Before she was totally out of earshot, she heard the doctor mutter to himself, "I do not play around."

The stars were still out while Lindy walked, easing her slight muscle cramps. Caldrin walked with her. Most of the hero students were fast asleep. No one seemed inclined to bother or aid the newcomer. Light greetings were exchanged with droopy-eyed hero trainees stuck with the night watch. After leading Lindy just outside of town to the top of a mound of dirt around the height of the one-story hovels in town, Caldrin handed Lindy two steel daggers and the sword she had taken from Sir Ren, along with a (for Lindy) knee-length rough hide coat. "These are for you. Remember, everything you gain as a hero is earned by your achievements."

Lindy looked longingly up at the moon. "Are we owned by the nation that raises us?"

Caldrin choked for a second. "That's right."

"And there are a king, nobles, knights, and peasants, in that order of authority?" Lindy pressed, still looking up to the sky.

Caldrin replied seriously. "There are few more ranks, but the king is at the top of this nation."

Lindy nodded. "This really is a medieval fantasy world."

"You are an odd one," Caldrin whispered.

"I feel like I have never been normal," Lindy murmured back as she reached out her hand as if to grip the moon. "I feel like I will enjoy my time in this world."

Seconds later a yell was heard from the main road. "Manticore attack!"

Lindy shrugged and swiftly put on her new coat, sticking the sheathed daggers in the strip keeping the coat closed and strapping the sword across her back. "Never a dull moment," Lindy muttered before vaulting to the roof of a nearby hovel and proceeding to hop from roof to roof in the direction of ever-worsening screams and the scent of blood.

Caldrin ran after Lindy. "Let the adults handle this one!"

Lindy yelled back as she raced even harder. "If the teachers die, who will take care of the students? No, I'll hold it off for you."

Soon Lindy spied shattered corpses, then after scampering up to a barn, she saw it. It was at least as long as an ogre was tall. Lindy was just in time to see Kelmo get snapped in half by the monster's jaws. Caldrin must have seen it too, because she cursed, "What's with my luck?" Her words had a different vibe to them.

Lindy leapt from the barn, drawing her sword. "You're lucky I'm here!" she yelled. The manticore's venomous tail shot up at its plummeting attacker. Lindy drew one of her daggers and stabbed into a gap in the monster's scorpion-like tail, then she used the tail's momentum to throw herself at the manticore's head. Lindy's sword stabbed into the monster's skull many inches before snapping in half. "That was new!" Lindy bellowed. As she gripped her hands together and raised them above her head, she dug her legs into the manticore's neck. With a wordless yell Lindy began to use her full power to pummel the monster's skull. The monster writhed in anguish from Lindy's onslaught, giving the adults an opening. Caldrin caused ice to cover the beast's limbs, locking it in place, and Haldin confused its eyes with illusions while he and Zender cut off the manticore's tail. It took all Lindy had to remain on the manticore's head. Each time she clobbered the monster they both winced. Cracks and snapping sounds came from both the monster and Lindy's own body but she kept going, trusting in her troll blood, toughness, and resolve to keep herelf in one piece. The teachers ran interference, taking away whatever shard of focus the monster had left as it stewed in its pain. Finally, the monster's skull caved in and Lindy ripped out its brain. She tossed the lump of meat to the ground and waited out the few minutes it took for the manticore to finish its death throes. Then Lindy collapsed onto the dead monster's back.

Caldrin called up, "You alive up there?"

"Not even a little bit. Give me a while to catch my breath," Lindy called back.

It took Lindy a full thirty seconds to get her breathing under control. When she hopped off the manticore's back she found Caldrin, Haldin, and Zender clustered around Kelmo's corpse. His eyes were still open and his guts spilled many feet from his upper half. A few bits of students were scattered about as well. The rest of the living kept clear. Even the birds had fled and had yet to return. When she saw Lindy, Caldrin rushed over and began shaking her. "What were you thinking?"

"Noblesse oblige?" Lindy replied in a bemused fashion that did not sit well with the adults.

"What language is that?" Zender asked.

A few seconds of thinking later, Haldin and Caldrin replied at nearly the same time.

"Jungle elvish," was Caldrin's statement, while peering at Lindy intently as if that would tell her why.

"Old sineesterion," Haldin began with certainty, but midway he trailed off, more focused on his aide's response than his own.

Lindy felt slightly embarrassed so she looked at her stats again. Finding something new, she whistled, "Wow, I am fearless now and got poison resistance: mild!" This managed to change the topic.

"That was certainly reckless," Caldrin agreed.

"With all the venom you have been exposed to in a short time, some poison resistance is unsurprising," was Zender's assessment.

Haldin raised his voice slightly. "That's enough. Lindy, find a tent and get some rest."

Lindy nodded, picked up what was left of her sword, and ripped her dagger out of the manticore's tail. She ripped off a strip of her rags and cleaned the gore from her blades, then resheathed them and skipped off. She found Genney huddled with a crowd of other students. "Ok, it's dead!" Lindy called. Her gore-covered body must have been either more confusing or spooky than she thought because everyone simply skittered back to whatever they had been doing.

All but Genney, who wetted a rag and began cleaning off Lindy's face. "How did you get this filth all over you?" Genney asked solemnly.

"I helped. So can I use your tent?" Lindy asked. She noted she did not feel awkward about being in another girl's room. This surprised her but she swiftly dismissed the thought as ridiculous, being in the body she was now.

"Ok, for what?" Genney agreed.

"I was told I need a nap," Lindy said, now feeling sheepish for having to say that out loud.

"Ok, but I will clean you off first," Genney proclaimed firmly, leaving Lindy no room for escape or argument. The older girl dragged her friend off to a tent and helped her undress. After wiping off the gore, Lindy was handed the blankets issued to one of the newly deceased. Soon after, Lindy was fast asleep.

3

Booted to Camp

The sun was just rising when Lindy woke up. Still half asleep, she loudly yawned. The other three children in the tent did not notice the disturbance right next to them. Lindy put her gear on, musty rags and all, then snuck out of the tent and walked over to the well. A few of the third shift of night duty guards were still roaming around. Some of them tentatively greeted Lindy even though her place among the heroes was ambiguous. Lindy was recognized as one of the main people responsible for slaying the manticore. No matter how the teachers tried to gloss over that, the hero trainees were perceptive enough to work out the details; they were all nearby, after all. Lindy began to stretch. Her limbs creaked; the healing had completed, but there was still some tingling and numbness. Lindy had destroyed her arms a few times over so she was more surprised they were working than anything else.

One of the night guards walked over to Lindy. "What's your name?" he asked.

Lindy looked up at the curious teenager. "Shouldn't you introduce yourself first?" she asked, raising one eyebrow to emphasize her question.

The boy's sloppy grin slacked off a bit. "Jatter of Byorn."

"Nice to meet you, Jatter of Byorn. I am called Lindy Shrew," said the only child in town that had power possibly on par with a hero teacher.

"So where did you learn to fight?" Jatter asked amicably. A few of the other guards had moved into range where they could clearly hear what was being said, while trying and failing to look like they were not listening in.

"Nowhere I can get to anymore," Lindy shrugged.

"So, like your instructor died. What was their name?" Jatter pressed.

"Manfred Endfield," Lindy sighed. She had taught herself much by modifying a few tricks she had learned in her past life. All those skills had been changed into new forms that did not resemble the first techniques she had picked up, so it was not a total lie, but most of all, explaining her past self to others all the time was getting annoying.

Jatter's face scrunched up. "I have not heard of him."

Lindy cracked her neck a few times and began to do sit-ups. "I don't remember a lot about him. Either way, he is long gone."

Jatter leaned over to watch the odd child before him, which Lindy found very rude. "How did he die?" Jatter asked.

"Fell off a bridge," Lindy spat.

Jatter's eyes narrowed. "It was serious question," he replied, now very disappointed and feeling like he had been strung along.

Lindy simply ignored Jatter until he stormed off. Before he could fully escape her, Lindy called after him. "Where I come from no longer exists. Finding your own way to be strong is the mightiest path. That much I know is true."

Jatter paused briefly but did not otherwise acknowledge the young oddity's advice. Then he left the square with a few of the other guards.

Caldrin slipped out of an alleyway and moved to sit on the lip of the well. "So are you going to stop telling everyone you meet about being reincarnated on Death's whimsy?" she asked.

Lindy sighed unhappily. "Well yeah. It takes too long."

Caldrin shook her head. "That too, but that much info could cause you problems if the wrong people knew."

"Nobles, bandit leaders, criminal masterminds, military commanders, and merchants. Ok, I'll be careful," Lindy replied.

"You are too clever at the oddest times. Anyway, you and I will be going to the kingdom's hero academy 3rd branch after breakfast." After hinting that Lindy was onto something, Caldrin walked back the way she had come.

Lindy soon walked out of the square seeking to avoid her soon-to-be fellow classmates. The only place in town living beings avoided was where the manticore had fallen. Kelmo and the non-monster casualties had been interred over a very tiring night. Only dried pools of nameless gore and rubble were left scattered about and at the center of it all lay the manticore's towering corpse. Lindy began aimlessly looking around. Soon she noticed many patches of deep green grass, most of which were under the manticore's body. Lindy was sure she had not seen any such plant matter after the monster had died, so she pulled up some of the grass and began to chew on it. It tasted slightly sweet with a sour citric acid kind of aftertaste. As her mouth became slightly numb and tingly Lindy mused over the flavor and kept harvesting the grass. After she had finished, Lindy clambered up onto the manticore's furry back and began watching the town wake up from what was now the highest point in the village, now that the few barns and its sole warehouse had fully collapsed from damage sustained in the fight.

Haldin swiftly moved around the town until he spied a small form on the manticore's back. He noted the grass that had sprung from the flood of blood and life energy the manticore had lost. He leapt up to the monster's back. Upon seeing Lindy surrounded by the monster's power fragments, he sighed and was about to check the child's pulse when she leapt up and looked at up at him. "Hey, is the chow ready?" she asked.

Haldin was mildly surprised that Lindy was showing no ill effects. "Yes it is." Lindy then nonchalantly began bundling up the manticore's power fragments with a braid made from the monster's hair. "You know those are poisonous, right?" Haldin asked. Lindy looked confused so the professor explained. "Sometimes when powerful monsters die, their power overflows and manifests in the world as something, in this case, moderately poisonous grass. Nothing about it is beneficial to beings like us."

Lindy shrugged. "But it tastes good." As if to prove her point, she pulled out yet another piece of the grass and stuck it in her mouth. After shifting it to one side she folded her arms and asked, "So breakfast is over there?"

Haldin followed the girl's tilted head to where a few tables and stew pots had been set up. "That's right, so get going," he told her. Before he could ask her to leave, Lindy took her bundle of grass and ran in the direction of the food line. Haldin jumped down and started working out how to harvest the rest of the manticore's body.

Meanwhile Lindy had leapt off a roof, landing at the end of the food line. One of the other girls who had been in the same tent was just front of her. When Lindy landed, over half the line and a few of the food servers looked over at her, but Lindy paid them no mind. After waving over to Genney, who was one of the people serving food, Lindy started focusing on chewing what was left of the strand of grass she had been working on. The child in front of her studied Lindy closely, then asked, "So you and our Sage seem close."

"Genney has been very nice. I'd like to be friends with her," Lindy listlessly answered.

"For an underclassman, you are hoping for a lot. Gen is the top mage in our grade," the girl said proudly, as if it was her own accomplishment.

"Gen's a nickname. Are you one of her buddies?" Lindy asked, peeking over at Genney who was being swamped by a large number of boys tying to get her to serve them.

"I am one of her disciples," the child firmly boasted.

"So, a groupie. You are sure Genney does not think of you as a friend?" Lindy asked. They were almost to the point of being served, given Genney's valiant performance taking the brunt of the orders in a flustered but nevertheless heroic effort.

The child took a bowl of thin stew, a slice of bread, and mug of faintly glowing vegetable juice. She pointed over to Genney and sighed, wavering off to one side as Lindy was served. "I can't compete with that."

Lindy was getting her tray under control and looked over at Genney. "She has it rough, but that's all the more reason for her to have girls her age she can talk to honestly."

The child looked shocked, then asked, "You think that would work?"

They found an out-of-the-way table. "You seriously think being swamped by a bunch of crazy jocks will be anything but stressful, especially for someone that nice and meek?" Lindy asked, digging into her bread. It was chewy for her but most of the other students seemed to be having trouble tearing off pieces.

"You think she is meek?" the child asked, sounding insulted on behalf of her idol.

"Yes. So what's with this juice?" Lindy asked, downing a sip from the mug.

"An energy booster. It's supposed to ward off fatigue," the girl said in a huff, then leaned over and whispered, "So being open and honest is all I need to do to be her friend?"

"Well, duh. Friends support each other. That's true for anyone," Lindy retorted with the confidence that came from the fragmented memories of her past life.

The girl thought hard about what the younger child she had dragged off had said. Finally choosing she had nothing to lose, the groupie stuck out her hand, stating, "You can call me Fraya Fields. Let's be friends."

Lindy finished savoring some of the soup that tasted far better than she thought it should. After shaking Fraya's hand she said, "I am Lindy. Let's try to be friends with Gen also." Then she turned around and spoke to the girl who had been standing behind her as she worked on the soup. "Hey buddy, what's up?"

Fraya had been so engrossed in her delusions that Genney had approached her unnoticed. Genney sat down heavily with her own tray of food. Lindy had a devilish grin and Fraya had temporally forgotten how to breathe. "You are both my friends." Genney seemed to pout before digging into her food. Lindy gave Fraya a thumbs up which Genney noticed from the corner of her eye with hint of gratitude, having worked out Lindy's trick.

The girls became silent and focused on eating to cover their shifting feelings. Genney thought *Am I really that intimidating?* Fraya thought *Am I really that shallow?* and Lindy thought *I should learn how to make this soup.* Fraya worked up her courage and asked her two mutual friends, "So what are your plans today?"

Genney slumped unhappily in her chair. "I will have to help with treating the townsfolk and healing the hunting teams."

Lindy did not answer immediately, choosing to take a deep gulp of the juice and carefully watching Fraya tense up. Lindy slammed her mug down, shaking the other two girls out of their funk. "I'll be setting off to a hero academy today. More than likely I will have to enroll." Genney looked over at Fraya and smiled, thinking *Lindy is a born leader. She knows our insecurities and how to deal with them.*

Fraya was shocked. "Wait, you're not even a hero, yet you killed a manticore!"

Lindy pointed at herself with a wooden spoon. "My not being enrolled should be an open secret by now."

"But no one believes that," Fraya shot back, not having the time or composure to care anymore about how she appeared.

"That's reasonable," Lindy nodded before Fraya could steady her mind. Lindy added a completely unreasonable aside. "Well, I did take down an adult dragon, too."

This was far too much for the other two. They leapt up, throwing back their seats and crowding Lindy. This caused the normal ruckus of the students eating to stop in an instant, which allowed Genney's shout to echo further still. "You killed an adult dragon?"

Lindy did not let the overwhelming mass of intensity pressing in all around her affect her mindset in any way. "Of course not," Lindy laughed. A few relieved breaths were soon cut brutally short when

Lindy smiled like a man-eating demon and said, "Gravity did. I only took its wing off."

Caldrin soon appeared behind Lindy and pulled the young girl to her feet. "Come on, it's a long walk."

As Lindy was being dragged away, Genney called out, "That's my best friend. Will I ever see her again?"

Caldrin did not stop and Lindy only shrugged until Fraya yelled out, "Same with me! Well, will we?"

Lindy looked up at her escort. Caldrin soon looked over her shoulder and said, "It's not my call, but you probably will. If this trouble maker goes anywhere, it will be at our academy." By then it seemed like all the eyes in the town were on them. Reflexively Caldrin scooped Lindy up.

Fraya let out a relieved sigh. She was so caught up in her inner feelings that she did not register when Genney put her hand on Fraya's shoulder. Lindy called back from her spot over Caldrin's shoulder. "Hey Fraya! I like how you speak your mind!" Unable to deal with all the eyes on them, Caldrin took off running until they arrived at the edge of town.

Caldrin set her charge back on solid ground. "Let's go," the half-elf said.

Lindy skipped after her escort. "Do we have rations this time?"

Caldrin took a small sack out of her backpack and tossed it over. Lindy dexterously perused the mound of supplies in the sack. "Ok. This will last three days?" she asked.

"With your body, five days easy, maybe even seven," Caldrin proclaimed. While keeping their eyes focused on the terrain, they walked along.

"I am still growing," Lindy scoffed. The rest of the day they walked in silence, Caldrin watching the land for dangers and places to camp and Lindy enjoying the scenery. The land slowly became flatter pockets of trees and small hills that dotted the land but at deceasing intervals. They ate bread, water, and jerky on the move. That night they still had not totally escaped the woodland and hills. Caldrin located a small cave she had been told about. When Lindy poked her head into it she sighed. "Something died in here," she noted.

"It's an old cave. Many things have," Caldrin agreed sternly.

"I'll take first watch," Lindy offered.

Caldrin lay her back to the wall of the cave and pulled out a blanket. "You sure? That's all the way until the moon is just past the top of the sky."

"A touch after midnight? I can do that. The thing is, if I go to sleep, know you may have a lot of trouble trying to wake me up," Lindy explained in a teasing manner.

"I'll be in your care but don't leave the cave," Caldrin yawned. Swiftly she had wrapped herself up in a thick blanket.

"What if I have to relieve myself?" Lindy asked.

Caldrin pointed at a corner far in the back of the cave. "Relax, we're both girls here."

"But only one of us is used to that," Lindy muttered, but her escort had already fallen fast asleep. Lindy sighed. Sitting down, she rested her back on the cave a few feet closer to the entrance than Caldrin.

Lindy jolted upright. Her danger sense suddenly was going berserk. Judging by the moon, midnight was still a few hours off. Swiftly finishing a half-eaten scrap of jerky, Lindy slowly got to her feet and readied a dagger in each hand. A fetid stink filled the cave, which easily roused Caldrin from her sleep. Before the older woman could ask what was going on, Lindy put her fingers to her lips. Anything moving around so obviously at night was either in great distress, reckless, overconfident, or had senses built for the dead of night and was very strong or simply uncaring of danger. None of those things were good, as all of them likely had something going for them, provided it was not an unmoving corpse. But that was a whole other can of worms.

Something came stomping over to the cave. The stink was only getting worse. Something green the size of an ogre with big red eyes and matted hair hanging from its back poked is head in and growled. "It's a troll." Caldrin trembled.

Lindy felt she could understand what the troll was trying to say. *Meat? Good, let me eat before dead things get mad.* Its words may have been vague but Lindy managed to piece together a meaning she felt fit. "Something else is around here. Get to the back of the cave." Caldrin seemed unconvinced but followed Lindy in, shimmying to the rear of the cave. This caused the troll to pause. Then it bent over and pressed in after them, ignoring the tight fit. As the troll pursued them its eyes were fixed not on its prey, but on the back wall. Lindy smirked *I knew it,* mentally congratulating herself. The rear of the of cave was pockmarked in many places, but if those pitted marks were ignored the wall would have been perfectly flat. "Hey teach, get to a corner." Lindy's vicious smirk convinced Caldrin that her young charge was on to something, and she obeyed.

Lindy looked right into the troll's eyes and kicked the rear of the cave as hard as she could. The rear wall crumbled and the troll froze. When the dust thinned, a hulking skeleton in heavy plate mail wielding a glowing long sword stepped from the small crypt that had been revealed. "What in the great tree is happening!" Caldrin swore.

Lindy stood up confidently and pointed over at the shaking troll. Looking into the twin pits of soul fire peeping out from deep in the ancient undead champion's helmet, she said, "He did it."

The skeleton's helm swiveled to peer at the troll. The living monster started to retreat slowly, its hulking mass working against it in the small cave. The skeleton's blade glowed and flailed about, hitting only air. It did not take a single step forward. The spots it had slashed shimmered and shot forward, slicing the troll to ribbons. Then the skeleton extended its empty arm and snapped its gauntleted fingers. The writhing troll corpse burst into flames. The bony menace swiveled to face Lindy. Raising its sword, it saluted her. "Father Death was right about you," it rasped.

"That I am an annoying pain?" Lindy asked.

The skeleton let out a dry cackle. "That too, but mostly that you are fun."

Lindy shrugged. "Well, either way, I've got friends in high places. Sorry for disturbing you."

The skeleton bent down and peered into Lindy's eyes. Then it pulled two old but spotless and glowing daggers from its back and placed them into Lindy's hands. "You need these more than me," it told her.

"Do you need anything for them?" Lindy asked empathetically.

"Talking to someone as an equal after all this time is enough for payment," the bag of bones gently explained.

"Cool. Well, my watch is over, so I will need to get some rest. Sorry but I've still got a long walk tomorrow," Lindy explained.

Caldrin shivered. "So I am up now," she trembled, peering over at the undead ancient.

"Perish the thought. You are my guests. I'll keep an eye out for the night," the skeleton told them.

Caldrin nodded but seemed unconvinced. Lindy took advantage of the uncomfortable stillness to take Caldrin's blanket and hide within it. In the morning the skeleton was gone and the rear wall was now smooth and spotless. Caldrin and Lindy had ended up huddled in the same blanket. Caldrin was still unnerved. She urged her traveling companion to pack up very fast. Lindy managed to tuck her new daggers into one of her coat's pockets after moving all the manticore power fragments into the other one.

When the road had shifted far enough to hide the cave within the thinning tree line, Caldrin firmly announced, "Last night did not happen."

"Right, I found two daggers yesterday. You let me keep them. Other than that, nothing of note happened at all," Lindy agreed.

Caldrin shook off some unhappy thoughts. "Ancestor, you are good at this."

The pair ate on the way again. Around midday Lindy was going to ask how far away they were. Caldrin said, "Two hours."

Two hours later they entered a massive swath of flat prairie land. When an arrow flew out at them from a ditch on the side of the road, no other hiding places were visible. Thirty men emerged out of the ditches and from under grass mats along the shoulders of the road. "Bandits?" Lindy asked.

A lean young man who looked by far the cruelest of the men around them sneered, "Give us everything of yours and you may live if we are in a good mood."

"Bandits," Caldrin affirmed, refusing to acknowledge the men around them.

The lean man clicked his tongue. "Kill the child and capture the pointy-eared one. Be as rough as you need to be."

Lindy began to laugh hysterically. "If I kill them, I get their stuff, right?"

"Well, normally," Caldrin began. Lindy pinched her escort while the bandits closed in. The half-elf cut to the chase. "Short version, yes." Lindy charged at the mob. Before she hit anyone, Caldrin called, "Keep one or two alive. I'll pay for whatever useful info we get from them." By the time she finished, five men had been gutted and three decapitated by Lindy. The last two standing had their skulls shattered by Lindy's punches. That left the ten on one side of the road and the ten in front of them.

Lindy tossed the daggers, axes, and swords of her defeated foes at the team on the side of the road. At first the cheap blades shattered before they arrived at their targets, throwing shards of iron all over their intended landing zone. "Keep your head down, teach. I got these punks." Lindy sneered, now sure she had worked out how much force she needed to use. Three men had been killed by all the shrapnel flying around. Still, her attack on the sides was taking a few seconds more than she felt comfortable with, so she tossed two large axes at the team of ten cautiously advancing on them from the front. As planned, the axes shattered above the ten bandits, including their leader. Lindy took their pause to defend themselves as an opportunity to scan their spokesman.

Jeffers

Human male age 19

Affiliation: Ernadon empire first heroes branch, iron mound
    syndicate (slavers, monster hunters, smugglers)

Job: mid rank hero

Status: commando of the Ernadon empire

Abilities: strength 490, vitality 431, mind 383, agility 397

Talents: inspire, alcohol tolerance: high, language com-
    mon Derndell/ common ernadon/ high ernadon, fear-
    lessness, poison immunity, residence mind reading:
    high, residence pain: high, shadow move, analysis de-
    fense: moderate

Skills: axe: expert, dagger: expert, literacy: journeyman,
    stealth: expert, tracking: journeyman, law: journey-
    man, survival: journeyman, intimidate: expert, barter:
    adept, torture: adept, first aid: apprentice, diplomacy:
    apprentice, bird handling: adept. poisoneering: begin-
    ner, athletics: beginner, tanning: beginner

Lindy tossed the rest of the cheap weapons at the men on the side
with less force, turning them into pin cushions. She charged at the nine
men in front. One had died. "Their boss is a foreign hero. Do we keep
him alive?"

"Memorize the data, then kill him," Caldrin ordered.

"You annoying…" Jeffers the bandit leader shouted. He had to cut
his rant short and jump to avoid Lindy's slash at his legs. Jeffers back-
pedaled to the rear of his men. "Hold off the runt!"

The bandits charged at Lindy but her danger sense was going crazy
again, although it seemed unlikely that anything with less than the
strength of a hero would be hazardous to her. Lindy tossed her normal
daggers into the dirt and drew her new glowing ones. She began to scan
the men running at her. After getting through half of them only paying
attention to their affiliation, job, and status, the only two things the men

had in common was they were all part of the Iron Mound Syndicate and they all had very criminal-sounding jobs and statuses. Lindy had kept her eye on Jeffers the entire time. When he vanished, she hopped to the side and unleashed a full-powered roundhouse kick. Jeffers appeared out of one of his men's shadows in front of Lindy, his axe in mid-swing and covered in green gunk. Lindy's kick connected with Jeffers's gut and split the air. The bandit troop and their leader were all split in half. The entire engagement had taken less than two minutes.

"You have the data?" Caldrin asked.

"That's right. Sorry, but I did not hold back enough to take anyone alive," Lindy sighed.

"I understand, but your new info better be worth it. Now loot their things and let's go." Caldrin nodded, her eyes thoughtful.

Lindy looted all the money she could find from the bodies. She took Jeffers's boots and gloves. While fishing around in the enemy hero's pockets she pulled out a few notes and a stamp marked with a complex emblem. Lindy handed the notes and stamp to Caldrin. "He was from Ernadon empire first heroes branch and was part of the Iron Mound Syndicate. A mid-rank hero and a commando for the Ernadon empire," Lindy stated.

Caldrin put the objects in an empty pouch. "Your life is never going to be dull, it seems."

"That's a huge underestimate." Lindy shrugged like it was someone else's problem. "So how much longer?"

"If we keep moving like we did, by the end of today," Caldrin answered. Lindy began to walk off but the half-elf stopped her. "Remember, you should keep what you are secret."

Lindy looked over her shoulder but kept walking, forcing Caldrin to jog after her until they were side by side again. "And what am I?"

"A lot, but the part about being on a first name basis with Death and having been knowingly reincarnated should be a secret you take to the grave."

Lindy began to ravenously eat through her supply of jerky, saying between the few intervals her mouth was empty, "My two new friends and your boss know all that. But you are wrong about one thing." Lindy took far longer to manage that sentence due to her focus on eating through her rations.

Caldrin waited for her charge to elaborate, but when Lindy did not divulge any more info and instead tore into the food with even more relish, Caldrin had to ask, "What am I wrong about?"

Lindy endured her escort's glare until five snack-sized portions of food were left. "My lifespan could far exceed yours."

Caldrin threw up her arms. "That's what I mean. Stop saying such crazy things."

It was Lindy's turn to glare at Caldrin. "I am very honest."

Caldrin took a few deep breaths. "All right, but by showing off your power, you are only going to give those in power far more ideas for how to exploit how unique you are."

"Does that come from personal experience?" Lindy asked.

"Yes. Humans are by far the majority in this kingdom. Its laws, especially the ones for the hero academies, are written for and by them. All the other races have to follow them. That includes slow-aging and very long-lived races like the elven varieties." Caldrin explained briefly but would not go into any more detail.

Two hours later, the sun had crossed behind the mountains. A young girl led by the aide of Haldin Gasteen approached the gates of a small castle with a large courtyard and very deep basement. This place had served as the home of the Derndell kingdom hero academy 3rd branch for a great many years. The night gate warden was waiting for them, his lookouts having long spotted the two travelers approaching. "Faywind. Is that Professor Gasteen's new find?" the warden asked sternly without malice or kindness.

"That's right, night warden," Caldrin agreed. "Is there someone else I need to report to?"

The warden grimaced. "Learn your colleagues' names." Without waiting for a reply he pointed up to one of the three towers within the walls. "The headmaster and his aides are waiting in tower number two. They want to see the new prospect and you immediately upon arrival."

"That's it?" Caldrin asked curiously. The warden nodded. So Caldrin grabbed Lindy's hand and said, "Come on, follow me."

They passed by the courtyard. Some students slightly older than the ones Lindy had met were sparring off to one side in the huge training field that took over the entire courtyard. An elf was watching over them but when he saw Caldrin he give the students a break and ran over to her. "That took a while," the elf-man said before noticing that Lindy was the only other one around. "So Haldin is not with you."

"Professor Gasteen sent us ahead." The way Caldrin emphasized the word 'professor' interested Lindy. Looking closely, the elf-man looked barely sixteen. Caldrin muscled her way past the man with Lindy in tow. Many of the older students watched them leave from the sidelines.

Long past the field they went through a thorough search at the front door of a tower. While ascending the narrow stairway, Lindy asked, "Formalities are big here. That man from before a friend of yours?"

"The man we met is a child. He turned thirty this year and became a hero at ten while appearing six. He is like my younger brother." Caldrin sighed.

Soon after, they arrived at a trap door that cut off access to the very top of the tower. Caldrin pulled a cord hanging from the ceiling. A glowing circle came from the door and rushed through the tower. After the magic circle was done probing the tower, the door latch clinked and a sullen voice echoed in their minds. "Enter," it commanded.

Lindy was pushed through the trap door, her guide following close behind. An old human man sat at a desk in a wide room that took up the last fifth of the tower. Books and arcane bobbles haphazardly took up most of the space. A lean middle-aged male human and a being that looked like a transformed female werewolf stood at either side of the desk. All three wore light and very expensive clothes. The werewolf had gold-trimmed goggles strapped to its head. "So you killed a dragon," the old man sighed. "Faywind, what is the meaning of this?"

Caldrin did not seem surprised. "Sir, what do you mean?"

The werewolf shook its head. It spoke calmly and without malice. "Secretary Faywind, you do survey work, not recruitment."

The middle-aged man added in a less forgiving manner, "And you lost a town."

Lindy groaned from beside Caldrin. "A dragon did it. Say what you mean."

The middle-aged man glared at Lindy. The werewolf seemed mildly intrigued and the old man grumbled. "We will get to you."

"A dragon fell on the town after setting it on fire. What more do you want?" Lindy grumbled back.

"Why you all ran," the old man stated firmly.

"She used my boss's sword to cut off the monster's wing." Caldrin pointed over at Lindy.

The werewolf and old man exchanged a questioning glance. After trading a nod, the werewolf soundlessly plodded over to one of the many random piles of things pressing in on them and picked out a sword. In a flash the werewolf stood towering over Lindy with the sword's hilt inches from her eyes. "You need to pick it up," the wolf-woman informed Lindy.

Lindy shrugged and drew the blade. It was a long sword that emanated a blue fire. Its edges were covered in runes. Lindy took a few steps back and juggled the blade between her hands. After a few tosses she got used to the sword's weight and center of gravity, and so began to spin the blade around in the air. The old man was holding his head. "That's enough." At his command the werewolf snatched the sword out of midair.

"Like a dragon," Lindy sighed.

The middle-aged man shook his head. "Dragons are beings that hoard all manner of things and burn towns whenever they feel like. More than one kingdom has been felled by those beasts."

Lindy laughed in her mind but she could not help herself from whispering, "They are very regal."

The middle-aged man did not seem pleased. "That dragon annihilated a town in part because of you what you were doing."

"Aiming for its chest." Lindy shrugged.

"And?" the old man asked.

"It tried to dodge, so my sword toss took off a wing," Lindy pouted.

The old man leaned back in his chair. "You will never get married like that."

A dull aura pulsed from Lindy. Things that sounded like tortured spirits echoed from the air around her. The effect lasted only a few seconds but it caused the four adults in the room to instinctively ready themselves for combat. Then Lindy took a deep breath and the aura receded back into her. "I exist to kill things, not play house," she sighed.

The old man recovered first. "Indeed you do. Most heroines try to get married off to nobles and join our reserves," he let slip.

"They try?" Lindy asked disappointed.

The werewolf and Caldrin looked uncomfortable with the subject. "Not all, but most," Caldrin managed to sneer.

"Anyway, is that child as powerful as you, instructor?" the middle-aged man asked.

"She may be a bit more powerful, although her technique is still unpolished," Caldrin allowed.

"We will put her in class 4S," the old man announced.

"We left them back in the Hardeen hills," Caldrin noted.

"They will be back in a day or two and have more open spaces than we were expecting," the middle-aged man said firmly, clearly considering the subject over.

"Plus, nothing good will come if we put a twelve-year-old transfer with the seniors," the werewolf elaborated.

"Faywind, you and Professor Gasteen will be helping oversee 4S. So I am leaving the new asset's accommodations to you. See that she is ready by the time her classmates return," the old man commanded.

A short way from the tower Lindy looked over her shoulder and asked dispassionately, "So who were they?"

Caldrin looked up at the sky in defeat and slowed down her speed. "The old human is the headmaster. He was a high-ranker. You will only be calling him headmaster, but if you must know, he is named Wallace Nut." Lindy burst out laughing and had to stop to hold her gut. The force of her laughter caused a light breeze to swirl around her. Caldrin got very embarrassed and dragged Lindy under a tall tower near a hedgerow. "Stop that. This is not funny," she whispered to her new student.

Lindy forced herself back under control. "Have you heard of a walnut?"

"Never," Caldrin replied, admonishing Lindy with a withering gaze. A walnut, Caldrin hypothesized, was not something from her world or went by another name, but slip-ups like that would put Lindy through a lot of pain. Whether the mind of the one inhabiting the little girl before her was like its body, still that of a child or far older, Caldrin felt obligated to try to help her out. However, Caldrin would not let herself get so invested that she would defend Lindy if she slipped up big time. After seeing that Lindy had gotten a hold of herself, Caldrin went on. "The lupine is in charge of inventory and the crafting departments. We call her Vexta. The other human does the public relations and accounting. He goes by Jeffery Derkin. He's the one you need to be most careful of. He is from a high-ranking noble family, so his pride and power are both up there, but what he has is not enough for him."

Lindy nodded. "So are political marriages using heroines normal?"

Caldrin leaned her back on the wall. "You really know nothing of the world. This is a dangerous world. Lots of people die. Humans are the most numerous right after plants, animals, and some weaker monsters. Weak heroes and those suited to noncombat roles are pushed into a reserve force. The line for human heroines to join the reserves is higher than the males, so all the strong fighters in the reserves are human females; however most of them become concubines or guards for nobles."

Lindy sighed. "Human beings do tend to let power and desires get to their heads, a lot often with less than stellar results."

"Do you intentionally mix words from other languages into your speech?" Caldrin asked. But when she saw Lindy's face half morph into a dazed look before becoming a wide grin, the half-elf put out her hand. "Forget I asked. The thing about heroes is their families get money from the government, but that assistance is prioritized to heroes' children. That and having individuals whose skill and power outclasses non-heroes close at hand is why complicated things happen."

Lindy glared at Caldrin. "You are wrong. It's greed and fear, both common and very powerful motivating factors."

Caldrin started to walk again towards a large gate set into the floor of the courtyard. "You are really cynical."

Lindy shrugged. "Why? Because I think a little greed will keep someone alive and a lot of hope is often a hindrance to living well?"

Caldrin groaned as they passed six guards standing at the wide stone steps leading underground. "I don't think I will ever get used to you."

"Well, you have the rest of your life for that. So, we will see," Lindy countered, which only made Caldrin feel even more out of her depth. *I really need to research any theories about other worlds* Caldrin told herself, knowing her own musings had hit a wall.

The first floor of the underground complex was thick with traps, methods of detection, security screening, and ways to touch at something's true nature, all both through physical and magical means. Caldrin's only hint was "Don't lie or fight for real here." They passed through a vault-like door to the next floor.

The next two floors were combat arenas and testing grounds. Magical and physical tests along with trials that closely mimicked field-work could all be done here, on top of duels and competitions. Again, Caldrin kept her review of this floor short. "The more active classes and tests are held on this floor." Lindy snickered quietly at her guide's demeanor but stopped long before that got on Caldrin's nerves enough to comment. Another vault-like door led to the next floor but this one seemed even more secure.

Floor four was a workshop and a dungeon to contain monsters. Small alchemy labs were dotted around the monster pens. "Don't goof off here," Caldrin told Lindy. A vault door thicker than the others crossed down to the next floor.

Floor five was the warehouse and cafeteria. Caldrin led Lindy to the cafeteria. Most of the staff and almost all the students were eating dinner at this time. Caldrin grabbed two salads and a two large bowls of stew plus a jug of tea, then handed them to Lindy on a tray and informed her, "Come on. I'll show you to your room for the next two or three years."

Lindy scampered after Caldrin, paying no mind to the unfounded rumors about her that had begun to spring up among the students. The sixth floor was cramped with dorm after dorm. "There are four to a dorm. I am assigning you to Genney's room. She lost two roommates, so I may shuffle another girl in when your classmates show up two days from now."

"So, what now?" Lindy asked.

Caldrin took a salad and stew from Lindy. "You eat and rest. I will be by early tomorrow, so get to bed soon. I will have a safe dropped off for your use before classes resume."

"So, are you going down to more floors?" Lindy asked.

"Yes, but all past the seventh are restricted areas to students," Caldrin answered levelly.

"So how long exactly will I be here?" Lindy asked.

Caldrin sighed and in an unfocused and disinterested way began quoting from memory the academy's cookie cutter line for that question. "As long as a student does not suffer a fatal event during their schooling, they will graduate into the kingdom's service. Any showing top-class skills will be allowed an apprenticeship with a senior hero for their last year of school." Caldrin grimaced. "I don't think you will die but still it would not be smart to show up your classmates too much if you can help it." With those parting words Caldrin Faywind left, passing through the fifth floor, the sixth floor dorms, the seventh floor dungeons, the eighth floor alchemy labs and armory, all the way to the ninth floor library. She had no need to go to the tenth and last floor where the emergency shelters, teleport pads, long range commutations, and scanning gear were set up.

Caldrin had many questions, the main unanswerable one being why Lindy let her full stats be seen. Analysis could only see stats less powerful than its rating unless the one being examined was completely unguarded. The main question Caldrin could answer now was what two of Lindy's abilities really did. Translation: all and full power strike: strength were not talents Caldrin was familiar with. She found full power strike rather quickly. One of the kingdom's five current legend-rank heroes had that ability and some extremely strong monsters did as well. With that ability activated, one was able to double one's striking force. It shared some traits with magic, as it tapped into the concepts the world was made of and the world spirits each embodied. It took almost the entire night to find a few sentences about translation: all in a decaying book in the library's highest security archives. It was a legendary ability that allowed its possessor to understand all spoken speech that possessed a distinct meaning and the intent of more basic communication when focusing. It was theorized that when paired with literacy, the possessor could read all languages as well. Caldrin took a two-hour nap in the library before getting up to shuffle to Lindy's room.

Lindy was sitting in her new room when she heard a firm knock. The room was large for one small child but would be a little snug with four teenagers. Lindy had woken up a full hour before Caldrin had come by. The habits from Manfred Endfield's life were still with her. Getting up early and shuffling off to work before sunrise had been a fact of life for Manfred regardless of his fatigue. Caldrin was surprised when Lindy opened the door. Her coat and rags had been mended. The gloves she had taken had been made smaller. Her face had been washed but she was barefoot. Caldrin had fully expected that she would need to unlock the door herself and drag Lindy out of bed. That expectation was swiftly quashed when the half-elf remembered *Oh right, this one is not mentally twelve.* Caldrin looked her pupil over a few times before asking, "Where is your footwear?"

Lindy shrugged and walked back into the room. She held up Jeffers's old boots in one hand. "Too big." Then raising her other hand, gripping her ragged shoes which were now more akin to strips of dirty yellow cloth than footwear, "Too little."

Caldrin resisted the urge to laugh at Lindy's antics. "Are you going to be all right like that?" Caldrin chose to suppress an unbidden thought about being glad she had gotten accustomed to Lindy's peculiar manner and gloating at how the more strait-laced teachers, in particular the human ones, would have to go through hell dealing with the simultaneously terrifying and innocent child.

Lindy stashed her two normal and two old magic daggers in some new pockets on her coat. "I'll live," Lindy shrugged.

Caldrin pretended not to notice Lindy arming herself. "You can sew?"

Lindy shook her head. "Not well. The materials I had were good and simple, so that did most of the work."

Caldrin led Lindy out of the room and locked the door. "Where did you get a needle and thread?"

"They were in the bottom of the sack you gave me," Lindy said, walking beside Caldrin. The hallway was just beginning to come alive with students trickling out of their rooms. Many eyes and ears followed Caldrin and Lindy.

Caldrin believed Lindy until ten minutes later in the slowly moving horde, all going to the cafeteria for breakfast a full hour before sunrise. By that time Lindy was right before Caldrin in line for food. A slowly forming suspicion bull rushed Caldrin's consciousness. "Wait!" she nearly shouted, forcing her words into a hissing whisper like a dying tea kettle. "Any needle would have been extremely cheap iron and I know the thread in the emergency suturing kit was no better than sackcloth."

Lindy looked up at Caldrin and smirked. "I never said that was what I wound up using. The iron needle broke first thing on my coat. Lucky that sword was good for something." Lindy slipped a small whittled bone needle into Caldrin's hand.

Many eavesdroppers were listening in now. Lindy got some bread and stew along with the energy drink like water. She waited for Caldrin by the doors. Luckily only a few people were going up to the surface at this time. In unspoken agreement, Lindy and Caldrin walked up to the training field and found an out-of-the-way spot in the spectator seating to sit down. Caldrin ignored her salad to look closely at the needle Lindy had handed over. "Is this manticore bone?" she asked incredulously.

Lindy finished a large bite of bread, then answered, "Nope, it's mine."

Caldrin almost dropped her self-warming mug of tea. "WHAT?!" she sputtered, totally disregarding appearances.

Lindy paused and took out a piece of her manticore power fragments and dispassionately stuck the poisonous substance into her mouth. Between chews Lindy explained. "It's mine. After bashing in that manticore's head my arms shattered a few times, so I had some bone shards to work with. The thread was strips I took from my new gloves."

Caldrin was at a loss for words. Then she grabbed Lindy's jaw and looked right into her eyes. "You are a child now. So please act like it."

"Hey new kid, fight me!" a boy around nineteen or seventeen yelled up at the stands. A few of the older students from the night before were clustered on the field.

Lindy used the distraction to slip out of Caldrin's hands. Unlike the teacher's aide, Lindy had seen this entire scenario coming. Lindy leapt up to the ledge of the seating and looked back at the half-elf. "To live in this world I must be ready for its cruelty." Then she smirked and looked down at the arrogant boy who had called up before. "Like right now," Lindy whispered so only Caldrin heard her. Lindy jumped. She fell a good five times her height, landing with a crash to stand unharmed before the still-overconfident boy. All his companions, however, were smart enough to back off in mild apprehension. "Fine, wooden swords and unarmed combat only; no magic. One round to knock out. Hand me a training sword so we can get this over with." The boy was too provoked by Lindy's confidence to question why she was even like that, so the boy tossed her one of the two wooden blades in his hands. Caldrin sat back and desperately tried to work out how she would play damage control this time.

The boy walked a few feet from the stands. "So what is your first name, kid?"

"It is polite to introduce yourself first, child." Lindy smiled nonchalantly.

"Whatever. Shrew, fight me!" the boy yelled, charging forward with his wooden sword raised with both hands high above his head.

"Get her, Cal!" one of the boy's companions called.

"Cal, is it? Is that your full name, kid?" Lindy smirked. Cal grimaced angrily. His face had long become flushed with rage. If not for doing things like walking, sewing, eating, and opening doors, Lindy would have been at a loss how to control her strength to the point where not killing someone on the level of hero-in-training would be likely. Lindy stepped in under the boy's guard and thrust her palm up into his chin, all the while being very careful to use somewhere around thirty percent of her strength. The boy's head rocketed back. His hand slackened, dropping his sword. Lindy hit the pommel of the falling chunk of wood, smashing it into the boy's foot. The boy groaned; his eyes dimmed slightly. Lindy saw Cal was far from knocked out yet, so she spun behind him with her leg out, tapping him in the back lightly by Lindy's standards. This sent Cal flying headfirst at the stands.

Caldrin hopped down from the spectator seating and caught Cal. "That was excessive, Lindy Shrew," she complained.

Lindy sat down on the ground and called back more than loud enough for Cal's entourage to hear. "Well, he was so intense I was not able to bring myself to hold back." Her acting would not work on anyone in their right mind. Luckily for her, Cal's friends' sense of what was possible had been shattered.

The only ones who knew otherwise on the field were Lindy and Caldrin. Even then it took Caldrin a few long seconds to translate Lindy's olive branch into more than white noise. Managing not to show gratitude, Caldrin sighed. "Well, you just beat the strongest student in this academy, so expect your life to get complicated. Now Lindy, help me bring him to the medical wing."

"Fine. I'll help lug this shameless braggart along," Lindy said solemnly, all while cackling like a maniac in her mind and doing a paper-thin job of hiding her real thoughts.

The academy had three medical wards, one on basement floor ten, one on basement floor three, and one on the second floor of the castle. Without another word or glance at the other students trickling onto the field, Caldrin led Lindy, who had Cal held over her head, up a side flight of stairs. Lindy bounded after the half-elf past many faculty offices and wide-eyed mostly awake academy staff. Caldrin threw open one heavy unlabeled door. Twenty beds were arranged in two even rows. A large man with rock for skin sat on a ball of something gelatinous. The man was in the middle of filling out some paperwork when Caldrin burst in. Without looking up the man said, "This is not a morgue. Move along."

Caldrin froze but Lindy dodged around her and tossed Cal on one of the beds. "Well, he is not dead yet, sir."

The rock man looked up, his eyes focused on Lindy as if noticing her for the first time. He said, "You don't seem to be among the living."

Lindy shrugged. "I don't care what you think. All of us here have a pulse but only two are hurt."

"Two?" Caldrin asked.

Lindy thought deeply and reviewed her stats. At some point life sense, aura: weakening, damage shield: decay had been added to her talents and necromancy: beginner had been added to her skills. Lindy focused on the life signs around her. "Three," she corrected.

"There are four in the room," Caldrin pointed out.

"No, there are five," Lindy said, pointing to the far side of the room "Fraya's there."

The rock man moved over to look over Cal in a single-minded manner. "So child, besides my new patient, who is the other wounded one?"

Lindy looked back at him. Caldrin was unsure who to glower at so she split the difference and alternated between Lindy and the academy's head doctor. "You are," Lindy said as if it was obvious.

"So you analyzed my curse," the doctor sighed.

Caldrin grabbed Lindy's shoulder. "I told you that was rude..."

Lindy rolled her eyes. "The aura that shows he is alive looks like a fraying ball of yarn. I don't need analysis to see that."

Caldrin turned her glare to the doctor. "It's an old petrifaction curse," the man said. "Now get out."

Caldrin began to leave. She tried to drag Lindy out but the small girl would not move, regardless of the force used. "Fraya Fields is a good friend of mine. Is the rest of her team back as well?"

For the second time the doctor looked up. He sighed. "They will be back in a few hours. Your friend was hurt on the way back and was rushed here. She will be fine. Now let me work."

4

Live Magic Fire

Lindy and Caldrin turned to leave. Before Lindy exited she whispered under her breath, "Death, do me a favor and don't take my friend Fraya Fields from me today." In the back of her mind something that existed for endings seemed to agree, while hinting that power always came at a price.

Caldrin led Lindy back to the side passage. When they had gotten past the offices and staff, she quietly asked, "What was that before?"

"Nothing. I am going to the gate to wait for my class," Lindy muttered firmly.

Caldrin blocked Lindy from advancing. "You requested something from a world spirit. There was power in your words. Why?"

Lindy's eyes hazed over. Her voice spoke into Caldrin's mind, making her very soul desire to hide. *Don't ask what you the living should not know.* Lindy's eyes snapped back. She stood unsteadily for a few moments then glared up at her escort and smirked. "What it said." Caldrin was too unnerved to stop Lindy now, and stood frozen as the little girl angrily moved to the gate.

So Fraya was going to die today, Lindy yelled with all her might into her mind.

Or tomorrow, the voice from before agreed. To most, the thing's voice would freeze their minds and souls, but to Lindy it was only annoying, even more so now that Lindy felt like she had ignored a prediction of hers in favor of her own desires. She got the price she knew was coming mercilessly shoved in her face.

How long does she have? Lindy demanded. A few seconds later she screamed again into her mind, *Answer me!*

Most of that depends on you, but she will die before two years is up no matter what, the voice replied in a huff.

That's more than I expected. Lindy sighed mentally. Ignoring the glances and murmurs from the training field, she walked at an unhurried pace while unconsciously causing all near her to feel weak, like something ancient and terrifying was all around them.

You are taking this well, the voice said.

Lindy took a deep breath. *I can't undo what's been done. So who are you?*

The voice began to laugh. *You, but you are tied to some old chump. I am a conduit to the concept of death. As long as you do what we need, you will stay in control and I will keep us alive.*

Lindy got to the main gate and brushed past the cowering guards. She found a windowsill in the gatehouse and sat down, keeping a vigil on the fields of grass all around. She continued to interrogate the presence in her mind. *So if we fail, I lose it and you come out to play?*

Their connection was strong. The more they talked the more Lindy could work out what the thing was doing. By now she could feel what its body language would be and what intents it wished to show her. To pass the time she noted one of the few guards still around her and analyzed him.

Jerrend

Human male age 20

Affiliation: Derndell kingdom hero academy 3rd branch, Derndell kingdom 8th army

Job: watchman

Status: corporal Derndell kingdom army

Abilities: strength 18, vitality 20, mind 16, agility 12

> Talents: keen sense sight, alcohol tolerance: mild, language common Derndell, resistance fear: mild, light sleeper, rally, true effort
> Skills: sword: journeyman, armor proficiency chain/leather: journeyman., athletics: expert, spear: journeyman, awareness: journeyman, smithing: beginner, survival: beginner, sewing: apprentice, barter: beginner

The voice waited for Lindy to stop looking over the man's stats. *If you fail, you disappear and I start over with the skills the first Lindy Shrew had before she was knocked out and we showed up.*

You want to live a long time? Lindy asked.

Yes, the voice told her.

Good, I'll call you Conduit. Now shut up and let me sulk, Lindy grumbled mentally. A few hours later the endless windswept green and light brown moving dots came into view. Her class was almost back. Lindy ran down to the ground floor of the gate and waited. Even then it took one glance from the sentries at the gate for her to stand just within the academy grounds, the abyss-like aura from before tucked away far under the surface of her bubbly smile. If anything, the shift in how Lindy seemed made those that had seen her anger earlier more wary of her, not less.

A few hours later, a little after midday, Haldin, Zender, Genney, and Jatter, along with most of the rest of the students Lindy had seen, walked in. All had a wound or three somewhere. "I hope the others are ok," Genney sighed as she collapsed right inside the gate, her face vacant.

"Fraya is in the main building's infirmary," Lindy offered from her seat on a crate stacked in the shadow of the gatehouse.

Until now, Lindy had gone unnoticed by the very tired new arrivals. Jatter bolted over and tried to grab Lindy. She hopped off her seat and Jatter crashed into the crates. Genney rushed over and tried to heal him but she was not able to muster enough power to heal the light abrasion Jatter had sustained.

"Who else is being treated?" Zender asked calmly.

Lindy shrugged. "Cal something or other."

A few of the girls became were giddy at Cal's name despite their wounds. "Was Lord Calen Derkin part of a relief force?" Zender inquired to one of the guards.

The man shook with fright and peeked over at Lindy who yawned and waved her hand as if to say none of this interested her. The man gulped. Now the eyes of the few students with a presence of mind left looked over at Lindy. "The new member of your class defeated him soundly," the guard managed to choke out, more afraid of Lindy than Calen's high-ranking noble family.

One of the giddy girls from before yelled in a panic. "She did what?"

Zender's calm facade cracked slightly. "She is in whose class now?"

Caldrin chose this moment to make her appearance. "That 12-year-old is in class 4S. She dueled Calen Derkin. He will take many weeks to heal." Caldrin paused, letting her petty revenge at the cleanup she had to go through from that duel sink in, then continued. "Professor Gasteen and Doctor Zender, the headmaster needs to see you now. Anyone who needs more medical treatment is to go to the ward on basement floor three."

"Genney, sort out anyone who needs more treatment and lead them down," Zender began, but then he saw Genney, who had knocked Lindy to the grass and was in the process of hugging her tightly while laughing and crying. Lindy for her part patted Genney's head. Lindy was behaving like a mother lovingly calming her young child. "Never mind," Zender sighed. "Jatter, Zoe, and Stelve, you get anyone that needs more treatment to the ward asap."

Two girls picked Jatter up and after shaking him awake they got to work. The panicked maiden from before walked over to glare down at Lindy. "So you hurt Cal bad."

"Nope. Only knocked him out," Lindy sighed.

Caldrin called back as she walked away. "Calen has a lot of broken bones. Lindy, hold back next time."

Many glares and more fearful glances were shot at Lindy. "I did hold back, like a lot," Lindy shouted. The glares got worse.

"That's a lie. You cheated!" the maiden argued.

"It's not like fighting a dragon. Why would I go all out?" Lindy argued.

"Because it's honorable," the girl retorted.

Lindy was not happy anymore, so she analyzed the new problem child before her.

Hanna Zigone

Female human age 16

Affiliation: Derndell kingdom hero academy 3rd branch, magma barons

Job: hero in training

Status: summoner

Abilities: strength 63, vitality 96. mind 211, agility 123

Blessing: universal fire shaping

Embodiments: favored of fire

Talents: language common Derndell/high Derndell/ unified explorer society code/ fire empress runes, fearlessness, heat immunity, empower magic, multi cast: three, enhanced trait: mana pool, analysis: moderate, perfect teeth, never bald

Skills: fire magic: expert, spear: adept, dagger: adept, intimidate: adept, etiquette: beginner, athletics: beginner, summoning spirits of fire: journeyman, ritual magic empowerment: adept. first aid: beginner

Lindy got up slowly, stared up at the older girl, and spoke very slowly. "If I went all out, one serious hit could kill half the senior class. I held back so no one would die and your crush could keep some dignity."

"Lindy, Hanna, stop fighting!" Genney pleaded.

"Fight me seriously," Hanna challenged, glaring at Lindy.

Lindy shrugged and began to walk to the training yard. "Show me what you can do and I might." Lindy glanced back at Genney. "Sorry about this. I know our pride is troubling you but don't worry, she will be fine."

Hanna rushed after Lindy. "Hold on. You arrived right before us, right? How were you not ambushed?" the summoner asked.

"Oh, thirty robbers, one of which was a mid-rank hero commando, attacked," Lindy listlessly replied.

"What happened to them?" one of their other classmates asked.

Lindy was barely listening and replied on reflex, "I killed them all."

"Impossible," Hanna retorted.

"Well, she did help kill that manticore," Genney volunteered.

"Says who?" Hanna asked.

"The professors," Genney replied proudly, as if she had saved the day in Lindy's place.

Finally what was left of their class arrived on the field. Lindy patted Hanna on the back. "Take your time," she advised, then walked to the far end of the grounds and began to look over her four knives.

"So how will we do this?" Hanna called over.

Lindy did not bother to look up. "This was your idea. Well, how about you summon something? If I pass out or surrender you win. If I kill it I win?"

Hanna nodded. "Fine, that works for me." She began to draw a complex rune-covered circle which soon calmed her down. "Who told you about me?"

"You seemed like a threat, so I analyzed you," Lindy admitted without a hint of remorse.

Hanna's face scrunched up but she accepted Lindy's reasoning. "Let me analyze you."

"Go ahead," Lindy answered. She really did not care who snuck a look at her stats. As far as Lindy was concerned, if they were a problem either they were weak enough for her to slice if needed, or too strong to do anything but escape from. No matter what, to Lindy there were two kinds of problems: those she could deal with now, and those she could not deal with yet. There was simply no point getting uptight with what she could not do yet, and no point regretting what she needed to do to accomplish what she must.

Hanna's countenance went white as a sheet. "You are powerful. I can't see just how high most of your skills are."

"Well, you still need to do your summoning thing," Lindy smirked.

"What, why?" Hanna paused. A few boos were hurled over from the now-packed stands. Her classmates and many other students who had heard of Lindy's fight but had not seen it were crammed into the stands. Perhaps tellingly, those who had seen her fight with Calen Derkin were nowhere to be seen. Vexta was in the audience. Given that she was watching, it seemed this duel had the tacit blessing of the faculty.

"Because you did not cool down before it got like this." Lindy smiled as if this had been her plan all along, which it partly was. After all, she had known that this might happen.

It took Hanna a few minutes to finish her extensive ritual summoning. Everyone could tell Hanna was going to use everything she knew to fight Lindy. "Ready?" Hanna asked.

Lindy got to her feet and put her knives away. "Don't hold back," she requested.

Hanna began a long incantation, pouring more mana than she had used on any one spell into the circle. Neither step was strictly speaking needed but she was doing all she could to empower and strengthen her summon. A cyclone of flames rose from the circle. Before it could move Lindy slashed her feet across the ground three times, kicking up walls of dirt that covered Hanna's summon. Lindy stood ready to fight more. "That's it?" she asked.

Flames turned the dirt to glassy flakes and the summon rose up even hotter than before. It had been reformed into a huge dense fiery net. "Not even close," Hanna grimaced. The net flew at Lindy, who kicked up waves of dust and air to blow the summon to pieces again. Chunks of fire expanded and formed into a huge lance that was roughly eighteen feet long. "Surrender," Hanna requested. She was smiling but her mana was almost empty. If she tried to use any more, either her power would eat into her body or she would faint.

Lindy took a lower stance. "You showed me yours, so I'll get a little bit serious. Come at me!" The lance rocketed at Lindy who was the only one not freaking out. Hanna could not stop the lance with her drained mana and even if she could, it would hit Lindy before it could come to a full stop. Hanna had acted on instinct as she had been taught, forgetting the other half of that lesson, which was to keep a calm and aware mindset. Lindy asked Conduit *Hey, could I borrow a few mindless spirits from you?*

Are you going to do something cool-looking and really dumb? Conduit asked.

"When have I not?" Lindy whispered to herself. Hundreds of disembodied ghosts rose from her body and Lindy had them encase the summon and crush it. After enough pressure the summon exploded and Hanna fainted. Some of the students had looks of recognition when they saw one or two of the spirits. After they were done, the ghosts returned to somewhere in Death's realm through Lindy's body and Conduit.

Vexta leapt from the stands and hoisted Lindy off her feet. Looking deep into the little girl's eyes, Vexta demanded, "Where did you get all those souls?"

Lindy did not struggle at all. "Spirits like me," she said.

"That's it?" Vexta growled. "Many of my students were there and I know they all passed on."

Faster than anyone in the field could follow, Lindy grabbed Vexta's head and dragged herself over to one of the lupine's furry ears. "Death is a good friend of mine. I borrowed a few spirits from its realm." Lindy relaxed her body and let go of Vexta, who no longer had the strength to hold Lindy. From the ground Lindy looked up at the lupine, who looked into Lindy's eyes, desperately searching for something in the girl's impassive and still poker face.

It did not take Vexta long to retreat. "Ok, that's all. Disperse!" she yelled before going back to her office to sulk and think on her next move. One thing was certain. Before anything else, Vexta needed to work out if she should tell anyone what she had been told.

Hanna knew she had been beaten although she could not agree with it yet due mostly to the heat of the moment and her adrenaline high. Genney stepped between the two combatants. "I am going to see Fraya. Are you two coming?"

Lindy was glad for Genney always helping. Even then this reinforced Lindy's desire to get stronger. Lindy was committed to getting to a point where she would always rely on herself and not call in any favors. "You two go," she told the two older children. Genney was about to try to play diplomat some more, but Lindy stopped her by nodding over to the complex glances of the students still around the field. "I still have to clean up here," Lindy explained.

Hanna left with Genney in a huff but before the fiery summoner walked more than three steps she muttered, "Don't die."

"I won't be dead even if I am killed," Lindy whispered back. Hanna and Genney stopped but before they could ask more, Lindy walked over to a small gathering mob of the angrier students. "Ok, so anyone else want to fight me?"

"That's right, you monster!" a girl yelled.

"One at a time then," Lindy smiled. It did not take foresight to see how crazy the combat field would be today, so Hanna hurriedly dragged Genney away.

"We should wait for an instructor," a boy commented with the scrap of rationality he had retained.

Lindy groaned. "You guys are so boring! Come on. I'll even hold back!"

The sole voice of rationality in the mob lost it. "Well, the instructors are always watching. Come on!"

A team of five upperclassman rushed Lindy. "If you gang up on me I will not be nice," Lindy warned. The charging mob grew to eight.

Lindy ducked under a punch. "Well ok then, the hard way it is," she growled. The mob tried to dog-pile her but Lindy dodged to one side and the students dropped on top of one another in a heap. Lindy leapt up and drop-kicked the clump of humanity. A great many bones shattered under her attack. The girl who had first spoken was in the process of aiming ice magic. A few others were aiming magic to attack and/or trap Lindy and some others were moving to heal their friends. "Stop or die," Lindy coldly requested.

"Never! You enslaved our friends!" the girl yelled.

"Idiots," Lindy sighed. A massive blast of power erupted from Lindy, destroying the field and those attacking her. The energy was not magic or a monster's innate attack, but something more. The combat field had turned to powder. Lindy now stood on the brick and steel ceiling of the first basement level. None of her attackers could be seen, as if they had disengaged. Lindy looked around her sadly and sat down waiting for the arrival of the staff.

Haldin and Caldrin arrived soon after. "What happened here?" Caldrin demanded. None of the witnesses could mange to speak, let alone think.

Lindy called up from ground zero. "Self defense."

Caldrin tried to get answers from those who had not tried to attack Lindy yet. Haldin walked over to the new crater and asked, "Where are your attackers then?"

Lindy picked up some of the dust scattered around her. "They are around here somewhere."

"Answer me seriously," Haldin commanded.

Lindy shrugged. "I decayed them." She blew on the dust. "They are mixed in here somewhere, I think." Caldrin and the students around the pit all vomited when they connected the dots.

"Stay there until the administrators decide what to do with you," Haldin gruffly told Lindy. There was no need to elaborate on what the consequences of disobeying that command of her own volition would be.

Lindy was mad but she understood logically that Haldin had every right to do what he was doing. "Fine, but for the record, some spirits willingly help me out. I don't force my will on them." There was a hint of irony in Lindy's solemn expression.

Haldin looked helplessly over to Caldrin. "I'll make sure no one approaches her and that she does not move from there. You go and report to the headmaster." Before Caldrin was even out of the training grounds Lindy had lain down fast asleep in defiance of the cooling air and hard ground.

Hanna along with the doctor was able to keep Genney from racing back to Lindy when the sounds of combat echoed all around the school like a recording of someone scratching a chalkboard being played from a stereo in the Grand Canyon.

When Caldrin arrived at the second tower Wallace Nut, Vexta, and Jeffery Derkin, along with almost all the school's former mid-rank heroes and half the low heroes turned professors and aides, were there. Jeffery was clearly in a much worse mood than normal, which was saying something given his normally foul temper. Caldrin would have found it interesting if said anger was not mainly being directed at her. "Where is your handler?" Jeffery asked coolly.

"Making sure Lindy does not move from the training grounds," Caldrin snapped. She was not in a frame of mind that would allow her to deal with niceties or give ground to bullshit.

"Watch it," Jeffery said.

"Oh, shut up," Vexta groaned. Caldrin would have enjoyed her superiors' fight but she knew some hard questions were coming, so instead she braced herself. Vexta glared over at Caldrin. "Lindy did something more insane, right? What's going on?"

Caldrin took a deep breath which annoyed those around her, who would rather be running around like madmen. "Eight fighters and at least five magic users have been slain during an attempted assault."

"Who started it?" Wallace demanded.

"The older students," Caldrin answered.

"That was after that little demon conjured the dead. The chief artificer was just telling us about it," Jeffery sneered. Wallace's gaze became harder.

One of Vexta's aides announced timidly, "We have the footage from Lindy Shrew's duels."

"Play all of it," Wallace ordered. Scrying and light magic combined to form a recording of Lindy's matches. There were some gasps but none of the professors spoke as the images played.

At the end Caldrin declared, "Trainee Shrew was clearly attacked by an unlawful mob."

"Your pet is a necromancer and killed many of her betters," Jeffery scowled.

"Not all uses of necromancy are illegal," Vexta growled, not happy with either side's argument.

"Caldrin Faywind, how do you expect us to deal with such a powerful being?" Wallace asked.

Caldrin had an epiphany and explained. "At best she is at the level of a powerful low-ranking hero. A few mid-ranks, or you alone headmaster, would be more than enough to subdue her."

"True, but what is she?" Vexta pressed, her fear of being overwhelmed and/or killed horribly by what she did not understand sooner rather than later suppressing her fear of probing the unknown and the dangers that could come with it.

Caldrin looked out a window at the sky. The entire academy seemed to come to a standstill. Then the half-elf sighed. "She says she is a reincarnation that met Death."

Vexta exploded at the explanation. She howled, "She is a priestess of Death?"

The other staff became very pale, to the point where Caldrin wondered if Lindy had cursed them to Death. Jeffery was white as a sheet for a few seconds before his face became deep red. *Please let him explode like a tomato* Caldrin prayed, but her wishes went unrequited. Instead Jeffery raged, "You knew what she was and did not tell us?"

Caldrin spoke before Wallace or anyone else could condemn her with more than their eyes. "Strictly speaking, I am not convinced she is a priestess, even if I fully believed everything she has said."

Wallace rubbed his temples. "Explain," he commanded unhappily.

Caldrin took a brief second to collect her thoughts. "Lindy Shrew is an anomaly. What she says and does far exceed what I can see as reasonable. Her fighting style and irreverent manner do not match what I would expect of a priestess. She is more lethal than nearly all the low-ranking heroes I have seen. All I know for certain is Lindy Shrew is a young human child with amnesia and possibly a personality disorder but as for what she is, well whatever she is, is not something I have ever seen before."

"That's not evidence," Jeffery whined.

Vexta ignored him. "Can we trust her?"

Wallace walked up to Caldrin. "Watch your anomaly closely from now on." Then he looked around. "Even if she is a little girl on a power trip, Lindy Shrew could be a very powerful asset for the kingdom in a few years. No one is to start fights with her during her time as a student. Caldrin Faywind will monitor our new problem child so she does not get out of line."

"Ok, but for tonight, can we start the curfew a little earlier? I don't want to give Lindy a chance to go nuts again," Caldrin asked.

Wallace grumbled. "All right. We need the students to calm down soon anyway. The rest of you, get all the students to their rooms, then find me again. It's going to be a long night."

Caldrin rushed off, not taking the time to care about the many kinds of glances she was getting from her coworkers. The training field was deserted. Only Lindy remained, snoring at the bottom of her crater. "Can you talk?" Caldrin asked in jungle elvish.

Lindy did not seem to notice Caldrin's tenseness. "That is what we are doing. What's the matter?" Lindy used the same dialect and accent Caldrin's mother had used. It was a very unusual variety. Caldrin the half-elf did not know of anyone else alive who spoke like that.

Caldrin knelt down on the lip of the crater. "Are you translating words all the time?"

Lindy opened one eye. Without moving her head she glared coldly to her far right up at Caldrin. Despite that, it seemed Lindy would begin to giggle at any moment. "I don't know what you are talking about."

Caldrin shook her head. "That should not even translate into any kind of elvish!"

Lindy begin to laugh. "One does not simply translate elvish."

After she calmed down, Caldrin spoke up. "Well let's get you to your dorm room."

Lindy leapt to her feet. "Ok, let's go," she said. Caldrin led Lindy back to her room. There were more guards and staff in the halls but none came near them.

When Caldrin knocked on the door Genney opened it. "Hello instructor and Lindy, is that you?" Genney ran over and hugged Lindy. "Are you ok?"

Hanna Zigone peeked out of the room. "This psycho is our new roommate? So who's number four?"

"Fraya. You all know her. Now get some rest," Caldrin said. Only when the girls had gone back to their room did Caldrin leave.

Genney asked Hanna, "Can't we be friends?"

Hanna groaned. "Look, the new kid will outlive all of us."

"And I am a bit crazy," Lindy agreed.

Hanna tried not to laugh but failed. "You are all right. I'll help you with class for a week. After all, you did beat me."

Lindy asked something Manfred Endfield had always wanted to know. "So what is magic and where does it come from?"

"You can use magic," Hanna answered, now slightly on guard. Lindy shrugged and sat on one of the only beds without an iron strongbox installed with a combination lock.

"Well, you are a priestess of Death, so necromancy is well within that concept." Genney nodded, seeming to understand something.

Hanna's eyes now held respect and awe but she was even more cautious now as well. "Is that true?" she stammered.

"I don't think so," Lindy said. She was slightly embarrassed. "But I may be something like that." Hanna was calm for all but a few seconds until Lindy finished her speaking. Genney was confused but very excited. Lindy looked over at the only priestess she knew of. "How is a priestess different from someone else?"

"Have you lived under a rock?" Hanna sneered.

"No, I reincarnated less than a few days ago," Lindy sighed.

Genney nodded in agreement. Hanna could no longer speak and simply fell into her bed. After giving their roommate plenty of time to hide under her noticeably more expensive sheets, Genney sat next to Lindy. "A priestess is the reincarnation of someone who a world spirit has taken a great liking to. We receive words of advice and tasks within our ability to handle. In return, the concepts our patron spirit controls are more readily available to us. As a rule, priestesses are born as they are."

"What about magic?" Lindy asked. Genney looked about to pout. "Tell me about magic and I'll talk to you more about myself," Lindy compromised. Genney was suddenly far happier than Lindy had expected.

"World spirits each govern an aspect of our world. These aspects are commonly called concepts and magic is drawn from those concepts. Ok, your turn." Genney was very impatient but her explanation was still very helpful

"The owner of this body was badly hurt because she could regenerate. The main consciousness right now is in part that of a forty-year-old man from another world. I have talked face-to-face with Death more than once. He is decent if annoying — sort of like myself, I guess. In return for staying alive, I work for him," Lindy explained.

Genney did not know what to say at first but she did feel sad for her friend and began to tear up little. Hanna peeked her head out of her bed. "So you are some overpowered old man?"

"I am mostly Lindy Shrew, even if my only memories from before being burned at the stake are of a man once called Manfred Endfield." Lindy sighed. Genney's love for her friend overpowered all else at that moment. She hugged Lindy tight and began to cry on her friend's behalf. Lindy could only support Genney and not struggle.

Hanna watched all this awkwardly. "So was Manfred Endfield a good man?"

"He was to himself. Most of his memories are vague but I know my words and actions are influenced by how he was and what he knew. In short, can anyone honestly say they are good? Isn't that a label people and societies use? Like in a war, both sides often believe they are right to some degree, so then who is truly right if the evidence can be seen in so many ways?"

Hanna quickly said "Never mind, good night." She then hid within her bed again.

Genney fell asleep soon after, so Lindy let her sleep on her bed while Lindy lay on the floor and was soon fast asleep.

Around the same time, headmaster Nut had just finished reading yet more reports of the Ernadon empire's undercover aggression. "A typhoon of death is coming but somehow I feel less safe here than I ever have on the battlefield," Wallace whispered.

"The new one. Lindy Shrew. Is she so dangerous that getting a legend-rank hero to help you is necessary?" one of the shadows asked.

"That's right. Interact with her. I will need someone of your rank to sort out how to deal with her." Wallace did not know when the still hidden individual had appeared, but he knew he could do nothing to someone that had remained so undetected and simply looked dejectedly at his desk. He did not even know who had been sent, although with its method of entry he could narrow down the possibilities significantly.

5

Arms from Alms

Hanna and Genney woke to the sound of their door echoing. Someone was knocking vigorously. Hanna grudgingly woke up. It was at least two hours before the start of their day. Caldrin was out of breath and wheezed without preamble, "Where is Lindy?"

Hanna took a moment to collect her thoughts, then another two moments to get over Caldrin's fevered manner. Hanna looked back into the gloom-filled room and upon not seeing her target answered sleepily. "You know I don't know." Caldrin paled and then Hanna woke up, now realizing what she had just said. "Oh shit." Hanna summed up the thoughts of everyone in earshot except Genney, who was still deep asleep and giggling like a lunatic on Lindy's bed.

A thin man appeared from behind Caldrin. The man looked over Genney like he was trying to sort out some very unusual event and working out if it was a crime or not. "What happened here last night?"

Hanna might find her roommates insufferable but she would protect their dignity, if only because she was stuck with them for now. "And you are?" Hanna asked.

"This is Evick Gillfoe. He a teacher in training sent to observe our classes. I was told to trust him," Caldrin answered, her words barely not sarcastic.

"He was a hero?" Hanna inquired. The man looked very young. Maybe twenty or so. Far too short a time to have any practical experience as a hero.

The man bowed slightly. "Evick Gillfoe, former master thief. Now possible teacher." Hanna nodded in understanding. Mages, convicted criminals, mercenaries, doctors, and other folk skilled in specialized or nonstandard things were sometimes used to train heroes despite not being heroes themselves. The felons always gave her and the general populace the most trouble to accept, although the mercenaries had more horror stories about them, not that many of those were ever made public knowledge. "So, what happened?" Evick asked again more sternly.

Hanna sighed. "The psycho and the giggling dullard spent a lot of time chatting. It kept me awake."

Evick opened his mouth to ask something when a stone in his breast pocket vibrated. The man's eyes went dull. After a while his senses returned. "She is in the crafting labs. Did Lindy Shrew pick her first class yet?" *That's not a sound sending tone, so is it for telepathy or possession?* Caldrin wondered. All of those were expensive but what she had narrowed it down to were both very hard to get, extremely expensive, and highly restricted at that moment. Caldrin knew *This man is no mere teacher or thief.*

Instructor Faywind shook her head. "Not as far as I know. She should not have had any time to do that yet. We have not even told her how classes work."

"This is going to be a long day," Evick grumbled.

"You have no idea," Hanna and Caldrin agreed in unison.

Caldrin followed Evick to floor four. Vexta (who Lindy thought of as a big-shot werewolf in clothes) met Caldrin and the academy's other sudden transfer. "He's the new guy?" Vexta asked.

"I am. So the problem child is here?" Evick asked.

"She is. Don't distract her," Vexta firmly commanded. She suddenly seemed more protective of Lindy than before.

"What happened?" Evick asked.

"I have a title, boy. It's chairwoman, don't forget," Vexta scoffed. Evick glanced at Caldrin. "Instructor Faywind has the most seniority among any of this facility's staff. So be polite to her." The lupine glowered. Only after seeing that her warning had been processed, she moved aside.

Caldrin led Evick and Vexta past pens overcrowded with goblins, elemental foxes, and a few large toads. All the creatures showed signs of experimentation. The bigger things were kept elsewhere. In one small workshop sat Lindy all alone and practically buried under a mound of metal bits; a few old crossbows lay disabled all around her. "Did you explain to her how classes work?" Caldrin asked long after she had given up guessing what Lindy was trying to do.

Vexta held up a slip of paper. It was a contract that Lindy had signed that stated that until Vexta or the heads of the school chose otherwise, Lindy would be working in the workshop and be instructed in tinkering through weapon making.

"Can she do it?" Caldrin whispered, sounding to all but herself like an overprotective aunt.

"I have no idea what she has in mind but that child has a plan. She has a few theoretical outlines and a lot of ambition but not the skills to make what she wants," Vexta murmured.

"And what does she want?" Evick asked.

"Silence," Lindy called over. She was lugging over a few pieces of wood and steel to a carving station.

"I'll keep the school updated on her progress," Vexta told the other two staff members before shooing them away.

A few days later and Lindy had not come back to her room. Genney stopped by only to find Lindy knee deep in many differently shaped bits of scrap metal. Instead of talking with her friend or dragging Lindy out, Genney began to bring Lindy's meals down to her. Two weeks into this, after more than a few total redesigns, Lindy presented Vexta with a very odd crossbow. The weapon had a detachable block of wood held near the trigger that held ten bolts. It had a grip near the front. The top was closed off. It had a handle on one side and the crossbow arms were set backwards. The weapon allowed ten or eleven shots to be fired, only needing the side handle to be pulled back to load a bolt from the block of wood. Lindy planned on trying to make a smaller version of the weapon. Vexta rushed off to show the headmaster Lindy's invention.

You know that weapon will take innumerable lives, Conduit informed Lindy.

Lives aren't numbers. At least not those that care for them. Lindy retorted back though their shared mental connection.

Don't tell me you are planning to make even more dangerous stuff, Conduit demanded.

I still have three things I want to build but I am not sharing them, Lindy listlessly huffed.

Ok, that should be fine, otherwise I'd force you to make some defenses. We can't have everyone die off at once, after all. Conduit agreed.

"True, no point in putting us out of a job or giving someone else an advantage over us." Lindy laughed out loud.

"Us?" Fraya asked from the doorway.

Lindy waved over to her friend. "Hey, I did not see you there, buddy."

Fraya squinted, then sighed. She was covered in bandages and walked with a small staff. It would still be around another month before she was back to full strength. "So Hanna misses you."

Lindy kept tinkering but found time to chuckle. "Not that she would tell me that. Thanks for passing that along."

"No problem. Can I watch?" Fraya asked. In response, Lindy picked up a thickly upholstered oil-stained chair with one hand, dumped the loose parts on it into an overflowing crate, and then went right back to her work.

Half an hour later Fraya inquired nervously, "So why are you staying here?"

"Because I heard putting in a lot of effort will help gain skills. Also, I need to finish a few weapons before going outside again," Lindy replied quietly with not even a third of her being paying attention anymore.

Another week passed. Lindy was still holed up in the workshop. An order had come down from the headmaster not to disturb her. Lindy's further improvements made the crossbow arms and new iron wire string encased in a box, adding half an inch between the ammo magazine and the arms, and making the loading system more substantial. The improved crossbow was dubbed the Storm Bow Mark 2. Lindy was forced to make a few more copies for the kingdom's tinkerers and weapon shops to examine, who viewed the storm bow with awe. Lindy's work was low quality but the design philosophies were seen as both completely insane and very innovative. In short, Lindy was now accepted as a genius. The headmaster had chosen to allow Lindy to use an entire workshop room for her own use, both to appease the kingdom's war industry that wanted to see what else Lindy would build, and to keep a terrifying psychopath locked up voluntarily. Lindy had even taken to using the cleaning systems in the monster dissection chambers to shower.

A few days before a month had passed Caldrin visited Lindy's workshop, which now had a sign bolted on the door that said in twelve different languages *Making stuff go away.* When the half-elf opened the door she saw Lindy ripping apart a miniaturized crossbow. A sheet of steel with some light scratches stuck in a heap of small crossbow bolts told a story Caldrin had no patience for at that moment. "I have been watched closely all the time. Was that your doing?" Lindy asked without tearing her gaze away from the gutted crossbow.

"You smell like blood," Caldrin noted.

"The bathing systems in this world will take some more getting used to." Lindy shrugged, picking up a few tools as she did.

"How was your last world different?" Caldrin asked, choosing to lean on one of the few uncluttered walls, which was around a grimy mat Lindy had been using to take naps.

"No magic, more death, less danger," Lindy replied. Before Caldrin could fully commit to delving into that philosophical quagmire, Lindy looked up and tossed five small cylinders to Caldrin. "I am going to need one of those charged with ice magic, three with wind, and one with fire."

Caldrin looked at the cylinders, noting power sealing stones and power amplifying stones within. Only deranged beings with a death wish would have such things next to one another. The stones were stable individually but together they had a reputation for being extremely volatile. "Ok fine, but what are you trying to accomplish?" The headmaster had told his staff to accommodate any request Lindy had when it came to making weapons. The more level-headed staff members fervently prayed that the freedom they had given a twelve-year-old enigma would not destroy them.

"I need a better power source for my three main projects," Lindy sighed.

"What do you gain?" Caldrin asked, fully aware the being before her was far more than she appeared or had let on.

"Influence, safety, and an armory of the best weapons around that only I will be able to use." Lindy's gaze was resolute and cold, her smirk chilling as if she had been sculpted out of the coldest ice.

"Influence and safety do not always go hand in hand," Caldrin cautioned. She then turned to leave.

"That's why I need to be feared and heavily armed with weapons of unknown workings and great power," Lindy whispered after the half-elf.

Caldrin shivered in fear but was glad Lindy let some of her presumably true self show at last. Before the door was opened Caldrin had to ask, "Why are you so open with me about yourself?"

Lindy had a plate of half-stale pastries in her hand. "Because having you help makes my plans simpler to accomplish. Plans that would take more time to finish and avenge if betrayed. If I had to do these alone, organizing the time tables would be way harder." Then Lindy began to snack on Genney's cooking. Caldrin was thankful Lindy had been so open (probably) and left to work on the task Lindy had given her.

For the next two and a half months Lindy cut herself off from the outside world. Finally, the lack of new data from spies, pleading, and observations forced the school administration's hand. Genney was on the way to drop off Lindy's food when Caldrin busted down Lindy's workshop door. Evick hid in the shadows spying. So far all the most-skilled spy in the kingdom could fathom was that he had no idea what she was building. The worst part was that no one Evick consulted with could work it out either. Lindy looked up from a workbench on which rested only three very odd devices.

Lindy had gotten a bit stronger over the nearly four mouths she had been in hiding.

Lindy Shrew

Female human age 13

Affiliation: hero!?

Embodiments: banished from death, living natural disaster

Job: hero to be

Status. common sense bane: extreme

Abilities: strength 383, vitality 501, mind 325, agility 462

Talents: translation: all. full power strike: strength. danger sense, innate map, skill retention: Manfred Endfield, photographic memory, sixth sense: intuition, toughness, favored environment: darkness, cold resistance: high, enhanced trait: willpower, analysis: extreme, good hair, quick learner. fearless, poison resistance: mild, life sense, aura: weakening, damage shield: decay

Mutation: troll blood (extra burnable, swift regeneration)

Curse: catastrophic encounters, heavily sleeper, light sensitively: mild

> Skills: sword: journeyman, dagger: master, unarmed: master, marksmanship: master, throwing: expert, athletics: expert, armor proficiency (leather/ cloth): adept, literacy: journeyman, history (other world): journeyman, intimidate (innate): adept, diplomacy: apprentice, awareness: expert, necromancy: beginner, tinkering: journeyman, magic tampering: beginner, counter spell: beginner

"It's a bit late for a birthday party," Lindy smirked. Somehow, she already seemed in full control of what was happening.

Caldrin looked around at the fully cleaned up room. Not a speck of junk was to be found. More importantly, no plans, dioramas, or any other documents were around either. It was clear Lindy knew what was going on and had totally prepared in advance. Caldrin managed to barely squeak out a scathing half compliment. "You are terrifying."

Lindy giggled sweetly but her smirk was even cleaner and sharper in her eyes. "There are far worse things than me in this world."

Caldrin had to do a double take; she could not agree with Lindy's self-assessment. "Like what?" the half-elf asked, hoping for an answer that would make Lindy seem less of a threat.

"No idea," Lindy shrugged before beginning to cackle.

Evick could no longer handle the strange turn of events. His frustration and fear caused him to break concealment and rush forward. Before he had fully taken his fifth step across the hallway to Lindy's door, the very same girl he was supposed to spy on and evaluate was before him. One small one-handed crossbow-like device without the arms or wires and with a magazine was in each of Lindy's hands. The one in her left was lighter and had less metal in its frame than the one in her right. Before Evick could say anything, he was hit twenty times in the chest. The left-handed weapon shot small darts at very high speed with wind magic and could hold ten darts at a time. The one in Lindy's right fired iron cylinders with a rounded front and a deep depression in the back. With a mix of ice and fire magic colliding, it could hold twenty such rounds. Evick was lucky Lindy chose to hold back, as the right-handed weapon was far more deadly and loud. Evick slumped down in a widening pool of his own blood. Lindy leaned in close to him and slowly mouthed the words *All things in time, lap dog*. Her right-handed weapon inches from Evick's jaw, the ambient heat alone was enough to feel like it was cooking him. A good five seconds after the attack had begun, Lindy's face became more childish. "Oh, you surprised me, sir. Let's get you some help."

A week later, Lindy, Hanna, Fraya, Genney, and Caldrin were in a cart heading to do some training in a trade city near the Ernadon empire. To everyone's surprise (although maybe not Lindy's), at Evick's insistence, Lindy got away with a light reprimand and was allowed to field test her new weapons. This was the assignment she and her room-mates had been handed. Lindy was being barred from the workshop until she could provide a full field report on her three new weapons and complete plans for making them.

Lindy's first prototype weapon was named the Lindy Special Version 1 pistol. The Long Barrel Express looked like a long iron tube stuck to a crossbow's stock with part of the top of the tube being able to slide back and forth. It fired small javelins with wind magic at farther range and with greater power and accuracy than other weapons. The Storm Hush was a one-handed crossbow that fired in complete silence. Lindy had performed a demonstration of the weapons for the headmaster and a few high-ranking engineers and their ace builders from the capital, only to then point out the weapons' flaws while the crowd was still dumb-founded by their terrifying and innovative power. Lindy pointed out how heavy the Lindy Special and Long Barrel Express were, as well as how volatile the compressed magic was, noting in particular how many specialized skills were needed to handle the weapons effectively, and the cost and complexity of large-scale manufacture, mainly in regards to the automatic reloading mechanisms and magic power sources. Lindy was then ordered to work out how to fix as many of those issues as she could while a few of the capital's best workshops poured all their staff into trying to work out how the weapons were made, let alone how to build a system to make more of them. That work's pace was effectively at a standstill without Lindy leading them by the nose.

Hanna was still slightly angry about being dragged along with Lindy but chose to make the best of it without letting on to anyone (including herself) that she was as upset as she appeared. "So how do you explain those things being your first real products?" Hanna asked, jamming her finger over at the bundle containing Lindy's pile of weapons. The fiery summoner's current frustration was aimed not as much at Lindy as she would have the rest believe, but at the shaking of their cart.

Lindy smugly replied. "I knew the theories behind these but did not have the skills to make them. So I had to practice before I gained enough experience creating these for it to look easy."

"Guys, get along please!" Fraya wailed hopelessly.

Fraya Fields
Female human age 15
Affiliation: Derndell kingdom hero academy 3rd branch
Job: hero in training
Status: scout
Abilities: strength 95, vitality 170. mind 83, agility 213
Talents: danger sense, sixth sense: attention, muted presence, selective forgettability, trackless, flurry of blows, wind walk, master parry, language (common Derndell/sprite/ranger sign)
Skills: counter strike: adept, dual wield: journeyman, sword: adept, athletics: adept, tracking: adept, stealth: journeyman, dagger: apprentice, bow: apprentice, herbalism: beginner, pick lock: beginner

That night the cart rested on one side of the road. Lindy was lying down on top of the cart looking up at the clear night sky. The rest of her companions and the driver were resting in the cart after eating preserved food and forgoing starting a fire. Hanna popped her head out of the heavy tarp draped around the cargo area and looked up. "Are you taking first watch?"

"I can keep watch all night," Lindy answered listlessly.

"You don't sound like it," Hanna retorted.

"Nothing dangerous to us and alive is close by right now. In fact, most living things are staying away from us. Seems like they are spooked," Lindy answered.

"I can't imagine why. It's not like any of us could intimidate a king-dom if we put some effort into it," Hanna retorted.

"True," Lindy laughed.

"You are dumb," Hanna grumbled.

"No, you are. Thinking I'd need to put in any effort," Lindy huffed.

"Well, I'll take first watch with you," Hanna groaned, rushing to pick up some jerky and a few blankets.

"Don't trust me?" Lindy asked mildly.

Hanna rushed out, tossed a small mound of blankets up to the top of the carriage, then tried to clamber up. Around half way up she slipped but Lindy swiftly leaned over and pulled Hanna up top. "I am too angry to sleep now," Hanna muttered.

"Don't get cocky," was all Caldrin managed to say before going back to sleep. She had been keeping watch all day, which was not something Caldrin had done that much in a long time, even by elf standards. It took all her concentration and their horses' natural inclination to give those with strong elvish blood some slack.

"Hey, so why do you still wear those rags?" Hanna asked, noting Lindy's unchanged wardrobe.

"No cash," Lindy sighed. Then she tensed up and Hanna was on guard after seeing Lindy's expression.

Soon after, Lindy was sure their chaperone was asleep, and fell into a deep slumber herself. "This one is such a pain," Hanna sighed, not noticing the small smile that had appeared on her face when she was certain Lindy was asleep.

Hours passed and Hanna nodded off a few times. Lindy bolted upright and gently hit the cart's roof, causing it to creak. "Look alive or play dead. Hostiles incoming. One is very strong." Then she leapt down. Four men walked seemingly out of nowhere.

"Who are you?" one of the well armed and rough looking men asked.

"It is polite to introduce yourself first," Lindy sneered.

Undaunted, the men drew closer. "I asked you the question, brat."

Caldrin hopped out of the carriage. "We are from the Derndell kingdom hero academy 3rd branch," she answered immediately.

"Is that so, Devil of the Tundra?" the man in the lead sneered. "Why don't you..." he began to add before Lindy cut him off.

"This one is one of that fool Jeffers's cohorts." Lindy groaned, glaring at all those around her.

Sam Graywind

Human male age 33

Affiliation: Ernadon empire 1st heroes branch, Iron mound syndicate (slavers, monster hunters, smugglers)

Job: mid-rank hero

Status: commando of the Ernadon Empire

Abilities: strength 600, vitality 220, mind 110, agility 373

Talents: language common (common Derndell/ common Ernadon / high Ernadon), fearlessness, poison immunity, mind reading: immunity, residence pain: high, analysis defense: moderate. fearlessness, boast spell, iron bones

Skills: fire magic: master, earth magic: expert, axe: master, leather/ chain armor: expert. riding: journeyman, pick lock: journeyman, tracking: expert, intimidate: expert, trap finding: expert

The men encircled Lindy and Caldrin. "It's like I am surrounded by idiots," Lindy sighed. One of the men tried to cast a binding spell on Caldrin but Lindy's hands glowed briefly, redirecting the spell's targets. Then roots twisted from the ground, only to ensnare the four men before they could complain to their suddenly worn-out main spell caster. All the men but Sam decayed to mush on the spot.

Sam ground his teeth and easily busted free from the bindings. Before anyone could move he had swiped Lindy off her feet, his axe at her neck. "You know I am almost a high-ranked hero," Sam muttered darkly.

"Your axe or monologuing will kill me soon. Do your worst." Lindy laughed.

"Nut case," Sam said coldly as he raised his axe and brought it back down. Before it could hit Lindy the axe shattered. Small lines of rust spread across the blade. The next thing Sam realized, his legs felt a bit weak and his arms numb. He stopped to wonder what was wrong with him, fully confident no one around him was a threat. The half-elf nicknamed Devil of the Tundra could only cause Sam's now-dead low-ranked hero some trouble if it and Lindy worked as a team. In his superiority complex, he believed his mage must have had something to do with the men's deaths. Which was why when the shards of his axe suddenly appeared jabbed all around his neck, Sam reacted far too slowly. Then a strange club-like device was pressed to his heart and the plains around them echoed with gunfire. Sam fell, his heart no more and his head held lazily by a small visibly angry girl who spat on his still-warm corpse.

"You're the nut case. Going after my friends. Only I get to cause them trouble!" Lindy looked at a spot a few feet from Sam's corpse at a hazy outline only she could see. "Still, that was some death wish. Have fun in hell. Just don't try to get drunk." Then the hazy specter dispersed to meet with the head bonehead.

"That seems a bit twisted," Fraya muttered shyly.

"Well, that's just how I am," Lindy said, puffing out her chest. Unamused glances were the only responses she got.

"So, what now?" Hanna asked coolly after a short but very awkward silence.

"How about we leave now?" the coachman asked, the danger of driving at night far less of a concern than the terror Lindy and the attackers had inspired.

"Well ok. If you can manage that," Caldrin agreed. The coachman rushed off to the cart, moving with more than professional haste. Lindy looked over the only remaining corpse of their attackers. After rescuing his coin purse she reduced his body to a few specks of dust.

"Why did you do that?" Hanna demanded.

Lindy sighed. "Because lugging around a corpse, especially of someone so important, would draw a lot of attention."

"Ok, but you could reanimate him," Hanna pressed.

I could, but only if it helped us fulfill your real job, Conduit whispered in Lindy's head.

"Nope." Lindy shook her head.

"But you did it before!" Hanna pressed.

Lindy suddenly hugged Hanna and whispered into her ear. "Was borrowed power. If it does not help Death then I can't borrow power," Lindy whispered.

Hanna pushed Lindy away. Her cheeks were a little red. "Why did you do that!" Hanna sputtered. Lindy shrugged and got into the cart. Hanna's head cleared up a little and she shouted, "Wait, does that mean that I lost to more than you?"

"Nope. I used something I don't plan to use often," Lindy replied. Lindy was deeply asleep before Hanna got into the cart.

Lindy was asleep for a few hours. The more time passed, the less comfortable she felt. Lindy's eyes opened suddenly but it was Conduit in control. *Something came up — we have to stop it* Conduit informed Lindy through their link. Lindy followed Genney's gaze. She was peering out at a glowing pillar of ghostly light shooting out from the summit of a hill. High city walls loomed on the horizon farther still. "You can see it?" Conduit spoke.

Genney looked back. "I feel like destiny is being twisted."

"So, you can sense the side effect. He found some interesting ones very early," Conduit replied.

"What?" Genney asked. Conduit made to jump from the coach. Genney griped Lindy's arm. "Who are you?" she asked.

Conduit easily twisted out of the panicked hold. "Ask this nutcase when she is in control again," Conduit grudgingly replied, then she flung Lindy's body out of the cart. The body's full might was put to good use, vaulting up the hill like some kind of human-sized jumping insect.

Fifteen steps were enough to vault across the plains and up the mini-mountain. The pillar of energy continued to expand. "What is that?" Lindy asked.

Conduit replied, "Unauthorized magic. Someone is trying to over-ride Death's authority." To an outside observer Lindy would look like a super powered little girl talking to herself.

"Ok, let's kill them," Lindy agreed.

Conduit crept up to a high stone wall that encompassed a small citadel from where the offending power was coming. "You aren't going to ask more?" she whispered.

"You aren't going to be a total psychopath and charge in like a mad-woman?" Lindy quietly snickered.

Conduit sighed and scaled the wall. *Let me be in control for this one,* she requested mentally.

After this I'll be back, Lindy agreed in the same way.

Men in robes with halberds roamed ground level in teams of three. Teams of two with crossbows kept watch from the ramparts. Conduit fearlessly tracked the guards, slipping by each team as she ran along the ramparts to a small walkway that led to a glass-domed citadel. Lindy's body neared the citadel. Conduit sneered *Zombie dogs, and a lot of necromancers will be our foes.* Conduit paused and thought, *Their boss is mine alone.*

Why? Lindy began before Conduit threw their body into the building via the glass ceiling.

An ornate glass-filled room full of glowing arcane dioramas, zombie dogs, and robed magic users was filled with an intense bloodlust that sapped their might. "Who goes there?" one mage yelled before all the minions erupted into fine sand.

Only Lindy, still piloted by Conduit, and a youngish necromancer in very orate robes were left. Even the magic runes had evaporated. "That is a poor choice. You just killed a lot of nobles," the necromancer boss grumbled angrily.

"Is that any way to greet a relative?" Conduit sneered.

"What?" the man asked.

WHAT? Lindy shouted in her mind.

Conduit pointed Lindy's Storm Hush Type 1 at the man. One of the old ornate magic daggers was kept loosely in her other hand. "You left me to die, bro."

The necromancer looked closer, squinting his eyes. "You are not Lindy."

"That's right. We are so much more than this body once was." Conduit smiled before finally breaking the last of the magic supporting the ritual.

The necromancer looked closer. "I see. But how are you here now?"

"Death gave us a deal to die for," Conduit sighed.

"That's your best joke?" Lindy yelled, finally finding her voice.

"Shut up," Conduit coughed. The necromancer raised an eyebrow. "Our village was burned down, by the way."

"Dragon?" the young man asked.

"Dragon," Conduit agreed. "So big bro, why did you and grandma leave me?"

"Power, power that you don't have," the young man sighed.

Conduit rolled her eyes and summoned a fog of dead souls from the necromancers she had killed. "Oh really? Looks like I have to be the hero."

"You a hero?" the man asked dubiously.

"Yes Ajax, a hero," Conduit grumbled.

The souls began to swirl, kicking up the shards from the dome in the phantom wind. The two siblings looked up. The ceiling was being broken apart even more, and glass rained down.

Ajax Shrew shielded himself with his clock. Lindy simply dissolved any glass that got near her, as if such an action was an afterthought. Ajax looked at the heavy mass of souls behind Lindy. "You want to join us and live forever?"

"As long as I work hard, I will live for as long as I want." Conduit smiled then fired a storm of crossbow bolts and exploding souls at Ajax. "Right now that means stopping and preferably killing you."

Ajax managed to summon a shield of ice that creaked, so Ajax had to endlessly reinforce it to keep himself protected. "What changed, sister?"

"I died before our neighbors even started to burn me at the stake." Conduit grinned evilly.

"You sound like a man." Ajax sighed, picking on the masculine-specific wording that Lindy's auto-translation used in that moment. A hole appeared in the space behind Ajax to swallow him up.

"You have no idea," Conduit shrugged. "Tell Grandma I will need to hunt her down, too."

"I'll be back for you," Ajax replied before disappearing.

"Pervert. Using all your power on a ritual and leaving none to protect yourself." Conduit shook her head. "Ok, number one, you have control."

Lindy's gaze refocused as Conduit shifted back inside her head. "I sense a story and much repressed anger behind this."

Conduit hissed back within their shared mind *Shut up.* For once the retort lacked any strength or bravado.

I'll clean out the grounds, buddy. Lindy mentally shrugged, knowing it was best to give her other self some space in their mind.

Lindy was back in control. She could hear the guards outside running around frantically. Upon punching one of the pillars, not even a dent was made. She then tried to disengage it, which only marred the pillar slightly. Ten halberd-wielding men burst into the room. "Who are you?" one of the men yelled. They seemed focused on Lindy and had not looked over the room yet.

Lindy felt nothing but curiosity that the pillars were strong enough to not be disintegrated, much like some of the stronger heroes she had run into. She gave the pillar all but a sliver of her attention. The guards' movements were the only thing besides the building she saw at that moment. Lindy blasted the pillar with much more focused disintegration, and it creaked slightly. She pointed her hand at the guards who had only now looked around the room and were moving to apprehend Lindy upon finding no other signs of life. All but one of the guards disappeared as if they had never existed. "Now what makes you so tough?" Lindy mused out loud absentmindedly to no one in particular.

"What?" the tall guard asked.

Lindy glanced over at the tall man, annoyed. "I was talking about this pillar." She shrugged and in the blink of an eye she was next to him, glaring up. "Well, mostly."

The man tried to leap back only to find Lindy had moved behind him. "What are you?" the man yelled, slashing widely with his halberd in a half circle. Another team of halberdiers and a few crossbowmen rushed in behind Lindy. "Quick, help me!" the tall man yelled. Lindy sighed and snapped his halberd in half before lightly jumping off the ground and kicking him into the onrushing reinforcements.

She looked at a few random cultists as they picked themselves up warily.

Davey Longfellow
Human male age 27
Affiliation: Ernadon empire eastern 2nd army, cult of the
    eternal wish
Job: man at arms
Status: Ernadon empire minor noble (2nd son of a lord)

Abilities: strength 40, vitality 35, mind 29, agility 16

Talents: language (common Derndell, common Ernadon / high Ernadon), menace, coordinate strike, good hearing, resistance acid/poison moderate.

Skills: sword: novice, armor proficiency (plate/ chain/ leather): adept athletics: journeyman. polearm: journeyman, cheat: adapt, intimidate (authority): journeyman, alchemy: expert, herbalist: journeyman, gamble: adapt, earth magic: beginner

Trayvar of Gelvo

Human male age 35

Affiliation: Derndell kingdom mercenarily guild branch, cult of the eternal wish

Job: sniper

Status: cult hireling

Abilities: strength 37, vitality 42, mind 17, agility 52

Talents: language common (common Derndell, unified explorer society code). danger sense. snap shot, rapid reload, pin shadow, trick shot, feign death, mimic voice

Skills: crossbow: expert, athletics: journeyman, acrobatics: journeyman. stealth: master, armor proficiency (leather): expert, gamble: beginner. fletching: adept, skinning: journeyman, dagger: adapt, throwing: journeyman, first aid: apprentice, poison: adapt

Lindy focused her power and disintegrated all but three men. Trayvar of Gelvo had avoided her strike. The tall man was still standing but was now missing an arm, and one of the other bowmen was more or less fine after eating Lindy's strike head on. "Now aren't you three interesting."

Lindy analyzed the tall man.

> **Mackliss Grin**
> Human male age 37
> Abilities: strength 93, vitality 132, mind 63, agility 42
> Affiliation: Derndell kingdom mercenarily guild branch, cult of the eternal wish
> Job: mercenary captain
> Status: cult strong man, leader of the crimson claws
> Talents: language common (common Derndell, eternal wish cant, unified explorer society code), goad, alcohol tolerance: high, expert parry, resist fear: moderate, cool mind, rapid strike
> Wound: missing two arms
> Skills: pole arm: master. armor proficiency (plate/ chain/ leather): expert, athletics: expert, smithing. beginner, tactics: expert, leadership: expert, diplomacy: adapt, intimidate (basic): adapt, law: beginner, first aid: beginner

Then the unscathed crossbowman.

> **Hazel of Leoniss**
> Human female age 28
> Aliases: Byron Smith an age 33 male human
> Affiliation: Ernadon empire eastern 2nd army, cult of the eternal wish
> Job: assassin
> Status: cult hireling
> Concealed status: presumed dead lesser Nobel (duchess) of the Ernadon empire
> Abilities: strength 165, vitality 252, mind 97, agility 347

Talents: language (common Derndell, unified explorer society code common ernadon/ high ernadon). fake status: moderate, analyses Resilience: high, snap shot, shadow step

Skills: crossbow: master, poison: expert, herbalism: adept

WARNING: 12 entries unreadable

Lindy began to laugh. The assassin fired five bolts in the span of a second. Lindy disintegrated three of the five before the power behind that reaction petered out. Lindy continued to cackle as she dove behind a pillar. "Very nice, much better. Now try harder to take me down," she howled, overcome with an adrenaline high and desire to test herself that only rarely had come over Manfred Endfield, but never at the same time before.

"Where are the casters!" Trayvar yelled. He was not yet in a full panic but was getting there.

"We need to beat that answer out of the kid," Mackliss cursed, grabbing a tall candle holder in his one arm. Lindy was very intrigued. After all, the captain should not have any arms left.

"She is too dangerous. Kill her," the assassin muttered before appearing next to Lindy with a dagger pressed inches from her face. Lindy struck the woman's stomach with a fully empowered palm strike. The assassin was sent flying at the far wall but reappeared next to her two comrades before she hit it.

"Are you ok?" Trayvar asked, now showing signs of panic.

The assassin spit a large blob of blood to the ground. "I am fine. Even someone like me can handle her strikes. We need to hold out until the casters teleport back. Someone this weak could not have done anything to the troops under Master Shrew's protection."

Lindy peered out from the pillar and caught the ten bolts fired at her. "You are quite good, former Duchess Hazel of Leoniss. Those two men are far weaker than you are."

"Who?" Mackliss asked. The other two did not seem to understand, either. So Lindy tossed the ten bolts in her hand across the room into Trayvar's chest. He died instantly.

"Not him. So how are you not disarmed yet, captain?" Lindy smiled

"My weapon is right here!" Mackliss shouted raising the candle stand. Lindy batted aside the next eight bolts. She leapt at Hazel and kicked the assassin into a wall. A second later she tore off Mackliss's arm.

The captain's arm was metallic and twitching. Lindy crushed it into a thin needle-like object, then impaled Mackliss through his heart and back. "Too bad, it was a nice arm," Lindy sighed.

"You monster!" Hazel shouted, prying herself from the wall.

Lindy tossed up her arms and complained. "Honestly, do any of my brother's underlings have a sense of humor?"

Hazel froze. "Brother?"

Lindy kept her insane grin. "See, this is what that dipshit Ajax gets for running from his sister and letting her die. What a dumb ass!" She paused. "You ever have the men in your family let things get real bad Hazel, or do you prefer Mr. Smith? It's just us now."

Hazel coughed up more blood. "I don't care what you say. Master Shrew is a just man."

"Fine. Not like what you think matters to me," Lindy muttered. Then she broke both of Hazel's arms and smashed the woman down into the ground by her head. "Any last words or anything to confess?"

"Could you tell Master Shrew I am sorry?" Hazel asked.

"Nope. Please let Death know to expect my fool brother. You can tell that bonehead that Lindy Shrew sent you. Oh, and ask Death if there are any good fantasy roleplaying games you can challenge him to. It might make you question your existence," Lindy mildly replied.

Lindy began to crush Hazel's head but then the woman panicked and asked, "Wait, who do you work for?"

Lindy put her face close to Hazel's. "The bonehead you will be seeing soon." Hazel's eyes began to widen but before she could say anything else her eyes and the rest of her head splattered all around her.

Just then Genney ran into the room. "Are you, you now?" Genney grabbed Lindy's shoulder and began to shake her.

"We saw some of the city guard rushing here. Let's go." Hanna grumbled.

"What did you do?" Fraya squeaked upon entering the room.

"Family squabble," Lindy explained as if it happened to someone else.

"You are insane. No way we can cover this up." Caldrin almost sobbed.

"I really wanted to go shopping for clothes soon!" Lindy pouted.

Caldrin held her head in her palm. "No, we wait here and try to explain ourselves."

"Yeah, Conduit is not going to be up for answering anything tonight," Lindy complained.

"That's why you changed?" Genney asked, looking over Lindy and starting to wipe off her friend's face with a towel.

"Yes, but this should not happen too often. It was close to a breach of contract," Lindy answered.

"I am afraid to ask, but what are you going to tell the city guard?" Caldrin asked.

Lindy cocked her head to one side, causing the towel to make a large bloody smudge on her cheek. "Death made me do it?" she answered with a wordless groan.

After Lindy's face was clean, the five young women walked down the hill. Caldrin, Lindy, and Freya could tell they had been spotted by a squadron of city guards on horseback. Soon after they were surrounded. "Identify yourselves!" the youngest man in the squadron yelled. Interestingly, his armor was the most well made.

Oh, he's one of them, Conduit grimaced.

One of what? Lindy mentally deadpanned back.

Someone that had found serendipitous natural ways to extend their life. It's a loophole so not something we need to kill him for, Conduit replied.

But I can kill him? Lindy asked, intrigued.

Well you are allowed to, but any other life extension we are required to eliminate on the spot. Just remember the lucky natural ones are all tricky bastards. Conduit sighed.

It took seconds for Lindy and Conduit to finish their chat. By then Caldrin had begun to respond to the guards. "Derndell kingdom hero academy 3rd branch. I am instructor Faywind. I am leading these four students on a field trip."

The man scrutinized the strangers. "What did you make of the light pillar from before?"

Genney spoke up, her nervous voice louder than needed. "Very bad. It destabilized all the life energy around here."

"Ok. So little lady, why do you stink of blood?" the young-looking man asked, inching his mount closer to Genney.

Lindy stepped in front of her friend. "Because I had a private chat with the cultists performing a very large ritual."

The young man looked over Lindy. In a disbelieving voice he asked, "You captured them all?"

"With a hundred well-armed men I could not hold back. One fled, the rest are dead by my hand." Lindy smiled.

The young man shook his head. "You can't cover for your friends. I will need to arrest you all." Hanna glared at Lindy while Caldrin relaxed, seeming to have expected this.

"Ok, so who are you, old man?" Lindy asked the talkative spokesman. Fraya and Genney looked at the leading guard's young visage, confused.

"I am not that old," the man asked.

"Says the thing that extended his life at least once. Good thing you found the loophole in Death's ban." Lindy grinned.

"What do you mean?" the man asked.

"Death is also my boss. Which is why I had to clean up that cult and could not get my classmates or instructor involved," Lindy said in a low voice sprinkled with conviction.

"So you say. But I still need to verify all of this," the talkative guard said.

"Whatever." Lindy shrugged. With a slight gesture half the guards including their spokesman led Lindy and company down the hill to the city. The other half went up to Lindy's latest killing ground.

"Should we disarm them, Lieutenant Quell?" one of the guards asked the young spokesman.

Lieutenant Quell looked back at Lindy, searching her eyes for something. Finding he was unable to read her, he looked back. "Not unless we can prove major wrongdoing. They are heroes, if nothing else. That much I can believe."

Hanna whispered in Lindy's ear. "Wasn't you being a priestess of Death a secret?"

Lindy whispered back without turning her head. "Yes, but it was going to be exposed at some point. Besides, that fact could help us now."

Genney nodded. "Well, recognizing you as a priestess is something any other true priestess could do very easily."

Lindy looked over at Genney. "Why?"

"Because your connection to the world spirit of Death is extremely dense and that power is still growing. Priestesses are familiar with being connected to a world spirit but your connection is constant and overwhelming for anyone not used to it," Genney explained.

By now, Quell and his team did not even hide that they were listening in. "So only another priestess like you could sense that. Which is why our new bodyguards are so useless." Lindy nodded. One of the guards nearly fell off his horse.

Caldrin grumbled. "Lindy Shrew, be more polite to our captors."

Lindy tried her best naïve and innocent impression which she totally failed at, making her appear even less sincere. "But calling them captors seems too malicious." Caldrin could only roll her eyes, while Hanna and Genney stiffened their smiles and Fraya broke out in a cold sweat.

The guards kept the four women surrounded through the thinly wooded mini-mountain and to the tall stone walls of a city at rest. One of the three men at the gate rushed over to Quell. "Sir, the governor requests your presence."

"I'll be with him soon," Quell said offhandedly.

Lindy asked sweetly, "But won't he be pissed if you blow him off like that?"

Quell led the women through the gates. "He will not know I am back."

"Because clearly he is only important enough to leave a message at an overworked guard post." Lindy shrugged.

Quell stopped his horse and turned around to look at Lindy. "How old are you really?"

"This body is thirteen. I have lived through another lifetime that I know of." Lindy yawned.

"I know what I am doing," Quell sneered decisively.

Lindy smirked. "Then let's hope nothing too unexpected happens." After that she allowed herself to be shoved into a wide cell in the basement of a guard post. Hanna and the others followed Lindy in with decent manners.

Lindy was soon asleep, leaning against a stone wall away from the grate-like window that allowed a poor view of the road above.

Lindy soon found herself face to skull with Death in a dark realm. "You still bored out of your cranium?"

"No. What are you playing at with that guardsman?" Death demanded.

"Hoping he will do something dumb. Why?" Lindy asked.

"Because far worse things are getting closer?" Death replied, taking a pair of dice out of an eye socket and spinning them between his fingers.

Lindy laughed. "You are really bored."

"No I am not. Simply end the undead horde coming toward you!" Death said unhappily.

Then Lindy woke up. "Oh you are cute," she said, meaning to make fun of Death, but instead meeting Fraya's wide-open eyes that were inches from her own. "Can't sleep?" Lindy asked her blushing companion.

Hanna looked over from across the room. "Where were you just now?"

Lindy smiled and looked away from Fraya who was trying to find another place to nap. "Saying hi to Death. Rest up. We will be in the middle of some trouble tomorrow."

"You mean our punishment for your deeds?" Hanna sighed.

"Nope. Undead horde," Lindy explained gleefully.

"What?" Hanna asked in a stony manner.

"Big undead army soon. Good night," Lindy shot back before going right back to sleep.

At late morning Hanna woke up. She had spent hours tossing and turning. Only Lindy was still sound asleep. Fraya kept close to the little death-defying terror. Caldrin peeked out of their window from time to time. Hanna fumed and Genney watched Fraya for a time before sinking into a troubled meditation. By late afternoon, Lindy was still snoring away with Fraya still watching her. No food had come and no intelligent beings had stopped by. When Lindy opened her eyes, Fraya was leaning over much like before. This time Lindy did not seem to mind. She walked over to the bars of their cell and waited, tapping her foot. A shambling guard trotted over. Seconds later Lindy moved in a blur, ripping out the man's throat, taking his sword, and stabbing him in the heart. Freya only stood up quietly. Genney continued to meditate, her brows now furrowed.

Hanna jumped out and asked angrily, "Why did you do that?"

Lindy ignored her friend's outburst and tore down the bars of their cell with brute strength. "What are you trying to do?" Caldrin asked. She was too used to Lindy's manic behavior to get flustered. If nothing else, Lindy always seemed to have a good plan and a solid idea of what was going on.

Genney opened her eyes. A short-lived pained smirk appeared on her face. "He was undead. Turned very recently. The enemy comes, right, my friend?"

Lindy frowned briefly before nodding. "That's right, and that army will be our ticket out of here."

Lieutenant Quell and five other men rushed into the dungeon only to find Lindy and friends reequipping their gear. Lindy kept the new rags she had been handed upon imprisonment as they were nicer than her old ones. "What is this about escaping?" Quell shouted.

Lindy looked out, now seeming slightly annoyed. "Nothing." Quell looked even madder and Lindy giggled. "I will wipe out that army to prove my friend's innocence and my sincerity."

Quell blocked the way out of the dungeon, his men helping seal off any escape routes. "What's stopping you from escaping if I agree?"

Lindy pointed to Hanna. "You still have them. Also, that army is as much your enemy as it is mine."

"So why not let them be worn down, then wipe them out?" Quell asked.

"Bad necromancers," Lindy yawned.

"Fine, but if you betray us the punishments will be worse," Quell agreed. Then he asked, "Did Death tell you to kill that army?"

Lindy began to tap her foot. "It only told me about it and not to annoy you."

Quell sighed. "You have been annoying me since we met."

Lindy's face became blank. "I know. You are even funnier to mess with than Hanna."

Quell sighed. "Let's get you to the main gate." He led Lindy and her team out to the street. Hanna was gripping Lindy's neck and being dragged along, her rage giving her tunnel vision to everything but getting back at her rival.

6

Unearthing Destiny

Quell was unamused but led Lindy, her companions, and a platoon of guards to the gate. The streets were already covered in bonfires in the making. Heaps of bodies were being piled up by hollow-eyed folks. The very wide cobblestone main thoroughfare was pocketed with many pools of blood. "They got here fast." Lindy appeared not the least bit put off.

"That is a very callous thing to say," a plump man covered in sweat and nice clothes replied, hobbling up to them. His left leg was covered by a large bandage. The man turned his beady eyes on Quell. "Why are the ones that caused this being released?" His words caused an ever-growing crowd to form.

"Well sir..." Quell nervously began.

Lindy stepped in front of the lieutenant and looked up at the large man. "Because your men can't handle a few undead." The fat man began to interrupt but Lindy raised her voice, blocking him. "I killed a lot of necromancers not far from here. They were up to no good. Your men did not stop them and now we are all paying for it because a little girl training to be a hero had to do your work for you!"

The fat man shouted. "Well if you had left them alone none of this would have happened!"

Lindy smirked, sneering loud enough for most of the still-growing crowd to hear. "Oh, you knew about them. How are you so well informed about infiltrators from the Ernadon empire and a large nefarious cult?"

The large man's face fell. "That's a loaded question."

Lindy shrugged and pushed by the man. "Well, I will be cleaning up this mess again by myself."

The large man tried to grab Lindy. "I am this city's governor. Be still, child!"

Without turning, Lindy dodged him. As she ran off, she called back. "We can talk after the obvious enemy is dealt with. Quell, if the other captives are harmed while I am away, I will no longer protect this place."

The governor looked at Quell. "Stop her!" he yelled.

Quell looked at Lindy's back, which was almost to the gate a good half mile away. "How? If she dies what do we lose?" It sounded like Quell felt that Lindy would not fail. Before the governor could move, a mob descended on him and Quell had to flee with Lindy's companions to make good on his promise. Even with their short contact and the reports from the men that scouted the last place Lindy decimated, Quell knew Lindy was not someone he wished to make truly angry, for his sake and his city.

Lindy rushed out of the gates. Close to a thousand undead were rushing to the gates as Lindy ran out. A skeleton on a zombie horse rushed her. The horse screeched, its rancid breath leaking. Lindy cut off the horse's head and yelled at the oncoming horde, "I am so done with this! Come on, die again by my hand!" With that, Lindy whispered to Conduit, "I'll kill them. You restrain any that get behind me, and keep track of anything that gets close."

On it Conduit replied within Lindy's mind as they dodged a dog pile of full plate-wearing skeletons. *But if my brother shows up, I take over and kill him* Conduit added. Lindy clad her hand in decaying power and thrust it through a mound of skeletons and iron.

Lindy sneered, a wild smile on her face. "Fine, but only after I work out some of my rage. I'll save our brother for you." A few undead rapidly shambled to her. Lindy hopped up and spun, kicking with her full enhanced might. The targets became a cloud of powder and small shards of bone that swept through the rest of the army.

Three wights rushed out of the horde. All three had a spark of intelligence. The one at the head of the team said with a hollow rasp, "Champion, I challenge you."

Lindy shot the two wights on either side of the new challenger with three pistol shots. Each of them stomped on the ground, causing the earth to shake and the undead nearing the gate to stumble. "Will you stop your army if I say yes?"

"I do not command this legion. Surrender, evildoer," the still "living" wight demanded.

A skeleton horseman rushed by Lindy a bit too closely. She shattered the rider with a backhand and tossed the horse into an onrushing swarm of its fellows. Lindy threw the horseman's lance like a javelin, impaling the wight in its chest. "Not happening."

The wight was sturdier than its fellows. It glared at Lindy. "You have no honor," the wight hissed. Lindy snatched up another lance and began to sweep it about with abandon, crudely smashing back those around her.

At the end of one arc Lindy smashed the lance into the wight's head. "I don't care," Lindy growled. Quell and Lindy's team along with most of the town guard watched the lone girl fight while the mob behind the walls strung up the now-former governor. None of the witnesses to Lindy's fight could find anything to say as they watched the small child hop around, slaying all before her within the rising cloud of dust and bone shards. More than once a lone skeleton would slip by Lindy only to pause and be shattered. Fraya, Caldrin, Quell, and a few of the sharper-eyed guards saw that happen more than once. Finally, Lindy could no longer hold in her rage, which deepened over time. Instead of subsiding, Lindy slashed out with both hands. Tendrils of decay whipped around from her fingers. The earth creaked. Plants, dust, bone, metal, wood, and stone all became nothing. With one wordless howl the skeleton army, all life and inanimate things, many feet of land under their feet, a few small hills, and the edges of the city's front wall all disappeared. Lindy howled once more from the crater she had made, then coughed and passed out.

When Lindy woke up she was at the bottom of a very deep pit. Hanna, Quell, and a few mages stood around her. "What did you do?" Hanna demanded.

Lindy felt very tried and woozy, maybe even a bit drunk. She looked up at the sky far above them. "What it looks like. I made a biiiigg hole. Whoopee!"

"Classic symptoms of over consumption. Perfect," Quell grumbled.

"Wwwhat'd you say?" Lindy slurred, as she tried to stand, only to fall back down.

"Well, why can't we use magic here?" one of the mages wailed.

Conduit's words filled Lindy's mind, causing her pain. *Over consumption. You used way too much power far too quickly and for far too long. You are far too weakened and ecstatic to be of any help. Oh, and when you decayed this place, it looks like you decayed the very mechanisms magic used to seep into this area.*

Lindy rolled around for a while, being ignored by those around her as they shouted up reports and requests for rope. "Magic routes are shot," Lindy managed to cough out. She leaned on one of the walls of the wide pit trying to stand.

Quell was within earshot. He looked over at Lindy and demanded, "Explain." That he seemed to expect a coherent response was ample evidence of how dire he felt their circumstances were.

Lindy managed to stand up. Leaning heavily on the oddly smooth wall, with a shaky hand she pointed to herself. "Too much decay," she muttered slowly. Then her eyes became clear for a few seconds as Conduit helped her cough out, "Affected by how magic flows here."

Hanna, who had been walking close by on her fifth trip around the pit, heard what Lindy had announced and shouted, drowning out the chaotic requests for aid being shouted up to the mob around the pit. "How were you going to get out if you destroyed the magic pathways?"

Some of the mages sent to drag Lindy out muttered. "How are we getting out of here?"

Lindy was still out of it. She shrugged and slurred her words heavily. "Don't know." Conduit was the most fed up now, so she took over for a bit. Lindy stood up straight and walked over to Hanna, who stumbled back at Lindy's sudden lucidity. "I can burrow a way out with my decay powers after I rest. After all, it's not magic." Then Lindy was back in control, falling into Hanna's arms and puking all over her friend.

"Who was that?" Quell managed to ask. He was already very suspicious of who or what Lindy really was. Even for a very young priestess Lindy was totally abnormal.

Hanna sighed. "Probably her other half. You'd have to ask one of them for the details."

"Don't you know?" Quell asked.

Hanna smiled grimly. "When she felt like sharing, yes. But those are her secrets." Quell and the mages clearly were not taking kindly to that. Lindy may have helped them but this was far too much. Hanna pointed around them at the pit they had leapt into in an effort to check on Lindy. "Do you really think someone who can do this is capable of any mercy?"

"She is your friend," one for the mages said.

Hanna looked the older man in the eyes. "Only because I do not anger her." Then she smiled sweetly. "You do know our only method of escaping here may be the same power that made this hole, right?" Hanna sighed, looking down at Lindy, who was still cradled protectively in her arms. Hanna thought, *Am I really letting myself be twisted in this girl's image?*

Half an hour later Lindy managed to stand up and stumble over to the nearest wall. Quell walked over to Lindy who was slowly stretching and grimacing in pain. "You are less of a monster than I thought," he said.

Lindy shook her head. "You are not qualified to tell me that. Plus, I am only like this because I was not careful with how swiftly I used my power."

"What do you mean?" one of the mages asked. His terror and despair, like most of those around, had dulled to a hollow fatalism.

Lindy sighed. "All of you step back." No one did. Lindy was still too worn out to hide her weakness. For once she chose not to censor herself. For one moment she stopped acting out her games, schemes, and obligations. The temperature in the hole dropped. Breath misted. When Lindy looked the people around her in the eyes, most fled to the other side of the pit. Lindy was annoyed but no one looked as her childish mask dropped for a few seconds. "I can tap into as much power as I want." She stomped on the ground. No one else made a sound. Lindy had their undivided attention. She stomped harder. The ground creaked and echoes filled the hole while small rocks fell from above. "If I paced myself I could do this and more. It would take a little longer and might not have this decaying effect on magic, but even then, I could do so much more than this." No one moved. "Anyway, let me save you all again." A small bubble of decay formed around Lindy and she began to walk into the wall. A passageway upward was left in her wake.

One of the mages scoffed. "We would not be down here if not for you."

Farther up the path the young terror had regained her inscrutable mask. "Without me, there would also be less of you. So be happy I am keeping it that way."

Hanna rushed after her rival. "Stop terrifying everyone."

"Oh, come on. They called me a monster but I can't act the part?" Lindy pouted.

The others were almost at the surface. Hanna was ten feet behind Lindy and right outside her decaying field. Quell and most of the braver or more desperate mages followed them. "Grow up. No one called you that!" Hanna retorted.

Lindy shook her head. "My sole use in this life is the same as a large explosive that can follow simple commands." Then she chuckled in a low sneer. "Well, when I listen, anyway."

Lindy's musings reminded her to check her stats.

Lindy Shrew

Female human age 13

Affiliation: hero!?

Embodiments: banished from death, living natural disaster

Job: hero to be

Status: common sense bane: extreme

Abilities: strength 405, vitality 519, mind 327, agility 482

Talents: translation: all. full power strike: strength. danger sense, innate map, skill retention: Manfred Endfield, photographic memory, sixth sense: intuition, toughness, favored environment: darkness, cold resistance: high, enhanced trait: willpower, analysis: extreme, good hair, quick learner. fearless, poison resistance: mild, life sense, aura: weakening, damage shield: decay, decay bolt, talent: (multi-tasking): adept, rapid reload, fearsome visage: moderate, selective decay: all, innate spell: chill blast, absorbed impact: mild, hair trigger aim, repost: debate

Mutation: troll blood (extra burnable, swift regeneration)

Curse: catastrophic encounters, heavily sleeper, light sensitively: mild

Skills: sword: journeyman, dagger: master, unarmed: master, marksmanship: master, throwing: expert, athletics: expert, armor proficiency (leather/ cloth): journeyman, literacy: journeyman, history (other world): journeyman, intimidate (innate): expert, diplomacy: adapt, awareness: expert, necromancy: journeyman, tinkering: expert, magic tampering: adapt, counter spell: journeyman, survival (woodland): beginner, cooking: beginner

Seconds later, Lindy opened a hole next to the pit. She had punched into local topography. No sooner than Lindy stepped back to ground level, Fraya leapt onto her, pushing Lindy down. Fraya clung to Lindy, giggling and bawling her eyes out at the same time. "Get a room, you two," Hanna groaned before taking a big lungful of the dusty air around them. "Freedom at last," Hanna smiled.

"Says the living weapon," Lindy managed to cough out before Fraya smothered her further.

"When were you two so close?" Genney asked from the side as Fraya and Lindy rolled around.

"Just now?" Lindy asked. Then she pretended to think. "Oh you mean like that? No idea."

Somehow Lindy managed to stand up, dragging Fraya up with her. "Before a room, I need to eat!" Lindy cackled.

"You emptied your guts all over me less than an hour ago!" Hanna wailed. All of a sudden, all eyes were on her. "So we need a bath first!" she added somewhat forcefully.

Quell had finished making sure everyone got out of the hole. "I can fulfill both of those requests and get you five out of my city by nightfall, but only if you swear not to destroy anything else."

Lindy escaped from Fraya's grasp. "Would you believe me if I gave you my word that your city was safe with me?"

Quell shook his head ruefully. "Not one bit. Let's get you all cleaned up, fed, and out of here before nightfall then."

"We also want one full set of clothes each," Lindy demanded shamelessly.

Quell sighed. "Fine. One army for some clothes and some hospitality for you not wrecking anything else."

"We have a deal." Lindy giggled like a child years younger than she looked. Only Fraya and Genney did not flee before Lindy's innocent (and battle worn) visage.

Quell and a few of his guards led Lindy and her comrades back into the city. The streets were a mess. Mass rioting had shifted to mass looting. Quell yelled at more than a few guards to arrest the looters, but he was smart enough to let the guards pocket small things along the way, and he never ordered the guards to arrest those they looked to be working with. In its own way this caused more looting and rioting, but the chaos in the city reduced significantly. "You have done this before," Lindy commented sagely.

Quell rolled his eyes. He had learned not to comment so as to avoid one snarky comeback or another. Before Lindy could bait him again they arrived at a solid and so far undamaged warehouse. "Take whatever you need from in there, then leave my city."

"Your city?" Caldrin asked dubiously.

"Yes, I live here, after all," Quell nodded.

"Oh. I thought you were aiming to take over the governorship of this city," Caldrin smirked without feeling.

"The governor would not give up this job, would he?" Fraya asked. She was holding one of Lindy's arms tightly.

"Well, the last governor is dead and very mad," Lindy sighed.

"Well, he was mad," Quell began. Then his confident expression dropped like a ton of bricks. "Wait, he is still mad?"

Lindy's eyes clouded over for a second. For a while fear of bickering had been filling her mind since the end of the battle. Lindy appeared near Death. In his realm the spirit of the governor and Death were playing chess. "So how many grim reapers play chess again?" Lindy asked, peering over the dead governor's shoulder. The man jumped, floating a few inches off what was supposed to be the ground, but given that Death's realm was a hazy black void with no sense of distance or mass, ground may have not been literally right.

"You died too?" the man shouted.

"Just visiting. So how are you?" Lindy asked.

Death grumbled. "Don't distract the man."

"Why chess? I thought a drinking contest would have suited this one better?" Lindy asked, pointedly looking at the governor's bulging gut. *How much ectoplasm is in that?* Lindy mused.

"Wait, that was an option?" the governor asked, looking up at Death. Now they both looked wronged.

"And listen to an angry drunk's ramblings? No thanks," Death complained.

"I only want good alcohol. I never drink to forget," the governor's spirit protested.

Lindy could have sworn Death was now grinning evilly even though he was fleshless. "Ok then," Death agreed.

"Well then, I am heading back to the land of the living," Lindy bowed.

Her eyes refocused. Fraya and Hanna were looking at her. They were in a moving cart packed with all sorts of things. "How long was I out?" Lindy asked. The governor's grumblings were more intense, to the point of giving Lindy a headache.

"So?" Hanna asked. "Where were you?"

"Saying hi to Death and the governor's ghost. He is pissed." Lindy smiled then she added, "I mean, very upset."

"Who?" Genney asked, peeking back from the coachman's seat. They were on the road now and it was almost nighttime.

"Both. The governor is drunk on terrible very alcoholic booze now, and Death has to listen to it," Lindy shrugged.

"That's cruel," Hanna sighed.

"You bet it is. Death made sure I can hear it," Lindy groaned.

"What is he saying?" Fraya asked, almost jumping on Lindy.

"No idea. Seems like Death did not account for distance so it is all very far off, vague, and echoes all around my mind," Lindy pouted.

Caldrin called from the driver's seat. "Sounds very annoying. Almost like that's what he wanted."

Lindy shook her head. "Yeah, it would do that."

"That sounds like something you would do," Hanna observed.

All five of them agreed with that. "That explains a lot," Genney muttered ominously.

Then Fraya leapt on Lindy and Hanna screeched, "What are you two doing?"

"How should I know?" Lindy squeaked. She was very confused, having only now noted Fraya's increasingly intense behavior.

Only Caldrin took note of Genney's words but did not comment on it. Instead the instructor yelled back, "I'm driving here, quit it."

Hours later they pulled off to the side of the road. Lindy began to modify the blueprints she had been tasked with improving. She worked out all the ways to make the three weapons cheaper to make, more reliable, simpler, and far less deadly. Most of this was by using small bits of naturally occurring elementally empowered crystals as cheaper power sources that had less shelf life, and components to disperse and accelerate the power rather than contain it within the weapons. If treated poorly, these weapons could be badly damaged, but as long as they were well treated they would work, so intensive use in the field would be difficult. After dinner Lindy went to sleep. Fraya followed after her.

Looking up at Fraya, who was trying to sneak up next to her, Lindy asked, "Why has your attitude to me changed?"

Fraya froze for a few seconds, then she sighed. After many more seconds Fraya answered. She looked very embarrassed. "I like you. If I stay with you I feel like I will get stronger as well."

Lindy sat up. She asked in a deadly serious manner, "Events around me will always be dangerous. Disasters find me. Anyone that is with me will likely die badly, sooner rather than later."

Fraya looked Lindy in the eyes and smiled sadly. "I know." Fraya inched closer. "If I am with you then my life will be worth living. My goals will be achieved with you, and I feel like I can escape those that would try to use me if I am by your side."

"So you are using me?" Lindy asked, wanting to see how far Fraya was willing to go for her stated goals.

"That's right. So let me help you with anything you need of me," Fraya answered without hesitation or doubt.

Lindy grinned. "Fine, but I will be the death of you."

Then she went to sleep. Before Lindy's consciousness had fully shut down for the night, she heard Fraya mutter, "If I die then it will be due to my own weaknesses. Being with you will be bittersweet. But I am only truly alive with you."

They left early the next morning, arriving at the school mid-afternoon. Lindy had a new close-fitting light gray coverall and a warmer brown coverall. She had chosen to wear the lighter one under her armor. Jerrend and the four watchmen stood by the gate, halting the cart. "Lindy Shrew, the headmaster requires that you report to him now," one of the men said.

Caldrin sighed. "Very well. I'll show her up soon."

The guards did not budge despite the nervous glances they were shooting at Lindy. Jerrend shrunk in on himself. "But we were told to send Cadet Shrew to the headmaster as soon as she arrived."

The warden walked out of an office set by the wall. "I'll lead the way," he offered.

Lindy leapt from the cart. After a lot of showy stretching, she looked up at the warden like she had just noticed him and laughed. "Make me." The warden staggered a bit when Lindy tried to stare him down. After feeling suitably entertained, Lindy chose to deal with the greedy grasping dullards that ran the place. She asked, "So which tower?" The warden did not manage to reply for a few seconds. Lindy let up on her glare and grumbled, "What tower is he in now?"

The warden pointed at three towers. "The rear one," he stammered.

"Good enough," Lindy glowered. Her face did a complete U-turn. "Well, see ya," she laughed, running off to the tower at full speed, a dirt cyclone spreading in her wake.

"She does not hold back, does she?" Jerrend muttered, collapsing on the ground like his fellows, now that they were no longer tense and scared out of their minds.

"That's why she is so awesome," Fraya giggled. No one thought she was wrong but all believed she was going slightly insane, given how happy Fraya seemed about something so terrifying.

Meanwhile Lindy was climbing up the side of the tower. At the top she pried open a window and slid in. Wallace Nut jumped up with a start from a desk. Jeffery Derkin looked over from a slightly smaller but no less ornate desk. "When did you arrive?" Jeffery asked.

"A few seconds before you asked that. Didn't you see?" Lindy asked, puzzled, tilting her head.

Wallace grumbled with feeling, leaning back in his posh chair. "Never mind. Give me your report." Lindy skipped over to the headmaster's desk, paying close attention to the presences she could not see but could feel like a cold blade in her back. After setting the new blueprints on top of the small mountain of paperwork the headmaster was trying to surmount, Lindy stepped back a few feet. "New and improved, I take it?" the headmaster asked wearily.

"They are much simpler to use and make but require more maintenance and have less power," Lindy told him.

"Then what good are they?" Jeffery Derkin demanded, fuming.

"Defense of city. How should I know?" Lindy shot back indifferently.

"You invented them!" Jeffery pressed.

"So all engineers must know how to fully implement their creations better than anyone? Do I look like any kind of military strategist to you?" Lindy replied cheerily.

"Not in the least," one of the hidden bodyguards around them muttered.

Lindy felt the air move from where the voice had come from. Once it settled she pointed to where it stopped. "That one gets what I mean."

Wallace slumped in his chair. "Cadet Shrew, you may go."

"Many thanks," Lindy nodded. She turned to exit from her entry point.

"One more thing," Wallace called after her. "Are these the best you can do?"

Lindy looked back at him, her face and voice now absolutely serious. The room tensed. "With the technology that exists now, yes. Those three things are already far too ahead of their time. The rest of the world must catch up a bit more before further improvements can be fashioned. Nothing in this world can handle that right now." Then Lindy leapt from the tower window, landing on one of the watchtowers along the wall. After a few more leaps she was back on the ground. Genney found her; the rest of their comrades arrived soon after.

"Let's get lunch," Caldrin offered. The girls all agreed. The security checks to get underground were swift but the number of guards seemed higher. Very few students were in the halls that Lindy's team passed. The lunch room was nearly deserted.

"Something is wrong," Lindy noted.

"I heard most of the student body left for field training soon after we did," Fraya explained before tearing into a large roast beef sandwich that was more vegetable than meat. Soon after she was lost in her own little world, seeing only the sandwich and Lindy, but otherwise being deaf and absent to her surroundings.

Right before they were done eating Caldrin told them, "We have a job assignment. We are heading out again at first light."

"So soon. Why?" Hanna inquired.

"Ernadon Empire agents may be inciting some small monsters. We need to investigate and capture the agents if we find them," Caldrin informed them.

"Why? We have only seen them twice and Lindy took care of them each time..." Hanna began before trailing off and glaring at Lindy, who was thoughtfully chewing on a slice of cake without a care in the world.

"I've fought them three times so far. The cultists had some of our countrymen, however," Lindy muttered.

"So, it's your fault I can't sleep in!" Hanna pouted.

Genney laughed. "You are letting your real feelings slip a little." Genney shook Fraya lightly. "Are you ok with this?" she asked her former groupie firmly.

The real world swiftly snapped back into focus for Fraya. She tensed up, but then relaxed after seeing no danger. "Yes, why would I not be?"

Genney seemed confused for a moment. Then her eyes lost a little focus. "Never mind. Let's do our best," she said without feeling before heading back to their room early.

Hanna, Fraya, and Caldrin did not understand what was going on. Hanna got up to chase after their friend but Lindy stopped her. "This job's going to be hard. Even more than what she saw," Lindy sighed.

"What she saw?" Hanna asked.

"What the Seer saw is not for us to know. Knowing could be far more dangerous than not," Lindy replied sternly.

"What if one of us dies?" Fraya asked.

"Then I'll see them off and put in a good word to my boss," Lindy shrugged.

"Meaning Death?" Hanna grumbled.

"Yes, so don't get too hung up. Being careless is almost as bad as trying to change fate," Lindy replied before falling asleep. Fraya had to move half of Lindy's cake so her face would not smash into it. Caldrin brought Lindy back to her room and Fraya got more cake.

Lindy woke up soon after to find Genney sitting in the dark, her face buried in a pillow. "Do you trust me?" Genney asked on the verge of tears.

Lindy sat next to her despondent friend, who flinched away. "I trust no one fully," Lindy swiftly answered. Genney began to cry. "But," Lindy went on, "I don't think you would betray me anytime soon."

Genney looked up at her friend, tears still running wild. "And if I did?"

"Your visions are that bad? Those last two really got you going." Lindy smiled, feeling like she could empathize with how the world spirits used their minions.

Genney only began to sob even more. "You knew? Why... why did you not tell me?"

"Because I don't want to know what the future may hold?" Lindy responded quizzically.

Genney grabbed her friend's collar and looked her friend in the eyes, their noses touching. "Not that you were told to kill me, right?"

Lindy wanted to look away from her friend's sad pleading gaze but doing so felt like it would be wrong, so Lindy took a deep breath. Genney skittered away a foot from her friend when the grim reaper's pet killer exhaled. "I have not been told that yet," Lindy explained. "So was that the one just now or the one in the dungeon?"

Genney looked away, now nervous and unsure. She closed her eyes and after a long time answered, "The dungeon. You know Hanna will likely die on this trip, right?"

Lindy noticed a skittering sound patter away from their door right after Genney said that. "Now I do, but I wish you had not told me."

Genney got a little mad. "Why can't you save her?"

Lindy got up. "I don't save, only kill. That's what being bound to Death for life entails. Whoever heard what you said may have other ideas." Then Lindy walked out of the room to her lab, her mind blank and needing a distraction.

"Oh no." Genney slumped down into her bed.

Good. Conduit's voice echoed in Lindy's mind. *Don't interfere in the affairs of the other world spirits.*

"I knew that already." Lindy sighed quietly in her small and now very empty workshop. "Someone cleared this place out," she grumbled.

Lindy slept in her workshop that night. In the morning Caldrin dragged Lindy to an awkward breakfast. Their cart left far before noon. Lindy chose to sleep. She dreamed of life back on Earth, the sort of dream she knew would be forgotten upon waking. Swiftly, however, her dream shattered. In its place stood Death and a tall glowing woman with three eyes holding a sundial and a pair of scissors. "So, you are his new plaything?" the woman sighed.

Lindy crossed her arms. "Are you Fate?" she demanded.

Displeased, the tall woman asked, "Why do you say that, young one?" Death was behind her, frantically making hand gestures for Lindy to shut up.

"Given last night, it would make sense for Genney's owner to formally complain to my keeper." Lindy smiled back evilly.

The tall woman grumbled, her hands in the air. "Ok fine. I am Fate. What will you do with what you were told?"

Lindy shrugged. "Why would I follow your prophecies?"

Fate shrunk down to a little over Lindy's height and glared at her. "Because you have reasons to."

"No I don't. You are not my boss. Keeping others alive past their time violates my agreement with Death." Lindy glared back.

"Do you want to save them?" Fate pressed.

"If they are saved, it will not be my doing. My role in this world is to serve the interests of Death itself. Not you, not me." Lindy was firm.

Fate was more unhappy but no longer mad. "If I told you that you could save them, then what?"

Lindy's glare froze over. "Don't mess with my life more than you have."

Fate shook her head in wonder. "Why do you reject me?"

Lindy's gaze thawed a bit. "Because the few free parts of my life are mine alone. That and besides shitty masterminds, what I hate most is to know what I am getting myself into."

"So you hate me?" Fate asked.

"My sense of self is built on relying on myself to live, no matter the life." Lindy smirked like she had won.

"Even if your nation wishes to scare you into working with them by using great force?" Fate smirked back in the same manner.

Lindy's face fell. "If they do then they will die. Goodbye." With that, Lindy forced herself back into her body.

When she was gone, Fate looked at Death. "You found a strange one."

"How many did you consign to my realm?" Death grumbled to himself.

Fate paused. "Oh crap. She was not joking, damn it!"

"So a lot." Death sighed, sitting down.

"Why are you nice to her?" Fate inquired.

Death looked in an arbitrary direction that was currently up. "Because that one reminds me of my past."

Back in the cart Lindy opened her eyes and spat. "Work keeps piling up."

"What?" Hanna asked.

"Keep focused, you guys. We are almost there," Fraya called from the front of the cart.

They rolled up to a small team of lightly wounded knights. One of the men walked up and saluted.

Sir Ashwall of Gail

Male elf age 115

Affiliation: Derndell kingdom, Derndell royal engineering corp, Derndell kingdom ministry of war

Job: Watchman

Status: knight of the realm, sworn to service of the Derndell kingdom hero academies, guard captain of the Derndell kingdom engineering corp's 3rd testing yards

Abilities: strength 36, vitality 32, mind 16, agility 22

Talents: resist fear/pain: high, language: common Derndell, master parry

Skills: sword: expert, armor proficiency pate/chain/ leather: journeyman, law: journeyman., athletics: journeyman, ride: journeyman, herbarium: beginner, smithing: beginner, gunnery: beginner, tracking: adept, diplomacy: journeyman

Ashwall stopped the horses and informed Lindy's team. "We spotted five enemy agents and three young basilisks in the forest. My men can't handle the basilisks. Please lead us in and hold off the monsters."

Lindy and Fraya led the way. Hanna and Genney walked a few feet behind them. Caldrin kept watch behind them. The men with Ashwall were a far ways behind her. Almost as soon as she stepped foot in the forest the air felt wrong to Lindy. The scent of blood was all over the place. Lindy felt cold like she might die again, but unlike her time as Manfred Endfield, for good. "Stay behind me and do not run off," Lindy whispered to Fraya who also could tell something was wrong long before Lindy did, but with far less clarity.

After half a mile of following the scent of blood they came upon a small hill of human and elf corpses, all in Derndell kingdom uniforms. Lindy stopped Fraya from advancing. When Caldrin ran over to see what was wrong, Lindy hissed, "Where are the escorts?"

Caldrin looked around. "I lost track of them. They should still be following us." She squinted in the forest's gloom. "Those aren't them, right?"

"It's too many to just be them," Hanna observed.

Genney stumbled to the ground. "We need to get out of here. It's a trap."

Out of the ground around the bodies three chimeras and a manticore burst from hidden pits. Lindy took out a pistol and dagger. "Run," she muttered just loud enough for her friends to hear. When she spoke the forest began to ice over. Without looking back Lindy lunged at the four monsters with unnatural speed.

Anti-magic field around the bodies. Someone is after you, Conduit informed Lindy.

Lindy shot the manticore in the head with two full magazines of ammo before sliding under its body, her arm clad in decaying power.

Lindy plunged her arm into the monster as she slid under it, opening up its belly. When she skated by its tail Lindy leapt into the air. With three swipes of her blade she cut off the manticore's tail, landing on its back, then sprang at one of the other monsters. A chimera swung down its own snake-headed tail. Lindy blocked with her knife but the taxed blade shattered. Right then a web of fire enveloped the other two chimeras and Fraya yelled out, "Hold on!" as she moved in front of Hanna.

Lindy turned in midair just in time to see Fraya dodge one claw swipe and get hit by another. Lindy landed, her eyes still glued to Fraya as her friend lost her right arm and leg to a chimera's jaws. In that moment Lindy lost her sense of time. Everything she had lived through as Manfred Endfield, the past Lindy, and the current one took over her field of vision. In the real world a full second passed and Lindy lurched, her eyes glazing over. She lost herself in the feeling of mindless destruction.

When Lindy's mind came back to itself the forest was cut down as if one massive blade had cleared it all away in one cruel swipe. Chunks of the corpse mound and monsters were scattered all over the place, all chopped into a fine sludge.

Hanna, Genney, and Caldrin were very much alive and trembling nearby. A limbless Sir Ashwall of Gail lay under Lindy's feet. He was weeping. "That's all I know," he was saying. "The king ordered us to do it. We were really only supposed to scare you into helping the war effort." Lindy bent down and snapped the man's neck.

Then she walked over to Fraya, whispering, "How is she?"

Begging to be reborn and remember you, Conduit replied.

"Let her and the boss know that I will destroy the ones responsible for this, and let her know I am sorry," Lindy grumbled. A single tear fell from her lips onto Fraya's chest.

Fraya's voice fluttered by Lindy's ear. *I am sorry too, and thank you.*

Lindy walked over to the rest of the team. "This time do not follow me," she snapped. After only three stepped back Lindy amended her demand. "On second thought, run away from me as far as you can."

Genney trembled. "What are you going to do?"

Lindy glanced back, her eyes suddenly dry. "Flatten those that get in my way. Goodbye." Then she put her full power into her legs and leapt into the sky.

Lindy bounded across the land. It took her six hours to arrive back at the academy. A few new carriages were parked in a courtyard and the rest of the place was nearly devoid of life. Ten lives were walking up to a tower when Lindy fell from above the walls and landed among them. The well-dressed humans froze. One female in armor had a sword out. Two men Lindy had seen before when showing off her inventions. The younger of the two mumbled, "Oh, you are back already?"

What's the plan? Conduit asked.

Lindy pulled a sword from one of the human's belts and cut all ten shocked officials around her in half. *Everyone here is responsible,* Lindy thought back, *so they die. Now help me slice this top-level down to my size.*

Fine, let them feel our rage, Conduit replied, the voice now almost indecipherable from Lindy's own.

Seconds later all the aboveground buildings had three-inch cuts decayed all the way through them at such an angle that they fell away from Lindy. A small dust storm billowed up from the academy grounds. Lindy jumped up high. After finding the tower the ten humans were walking to among the rubble, Lindy barreled through one of its windows. Wallace Nut was alone and slumped among many ornamental swords and books. A few of the swords had impaled him. Before the man could regain consciousness Lindy cut off his head. Crawling out of the room was annoying, as the cylindrical walls had become the floor. Five steps from the tower Lindy's danger sense was suddenly manic. She ducked in time for the sword that arced over her to take a few hairs, but not her head.

"Impressive," a wizened voice praised coolly.

Lindy rolled forward a few paces and spun around to find a solidly built wizened bald man sporting a gray goatee and shining silver armor. His rune-covered broadsword hung at his side.

Matric Linch

Human male age 85

Affiliation: Derndell kingdom

Job: elite hero

Status: champion of the realm, sworn to service of King Jay master of the Derndell kingdom

Abilities: strength 1345, vitality 983, mind 1022, agility 789

Talents: pain/seduction/petrifaction: immunity, fearlessness, alcohol tolerance: high, language: common Derndell/high Derndell/ gnomish trade tong, rock spirit, silent cast, shade step, double slash, dual cast, maximize magic output, aura shield, erase aura: self, piercing voice, commanding presence, intuit schemes, target lock on, prey track, petrifying touch

Skills: sword: master, armor proficiency pate/ chain/ leather/ cloth: master. law: expert, dagger: expert, athletics: master, earth magic: extreme, spear: expert, duel wield: expert, tracking: expert, herbalist: master, first aid: master, survival (all): expert, riding: journeyman, barter: journeyman, tactics siege/ assault/ infiltration: expert, leadership: master, stealth: journeyman

"Oh shit," Lindy managed to squeak before Matric Linch grabbed her head and turned her to stone.

Part Two

7

Stone Cold

An old man walked into the resting lodge for heroes in the city of Forlest, capital of the Derndell kingdom. The guards spared the man a glance. Most visitors would have been stopped, but the old man was a human of great influence. That, and he had an appointment. The old man was a high-ranking alchemist named Ajax Shrew. He had been working for this moment for the thirty years his sister had been silent.

The Zigone sisters were born into house Derkin by two mistresses. Their mothers were Genney the sage and Hanna Zigone. The father had been Calen Derkin. Genney had died giving birth to a boy who had passed away as well. Hanna managed to get the two daughters certified as heroes.

Frost Zigone was Genney's daughter. She was seen as lazy, indifferent, and quiet. Frost was pale; her white hair and gray eyes further made her look like some kind of apparition.

Fall Zigone was Hanna's daughter. Mother and daughter were well known to be equally fiery. Fall's bright red hair, light bronze skin, and black eyes only helped enhance that image.

The two young heroes were skilled in magic and close combat. They sat at an out-of-the-way table on the second floor of the lodge. Fall had been keeping watch the whole time while Frost napped soundly, her legs on the table. Ajax found the two heroes swiftly and sat himself at their table without a greeting. Fall seemed a bit upset. Frost opened her eyes and sighed. Any feelings she had stayed hidden behind the listless guise she had never dropped. Ajax broke the silence. "I look forward to working with you."

Fall shook her head. "No way are we working for you until the contract is explained."

Ajax's smile was hidden behind his massive beard. He slowly rested his head in his palms and his elbows on the table. "I need to be escorted to the former 3rd hero academy."

Fall sneered. "That zone's forbidden."

Frost sighed. "They're called the Dark Stone ruins now, and we are not going."

Ajax leaned back in his chair casually and shrugged. "The Dark Stone ruins will no longer be forbidden territory by the end of the week." For a split-second Frost's eyebrows twitched.

"Says who?" Frost asked with a yawn while stretching.

"The king and new champion," Ajax chuckled. For the first time Frost looked closely at Ajax, her eyes seemingly without focus. Fall and her mother were the only ones who knew that's how Frost glared.

"Why us? Exploring is an adventurer's job," Fall piped up irritably.

"It could be dangerous. The magic death storm around the ruins will still have some power for a few months. Who knows what that runaway magic has spawned? Plus there will be salvage teams sent by many lords." Ajax groaned.

Fall threw her arms up, annoyed. "Then get some mercenaries." While heroes handled the most life-threatening tasks, most either did combat or research. Heroes were the most powerful of their kind and primarily worked for the state. Mercenaries killed for a living, as well as taking escort tasks like adventurers, all for cash. Adventurers killed mainly monsters and animals, gathered plants, did errands, did limited escort tasks through monster territory, and mapped out the unknown, in general doing odd jobs that were beneath the heroes and not worth mercenaries' time.

Ajax shook his head. "I need to get to the center of the storm before anyone else. Your father is letting me borrow you two for this."

Frost looked in danger of walking off to a nearby window. "We know that. Why us?"

"Your mothers knew the ones I am seeking," Ajax relayed, all levity gone.

Fall rolled her eyes. "So it's our bloodline?" her expression full of disgust.

"Nothing can live in that storm for long," Frost muttered.

Ajax replied acidly. "My sister can't be killed by Death. I need to find her to work out why before she moves."

"Your sister was Lindy Shrew? She died frozen in stone. She made the 3rd academy a forbidden zone. She is dead." Frost spoke quickly.

"All but that last part is right. I don't know exactly how or why but she still lives, frozen in stone or not," Ajax replied sternly.

"Pay us double and you have a deal, but if that monster still lives it dies by our hand. Our mother's honor demands it," Fall replied, in a tone making it clear her words were anything but a request.

"And tell us how they knew that monster," Frost added, still not willing to believe Ajax was telling them what he was really after, let alone about their mothers.

"It's a long story," Ajax noted.

"It's a long trip," Fall snapped, walking away.

Frost got up to follow her sister. "We'll be ready tomorrow. You prepare transport and pay. If you cheat us, you die."

After the young heroes had left Ajax grinned evilly, mumbling to himself. "It's been far too long for a rematch. I can't wait to see you again, dear sister."

Before the sun had risen, Fall and Frost stood right outside the city gates. Frost yawned. A mace hung from her belt, shield strapped to her right arm. She wore a full suit of silvery chainmail over light padded wool but none of it made a sound as she moved. Fall was encased in armor made from red-stained hydra leather. Her bastard sword possessed a thin dark blade with small serrations. The pommel was a large spike. Neither woman looked happy but both were alert and ready for anything.

Ajax drove a cart slowly up to his guards. "Get in," was his first order.

The heroes did as they were told. Frost sat next to Ajax and Fall sat in back of the cart. They stayed on high alert for anything funny from the lands, the sky, and their employer. After a few hours Fall spoke up without stopping her vigil. "So did our mothers really know Lindy Shrew?"

"They were in the same team. As far as I could gather, they were close friends," Ajax explained.

"But then she went mad and our mothers got blamed. They had to hide with father just to stay alive," Frost nearly pouted.

"I had heard another one: their friend was killed in some heavy-handed scare tactics. Then my sister went crazier than normal," Ajax said.

"Fraya," Frost whispered to herself.

Ajax's wise teaching manner was thrown off for a few seconds. "That's right," he coughed.

"Still, why would Lindy Shrew still live?" Fall demanded.

Ajax shrugged. "All I know is she is practically immortal. I can't believe she is dead until I see the body."

"The death storm strips everything to bone if they are lucky, less if they are not," Frost said in an expressionless accusatory tone.

Fall nodded. "That's right. Even the mages that sealed off that area died in droves. So how is your sister any better?"

"She is not suicidal," Ajax told them firmly.

Fall grimaced. "If that monster lives, I will be sorely temped to flay it alive." She then began snacking on some beef jerky and ignored Ajax, as if to forestall new commands.

Ajax looked over at Frost. "How do you feel?"

"The job comes first. However, I don't get in my sister's way," Frost replied lackadaisically, but in her mind her doubts and insecurities mounted as they always did during a job. Frost forced her discomfort into heightening her focus. They still had close to a week to travel.

Over many days the roads became more and more unkempt. Frost and Fall did their jobs well, hunting, keeping vigilant, and maintaining their gear, all done with precision as their pride demanded. The roving monsters and barbaric beings thinned out the closer they came to the Dark Stone ruins.

Half a mile out on the now-barren plains Ajax stopped the cart. "Set up camp," he ordered.

Fall spread her arms wide as if to show off the desolation all around them. "And hunt what exactly?"

Frost sighed and took out a pouch of dried berries, nuts, and jerky along with a tanned goat's stomach filled with fermenting milk and honey. "Food for a day," she said, handing her sister the food. When Fall's hands grabbed the bags, Frost still held on. "Take half," Frost reminded before looking over at Ajax, who was taking a steaming fresh sandwich out of a magic bag. "None for you," she added.

Ajax shrugged, grinning wolfishly. "The seals will be down before nightfall. Then we move in when the smog thins enough."

Fall, who had begun to unroll a tent, stopped. "Tell us that first!"

Before Ajax could respond, Frost's eyebrows shot up. "How do you know it will be safe?"

Ajax ate his sandwich slowly. Fall packed up the cart as Frost watched the area and ate. Soon Fall ate her fill, pocketing some food while the two heroes kept watch. Sometime after they had finished eating, Ajax was on his second cold ale and Fall's mouth was a thin angry line. *Wizards are all showoffs. At least mum was not pompous about it,* she thought.

Finally Ajax spoke. "I did tests. How else would the kingdom know this plan will work?"

Fall rolled her eyes. "If someone else did the tests," she muttered.

Frost glanced at her sister. *Don't tell him that, sis,* she sighed mentally. "These expeditions are your doing?" Frost asked, pointing off to the carts far closer to the barrier.

"A byproduct," Ajax responded.

"What will happen to them?" Fall asked. A mad glint surfaced briefly in Ajax's eyes.

"Nothing good," Frost whispered. Fall got the message and stayed quiet. Both heroes eyed the other teams nervously during their patrols around the cart. For his part Ajax stared intently at the column of man-eating smog that was contained by powerful wards and hid all that remained of the 3rd hero academy. Ajax had tracked his sister's bizarre multiple souls and knew they had not left this forbidden zone. Where Ajax had failed and his grandmother succeeded, somehow the once talentless Lindy Shrew had outdone them and all other necromancers in the pursuit of being truly undying. On this point the other members of the Shrew family, who for ages had devoted themselves to the secrets of necromancy, agreed.

A little after noon large runic formations set around the barrier flashed with light, then slowly dimmed. Fall watched as the other teams rushed forward. Frost noted that Ajax no longer hid the mad smirk that had been creeping across his face. Only Ajax and the Zigone sisters had not moved from their camp when the formations fully powered down. Frost's cold gaze shifted to panic when she sensed what was coming. Some of the other teams had members that panicked as well, but they were too close to the danger zone to save themselves. Frost conjured up a small barrier and flung herself and her sister inside. Some of the scattered hirelings tried to run but they were all far too close to the barrier when it burst. The remnants of the Death Storm rushed out, corroding away the flesh from bone, then turning bone to nothing. It left any magic item drained. Most leather was consumed as well. Horses, elves, lupines, dwarves, and humans were all equally vulnerable to the smog. In the brief instance the smog's victims knew, despite their terror, that they were not alone in the fate that claimed them. The smog ballooned out but did not reach Ajax. However, a baleful glowing skull did appear for a heartbeat, seeming to glower at him. Minutes passed and the smog thinned. Some random bones, rusted metal, and a few gold teeth were all that was left of the other teams.

Only when Frost deemed the smog had thinned enough for herself and her sister to move with slight discomfort did she disengage the barrier. Ajax looked at his guards from the cart. He was totally unharmed but a sinister glow now emitted from beneath his robes. "You said this area was safe!" Fall howled, wincing at the feeling of pinpricks on her skin. Both heroes' bodies felt painfully numb. Ajax glanced at Frost briefly, then shrugged. "This was slightly more intense than expected but since magic works here, still well within an acceptable margin of error."

"Did you tell the other teams about the safe zone?" Fall sneered sarcastically.

"Of course not; the full report on this place is classified. Random treasure hunters can't be told such things. Still, I did tell the king how dangerous this place could be. It seems they did not plan for the third worst case like I did," Ajax mused.

Frost looked at the field, now outwardly back to her detached self. "What was the first worst case?"

"All the land being eaten up," Ajax said indifferently.

Fall wanted to rage more at her employer but stopped herself. Fall chose to focus on the job at hand because getting mad now would not help them or change things. However, somehow her opinion of Ajax fell farther than she knew it could. "Can we move into the ruins yet? I doubt staying around here is healthy," Fall asked, not bothering to hide her disgust but managing to hide her anger.

The three raced down the hill. Frost cast a glance at their horse bound to their cart. Ajax gleefully focused single-mindedly on the ruins still enveloped in a light covering of flesh-eating mist.

8

Spark of Shadow

After thirty years working in Death's realm handling administrative tasks and running errands to other world spirit's realms, Lindy had gotten her first two-minute coffee break. The coffee was dry, bland, and foul in every way. "I should not have been looking forward to this," she sighed. Death had Lindy working overtime in what was the stopping point for all souls within five universes. Even if the workload seemed like hell, Lindy thought it could be worse. Not that she wanted to find out.

With five seconds left on her break, Death showed up. "Go back," it said. Lindy pointed at the alarm clock sitting on a can of lukewarm foul coffee. Death crossed its arms. "This is your get out of jail free card. Now return to your body."

Lindy sighed, holding up her mug of coffee. "One for the road?"

Death shook its head. "No."

"Why?" Lindy pressed.

Death glared at her. "Because I could not make it worse."

Lindy giggled as she faded from Death's realm. "Good, you are learning."

After Lindy had dispersed, Death sighed. "No, I am remembering my rebellious phase."

The first thing Lindy did when her eyes opened was to smash her way out of the stone shell that covered her and check her stats.

Lindy Reaper
Female human age: forever 20
Affiliation: realm of death
Embodiments: kicked out by death, semi-eternal calamity
Job: Reaper
Status: common sense bane: extreme
Abilities: strength 805, vitality 1032, mind 611, agility 1003
Talents: translation: all, full power strike: strength, danger sense, innate map, skill retention: Manfred Endfield, photographic memory, sixth sense: intuition, extra toughness, favored environment: darkness, cold resistance: high, highly enhanced trait: willpower, analysis: extreme, good hair, quick learner, fearless, poison resistance: moderate, presence sense, aura: weakening, damage shield: decay, decay bolt, adept talent: multi tasking, rapid reload, fearsome visage: moderate, selective decay: all, innate spell: chill blast, absorbed impact: moderate, hair trigger aim, repost: debate, realm authority (death): minor, shadow shift, six fold strike, perception tampering field, find soul, see soul
Mutation: troll blood (extra burnable, swift regeneration), un-aging
Curse: catastrophic encounters, heavily sleeper, light sensitively: mild,
Skills: sword: journeyman, dagger: master, unarmed: master, marksmanship: master, throwing: expert, athletics: master, armor proficiency (leather/ cloth): expert, literacy: journeyman, history (other world): journeyman, intimidate (innate): expert, diplomacy: journeyman, awareness: expert, necromancy: extreme, tinkering: expert, magic tampering: master, counter spell: expert, survival (woodland): journeyman, cook-

ing: journeyman, acrobatics: expert, stealth: journeyman

If anyone had watched Lindy break out of the statue that had once been her, it would have looked like she expanded out of it. Her clothing, however, no longer fit. Lindy's growth tore her armor; the clothes now covered far less of her, and were on the tight side. Lindy was far taller than she had been. She had a lean build, sharp eyes, and a relaxed jovial air about her. It was then Lindy looked around. The academy was gone; dust and smoke were all around. As she was getting her bearings a red-haired young woman burst out of the fog. She glared at Lindy. Right behind her a pale well-armored young woman raced forward. Lastly an old man raced into sight. "Brother, it's been far too long," Lindy sneered.

Ajax looked at his long-lost sister. "Those three souls are all fused now?"

Lindy looked inside herself. Conduit, Manfred Endfield, and Lindy Shrew were indeed all in a single mass. "So it appears," Lindy nodded.

The red-haired hero rushed forward. "Die!" she bellowed.

The pale one called out lazily, "We need her alive, sis."

"That's right, Frost Zigone. Stand down, Fall." Ajax grinned evilly.

"Zigone?" Lindy asked.

"Hanna Zigone and Genney the sage are our mothers," Frost nodded.

"The ones you betrayed," Fall added, trembling with rage.

"For what it's worth, I am glad they lived so long," Lindy informed her visitors.

"My mother died," Frost added coldly.

"I know," Lindy nodded. In an effort to stall any violence she added swiftly, "I see Genney all the time at the inter-departmental meetings." Genney had indeed taken to handling many administrative tasks for the world spirit. Fate, in fact all the world spirits but Death, had teams of support staff. Death, however, only had Lindy.

"What?" Ajax asked greedily.

"Genney works for Fate. I see her all the time." Lindy sighed, then she pointed to the sisters. "I know all of our embarrassing childhood moments."

Fall gripped her sword tightly. "You spied on us?"

Lindy shrugged. "Genney told me, and she does spy on you two when she is not working."

"You work for Death?" Ajax asked, trying to salvage the derailed conversation back to what he really wanted to know.

"The hours are lethal," Lindy replied in a snarky tone. Then she clapped. "Next question!"

Frost, who had been looking closely at Lindy for a while, asked, "Have I met you before?"

Lindy looked closely at Frost. Lindy's pulse and heart rate spiked for a second when she saw Frost was Fraya reincarnated. "Are you hitting on me?" Lindy smiled. Frost shook her head, unsure why she had suddenly asked such an unlikely question.

"Why do you look so young?" Ajax pressed energetically, now letting his real desires peek out.

"Don't ask a woman her age. If you must know, I am forever twenty." Lindy laughed.

All this time Lindy had been on high alert. She was the first to notice footsteps drawing closer. One of Lindy's feet slammed down. A rusted blade once welded by Matric Linch flew up from the ash-covered ground and into Lindy's hand. "I think I'll see how being a mercenary suits me. Failing that, I could always moonlight as an assassin." Fall charged at Lindy but before the fiery hero had taken three steps, Lindy's entire body faded away exactly like a shadow being snuffed out by the sun.

Frost and Ajax both picked up on Lindy's not-so-subtle hint. Fall, however, raged. "Where did she go!"

Ajax shook his head, seemingly surprised by how badly Fall's rage had caused to her lose sight of anything but killing Lindy. "She told us where to find her," he grumbled.

Frost began to look around, only now sensing a team of new arrivals. "Who got away?" the red-robed woman asked. Three mid-level heroes walked behind her.

When some ash shifted, Fall looked right at the red-robed woman. At the same time Fall went out of her way to pretend not to see the three other heroes around her age. "Mum, why are you here?" Fall asked.

The red woman was well known as Hanna Zigone, more often called the flame weaver. The three heroes with her were two sons and one daughter of house Derkin, but unlike Frost and Fall they were publicly acknowledged children of the house. "Who else was here?" Hanna asked patiently. Her eyes narrowed at Fall's drawn sword.

Ajax shook his head sadly. "It appears Lindy Shrew still lives. We could not stop her from running away."

A small complicated smile broke past Hanna's perpetually serious countenance. "She lives again. Are you going to tell the king about this, Ajax Shrew?"

Ajax nodded. "Of course. I'd rather keep my head."

"Good." Hanna nodded, then glanced at the three youngish heroes filled with arrogance and righteous indignation behind her. "We still need to search for the academy's underground. Let's go." One of the men tried to jostle Frost as he passed, only to find Frost was more like an iron wall. Neither Frost nor the young man showed they had noticed the collision. Soon after, Hanna and her tag-alongs vanished in the swirling ash all around them. The ash cloud continued to thicken in the air now that airflow had returned to this place.

Ajax watched Hanna's team leave then he turned around, now in a very good mood. "Ok, we are heading back to the capital."

Fall had been looking around trying to find a trace of Lindy. "What then?" she asked, not looking up from her work.

"This job is over when I enter the capital." Ajax shrugged, still walking to the cart.

Fall ran after him. Frost tried to stop her sister from doing anything rash. "Were you planning to capture or kill that woman?" Fall snapped.

Ajax glanced back. "I need to learn her secrets. Killing her might not let me learn all of them."

After a long silence the three returned to the cart. "Keeping her alive and secret should be a capital crime," Fall muttered upon climbing into the cargo bay and sulking.

Ajax channeled some magic into the horses that forced them to move. "But if the kingdom gets her, you will not be able to kill her yourself. I'll still need to tell them but do tell me if you find her first," he pointed out. Ajax needed to rush back to get his supporters to look for Lindy. Despite all of this, Frost still looked unmoved, but inside she was a mess. *Why do I feel like I know Lindy Shrew, why does my heart race when I think of her now, why... why don't I want her dead?* Those thoughts and more ran through her head. Close to the capital where bandit teams and monsters appeared from time to time the land was still. Animals moved warily and no dangers appeared although signs of small skirmishes lay here and there along the road Ajax took.

A day after Lindy escaped from confinement she was resting a few miles from Ajax's encampment for the night. At this time they were on the border of the dead zone around the old academy. Some animals and many plants were around, but nothing that needed lots of food or loot moved along the overgrown grove they had found themselves in. Lindy woke up when she noticed three people sneaking up on her from far deeper in the grove. A large man tried to sneak up on Lindy who was not pretending to sleep. "You think she has any food on her?" the man asked.

A woman whispered. "Shut up! Don't startle her." She moved to the side, hiding behind a tree between Lindy and Ajax's camp.

A lean man walked up to Lindy and asked softly, "Hey, are you awake?"

Lindy opened one eye. Looking up at the young man she was surprised at recognizing the man's soul but did not show it. "Who are you?" Lindy asked indifferently, keeping tabs on all the newcomers' movements.

"You can call me Theodore. My friends call me Quell," the young man said.

Lindy smirked. "Not a lieutenant anymore then. I thought you would be a governor by now, old man."

Theodore shook his head. "I don't know what you mean," he said.

Lindy chuckled. The large man behind her flinched. "You got younger again but have not died since I last saw you. What's it been, thirty years, maybe more?" Lindy explained.

The woman came out from behind the tree, her hand on a sheathed dagger. Lindy noticed she was a half-elf who could be even older than Quell, but not by much if her age was natural. "How do you know Sir Quell?" To Lindy's amusement the half-elf was clearly jealous.

Forcing herself not to laugh, Lindy pointed to the camp far behind the half-elf. "I am tracking those heroes. Your love interest arrested me a long time ago. I have no other connection to him."

Quell snapped quietly. "Must have been an impressive arrest. What did you do?"

Without warning the large man rushed at Lindy. "Rob her already," the man growled. A wave of cold rushed out from Lindy who was still seated, freezing the man solid. In the blink of an eye Lindy melded into the shadows. Appearing behind the large man, she chopped with her hand and the man's frozen head flew off into Quell's hands.

"I killed off a cult, instigated a riot, took down an undead army, and made a very big hole in less than two days." Lindy looked at Quell, who did not seem the least bit fearful.

"Lindy Shrew, you died," Quell said, tossing the man's head to the ground. The half-elf looked terrified at the mention of Lindy's name.

"And yet Death still inflicts me on this world. Oh, my last name is Reaper now," Lindy smiled.

"Y- you are the hero killer?" the half-elf stammered, now terrified.

Lindy looked the woman in the eyes. "Maybe. What of it?"

"Maybe?" The half-elf choked down an incredulous shriek.

Quell looked at his living companion. "Hazel, save the hysterics." Then he looked at Lindy. "You owe me. Help us kill some bandits and I'll call it even."

"Does he count?" Lindy asked, pointing at the frozen headless corpse. Quell simply glared at her. Lindy pouted. "You are less fun now." Her face went from childish to dead serious in an instant. Now not even Quell could keep up or feel he knew Lindy's true mood. "Help me be a mercenary right after that and we have a deal."

"I don't owe you anything," Quell sneered.

Lindy laughed, grabbing Hazel. "Her life, your life, the governorship of a city you failed to keep."

Quell's face stiffened. "Fine, deal if you help us."

Lindy released Hazel who had gone very pale and patted Quell on the shoulder. He flinched. "I always keep my promises, old man," Lindy whispered.

Hazel nodded robotically. "L- let's go."

Lindy took one more glance at Ajax's camp, which was not stirring. "Yes, let's."

Hazel led the way. A little over half a mile away was a small hill with a large chunk missing on one side. Fifty bandits hid there, looking over the spoils from their most recent raid. By the looks of it, a modestly well-to-do merchant and his escort had been robbed of all their worldly possessions. Deep in a dark grove Quell muttered, "That is a lot of bandits."

"Too many," Hazel agreed.

Lindy rolled her eyes. "Fine, I'll do it. Wait here."

"Wait, you can't," Hazel said. What the half-elf soon realized was that Lindy had left before Hazel had even noticed the terrifying hero had spoken.

The bandit handing out the loot, one flunky, and the three most self-important-looking bandits all died in a torrent of gore. "Attack!" a bandit yelled.

"Ambush!" Lindy yelled back. Six more men lost limbs and heads. Lindy stood in place, her speed giving the illusion that she had not moved at all.

"Attack all together and we can surely kill that thing," an oddly naïve-looking bandit yelled heroically. As soon as he finished, the man decomposed into ash within seconds. Half a minute later every bandit had died by Lindy's hand. Her job was made far simpler when nearly all of Quell's targets rushed her.

Watching the scene, Hazel threw up. Quell sighed. "I am helping that monster because she terrifies me."

"Can't we report her to the kingdom after we finish the deal?" Hazel asked, shaking, her flesh pale and her eyes skittish.

Lindy appeared next to Hazel and whispered into her ear. "If you did, I would kill anything between us until you both died as well."

Quell nodded. "I know you would." Then Hazel fainted in abject terror. Quell glared at Lindy. "Was that really necessary?"

"Well it's not like I lied," Lindy groaned before wiping Hazel's mouth with her own shirt, then hoisting the half-elf over one shoulder. "So what now?" Lindy asked.

Quell looked around. "I loot this camp. You stand watch. Then we find a new campsite."

Lindy smiled. "No problem." Quell maintained an unreadable expression.

The next few days Lindy hunted the targets Quell picked out. Hazel slowly became barely numb enough to not faint in Lindy's presence. Along the way Lindy kept an eye on Frost and her companions. One night Hazel asked, "That pale child. Why are you so focused on her?"

"Love at first sight," Lindy shrugged, not bothering to swallow a lump of bread as she spoke.

"Something as inhuman as you should never feel love," Hazel shouted, no longer able to keep her fear under control. Given that Hazel could not escape from Lindy, let along wound her physically, a verbal assault was all she had to fall back on.

Lindy looked down at the bowl of beans, beets, cabbage, and jerky she had been enjoying. "Living beings can be extremely vicious and complex. I am very unusual but I have retained some of my human feelings."

Hazel took a deep breath. "The world of humans and elves is not that kind of place."

Lindy looked deep into Hazel's eyes with a look of pity. "When an ogre, troll, or dragon eats someone, are they a monster?"

Quell shook his head. "Those are always monsters."

Lindy leaned her back onto a tree and closed her eyes. She sighed then stooped forward, picking up a scrap of jerky and holding it up. "Then would whatever this was think of us as monsters?"

"Of course not. They can't think that far," Hazel answered angrily.

Lindy smiled evilly. "Then aren't you worse than a man-eating monster?"

Hazel focused on what she wanted to from Lindy's argument. "If you don't want to be called a monster, then why eat?"

"To live. There is a lot to this world and not all of it is kind. Some of that is inescapable; others are built in, and so on." Lindy sighed like someone well over twice her true age.

"So which one do you love?" Quell asked.

"She is called Frost in this life," Lindy muttered, for once showing some pain on her face.

"If you knew her then, you mean Fraya?" Quell inquired.

"Names don't make a life," Lindy grumbled before getting up and leaping into a tree. "I'll take first watch," she volunteered.

A few more days of hunting later, Lindy had looted some close-fitting clothes, some light leather armor, a backpack and a long hooded cloak that fit her, all in dark colors. Quell and Hazel stood next to Lindy in a line of a good forty other groups waiting for the security check at the gates. The day before they had watched from a hidden rocky outcrop as Ajax and company entered the gates. Quell whispered to Lindy, "So are you going to look for your ex?"

Lindy shook her head grimly. "No. Fraya is long gone. Frost has different goals, desires, values, and experiences. They are not the same person nor do I wish them to be."

"But you loved her, right?" Hazel asked.

Lindy looked up at the sky. "Frost is young. Her past life should not define her. So I am not going to confront her with her past self, because I care."

"Is that why?" Hazel pondered gruffly.

Lindy threw her hands up into the air. "Not that I have looked, but you are almost certainly older than I am. How is that hard to understand?"

They were nearing the gate when Lindy finished that memory. The line had extended far behind them by now, owing to it being early morning. The produce shops had carts coming in with their stock for the day. Hazel took a deep breath and said something she had been thinking since she met Lindy. "You are too far outside the bounds of common sense. Don't judge others by those standards." Lindy was glad Hazel had gotten more confident talking to her, even if Hazel was using her discomfort and rage to overcome the hesitation and terror that had held her back for most of the trip.

At the gate three groups were screened at a time. Quell and Hazel handed over small wooden cards bearing their names, a symbol of a yellow stack of gold and a small red dot of preserved blood that glowed with life when near its owner. Quell shoved Lindy up to the guard. "This one is with us as well. She will have a mercenary ID by the end of the day."

Rolling his eyes, the guard grumbled and held out his hand. "Ten silver."

Quell slammed a bundle of twelve silver coins into the man's hand. "The security is a lot tighter than it was last week. What happened?"

The guard glanced at the coins in his palm. Putting two silvers into a bulging pocket and the rest in a strong box, the guard shrugged. "We do as we are told. So far my post has been on high alert for five days. No one is telling us anything. Word is some big new ruin has blue bloods in a panic." The man sighed, then taking out a sheet of worn dirt-smeared paper the man asked Lindy, "State your name, occupation, and business in the city."

Out of the corner of her eye Lindy spied a thin stern-looking officer standing in the shadows behind the guard. "Most people call me Reaper. That is also my current profession. I am to be a well-known mercenary as soon as possible."

The guard looked back at the officer, who nodded back. The guard then handed Quell and Hazel their cards. "Move along, you three," the man told them unenthusiastically as he looked back over the still-growing line behind them.

Quell led Lindy over hard dirt-packed streets with tall wooden buildings and stinking alleyways. Hazel noticed a flicker of disappointment in Lindy's eyes. "First time in a city?" she tried to sneer but lacked the energy to really make her annoyance come across.

"I was expecting more high-level fantasy here. I mean dragons and magic exist, but this is just so..." Lindy paused, looking around. "Normal," she finished.

"The noble quarter has stone roads maintained by earth magic," Quell told Lindy, who was still a bit distant from her expectations being let down so far. Grasping at straws, Quell added, "Long distance communication is used by our leaders to stay informed."

Perking up, Lindy asked, "How much exercise do the nobles get?"

Hazel sighed and shrugged. "Most don't, so we get paid and the world keeps turning."

Lindy watched some homeless urchins escape down an alleyway from a slightly older boy in a shopkeeper's outfit. "Some things never change, no matter the world." Lindy shook her head.

The walk took them by the military buildings, past more gates, by slightly nicer homes, and then to shops. Quell stopped after the stalls, near what looked like a second line of military facilities. "So why work as a mercenary?" Quell asked.

Lindy smirked. "It's a living."

"Right, can't die," Quell nodded.

Lindy glared at him. "Only because I have not tried. Dying is not fun. All of my deaths have been fast and violent."

"But you still died," Hazel noted.

"I don't stay dead," Lindy replied, absently looking at her hand. "I'm beginning to think living forever may be a fate worse than death," Lindy whispered wistfully to herself.

"Well, whatever, we are here." Quell pointed to the top of a squat building slightly removed from the military structures. "I don't want anything more to do with you, Lindy Shrew, hero killer."

Lindy brushed past him. "That may be best. Although most of my prey will not be heroes." At the door Lindy looked back at her two unwilling aides. "Oh, and old man, be careful if you extend your life more. The loophole you have been using is currently under review."

"Well now I know Death is not omnipotent," Quell smirked provocatively.

Lindy laughed. "I am not allowed to comment on that, but I can say its realm is a very boring place. I keep telling that bonehead to relax a little but nope, being overworked forever is life for those like me and that one." Before Quell could reorder his thoughts Lindy marched into the building. Small meeting rooms took up most of the first floor. A mid-sized lobby and a small reception desk were the only other things on that level. "No bar. That's new."

A large man at the reception desk looked up from some papers he was shuffling. "Bar fights would get too out of hand. The adventurers' HQ is in the market district. They get more than enough of that."

"So this is where I sign up to be a mercenary?" Lindy asked amicably.

The man held out a hand. "Your referral letter?" to which Lindy allowed an expression of surprise onto her normally impassive or jovial face. To her shock she found other expressions were harder to do well, so she used her surprise at failing to make an expression help her act along. The man went back to his papers. "Then bring your sponsor. We work in units. If no unit will hire you then tough luck."

Lindy asked innocently, "Can I make my own unit?"

The man grumpily looked up. "Units have three members minimum. Can you even fight?"

Lindy giggled. "Only a hero could beat me."

Then man was now very annoyed. "Stop wasting my time."

Lindy dropped her naïve act and glared at the man as twenty specters appeared around her. "Say that again," she challenged.

"High level magic is not enough to allow for an exception, so send those dead souls back," a smaller man called from a meeting room. Its door stood ajar.

Lindy could almost see the power of the smaller man. "These are bodies made of deathly energy. I don't need souls for them. Are you the most powerful fighter here?" The specters dispersed without sound or fanfare as if they had never existed.

"Not even close," the smaller man replied calmly despite the small amount of bloodlust and rage Lindy was letting show.

Lu Limore

Male human age 34

Affiliation: Derndell kingdom mercenary union

Job: blade master

Status: Derndell kingdom mercenary, leader of the Eternal
unit, master of sword craft lower old imperial style

Abilities: strength 418, vitality 347, mind 122, agility 211
Talents: fearless, language (common Derndell), master parry, hero power: unlock, true event sight: 10 second precognition, forceful blow, subdue, enhanced trait: awareness, good teeth, strong sword. tough sword, flurry of blows, extended lifespan 1 time minor
Skills: sword: master, armor proficiency (plate/ chain/ leather): expert. Athletics: expert, repost: expert, duel wield: expert, search: journeyman, tactics: skirmish: journeyman, smithing: journeyman, intimidate (force of presence): journeyman, diplomacy: adept, etiquette: beginner, tracking: beginner, survival (woodland/ plains/ mountains): journeyman, climb: adept

"Lies," Lindy retorted.

"You are stronger than I am," Lu shot back.

"That's right. Your stats are far below mine," Lindy grinned.

The man at the counter had been listening but he could no longer stay silent. "Limore, how do you know this brat is stronger?"

"I have fought enough times to know she could kill me easily. Are you a hero, miss?" Lu asked. He was paying the receptionist just enough attention to still be vaguely aware of him.

"I am not heroic," Lindy replied evenly.

"You are sinister. I think I'm in love," Lu chuckled.

Lindy was at a loss. "That's not something you say upon first meeting someone."

"It's not?" Lu asked. He seemed confused.

Lindy looked at the man blankly. "Are you hiring?"

"Do you want to join?" Lu asked, walking up to Lindy. A few more heads were now poking out of some of the meeting rooms.

Lindy extended her hand. "Let me work alone as much as possible and I would have no problem working with you for Eternity."

Lu shook Lindy's hand. "Ok deal, vice leader."

This guy really throws me off. Oh well, this should be fun for a while, Lindy thought, looking at the ashen faces all around her.

Lu waved to the receptionist as he dragged Lindy. Hung on the door he exited from was a plank showing a skeletal hand reaching into the air from a mound of dirt. "Pops, take care of the paperwork for us. Thanks. Bye." Lu called before pushing Lindy into a room with three of his subordinates and shutting the door.

In the cramped meeting room sat twenty gruff-looking mercenaries. Each one wore the same symbol displayed on the door somewhere on their person. "Who's the newbie?" a thin young arrogant-looking man asked.

"Our new vice leader," Lu told them.

"So you like those kinds of women, boss?" someone well-hidden in thick heavy robes asked. Its voice was rough but light.

"At least choose the replacement from one of us," a middle-aged wall of muscle asked jovially. His eyes, however, were sharp and judgmental.

A small man with a monocle spoke up. "The so-called newbie is likely as strong or stronger than our leader."

"What Salver said, and more importantly, so how young are you, brat?" the young man from before asked.

"Tomayis, don't tell me you can't even analyze that," the robed one complained.

"I can't believe I am saying this, but neither can I, Cal," the small man sighed.

Lindy looked at the ceiling, somewhat regretting her choice to join these apparent boisterous morons, but at the same time looking forward to the mischief she could cause with them. "For the past thirty or so years I have not been a day over twenty."

"As bad as I am at math, even I know something is off about that," the large man groaned, his head clearly hurting. Lindy watched the other members around them. Two members sat near Cal, three more by the young braggart Tomayis, five sat around the small man, and five with the large man. Judging by the others' attitudes, these were the other leaders of the unit, or at least the spokesmen of factions or teams within it.

"That's true," the small man replied.

"So, this one is stronger than you, boss?" the large man asked.

"That's right Yern, she is," Lu smiled.

"So what's her name?" Cal asked a little forcefully.

> Calanya Fulbrin
>
> Female elf age 297
>
> Affiliation: Derndell kingdom mercenary union
>
> Job: arch mage
>
> Status: Derndell kingdom mercenary, mage cell head of the eternal unit, honorary grand magus of greenwood builders union
>
> Abilities: strength 97, vitality 62, mind 170, agility 75
>
> Talents: language (common Derndell/ high Elven/ greenwood mage sect cant. spirit cant). subdue, enhanced trait: awareness, good teeth, soul sight, empower magic, empower object, limited swift enchantment, high tier magic sense, discern lies
>
> Skills: earth magic: expert, armor use (cloth): adept, absorb impact: journeyman, healing magic: master, lighting magic: expert, literacy: expert, metal magic: journeyman, mace: journeyman, athletics: adept, cooking: beginner, weaving: adept, sewing: journeyman

Lindy chuckled, drawing more than a few annoyed gazes. "Ok Calanya, I am glad I'm not the lone female here. I'm Lindy Reaper and you are stronger than these guys, right?"

Cal tore off her hood. Scars and burns covered her face and exposed parts of her arms. The elf's pointed ears had long been cut down. "You analyzed me," she said, narrowing her eyes.

"That's right. If I was going all out you might last three seconds. If I took my time, 25 seconds tops." Lindy smiled lightly, which made her expression all the more menacing. Cal shot a glance at Lu. For less than a second Cal's expression was one of loneliness and disappointment. Lindy pretended not to notice and looked over at Lu. "I am not attracted to men. You still want me to help out?" she asked.

Yern growled. "That's rude to our boss, twerp."

Lu looked closely at Lindy before firmly and steadfastly telling her, "I need your power to make my unit famous and rich. No one here is allowed to romance another member of the unit."

Lindy studied Lu for a few seconds before nodding. "Good answer. Fine, I'll help your unit for a while."

Salver looked closely at his new sub leader. "Still, Lindy has never been a common name. It's pretty much a faux pas to name a child Lindy now. What with that being the name of an infamous traitor."

Lindy looked at the man. "Lindy is a common name for those with my blood, and that traitor does not exist anymore." Cal narrowed her eyes but did no more than that. "So how did the last second-in-command die?" Lindy asked.

"Manticores," Tomayis spat.

"Indeed, what the idiot said. Manticores, a whole legion of them," Salver nodded.

"Always with the fucking manticores," Lindy muttered. Then her eyes seemed to glow with an inner fire of willpower. Her mischievous childlike visage crumbled like bad plaster over a statue. An oppressive murderous intensity took the place of Lindy's jovial self. "Where is this legion of monsters?"

"Why are you so mad?" Tomayis asked fearfully.

"I have more than a few bones to pick with those cliché big bad monster wannabes," Lindy hissed.

"Spirits. What did they do to you?" Cal whimpered.

"Killed my girlfriend, almost ate me a few times, killed my friends' future lackeys, shattered my arms, and I only got like two good meals out of them!" Lindy yelled. By the end of her rant she was gasping for breath. Lu put his hand on her shoulder. A few minutes later Lindy was back to her normal self, but with sweat now drenching her.

"If you hunt them now, we can't help you. There are too many of them," Lu told his newest recruit kindly.

Lindy took a deep breath and nodded. "That's fine. Those monsters were a mission target, right? I will end them all for my sanity and the unit's honor."

"All right. Cal, get her washed up. Salver and Tomayis, you guys get as much data on that mission as you can. When you're done pass it to the Eternals second-in-command. That's it. You lot, get going," Lu commanded, ending the meeting.

Calanya took Lindy's hand and nearly dragged her to a small washroom. The room had a hand pump, a few buckets, a stool, and some greeting on a mat. Tossing the new vice leader inside, Cal waited outside the door while Lindy hummed. This was the second time in Cal's long life that she found such peacefulness oppressive, so she asked, "So are you really our ally?"

Lindy's humming stopped suddenly, leaving an eerie silence that seemed to flow around the building unnaturally. "If I said I was, would you be my ally?" Lindy asked after some thought.

"If I felt I could trust you more, then yes," Cal answered.

"Do you trust anyone completely with everything?" Lindy shot back, now seriously inquisitive.

"Only the unit leader. The rest I trust with my life but not how I live," Cal answered within seconds.

"I trust no one completely but I will help our unit live well," Lindy replied, walking out of the washroom. The dirt she had accumulated was gone and her hair which had grown long and matted when her body had broken out from her prison was now short and even.

Cal was stunned when Lindy smiled. The only words that came to mind were dignified and cute, but when she scowled, now Cal knew only the word 'terrifying' would fit. Cal needed to know how Lindy could be both the life of a party and the kind of person that would make a crowd's blood freeze in terror. "Will you tell me where you are from?"

"Nope. Will you tell me where I can find a workshop?" Lindy smiled, opening her cloak to reveal her Lindy Special Version 1 pistol, Storm Hush Type 1, and Long Barrel Express. They were no longer as easy for her to wield, given Lindy's increase in size and some stone pieces that were stuck to them.

Calanya looked closer. "That's not a storm bow," she said, looking at Lindy's mini version of it.

"So, tinkering workshop?" Lindy pressed.

Cal looked into Lindy's eyes for a few seconds. "I know a place but I can't promise they will let you in," she said.

"Can we go now?" Lindy asked, her voice firm, but it was the gleeful twinkle in Lindy's eyes that make Cal apprehensive.

"Sure, but don't destroy anything," Cal grumbled. Despite her annoyance, Cal was inwardly enjoying how free Lindy seemed.

Calanya led Lindy out the back door to a small squat building. Past the door was a small staircase leading down. Lindy smirked upon noticing the building was sunk into the ground "How many workshops have you guys lost so far?" she asked.

"Not a one!" a small bearded man yelled at her from the first basement level.

"Three that I know of," Cal corrected.

"Damn elves," the small man sighed.

Lindy rolled her eyes and took out her pistol. "I need to repair a few weapons. Can I borrow a workbench?"

The small man froze seeing her weapon. "That's one of the originals."

Cal looked over at Lindy quizzically, not getting the significance. "So can I use a workbench?"

"I don't have the skill to fix that," the small man told her.

"I'm the one fixing it. No one touches my weapons," Lindy grumbled. Some of her inner bloodlust leaked out.

Cal got a cold sweat and backed away from Lindy but the small man did not notice, too entrapped in his own little world. "Can I watch you maintain that?"

Lindy took out her other two creations. "You can watch me work on all three if you like. As long as I can work in peace and quiet."

The small man bolted away. "Follow me," he bellowed.

Lindy sighed, looking at Calanya. "So who is he?"

"A dwarf," Cal told her. Lindy sharpened her gaze. Cal relented. "He's called Maklin Steelfoot," she said.

The women were led past some tables filled with a haphazard arrangement of tools and supplies to a line of private rooms. Maklin led them inside one of the back rooms where two older dwarves sat eating lunch. Their guide had to loudly clear his throat a few times before the two elders looked up. The oldest-looking dwarf peered at Lindy's three personal inventions and proclaimed, "I can't fix those."

"But I can," Lindy huffed. The room they were in was neat enough. Shelves filled with half-sorted materials covered the walls. "Mind if I use this to repair these myself?"

"I'd like to see you try," the oldest elder said gruffly.

Lindy shrugged. "Fine, but don't invite anyone else."

The younger elder smiled. "Fine. If you completely repair those, we won't charge you for anything this time."

The older elder held out his hand. "Fixell Shadesmith at your service."

Lindy shook the man's hand lightly. "Lindy Reaper." Fixell looked over at Cal, narrowing his eyes. "She's with me. I'm her boss," Lindy added.

Shadesmith nodded impassively then turned to the other elder. "Grix Fellscrew, clean that table!"

Grix was a little mad but after a long glance at Lindy's bundle of gear he saluted. "At once, grandmaster."

Lindy smirked to herself, placing her three old weapons on the table. Grabbing a few scattered tools and rapidly cleaning the gear, then regenerating any cracks in the weapons using a few small runes designed to synthesize monster parts into alloys, Lindy used her own blood empowered by necromancy.

Shadesmith watched in awe. Lindy's speed was due mainly to her stats and the fact that she was the inventor and creator of the three relics. Her work was precise and did nothing to diminish the potential carnage the weapons were able to unleash. Grix looked at Lindy's pistol. "Is that an original officer-grade handgun?"

"It is an original of its kind," Lindy allowed.

"With no replacement parts?" Grix pressed.

"Not yet," Lindy told him absentmindedly, far too engrossed in her work to pay the world around her much attention.

"How old are these?" Grix pressed madly.

"Around thirty years," Lindy replied lazily.

"Are they usable?" Shadesmith inquired, his greed for knowledge overriding anything else.

"They will be," Lindy smiled to herself.

"Shame they will not be in peak condition," Shadesmith sighed. What Lindy did not know was her originals had been copied heavily. Most of those copies broke fast. The downgraded ones had been mass produced and were even more volatile than she had anticipated. Repairs often reduced the weapons to being even worse off. Most of the originals had been broken down and either badly reassembled or had their parts installed in new poorly made versions.

"Oh, these will be good as new," Lindy said. This was the last thing she should have told them. Ignorance and tunnel vision caused her misstep.

Calanya blocked the dwarves' view of Lindy. The new vice leader of Eternal asked, "That's enough. How much do we owe?"

Fixell looked around the room. "We have seen enough. As agreed, no cost. I can't charge you for a few minutes well spent."

Grix walked to the exit. "I'll lead you lovelies out."

Lindy followed after Grix. Calanya leaned over to Lindy. "What blood did you use for that rune?" Grix perked up. He had been observing Lindy closely, trying to gather as much info as he could since she showed off her weapons.

Lindy shrugged. "Mine." The two with her stumbled.

"What are you, some kind of monster?" Calanya asked awkwardly.

"You think I'm not?" Lindy retorted. She inflected her words like a joke but her tone was dead serious.

"Fair point," Calanya sighed, deflating. Since Lindy had analyzed her, Calanya only saw her new superior as a monster. This new event simply made that impression less metaphorical.

They arrived at the main counter and Grix ran off on some errand.

"Tell the boys I'll need that info soon," Lindy called, walking out of the door.

"Where are you going?" Calanya called after her.

"Hunting," Lindy called back. After a few steps she turned around and giggled at Calanya's horrified expression. "Food shopping. I'll be back here early tomorrow morning."

9

Gilded Rust

Late that night Hanna Zigone and Quell of the Golden Horde sat in the back of an expensive restaurant that prioritized their customers' privacy. "This better be really important," Hanna scowled, the full force of her considerable focus trained on Quell, which was bad for anyone's health.

"Lindy's back," Quell groaned absently, swirling a spoon in a bowl of soup he could afford if he used ten years' worth of his earnings.

Hanna snapped out of her internal musings. "Say that again."

"Lindy's alive," Quell snapped, grinding his teeth. His shoulders twitched with the memory of his recent encounter.

"Who else have you told?" Hanna asked. She let a smile slip. *Ok, she's not dead for good yet, what an unlucky child. Perhaps that rat Ajax really did see her,* Hanna mused to herself.

"You are the only one I am going to tell. Even that might be enough for that psycho to hunt me down." Quell shook.

"Anything new with her?" Hanna inquired, somehow more amused than angry now that she knew Lindy was most likely back.

"She looks older and seemed to think her girlfriend was back and that past flame might be one of your daughters," Quell slumped into his chair.

That was not something Hanna could let go. Lindy's escapades were one thing but getting her family involved in those deadly daredevil escapades was something else entirely. At least Lindy could recover from dying, if Ajax was to be believed. "Which one?"

"Frost," Quell replied, his energy drained.

"Looks like things will get chaotic again." Hanna shook her head, now working out how to let herself and her daughters survive Lindy's existence physically and socially. The politics around Lindy being alive again was going to be a powder keg. Hanna had to make sure she and her daughters did not get burned by it.

"Where is she now?" Hanna finally asked. After the appetizers and main dish were long gone, a small slice of pie was laid before her.

"She was looking to become a mercenary," Quell replied. One look at the gleam in Hanna's eyes and Quell easily added, "No, I don't know which unit if any recruited her, and there is no way I will spy on Lindy Reaper." After saying that, Quell bent over in agony. *Shit, the psycho did something to me* he realized.

"Lindy Reaper?" Hanna asked, not seeming to take note of Quell's suffering.

"That's what she is called now. I am certain it's the same one. Please dispel the trap she set on me," Quell pleaded.

"Frost, Fall, treat this man. After that, tell me what really happened," Hanna called over to some curtains. Her daughters swiftly showed themselves and managed to treat Quell's pain but not the cause. After that, Quell fled the scene and the young heroes fearfully told their mother the full truthful account of their trip with Ajax Shrew.

Early the next morning Lindy walked out of the back room of an herbalist's shop. The owner of the shop was a human and married to Calanya's half-elf niece. The shop was in the shopping district and close to some military buildings. "That was a good couch. Too bad I am incorporeal. Wait, what?" Lindy muttered to herself. "No, Conduit is incorporeal, I am full-bodied." Lindy nodded to herself, now lost in her thoughts. She bumped into a large man wearing a badge displaying a yellow stack of gold.

The man tried to grab Lindy. Even impaired, Lindy dodged around the man without noticing what had happened. The man yelled out, "Hey, get back here kid!" Lindy did not stop.

Hazel stood a few feet from Lindy at a food stall. Hazel swiftly finished the bite of an apple she had been savoring and called out, "Rec, don't push that one."

The large man and a few of his cronies sneered, rushing after Lindy. The one careful member of Rec's team slowed down and asked, "Why?"

"She is really dangerous," Hazel replied in a fearful manner.

"The bosses said to rob that mark though. Something about priceless weapons," the careful and well-paid thug said.

"Don't die too fast then," Hazel called after the man, now more disgusted with her unit than ever before. After finishing her shopping Hazel ran back to the apartment Quell had been hiding in, enduring intense agony every few hours. *We have to escape the unit and this nation before that psycho blows it all up,* Hazel realized.

A little way into the housing district, Rec caught up with Lindy. This time he and four subordinates grabbed at her. The last two men glared at the passersby, getting them to distance themselves from the scene. Before she could process what was going on, Lindy cut open the bellies of three of the subordinates. "You punk, how dare you!" Rec yelled.

Finally, Lindy snapped out of her musings and looked around. Then she glared at Rec. "What's going on, are you mugging me?"

"Our bosses demand all of your weapons now!" Rec yelled. A crowd began to gather, watching the fight unfold.

"On what authority?" Lindy sneered. The street and buildings began to ice over and the sky suddenly became dark.

Rec puffed out his chest. "We are nobles!" Lindy tore off the head of another of her assailants.

"You are as noble as I am heroic," Lindy scoffed, tossing the head away in disgust.

"You are no hero," Rec growled.

"That's right. I am at best some kind of villain, you scoundrel." Lindy sneered, a bloodthirsty grin growling on her face.

Suddenly a lazy voice yelled out, "Lindy Reaper, stop this now, please." Frost jumped down from a carriage. Fall was gawking from within the carriage. Hanna sat beside her daughter nursing a headache.

"Sup old friend. What's new?" Lindy greeted Hanna casually. Lindy's aura was now the picture of calm even with all the blood spatter on her.

"Not well, Lindy," Hanna sighed, then she glared at Rec. "Sir Zu Recodin, stop harassing my sister."

"What sister?" Zu 'Rec' Recodin asked. It was common knowledge the only person Hanna ever called sister was Genney the sage, but she was long dead.

"That fool is my sister. She disappeared before you were even born. Now both of you stop fighting," Hanna demanded.

"You are called Lindy?" Rec asked his target.

"That's right," Lindy smiled, bobbing her head. The sky regained its shine, somehow making Lindy look very cute.

"Are you that Lindy?" Rec asked. Hanna held her breath.

"You mean Lindy Shrew? Nope, she's long dead," Lindy replied guilelessly. Her sudden cheerfulness unnerved almost everyone who had seen her fight.

"How do you know that for sure?" Fall huffed. Frost and Hanna both looked at Fall, wordlessly telling her to shut up.

Lindy skipped past Frost and up to the carriage. This made Frost feel somewhat sad. *Am I really that other person? No, I am myself,* Frost thought. "Because Lindy is a title in my line. I am Lindy Reaper. There can't be a Lindy Shrew because I succeeded her." Lindy winked so only Fall and Hanna could see.

"See, she is the descendant of that Lindy," Hanna called over. All of a sudden, panic erupted. After much yelling and pushing, Frost, Fall, Hanna, Lindy, two horses, a few corpses, some rats, a pigeon, and Rec were the only ones still around.

"Ok, don't do that again," Lindy sighed.

Hanna grumbled. "This will be so much more paperwork."

Rec looked around. "Can I go now?" Hanna dismissed him with a wave.

After giving Lindy a once-over a thin smile appeared on Hanna's face. "Vice leader already. You are moving up in the world."

Lindy shrugged. "Not as much as you. Anyway, I got to go."

"Where?" Fall snapped.

"Hunting?" Lindy replied.

"Why?" Fall pressed.

"Need food badly," Lindy said, seemingly as if that was the sole reason anyone would go hunting.

"Oh. What are you after?" Frost asked, the ice in her voice thawing just a little.

"Manticores," Lindy said proudly.

"To eat?" Fall asked slowly.

"You have not changed," Hanna cut in. "Go, but do not cause problems for my daughters."

"Fine, but I promised Genney that I'll defend them if needed," Lindy said as she ran off. Hanna's headache got worse and Frost blushed a little.

Hanna and her daughters followed Lindy from a far distance. Near the gate a middle-aged man trotted up to Lindy. "Hey miss, spare a coin?" the man asked. Everything about the man rubbed Lindy the wrong way.

Wisdom Longteeth

Human male age 43

Affiliation: Derndell kingdom imperial rust thieves guild

Job: beggar

Status: village idiot

Abilities: strength 11, vitality 20, mind 90, agility 32

> Talents: mist like presence, alcohol tolerance: high, language common (Derndell/ imperial rust sign), enhanced trait: intuition, nonthreatening, trick moves, misdirection (attack/words/action)
> Curse: annoying to everything, pitiful to everyone
> Skills: armor proficiency (cloth/leather): adept. law: beginner. lie: expert, dagger: adept, athletics: journeyman, diplomacy: adept, bribe: beginner, stealth: expert, extort: journeyman

Lindy took out a small silver coin and held it up. Wisdom's eyes gleamed seeing the coin. Just as fast as Lindy retrieved the coin, she firmly clenched it in her first. "Word of advice. Learn how to haggle."

Wisdom looked at Lindy in a blatantly guarded manner. No one had ever looked him in the eyes. He got pocket change in a steady stream but those that handed him their cash cither did not seem to realize he was there or could not bring themselves to look at him. "Why?" he asked.

"Because you are a smart man. You could make a much better living negotiating with others." Lindy tapped the man on the shoulder. "You are alive and have very little left to lose. Try to be more greedy and cunning. After all, it would be a shame to not enjoy the benefits of living."

Lindy walked off. Wisdom was confused but more than that, his pride was ignited. Lindy had crossed the one line Wisdom would not let anyone cross: saying he could do more, which he could not believe. "What's so good about living!" he yelled at her.

Lindy tossed Wisdom the coin she had been holding. "Even if you get another life, your experiences in this life belong to you alone. If you don't give this life your all, why do you even try to survive?" Wisdom started to walk off when he felt a life-threatening glare directed his way.

Wisdom turned around, seeing Lindy glaring at him. "Well, what's your excuse?" she asked.

"Living is not that simple," Wisdom muttered.

"Do you give your life your full effort? Do you have dreams and ambitions? Do you want to win at life?" Lindy asked sternly.

"Of course I do! I still have my dignity!" Wisdom shouted angrily.

Lindy rolled her eyes and tossed Wisdom another silver coin, which he caught awkwardly. "Remember that feeling," she called.

Wisdom ran after the odd woman. "Wait, what are you?"

Lindy looked back at the interesting man who somehow could still affect her mood with abilities she could not fully understand and he did not appear to know about. "My self, just like you," Lindy laughed. Lindy used the shadows to directly whisper into Wisdom's ear. "Also, I am the one and only Death's Herald."

Wisdom was not fearful as this whole encounter seemed surreal to him. "Do you come to kill me, miss?" he asked.

Lindy appeared next to him and shook her head. "No. Your life is worth keeping around for a bit longer. If you live it well, soon it will be worth much more."

"Why?" Wisdom asked.

"You amuse me," Lindy shrugged.

Wisdom's eyes went bloodshot. "Then kill me now!"

Lindy grabbed Wisdom by his messy shirt. "No. You are strong, good, and most of all, not annoying. You could do a lot for this world." Then she tossed him to the ground. "Life is not meant to be easy. Everything worth something takes effort. Even the attempt at living has purpose!"

Wisdom looked up at Lindy angrily. "Cheap words. My attempts mean nothing!"

Lindy sighed and dragged Wisdom to his feet. "Nothing is free in life. Trust me, dying means your round in this game is up. Living is worth the attempt because if nothing else, it is something we all share. Also, wealth and living well are not the same thing."

Lindy walked off in a huff. Wisdom had one parting shot. "Why are you telling me all of this?"

"Because you don't pretend to be someone else. Unlike everyone else I have seen today, you alone have dignity. Keep it up, Mr. Longtooth," Lindy called back, her words skipping the thick crowd around them and resonating only with Wisdom.

"It's Longteeth," Wisdom yelled after Lindy.

"I know," Lindy snickered quietly to herself. Her mood finally stabilized and became battle ready. *I really missed not being able to bicker with and support someone honestly without holding back.* Lindy sighed in the dank void where she exiled the feelings that made her feel weak.

Lindy plugged into the mass of traffic. One of the city gates loomed over the rooftops, carts, and heads all around. Seeing a familiar soul near the gate, Lindy jumped though the shadows into an alley right behind Salver. Lindy walked up to him casually. Leaning over to him, Lindy was about to whisper into Salver's ear, but he twisted around and brought up a knife. Lindy caught his blade and reduced it to rusted sand. "Hello to you too," Lindy smirked, enjoying Salver's confused and horrified gaze.

"Where did you come from!" Salver asked shakenly.

"That way," Lindy pointed over to the back of the dead-end alleyway.

"That's impossible," Salver said, still in shock.

Lindy held out her hand. "Data now." She knew Hanna was getting closer to knowing her plans and uncovering all her deeds and that frightened Lindy. The only thing she truly feared was getting those she cared about tangled up in her own fate.

Salver was still frozen. "Are you..." he started shaking.

Lindy activated her weakening aura over her hands and grabbed Salver's shoulders. Glaring into his eyes she pleaded, "Info now."

Salver looked like he was spasming now. He managed a shaky nod and took out a small stack of papers. "This is all I could get so far. I should have more soon."

Lindy snatched the small stack from him and skimmed through it. Everyone near the gate felt panicked. Some of the guards zeroed in on Lindy and began to creep over. "This is enough." Lindy nodded. The oppressive air around her vanished in an instant. "Thanks." Lindy then took out her new ID that was tucked into the papers. "I'll eliminate all those that harm our comrades." With that oath still echoing in the mobbed street, Lindy put all her power into her legs and leapt over the wall.

Soon after, a small team of the bravest guards at the gate tackled Salver. Fall appeared before he could be dragged off. Fall blocked the annoyed guards, slowly fishing out a seal bearing the crest of House Derkin. "That man will answer to my family."

Tomayis had arrived right after Lindy had left the city. Not able to take any more, he pushed into the small clearing made by a hoard of spectators. "Hey, he's one of mine!"

Hanna and Frost had followed Tomayis into the confrontation, tying to use his arrogant and annoyed appearance to ease their passage, not realizing the force of their presence was helping him instead. Hanna kicked the thin man to the ground, looking far more annoyed than he did. "Explain please." Everyone knew she was not asking and that she was fully prepared to break the man's arm and burn him to ash if she got any more unhappy after losing Lindy again.

The guards were about to object when Fall tossed Salver's ID over. "Mom, catch," she called. The crowd froze, only now realizing just how important Hanna was.

Hanna caught it with her free arm and frowned. She glared at Tomayis, whose arm was creaking. "Young man, did your unit hire an annoying overpowered young lady a few days ago?"

"Who wants to know?" Tomayis asked, his teeth bracing against the pain.

Frost noticed a stack of papers peeking from Tomayis's pocket. Grabbing it, Fall took one look at the map and handed it over to her mother, who dropped Tomayis.

"That moron! The nursery, really?" Hanna fumed. She bent down to Tomayis, holding up the map for him. "What does that idiot want here?" The way Hanna cursed Lindy's existence was somehow lonely and endearing.

"We lost a few teams there on a job. She went there for food and to avenge us and some former lover, she said!" Salver confessed.

"Shit," Hanna groaned. "Fall, Frost, follow me. We need to see the king."

The three women began to walk away. The guards started to manhandle the two troublemakers left behind. Tomayis called out, "What did our vice leader do to you?"

Hanna did not turn around. Biting her lip she whispered, "She left me." Frost and Fall stopped for half a step, surprised at their mother's vulnerable appearance. Hanna composed her outward self swiftly and called back. "And those two are free to go. You don't want to make their new friend mad, trust me."

The guards Tomayis and Salver stopped mid-move, not able to believe what they were hearing. Frost looked back. "You really don't." Fragmented images of a former life spent with a small, captivating, overpowered, and careless girl came to Frost in a jumbled mess. Frost's voice was cold but a small tear fell from her face, freezing before it hit the ground.

"Sis?" Fall whispered.

Frost closed her eyes for a few seconds and sighed lightly. "I'm fine. Just an old dream, nothing real." The three women got to their carriage. Fall took over for the driver who they left to run back with a report to the main house.

Hanna examined Frost's face. *You can't lie to your heart, my child, but I wish we could,* she thought.

An hour later and six miles out, Lindy had arrived at her destination. Around the same time Hanna was admitted into an emergency audience with the Jay the King. His war marshal, champion, and spymaster were in the room as well. The court wizard and hunt master were listening in through remote viewing magic. Despite the immensely powerful and old barrier surrounding the room, this meant the kingdom's most powerful fighters and advisors were sitting in on the meeting. Ajax Shrew was in the room as well. After the normal shows of respect and fealty, King Jay allowed Hanna to stand. From the tall raised dais Jay looked down at the woman reviled by some and pitied by more. "You have news about the traitor?"

Hanna was used to hearing insults and slander directed at Lindy. She had cursed Lindy plenty over the years. To this day she did not believe all of the attacks on Lindy's character were totally wrong, but now after seeing Lindy again, seemingly the same girl from so many long years before if a bit taller, Hanna felt a bit annoyed at anyone but her slandering Lindy. "I have seen her, sire."

The new champion, a man called Randull Lorn, a master of close combat with magic like all the champions before, was still trying to prove himself. "Why did you not report this before?"

Hanna sighed, lying. "I learned of this late last night and wished to confirm that rumor before bringing it to our master."

"Well then, where is she now?" the spymaster asked from within his jacket. No one but the king knew what let alone who the spymaster was, given his gravelly voice that seemed to shift its origin point in the room randomly like vapor, regardless of where he was standing. The thick overcoat and hood covered in shadow magic he always wore only aided the mystery. The spymaster was called Dusk Nightcrow.

"She was headed to the manticore nursery. That was an hour ago," Hanna informed them.

"Why? Vengeance maybe?" The court wizard was a female pixy called Wisp.

"Food seemed to be her main objective. Vengeance was also part of it, for the love of her life and for the mercenary band she now helps lead," Hanna said.

"So that's where she went," Ajax muttered.

"You knew too?" Dusk said, seemingly to no one in particular.

Quick to throw her old friend's foe under the cart, Hanna announced, "From what I could gather, Mr. Shrew knew of his sister's return before I did."

"But a mercenary. We could use that," said the war marshal, the kingdom's best warrior and general, a hulking man with ogre blood named Grgen Smalsh.

"I concur. We could hire her for all kinds of things," said the hunt master, a half-elf of noble blood on both sides of her lineage called Anna Faywind, who happened to be Caldrin Faywind's niece three times removed on the elven side.

King Jay suddenly felt even older. "Hanna Zigone, do you believe Lindy Shrew would obey us in that manner?"

Hanna sighed. "If the offer was good enough and did not harm what she wished to protect, that one would do just about anything. She goes by Lindy Reaper, vice leader of the Eternal."

"Can we lose that nursery and those guarding it?" the king sighed.

"We have more than enough data for the next phase, Your Majesty. Even if the two summoned heroes are killed, it will not impact our plans," Anna Faywind reported.

"As long as that monster does not take her anger out on the kingdom, we will try to work with her closely. Do not let the Eternal unit out of the kingdom. We need that mad genius working for this kingdom. So watch them, but spare no effort at keeping Lindy Reaper and her unit comfortable. Do not antagonize her, but remember she is very dangerous and even more, useful. If Lindy Reaper looks to turn traitor or harm the kingdom let me know immediately, no matter what," the king decreed.

Meanwhile Lindy arrived at a large-scale dome-shaped magic barrier. The barrier was strong but visibly simple to find, merely reflecting the land directly outside. It had no subtlety, given how stupidly huge the barrier was. "Must have looked good on paper," Lindy scoffed, controlling a small chunk of the barrier's power to open up a path inside. On the other side was a polluted waste dump. Many small dens were scattered around, hollowed out from the muck and debris. Scores of manticores in all sizes frolicked and rampaged around, slaves to their whims, boredom, and instincts.

Two teenage male and female humans were seated a few steps from where Lindy entered. Somehow they were enjoying a picnic. The female at least had a near permanent scowl. Given her environment Lindy believed that much was normal. The pair's glossy equipment, however, was not. The female was the first to spot Lindy. She jumped back. "You lot are early," she said, looking around. "Where are the rest of you?"

Mia Fellborn

Female ?? age 32

Affiliation: Derndell kingdom assault team

Job: high hero

Status: outworlder, summoned being, indentured hero

Abilities: strength 985, vitality 1903, mind 2806, agility 2021

Talents: translation: all. empower magic, quick cast, innate spell: force. ritual magic, rune magic, analysis: high, resist: (fear/ heat/ poison/mind control/illusion): high, takedown, shape spell, anti magic: mastery, swift run, soundless step, never bald, extended life span, toughness: high, sense danger

Skill: healing magic: master, fire magic: master, earth magic: master, lava magic: expert, water magic: expert, cooking: expert, survival(all): journeyman, bluff: expert, empathy: adapt, perception: expert, armor use (cloth/leather): expert, staff: journeyman, hand to hand: expert, herbalism: expert. control magic: expert, sewing: adept

Mia looked no more than 20 years of age.

Valor the Merciless

Male ?? age 35

Affiliation: Derndell kingdom assault team

Job: high hero

Status: outworlder, summoned being, indentured hero

Abilities: strength 2506, vitality 2490, mind 1043, agility 1211

Talents: translation: all, good teeth, power strike, swift charge, flurry of blows, advanced danger sense, stunning strike, resist magic: moderate, resist: (pain/ fear/ poison) extreme. see truth, see magic, blink strike, rapid parity, improved trait: reaction speed, extended life span, toughness: high

Skills: armor proficiency (cloth/leather/chain): master, sword: master, dagger: expert, athletics: master: repost: master. survival(all): expert, blather: journeyman, intimidate (presence): expert

The boy too looked to be is his early 20s.

"So, you are not from here either?" Lindy commented reflexively.

Valor called back to his partner. "Friend of yours?"

Mia was heavily on guard. "You don't know her either?" she asked

Even though Lindy could understand what they said, the language the pair used seemed to buzz painfully in her mind. The words the pair used with each other consisted of clicks and whistles, mostly. "Ok, that rules out Earth as your home world."

Mia squinted her eyes at Lindy. "She has the same translation ability."

"And I can see all your stats," Lindy laughed. That if nothing else put Valor and Mia in combat mode.

"Why are you here?" the boy asked.

"To kill off the monsters here," Lindy smiled acidly.

"Just another bandit," Mia huffed.

"I am a mercenary," Lindy sneered.

"We follow orders," Valor growled.

"Right, so go away," Mia added. It seemed she had picked up on how powerful Lindy was.

"I made an oath to my unit. That, and I need to know if a pack was sent off from here thirty years ago," Lindy said.

"I can't let you do that," Valor said.

Lindy jumped to the rear of the pair's formation behind Mia. Before either of her opponents knew what was going on, Mia had collapsed, her magic power draining out of her. "One on one then, young man," Lindy spat.

"Nothing about you is just," Valor shouted.

"You are far too naïve," Lindy sighed.

Valor yelled, "Justice is mine!" Drawing a long thin translucent sword, the hero channeled magic into the blade, tinting it blue.

Lindy felt that the power in the sword was dangerous. "Nice blade," she praised, ducking a slice. The sword passed through a tree as if it were a phantom. The tree did not have a single mark on it. Valor swung the blade down at Lindy's back. She tried to parry the blade but it passed through her dagger just like the tree. Lindy swung out a leg, knocking Valor on his back. She then pulled out her pistol and empted its magazine into the boy's sword arm. Valor yelled out loudly.

Lindy tried to pick up Valor's sword but her fingers passed through it. Valor sneered past his pain. "Transcendence picks its wielders." Lindy stuck her three daggers into Valor's other arm, pinning it down. She then emptied the sword of Valor's magic and thrust her own magic into the blade.

Transcendence became inky black and leapt into Lindy's hand. "Looks like he likes me," she retorted in good humor. She thrust the sword under Valor's chin. "Now what does it do?"

"Why would I tell you!" Valor groaned. Lindy spun the blade down and placed it a few inches over Mia's heart. Lindy looked back at Valor and raised one eyebrow. "Fine. It cuts whatever I want and passes through what I don't want to harm." Lindy nodded and thrust the sword down. It passed though Mia but did no harm. Lindy smiled evilly like a child being challenged to a mud fight.

Lindy then slashed the sword at a patch of trees a few feet away. The trees fell down, cut cleanly in half without even being touched by the sword. "It cuts whatever I want it to and does not harm what I don't want to hit."

Valor looked very shocked. "It can do that?"

"So it appears." Lindy shrugged, snagging Transcendence's sheath and walking farther into the monster nursery.

"Wait, what about us?" Valor yelled.

"I don't have time for you," Lindy called back, cutting down a few small manticores with her new toy.

Lindy kept up her hunt methodically, cutting apart large numbers of juvenile and younger manticores. A small number of adult monsters appeared from deeper in. Even fewer heavily robed humanoids trailed after them. Lindy had slain most of the hive at this point. She was not enjoying how simple her slaughter had been so she cut down a tree and sat on its stump, reanimating the dead in the breeding ground. All the pieces of Lindy's current victims awkwardly sprang to un-life, cutting down the few living beings barring their master's way into the depths of the nursery. After the dead were done, Lindy released her flesh puppets from their strings. The last two beings were on their way to her.

A tall man in a thick robe and a very big manticore approached over the dead. Lindy waved at the man. "So who are you supposed to be?" she asked.

"You first," the man gruffly challenged.

Lindy lashed out with Transcendence, cutting off the man's legs and destroying the blood pathways next to his new stumps. Ignoring the man's screaming, Lindy looked up at easily the biggest manticore she had ever seen. Sensing something off about the beast before her, Lindy waved casually at it. "Hey, come here often?" she cooed as if talking to a small timid house pet.

"Kill!!!" the manticore replied in a deep tone. If she had not listened closely, it would have been nothing more then a blood chilling roar. Lindy sighed to herself, not affected by the monster's attempt at intimidation. *I am so cold-blooded that something like this makes me feel nothing,* Lindy grumbled introspectively. "You die now!!" the manticore yelled a little more clearly as it leapt at her.

Lindy sighed, rolling under the beast and cutting open its belly. "So I was not hearing things," she mumbled. The monster sailed over her, bleeding heavily. Lindy took up the Long Barrel Express and leveled it at the monster's backside. She fired one spear into its tail before the manticore twirled around, glaring. Lindy smiled. "Good, you can fight," she laughed, thankful for her chance at some stress relief and wondering how sickened she would be with herself after. The beast rushed her again. Lindy ducked under its jaws and cut off its head. Nonetheless the beast stood twitching, so Lindy thrust her hand into its neck and stilled its heart with necromancy. Lindy bitterly watched the beast crash to the ground. "Damn it," she spat. Looking up at the sky, Lindy yelled to no one and nothing in particular, "A challenge would be nice!" She began to cackle at the irony of her actions. "Granting wishes must be the pits," Lindy grumbled. Her rage was now the only thing keeping her painful memories and insecurities under control.

Lindy sighed to herself, looking over at the legless man and finding that he was dying from shock. "Today is not my day," she intoned deeply. "You got that right," she added before looking around. After realizing she had been talking to herself, Lindy shook her head. "Talking to myself. As if it was not already clear I was out of my mind." She walked into the center of the nursery.

Soon after she found a cabin. "The three of us are all insane in here," said Lindy, shaking her head. "Oh right, Conduit, me, and the other guy are all here, in me? Wait, I was the guy," she rambled before clutching her head and yelling "Shut up, we are me!"

Storming into the cabin, Lindy grabbed the few papers not stuck in the raging fireplace and ran out of the monster sanctuary.

It was late afternoon by the time Lindy leapt back into the capital. She staggered down the main street, fully aware that Fall had been trailing her since the moment Lindy had ducked out of an alleyway by the main gate. Normally Lindy would feel something about the person following her, wanting to mess with them or hunt them depending on circumstances, but right now Lindy's mind was in so much chaos she could barely walk. In short, her inner turmoil was her only focus. Her plans, tasks, musings, and grievances — none of that mattered right then, only her pain and the three personalities forcibly trying to mesh into one, all in her head. Staggering into a random pub, Lindy did not see the looks of concern or hear catcalls directed her way as she found a seat at the bar. Looking up at the aging bartender looming before her, Lindy smiled painfully. "Whatever is strongest." She scoffed at her own weakness, plopping a small gold coin before the man.

The man studied Lindy's eyes, searching for something. Looking satisfied he nodded, pulling a large bottle from under the counter and setting it in place of the coin. "I'll get you something solid as well," the man noted, gently pulling aside a waitress and getting her to rush to the kitchen. The bar had been still since Lindy had flashed her coin.

A thin scoundrel slinked up to Lindy. "Hey gorgeous, trouble sleeping?"

Even with her mood so dark Lindy had to scoff merrily at how pathetic the man seemed. "Don't use me to stroke your own ego," she told him flatly.

The man's face fell, his shock and anger plain. Taking out a small card, he shoved it into Lindy's face. "Do you know who I am?" he asked acidly. The man's shameful display only proved Lindy's point.

"I do now," Lindy groaned. "Golden Horde team leader," she whistled. When the man was grinning, Lindy took out her own card and waved it in the man's face. "I outrank you."

The man's face fell. "You are not a noble."

Lindy sighed and took a deep swig of her drink. It went straight to her head. "Your noble buddies tried to rob me this morning. Where's the nobility in that?" The man moved to speak but Lindy stopped him. "Shut up, sit down, and listen to my monologue."

The man ran away and the waitress placed a thin sandwich before Lindy, taking the man's spot. "That's a nice sword," she said, pointing to Transcendence.

"Thanks. It's new," Lindy nodded, drinking more.

"But is it yours?" the waitress asked.

"How would you know?" Lindy asked.

"I'm a priestess of War," the waitress said.

"Neat. One of the voices in my head is Death," Lindy revealed, putting out her hand to shake.

"That's rare." The waitress smiled a thin fake smile, shaking Lindy's hand. "Now where did you get that blade?" the young woman pressed.

"Answer a question of mine first," Lindy said between mouthfuls of sandwich.

"Fine. One question," the woman agreed with bold confidence.

"It's two questions but they may have one answer. In this world why are those born with great power beyond other children called heroes regardless of their moral character, and why are nobles called noble regardless of how just and good they act?" Lindy griped.

"I'm not touching that second one. What does morality have to do with heroism?" the waitress asked.

Lindy rolled her eyes. "Everything." She spoke painfully slow. "In my last world," Lindy finished in a flash.

"I don't get it," the waitress sighed.

"Neither do I," Fall answered from behind Lindy.

The waitress looked over at Fall. "Who are you?"

"Fall Zigone, house Derkin. You?" Lindy's stalker demanded.

"Warfelula Erstbow," the waitress/priestess of War replied.

Fall pulled up a stool next to Lindy. No one stopped her after seeing the three women together. "I've heard of you," Fall said.

Warfelula looked back at Lindy. "Last time. From where did you get that blade?"

Lindy finished the last of her drink, now feeling slightly giddy. "From some fools who did not stand a chance against me even when they outnumbered me."

"Is that true?" Warfelula asked, not seeming to believe Lindy.

"Yup. Valor made one good attack before I subdued him. Mia did not even manage that," Lindy said, hiccupping.

"Even for a priestess of Death, taking out a powerful hero like that is a bit much," Warfelula said.

"Lindy, I thought you were the only priestess of Death," Fall blurted out. Warfelula's face fell a bit at the mention of Lindy's name.

Lindy willed herself to sense other beings serving Death directly, finding that in this world she was the only one. Lindy sighed. "Looks like that deal is still good." Then she hobbled to her feet. "Are we good now?" Lindy asked Warfelula.

The priestess of War shook her head. "No, but we are even."

"Wonderful," Lindy sighed, staggering out of the bar and back down the street.

Fall rushed after her target. Her sister Frost had been acting off ever since meeting Lindy and it had only gotten worse. Lindy was an enigma. Hanna would not share details about her childhood with Lindy for anyone now. So, taking matters into her own hands, Fall had chosen to stalk Lindy and assess what she was really like. Three things confused Fall. Why her mother and sister did not appear to resent Lindy now that they had met her. Why the kingdom which had levied so many horrible crimes against Lindy was not pressing them now that Lindy had returned. But most of all, why Fall's perception of Lindy and how that infamous hero appeared were so different. All her life Fall had built up an image of a chaotic larger-than-life psychopath who betrayed anyone as soon as they trusted her. Lindy was a chaotic enigma but it was hard to see her as completely evil now.

Lindy hobbled down the street towards the mercenary guild. Fall had been tailing Lindy for close to five minutes and was getting bored of watching her staggering around. When Lindy passed by a closed-up warehouse near a potter's shop and a thin alleyway, Fall glanced at a clocksmith's shop across the street. When she looked back Lindy was gone. Looking around swiftly, Fall bolted down the alleyway where she had last seen her. The alley was tight but short, leading into a small courtyard. Fall froze at the edge of the alley and watched three men stand glaring at Lindy, who was just getting off the ground and nonchalantly dusting herself off.

Sir Zu Recodin, Jalthrow Gerin the vice leader from the bar, and a tall hook-nosed man Fall did not recognize leered at Lindy. After checking herself over Lindy sighed, "I meant to do that."

"Do what?" Zu sneered confidently.

Lindy studied the men with a pitying gaze, seemingly no longer drunk. "Falling into this amateurish trap."

Jalthrow shook his head. "That's not how this works. Hand over your weapons."

"No," Lindy said, crossing her arms.

The tall man stomped over and leaned over his mark. "This is for your own good."

Lindy rolled her eyes at the tall man. He disintegrated; a small pile of dust flew away on a stiff gust. Zu sputtered, "What did you do that for?"

Lindy glared at the men and laughed. "The only thing worse than dying like a hero is taking your life for granted."

"What?" Zu howled. Jalthrow began to inch away towards Fall without turning around.

"Dying like a hero. Basically, charging forward and showing off," Lindy leered. Then she vanished, reappearing under the porch of the potter's shop next to Fall and dashing up to Jalthrow, impaling him in the back with her hand. Lindy then dashed up to Zu, who had yet to react, and cut him in half with a knife. Looking over the men's corpses, she reduced them to dirt, then spat on the ashes. "Amateurs," Lindy growled.

Fall came out of hiding. "You have some odd thoughts about heroes."

"I could same the same about this world." Lindy shrugged as she faded into the shadows, only to reappear by the clocksmith's.

By the time Fall rushed back to the street, Lindy was long gone. Soon after losing her stalker Lindy entered the mercenary guild. Tomayis was standing near the counter, a block of ice wrapped in a towel held to his cheek. When the young man looked up he blinked a few times, seeming to believe he was hallucinating. Lindy looked very clean and was back far too early. "You know, when someone rejects you it's not an invitation to hit on them more," Lindy smiled.

Lindy's voice snapped Tomayis out of his stupor. "You failed. That's too bad."

Lindy shook her head, patting her new sword. "Oh, I killed a lot. Even got a new sword."

"How many?" Cal asked, walking out of a meeting room fully robed but staggering like a drunk.

"Two lived," Lindy smiled.

"That's too bad," Tomayis sighed.

"Well, the other hundred plus fools died," Lindy shrugged.

"So why did you let two live?" Lu chimed in, walking out from the same meeting room.

"Because they were heroes linked closely to this kingdom," Lindy grumbled.

"How do you think they will respond?" Lu asked seriously for once.

"I can keep them from doing anything they'd regret," Lindy smiled.

Lu leaned on a wall. "You are something else."

"So, no one thinks it's weird she took on two heroes?" Tomayis asked.

"That's right," Lindy said, feeling a bit annoyed.

Cal dragged Lindy into their meeting. Lu followed, shutting the door behind them. "How powerful were these heroes?" Cal pressed.

After Lindy sat down on a small bench she replied. "Two high heroes. They had very good gear as well."

"And you won?" Lu asked, sounding more impressed than skeptical.

"I could have killed them both but that would have caused problems," Lindy complained.

Cal looked closely at Lindy. "What we really need to know is just what are you to the Derndell kingdom?"

"Something they do not want to fight. Hope to control. But has hurt them a lot," Lindy blandly said. Then pulling out her pistol. "I also invented this and the storm bows."

"What?" Cal yelled.

Lu locked the door and looked over Lindy. "That's a little more than I expected. So what do you need from us?" Cal looked at their leader incredulously.

"I need a paying job. Fighting is how I'd like to make a living. Also don't tell anyone about the things I have and will make," Lindy said. Looking at the ceiling in an unfocused state she was monitoring her words closely now.

"Then comrade I'll have to find something insane for you to fight," Lu nodded thoughtfully.

"Is that ok?" Lindy and Cal asked at once, not seeming to notice the other had spoken.

"It should be, but if a kingdom starts a personal war with you there is only so much your unit members can do for you," Lu said after thinking hard.

Lindy got up and patted Lu on the shoulder. "If it looks like I will drag you all down with me, feel free to disavow me."

"I can't do that," Lu said strongly. Cal shook at his words.

Lindy glared at them. "You can and you will. Our subordinates need to live well too. I will be responsible for a lot of killing but I really do not want the blood of the Eternal on my hands," she sighed. "Besides, unlike you two, I can't die."

Lindy fell into a shadow escaping the building. Cal sputtered, "Really?" When she realized the vice leader had escaped Cal chose to keep the rest of her words to herself.

Lu looked at where his ally had left from. "Don't tell the others what she told us."

Cal looked at the love of her life and sighed. "If that's what you want."

10 |

Collapsing the Balance

Lindy spent the next day holed up in her room nursing a hangover. Cal visited her twice, only staying long enough to see how her superior was feeling. To pass the time from her bed Lindy observed the sea of souls in the city. She found it cute that Frost stayed close to the room Lindy was renting.

The day after, Lindy found Grgen Smalsh outside her building. "Lindy Shrew?" the man asked. Lindy looked at Grgen closely.

> **Grgen Smalsh**
> Male half ogre age 31
> Affiliation: Derndell kingdom
> Job: Legendary hero
> Status: King's War Marshal
> Abilities: strength 10,056, vitality 10,092, mind 8,112, agility 7,970
> Talents: unknown
> Skills: unknown

Lindy was planning to walk by the huge man but upon seeing his stats she asked acidly, "What does the king's War Marshal want with me?"

"The king demands an audience," Grgen said sternly.

"And I will answer that why?" Lindy sneered. The man's ego was so inflated it may as well have its own gravity, which she found insipid at best.

"Because you are a citizen of his realm and I could catch you by force," Grgen grumbled, not enjoying Lindy's lack of awe and deference.

Lindy thought quickly. "You are technically right. Fine, lead the way," she nodded.

Grgen pointed up to the castle. "Go that way."

Lindy laughed. "And the guards will just let me in?"

"They will if you are Lindy Shrew," Grgen said, seeming to believe he was being made light of.

Lindy pointed at her chest. "I am Lindy Reaper. Never call me Shrew again. That name no longer binds me."

Grgen's eyes twitched. He could tell Lindy was willing to fight to the death if he called her Shrew again. "With me, then," he offered. Originally, he wanted Lindy to walk in front, but by now Grgen had lost far more time than he liked and even if Lindy was not a threat to him, she still freaked him out.

Grgen led Lindy to a four-legged lizard slightly bigger than a large horse. The war marshal stepped onto the beast's back. "Get on," he said.

"What is that?" Lindy asked.

It took Grgen a few moments to realize Lindy was taking about his mount, causing his guard and opinion of her to lower. "A draklin. Come on."

When Lindy got behind Grgen he slapped the draklin once and it sped off. The beast was faster than most animals. Grgen's skillful handling was all that allowed them to avoid crashing into the many carts and cursing people they passed. Moving past the second military line and the nobles' quarter, only the palace towered over them. Round towers, squat thick walls, and deep stone blocky buildings plus even more walls within met Lindy's discerning gaze. The wards cast and carved on the buildings were very powerful as well. It would take Lindy far longer than she felt comfortable with if she ever tried to break past those wards while the local garrisons still lived. "Impressive," Lindy nodded to herself.

Grgen looked at Lindy, surprised at her sudden change of tone. "It is our prized impregnable bastion." Lindy coughed trying to hide her chuckle but the war marshal caught her. "What's so funny?" he glared.

Lindy looked up at the large man who had stopped his mount before a stone bridge leading over the castle moat. "It's not impregnable, just very annoying to break."

Grgen allowed a small smile onto his face. Lindy was right after all. "Indeed, it would take a massive army at least half a year to break past."

Lindy scoffed. "Even I could take that down in less than a day with good conditions. You, however, would only be stopped by the worst events."

Grgen was slightly embarrassed. For all her flaws, he saw Lindy was indeed very clever. "There are not many with my level of power. Only Wisp the court wizard is my match. In this kingdom there is a treaty that prevents those like me from invading other nations."

Lindy was dragged past many flashily armored knights and dimly lit marble hallways. Only after getting a few floors underground was she pushed inside a large room. The king's top aides, the king, and Ajax Shrew were all assembled in the room.

Lindy looked around, not recognizing most of the faces. She could see how powerful and relaxed most in the room were and how over-confident the rest were. She knew these were all core members of the kingdom. "Wow, I hope you left some of the big shots out of this," Lindy whistled.

The king laughed. "And why would we do that, Lindy Shrew?"

"Because eliminating this kingdom's powerbase could be achieved by destroying one location," Lindy sighed. Before most of the powerless fools in the room could gasp and the powerful ones could attack, Lindy was crushed into the ground by an unseen force.

"We can't have you do that," Wisp the forceful court wizard giggled.

"It was tactical advice, you idiot," Lindy sneered, spitting some blood to the ground and ripping apart the spell by decaying its magic.

The champion Randull Lorn stepped in front of King Jay, shielding him as Lindy got up and dusted herself off. Now the powerful ones were tense and the weak fools had either collapsed or were sneering back at Lindy like the fools they were. Lindy looked at the king mildly. "So what did you want?"

"Don't insult your king!" Randull yelled. Lindy looked into the champion's eyes, gauging his power, noting that among the six powerful presences only Ajax Shrew was weaker.

"He is not my king after killing me once and trying to kill me another time, all in a day, I might add," Lindy replied calmly.

"That changes nothing," the shadowy form of Dusk Nightcrow hissed from the back.

"And my best friend died. Those were the major things," Lindy scoffed.

"I heard about that. You had a really bad day that time but you still owe the kingdom, so hear us out," Anna Faywind asked.

Lindy did not respond, instead looking over at the king and folding her arms over her chest. After a few moments of silence she began tapping her foot on the marble floor. The king cleared his throat loudly and Lindy stopped tapping her foot. Only then did the king glare at her. "I'll get right to the point. Make us more weapons and design better ones," he demanded, haughtily looking insulted.

Lindy looked over the king's face feeling that firstly, giving one kingdom too much power was very bad for the balance she was supposed to maintain in this world, and secondly, that King Jay was very likely to stab her in the back again. Lindy shook her head. "No way. I serve Death, not you."

Without batting an eye, the kind coolly commanded, "Kill her."

Grgen Smalsh stabbed a sword though Lindy's chest and heart from her back. "Even I can die from something like this. Goodbye, little fool," he intoned.

Lindy coughed up more blood and slid to the floor. "I'll remember that for next time." Then her vision hazed and Conduit's far-off voice whispered in her mind, *One last favor before our three minds are one.* Lindy knew something big was coming and looked up at the king. She raised a trembling hand out of her own blood and pointed at King Jay. "Fool, now we are enemies."

"And you are dead," the king spat, turning around.

Lindy laughed, her voice echoing unnaturally in the room. The king and all the powerless fools around him fell lifelessly to the ground. Lindy's head surveyed the powerful beings in the room. Conduit's unearthly voice echoed in the minds of those still alive in the Derndell kingdom capital. "I'll be back for the rest of you."

Soon after, panic filled the Derndell kingdom and Lindy, now fully of one mind, appeared as a small cloud of dark smoke in Death's realm. "So, you died," Death grumbled.

"And I need a favor," Lindy's ghostly voice howled.

"Why me?" Death seemed to sigh despite his lack of lungs.

"Because you are my boss and my failures reflect on you?" Lindy asked, only now noticing something sitting next to Death. It looked like a mass of red fur in the shape of a massive man and clad in simple steel armor, the fur poking past the joints like rogue stuffing. The two beings were hunched over a chess board. Lindy looked closer at the giant. "War, I presume?"

The mass of steel and fur nodded. "That's right, little one. How did you know?"

"I met one of your priestesses and got my hand on a relic that may be connected to you. They both smelled the same as you," Lindy replied.

"But you are a small ghost right now," the man-thing pointed out reasonably.

"Says the spirit being, all buddy-buddy with a skeleton that acts like it has organs, can talk and move, but most of all loves to sigh like an old man," Lindy humphed.

"I am your boss!" Death grumbled.

"And you are not working!" Lindy replied.

"My un-life is hell," Death sighed again.

"Hey, home is where the heart is!" Lindy snidely answered.

"I see what you mean. So what do you want from me?" War asked.

"Tell me how to make strong walls that will dispel attack magic on contact," Lindy demanded.

"Why?" War asked thoughtfully.

"To restore the balance," Lindy replied.

"The balance you broke," Death whispered to itself.

"And yet I still live?" Lindy said, phrasing the observation like a question.

"You will be the death of me," Death complained.

"Ok, that one is way too easy to make fun of, so I am not even going to try," Lindy said, sounding disappointed.

"Fish bones in runic shapes set in clay laced with counter runes, mix lime and ash in for good measure. The more contradicting anti-magic enchantments and purer materials the better. As for what the runes look like, I'll let you work that out," War replied, holding back laughter.

Death glanced at Lindy sheepishly. "So what will you do now?"

"Remake myself from the body of a freshly killed troll. Help power up some kingdom on bad terms with the last one and wipe the Derndell kingdom out, cities and all," Lindy boldly said.

"That will throw off the propulsion ratios we were trying to keep," Death said.

"Oh, I'll make sure to drag a few elves and dwarves down too. Might need to include a dragon or two as well. One elf for every ten humans and five dwarves, right?" Lindy replied.

"No. Given how the humans and dwarves on your world are lowering their average life expectancy by pollution and malnutrition, you might have to let a few more elves die after factoring in post-war birth-rates," Death informed her.

"Ok, sounds good." Lindy nodded, mildly surprised how easily those calculations came to her now that Conduit was fully part of her. "I'll make sure to leave enough alive to sustain civilization and a workable population, as long as no one goes really overboard."

"Just keep your machinations within a good margin of error and be more careful with the toys you hand out." War spoke up, now very serious.

"Oh, don't worry. That's one lesson I've learned well," Lindy said.

"Well, get going," Death told its favorite lackey.

"See ya, chief," Lindy told Death as she disappeared from her boss's realm back to her posting.

As soon as Lindy left, Fate and the world spirits overseeing fire, water, earth, and air all poked their heads back into Death's realm. "Is the brat gone?" Fate asked.

"For now, let's party. I only have ten minutes of my half-hour break left," Death replied.

"Our work hours are hell," Fire sputtered.

"Don't you start too!" Death complained.

"But you like it when that subordinate of yours does that," Air said breezily.

Death grabbed a huge foul-tasting beer that would never get him drunk even if he had a stomach. "Don't ask. It's complicated," and preceded to drown the floor in his sorrows under the jealous glare of Fate.

"You know that brat will likely cause most of the destruction in the coming conflict," Fire sputtered.

"No skin off my back," Death shrugged.

"Your reasons for supporting that one are hazy at best," Air said. A gong sounded from nowhere all around Death's realm, signaling break time was over. "Tell us next time," Air said, dissipating back to its own realm.

Somewhere in the kingdom of Otten a freshly killed swamp troll burst open. Its bones skewered the team of adventurers that had killed it. A figure that was Lindy but did not look quite like the last Lindy crawled out of the troll's corpse.

The Lindy

Female (shadow touched) human age: forever 20

Affiliation: realm of death

Embodiments: kicked out by Death, eternal calamity

Job: Reaper

Status: common sense bane: extreme, death's agent

Abilities: strength 8620, vitality 9705, mind 8902, agility 10001

Talents: translation: all, full power strike: strength, danger sense, innate map, skill retention: Manfred Endfield, photographic memory, sixth sense: intuition, extra toughness, favored environment: darkness, cold resistance: high, highly enhanced trait: willpower, analysis: extreme, good hair, quick learner, fearless, poison resistance: high, presence sense, aura: weakening, damage shield: decay, decay bolt, adept talent: multi tasking, rapid reload, fearsome visage: moderate, selective decay: all, innate spell: chill blast, absorb impact: moderate, hair trigger aim, riposte: debate, realm authority (death): moderate, shadow shift, six fold strike, perception tampering field, find soul, see soul, sense lifespan, attuned to purpose, shadow from, plains walk: deaths realm and back, full power burst weakening/ decay/cold, siphon soul, suppresses kindnesses: self full

Mutation: troll blood (extra burnable, swift regeneration), un-aging, mutagenic blood

Curse: catastrophic encounters, heavily sleeper, light sensitively: mild,

Skills: sword: master, dagger: master, unarmed: master, marksmanship: master, throwing: expert, athletics: master, armor proficiency (leather/cloth) expert, literacy: journeyman, history: (other world) journeyman, intimidate (innate): expert, diplomacy journeyman, awareness: expert, necromancy: extreme, tinkering: master, magic tampering: extreme, counter spell: master, survival woodland: journeyman, cooking: journeyman, acrobatics expert, stealth: expert, shadow magic: expert, laws of death: extreme

"Ok. Should be enough to fight a legendary." Lindy grinned, taking the money from the dead team around her, the clothes from the female archer in the team, and the cloak from the best-dressed fighter in the team. Lindy walked out of the forest she had appeared in. As she walked, the land died. Her rebirth had sucked most of the forest dry of life. At her hip rested Transcendence and the Lindy Special. Luckily Lindy found a road with carts mostly going in the same direction. Lindy hailed one of the carts. "Where's everyone going?"

"The festival," a short female in red robes said.

"Looks like a big deal," Lindy commented, walking alongside the cart the red-robed young woman drove.

"It is, but no one has finished the king's challenge yet," the young woman replied. Lindy listened to the background noise around her as well. The word Derndell was spoken in hushed fearful whispers.

"Which one?" Lindy pressed.

The young woman rolled her eyes but upon seeing Lindy's pistol she almost fell over. "To make that."

Smiling inwardly, Lindy huffed angrily. "Right. Those bastards are using my sister's inventions."

The young woman nearly screamed. "Your sister made those evil things?"

Many eyes gathered on Lindy. Slowly showing off her pistol to the crowd, Lindy replied firmly. "My sister invented the first versions of this. All she got for it was a sword through the heart."

"Can you build them?" the young woman asked.

"Among other things," Lindy smirked.

"What's a skilled artificer doing out here then?" a middle-aged man yelled from the crowd.

"I'm a mercenary by trade," Lindy called back, rolling her eyes.

"Get on. I'll take you to the festival. Prove your skills there," the young woman nearly ordered Lindy.

Taking the young woman's hand Lindy asked, "And you are?"

"Third princess Salvea Oat, kingdom of Otten," Salvea said. "You?"

"Lindy." Salvea and some of the crowd stiffened up at Lindy's introduction. "It's a traditional name in my family."

The road was packed but the young woman managed to pass any cart with only a nod. She looked over at Lindy. "Where have you been for the past ten years?"

"What?" Lindy asked. They were now moving at a good clip. The road was well maintained, but its borders heavily wooded and slightly hilly. Despite the rough surroundings, over a half a day of travel they had been able to get much higher up.

"The war with the Derndell kingdom. The one where they have been invading all round us?" the young woman asked, seemingly amused. As far as Lindy could tell, this young woman had no reason to be laughing about this, which put Lindy on guard.

"You say that like I should have done something sooner," Lindy sighed.

"You killed a king and most of his family. Some brat with too much to prove got the crown and here we are," the young woman shrugged. Her inflections made it sound like she was now speaking a very different language.

Lindy switched to this new language, answering, "Who are you?"

"I asked first," the young woman replied, back to her normal tone.

Lindy looked over the young woman in all the ways available to her, lastly peering at her soul and finding two. "But you only introduced half of yourself."

The young woman grinned evilly. "Caldrin Foxfoot, elven chieftess, killed by heroes from the Derndell kingdom."

"Right now, my name is The Lindy. I have been called Lindy Reaper, Lindy Shrew, Conduit, Manfred Endfield, and a fool. I am Death's agent on this world. Right now I want to turn the Derndell kingdom to dust."

Caldrin paled. "What did they do to you?"

"They were very rude. Would you like walls immune to most attack magic?" Lindy asked dutifully. She might have well been cackling given how gleefully her eyes shone.

The young woman became even more pale. "The elf talked to you."

"The one in you did," Lindy nodded.

Salvea bowed slightly, hiding her body moments with her robe so no passerby could see. "Please don't tell anyone about her or destroy her."

"Chieftess Foxfoot has leave to be in this world. As long as neither of you tell anyone who I have been, then I'll keep that secret," Lindy agreed.

Roughly an hour later a large explosion of wood and horse bits erupted far down the road. Cries of "hydra" echoed soon after, followed by many fleeing beings, some with two legs, some with four legs, and a few with one. The lucky few two-legged runners escaped on horseback. Salvea caught one of the more dusty but less bloody runners. "Hydra?" she asked, pointing over at the sounds of sobbing and chomping. The dust-covered being of indeterminate gender nodded and resumed its flight.

Salvea pointed to a few men in carts close to hers. They wore armor under thick robes. She pointed again in the direction of the new roadblock. "Kill it." Then looking over at some hardy folks that smelled of magic, she added, "Rescue," still pointing off into the distance.

Before the troops could get very far, Lindy looked at the growing dust cloud around the first explosion. "I could kill anything around here before help arrived."

The princess looked at her, now mildly annoyed. "Then kill the monster." Lindy really wanted to ask if Salvea meant her or the hydra but refrained because she did not want to piss the princess off just yet.

"Ok," Lindy shrugged. Still sitting down, Lindy covered the dust cloud in an orb of shadows. "When I get back you will need to explain how the syntax of your language works. It sounds very literal and abrupt."

Lindy sounded very confident and interested so the princess chose to not take offence. *She is auto-translating,* the voice in Princess Oat's head informed her. "Ok, be fast," the princess sighed.

Lindy's childish smile reached from ear to ear. Then she disappeared, jumping into the shadows she had created. To any normal observer it would look like Lindy had suddenly teleported without causing so much as a ripple in the air. The princess briefly considered Lindy being an illusion or figment of her imagination, possibly caused by the freeloader in her mind, but the ball of shadow and screeching coming from within it made her reassess that assumption. Meanwhile Lindy was gleefully jumping around, moving anywhere within the huge ball of shadow at will, even going so far as to alter her substance to be ethereal temporarily when attacked. Admittedly it was not a hard fight, but Lindy did get a chance to test some techniques, so it was not all bad for her. What made Lindy the most excited was that hydra meat had to be a little poisonous, right? In Lindy's mind that equaled tasty although it had been years since her last taste of poisonous monster. The hydra was cut into small slabs and its meat was decayed into jerky on the spot, thus preventing it from regenerating too well. When she was done, Lindy dispelled the ball of shadow. Finding the princess and her hidden guards right outside, Lindy sat on a mound of dried hydra steaks and began eating thoughtfully.

"Can we?" one of the guards asked, moving to the meat.

"It's mine," Lindy warned acidly, none too pleased with how mild the meat tasted, only now realizing that with how powerful she had become, now only supremely powerful toxins could give her a buzz.

Salvea held her men back while looking up at Lindy. "Hydra skin is very valuable."

Lindy bit into a large chunk of meat, confirming that dried fatty hydra skin was delicious. "No, it's the best part."

"What do you need it for?" Salvea asked.

"Food. I'm really hungry." Lindy scowled, getting a little annoyed at the folks interrupting her meal and not noticing that she had shifted priorities.

To all around her Lindy appeared to be nothing more then an ultra-powerful slob but Salvea waved her men to the road. "Clean up the damage."

When the princess reached for one of the steaks, Lindy warned her. "Those should be very poisonous." The princess looked up at Lindy and gestured for her to continue. "I did not remove the poisons. It looks like someone as powerful as me is not troubled by this level of toxin." Salvea would have rolled her eyes if not for the speed of Lindy's solo hydra slaying.

It took around an hour to move the debris and get the travelers under control. While the guards and princess were working, Lindy was finishing close to a fourth of the hydra, not counting the heads. As she ate, Lindy extracted what was left of each head's mind, imbuing the last strands of the monster's life force and twelve minds into small snake-shaped shadows.

Shadow Born Serpent

Elite shadow pet (serpent)

Job: specter

Status: remodeled hydra bits

Abilities: strength 2232, vitality 1310, mind 562, agility 2832

Talents: decaying bite, heat sense, tremor sense, burrow, shadow shift, immunity (cold/poison/electricity), latch on, echolocation, reshape shelf, cold touch, wakening aura: mild, swarm, danger sense: selective, endowment (ethereal form)-selective, telepathy: master

Skills: athletics: expert, bite: expert, intimidate: master, shadow magic: journeymen, stealth: expert, tracking: master

The first thing Lindy's new pets did was hide in her shadow and choose to exempt her from their danger sense; otherwise they would lose what little remained of their mental state. The princess returned from her tasks. The hydra skulls were now fleshless, hidden under the pile of meat. "You ready?" Salvea asked.

Lindy destroyed the venom left in her kill's flesh and jumped down. "Give away the rest. It's safe."

"It is?" Salvea asked.

"No venom left." Lindy nodded.

"Let's go," Salvea sighed, leading Lindy back to their carriage while pointing at the pile of meat. "All good, free," she said, pointing at the mound of meat. The two women and some of the princess's guards left before those left behind gained the courage to leap at the food. Even if wartime rationing had hit them hard, no one was so desperate to eat meat that was filled with deadly poison, at least not knowingly, or yet.

A few hours later, as the sun was setting before them, Lindy and the princess arrived at a midsized city nestled within a cleft of a mountain. The sun tinged the city red but a great many deep shadows rose to prominence as well. "Nice place," Lindy nodded.

"It looks nefarious," Princess Oat said, rolling her eyes.

"Still better than where I died last," Lindy shrugged.

"Why?" the princess asked, pulling up to the city's iron gate.

"Somewhere that looks bad is much better than somewhere that pretends it is good," Lindy replied half-heartedly. The princess squinted at her companion before pulling down her hood, showing off a small crest and racing past the guards as soon as the gate creaked open.

Lindy looked around, seeing a small tavern with an oddly familiar soul racing into an alley beside it. "Let me off here," Lindy requested.

The princess slowed down. "Not coming to the palace?" Luckily the night crowd was not thick given the depressed wartime mood.

"No. When is the competition?" Lindy asked.

"Late tomorrow." The princess relented, stopping the carriage a few buildings past the inn.

Lindy jumped down, asking casually, "Good. What else?"

This time Caldrin summed up what her strange passenger had told her. "You are related to the past Lindys and your relative made the firearms we are being destroyed by. You are a powerful mercenary who feels betrayed by those fools and would like to help us."

Lindy nodded. "That's right." Then she disappeared from the street, appearing right behind the fleeing figure she had seen. "Been awhile, instructor," Lindy said in common Derndell.

The fleeing figure wore a thick cloak with a very deep hood. It stopped but did not turn around. "What?" it asked in the language Salvea had been using.

"You know, when I died last time your niece just stood there," Lindy said. The cloaked figure flinched sharply. Lindy prepared to cast a barrier at any moment. "Anna Faywind is your niece, right? Is she still the hunt master?" Lindy continued nonchalantly.

"Who are you?" the cloaked figure asked, turning to peer at Lindy.

"This time I go by The Lindy. No longer Shrew or Reaper. At least I got a few new abilities from my name change. It's a shame I had to leave behind a body that time." Lindy shrugged.

"Frost still has not gotten over that." The cloaked figure let down its hood, revealing the face of Caldrin Faywind, who sported a few gray hairs now. She now spoke in jungle elfish. "So why now?"

Lindy smiled, knowing what her old teacher meant. "Just got back. Got an earful from Death, War, Fate, Fire, Water, Earth, and Air."

Caldrin let out a long sigh. "So it is you. What are your plans?"

"Destroy the kingdom that killed me." Lindy shrugged like it was not a big deal.

Caldrin twitched. "Whatever happened to maintaining the balance?"

"Just need to tweak some numbers and it'll be fine," Lindy said with extra slowness, drawing out each word.

"That sounds very convenient," Caldrin said. She covered Lindy's legs in ice and tossed nine shards of ice at Lindy's face. Three other cloaked figures charged at Lindy from the rooftops shadowing the alleyway.

Lindy scanned her attackers.

Caldrin Faywind

Female half-elf age 139

Affiliation: Derndell kingdom commandos

Job: hero journeyman

Status: commando senior sergeant

Abilities: strength 134, vitality 201, mind 235, agility 290

Talents: analysis: moderate, resistance (mind control): high, keen senses: all, detect lies: high, unerring strike, truth sense, analysis resistance: moderate, language (common Derndell/ old magic/ jungle elfish/ Oatesseion low/ Oatesseion common)

Skills: armor use (plate/ leather/ cloth): journeyman, dagger: adept, ice magic: expert, healing magic: journeyman, spirit magic: adept, counter spell: adept, read lips: beginner, stealth: adept, survival: journeyman, tracking: beginner, literacy: adept, journeyman: adept, bow: adept, club: adept. staff: adept, counter attack: journeyman, torturer: beginner

The most powerful of her ambusher's stats read as:

Julieous Samson

Male human age 23

Affiliation: Derndell kingdom commandos

Job: agent

> Status: commando corporal
> Abilities: strength 50, vitality 42. mind 32, agility 68
> Talents: silent steps, no tracks, forgettable visage, good
>   teeth, keen sense: all
> Skills: armor use (leather/cloth): adept, stealth: expert,
>   bluff (lie): journeyman, counter attack: adept, knife:
>   journeyman, read lips: journeyman, cooking: adept,
>   ride: beginner, tracking: beginner, literacy: beginner

Lindy shook her head. Her weakening aura erupted in full force, causing her attackers to collapse. Shattering the magic binding her, Lindy summoned her twelve shadow-born serpents, who fully consumed Caldrin's backup alive.

Caldrin went pale. "Why?"

Lindy smirked. "I could kill a legendary existence now." Then she knelt down, ignoring her servants munching and the wailing of their food. Looking her old teacher in the eyes, Lindy said coolly, "I'll let you live if you leave this kingdom and deliver a message."

"And if I say no?" Caldrin asked, not trembling in the least.

Lindy kept smirking. She could see Caldrin was trying to get free info. "Then you die worse than your lackeys. I am letting you live for old time's sake. Cross me again and I will not show mercy. Plus I really need you to relay my threat." Lindy paused, then laughed. "Sorry, sorry, message, not threat."

Caldrin looked over Lindy, barely seeing her mature, strong-willed, genius, skilled, and childish pupil who had long surpassed her. All she saw now was a conniving bloodthirsty lunatic hell-bent on revenge. *What have we created?* Caldrin asked herself, well aware that Lindy's manic state was her kingdom's fault. "Ok, fine, what's the message?" Caldrin asked, ignoring the pleading gazes of her rapidly dying underlings.

"Tell the fools that watched me die that I will fulfill my promise," Lindy replied.

"That's it? What about Frost?" Caldrin asked suddenly.

Lindy got up and looked at the darkening sky sadly, the last rays of red light streaking past her face. "Tell her I messed up and am sorry. Now get out of this kingdom immediately." Caldrin slowly got up, not looking back at her more-than-half-eaten subordinates, and fled without a word. Some minutes later Caldrin's helpers had been eaten and Lindy's servants had slithered back into her shadow. Ever since Caldrin had asked about Frost, Lindy had been absently gazing at the sky, a slight grimace filled with self-loathing twitching on her face. "Well shit," Lindy finally grumbled, summing up her mood and walking to the inn. No guards were anywhere to be seen, causing Lindy to shake her head at how bad public security had gotten. "Must have been some draft," Lindy sighed, pushing her way into the inn.

Right by the door the inn's restaurant area was bustling. Families came and went rapidly. Lindy found one of the few spots at the bar and took a seat next to a sobbing drunk. Half a minute later a wizened bartender stood before her. "Is it always like this?" Lindy asked dubiously.

"Of course not," the bartender sighed. "For the first time in years we have a surplus of meat."

"Is it hydra?" Lindy asked.

"Not only that, but completely free of venom as well," the bartender bragged, as if he had killed that multi-headed snake.

"Have you made stew out of it yet?" Lindy asked, mildly unimpressed.

"The first batch was completed recently," the weary but bubbly man boasted.

"I'll have as big a serving of that as you sell and the most bitter beer you have," Lindy smirked, finding the man absurd and funny.

"Money up front," the man replied.

"How much?" Lindy smirked again. "Does that stew even have a price yet?"

"Then as much as you think it's worth," the man sighed.

"Can you do that?" Lindy shot back.

"How are we supposed to price something as crazy as a non-venomous hydra? Before we had maybe some chicken every month or two, but now even if we give the meat away we will still have leftovers," the drunk next to Lindy grumbled.

"Fine." Lindy dropped two gold coins on the counter. The busy tavern slowly went silent and the bartender froze, panicked. "I will also need a place to rest for a week. This is an inn, right?"

"Miss, that's still too much." A waitress ran over. "Before the war our beef stew was under a silver coin."

"What beef? Back then, that stew was all cabbage!" the drunk groaned.

Lindy rolled her eyes; she had only gold coins, not silver. "So if the stew now has a lot of meat in it and meat is normally in such huge demand, won't that mean the price is higher anyway? It's not like meat keeps forever, and there are tons of it in circulation so you will need to use what you have sooner rather than later." The room somehow became more still. Sneering evilly she added, "If you guys don't have a spare room then you can give me back the change you think I am owed." The waitress almost fainted.

"Fine. Two large bowls of stew, three of our most bitter beers, and a week in the best room," the bartender stipulated.

"Deal," Lindy cackled.

A large hand gripped the bar next to Lindy. The wood cracked and the bartender swore. "Do I know you?" a tipsy dwarf asked.

Lindy squinted, recognizing the man. "Maklin Steelfoot. It's been too long," she smiled.

"Who are you again?" Maklin hiccupped.

Grix Fellscrew walked over and tried to drag his friend away. "Hold up. What's with your companion?" Lindy asked.

"Our elder was killed," Grix snapped.

"Fixell got taken down? Wow. Did you three work out one of Lindy Reaper's four weapons yet?" Lindy whistled. Again the tavern went still.

Maklin showed fear but Grix was enraged. "Its six, six weapons!"

The drunk next to Lindy perked up. "No, it's three. Two pistols and the Storm Bow."

Lindy began to laugh once more. This time the light in the room flickered. Shadows grew in spots filled with light and everyone around her felt as if their very souls wished to flee in terror, but no one could muster the energy to move. Most could barely even think. Even so, a few spirits did attempt to flee their own living bodies. What felt like centuries lasted a split second before Lindy pulled out her own pistol and the pressure stopped. Lowering her mirth to a wry giggle, Lindy held the first pistol made in this world before the dwarves. "This is one of them. Then there's the Storm Hush and Long Barrel Express, and the Storm Bows."

Maklin fell to the ground. "You killed the reaper?"

"My sister was killed by the Derndell kingdom. I am more than she was," Lindy replied coolly. All magic in the room began to fade.

"Fine, we get it. Now get out," the bartender pleaded.

The drunk next to Lindy looked around the panicked room but no one else could move. Even then he could only move his neck a few inches. "Kid, you were the one who killed the hydra we are eating, right?"

Lindy slowly got her powers under control once more. After a deep sigh to steady the sudden emotional outburst that had let her powers seep out unconsciously, she nodded. "I got rid of the venom, too." Then she smiled sweetly at the bartender. "You are welcome, by the way."

"Fine. You can stay. Just don't do wreak havoc like that again," the bartender agreed. Grix, who had once sold out Lindy to the Golden Horde, shook his head. He knew far too well how many ways Lindy Reaper could cause mayhem. As far as he could tell, that one's self-proclaimed sister was far more dangerous and unpredictable. For the first time in his life, Grix swore to himself never to anger those with the blood of that Lindy. After all, if getting this new one very annoyed could temporarily annihilate the minds in a packed inn, what would happen if she got mad? Grix was sure he would not like the answer to that one bit regardless of who Lindy set her sights on.

After finishing her meal Lindy used the bartender's troubled expression to read the room. Seeing that her presence was still off-putting, Lindy retreated to her room. The room was clean and walled with something like pine. The bed was small but used wool in the mattress. A small washbasin with a reflective steel plate mirror hanging over it was all her room had, but even then, Lindy could tell why this was the best room. While these furnishings were not rare before she had died last, they were still hard to find and on the low side of pricey, even for a popular inn. No water graced the basin yet, so Lindy looked at her reflection, something she rarely had the chance to do in this world. The first thing that hit her was how pale she looked. Then she shivered upon seeing her eyes. "When did I look so tired and dangerous?" she said. After a few seconds Lindy had enough and turned away. *That's not right. Dead to the world is more spot on. Will I always look this unhealthy? Is it a necromancer thing?* she brooded in her mind. Only after taking off all but her pants and shirt did Lindy collapse into bed. "I need to sleep," she moaned.

A hard dull thump shook the building. Before Lindy could think, all her clothes were on and she was glaring around an empty dining room. "An explosion from where?" she mumbled to herself, only now awake enough to consciously want to find out what was happening and if it was dangerous to her. If it was not, she would go back to bed. If it was, she would annihilate it with extreme prejudice, then go back to bed.

The waitress was the next to run out, followed by the talkative drunk from before who was still getting into his pants. If Lindy had been feeling herself she would have let loose a wisecrack or three at them. "What's going on?" a faster maybe young teenager asked from the balcony. Lindy tried to discern why he spoke up first.

That's not brave. Foolhardy then. Wait, why did I think that just from his age? He's a kid but that's an adult in this world. Crap, now is not the time. Lindy thought. Noticing that no one else was showing up and that all eyes were on her, Lindy shrugged. "Hell if I know. I just got here. That was an explosion. Something cut most of the force. If it was anything less I'd still be sleeping."

"You really are something else," the now sober male still labeled as that drunk said, clearly nursing a wicked handover.

"That blast must not be doing your head any favors. You almost look worse than me," Lindy snickered, no longer able to hold back.

"How rude!" the waitress yelled. *If anyone was still sleeping they were up now.* That realization alone made it hard for Lindy to stop giggling.

"Will she be all right?" the teenager called down worriedly.

Lindy waved off his concern. "It's been a rough few years. I needed a good laugh." She replied inwardly, glad for the confused looks she got. *That's right, this eternity is mine alone, young ones,* Lindy noted lonesomely. She dispersed, reforming above a crumbled carpet many feet away, which she tossed off, revealing a trap door. Before anyone could blink, Lindy wrenched open the trap door, yanking out Grix and Maklin accompanied by the sound of an iron bar snapping. Grix had recently lost three fingers. A blood-slick key was held in his hands. "You guys failed, huh?" She set the two men down.

The drunk ran over. "Let me try to heal him."

"We need to win the competition." Maklin shook, fear of something worse than dismemberment in his eyes. Lindy ignored him.

"Oh, you can heal?" Lindy asked.

"I am training in healing magic. It's not to the level of a skill yet but I can stop most bleeding," the former drunk replied, already working on doing some magical first aid on Grix.

"Oh, that's how it works. So what's your name, kid?" Lindy asked. Maklin had busied himself with glaring at the two of them for ignoring him.

"Jeffrey Orion Kingslee. You can call me Jefforex," the drunk nodded. "And I am older."

"No you're not," Grix, Lindy, and Maklin replied as one.

The waitress walked over to Lindy and looked deep into her eyes. The young woman's eyes glowed for a few seconds. "Wow, you are an odd one." The statement was said in a matter-of-fact even tone, not something one would often use to make fun of someone. "Jillean Venlee or Jillvee, your pick. We are friends now. So how old?"

"Fifty, maybe eighty? I lost count like forty years ago," Lindy grumbled, then she stopped. Clearing her throat solemnly she added, "I mean I never really thought about that for so long." Her evasive chuckle at the end ruined the weighty atmosphere that had filled the room.

"That's her all right. You don't have any sisters, do you?" Grix coughed, his fingers now healed.

"I am that easy to see through? All that work for nothing, dammit!" Lindy muttered. "Oh, also you may have something up with your lungs if you took your experiment to the face."

"How do you know that?" Jefforex asked. Seconds passed and his hands leapt onto Lindy's shoulders. "Wait. You are that Lindy and you also can do translation: all?"

"In speech it's translate all and yes. Now don't tell anyone." Lindy sighed gently, prying off the man's hands, taking care to not cripple him. A scan of the room was enough to tell Lindy the teenager had long fled. Two men were walking over from a back room. "Anyway I am going to back to sleep. So only warning — don't spread around who I am." With that she walked off.

"You are getting soft." Grix shook his head, then a coughing fit started. "Is that blood?" he asked before collapsing onto the ground, out cold. Lindy did not stop moving until she was back in bed fast asleep.

11

Test Testing

The next morning, Lindy woke up just as the sun began to pour into the city, reflecting off the mountains high above and into the metal in the street. More than one row of spears moved past her window, shining light right into Lindy's eyes. "Why?" Lindy asked the ceiling. Soon after the spearmen went past the window they noticed that the top foot of their spears had decayed to dust. Lindy ignored the shouts and panic from the street, focusing instead on rolling out of bed and lazily getting dressed. Only after taking out her old pistol and the sword Transcendence from her shadow and looking them over did Lindy truly feel ready to face the day. Tossing her beloved weapons back into her shadow, she nearly hit one of the serpents within, but none of her creations were stupid enough to complain. She was their master, after all. In their eyes no one could possibly terrify them as much as Lindy.

As she arrived at the ground floor, a few eyes followed Lindy before swiftly going elsewhere. "Good morning. Are you going to watch the artificers compete?" the bartender asked.

"I was going to see if I could try my luck at winning it." Lindy shrugged.

The bartender frowned his brow and tossed her an apple. "Well, the preliminaries start soon. You will be late."

"The two dwarves from last night will be there, right?" Lindy asked, calmly eating the apple.

"Well of course," the bartender nodded.

"I'll get them to lend me a hand," Lindy smirked to herself. Upon seeing the bartender scowl Lindy began to cackle. She merged into the room's many shadows, only to step out of Grix's shadow less than a second later, finding herself in a packed square. Stands had been set all around it. A flashy booth was set at one end. Before each team of contestants was one table with the same set of parts.

When Lindy appeared still cackling, the entire stadium froze. A man sitting within the fancy booth had been in the middle of an impassioned speech when Lindy appeared. "Who are you?" a team of brawny guards yelled out in perfect sync like they had spent the entire night practicing.

"Get the late newcomer to table two," Princess Salvea Oat yelled out of the flashy booth.

The crowd began to murmur wildly but the contestants began to closely examine Lindy. She was led under heavy guard to the table right in front of the fancy booth. "Contestant two. Your name is Lindy, correct? Your sister invented the handguns that plague my kingdom, is that right?" asked the man who had been speaking when she arrived.

"Yes, one of my sisters did that. She was killed when she asked to be paid for her work," Lindy said, inclining her head slightly.

"She must have had a good life," the stately man pressed.

"She had no freedom. Her genius only chained her down even more. In the end, Sis took almost all the royal family of Derndell with her," Lindy spat.

"Do you fear being chained as well?" the man asked. No one else in the stadium was making any noise now.

"I am far more powerful than my sister. She was a hero but I am less heroic than she was." Lindy grinned, narrowing her eyes as if to ask *Why are you making a big production out of my cover story?*

The man shivered but his fear did not creep into his voice. "So you hate the Derndell kingdom?"

"Yes, and I will see that entire land burn. Although I would appreciate being paid for such hard labor," Lindy nodded.

"You have my word as king of Otten to grant you asylum and work as a mercenary, no matter the outcome of this test," the man said. Then he whispered just loud enough for Lindy to pick up on, thanks to her sky-high stats. "Thanks for such propaganda."

A familiar man walked out from the cluster of guards at the stadium entrance. "I am Commander Kingslee. Contestants, using the parts before you, construct a working Derndell kingdom model firearm as flawlessly as possible."

The few seconds of solemnness and contemplation were shattered when Grix sighed deeply. Seeing all eyes on him, he inquired, "So making any working firearm is not all right? It has to be a working copy?"

The king spoke before anyone one else could voice their building rage. "Are you saying you are confident that your team can make something that miraculous?"

Grix took a deep breath. "No I can't." He glanced over at Lindy and grimaced. "But that does not make it impossible."

There intervened a long pause that may have taken half an hour as all those present digested what had been said, save for Lindy, who was napping, seemingly passed out on her workbench. Kingslee was the first to address those gathered with anything coherent. "As long as it has comparable power to the Derndell kingdom model and is safe to use, then that should be fine. But you are still limited to only the parts you were given and your own capabilities." Kingslee bowed before the king's booth. "Is that all right, your majesty?"

The king nodded, still not over himself and concerned with how lightly Lindy was taking all this. "Very well."

Lindy shot up and raised her hand. "I need a smelter."

"I told you to use what you were given," Kingslee shot back.

Lindy's evil grin shook the hearts of all who saw her. "Good sir, a smelter is a tool, not a part."

"Do you have one with you?" Kingslee demanded sternly.

Lindy looked over her shoulder. "Yo, Grix old buddy, your smelter still works, right? Can I borrow it?"

"I am not getting it for you," Girx groaned.

The audience laughed until a hole of shadow appeared over Lindy's right arm. "Ok thanks. That's the third time you have helped me today." So saying, out of the shadow Lindy single-handedly pulled a burning smelter with fuel, which was twice as big as she. Setting her borrowed tool next to her table with a crash, Lindy threw off her coat and rolled up her sleeves. "All set." She grinned like a crafting maniac.

Grix ran over to her. "What happened to the ingots I set in there?"

"I left them back in the basement?" Lindy answered quizzically like she did not get why he was so worked up.

"You what?" he yelled.

"Are impurities present?" Kingslee asked suspiciously.

"No, I destroyed those," Lindy replied like she still did not get it.

Without needing to be asked, Jefforex's other half ran over and cast a powerful searching spell. "It's clean, too clean," Jillvee pronounced.

"Sergeant Venlee, explain," Salvea asked.

"Princess, nothing foreign to a smelter save low grade kindling is present," Jillvee replied, quaking.

Salvea turned to Lindy. "How?" she demanded.

Lindy raised one hand. Half a second later not a speck of dust was anywhere in the square. The ground and spectators were all equally spotless. "Sort of like that," Lindy shrugged.

"And?" Salvea pressed.

"It's only targeted decay. All dust is gone," Lindy said. Any contestant that wanted to protest Lindy hogging the spotlight swallowed their pride and chose to not speak up after Lindy so casually disclosed her trick.

Kingslee shook his head in resignation then yelled, "Ok nothing else, good. Start!"

Lindy promptly crushed together the barrel, a few of the loading mechanism parts, and most of the shell into the smelter. She watched the smelter and got to work slowly etching things onto the parts as they cooked. At the same time, she was ripping apart the magazine and welding it into a different shape with some drips of molten metal fished from the smelter.

A low whistling began to fill the yard. Most of the contestants did not pick up on it as they were far too preoccupied sweating over their work. The ones who had done this for years knew roughly how to put together the parts but no one had yet worked out how to enchant them correctly. Suddenly one table's half-finished project began to shake and creak. Before the team working on it could leap away from the impending detonation, the device lost its glow. Only after confirming that all magic power had left the weapon did a small team whose sole job was picking up after the occasional self-destructing prototype run over. Only Salvea and Caldrin Foxfoot noticed that Lindy had been the one to eliminate the out-of-control power swirling around the weapon. Such accidents happened a few times each festival but most were caused by new teams. The two responsible this time had been long-term contestants, but had rushed upon noticing how swiftly Lindy was working.

Before that frenzy died down Lindy waved over Kingslee. "What do we do when we are done?" she whispered.

"You finished?" Kingslee asked a little too loudly. The frenzy shifted to Lindy. Jefforex regretted his mistake but chose to act like he did not notice it. "Are you sure you are done?" he asked.

"Yup," Lindy beamed innocently. The few who knew her got chills from how pure Lindy looked at that moment. A few even had flashbacks to the mildly psychopathic moments they had seen her cause.

Jefforex picked up the weapon. "And it is stable?" By now no one was getting any work done. All listened to the commander's interrogation.

"Well yes, it is very stable. The skills needed to fire it properly should be very low as well, but its power might be on the high side. The weapon is fine to test but no one weak should fire it," Lindy said, seeming to dodge the question.

"So, it's a dud." Jefforex sighed, disappointed. The other contestants' turmoil turned to glee.

"Hey, it's not my fault nothing was provided to adjust the recoil." Lindy shrugged.

Jefforex paused. "How much recoil?"

Lindy thought hard and fast. "Roughly a cannon less than two of those." Then she scratched her head and added sheepishly, "Right, you don't have those. Um, like a small ballista without wheels maybe? Either way, far too much for weak arms or feet to handle."

"But the weapon is fine?" Jefforex asked.

Lindy crossed her arms, seemly insulted. "That's right. More powerful, simpler, and far more reliable than what my sister made. I could fix the kick it has but not with what I was given."

"Why make something so crazy?" one of the competitors heckled.

"Because it is funnier that way," Lindy replied. No one said anything and Lindy sighed. "The look on most of your faces makes this all worth it?"

Chaos reigned; things were smashed. Before the sudden riot could truly erupt, Jefforex pointed Lindy's invention at one of the targets set up around the stadium. He chose the one furthest removed from intelligent life and fired. Commander Kingslee was tossed through the air; his arm stung. Jefforex landed in a heap on the other side of the area. He looked up and all of a sudden his pain was the farthest thing from his mind. The target was gone; the wall around it was as well. A good fifteen feet had been gouged out of the ground all along the firing line, including a good chunk of the street outside. The weapon itself was cool to the touch and more than ready to fire a few more times before it needed to be reloaded. The arena was silent. No one besides Lindy could still think straight. "Well, that was more than expected." Lindy's grumble was full of disappointment and was the only sound heard for a great many minutes.

Lindy's show made a few contestants quit on the spot. Many others rushed to finish, only to end up a little singed from their own constructs. A few did build a complete version of what they were asked but none of those fired. At midnight the contest was done and Lindy was unceremoniously woken up for the closing ceremony by Salvea Oat, who had to shake Lindy more than once. Upon seeing that Lindy was more or less awake, the king spoke. "Well done, all of you! The first winner of this contest is the master artificer known only as Lindy." The king's shout seemed to echo throughout the still sleepless city. He looked down at Lindy from his podium, causing the ageless deathbringer to smirk. "Do I have that right, miss?" the king of Otten called.

Lindy slowly stood up. Only she and the king now stood. All others around them were kneeling. "Not quite. Technically my name is The Lindy, but I would like to be called Lindy. Also I am a mercenary first, inventor second."

The stillness deepened. The king coughed and asked, "Would you share your wisdom with the craftsmen of this kingdom?" The king's words seemed to shift between different languages but Lindy did not know which was which.

"I can share some things. Others, either only I will build or will not do at all. I will need a secluded workshop and to be well paid," Lindy said.

Salvea would have flung herself at Lindy if Jefforex had not held her back. Jillvee was screaming, "You animal! Don't you hate those Derndell monsters as well? You are helping them this way!"

The king nodded. "That's a good..." he started.

Lindy sighed loudly enough to stop everyone in sight. Suddenly she seemed older than any human present. Her pain, rage, and force of will took hold of the world and shook the hearts of all present. Her display caused more than a few to pass out. All living beings in the capital of Otten were plunged into a soundless timelessness far more maddening and still than the idea of total silence was able to represent. "First of all..." Each syllable Lindy spoke rattled the souls of those that heard it; none could escape her onslaught. "I have the power to wipe out everything on this continent, including the bedrock itself. However, there are some oaths I would prefer not to break." Lindy's eyes blazed with a chilling disregard for her listeners. "Next. I am a mercenary, meaning

I expect to be paid for my work." By now Lindy's voice was flat and echoed like a blast wave. "And lastly, there are many things that, while they can be made, they cannot be handled in this era. The firearms you fear are but an example of this." Lindy then spun on her heel, looking each being around her in the eyes. "Things far more terrible than pistols can be made, but to use them in this era could very easily kill off all life in this world long before I do." A dark crimson haze engulfed the city. It spilled from Lindy as she raged, yelling, "Well just try to slay me! Yes, Derndell is my foe, but its people are merely its pawns and rulers. I have not been cleared to flatten it. So here we are! Well, come at me! I will not die so soon after the last time. Come at me!" Lindy raged at the crowd. Only a handful were still conscious.

Finally the king managed to stand before Lindy and prostrated himself before her. "Please, still your wrath. I accept your terms. Just stop your rage, please!" he begged in tears, blood dribbling from his eyes and lips.

Lindy's eyes were bloodshot. She looked down at the king as if not understanding where or even who she was, so lost was Lindy within her grief and rage. Only the king showing signs of life moved Lindy to pause. She took a deep breath and covered her eyes with one hand. A wide mad grin formed slowly. "Very well," Lindy whispered. Her aura once again was sucked within the darkest most hidden places of her mind. Lindy then nonchalantly stretched. "Ok, how about I help you build a wall that is permanently imbued with anti-magic and then teach how to render the guns of the Derndell kingdom unable to fire? If those fools over there work out how to make the two inventions I left behind, then I can add something else to the list," she mused innocently, not even taking note of all the people passed out around her.

The king bobbed his head many times. He rose to find dust on his robes. "That would be fantastic," he said. "Of course you will receive a princely sum in return," he added, nearly whimpering.

"A place to work, enough money to eat, clothe, and supply myself, along with a rent-free workshop somewhere out of the way and to be hired as a frontline fighter whenever possible when your nation fights the Derndell kingdom. That is all I need."

"That's it?" Jefforex yelled. Only he and the king were still able to stand, let alone think.

Lindy looked up at the night sky. "They are my worst foes and above all my greatest disappointment to date. I do not wish all in that land ill but I must set right their twisted path. After all, I did a lot to set them on their road."

"Who and what are you really?" the king asked. Lindy looked him deep in the eyes, her gaze gentle and apologetic. "Tell me. It is only fair. After all, I am entrusting my kingdom's future to you."

"A human that may outlive all but this world. Lindy Shrew and Lindy Reaper have been my more well-known past names. See that you tell no one of this," Lindy replied. Her eyes, while still kind, carried a hint of worry.

"Tell me why," the king requested.

"I would like to be judged on who I am now. Or maybe I want to choose those that know my past. The life I live will always be filled with murder and pain. It is not something I share lightly."

"Very well. I can respect that," the king growled.

"Well then, I'm off. The commander and his sergeant know where I am staying. Sorry for the mess," Lindy told her new employer. Then she skipped off while humming something she identified as an old marching tune, but could not recall where she had learned it.

"Dead if we don't but maybe dead if we do. Why is life such a tightrope?" The king sighed, looking around at his still-passed-out citizens and daughter.

"At least we have a fighting chance now, as long as no one angers that monster," Jefforex agreed.

"Get some men to clean this up. I need to sit down," the king ordered his commander. Jefforex ran off while the King pulled over a crate and turned Lindy's newest creation over in his hands. "Now then, what did she do differently?" he asked the night, taking one glance at the smelter before discarding it from his thoughts. *That frivolous lunatic is far too clever to leave traces where she wants none to remain. Well at least she is honest. I can work with that.* The King of Otten mused long into that sleepless night.

When Lindy got back to her inn only the bartender and a younger waitress were there. Seeing her stumble in, the bartender called over. "No one passed this time?" He seemed to realize Lindy could understand the everyday language of this kingdom even if she was clearly a foreigner.

A small sad smile flashed across her face as Lindy shook her head. "Win or lose, this war will still get worse."

The bartender was slightly annoyed at Lindy's crass words but dealing with drunks was an occupational hazard, so this much was nothing. He had seen plenty of soldiers and adventurers drink themselves silly after losing most of their team. "Do you need dinner now?" he asked.

"I'm not hungry," Lindy sighed, already halfway up the stairs. Not even bothering to get undressed, she fell into bed. Near midnight Lindy's eyes shot open. She had subconsciously been observing the Otten kingdom using her link to Death's domain to spy on the land of the living. It was made distressingly simple. All she had to do was perceive the world through a preexisting link. *That was fast. Instructor must have fled to a camp. That is something she would do. Should I tell the people of Otten? No, I can't. That would mess up the balance even more. I can't give others advantages to live; it's only allowed when done equally. So if I told Otten about this they would try to keep using me like that, but then I'd have to do the same thing for Derndell, which would put me in a bad spot. But if I kept doing that then this war would take way too long and I can't serve a kingdom; that's also against the rules. Shit, why me? What kind of man was Manfred Endfield? Hold on. If I had never made the pistol and escaped from Derndell would it be this bad... No, it would be worse. I was far too powerful even in the academy. They would have tried to use me. Without this war I would have never been able to get this kind of support. Why is war the lesser of two evils in this, that is bullshit! Death, all these rules are messed up! I understand logically why they are needed but this is such a pain!* At the end of Lindy's mental rant she groaned. "But even then, I still want to live. Fraya, just what did you see in me? Frost and whoever else you become, I know my life is far too messed up. Please do better than me." Lindy cried herself to sleep.

Mid-morning Lindy was woken up by loud rapping on her door. She leapt up and threw open the door, her old pistol up and her sword held in a reverse grip. Lindy stopped her attack short, now awake and seeing that Salvea Oat had been the one trying to get her attention. Lindy tossed her weapons back into her shadow. "I was having a nightmare."

"Oh, ok. Are you feeling better?" Salvea asked.

"No, but I will live. What's up?" Lindy asked.

"Dad wants to see you," Salvea replied.

"Fine. When?" Lindy asked, walking into her room and stretching.

"Now. Come with me," Salvea said. They had fallen into the same speech pattern. If anyone was nearby, Lindy's accent would have sounded nearly the same as the princess's.

The third princess led Lindy to a carriage where two other female humans were waiting. Lindy chose to ignore them and sat silently thinking about her next twenty or so steps as well as updating the mental checklist of schemes she needed to work on. One of the strangers was maybe a year older than Salvea; the other was a few years younger. Lindy absently noted when the older one moved to look closely at her. "You are kind of young for our last hope."

Lindy rolled her eyes. "If I am the last hope then I could not be middle-aged."

"Why?" the younger one asked.

Lindy sighed. "Kid, you know how a draft works?"

"Yes," the little girl said.

"So what happens when you don't have any able-bodied cannon fodder left?" Lindy replied.

"What's a cannon?" the little girl asked. Only then did Lindy notice she had used the English word for cannon. *Right, that's not a thing yet. Wait, so do they really not have an equivalent?* Lindy mused.

"Is she always this way?" the older sister asked Salvea.

"Mostly." Salvea nodded. Looking Lindy in the eye, the third princess added, "Meet first princess Wallmeana Oat and fourth princess Covell Oat, my sisters."

"The smaller one's Covell?" Lindy asked.

"I'm not that small!" Covell humphed but a flicker of power flowed around the small child's hands. The pulse beat like a drum. No one else seemed to notice the deep well of might the young girl contained. Even then only Lindy and a few others would know just what that pulse was connected to from a glance.

"Be nice," Wallmeana scolded, not making it clear who she was addressing.

Lindy bent over and whispered into Covell's ear. "Ever met a man named War?"

"Who?" Covell asked, tilting her head, but Lindy could tell the little girl's soul was far too old for such a young body, and that she was not nearly as naïve as she appeared.

"I heard Death once took a man from a world called Earth and stuck his soul in a young girl in this world. Ever since then it's one disaster after another for that poor traveler." Lindy shrugged, leaning back in her seat. Covell winced slightly at the name Earth.

"Is that true?" Covell asked.

"Well, that psycho is a close friend of mine," Lindy said, wearing a big shit-eating grin.

"I see." Covell nodded in a bland manner. Even Lindy could not tell if the child was really not interested or feeling something else. Neither Salvea nor Wallmeana was able to decipher the true meaning of their fellow passenger's exchange.

Silence prevailed until the carriage arrived at a small but very fancy villa. "Let's go," Salvea requested. Lindy hopped out after the third princess. The other two exited after. Only Wallmeana seemed unhappy.

Jillean Venlee greeted Lindy and her escorts. A few powerful mages disguised as maids stood to one side. Soon after, Lindy found herself in a small room being bound into a fancy gray dress. As soon as that was done she was rushed into a dining room with a very long table. The king and a regal woman around his age remained seated. The three princesses stood up from their seats. A small boy looked around, fidgeting. Covell had to drag the boy down from his seat. Jeffrey Orion Kingslee stood behind the king. The only one to approach Lindy and the two so-called maids leading her was a young very handsome man. The man bowed and extended his hand. "Hello miss. Please, this way." Lindy rolled her eyes before the young man stood back up. Wallmeana grumbled wordlessly. Covell simply shook her head in disgust. The last two children in the room paid the man's gesture no heed.

"You have me at a loss, sir." Lindy smiled outwardly when the man took her hand. He tried to lead her to a seat but Lindy stood as if she was suddenly an immovable object. The maids tensed. "Who are you?" Lindy asked the young man.

The young man looked at Wallmeana, who shrugged. The king appeared unhappy at this development. "Your fiancé? Count Jethrow Fin?" he explained, now inwardly unsure if this was a good idea.

Lindy chuckled. "No you aren't." She looked over her shoulder at the tense maids. "Magic of that level can't do anything to me." Venlee along with many more mages burst out of a side room. Time in the room seemed to freeze. Lindy shrugged. "I am not interested in men. More importantly, I am not allowed to bind myself to any nation." With that Lindy walked past the panicked and fearful humans all around her until she stood over the small boy. "Hey kid, mind if we switch seats?"

"Why?" the small prince asked, still clueless as to what was going on.

Before the boy could move Covell picked him up and moved him to one side, then turned the boy's head to face Jethrow Fin. The boy's face lit up and he trotted over to the sour looking Count Fin. "Have a seat," Covell invited Lindy.

The king waved off his guards and studied Lindy closely. "You can't bind yourself to us?"

"Nope. That would upset the balance," Lindy replied neutrally.

"Explain," the king demanded.

"I am the only priestess of Death on this world. I am using you to restore the balance by giving you power on par with what the Derndell kingdom was given." Lindy sighed.

"Is this not for revenge?" Jethrow asked.

Lindy took a salad from the hands of a trembling fake maid. "Well they did kill me once, tried another one or two times and did a lot of other things to piss me off. I would not have agreed to fight them otherwise."

Covell looked closely at Lindy, who was enjoying topping the salad with all kinds of oils. "How old are you really?"

Lindy chewed thoughtfully before swallowing a big bite of salad. "Let's see. This second body of mine will always be 20 like the last one, but mentally I have no idea — 12 maybe? I have lived for way too long. Let's see, maybe 90 something?"

Covell groaned. "So are you from Earth?" the question was asked in French, which was certainly not a language native to this world.

The king sighed, seeming to believe his youngest daughter was something of a mental case. Wallmeana started to roll her eyes but stopped when Lindy replied back to Covell's question in French. "One of my lives was. My core was once three different souls. War chose an interesting one. Next time you two talk, could you see about renaming Transcendence to The End?" Fin looked at Lindy with a start but Lindy told him in his native language, "Your name means 'end' in this language."

Covell grumbled. "You did that on purpose!"

Suddenly one of the mages ran over to Kingslee and whispered into his ear. "What, a battalion got that far?" Kingslee sputtered.

Lindy closed her eyes and looked over at the enemy unit from high above. "Wow, that is far. They got a small castle already." Ten maids suddenly surrounded Lindy and tried to trap her with magic. Lindy opened her eyes. All of a sudden no magic in the entire Otten capital worked. "One last reminder — you lot are too weak," Lindy said, getting out of her seat. Kingslee released a sonic pulse at her but it dissipated, leaving not even an echo. "Hey, if I wipe out those enemies, could you try to work with me and not pull crap like this again?" Lindy asked.

The king held his head. "Do I have a choice?"

"I could go to another nation?" Lindy said it like a question but they all knew it was promise and a threat.

"Why should we listen to you?" Fin asked. He was embarrassed but was holding in most of his anger. He knew the king might get rid of him so the kingdom could acquire Lindy's technology, but right then Fin's pride was more important.

"I will work with this nation, not for them, as long as I am treated in good faith," Lindy replied absently. This was her ultimatum.

"Fine. How many troops do you need?" the king asked.

"I can do this myself. Who should I report to after I am done?" Lindy asked, looking around.

"Me," Kingslee replied.

"Ok, see you in a few hours." Lindy shrugged before walking through her own shadow directly to a tall hill overlooking the fortress that Otten's foes had just seized.

Swiftly looking over how the guards were stationed, Lindy nodded. "Might as well take time to enjoy this," she muttered. No matter how icy her calm looked, deep down Lindy was still extremely annoyed. She vanished into the darkness, appearing right behind one of the three hundred and five enemy soldiers in and around the castle. With a flick of her wrist the man lost his head. After pilfering the grunt's dagger she appeared behind yet another guard and severed his spine with her stolen dagger, replacing her weapon with the dying man's knife. Lindy repeated this process close to a hundred times. First the sentries, then the patrols, then the search parties were all killed off without a sound. Finally the enemy commander recalled all his troops to the castle court-yard. Some junior officers looked over the troops, checking if there was an imposter in their ranks. At this point Lindy was as cool-headed as she was bored. She observed the orderly line of troops getting yelled at. After no issues were found only then did the commander show up with two young aides by his side.

Jerrend

Human male age 61

Affiliation: Derndell kingdom 8th army

Job: siege specialist

Status: Major Derndell kingdom army

Abilities: strength 39, vitality 46, mind 50, agility 27

Sickness: ash wasting (source Lindy Shrew)

Talents: keen sense (sight/hearing), alcohol tolerance: high, language: common Derndell, resistance fear/mind control/seduction/intimidation/hunger: mild, light sleeper, rally, true effort, swift thinking, subdue, toughness, move till dead. swift command, see invisible

Curse: no sense of pain

Skills: sword: master, armor proficiency (chain/leather/plate): expert, athletics: master, spear: expert, awareness: expert, smithing: expert, survival: journeyman, sewing: journeyman, barter: journeyman, leadership: expert, intimidate: journeyman, tactics (all): journeyman, drive: journeyman, accounting: expert, literacy: journeyman, provisioning: master

Lindy leapt into the middle of the enemy formation. The ground shattered; all those near her died. "Artillery! Spread out!" Jerrend yelled. Over the screams Lindy began to cackle. Drawing Transcendence, she swung lazily at a wall and close to eighty men were all cut in half by the attack. "Show yourself!" the commander yelled.

Lindy revived both halves of the men she had cut in half and had them turn on their former comrades. She walked out of the dust storm still billowing up from her landing. Two junior officers were shot in the face by her pistol then another one lost his head, much like cork getting separated from a bottle of champagne. "What are you?" the commander yelled upon seeing Lindy in her still spotless dress.

"Hold that thought," Lindy sighed. In the time she spoke, the three men she had killed before and the eighty zombies she had slain largely due to the soldiers' panic rose from the dead to aid in the cleanup of the living. "I'm sorry, where were we? It's been a long night," Lindy asked the commander, managing an awkward curtsey.

"What do you want and who are you?" the man asked.

Lindy looked closely at the commander, making him shudder. "Oh, I remember now. You were that watchman from the 3rd branch hero academy." It really had taken Lindy a while to place the man.

"Who are you?" the man repeated more strongly this time.

"Oh it's me, Lindy. You should go back to your kingdom with your helpers." Lindy shrugged.

"Lindy! The one that destroyed the 3rd branch?" Jerrend shouted before breathing hard a few times. "Why are you letting us all go?"

"Because only you three are left?" Lindy told him like it should be obvious and in all honesty it really should have been, but Jerrend had all his attention on Lindy so he had not noticed.

"Ok, but why?" Jerrend pressed.

"Just tell whoever is in charge that I will pay back the Derndell kingdom for all the wrongs it's dealt me." Lindy nodded to herself. She held out her hand to shake. "Deal?"

Jerrend looked at her hand like it was some kind of WMD (he was not truly wrong) and walked past her, dragging his two aides along. "I'll tell them what about my troops?"

"I'll dispose of them. Watch out for any patrols," Lindy told him. When Jerrend was far out of sight Lindy turned the zombies to dust and moved into a shadow repairing next to Kingslee who was still with the king in the dining room. "Done," Lindy reported.

"Done?" the king asked, more shocked by Lindy's words than her sudden appearance, unlike his guards who were panicking to surround her.

"So when do I get my workshop?" Lindy asked, not taking note of the sour-faced mages all around her.

"After I confirm what you said is true, we will hire you as an adviser with no permanent ties to the kingdom," the king groaned.

"Great. So can I keep the dress?" Lindy asked.

"Fine," the king murmured half-heartedly. He had yet to work out how to deal with Lindy, let alone keep a straight face around her. She was blunt and gave him a hard time politically but the worst thing was she had yet to be wrong. The king was unsure whether he should feel happy about that or not, so he chose to find dealing with Lindy tiring but necessary.

"Ok, I'll go back to the inn. Let Covell know I would love to talk to her again." With that, Lindy slipped into a shadow yet again.

"I need a hard drink. Commander Kingslee, join me," the king commanded.

"I couldn't, sire," Jefforex said.

"That was not a request," the king told his most trusted commander. The two men got a bit tipsy and complained bitterly about how much work Lindy was pushing onto them. None of the maids were amused.

Lindy spent three months setting up her workshop named The Merchant of Death in an out-of-the-way village. Setting up supply lines for both materials and secret blueprints was a terrible headache for the kingdom of Otten as a whole but they had to endure it to have a fighting chance. Apprentices came and went, absorbing very little of the knowledge Lindy tried to impart. The fine detail work of magic pathways and calibration for her firearms with anything better than a deplorable success rate was very rare. One of the more skilled students she taught in the time her workshop was being built was a young man called Danith Fin. He was a distant relative of Jethrow Fin and likely some kind of agent. Lindy was appalled when a few very powerful nobles discredited the non-noble artificers in the kingdom for not understanding Lindy's instructions. Those same nobles pressured the king to appoint Danith Fin as Lindy's official aide. In private the king often apologized to Lindy, explaining that if he tried to overturn the "help" of Danith Fin, his nobles would cause some minor havoc. Lindy allowed the annoyance to help while swearing to keep him at arm's length. However, the king was forced to agree that if some other noble tried to get in her way again, his entire family would be wiped from existence by Lindy herself.

Jerrend lost one of his aides, who died after being wounded when leading their pursuers away on a stolen horse.

Around the time of this drama, Jerrend and his last aide, along with Caldrin Faywind, arrived in the Derndell kingdom capital after relaying their reports to the young king of Derndell. The most powerful retainers in Derndell along with Ajax Shrew were called to a meeting. The new king was called Gerrad the Second of Derndell. His mother was from a merchant family and had been merely a disposable mistress until all the highborn in the royal family were killed off. Afterwards the eldest remaining male heir was a boy named Grin who had rebranded himself as Gerrad. When his aides stepped in, Gerrad shouted, "The monster you all let kill my father is back."

The aides all looked at Ajax, who shook his head. "I believe you, but her old soul is not back, meaning something very odd is at work and I can't track her."

"Then what use are you?" Gerrad asked.

"Very little right now, my king." Ajax bowed.

Gerrad took a deep breath and addressed his aides. "Find a way to kill the demon called Lindy for good this time." After a long pause the king looked around. "That's all. Now go," he added.

Around the same time as the Derndell kingdom restarted its hostilities with Lindy the individual in question was enjoying a light ale on her new workshop's porch. Covell, who up until then had been avoiding her, arrived for their first meeting. The young princess's guards had been left at a nearby inn. Lindy handed her guest a mug of apple cider. Only after Lindy secured a thick screen on the porch did Covell let down her hood. "That story about your sister being Lindy Shrew is a lie," she commented.

Lindy looked over the technically young person. "Why do you say that?"

"You gave far too much away." Covell sighed, now appearing far older than she physically was. "So drop the act. I know you are Lindy Shrew."

Lindy and Covell studied each other for a time. "I was, but you are one of War's agents and remember a life on another world."

Covell sputtered mid-drink. "Why do you say that?"

"I am crazy, not stupid," Lindy replied.

"Well fine, but are you from Earth as well?" Covell asked.

"One of me was, but I only remember knowledge from when that body died," Lindy replied wistfully.

"Did you have a name?" Covell pressed.

"Manfred Endfield," Lindy replied. "What about you?"

Covell stuttered, "First tell me how you died."

Lindy shrugged and replied all she could recall about Manfred Endfield's flight from a cold bridge. At the end, Covell was in shock for a few minutes, then she threw her arms up. "Why did you have to be my uncle?"

Lindy did a double take. "Say that again?"

Covell took a few deep breaths "I had an uncle back on Earth named Manfred Endfield. He died before I was born. I was told it was suicide but it sounds more like you were careless."

A torrent of thoughts erupted in Lindy's brain. She had so many questions, so throwing caution to the wind she picked one question at random. "I thought you were French."

The look at Covell's face disappointedly said she expected Lindy to blurt out something like that. "My dad was Canadian," Covell explained.

"So your mother was my sister? Was she older or younger?" Lindy asked swiftly.

"Younger. You really don't remember you past life?" Covell pressed.

"Not that one." Lindy shook her head.

"Is that so? Your infamy was still going strong when I was alive," Covell said.

"How long did you last?" Lindy asked.

Covell shrugged. "Eightyish."

"Oh, good job," Lindy nodded.

"You don't want to hear about your past?" Covell asked.

"Nope. That said, if you need anything, let me know," Lindy sighed deeply.

"Ok thanks," Covell said before forcing out the word, "Uncle."

"Man, I am not going to get used to that," Lindy laughed.

"How about first names from now on?" Covell suggested unhappily.

"That works." Lindy nodded before holding out her hand to shake. "It's nice meeting you, Covell."

"Call me Venessa, Mr. Manfred," Covell requested mean-spiritedly.

"Fine," Lindy grinned, rubbing Covell's head. Neither was willing to admit they felt happy about meeting this way.

Covell got up. "By the way, do you know anything about an exploding troll killing some people?"

Lindy vaguely recalled such an event. "Why?" She felt sure that after a few minutes she could retrieve the memory she felt was in her mind somewhere.

"Because Comander Kingslee was training a team of adventurers to be royal guards," Covell explained.

"And that's why he was drunk and practicing healing magic?" Lindy asked.

"Maybe. Either way, he is still upset about them dying," Covell replied.

"Thank you for telling me," Lindy said.

Covell took one last glance at Lindy and sighed. "I see you are the same as the stories, Manfred."

"All of them?" Lindy asked.

"Close enough. But is this how you want to be?" Covell asked back.

"If I could, I'd like to stay in the shadows doing what I need to do. But this time I'll need to get my hands really dirty before I can pretend to be clean again," Lindy grumbled.

"You have not changed," Covell shrugged.

"That's not true, and you know it, short stuff," Lindy heckled as Covell made her escape out of town.

Months passed and Lindy got into a daily routine. She was truly bored but the feeling of drudgery felt nostalgic, so she worked even harder than she had promised. Disciples came and went. For her students Lindy explained both verbally and with step-by-step examples how to make her inventions. One in fifty showed some grasp of what she taught. Before Lindy, the artificers of this world had never made anything more than small curiosities and lab equipment used by far more prestigious professions. The artificers' pride slowly formed for the first time. Many had always enjoyed their supporting role but now they held center stage in world events. Few shied away from it. Every so often Lindy went to view new walls being built, walls that could repel most magic. Other than that, she spent far more time than she liked turning down dates and party inventions. What Lindy most enjoyed was flaying alive the few foreign spies she found.

Nearly a year of work passed quickly. One day Lindy received two unannounced visitors. This was not uncommon but most who looked for her now sent expendable messengers.

The first to arrive was a young count. Lindy was on her lunch break so she met with the man promptly. Before she was able to introduce herself the man demanded, "I want to commission a firearm."

"Why?" Lindy said, sighing in her mind.

The young man's gaze hardened. "Let your supervisor ask that."

A long silence ensued before Lindy realized what the young man was getting at. It had been a very long time since someone was not afraid of her. "I am the owner of this shop. Tell me."

The young man looked over Lindy then shook his head. "You are far too young to be The Lindy."

Lindy could only grumble. "Not everyone ages like a normal person."

The count glanced at the trembling apprentices around him. His gaze softened. "Oh, my apologies then. I did not know you were an elf." Lindy only smirked at the man's poor effort at gaining information. The young man went on as if nothing happened. "The weapons being issued to the army are far too bland-looking and embellishing them does not work."

"How so?" Lindy asked, only now interested.

"The balance is thrown off, the weapon explodes, or both." The young man grumbled at his apparent failures.

"Ask the king if we can make a custom one for you then," Lindy told him.

"I can't ask you directly?" the young man shot back, unhappy but not arrogant anymore.

"I make weapons for the Otten kingdom's war effort. Anything that may halt that even for a few hours must go through the king," Lindy told him.

The young man's face darkened. "So I am a spy, is that it?" he spat.

Lindy could only roll her eyes. "If you were a spy you would already be dead. My agreement is with the king of Otten. Anything more than what was agreed upon must go through him."

The young man took a deep breath. "Why?"

"Because Derndell must perish. That is the only reason I am doing this," Lindy replied. The young man shivered and rushed out. A few of Lindy's apprentices had collapsed in terror. At that moment Jefforex entered the workshop. Lindy looked over at her still-standing students and pointed at the floor. "Hey, clean them up," she ordered. A few more fainted.

"What did I miss?" Jefforex asked incredulously.

"I may have released too much power just now." Lindy shrugged.

Lindy slid over the mug of ale her last guest had not touched. "What did Count Griff want?" Jefforex asked before taking a sip of ale.

"A custom firearm. Seems like he tried to modify some of his own army's and lost some," Lindy lightly replied. Jefforex spat ale from his nose from shock.

"What?" he shouted then after a deep breath. "I thought he was going to demand you marry him."

"Why?" Lindy asked.

"Because that's what the house backing him is plotting. I came to warn you and ask that you don't kill them all," Jefforex replied.

Lindy spat out the water she was in the middle of sipping all over the table that Jefforex was trying to wipe down. "Et tu, water," she said to herself. "If they let me ignore them or take no for an answer then I won't go after them," Lindy promised.

"Says the immortal assassin." Jefforex shook his head, clearly not believing Lindy's vow of non-violence.

"That's defamation of character!" Lindy swore. "And who told you that!"

"So you are that Lindy." Jefforex smiled.

"But I have not killed enough to be an assassin," Lindy lamented.

"Then what's your body count?" Jefforex asked while biting his lip and dreading the answer.

"Not counting manticores, chimeras, and hydras? Fewer than three hundred intelligent life forms, I think," Lindy pondered.

Jefforex shook his head in exasperation. "And that's not enough to be an assassin."

"Almost none of those were sneak attacks!" Lindy defended herself and in the process derailed the conversation further.

"Really?" Jefforex asked blandly.

"Absolutely. It's not a sneak attack if you start yelling before killing a squad or five," Lindy said.

"Well, assassin is still nicer than psychopath," Jefforex retorted. Before his words died down in the ears of his audience, all of Lindy's students fled the building en masse. "What did you do to them?" he asked, looking out the door.

"Nothing weird," said Lindy, who was perhaps the single strangest being on the world she called home. "Anyway, what's the most venomous thing you know of?"

"A dark wyrm. The older the worse it is. Why?" Jefforex said warily. He began to feel sympathetic to Lindy's students.

"Because none of the poisonous things I can find taste that great," Lindy lamented.

"You don't feed poisonous things to anyone, do you?" Jefforex asked, holding his sword and planning an escape route.

"Of course not!" Lindy shouted. Jefforex jumped from his seat. "I'd never let anyone take from my stash!" Then she looked up at her conversation prisoner. "Hey, can you show me how this place's common alphabet works?"

Jefforex slumped into his chair and took a pen and strip of hide Lindy had handed him. He drew a diagonal line and a few squiggles on the top and bottom of it then a blank diagonal line next to it. "That says immortal assassin. The written word is based on a few key ideas, names, and titles. Everything else is part of that and can be used to make or copy other ideas. A blank base on the bottom shows the end of an idea." He drew five filled diagonal lines and one half-filled one. "This was your response. It says that's completely untrue and beside the point, so don't slander me."

"What you said is not what I heard." Lindy shook her head.

"Auto-translate can do that," Jefforex nodded. "It would also explain why you sound so long-winded."

"This world is nuts," Lindy sighed. Then looking at her open back door she yelled, "Ok, back to work now!" The students rushed in and Lindy looked back at her guest. "If that's all, I need to get back to work."

"Right. Have fun." Jefforex nodded.

"Right, no pressure," Lindy muttered.

12

Treading the Abyss

After a good eight months of production, the quota on weapons and walls had almost been achieved. If the question was what allowed the walls to be built up so fast, the words magic and feudalism explained a lot. At that point Lindy felt it was a good time to fulfill yet another part of her agreement. One day she put on a bulky cloak and transported herself to the biggest training field in the capital of Otten, which was just inside the newly built walls. Suddenly appearing in the heavily guarded training grounds used to train large teams in the use of high-powered ranged weapons centuries ahead of their time led to a predictable result. As soon as Lindy appeared, ten weapons fired at her. The bullets turned to rust midflight and were swept up by the wind, and the weapons used on her lost all power. Various profanities and questions hurtled back and forth from the team of ten that had shot at her. "Identify yourself!" yelled Jillvee, who was in charge of the field at this time, rushing over.

Lindy pulled off her cloak's hood. "They are getting good," she smirked.

"Lindy, you can't just appear in a restricted area like that!" Jillvee nearly howled.

"That's a problem for tomorrow," said Lindy. "So when can I teach how to render weapons like these unusable?" she asked, ignoring the indignance, fear, and anger around her.

One of the men who had shot her looked at his weapon. "Unusable?" he murmured.

Lindy sighed, fading into her own shadow and jumping out of the worried man's. Upon touching the man's firearm Lindy announced, "Ok, that will work now. Our enemies have similar weapons."

"Can anyone counter that?" Jillvee demanded. She had given up restoring order for now, although the fear Lindy caused so effortlessly went a long way to getting the troops under control, much to the officer's chagrin.

"If you know the trick and the opponent half-assed it, yes," Lindy nodded seriously.

"Who half-asses and attacks!" Jillvee demanded.

Lindy looked at the other woman with pity. "Idiots, overconfident lunatics, overpowered lunatics, and puppies," Lindy replied.

"Forget I asked. Come back early tomorrow," Jillvee sighed.

"No problem," Lindy nodded, then she leapt over the wall into the city. Shouts and even more profanity followed her for a time.

"Who was that, ma'am?" one of the officers asked Jillvee.

"The most dangerous enigma ever," Jillvee muttered before getting back to work.

Lindy wandered around for hours. She noticed Maklin and Grix sitting with a woman that looked far too familiar.

Frost Zigone
Human female age 31
Affiliation: Derndell kingdom nobility
Job: mid-level hero
Status: Derndell kingdom diplomat, shunned
Abilities: strength 328, vitality 403, mind 340, agility 292
Talents: translate: all, resistance (mind control/intimidation): moderate, true effort, swift thinking, subdue, toughness, immunity: (seduction/fear), calming presence, watchfulness, acute sight/hearing: mild, all-out

attack, bulwark, true guard, absorb force, roll with hits: all, swift step, substitution: bodyguard style, limited precognition: attacks only, rally, empower spell, charm, see truth, hide feelings, still mind.

Unnatural state: beyond limits (permanent)

Skills: mace: master, armor proficiency (chain/ leather/ plate): master, athletics: master, awareness: master, smithing: journeyman, survival: journeyman, barter: journeyman, leadership: master, literacy: expert, ride: expert, ice magic: extreme, rune craft: expert, unarmed: expert, shield use: extreme, time magic: journeyman, diplomacy (all): expert, etiquette: journeyman, intimidate (force of presence): expert

"Shit," Lindy swore, trying to flee before those three old acquaintances noticed her.

Before she could flee, Grix saw her out of the corner of his eye and began choking on his coffee. Before Lindy could take so much as a single step, Frost appeared behind her, gripping Lindy's shoulder. "Turn around," Frost asked hopefully. Lindy did as she was asked and Frost's face fell in disappointment as her hand dropped from Lindy's shoulder. "Sorry, you looked so familiar from the back."

"Right," Lindy nodded stiffly and turned to run.

"Lindy, why are you back?" Grix coughed. Both Lindy and Frost snapped around to glare at the dwarf. Then they looked back at each other.

"You look great, by the way," Lindy said, her face reddening.

"Who are you and where are you from?" Frost asked.

"Lindy, back from the dead? So are you Fraya or Frost?" Lindy sighed. The next thing she knew Frost had tackled her to the ground.

"Idiot!" Frost yelled, gripping Lindy tightly and pressing her against the cobblestones.

"You could break someone like that. Let's talk about this like adults!" Lindy pouted.

Soon after, Lindy found herself sitting with Grix, Maklin, and Frost. "What are you doing here and what happened to you?" Frost shouted after composing her thoughts.

Lindy held up her hand. "Hold on." She took out a drawing of a steam-powered train and handed it to Maklin. "There may be a market for this. Now go away." It took Maklin one look at the drawing to drag Grix away. "I was killed and had to make a new body. I've been in this one for close to a year. Now what are you doing here?"

"Trying to start peace talks," Frost grumbled. Then her expression seemed to freeze over. "Wait, who killed you?"

"The last king of Derndell," Lindy shrugged.

Frost jumped out of her chair. "That is not ok," she muttered.

Lindy did not stop talking despite her old girlfriend's outburst. "So I killed him and almost everyone else in the room where they executed me. I am helping the Otten kingdom to wipe my old homeland off the map."

Lindy looked up at Frost, tying to gauge her feeling on this, only to realize that Frost had gotten even better at hiding her emotions. "What about my sister and her kids?" Frost asked after a while.

"Wow, time really flies. Well, if I find them I am willing to keep them alive," Lindy replied.

"Ok thanks. So how can I help you?" Frost asked, leaning over Lindy.

"Won't helping me cause even more issues for your family?" Lindy asked, only to see Frost's face cloud over for a few seconds. "That's what I thought; don't fight, and keep your family safe. I'll do what I can to keep our family members alive."

"But then I can't help you enough," Frost grumbled.

"Killing is easy; protecting is hard. Keep Fall, her kids, and your mother alive and out of combat, and I will be able to fight with a clearer mind," Lindy replied.

"Are you ok?" Frost asked.

Lindy leaned back in her chair and took a deep breath. "No. This sucks. If I did not draw so much attention to myself then all of this would be unnecessary and I could assassinate in peace but noooo, I just had to invent the gun way before it should have been made."

"And that's why all this happened?" Frost asked, suddenly mad.

"More or less," Lindy nodded. "But you can't kill me, even now."

Frost cancelled the spell she had been slowly building. "I still love you and you don't seem to be mind-controlled." She began to walk away before looking back at Lindy who was peering over the bill with frowned brow. "But I will still try to stop this war through peaceful means."

"And you are leaving me the bill. Why?" Lindy called after Frost.

"Because you would go on a rampage either way. I need some payback." Frost waved back before disappearing into the bustling market.

Lindy shook her head, a smirk wide on her face. "Interesting. She has a sense of humor now." After leaving a coin worth a good ten times the cost of the bill, Lindy slipped into the shadows and out of the city.

Frost left the city after a week. Lindy spent a month training all those sent to her. She worked feverishly to control her might to near-normal levels so no one died.

Soon Frost returned to the kingdom. Ajax Shrew met her at the gates to the city. "How did it go?" he asked mildly. Somehow, whenever it seemed someone was looking down on Lindy, Frost got very annoyed. That feeling had gotten even more intense after meeting Lindy again.

Ajax and the king of the Derndell kingdom annoyed Frost more than anyone else. "Lindy's still live. And the Otten kingdom only wants war with us," she reported.

"They are not afraid?" Wisp asked, removing an illusion spell. The guards and townsfolk around the gate disappeared as if they were never truly there. Ajax, Wisp, the young king Gerrad, Grgen Smalsh, Randull Lorn, and Nightcrow were the ones who had really been there all along.

"They believe that with Lindy's help the damage Otten can do will be enough to make us back down," Frost replied.

Gerrad huffed. "We all know that's not true. Why did you fail to make them see that?"

"Because there was no doubt in their minds that they are right. Much like there is no doubt in my mind that they should not fight us," Frost sighed. She left out that she believed her own kingdom should not fight too, on the grounds that Lindy never made idle threats.

"So, we will just crush them," Grgen nodded.

"Lindy is close to Legendary rank and has been making a new weapon and walls," Frost added.

"Why did you not kill her then!" Gerrad shouted.

Frost took a very deep breath and used her magic to cool down her boiling blood. "I am not that powerful." Then after a glance around she asked, "Where is the hunt master?"

"Anna Faywind and her aunt fled. They may be rebelling," Ajax replied. Only Wisp glared at him; none of the other advisors had much of a response. "Two dwarf holds also declared war on us. Including the Otten kingdom, four human nations are making hostile movements. Lastly, three dragons have been causing havoc around our borders."

"And we are to fight them alone?" Frost asked.

"Only the Otten kingdom and Faywood elves appear to be truly serious. We will be fine," Gerrad sneered.

"Then guard your heart well," Randull muttered. Nightcrow twitched but did not appear to disagree, although Nightcrow had been wearing even more layers as of late, making it impossible to get a read.

Nightcrow acted like nothing out of the ordinary was going on. "How did you identify Lindy Shrew?" he asked.

Frost took a few moments to calm herself down even more and organize her thoughts. Now she was certain that what Lindy had told her was not some kind of sick joke. The bastards in front of her had killed off the one she cared about most for their own greed. "Her name is The Lindy now. Her personality is more or less the same and she remembers all that has happened to her. However, Lindy's current body looks different."

Ajax seemed to glow with an intense hunger to know Lindy's secrets. Gerrad grumbled at his advisers. "Well then, we all know what the threats are, so go and kill those problems."

Frost was dragged away by Ajax and Nightcrow to allegedly compile an image of the new Lindy and unofficially for some light interrogation.

One day Lindy was called to the Otten palace. When she arrived, a small female waved to her from the palace gates' guardroom. "Manfred," she cooed.

"Don't say it like that," Lindy cringed, speaking in French again.

Covell dropped her act. "The war's about to start," she said seriously. "Are you ready?"

"As your war's your job, killing is mine," Lindy retorted.

"Yup. I raised as much cash as humanly possible for the war effort," Covell replied with a yawn.

"Rough night?" Lindy snickered in English, making the guards suspicious but not enraged as Covell led her inside.

"Running a military industrial complex is exhausting. Plus my body is still a child's. What did you expect, uncle?" Covell retorted in their past world's languages.

The long hallway resounded with footsteps but Lindy did not hear them. Her thoughts consumed her for a time. The deeper into the castle, the fewer people they passed. At a large door Covell had to pinch Lindy, who was able to wake herself up and realize what was going on before she destroyed the entire city. "About our real jobs: weapons, economy, diplomacy, and politics are all part of war. Malice and greed are only part of what I work to create, use, and control. What about you? What do you mean to Death?"

Lindy sighed. A far-off look glassed over her eyes. "Life, death, rebirth, annihilation, chaos, endings, beginnings. I keep things alive, destroy those that try to work against that order, and keep the world in flux. I am the embodiment of shifting and changing."

"So you are a hero of justice?" Covell asked. She did not believe Lindy had anything to do with justice in this world or the last.

Lindy looked at Covell like she was insane. "I help keep this world alive and spinning, but I am not just. My work is harsh and evil. I think Death puts up with me because I can do this job without shattering, all while smiling and skipping around like the deranged lunatic I am."

"As long as you know that," Covell muttered, now not quite sure how evil Lindy really was. "Let's go."

"Let's," Lindy agreed, a few tears becoming vapor before Covell could get a clear look at her uncle's face. They opened the war room door together.

The king of Otten, Wallmeana Oat, Salvea Oat, Jillean Venlee, Jeffrey Orion Kingslee and a few high-ranking officers were all in the room looking over a large map. A few heads looked up when the doors opened. Covell coughed loudly. When that only made the few heads that had looked up turn back to the map, she knocked loudly on the door. "Master Lindy is here."

One of the generals tried to wave Covell and Lindy away. "This is the war room. Don't bring outsiders in."

Lindy looked at her guide. "The war room. Did War ok using his name?"

"No?" Covell replied, clearly unsure if that was true.

Lindy sighed. "Well, for a big red ape he seems jovial, so I suppose it's fine."

Jillean could not let that go. She crushed a map case in her hands. "Don't make up such tales."

Lindy shut up, seeming to remember all the effort in remaining low key. "She is not lying. They have met," Salvea said, her face suddenly vacant.

"Who, when?" Wallmeana stammered.

"Oh," Lindy said lamely. "Well, Death is my boss and I have talked with Fate and War a few times." Then she stopped and slapped her face. The wind pressure from that slammed the heavy doors closed and scattered many pages. "But that's a secret."

The room was still for a few seconds and papers rained. "So you really are Lindy Shrew," Jeffrey sighed.

"That monster is her?" Jillean asked

"You?" Wallmeana added, her legs weak and shaking.

"And that's why it's a secret. Also, I *was* Lindy Shrew. That name belongs to a body from years ago." Lindy shook her head.

"Why do you need us again?" the King of Otten asked, although more to let Lindy explain herself to the officers rather than believing his words would change things at all.

"Look, I am bending the rules as it is to help you all. I'll serve as a unit of a hundred soldiers, and take care of any mid-level or higher heroes. However, if I fight a team of high-level heroes or a legendary rank, I will not hold back. So pulling away from such a fight would save many lives," Lindy explained.

"But you armed those Derndell kingdom bastards with the power they are showing off now," Wallmeana shouted.

"And that's why we are even talking about this. I help you all to fix this mess or I find another kingdom to help. I feel like dwarves and I could be very good friends," Lindy replied emotionlessly.

"Not a word of our ally's connection to Death is to leave this room," the King decreed tiredly.

Turning to leave, Lindy added, "Well, come and get me when the war's on." No one stopped her.

Covell and Salvea left the room briskly and rushed after their kingdom's greatest benefiter and terror.

"Wait. You talk with Death a lot, right?" Salvea called.

"Death and I are well acquainted," Lindy smirked.

Covell stopped her now giddy sister from asking a follow-up. "What do you mean well acquainted?"

"First name basis and nicknames. I call it Death and it calls me crazy," Lindy replied, failing to suppress a grin.

"He's messing with you," Covell gowned.

"Oh, wait, he?" Salvea said.

"So why did you want to know?" Lindy asked, genuinely curious and still wary about why someone would want to know all about the humorous manifestation of death (not realizing most would never want to laugh in that giant's face).

"Dying again scares us," Salvea sighed.

"Well, sure it does. Wait — again?" Covell asked.

"I've seen more death than you can imagine," Lindy began gravely. "Part of me was even at a grim reaper convention. Trust me, waiting tables in an endless expanse of those boneheads is a fate worse than dealing with one of them." After a few seconds, Lindy realized why that one memory of Conduit's was so strong. *Why do all of them have such terrible outdated jokes?* she mused.

"That's it?" Salvea asked.

"Live as well as you can, grow well, don't go totally insane, and have at least one being remember you when you die. Do that, and you have done well," Lindy shot back.

"You make it sound so simple," Covell groaned.

"Cut your uncle some slack. At least you three have me to remember you," Lindy sighed, ignoring the dubious looks the two sisters were giving each other. Lindy added, "And Foxfoot, if you ever want my help, have Salvea let me know," Lindy said.

Salvea's eyes clouded up. "Try Caldrin next time. It's not fair to only use their first names."

Lindy grinned as Covell grabbed her sister, shouting, "What was that?"

Salvea yelled down the hall at Lindy's rapidly retreating back. "That was our secret!"

"Live with no regrets. I am sure my niece would love to share a few of her own secrets in exchange," Lindy yelled back as she bounded around the bend, evading Covell's glare and entering a shadowy portal leading right back to her lab.

That night Covell sat with Salvea in the older sister's room, although only Covell sunk into the fluffy chairs. A small coffee table separated them. For a long time after their tea had cooled the sisters glared at each other, viewing one another like strangers. Finally Covell groaned. "Fine, as the older one of us, I'll answer your questions first."

"How are you related to Lindy?" Salvea asked. Her voice was pure resentment and confusion.

"Lindy has three souls stuffed into one body but as far as I can tell they have been mashed together into a single mass. One of those souls was my uncle in my past life in another world," Covell replied, listing off facts casually, then she leered. "And given that I remember most of my one hundred and one years spent in that other world, I am older."

"Priestesses don't remember their pasts," Salvea noted firmly.

"Right about that, I'm kind of a special case," Covell said, stuffing some scones into her mouth bashfully. After a long time chewing and thinking, she began, "When I died and met my world's Death, this world's Death was there as well. They were having a drinking contest. The one from this world was still totally sober and very unhappy. After hearing that they were complaining about my uncle, I got mad at him as well. So the drunk fool from my old world sent me to this world, but he messed up, and I ended up in a realm of endless burning blood and gold where I met War. And after telling him some stories about my years as an accountant, well, the next thing I knew I was in a two-year-old's body."

"Sound like you hated your uncle," Salvea noted suspiciously.

"I still do!" Covell replied, raising her voice. Then a few deep breaths later she finished off their tea. "Lindy is not just my uncle; she is our best shot at living if he does not remember his past life."

Silence reigned for a time. "Go on," Foxfoot prodded.

Covell could see her sister's expression glaze over and was content to press her for details as payment for spilling her own secrets. Covell took a deep breath and explained. "Manfred Endfield, my uncle, was a, let's say, healer in a powerful..." She paused. "...Kingdom's military. He was in a very big war. Two times his platoon was almost all killed off. Both times by..." She paused again, looking thoughtful and uncertain. "You know what? Even explaining these in terms those from this time would understand is hard. Anyway, weapons able to wipe out a lot of things at once fired from places their weapons could not hit. Killed off almost everyone he worked with twice. After that he was forced to quit due to his mind snapping. The sight of blood terrified him and his memories sometimes came back, tormenting him. He became a repairman working on devices of a complexity far above what we have here. He tried to design weapons in secret and became an angry loner. After a big argument at his father's funeral he left and slipped off a bridge to his death. My uncle was very infamous. Even then I was an old woman."

"So he went from a healer of men to a healer of artificed things?" Salvea asked.

Covell looked up at the ceiling and sighed. "In a manner of speaking. So what's the story of the thing living in your head?"

Foxfoot replied. "I was an elf who died with her village when humans raided us. Only my soul remained, left alone in this world. When the primary mind and this body were very young they stumbled upon me. Most of my substantial power had faded by then, but enough was left to share this child's body."

"What are you called, and do you intend harm to your current host?" Covell asked evenly.

"Those that struck down my village are long dead. I do not blame her or any living humans. Besides, Salvea and I have an understanding and I like her. I mean no harm to the one who allowed me to look for peace," Foxfoot replied.

"Keep that promise or else," Covell grumbled.

Salvea's eyes regained their normal luster. "What promise?" she asked. Looking around, then noting most of the snacks she had set out were gone, Salvea culled up into a ball. "Um, sis, what did the other one say?"

"What other one?" Covell asked, tilting her head to one side.

"Um..." Salvea stammered incoherently, peeking out from behind her legs.

"Hahahaha..." Covell shook with laughter. "Don't worry. It is not my enemy and I will not tell anyone unless it does anything to you that I don't like," Covell replied. She swore that this would be the last time she tried acting like her long-dead uncle's newer cuter self, because it would be bad if she got to enjoy this persona any more than she did already.

Early the next day a lone figure stood outside a dwarven keep. The fortress city was cut deep into a cliff face high above the world. Crags of marble and granite jutted like the fangs of some massive maw. The red clouds of morning and redder sky had just begun to chase away the night and stars. The ground shifted in a riot of red-orange and shadow, showing the war of the color palette above was still being contested. Suddenly out of one shadow sprang a single human who skipped a few steps to the massive city gates. Three heavy knocks struck the door, denting it. The echoes shook the dwarven city like no siege engine ever had. Minutes ticked by. A single hair-covered face peered out of a small window. "Who are you?"

Lindy checked.

Tomorrow Lindy

Female (shadow touched) human age: forever 20

Affiliation: realm of death

Embodiments: kicked out by death, eternal calamity

Job: Reaper

Status: common sense bane: extreme, death's agent

Abilities: strength 8650, vitality 9723, mind 9000, agility 10002

Talents: translation: all, full power strike: strength, danger sense, innate map, skill retention: Manfred Endfield, photographic memory, sixth sense: intuition, extra toughness, favored environment: darkness, cold resistance: high, highly enhanced trait: willpower, analysis: extreme, good hair, quick learner, fearless, body of poison, presence sense, aura: weakening, damage shield:

decay, decay bolt, adept talent: multi tasking, rapid reload, fearsome visage: moderate, selective decay: all, innate spell: chill blast, absorbed impact: moderate, hair trigger aim, repost: debate, realm authority (death): moderate, shadow shift, six fold strike, perception tampering field, find soul, see soul, sense lifespan, attuned to purpose, shadow from, plains walk: deaths realm and back, full power burst (weakening/decay/cold), siphon soul, suppress kindnesses (self): full, suppress power: any, track soul, find living, alcohol residence: mild

Mutation: troll blood (extra burnable, swift regeneration), un-aging. mutagenic blood

Curse: catastrophic encounters, heavily sleeper, light sensitively: mild

Skills: Sword: master, dagger: master, unarmed: master, marksmanship: master, throwing: expert, athletics: master, armor proficiency (leather/cloth): expert, literacy: expert, history (other world): journeyman, intimidate (innate): extreme, diplomacy: journeyman, awareness: expert, necromancy: extreme, tinkering: master, magic tampering: extreme, counter spell: master, survival (woodland): journeyman, cooking: journeyman, acrobatics: expert, stealth: expert, shadow magic: expert, laws of death: extreme

"Looks like right now I'm Tomorrow Lindy?" Lindy said, sounding bemused. Then her face fell. *Oh that's why* she thought, remembering a conversation months before.

"What do you mean, right now?" the furry tufts asked.

"Well this is embarrassing. I just looked at my stats and my name is different. It must have changed since the last time I looked," Lindy said in a tone of voice that could have easily been smug and proud.

"Well, have a nice day," the tufts called down before withdrawing.

"Wait!" Lindy yelled, punching the door. No response was given so she stamped her foot and a crack split the ground, making a large cleft under the massive door.

Soon after a mound of hair with a steel cap peeked out of the hole with a pair of beady eyes. "Why are you still here?" it asked.

"Is this kingdom going to war with the Derndell kingdom soon?" Lindy asked, grinning.

 The hair blinked. "No?" it asked.

Lindy's smile grew bigger and crueler but her eyes dimmed. She rolled up her sleeves and rolled her shoulders, theatrically taking a step forward. "You know what I don't like? That door. It's been looking at me weird."

"Doors don't do that," the mound of hair informed Lindy solemnly.

Suddenly a new head poked out of the cleft Lindy had made and yelled, "Hold it! Shit, Lindy, stop! Please calm down."

"Maklin. It's been too long," Lindy giggled.

"You know her?" the first furball asked.

"Yes, you moron! That's the horrible monster I have been telling you about," Maklin whispered as Lindy inched closer.

"We can't let monsters in. The manual says so," the furball said.

More faces popped out of the hole. "That's right," one said. The others may have nodded, but with all the hair covering the new arrivals it was hard to tell.

"It also says follow the orders of your superiors," Maklin snapped.

"But you ain't our boss," another head chimed in, but now Lindy was peering down at all of them.

"The king told me that everything having to do with Lindy is my responsibility," Maklin said.

"That one's called Tomorrow Lindy, though," the first ball of fur said.

Maklin rifled through his pockets. Taking out a note covered in wine stains, he shoved it in the first furball's face. "It says so here. Also this one is only dangerous if you anger her." He looked up at Lindy and implored timidly, "Right?"

"Mostly," Lindy smiled. After a long pause she added, "If you guys are going to war with the Derndell kingdom, I'll give you a new weapon plan."

"Why would you care if we were?" furball #1 asked.

"Because they think you are, and that means this place is a target anyway," Lindy smirked.

"Our gate can hold them!" one of the furballs shouted before looking down at the metal bucket. He was standing in the cleft Lindy had opened under the gate. "Oh right."

"Maklin, are all your guards this dumb?" Lindy asked.

"Yes. All the smart ones are either officers or craftsmen." Maklin nodded somberly.

"Except him?" Lindy asked, pointing to furball #1.

"Oh Cragoaf the drunk. This is a Monday so..." Maklin began, then stopped and looked at furball #1, better know as Cragoaf. "Why are you so out of it today?"

"Because I'm drunk, stupid!" Cragoaf replied.

Maklin's face fell. "It's in the name," Lindy hinted.

Maklin looked up at Lindy. He clearly had a migraine now. "Just come with me, Lindy. I'll get this idiot demoted later."

Maklin led the way into the fortress of the Igorein clan through the cleft under the gate. They walked past three checkpoints shaped from the mountain before even seeing the city. At the last checkpoint stood an angry beardless dwarf in well-made full plate mail. It held a war hammer as tall as it was in one hand. A battle axe of the same size was strapped to its back. "Is this the attacker?" it asked.

"No general. This is our unannounced guest. The guards chose to deny her entry without telling me," Maklin answered stoically.

"So they did their job and our gate got wrecked? Why is she here?" the general asked.

"Because I am Lindy?" Lindy asked.

Maklin looked at his commander, who was glaring at the sole source of his bad luck, then at Lindy, who was looking over the price list for tolls. "The guards were drunk and I had told them that this lunatic is too much for them."

The general shook its head. "And that's surprising how?"

"True, but they were all drunk!" Maklin sighed deeply.

"One was sober," Lindy added, still fixated on how tolls were calculated by weight and height. After a few seconds she added, "He was the one supplying buckets."

Seeing that this was not getting anywhere or unnerving the newcomer, the general folded its arms. "And why is a human female here, anyway?"

Lindy turned one eye to look at the general.

Zoea Jarvellkon the 89th

Dwarf female age 13

Affiliation: Igorein clan

Job: The boss lady

Status: commander of the Igorein clan

Abilities: strength 589, vitality 1201, mind 600, agility 312

Talents: translate: all, resistance mind control: high, true effort, subdue, toughness, immunity: fear/intimidation/drunkenness, all out attack, bulwark, rally, hide feelings, one handed wielding: all huge weapons, whirlwind attack, danger sense, queen of stubbornness, shattering smash, full power strike: strength, innate map, supreme toughness, high enhanced trait: willpower, analysis: extreme, hide stats: moderate, rage

Curse: can't craft new objects

Skills: mace: extreme, axe: extreme, armor proficiency (chain/ leather/plate): master, athletics: journeyman, awareness: master, smithing: master, leadership: master, literacy: expert, rune craft: expert, unarmed:

expert, intimidate (force of will): master. sense weakness: journeyman, stone cutting: journeyman, teaching: journeyman, mending: apprentice, first aid: apprentice

"Can I call you Zoea?" Lindy asked. Catching the hammer Zoea Jarvellkon swung at her foot, Lindy went on. "Ok then, boss lady Jarvellkon. I have an exclusive invention to give your clan."

"We aren't buying it," Zoea snarled, trying but failing to retrieve her hammer.

"No problem; it's free." Lindy laughed. "Hey Maklin old buddy, what's a mythical dwarf chick doing here?"

"We are a matriarchal society. The men go out into the world. Sometimes the women lead us and keep the cities running." Maklin replied, slowly backing away.

"She called me a chick! I am not a small bird!" Zoea raged, drawing her axe with one hand.

"Oh so that translated literally weird." Lindy sighed. "Well ok," she shrugged, her eyes grinning, before turning the axe into a clump of rust.

"Kill this fool!" Zoea yelled.

A new voice sternly commanded, "Stand down." Walking up to the checkpoint was a young female dwarf in heavy robes followed by older dwarf women and a few heavily armed female guards. The child ruler looked at Zoea and sighed in an exasperated way. "That means you too, sister." A few of the elders hissed in agreement. Before the reinforcements could spread out in a properly authoritative way the young dwarf walked up to the human in the room. "I am the leader of this clan. Who are you?"

Lindy bowed lightly. "Right now I go by Tomorrow Lindy, but you can call me Lindy. That name has not changed in many years."

The child ruler folded her arms. "You started the war. Why are you here?"

Lindy rolled her eyes and pulled off the list of tolls from the wall. On the back of the list was a hastily drawn formula for explosives using gunpowder and fire crystals. It had taken Lindy months to work out how to make usable blasting power from her otherworldly knowledge. Ignoring the drawn weapons around her, Lindy tossed the formula though a shadowy rift. Before anyone could move, the formula was in the young leader's clenched fist.

"What do you want for this?" the leader asked, her forehead slick with sweat. With what she had just seen, she knew Lindy could easily kill her and escape at the very least. Knowing the reports about Lindy, it could be far worse than that.

"Rune lord!" the crowd all around the room shouted, rushing at Lindy. They were out for blood. "Stand down, all of you!" the clan's leader shrieked. Most stopped; some did not have time to. The rest watched Lindy beat their armored comrades senseless with her fists. The rune lord added, "Lady Lindy could kill us all with little effort if she wanted to." The rune lord of the Igorein clan calling another Lady froze all her clansmen. "So what is the price?" the rune lord asked, tapping her foot, thankful no one had died yet. She had broken into a cold sweat despite the very real possibility of her entire mountain and clan being wiped from existence. The rune lord burned with an unshakable craftsman's zeal.

"I want nothing," Lindy smirked knowingly.

The rune lord took a deep breath to center herself. "Then who does?"

"No one I am talking to," Lindy replied lightly.

"You want to make us a target," the rune lord muttered sadly.

"You already are. I am helping you defend yourselves," Lindy explained like it did not matter what they thought.

"You think Derndell kingdom will not stop with the human nations?" the rune lord nodded, her eyes holding a stubborn glint of pride and wrath.

"Well, they are unbelievably greedy. Killing me once or twice only made them worse," Lindy answered without a hint of irony.

"But you gave them their weapons," the rune lord countered.

"And then they went mad and did not let anyone share those plans. That broke the balance I need to keep. That's why that plan is free," Lindy explained.

The rune lord looked up into Lindy's eyes for close to a minute. "Very well. I believe you," she said sternly. After one more look at the plans she asked, "Do you have time for tea?"

"Maybe after the war? I still have to hand out some other plans," Lindy smirked.

The rune lord deflated like the child she was for the first time all but Zoea and a few of the oldest elders could recall. "The plan you have is the only copy I will ever make. Just be careful testing it. Shockwaves and large explosions should be surprisingly easy to make with that formula."

"Ok. Thank you very much, bigger sis!" the rune lord giggled.

On her way out Lindy patted Zoea on the shoulder. "Hang in there," Lindy told her.

Near the first checkpoint a spirit crept up behind her. "Grix, I see you are upwardly mobile now," Lindy noted.

"I am dead," the ghost of Grix replied sullenly.

"Well remember to volunteer to test that cute rune lord's new blasting power," Lindy laughed.

"Rune Lord Sasha Jarvellkon the Third is not your toy," Grix snapped.

Lindy glared at the floating dead man. "Then keep her in once piece, otherwise I will not send you into the realm of Death gently."

Grix shuttered his incorporeal form, shifting though degrees of visibility. "Fine," he huffed before floating away. After the screams from the third gate died down and Lindy made sure no one else died, she stepped into the shadows once more. "Next stop: the Faywind clan. I hope Teach and that lunatic relative of hers are not around."

13

Death's Remix

The moment Lindy appeared at the edge of a huge forest she saw that logging efforts had taken a bite from the allegedly neutral ground. Three elven clans called this one sea of green home. Of those, only a few members of the Faywind clan left their woodland sanctuaries. Lindy could see the souls of many things in the woodland, but her soul sight was blocked partway in, around the elves who were making a beeline to watchtowers set along the tree line. Grinning wickedly, Lindy walked slowly to the current edge of the woodland and yelled up to the trees, "Hey, any of you fools seen Anna?"

An owl hoot was her only reply. "Fine," Lindy sighed. She pointed at Anna Faywind who was huddled with two elves. "Since when did you leave the Derndell kingdom?"

A volley of arrows erupted from the trees. All the arrows fired became mulch. "Is that any way to treat an old rival, Anna? What would your aunt say about you attacking one of her most memorable pupils?" Lindy laughed and stomped down once with her full might. She removed her perception tampering and activated her fearsome visage at full power. The woods creaked dangerously. A cacophony of screams, vomiting, and crashes resounded even above the mini-earthquake.

A bedraggled half-elf limped from the woods, her eyes murderous. "World spirits be dammed. Lindy, are you insane?"

"Oh, now you know me." Lindy rolled her eyes. "And don't ask questions you know the answer to." She tossed her old enemy a disk that was sharpened on the outside and a thin leather rope. "There — a new weapon you can use with or without the sling. Oh, and adding those enchanting runes your new friends like so much might be a good idea."

"Just like that. You wrecked so much then hand me a weapon? What are you after?" Anna spat.

"At least I am not so foolish as to follow the Derndell kingdom. Those assholes are the worst, wrecking a neutral zone without caring about the consequences," Lindy smirked.

"What do you mean?" Anna asked.

Caldrin Faywind walked out of the damaged tree line. "She means we will be forced to choose a side. Lose the forest or fight." Lindy clapped and Anna gasped. "Lindy, I did not raise you to be such a psychopath."

"True. I put far more thought into the chaos I cause now," Lindy answered proudly, while her heart broke a little.

A lich made its way out of the forest after Caldrin. "So you are part of my granddaughter."

Something in Lindy's soul shrieked and hid itself. "Which third is part of what would be pure semantics at this point. You are the mastermind behind Ajax, right?"

"I was. So who are you?" the lich asked.

"To you, a stranger," Lindy answered coolly. The part that was Manfred Endfield was the only mentality present.

"So you feel nothing for your family?" the lich asked.

"I don't even know your name. That died with Lindy right before the rest of us showed up. Nothing here is yours," Lindy snapped.

"This mage is Frelda Shrew. She was just leaving," Caldrin said.

Frelda Shrew: lich, necromancer, torturer, schemer, and a relative of Lindy when she was whole and always feeling agony due to her family. The being that had inadvertently put Lindy on this path by abandoning her took one look around at the hostile glances it was getting. "I still want to know how you are alive, my child, but I'll ask again next time." Before that one-sided proclamation could be answered, Frelda winked out of existence much like Lindy was able to do.

Lindy fell to her knees as the rest of her woke up again. "Hey, are you ok?" Anna called over.

Lindy took a deep breath and yelled at the sky. "What is with all this crap!" For once she was baring her true feelings in public. Then she too disappeared from the woodland, only to reappear a few feet above her workshop's bed, where she literally fell asleep.

While Lindy brooded over how messed up the past was while temporarily forgetting the good things in it, Frelda Shrew was in her lab far under the Derndell kingdom's capital. Technically it was the most secure lab in the deepest room loaned to Ajax Shrew, but no puppeteer who had lived even half as long as Frelda would care about such things. The Derndell kingdom was under her control now, even if no one else knew it. In the room lay Wisp, Hanna Zigone, and Xana, the mother of king Gerrad. All were fast asleep as curses were branded into their very souls. "So Death really did find my replacement. But of all the possibilities he choose that failure," Frelda hissed.

"So you met her?" Ajax asked from the doorway.

Frelda's feelings were not steady. Betrayal, jealousy, confusion, and disbelief ran though her like an icy needle. Any one of those should have been impossible for an undead sage like her. Worst of all was the feeling that she had been cheated and her entire life and unlife were one huge joke, now that Lindy had stolen what Frelda had always wanted. It did not help that other beings had given Lindy the power Frelda had spent ages fighting for. "Speak when spoken to, fool."

"The brat wants to go to war immediately," Ajax replied, not moving an inch. Neither cared about freely disrespecting the child ruler they officially served. Frelda knew Ajax had heard her but also understood why he took the risk to talk when she was so mad.

Looking over the first serious power players to be put fully under her control, Frelda nodded. "Fine, then put Lindy's friends in the front line."

Ajax smirked. "The brat did that already. He even ordered they bring him Lindy's head."

"Good," Frelda said. Ajax turned but before he got very far Frelda spoke up. In a moment of weakness that she told herself was purely for research purposes, she asked, "Why don't you call her your sister anymore to my face?"

"That thing is not my sister. It is so much more than she could ever have been," Ajax replied quickly.

"Then is she like me?" Frelda said.

Ajax turned around but when he saw his grandmother's clenched jaw he shook his head. "I don't know. Both of you are impossible for me to figure out."

Two days later Lindy came out of her room for the first time since her trip. When Danith Fin saw her come into the workshop he stammered, "Master, the war's begun." Lindy took a note from the young man's flustered hands. It was a mustering order.

"No rest for the wicked it seems. Shop's yours. Live well." Lindy smirked sadly, tapping her awkward aide on the shoulder.

"Please come back after we win, ma'am," Danith pleaded.

"If you ever man up and get yourself a good wife, I'll think about it." Lindy snickered at the man who had tried to win her heart, even when his own heart was not in it. "I can't die but you can watch your back, kid. This world is a cruel place." Lindy slipped into a shadow before Danith could express himself anymore.

Coming out of a shadow, Lindy tripped and fell onto Jillean Venlee, who looked up at Lindy coolly. "You are late," Jillean grumbled.

Lindy leapt up. "Jillvee, it's been too long. What now?"

"You come to the front and shut up while my dad talks," Covell said, breathlessly running over. "So how did your plot go?" she wheezed.

"Some of the dwarves and elves may help us," Lindy shrugged.

"How did you manage that?" Jillvee asked.

Covell looked Lindy in the eyes and they answered in unison. "You don't want to know."

"Right; dumb question. Let's go and stay silent," Jillvee nodded, grabbing Lindy's hand.

Lindy snatched Covell's hand. "Come on then." When the princess did not resist, Jillvee raised her eyebrows briefly but led the way regardless of her misgivings. After all, she was not paid to question her leaders.

Lindy was led past rows upon rows of officers. In the kingdom of Otten, anyone commanding one hundred troops or more was some kind of officer. More than a few eyebrows were raised as Jillvee pulled Lindy and Covell.

The closer they got to the stage the higher the rank of officer. Lieutenants led platoons of one hundred men. Captains led companies of five hundred and four. Commanders led regiments of one thousand five hundred and ten, including a supply unit. At the top were generals, each in charge of an army numbering fifteen thousand one hundred and ten. Most battles did not need a full army, so seniority and military/noble rank were how overall authority was calculated, often at the whims of the highest-ranked officer in the field. It should be noted that platoons and companies were staffed by either nobles or commoners. Only regiments and above were mixed units.

On the stage were the exceptions: the king, Jefforex, commanders of small but very elite units, the top mages employed by the king, and Salvea Oat. Lindy too was dragged onto the stage. Jillvee turned to whisper some last-minute advice but froze upon seeing Covell slung over Lindy's shoulder. "What, she can't walk as fast as us?" Lindy said expressionlessly like it was stupid to think anything else.

Lindy gently placed Covell down and bowed deeply to her. "Apologies for the rough handling, my lady." Jefforex, who had walked over, could only grit his teeth and sigh when Covell rolled her eyes in exasperation without anger.

Jefforex nodded over to an empty spot slightly behind Salvea. The three royals, Jefforex, and Jillvee were the only ones at the front of the well-guarded stage, the other high-ranking officers being arrayed behind them. In similar fashion to their audience, most of the less experienced participants had their minds short-circuit for a brief second trying to work out who this rude young lady was. Those that Lindy had trained, however, shivered reflexively in fear.

After one sidelong glance at the still emotionally unruffled Covell, the king cleared his throat and began a speech that few would recall because most of the audience watched Lindy sleep through it.

The king's speech was as follows. "My brave officers, we all know why we are here. The Derndell raiders have come to our borders. Over these hard years we have lost many loved ones. I myself have lost close family members. We have had enough and with the help of our neighbors and the hard work you all have put in to reinforce my forces, we are ready to crush the warmongering of Derndell. It is a fact that we are right and our revenge is just! The months to come will find us victorious!" The king looked over at Lindy who after being elbowed hard by Covell a few times woke up. Lindy's grogginess seemed to disappear when her eyes met the king's. "Care to share a few words, hero?" he asked.

Looking out onto the crowd most eyes were still on Lindy. She sighed and released a fourth of her fearsome visage. Three of the men behind her managed to draw their blades. One lieutenant in the back, Jefforex, and Jillvee got ready for combat. Nearly half of those in the audience fell to their knees. If Jefforex had not subtly supported the king he would have nearly fainted. A few lieutenants really did faint, foaming at the mouth. A few seconds later, Lindy withdrew her visage and life slowly returned to the field. "Well that was…" Lindy began, then paused, allowing around fifty birds to fall into the field dead after dying of fright in midair. "Good enough," Lindy sighed. "Just a reminder. If you can't take that pressure, a hero on the higher end of mid-tier will have no problem killing you. Remember this feeling if you come across a foe that makes you feel like that, or worse, get support. I am not saying this so you will live but so you will use your lives well. You all fight for this kingdom so do not sell your lives cheaply. Unless you kill at least two foes you have not done your job." Then she looked around the crowd. "And for those that I trained, if you mess up what I taught you, your time in Death's realm will be even worse than normal." A few more men fainted on the spot at Lindy's last remark. Then she walked back next to Covell.

"So how was my dad's speech?" Covell asked, surveying the mayhem on the field as men called for medical aid.

"Cliché," Lindy whispered back.

"On our last world you better believe it. You remember yourself yet?" Covell asked, lowering her voice even more.

A few men were glaring at them so Lindy shook her head and spoke in a normal tone. "Nope. Some things seem just that basic."

Jefforex walked up to the pair. "Having fun?"

"No?" Lindy asked.

Jefforex sighed. "Come with me. The expedition force heads out tomorrow. That includes you."

Lindy really wanted to give Jefforex a hard time about not specifying who was going where, but thought better of it. "Fine, lead the way."

Covell looked at Lindy oddly. It was obvious to all but her former uncle that Lindy wanted to get a few verbal jabs in but was restraining herself. "Just stay the you in this world."

"Not like I will get my old memories back," Lindy shrugged, following Jefforex with Covell close behind.

"That's not what I am afraid of," Covell whispered, wondering if that was true.

Lindy looked over her shoulder at her only connection to the life lived as Manfred Endfield. "Just dying will not kill me."

"You are immortal," Jefforex sneered.

"I don't age but I think it is possible for me to die for good. That's why I try to live and enjoy what I have. Being angry and stressed most of the time is not a good way to go." Lindy nodded solemnly before skipping in front of Jefforex and into the camp they had arrived at. "This my new digs?"

"Um, what?" Jefforex asked, not knowing how to respond.

"Yes. Good night, uncle," Covell replied with a feeling of loss she could not place or reconcile.

Lindy bolted over to Jillvee who was in the center of the camp sorting out what went where. "Hey sarge, where do you need me?"

Lindy began bustling around the camp like a whirlwind as Jefforex looked on with Covell from outside. "Uncle?" he asked.

"It's a long story," Covell muttered.

"Should I get her to stop?" Jefforex asked.

Covell shook her head. "No, he is who he is. It was my choice to think of Lindy as family. As long as you keep this a secret nothing will happen." With that she began to walk back home.

"That is a threat, right?" Jefforex sighed.

"And trying to stop that one will never be a fun experience for anyone but her," Covell called back as she speeded her retreat to a jog.

The next morning Lindy awoke to the carts being loaded. Grabbing a chunk of bread from a table lined with thick salty soup and hard bread, Lindy walked over to Jillvee, who was in the center of the chaos. "Need help?"

Jillean Venlee looked over. "Your firearms have anything we need to be careful about?"

"Load them like they were shipped and you will be fine. The gunners would know what I mean," Lindy mumbled between the bread she had stuffed in her mouth.

"Well they're occupied," Jillvee sneered.

"Fine, I'll do it. Where's the gear?" Lindy sighed. Jillvee pointed over to a stack of crates laid on the damp ground.

"Well that's not good." Lindy shook her head, making her way over to the boxes.

Lindy was left to her own devices for the morning. When the packing was done, Jillvee walked over with the lieutenant from the assembly who had not been affected by the terror that was Lindy. "Any problems?" Jillvee asked. Lindy pointed at a muddy puddle. "You don't like water?" Jillvee asked.

"Keep the weapons dry and clean," Lindy said evenly.

"Tell us that next time," Jillvee said.

"I did, and that's written on the shipping documents I sent out all the firearms with," Lindy grumbled.

"Excuse me, but the inventor of our new weapons is coming with us?" the lieutenant asked.

Jillvee patted the man on the shoulder. "This is Felix Aesin. He will be leading your bodyguards."

"My watcher, you mean?" Lindy smiled. "Lieutenant, don't get in my way when the fighting starts."

"I can't do that. My job is to defend you," Felix retorted stoically.

"If something that I can't handle shows up then we are all dead," Lindy grinned evilly.

Felix looked confused. Jillvee just shook her head, saying, "She is not joking. This one could likely kill the entire expedition force without collapsing from exhaustion."

Felix looked mildly shaken. "Then it's a good thing I'm being paid to keep as many of you as I want alive." Lindy shrugged.

"Just take this seriously," Jillvee angrily retorted before storming off.

When the packing was done, Jillvee yelled, "All assemble!"

Felix told Lindy from his spot a few steps behind, "We are with the gunners."

The only response he got was a nod. After a few more steps Lindy reached behind her and tossed Felix in front of her.

Felix Aesin

Human male age 22

Affiliation: kingdom of Otten army. Sildrin trade union in-
    telligence agency

Job: agent

Status: two faced

Abilities: strength 212, vitality 233, mind 312, agility 358

Talents: forgettable, single minded, translate: all, obscure status. honest face, fearless, immunity (poison/drunkenness), steadfast, fluty of blows, master retort, quick load, inspire trust, innate spell: short range teleport

Skills: Athletics: expert, acrobatics: expert, sword: journeyman, spear: expert, dagger: journeyman, lie (spin truth): journeyman, ride: adept, gunnery: adept, stealth: journeyman, bribe: expert, lock pick: master, alchemy: expert, persuade: master, seduce: journeyman, bow: journeyman, torture: expert

"Lead the way like this. I don't trust those with two masters," Lindy whispered into Felix's ear.

"Nonsense. I would never betray this kingdom, ma'am," Felix sputtered quietly as he walked stiffly.

"Your skills show you are a bad man. More importantly, your two employers could easily go to war," Lindy muttered.

Felix stopped and sighed. "Why? Did you look at my stats?"

"I don't trust anyone," Lindy smiled.

"But you serve at least two masters?" Felix replied.

"Myself, Death, and Otten, you mean? Even if that was true, I would never trust myself," Lindy nodded.

"What?" Felix asked.

"Keep walking," Lindy said, rolling her eyes and pushing her bodyguard along. "I do what I must but mostly what I feel like. If you know anything about my history then you know why I don't trust."

"Do you want to know if Otten knows about my other employers?" Felix sighed.

"Don't get in my way and I will not care," Lindy smirked. When she neared the cart a huge energy wave washed over her. The wave reminded her keenly of War, the world spirit, but no one else seemed to notice.

Lindy searched for the wave's source and found the Igorein clan's hold. "I am going to stay in this wagon's shadow. See you when we get to the battlefield," Lindy told Felix before stepping into the wagon's shadow and out to the Igorein clan's ruined front door.

Zoea Jarvellkon stood outside the door, overlooking the work of tearing down the door that Lindy had undermined. A large crack ran through the door. "It's you," Zoea noted.

"Something crazy happened here," Lindy said. A few dwarves looked up at her and nodded. "Something besides me," Lindy smirked.

"I don't know what you are talking about," Zoea huffed, but Lindy could feel a vortex of energy spilling from the ground under her feet.

"If that's true then someone just delved far too deep," Lindy muttered.

"Again, nothing odd happened," Zoea nearly shouted.

"Then it happened when you were out here," Lindy shrugged.

Zoea called over to a worker running past her with an empty bucket. "You get to the administrative block. I need to know if anything unusual happened." When the messenger had run off Zoea looked over at Lindy. "Happy now?"

"No. I'll wait," Lindy replied, sitting down on the ground.

A good three minutes passed when Lindy noticed a slight pressure signifying someone studying her closely, which was spooky because the dwarves were doing everything they could to avoid her, which meant it was something else. Faint life signs drifted in the sky behind Lindy's spot on the ground. Shooting a wave of ice at the nearly invisible presence, Lindy smirked, her boredom gone for now.

The presence crashed into the ground. Three more life signs broke through the earth at the same time, an ice chink missing them by inches. "Crap. When did the wet noodle get here!" a startled shriek said.

By now the ruckus had attracted the gazes of the dwarves. Zoea rushed over. "Lindy, what did you do?"

"Shut down magic around here. The hot brat tried to teleport in," Lindy shrugged. Her face then scrunched up. "Wait, why did I think of heat just now?"

"Because Fire is my boss?" A lean female in very light clothing groaned from the ground. She had landed on her back when her magic neared Lindy.

"Oh, so Air was the sneaky one?" Lindy replied, not turning to look at the dust cloud.

"Friends of yours?" Zoea asked. She was unamused.

"Coworkers in other departments. We just met." A very thin woman in leather armor adorned with feathers sighed softly. Her voice, however, carried very far.

"So your boss is Air?" Lindy asked, turning around.

"That's right. I'm Falcon," the woman nodded, holding out her hand. Lindy sucked herself into her own shadow, only to appear above the hole the last two visitors occupied.

In the dusty hole a female dwarf in heavy work clothes, dense metal in dense metal, grumbled. "Gravel and Marsh."

An elf wrapped in thick robes that obscured all but her face nodded. "I'd be Marsh. You're Death's new tool, right?"

"Something like that," Lindy grinned. Then she looked back at Zoea. "I'll make sure these four don't do anything too crazy as I wait."

"Landra," the fire priestess murmured before jumping to her feet.

"Ok, firebrand. I go by Lindy," Lindy sneered.

"I am not called firebrand, you insufferable lunatic." Landra snarled more from pain and embarrassment from her fall than anger.

"She knows. Among you humans she is the oldest one here," Gravel sullenly pointed out.

"I thought Falcon was older," Landra asked.

"If the rumors are to be believed, Death's gofer does not age," Falcon gently murmured.

"I may be getting close to one hundred but honestly, after fifty I stopped counting." Lindy nodded. "So you guys feel that crazy wave of power too?"

"Of course. What was that?" Landra asked, shifting her focus swiftly.

"So besides the hot airhead, anyone else want to speak up?" Lindy sighed, only managing to hide her glee from Landra.

"That power wave was something related to War. It was far too much of that concept's power to be anything else. Fate is chewing out the world spirits now, but War so far is getting the worst of it," Marsh nodded.

"Well, it was just unearthed. I think it's a slab of metal. I was in the process of getting permission to check it out when you all showed up," Lindy nodded.

"You know what it is and can get access legally?" Marsh asked.

"I say we let the newbie try her hand at it as long as she shares the info after," Gravel said.

"I would if this jerk would let me teleport," Landra grumbled.

"I'll see what's what and let you all know. My business partners live here, after all," Lindy answered.

Gravel perked up at the word business. "What do you sell them?"

"Plans for explosives," Lindy shrugged.

"Something like that would never gain War's favor," Landra noted.

"Landslides are more impressive," Gravel agreed.

"I know this world has small-scale explosives but that's a bit harsh. That red ape would love something big and fiery if they scaled it up... Well crap, I hope they don't do that," Lindy said to herself.

"If someone used your plans to make the biggest explosive that could be feasibly built, what kind of damage are we talking about?" Gravel asked, her voice rising an octave.

"This mountain to dust and house-sized boulders? Actually maybe a few mountains," Lindy whispered.

"I can't even imagine that would be popular or sane," Marsh said.

"Sane? Not a chance. Popular? Hell yes. I think things like that would get huge crowds no matter what," Lindy replied.

"And that could draw some of War's power. This is bad," Marsh pointed out.

"Well we know that might be the case, so I'll call this a win, not a victory," Gravel stoically said.

"And she being an outworlder is ok?" Landra asked fiercely.

"Above our pay grade, kid. Complain to your boss if you want," Gravel shrugged.

Rune lord Sasha Jarvellkon the Third rushed out of her kingdom and up to the gathering of priestesses. "Sis!" the rune lord called before looking around. "Who are they?"

"They work for other world spirits," Lindy replied calmly.

"We could have remained undetected if not for you," Landra muttered.

Sasha's soft gaze turned hard. Falcon sighed. "Hiding our link to the world spirits is safest. The energy that drew us here is deep under-ground."

After a long silence Sasha replied sternly. "I can understand that, but only my sister is allowed in."

The crowd looked around. "She means me. And no, not by blood," Lindy snickered.

"Well that's what we agreed on but let us know what you find out," Marsh replied, jumping out of the hole and unpacking a picnic on the ground.

Lindy looked over at Sasha, who seemed unhappy, and the rest. "If it's not a state secret, fine. But I'll report to Death about the power we felt."

Sasha led Lindy into the dwarven stronghold. "What energy did you feel?"

"War's. Too much energy in one place can cause problems. That's why I need to look," Lindy replied.

Sasha paused. "Any energy?" she asked quizzically. Her concern was well hidden but not invisible.

"Energy related to the concepts. No resident of this world could output that level of power," Lindy smiled.

Sasha looked at Lindy's expression. "What are you doing?"

"Smiling reassuringly?" Lindy asked back.

"Practice more," Sasha said in huff Lindy found cute.

"That bad?" Lindy laughed.

"Worse," Sasha replied, her posture stiffening.

"Well, it's been a while since I've tried being this nice." Lindy nodded, pretending not to see Sasha nearly fall over as her entire body calmed down.

Sasha led her honorary big sister past the point Lindy had gone before, past more gates and a military complex. Later they came to three branching paths labeled mine, fortress/admin, and living/market. "It may just be me but your administrative district is simple to find," Lindy noted.

"That's why it's well defended. The hope is that an enemy rushes that instead of residential," Sasha replied, turning into the mining passage and up to a pulley attached to a wooden plate and a mob of burlier-than-normal dwarves. "Anything new?" Sasha called out to the oldest of the pulley crew.

"Some more echoes but nothing else," the graybeard replied stoically.

"My bodyguard and I are going down," Sasha informed the man.

The old man grimaced tightly within his typically neutral and solemn visage. "The scout teams are not back yet."

"I can see that," Sasha nodded. "Now get to work."

"You are lugging one human as your guard?" the old man asked evenly.

"Yes, now get to work," Sasha grumbled sternly. Even in her annoyance she was regal.

Lindy silently got on the hand-pulled elevator with the rune lord. Ignoring the looks of the pulley crew, Lindy focused her senses on the tunnels far below. War's energy surged like a tidal wave. A few tunnels passed by in the shaft before Sasha nudged Lindy hard. She had been trying to get her big sister's attention for a while. "Hey, how bad is this?" the young ruler asked.

"Worse than I thought. There's a lot of power down here." Just then a smell of wet iron, acid, and rot sucker punched her senses. "The ones that were here before will not be whole."

"What?" Sasha asked, for once sounding like what she was, a very young woman shouldering the weight, expectations, and destiny of her people.

"Anyone lucky is getting out of here with their body whole but their mind torn to ribbons. The rest will be dead or crippled, mind and body, one way or another." Lindy sighed, her body and mind now prepped for combat. "Stay next to me no matter what," Lindy said, letting a good third of her combat-ready psyche leak out. *Seems like my sense of combat is not of this world* Lindy grinned to herself, not allowing her levity to seep out and ruin the gravitas of the moment or relax her too much.

Sasha took a few seconds to steady her mind. "How could this happen?" she finally asked in a way that seemed almost arrogant, but her feet were shaking.

"That's what I'd like to know," Lindy replied. "Jobs like mine should prevent things like this from happening. Priestesses go where their bosses can't because world spirits like Death and the rest would track in too much power for this reality to contain." Then the elevator touched down at the deepest part. Lindy smirked at the irony. "Stay close no matter what. The energies I wield should force most of this uncontrolled war essence to keep some distance."

Sasha walked two steps behind Lindy and out to a roughhewn but well supported maze of tunnels. "So it's afraid of you."

"Everything else is. Why not an incorporeal essence of bloodlust, madness, and greed?" Lindy shrugged, her sword Transcendence in her hands and the powers of Death's realm crammed into it and the local area. War's wild energies pushed on the barrier, preventing Lindy's powers from getting too far away from her.

Sasha took a deep breath and spied the upper half of a dwarven miner. Through her gagging the young leader managed to croak, "I'll guide you to the new sections in the back, so keep an eye out."

"No problem," Lindy nodded, working hard to keep power use to a comfortable level. The hardest part was not letting the strain she was feeling show too much in her voice but lucky or not, Sasha had too much on her mind to notice and far too much confidence in the one she chose as her big sister.

The two women followed a scattered path of body parts deeper into the cramped mine tunnels. Sasha kept her eyes on Lindy's back. After some time the women stopped. The sound of metal hitting metal echoed from close by. Lindy motioned for the rune lord to be silent and they crept down the hallway to a bend in the shaft. Lindy peeked around the corner and into what had become a charnel house. The room looked like a natural cave. One wall had collapsed, revealing a massive shard of worked metal. One man was hitting it with a broken sword while another broke the bones around it. Neither war-maddened dwarf paid attention to the other and both stayed next to opposite walls.

Lindy hefted Sasha onto her back and charged the sword-wielder. This allowed her to easily knock the man out. The other dwarf looked up from breaking bones and began tossing scrap from the mound of corpses. Lindy tossed some of the scrap back, finally landing a clean hit, knocking out the other dwarf.

"What is that?" Sasha asked, looking up at the only thing besides Lindy's back she could see. Her focus was on the shard of steel-like metal that took up one whole wall.

Lindy tapped on the metal but soon noticed what most would see as thick red rope, but Lindy knew it was one of War's hairs. "A shard of War's armor and a few hairs."

"A few hairs made my men lose their minds like this?" Sasha asked incredulously.

"Do you understand why the world spirits don't come to this world in the flesh?" Lindy asked.

"No," Sasha said automatically. Then after a few more seconds, "Wait, this could have been worse?"

"It could always be worse. If my boss visited anywhere on this world in person, a lot of planets would stop existing, including this one. If that happened no one and nothing would be left on this world," Lindy explained.

"How do we deal with this then?" Sasha asked.

"We do nothing. I try to dampen the energy in this junk," Lindy grumbled. She held out a chunk of hard military-issue bread to her self-proclaimed little sister.

"What?" Sasha asked.

"This will take a few days. Don't worry, I brought food." Lindy's snake pets crawled out of her shadow and got to work binding the other two dwarves.

Sasha looked around the gore-covered nightmare of a room. "I have to stay here?"

"For half a day or so, yes. After a day at most, this will be weak enough for me to teleport you out. When you get back send a message to the Otten expeditionary force that I may be slightly delayed," Lindy answered.

"We can't go back and report now?" Sasha asked.

"I can't let this energy spread more," Lindy explained.

"That would be bad," Sasha replied. "I see it could be worse but I never thought there was something you feared," she sighed.

"Losing those I care about hurts a lot," Lindy nodded. She was putting far more of her power into fighting War's powers than was smart, but Lindy wanted to fix this soon. Risking herself like this made Lindy's cold heart warm a little. "The world spirits annoy me a lot. Well, only Death and War are that bad. The rest are a bit too spacey for my liking. If I did not know any better I would call them gods, but they are more like bored caretakers with far too much power and infinite time."

Lindy hoped her words would distract Sasha long enough to get though the day without picking up on the strain Lindy was under.

I don't deserve to be worried about others or have others care about me. Still I should repay that kindness sometimes. Feels like none of my lives have been good ones. At least I will carry the pain I cause others as my own. It would be so much simpler if the world was my enemy. Seems like I tried that before and failed badly. Wait, are these the feelings from a past life? Shit, focus you fool, focus. Keep the kid and her people safe, then run. Ok good plan me, thanks me. Lindy thought.

Lindy lost track of time. The chunk of metal continued to seep power, which complicated things. More power dispersed all around her, necessitating more focus to keep it contained. It was slow taxing work. Eventually Lindy managed to suppress the warring power and was able to exert her control on the outside world again. First she reopened her link to Death's realm and looked down on the army she had left. After making sure Sasha was still alive and free of the corruption from War's uncontrolled powers, Lindy sent Sasha, who at some point had gone to sleep due to exhaustion, to her room in the city.

Over time the metal weakened and Lindy realized that the more physical contact she had with it, the faster she could purge its power. So Lindy replaced a person-sized chunk of the metal with herself, using a lot of power and teleportation. When the metal was no longer a corrupting influence Lindy rested for a day within it, then teleported the chunk to the surface. The few inches of metal around her skin had become charged with her and War's energy, turning it an inky black. When Lindy left the huge metal shard the inky metal stayed on her like a second skin. The metal seized up and in a moment of panic and claustrophobia Lindy's skin began to crack, oozing blood, which changed the metal into something terrifying and armor-like. Now able to move in her prison Lindy waved to Falcon, who was standing nearby. "It's safe enough now. Think we can hand this shard over to the locals?"

Falcon looked up and held out her hand. "Yes, it should be fine." Her eyebrows furrowed.

Gravel walked out of a tent. "What's the matter?" Then she stopped, looking up at the chunk of dull otherworldly metal. "Is that what I think it is?"

"You tell me. I can't read minds," Lindy shrugged from within her new shell.

"Why?" Gravel asked.

"Because I am not all-powerful," Lindy smirked.

"Right. That's from War, or at least not from this kingdom," Gravel retorted. By this point a crowd was rushing out from the hold.

"It's not found naturally in this reality. Although I use the word naturally loosely," Lindy replied, grinning widely.

"You sure you can't read minds?" Gravel pressed.

"Not yet," Lindy laughed, now the center of a crowd. "But I'll have all the time in this universe if I play my cards right."

"Marsh, you read minds, right?" Landra asked, looking at the back of the silent crowd to the place with the least presence. It felt like smoke hiding in a shadow within a deep unlit well.

"I am not reading her mind," Marsh sighed, her voice cutting across the crowd like a gentle ripple.

"You read Gravel's all the time," Landra huffed.

"Lindy's mind is a death trap to the sane. No way is anyone grounded getting out of there in one piece," Marsh retorted. Many in the crowd nodded in agreement.

"But mine was fine," Landra said innocently.

Lindy cackled. "Simple minded, emotional, and naïve like me when I was someone else and very young."

"Well excuse me. Not everyone can be some lunatic from another world," Landra exploded.

"Close enough," Lindy wheezed, slowly calming down. "But try to stay you. Those innocent and true to themselves are far too rare in any world. It seems even more so when time takes its price for your existence."

"Time? Who's that?" Zoea asked from the front of the gathering.

Lindy took a deep breath to keep from snapping. She was tired and getting even more irritated dealing with the ensuing chaos that was at the very least her own fault. "A euphemism, as far as I know."

"What?" a few muttering voices asked.

"More importantly, is that you, sister?" Sasha asked.

Lindy focused her mind for a moment, transporting her new armor into her shadow. "Yes." After a pause to examine and soften her expression, "That chunk of metal may make a nice door. It's all yours, sis. Reminder to wait a month before letting anyone get near that tunnel."

"That long?" Sasha asked, clearly remembering the many dead and few living still down there.

"Normally this whole place would be locked down for years, if not centuries. Death's representative did very well. Two weeks may be enough without any bad side effects, but longer than that is prudent. This energy plays by its own rules, after all," Falcon explained.

"She's right. That stuff has a mind of its own and does not play well with anyone besides those it loves absolutely. Fate's and War's energies are more choosy than most," Gravel noted as the sole dwarf among the hold's mysterious and odd visitors. Her kinship with the locals made them give more weight to her words.

"Well I have got a war to get back to. Have fun, everyone," Lindy whispered before sinking into her own shadow.

"Right. You too," Falcon said.

"Killing is not fun; it's work. Although that might just be what I tell myself to keep from going crazier," Lindy retorted ruefully. "Although a good chicken dinner and wine is still something else." Lindy's side note lingered far longer than she did.

"What just happened?" Landra asked after a time of seemingly endless silence.

"With Lindy, anything, nothing, or something else," Zoea replied as she collapsed to the ground, only now giving in to the fear Lindy had caused in her.

Fools and Heroes

Lindy arrived out of Jillvee's shadow and blocked a sword aimed at her back. They were on a small hill beside a thin line of foes. A good half a mile off, the entire field was a chaotic mishmash of troops fighting wildly, isolated or in small groups. A ruined camp sat atop the hill where Jillvee fought. "Wow. Well this is..." Lindy began by slicing apart ten men in uniforms she did not recognize. For the first time in ages Lindy was at a loss for words.

"The ones in red are theirs," Jillvee said unhelpfully.

"But they are all in red!" Lindy groaned.

Jillvee finished off her single opponent. "Blood does not count!" Then she spun around and accidentally slapped Lindy in the face, which nearly broke Jillvee's hand.

"I had an emergency to take care of." Lindy shrugged, taking a quick glance at the battlefield. "But wow, you guys suck."

Felix Aesin rushed down from the hill. "Miss, they do have a legendary rank foe and we are outnumbered severely."

Lindy peered at the souls within the enemy line. "Wisp," she spat, finding a familiar soul with a few more knick-knacks stuffed inside.

"Fine. Get as many troops as possible to fall back now. This is going to be messy and I will not be holding back much." Lindy huffed, encasing herself in her new armor.

Before anyone even remotely normal could react, serpents sprang from the shadows, biting into the Derndell troops while cries of "retreat" sounded from the Otten army's rear lines and chorused inward, mixing with the cries of agony that sprang from their foes. With this chaotic cacophony, only one soul walked out into the killing field from the Otten rear lines while all those that could streamed out. Men fell to blasts of magic, a pitch-black sword, fists, feet, and head-butts from the armored newcomer.

When Lindy had gotten to the center of the field, one dainty figure floated out from the opposing camp. "My, my, who are you, dear?"

"Wisp," Lindy sneered.

"Oh Lindy dear, come to join us?" Wisp smirked. Her face, not accustomed to such an expression, did not manage quite the right shape. Wisp's sneer looked sad and wooden like someone putting up a front for the first time but her eyes were deadly serious.

"No thanks," Lindy replied, deflecting a gust of wind shot at her. "My soul is twisted enough, thank you."

Wisp's eyebrows quivered. In the few seconds she was distracted, all the bodies left on the battlefield sprang up and dogpiled her. Many were torn apart but a small fraction were blown to bits. Wisp's mind and soul collapsed in on themselves because Lindy used implanted parts that contained poorly intertwined bits of Wisp's tattered soul to rip the entire construct asunder. Only one hundred were slain or re-slain from the multitude under Lindy's control. Lindy's flair for the dramatic, which she liked to think seldom reared its head, unnecessarily compelled her to casually point at the enemy lines and shout, "Get 'em!"

It was over in hours. The undead were allowed to de-animate and the others who still lived had changed into something not quite human, or half-elf as the case may be. "You are all shades and my servants. Do you understand?"

The newly minted beings had become something like Lindy's snake pets but on a much wider scale. "To do what exactly?" one of the shades asked Lindy. The transformed had kept most of their free will and skills intact, but had lost the memories of their lives and been shackled to Lindy's will. The shades would do anything for Lindy regardless of their own options.

"For now, fight for me. After that I will ensure those that still live will have a home and land to do with as they wish. You will all serve me until then," Lindy replied sternly.

"As you wish," came the thunderous reply from her new army.

Jillvee rushed over to Lindy. The rest of the Otten troops were too spooked to move from a large hill. "What did you do?" she railed. The shades drew their blades as one.

"Stand down," she waved absently at her army. "I made back-up."

"Gendree, are you ok with this?" Jillvee called over to one of the shades.

"I am Gendree. Who are you?" came the reply.

"They aren't who they were. I did tell you to retreat, remember?" Lindy said.

"But this is not right!" Jillvee snapped, stomping her foot.

"Well duh, this is war!" Lindy snapped back, rolling her eyes. An ache formed in her gut. *Am I ok with this? Is it good or bad that I don't know?* Lindy mused.

In the tent that had suffered the least, Lindy, Jillvee, Felix, and a few other officers were looking over a map and a list of their supplies. "We have too many prisoners," one man said.

"If you are talking about my army of shades, they are reinforcements," Lindy countered.

"Can you guarantee this new army's loyalty?" a younger officer asked.

"As long as I am in command of them and they are kept away from this army, then absolutely," Lindy allowed.

"That's a lot to accept. Some of those troops were ours. Are you saying they can't be retuned to their units?" Jillvee hissed in the most diplomatic way she could manage.

"Their minds and bodies have been modified. They do not remember who they were but I will need to observe them in case any mental breakdowns happen," Lindy sighed.

Jillvee slammed her hands on the table, no longer able to maintain her veneer of calm. "You made them that way. Why?"

"Because this was the best outcome. Remember, I did say to run." Lindy shrugged innocently.

Jillvee grabbed Lindy's shirt and lifted her off the ground. The target of her rage did not resist. "How could this be worse?"

Lindy looked around the room, her eyes stern. "We could all be dead or everyone on that battlefield could be dead. If I really pushed myself I could make a wasteland. We were lucky," she grumbled.

"And that is playing by the rules?" Felix inquired.

Lindy, who was still suspended in the air and outwardly untroubled, looked over at her aide. "That's right. As long as I keep to the agreement and heed the orders given by this army, it should be fine. This does not technically infringe on my agreement with Death or the rules I am bound by."

Jillvee dropped Lindy back to the ground. Another old officer spoke up. "So the plan is still in motion?"

"It is. We keep up our advance," Jillvee nodded.

"We may need to pillage some food. We have more troops than expected at this point and the shades may need more or less calories than before," Lindy replied, grinning from the ground.

"What are calories?" Felix asked.

"Right, that's not understood here yet. It's energy from food. Does that make sense?" Lindy replied thoughtfully with some exaggerated gestures.

"That is most helpful," Felix replied, thankful for all the information he now had to send off to his real bosses.

Jillvee looked down at Lindy. "You are terrible, you know that."

Lindy snickered. "If I thought I was good..." Then her face fell. "I'd cause far more carnage than I do." Then Lindy grumbled, "Well, back to your shadow." Lindy seeped into Jillvee's shadow and went to sleep surrounded by the darkness.

"You are close," a young officer observed.

"Maybe, but I only get the glory she does not want, and that woman's attention does far more harm than good," Jillvee spat.

"That sounds normal to me," the young man replied.

"Maybe, but no whirlwind is as chaotic as that dervish," Felix noted quietly, unknowingly slipping in some choice words from his homeland.

Around four in the morning when the camp at large began to stir, Lindy hopped out of Jillvee's shadow and into her tent. Jillvee woke up in an instant and while still waking up lunged at Lindy with the sword that was kept next to her sleeping bag. Lindy caught her attacker's blade with both hands, snapping it apart on reflex. "What the crap!" Lindy complained.

Jillvee's eyes slowly came to life. "What are you doing in my tent!" she howled.

"Waking up! What else?" Lindy asked back, visibly annoyed and confused. Two female guards rushed into the tent and froze, unsure of what to do.

"Then what are you doing in my room!" Jillvee yelled back.

"I was living in your shadow, dufus," Lindy snapped back, her tone taking on a stern tutor's vibe.

"What's a dufus?" Jillvee started before blinking hard a few times to clear her head and yelling. "Wait, why are you taking it for granted that my shadow is where you live?"

"I am not, but I was too lazy to switch to another one!" Lindy replied.

"Then don't take it for granted!" Jillvee snapped, her mind still far from steeled.

"Oh well then," Lindy began. Then pausing, she looked around at the tense guards and Jillvee who was out of breath and still very enraged. "Right, my bad. So where should I be sleeping?"

"With your army. Now get out!" Jillvee yelled.

Lindy's shadow lengthened and the broken sword was consumed into it. "I'll get that fixed up for you and see to my troops. Thanks for putting up with someone as crazy as me." With that she left, putting on a brave face and thinking hard about just how out of touch she was. Lindy absentmindedly looked over at one of the guards that had burst in. "Which direction is this camp's quartermaster and the other army?"

Neither guard managed to hide their discomfort and pointed in the same direction. "Both are that way," one said, then swiftly marched in the opposite direction. The other took up position right outside Jillvee's tent.

Lindy looked back at the tent. "The sword should be fixed within the day." She smiled, then walked off to find the camp's quartermaster in the hopes of borrowing some tools.

Lindy found the quartermaster surrounded by messengers from many different units. She slinked away to a bare patch of dirt behind a few tents where the rations and supplies were kept. Lindy took out a few magic stones from her shadow. Lindy removed the sword's handle and dug out a chunk of dirt, making it into mud. She pressed the sword parts into the mud. After making a few adjustments like hardening the mud, she turned the sword blade into metallic dust and melted it. The hard mud served as a mold. Lindy pressed a few random anti-magic runes all over the cooling blade in as haphazard a way as possible, mucking about with temperamental energy and water stones. She secured the old handle. After a test swing Lindy sent the sword back to Jillvee through her shadow.

Lindy walked to a new camp a short but obviously separate distance away. A few human troops were arguing with the shades when Lindy walked up.

"Allen, come on," one human said.

"I have my orders," a shade replied.

"Tellen, what's with you?" another human asked.

"I don't know you," another shade said.

Other such conversations bubbled over to her.

"Hey, this camp is not for normal humans. Get going!" Lindy yelled over the hubbub.

"Let's go bro," a lanky man said, trying to pull away one of the shades. The shade did not budge no matter how hard the lanky man pulled.

"Again, who are you?" the shade asked the lanky man.

The human man's stats read as:

> Hayveen of Camp 13
> Human male age 19
> Affiliation: Otten army
> Job: infantry
> Status: mid weight shieldman
> Abilities: strength 15, vitality 20, mind 8, agility 5.
> Talents: alcohol tolerance: moderate, language (common Otten), stunning hit, dig in, brace for impact, minor luck, fast healing
> Skills: Sword: journeyman, armor proficiency (chain/leather): journeyman. dagger: beginner, athletics: journeyman, smithing: repair beginner, gambling: apprentice, coordinate: journeyman

The new shade, however:

> Tellen of You Are Here
> Shade (human) male age 23
> Affiliation: Lindy's private army
> Job: meat shield
> Status: that guy
> Abilities: strength 38, vitality 37, mind 22, agility 39.
> Blessing: immunity necromancy

Curse: incompetence necromancy, mindless obedience
creator (Lindy)
Talents: language (common Otten), bull rush, impactful
strike, fearlessness, stubborn
Skills: energy control: adept, spear: journeyman, first aid:
beginner, athletics: expert, acrobatics: journeyman, armor proficiency (chain/ leather): journeyman, thrown
weapon: adept, brewer: beginner, cooking: beginner,
tracking: apprentice

"Ok troops, toss 'em out. No killing!" Lindy hollered. The shades then tossed the humans out of their camp. After much grumbling and many hateful glares at Lindy, the humans left. "Ok now. Training," Lindy announced. She put shades into teams that switched members around after each drill until she found which units worked best with each other after two full rotations.

Late noon Jillvee and some bodyguards came over. "We are going to march soon."

Lindy clapped loudly. "Pack up!" No sooner than Lindy's echoes died out, the shades had put all their camp's supplies into a few of their members' shadows.

"We have more of you. Lovely," Jillvee grumbled.

"Only the finest half-baked imitations for you, my lady," Lindy bowed.

"That's rude," Jillvee hissed.

"Right, so don't expect them to take down a legendary without me," Lindy added.

Jillvee did not have any counter for that, so she left.

Lindy sat down on the grass and sighed, looking up at the sky. "Looks like I am going to be a necessary evil no matter what I do, as long as I live in this half-life," she muttered. Normally Lindy would not voice these feelings to anyone other than Death or Fate, but Lindy had forced herself to think of the shades as tools, if only to preserve her dwindling sanity.

Ten of the nearly one thousand two hundred soldiers Lindy had changed walked up to her. One of the shades that had fought in the Derndell army spoke up. "Excuse us, master?" she asked.

"You will address me as commander," Lindy grumbled, throwing her back onto the grass and looking for interesting clouds.

"Right, commander. Who were we?" a male shade said.

"Fools." Lindy sighed very deeply, tying to sound irritated rather than upset with herself.

Rolling over to her side, Lindy looked up at the first shade in the group to speak. "Look, all of you guys got caught up in a spell of mine. It was either that or we all died. I made you all into what you are. Like it or not, you will all fight for me until this war is over. I'll do what I can to keep you all alive. I owe you all that much, but cross me and nothing will be left of you. And I mean *nothing*." Lindy looked at the gathering crowd of her army. Given that they had nothing else to do until the Otten army finished packing, she let her troops mull around within her camp's perimeter.

One of the former Otten knights spoke up. He was on the older side. "Were we your friends or enemies?"

Lindy sat up, her face blank. "You all were and still are my charges. If you wanted to know whose side you were on..." Her lips twitched trying to smirk but failing, Lindy pointed over to the Otten camp. "The Otten kingdom is who I am working for right now. Two armies fought in the last clash. Look at what you were wearing when you woke up and use your heads."

Jillvee ran up to Lindy's camp. "Lindy, follow us out. You're the rear guard."

Lindy leapt to her feat. "Form up!" she bellowed. The shades all lined up swiftly, no matter their thoughts and will. *After this is over I'll need to be careful not to take advantage of these guys. Wait, is their condition genetic? Fuck, this is going to mess this place up even more. Well let's deal with the here and now. Right, I'll put off dealing with that until after. Putting off planning for sudden world-altering changes is always a good idea. I am so screwed. Well, Death's not complaining yet. Let's see if I can get away with this and maybe a bit more.* Lindy thought as they marched.

The march lasted for five days. Each day around dusk they would set up two camps, post guards, fix what was broken, have a good meal, prepare rations for the next day's march, and do some light combat drills. The shades put the most effort into their tasks. A small part of Lindy was posted right before Death's realm, at the barrier separating this universe from Death's seemingly much larger realm; that said, the laws of space and time did not apply to the realms of Death and those like it. After working out that distance was completely irrelevant, even with the five universes her boss watched over, Lindy gave up working out how any of this made any sense. Despite that, the seeming omnipotence this vantage point gave her was useful for monitoring the world.

Near the end of the fifth day Death's voice shook the fragment Lindy had been using as her eyes in the sky. "Those new things will need a lot of paperwork," it said.

Lindy let a few more bits of herself flood into the shard she was seeing through. "Is that all? Well, no way I can make a habit of this now, but should you be here?"

Death was still technically within its realm but only just. "This would be fine," it said as a few trees began to wilt.

"Ok, what do you want?" Lindy asked.

"War's dead," Fate answered, floating up from behind Death.

"And?" Lindy asked.

"And his aides are overworked now," Death replied.

"Ok, what else?" Lindy asked.

"We came to tell you because of how close you were to the victims this time," Fate reported.

"But he's War!" Lindy snapped, not understanding what was going on.

"And I am Death!" Death replied.

"Exactly. Even Fate has victims, depending on who you ask," Lindy agreed.

"Grog, what's with you? None of the other Deaths would be this roundabout!" Fate snapped, then fled.

"Grog?" Lindy asked Death, who was clicking its jaw.

"My name in your last world's stone age," Death replied.

"Right, but at that convention where Conduit worked, some of the other Deaths were real jerks," Lindy agreed.

"And me being from your Earth is not weird to you?" Death pressed.

"My first day here a man called The Just almost burned me at the stake because he was an ass, and I got a dragon to impale itself to death. So no, you are not being weird," Lindy shrugged.

"Fair enough. But what are you going to do about the ambush down there?" Death asked, pointing at the team of men sneaking up on the camp with weapons drawn.

"I'll get my troops ready then see what the main armies are going to do. What are you going to do?" Even if her shard looked like a small mote of light it still seemed to shrug by hopping around, which to Death amounted to a cool party trick.

"I am not helping you," Death said, its tone filled with warning.

"I mean about Fate. Bribe, console, or both? Leaving a woman out to dry like that is low no matter who you are," Lindy said. Death swiftly retreated into its realm and Lindy went back to getting ready for the upcoming fight.

As Lindy spoke with Death her body motioned to the shades, informing them of the ambush, number of foes, and the distance between her and the closest enemy. Her army spread out while keeping the center guarded and in view. Soon after, the first ambusher was taken down before the human army could react.

Felix Aesin, who had been marching behind Lindy, rushed up to her. "What's going on?"

Lindy pointed to the trees on both sides and shrugged. "Bad ambush."

"There's no good ambush," Jillvee shouted from a cart away.

Lindy groaned. "I meant the skill of our attackers." Then she looked at Felix. "This should be a good learning experience. The troops are far too green."

"They have been trained well," Felix commented, standing up for the men around him as Jillvee organized their response.

Lindy tossed a few rocks into the trees, killing off a few enemies that were a cut above the rest. "Some things are best learned from doing and not breaking too badly," she retorted. Noting a few men that were in positions that obstructed their ally's line of sight, Lindy went around and dragged the men who were slightly out of formation back into a proper mutually supportive defensive line. Jillvee was a little aggrieved at Lindy's antics but allowed her actions in the name of training and keeping more of the troops alive.

After the fight a quick treatment of wounds was conducted. Anyone with trouble moving was set in a cart with a medic and the march resumed. Without anyone noticing, Lindy let her pet snakes eat the bodies of the dead enemies once the bodies were out of sight.

Two days later they arrived at a city. It boasted high walls and many smokestacks spewing steam. "Where are we?" Lindy asked Jillvee as they observed the city from a distance, the troops around them setting up for a siege.

"Former Ernadon empire territory. This is a trade city called Abyss of Lin," Jillvee replied.

Lindy could feel that magic spells were nearly impossible to call on in and around the city. "Will the lack of magic be an issue?" she asked.

"No, but it seems the Abyss is worse now," Jillvee nodded. After a short pause she added, "The Abyss is named after the huge hole near it that keeps expanding and cancels out magic."

"I know. I made it." Lindy shrugged.

Jillvee clenched her hand hard then took a deep breath. "You know what? I don't care anymore."

"I'll handle my troops. Are we just backing up you guys?" Lindy asked.

"Until I say otherwise or something major happens, yes," Jillvee nodded.

"Got it. My guys will keep you all covered," Lindy said as she dashed off to the shades, who were lining up and setting up siege equipment.

As the battering rams and barricades were being constructed from the forests and earth around them, soldiers on Abyss's city walls started slowly to prep and fire cannons. Lindy and many of the skilled mages in the Otten expeditionary force noticed that their cannons were not using magic to lob stone balls slightly larger than a person's head. Lindy and fewer than a handful of others knew how odd this was. "The fools worked that out damn fast," Lindy noted with a trace of admiration. In her mind she could only feel regret. *This is my fault, too. Being used to this now does not make me happy.* Lindy mused as she turned all the incoming projectiles to dust before they landed.

"Get to work double time!" Lindy roared at her army. "I'll hold off the missiles." Seeing what she was doing, Jillvee ordered her units to pick up the pace and sent a messenger to Lindy.

Less than a minute later a man covered in cold sweat rushed up to Lindy. "Commander Tomorrow, how long can you keep up your support?"

"All day," Lindy grumbled. The man frowned. "And most of the night if they keep up with the maximum firepower from those cannons and the arrows stay around the same mass. As long as both Otten armies stay in the same positions and no larger weapons are fired this way, I will manage."

"How likely is it that they will use bigger weapons?" the man asked, taking great pains to memorize all of what Lindy was saying.

"Not." Lindy began to chide the man. Then she swore "Shit" and yelled across the battlefield "Incoming!" Her men scattered as five massive boulders were tossed over the walls from trebuchets. The bigger problem was both that the incoming fire from steam-powered cannons and archers picked up slightly and the new boulders had powered magic runes covering them. *Well that's a loophole. Still, even one minor rune would drain a skilled mage dry. Let's hope they run out of those soon.* Lindy mused as she called out, "Gunner teams, disrupt those runes!" Even then Lindy only managed to take out one boulder and the smaller missiles. Most of the runes were not disrupted. In time, there was large-scale damage. Close to two hundred died resulting from that one attack.

Lindy snapped her head over to the messenger who was cowering next to her. "You. I am requesting permission to take down the cannons and make a few holes in the walls. Get me a response ASAP. Now go!" The arrows were still coming in and soon after the cannons opened up again. Lindy spat angrily. "It would be so much simpler if we did not need to take this city intact for the rest of the army." No one heard her grumble over the screams, perforated constructs, and incoming fire, but all could sympathize with her complaint, no matter how unhappy they would be to hear such a powerful commander being so human in the midst of this carnage.

After what seemed like seconds but was likely closer to half an hour, Lindy could feel the arrow barrage lessening and new boulders being charged with power. As she was debating how justified it would be to just crush it all, her two messengers rushed up to her, panting. "You are to take the walls in as intact a fashion as possible and open the gates," the slightly faster messenger informed Lindy between gasps.

"I'll start that now. Should take a few minutes but after this I will be taking a rest, so make sure your commander knows not to expect much help from me for the rest of the day unless something really insane happens." The messengers took off running back to the other camp. Lindy looked over to a team of shades that were on standby. "Go with them," she ordered, and without looking back Lindy took off sprinting alone at the walls.

Her inky armor rose around her, a dark mist seeping out of it. To those watching it looked as if a lone young woman was rushing at the walls wearing her own shadow without any backup or support. Lindy reduced all shots fired around her to dust, leading to more focused fire being directed at her as it dawned on the wall's commanders that the young-looking human rushing at them was one of those, if not the one, that had been hampering their fusillade. The cloud of dust around Lindy expanded, which only caused a lack of visibility for a few seconds. Lindy sped up, taking advantage of the archers' momentary pause while trying to find their target. After all, they had used far more arrows than had been planned for the first day of the siege.

Lindy shot out of the dust cloud and scrabbled up the walls, making small footholds in the wall. When she landed upon the walls it was a slaughter. Lindy limited her attack power to that of someone with 200 in their stats. Only one foe did not die in one hit and it was a soul she recognized. After knocking the man out, Lindy reduced all the living matter left on the walls beside her and the man to goo. With two chops she put some extra force into it. The gate fell over now that its hinges were severed. Lindy kicked the man awake as the city was flooded with her allies and shades. "Lu, how's Calanya been doing?"

Lu Limore groggily looked up, taking in the sounds of war from within the city. "How do you know my wife?"

Lindy took off her helmet and grimaced in a way she once had. Her eyes, however, made it clear she was playing with him. "That's how you greet your old vice leader?" After deflecting a few arrows shot from a church steeple and a few smoke stacks, Lindy called down to the shades below her. "Remember to hunt down the snipers. Go house to house."

"It's on, boys. Let's do this!" one of the Otten troops called out. The shades simply shrugged and a few units began combing the buildings as the rest took to the streets.

"Oh, you outrank me now," Lu observed. "I am the only one in the Eternal that still remembers you, Lindy." Lu sighed wistfully.

"All dead?" Lindy asked, letting some pity into her voice and making a mental reminder to allow herself to feel the rest of her pity after the battle.

"Or retired, but yes, almost all dead. We have more members now but I still missed you," Lu nodded.

Lindy sighed deeply. "Well, you still throw me off. Somehow I am glad that has not changed. So, death or capture?"

Screams had begun and stillness had become less common within the city. "You do understand most of my men are in this city, right?" Lu asked, seemly resigned to his fate and exasperated at their loss and Lindy's casual displays. But even then, taking all of this as par for the course, having lost such a fight.

"Right. Well, I am sorry for your loss," Lindy nodded sincerely.

"You really mean that," Lu sighed. He was wounded badly and did not want to be healed by the Otten army. "Kill me. I am far too old for this."

"You and me both," Lindy shrugged while drawing her pistol from a shadowy hole.

Lu shut his eyes. "This brings back memories. If you meet Calanya or my daughter, please be gentle."

"I'll do what I can," Lindy replied, her heart temporarily purged of grief or regret as she blew apart an old friend's heart.

The battle was slowly dying down so Lindy crept up to the top of a tower and sat down looking over a city she did not recognize, next to a huge slowly expanding hole she knew all too well. This city had been contested by the Ernadon and Derndell empires. Ernadon had lost badly. The Abyss of Lin, as it had become known, was far more cramped than it had been so many years before. Steam and coal power ruled the town. The Abyss had become a massive coal mine complete with a train track and simple trains. Lindy did not know whether to be amused or mildly insulted by the city's new name.

Half an hour later Jillvee was rounding up the prisoners, most of whom were locals. Within the next couple of days food stores were raided. Engineers were found, with extra focus being put on those that had made the steam powered cannons on the walls. *Very smart, Jillvee. Hopefully those cannons are not my problem.* Lindy mused from the perch she planned to camp out on until the army was ready to march. At some point her name had spread throughout the occupied city. Older locals would glare up at the tower roof Lindy had claimed. Some of the braver young folks would wave up at her from places they thought no one else could see. Fame really is a double-edged sword. *I really need to change my face after this war,* Lindy thought.

Three days later order had been fully restored but normality was still likely years away. Jillvee managed to clamber up to Lindy's temporary home. "I need you to look over some of the steam shots."

"The what?" Lindy asked.

"The big hot water things on the walls," Jillvee tried to explain eloquently, failing miserably.

"The cannons? No can do. I did not design those." Lindy shrugged.

"But you know about them," Jillvee stated in an accusatory tone.

"I know about things like them and those may have been inspired by two or more of my gifts, but I will not interfere," Lindy retorted.

"The balance?" Jillvee asked.

"More or less. I am not allowed to meddle too much with the lives others live." Lindy sighed, knowing full that that rule had been loosely applied but not wanting to test Death or Fate's patience much more than she had.

"Right. Death." Jillvee nodded, not seeming to fully accept Lindy's reply. Then she tossed Lindy a lump of dark mineral-like substance. "They call that coal."

"Death also takes care of births, you know, but kindness is not in my job description," Lindy grumbled. "So the coal, what about it?"

"It's called coal," Jillvee admonished. Listening closer, Lindy could tell that what Jillvee said and what she said, while translated the same, were very different.

"Coal?" Lindy tried this time getting the less complex inflection down.

"Right. So do you know what it is?" Jillvee asked.

"I know about something like it. That was a fuel source that could make living things sick from its fumes." Lindy tossed back the clump of matter.

"Ok, well, keep up the good work," Jillvee sighed.

Eight days after the Abyss of Lin was taken, three armies appeared outside the gates: a dwarven army, an elven army, and the main army of Otten, plus a red dragon. A small delegation from what was left of the Ernadon royal family showed up as well.

Outside the gates the dragon, Covell, and a young man from the Ernadon royal family were arguing.

"It is and always has been a city of the Ernadon people," the young man was saying firmly.

"A people without a kingdom or a means to defend themselves," Covell replied just as firmly.

"Sis, over here!" a lump of metal and padding shouted over from the dwarven army as Lindy leapt down to the massive gathering.

"Hey Sasha," Lindy waved back.

Sasha rushed over, somehow making good time despite looking like a small lumpy snowman made of mithril, or legend ore, as most languages called it on this world. Sasha tossed over a few small orbs that were obviously grenades to Lindy. "I made those. How are they, sis?" Only then did Sasha look up at the walls and stop. She pointed at the cannons. If her army had not been within eyesight, Lindy was sure Sasha would be jumping up and down in glee. "What are those?"

"More of your death machines?" Anna Faywind asked spitefully.

"Oh, those are based on a few of mine, but I did not invent them," Lindy replied in jovial manner, appearing to enjoy the attention.

"You and your crazy stunts. You really need to act your age, Lindy." Anna grumbled.

The young man from Ernadon and the dragon looked up from their argument and spoke at once.

"You made me lose my birthright," the young man raged.

"You killed my younger brother," the red dragon chuckled.

"I have wounded a dragon badly once, but I have never crushed a kingdom yet," Lindy sighed, letting her happy-go-lucky mask slip for a second. Only Covell and the dragon picked up on that.

"I demand this woman be executed!" the young man shouted.

"For the last time, no. Only another nation can ask for what you are demanding. As the former Ernadon empire no longer exists, I have no reason to help you," Covell nearly spat.

"You and Princess Salvea were engaged to my brothers," the young man raved.

"Which is why we are even speaking. If you are only here to make demands, then go away," Covell said, finally snapping.

"Dragon, kill that fool!" the young man yelled, pointing at Lindy.

The red dragon swiftly stomped on the last of the Ernadon royal family and their retainers. "I don't hate the strong, but whiny cowards upset me," the dragon explained after making sure its paw was free of gore and the men were dead.

All eyes tuned to Lindy. "What? A dragon did it," she said calmly.

"Yes, but a Lindy made me do it," the dragon smiled.

The armies took a few steps back from the dragon but Lindy laughed, seemingly the only one to recognize the dragon's humor. "Right. Well, as catchy as that is, I hope it does not become too popular."

Covell peered behind her uncle. "Who are they?" she asked, looking at Lindy's army who wore the tattered gear they had in life.

"Deserters," Anna said firmly, but the way she glared indicated it was more of a question.

"I may have made more of me," Lindy replied, not thrilled with the conversation's new direction.

"So I have brothers?" Sasha asked meekly.

"Not quite. They have some powers like mine but far less powerful due to some meddling on my part," Lindy explained.

"So lab rats?" Covell asked in English. This drew many stares from those around them but for one, Covell did not seem to mind at all.

"It was a spur of the moment reflex when I fought a legendary-rank enemy." Lindy nodded back in the same otherworldly language.

"Does Death know, and how are they even following you?" Covell snapped back in English.

"Well, War is dead. My big boss in the sky might be too over-worked right now to notice. Seems like as a side effect mind control and memory loss are an issue with the shades. I really don't like ordering them around." Lindy switched to French mid-way.

"Why are you always doing shit like this!" Covell yelled back in French. By this point all those without auto-translation had confirmed they had no idea what Lindy and Covell were saying, but the real clever ones in the crowd could tell at least two languages were being used.

Sasha stormed up to Covell and demanded in her native tongue, "Who are you to my sister?"

One of Covell's aides rushed over and began translating for her. One of Sasha's guards and a translator rushed over to support their leader. The guard glanced at Lindy who gestured she was sorry for the trouble. The guard only sighed but his mood seemed to improve. "She's my uncle," was Covell's official stance on the matter. This put Lindy even more in the spotlight.

After Sasha's translator repeated Covell's words three times, and before anyone could really process the impact of this revelation, the young rune lord exploded in Covell's native tongue, "That makes no sense, human. Explain!"

Covell very nearly rolled her eyes at a world leader with even more control over a nation than she had. "Manfred, you explain," Lindy's niece demanded.

A few heads looked around before Lindy cleared her throat. "It's Lindy now. I know part of me that died one lifetime ago was once a man from another world named Manfred Endfield. Unlike myself, Covell remembers more of that past than I do, but I was her uncle in that past life and she keeps calling me uncle. If I died in other lives, I don't recall them." Then Lindy grumbled. "I don't like being reminded of my other lives."

No one needed a translator for Lindy's words because her words reached all equally and the effect on the crowd was pandemonium until the dragon roared, "Shut up!" and everyone calmed down in a hurry.

"What!" Covell yelled, blood coming from her ears as a half-deaf mage used magic to heal her. "Mi-fa-so-la-ti-do," Covell repeated a few times before nodding in satisfaction and waving the healer off. Then she looked up at the dragon. "What the hell!"

"Oh, you are related," Sasha spoke up. The physically young princess's outburst served to dispel all her doubts.

"Well if I am now some kind of royal, do I get a city?" Lindy asked, hoping she would be yelled at and this incident forgotten.

"You are not a royal!" Jillvee fumed.

"But she has point," Covell mused.

"How about that one?" Sasha asked, waving at the city before them, whose residents were peering out of the walls and directing intense bloodlust at Lindy.

"Sounds good to me," the dragon nodded.

"Why?" Lindy fumed, no longer pretending to be calm. A few of the residents in the city echoed her comments, which made Lindy feel even more conflicted.

"Because it's funny," the dragon declared mirthfully.

"And you deserve it," Sasha added mirthlessly.

"Fine. But no city of mine will owe taxes for as long as I live," Lindy agreed.

"But you are immortal," Jillvee snapped.

"And?" Lindy smirked, slowly easing herself with the mind games she so loved.

"Well, we will get plenty of other cities to go around. I need a rest and dinner. After we are all prepped we march as one. Objections?" Covell asked. No objections were forthcoming.

"I will need to see to getting my army some uniform gear and working out how much to charge you all for food," Lindy smirked before racing off to coordinate a city-wide price hike for nonresidents that even the locals could love.

15

Haven of Fools

None of the army could locate Lindy for the entire night but in the morning her new city was many times wealthier than it had been the day before. The prices for visitors all had a fifty percent markup on top of wartime costs, but a deal of buy-two-get-both with only a twenty percent markup if one went to Lindy's army was enacted. In short, Lindy's shades got all their new gear and uniforms for free as well as getting a hefty pay increase, although they had been working for free until now. The new pay was about what they would have been getting as normal human militia, so it could be argued the shades were still vastly underpaid.

Four days later Lindy's troops were all set and other nations had begun their own invasions of Derndell. She left half her army in the newly rechristened City of Smog. On the march to the city, Lindy walked up to Zoea, who had been put in charge of the dwarven army. Sasha was geeking out over all the stuff in Lindy's City of Smog. "So how many targets do we have to take down?" Lindy asked.

"Two forts and one town before the main capital. The other nations are cutting paths of their own. Those three targets are out of the way of the other forces but not out of our way. If any big shots show up..." Zoea explained.

"They are all mine, if the rest of you are too weak or in the middle of something," Lindy interrupted.

"I'll take that as a challenge," a human-looking woman with a long red scaly tail and clawed digits huffed. Ten others like her of different genders and ages floated around her, levitating a short space above ground.

"Who are you?" Lindy asked.

"This is not my final form," the odd being said. Then she spat a gob of fire to one side of the road. Her tail swished, covering the fire with dirt before it got out of control.

"Oh, Big Red. I did not recognize you," Lindy smiled.

Some of those floating around the dragon in human-like form snickered but quickly stifled their laughter when their spokeswoman glared at them. "Call me Daffodil."

"Like the flower?" Lindy asked.

The dragon tilted her head and was lost deep in thought for a while as if trying hard to remember something. "Yes," she nodded finally. "As the eldest child in our nest, I have been tasked with leading the youngest whelps into battle."

"Ok. So why are you all fighting?" Lindy asked.

"To beat up some dark wyrms," one of the whelps answered haughtily.

"Oh. How do they taste?" Lindy replied.

"Why would we eat them?" the brat answered, honestly confused.

"Right, that would be cannibalism, I guess. Sorry," Lindy nodded.

"Right. So we don't eat those poisonous snakes," Daffodil replied, seemingly mollified by Lindy's apology.

"Well then, more for me, so let me kill at least one," Lindy nodded.

"No!!" Daffodil yelled. Then she leaned in close and whispered into Lindy's ear, "Don't get caught eating any dragons in front of my siblings, ok?"

Lindy grinned. "Ok kids. No eating humans, elves or dwarves during the war, ok?"

"Why? Dwarves taste like gold," one of the young girls asked, eyeing one of the sappers nearby, who froze and had to be dragged along by some of his fellows.

"Because that would be like me eating one of you in front of your family," Lindy explained calmly.

The dragon child did a double take. "But no human could kill us."

"Who said I was human?" Lindy laughed.

"And you did kill Bubbles," Daffodil nodded.

"Who the fuck is Bubbles?" Lindy asked.

"That brother I told you about," Daffodil grimaced.

"She killed big bro Bubbles. Oh my death," one of the dragon whelps observed, now panicking.

"So how do you get named?" Zoea asked.

"Mom has a big book. She picks from there." One of the dragons spoke up, seeming unafraid, even if her floating was slightly more erratic now.

"It's called an encyclopedia," Daffodil added.

"Have you read it?" Lindy asked.

"Nope. It's in a language from Mom's home land," Daffodil sighed.

"Oh. What language?" Lindy asked.

"Swedish," Daffodil replied.

"So her home land is Earth?" Lindy asked dubiously.

"It's called Dirt," Daffodil replied "Only mom, dad, and I were born there."

The march did not stop except for nine hours each night. In less than a week they arrived at a fortress.

As the troops prepared for a siege, the commanders and their guards hung back a short ways, getting a last-minute meal and intending to sort out what army would do what. Before they could properly begin the talk Daffodil said, "Let me and the pups play first." She clearly meant it as a formality.

"This is no game," Jillvee shot back.

"As long as you and yours mess up the walls, then go for it," Lindy shrugged. Zoea and Covell took a short time to think before nodding in agreement.

Jillvee looked around for some support but Anna summed up the others' thoughts. "As long as they don't bite off more than they can chew, my troops will have less enemy fire on them."

"I'd still like some of my troops inside the walls before everything burns down," Lindy muttered.

"Ok," the commanders and dragon agreed, not wanting to miss evaluating the threat the shades posed.

"Then I'll bring down the gate while the dragons have fun," Lindy promised.

"How?" Daffodil asked. The glow in her eyes reminded all present that a fire dragon was literally and figuratively the biggest natural born pyromaniac on the planet.

"By rusting the hinges to nothing," Lindy said, sounding bored but watching all present intently. For all her jokes and bluster, Lindy was a haunted but clever one-woman legion with trust issues.

"Oh, where's the fun in that?" Daffodil pressed, clearly disappointed. If not for the professional and somber setting, Jillvee would be loudly questioning the dragon's judgment behind its back.

"It will make a very loud bang and plenty of dust. Plus keeping most of the door intact means one less massive door to lug over." Lindy laughed.

Daffodil asked, "You think I'm an idiot, right?" No smile graced her face.

"Not quite. I simply don't expect you to fully understand or care about the smaller races' needs." Lindy sneered back playfully. All the other commanders were holding their heads and wishing the two terrors would shut up.

"As it should be," Daffodil snickered teasingly as she and Lindy exchanged a vigorous handshake.

The dragons walked to the rear lines. As they did, a man in a helmet as gaudy and big as his ego yelled from the fort's parapets. His shout was amplified may times over. "Lindy Shrew of the Derndell kingdom! By the emperor's order, fight for the Derndell kingdom."

By the time the dragons had finished transforming, all eyes in the allied army turned to Lindy, including the still grounded dragons and the man on the parapet. Lindy rolled her eyes as her armor spilled from her shadow, fitting itself to her. She drew Transcendence and her old pistol. Twelve pitch-black snakes the length of her legs and with the same thickness as her arms burst from her shadow.

Shadow Born Serpent
Elite shadow pet (serpent)
Job: specter
Status: servants of the one true Lindy
Abilities: strength 4000, vitality 1672, mind 895, agility 4322
Talents: decaying bite, heat sense, echolocation, tremor sense, burrow, shadow shift, immunity cold/poison/electricity/harmful mental effects out side of pact, latch on, echolocation, reshape shelf, cold touch, wakening aura: major. swarm, danger sense: selective. constrict, inflict primal terror, unyielding
Endowment: ethereal form: selective, telepathy: master, share rage: Lindy, take hit: for master only
Curse: removed from death
Skills: Athletics: master, bite: master, intimidate: master, shadow magic: expert, stealth: expert, tracking: master, absorb impact: journeymen, riposte: adept

The entire field seemed to freeze in fear. Lindy motioned to one of the shade's skilled wind mages. When no one moved, Lindy made an obscene gesture at the parapets before stomping over and grabbing the wind mage. "Amplify my voice," Lindy snarled.

Lindy tuned back to the parapets, her serpent pets conspicuously absent. "No Lindy by the name of Shrew is here, so prepare to die!" As she spoke, the man on the parapets seemed to be fighting something. By the time she finished speaking, they were all dead. "Or not?" Lindy shrugged, her voice still booming. The gate crashed to the ground, its hinges now dust. As she waved to the dragons, Lindy's voice echoed even louder across the land. "Sick 'em, kids." Then she sat down and the dragons shot past her head, howling both to hype themselves up and to shake off their fear of Lindy. In contrast, the shades rushed silently into the fortress. Lindy tossed the mage after the rest of her army. "Off you go!" Her voice shook the ground. A shade ran after his comrades and Lindy lay on the grass. "Kids are such a pain," she muttered. No one could see her face but from her voice, most believed she was smiling fondly. The yells of pain and rage, and smells of fire and gore followed. The fort was fully captured in half a day. Not one of those who had called the fort home the day before was left alive.

"Thanks for keeping our casualties so low, uncle," Covell praised, looking down at Lindy, who had yet to move from the grass. Her snakes had gone back into her shadow after the parapets were cleared the first time.

"Well, the next two targets have nothing do with me unless the rest of you get killed off," Lindy replied sourly.

"Why?" Covell's tone did a complete 180 from joy to deep malice.

"My troops fought two or three battles while the rest watched. Show me that my allies are not ornaments," Lindy scoffed back unfazed.

Covell took a deep breath and sat next to the thing that in part had once been her uncle in another life. "So that's how you feel. I thought you wanted to be a hero."

"I want anonymity," Lindy grumbled deeply, her voice filled with self-loathing.

"That's surprising for a drama queen like you, uncle," Covell snapped.

Lindy sat up and took off her helmet. A spot of dried blood cracked from her lips as she spoke. "Look, I will do wrong by everyone I know at some point. Hell, that's basically my job now. The last thing anyone needs is to remember all the evil crap I have done. Heroes need to give hope. All I give is pain."

Covell grabbed the sides of Lindy's head. Leaning in, she glared right into Lindy's eyes. "So you are going to run away again?" the young princess asked.

"I kill, and should do so from the shadows. Eternity as a boogeyman seems fitting," Lindy said softly. Then she batted away Covell's hands gently, but that still caused the child much pain. "I don't remember Manfred Endfield's life, but I am sure he was as bad as me. Don't do the evil I do or have done. Cool?"

"How used to killing are you?" Covell asked, her eyes now moist.

"Getting used to taking a life is the second thing I never want to do. That's a fate worse than dying, after all. So never take life for granted or shrug off killing others."

"What's the first?" Covell asked as Lindy stood up.

"Lying," Lindy murmured bluntly.

"That's it?" Covell asked, unable to stop herself.

"That's right," Lindy answered, putting her helmet back on and walking by Jillvee, who was rushing over.

Jillvee watched as Lindy walked into the deadly still-burning fortress. "What?" Covell snapped, her mask of calm control back in its place.

"Was she crying?" Jillvee asked.

"Your guess is as good as mine," Covell grumbled. Tightness pulsed in her chest for no reason she knew of. After Jillvee helped her up Covell asked, "What do the shades have that our army does not?"

"Power and experience," Jillvee answered almost immediately, looking over the burning fortress with conviction as if replaying the entire battle in her mind.

"Speaking of where are the shades…" Covell asked, only now noticing the absence of an entire army.

"The first funeral of the day," Jillvee answered.

"How many did we lose?" Covell asked, feeling tired but calling upon her fifth wind. She had used up her second wind many hours before.

"Us? No one. The dragons lost one and the shades lost a little under two hundred. The enemy lost close to five thousand that we know of. Most of the enemy bodies are ash or something equally unidentifiable. By tonight we expect over two hundred shades to have died in this battle."

"Statistically that's amazing," Covell nodded. Then she noticed the cloud that was sitting over Jillvee's face. "What?" the princess asked.

"I am going to speak frankly, princess. I will accept any penalty you see fit to dole out after. Never say anything like that again, especially on a battlefield. True, we did not lose anyone, but the other armies know that the shades died in their place. No one is a number out here. All right?"

"You are right. I seem to have forgotten that," Covell nodded, remembering back to the talk she just had with her uncle.

Lindy walked into a small clearing. The shades and a few half-elven and human gunners she had trained along with three elven army sergeants were gathered around the shades that had died in combat. A pyre had been erected on which the bodies were stacked. Lindy sighed and looked over at the nearest living shade. "How did we lose so many?"

"You are their commander. You should know," one of the elves muttered.

Lindy turned around and looked the elf-man in the eyes. The intensity and stillness in her gaze made the man afraid but unable to look away. "I could name at least five general things and many more individual mistakes, but just because I know does my army no good if they are clueless." She turned back to look over the shade she had addressed, her gaze now far more intense.

"They had a new weapon. It shot iron spikes the size of a man," the shade replied as he shook slightly.

"Right. Half of these deaths were from those spikes. Only two who got hit by them are still hanging on," Lindy said as she waved at the pyre. Then looking around, the air became cold and her voice hollow. "The main cause of death in this battle was none of you covered each other well enough. Not one of you is immortal. We will be sitting out the next two battles to watch the other armies' teamwork." Then with a breezy smile the chill was gone. "If any," Lindy added with a chuckle.

When the pyre was lit, Lindy looked up into the sky, alone with her thoughts in the middle of her army. As more of her troops died from their wounds they were brought to the pyre. Only Lindy remained when the last body was tossed in at mid-morning the day after the battle. Covell and Jillvee watched as Lindy tried to pray, without knowing or remembering where or why those motions were automatic to her in moments like this. "What is she doing?" Jillvee whispered.

"Trying to respect the dead in an old way," Covell muttered, her eyes glued to the woman who would be forever young and more often than not covered in gore. That this thing was all that Manfred Endfield, Conduit, and a lonely little girl called Lindy had become after being stuffed into one soul was too cruel, even for what Manfred Endfield had done in a past life and world. Covell knew that whatever those three had done, their life now was likely far worse than any mortal could deserve. There was no way this was fitting for their combined sins. At least it was not fair for her uncle. At that realization, Covell shivered and waked away. "So is this my hell?" she whispered too softly for anyone but her heart to hear as it cracked.

A few hours later the army moved out. They spread out in formation across the farmland that started beyond the last fort. It took a day and a half with a few short rests to reach their next target. The town was a trading hub at the center of four roads that led to smaller farming villages. The shades hung back but Lindy walked in the rear as the rest of the army approached. Suddenly a rain of iron poles hit the front lines. "Where did they get those?" Jillvee asked.

"Not me. So no free stuff," Lindy shrugged at her side.

Anna grumbled. "They could not make your weapons so they made them bigger and safer."

"You mean more unwieldy and shoddier. My weapons are reliable. Those are impractical trash," Lindy answered as more men fell.

"Then how do we fight it?" Zoea inquired.

"Well those are really heavy. They either have to be fixed to a platform or a hero can lug them around. A low-rank hero would still have trouble with the recoil so a mid-rank or higher would be best. However, loading would still be difficult. Having a loader or two following them around would speed things up. You could also set the town on fire if needed," Lindy explained.

"Scorched earth is a last resort," Jillvee nodded. "The armies should encircle the town and charge in at the same time."

"Fine by me," Zoea agreed. "But you humans should move to a side. We can take the front."

"Far more of my army is engaged than yours. It would take too much time to change our angle. But move fast." Jillvee shook her head.

"Ok, but don't expect us to be swift," Zoea scoffed.

"What's the signal for the attack?" Anna asked. Most of her forces had moved out already.

"Fire breath in the sky?" Daffodil suggested.

"Ok," Anna agreed before running after her army with her bodyguards and a few teams of lighter infantry.

"I'd still like a diversion. Dwarves are not built for charging over open ground," Zoea sighed as her forces rushed off.

"No one is," Lindy nodded. "How about I place a few mines where the enemy would likely move to intercept or keep watch?"

"Is that ok?" Jillvee asked.

"It's not fighting, and could be dangerous for everyone if you are not careful," Lindy shrugged.

Zoea swore under her breath, Daffodil tilted her head wondering why smaller beings dying was so important, and Jillvee scoffed. "Right. Still up to us how many die. We should only do that on the dwarves' side. Any one that flees the town from the side we can't cover, the dragons can deal with."

"Ok. I'll need two bags of mines," Lindy informed Zoea.

A nearby sapper rushed over at Zoea's urging and meekly handed two bags to Lindy. Zoea turned to Jillvee. "Our advance will be slower in the town but it should draw more attention, so make sure to hit as many of our attackers in the back as possible." With that, the rest of the dwarven force shambled off.

Lindy dispersed into her own shadow to plant mines and look for Calanya and her child. If they were here Lindy would try to keep her promise to Lu. What little humanity Lindy still had compelled her to do that much.

As the armies got in position Lindy crept across rooftops, placing mines in the ground using shadows. The dwarves were the last in position. The Derndell kingdom forces were tired and running around, having spent long hours on watch and relocating to the other forces' movements. A few stepped on the mines Lindy was setting and so the chaos started. Daffodil, now back in her full dragon form, blew a pillar of fire into the sky. The signal was early but Lindy knew now was the time to strike. Men ran to the dwarven side only to die deaths they did not understand. The elves kept their attackers away with arrows and magic. The Otten shield wall and firearms kept the Derndell forces corralled. The dragons took that last spot, keeping at a distance. Their breath could hit farther than any of the enemy shots. Lindy watched all of this from the shadows. She could not resist tripping a few Derndell soldiers who were fighting well. As she stalked the battlefield, remaining hidden, she came to the center of town where a few women and children huddled. Lindy felt like the town had not been used for its intended purpose so any one in it likely had something to do with the army.

Lindy's sympathy was muted. Officers and messengers scurried to and fro in the town center. A small cry came from one of the buildings but no one paid attention. In fact, many of the women purposefully ignored the sound, but not due to fear, inferred Lindy as she scuttled to the side building. A lupine man stood over the body of a thickly robed woman; a half-elf female clung to her. All three had black uniforms with the eternal mercenaries' symbol; the man held a bloody sword. The woman would not survive the deep and wide chest wound. The young half-elf was enraged and firm, but not mindlessly so. She kept a close eye on her surroundings, which impressed Lindy. "Why?" was all the half-elf asked.

"Orders are orders," the man spat, raising his blade. Before he could strike the half-elf, he was cut clean in half by a dagger that flew out of nowhere. The man was turned to dust. The half-elf had aimed at the man's heart but was unable to hit him before he died.

"Well, that's underwhelming," something in the house grumbled, causing the half-elf to look around, ready to protect her fatally wounded mother and unwilling to believe that soon she would be orphaned.

The woman coughed up blood. "I know that voice."

"I can't believe my ears, either. You have not aged a day, Calanya," the voice replied from nowhere the half-elf could find.

"That's low, Lindy, even for you," Calanya sighed. "I am dying," she stated. This was something Lindy knew well and the half-elf knew but could not accept.

"Mom, why?" the half-elf asked.

"So this is Lu's kid?" Lindy asked.

"What does my father have to do with this!" the half-elf spat, looking around, still unable to find anyone to vent at.

Suddenly the young half-elf's arms were pinned behind her back by an incredible force. "I'll take that as a yes."

Calanya looked up. Even with her hazy eyes, the being that now appeared to be restraining her daughter had very different looks than the shortest-serving vice-commander in the Eternal Mercenaries. "New face?" Calanya asked.

"New body. Lost the last one," Lindy replied.

"How's my husband?" Calanya asked.

"Dead. I did offer to spare him but he wanted to follow his men," Lindy sighed. The half-elf began to kick.

"Why are you here?" Calanya asked, using the last of her strength to hear Lindy's answer.

"To save you both of you. But looks like I'll have to make do with your daughter," Lindy said. The half-elf could not believe how calm her mother was being and went limp, now realizing nothing she did would harm this newcomer.

"Take good care of her," Calanya muttered. She then allowed herself to die.

"Ok," Lindy nodded, placing the young woman on her shoulder. "Ok kid, you are stuck with me for the rest of your life. What's your name?"

"Zandra. Who are you to my parents?" the half-elf spat.

"A lot of things. Right now, your caretaker," Lindy said as she sped from the town, dodging around soldiers before they could react.

When Lindy got to her army she put Zandra down, who promptly lost her battle with motion sickness and began vomiting into the grass. A few shades waved their weapons in the young half-elf's face. "She's under my care," Lindy noted casually. The shades however, shivered in terror and promptly brought Zandra a chair, an entire barrel of clean water, and a large clean rag. Zandra spent a few seconds watching Lindy, who seemed to be ignoring her, but Zandra could not shake the feeling that Lindy was still watching her closely.

"Who is she really?" Zandra asked, but not neither Lindy nor any of the shades answered her.

The fighting ended a few hours later. Soon after, Covell marched over from her camp and asked Lindy, "You went in?"

"The village during the fight? Yes, I did," Lindy nodded.

Covell looked over at Zandra. "Who's the new guinea pig?"

Lindy walked between the two young women and introduced them with a straight face. "Zandra, my ward as of a few hours ago. She will be aiding me in a sociology experiment. Covell, an Otten princess."

"Nice to meet you," Covell said, extending her hand to the newcomer.

Zandra and the princess shook hands then the half-elf asked, "Wait, that's it? What's going on?"

"She is still in shock," Covell sighed, looking at Lindy reproachfully. "Zandra, you will get used to my uncle. Don't think too hard about what she does or says and you may keep your sanity."

"So what happened to my dad and his unit?" Zandra asked.

"Dead, most likely," Daffodil replied, landing lightly in her full dragon form.

"I did explain that already," Lindy added with a shrug. This earned her a few glares.

"And you killed him?" Zandra asked, looking around the camp. The shades had formed a shield wall around Lindy and company.

"He did refuse to surrender," Lindy replied sullenly.

"How many of my comrades did you kill?" Zandra asked, her voice hard.

"You mean the Eternal Mercenaries? All of them I have seen in this war except you and your mother," Lindy said as she began eating a sandwich one of her men had handed her.

Zandra stepped forward and tried to punch Lindy in the jaw. Lindy simply smiled, deflecting the straight lunge with one hand as she ate the sandwich with the other. A few of her allies moved to intervene but Lindy signaled with her eyes for them to not get involved. Zandra tried a few more punches and kicks, heedless of the armies around her. Lindy dodged or deflected each hit. Each deflection caused the half-elf to stumble. Finally Lindy lightly dodged a low bear hug and Zandra fell face-first to the ground. "Feel better yet?" Lindy asked, looking down at her charge.

Zandra lay there, her face in the mud. Gasping for breath and crying, she asked, "Why don't you kill me?"

Lindy knelt down and patted Zandra's head. "Because just like most of the beings I have killed, you are not my enemy."

"But you still killed them," Zandra replied.

"If someone was paid to kill me, would they be my enemy?" Lindy asked.

"Yes," Zandra replied, her voice hardening between sobs.

"If they are reckless fools, then maybe. Your parents and I did what we must. I could not save them but I can keep you alive." Lindy sighed, looking up to the sky.

Zandra shot up and tackled Lindy to the ground. "You killed them!"

Lindy looked up at the tired sad woman with cold eyes. "Your own forces killed Calanya. Your parents were my friends."

"Why?" Zandra repeated over and over as Lindy stroked her back.

"Such is war," Lindy whispered, more to herself than anyone else.

Soon after the fight the army marched on, more spread out than before. Outriders and scouts orbited the main force. In normal times, their next target would have been a day and a half away. It took two days, even with speeding up and a few more rests than most travelers. As the preparation for their siege began a meeting was held for the army's leaders. "This will take too long for my liking," Anna noted, looking at a map she had made from her memories and the scouts' info.

"A few spies stopped reporting in," Covell added.

"Mind control is messed up." Lindy nodded.

"You knew?" Covell asked, unaware that Lindy had noticed how some prisoners turn into spies through less than ethical magic on both sides.

"Back on topic: how are you getting in?" Lindy bluntly dodged the question with the elegance of a wrecking wall through a ten-story-tall hard pastry.

"Taking out their commanders would work, right?" Zoea asked.

"But who could do that?" Daffodil asked, patting Lindy on the shoulder. "Oh right, the teleporter," she smiled.

All eyes moved to Lindy. "This is outside the agreement," Lindy said.

"Please," Covell said innocently.

"It would help," Anna added.

"If you all pay me now, then fine." Lindy sighed then she held out her hand and grinned at the blank gazes. "It's an assassination job, after all."

Covell went to the back of the tent and took out a huge sack of gold. "Half of this."

"Two thirds." Lindy grinned.

"One third now, the other after," Covell countered.

"Pay in full now. It will be done in half a day," Lindy replied. Her widening smirk was unnerving.

Covell set the sack at Lindy's feet. "Fine. Kill all the officers."

The sack of gold shrunk suddenly. "I'm off to kill the dragon and general." Then after a meaningful pause, "See you in half a day." Lindy laughed.

"I said all officers," Covell snapped.

"I am already doing this for less than the going rate. Most of their officers are mid-tier heroes." Lindy shrugged before sinking into her shadow.

"I can't fucking believe him. Why now!" Covell began to rage.

"She is right about the going rates, and I can see the officers being that powerful," Anna grumbled.

"And you never said anything about it?" Zoea prodded.

"None of our spies or scouts got back with info like that," Anna said after taking a deep breath.

"So the old one knows more than she is saying." Zoea fumed in resignation, more for her own benefit than anything else.

"Yes," the others agreed.

"Wait, did she say a dragon?" Daffodil asked, spinning around.

Covell sat down heavily. "That's right. You cost me a few dead officers and a lot of gold."

"But that was my kill!" Daffodil yelled, trying to rush out of the tent before being dogpiled by Anna and Zoea.

"And Lindy killing it means less damage to us and the fort," Covell replied.

"And she would minimize the damage because she was being spiteful?" Daffodil snapped.

"More than you," Covell replied.

Tossing aside the dwarf and elf commanders, Daffodil stood up and shook her head. "That's such a waste. That man, woman? Whatever it is can do far more damage than I ever could."

Lindy's head popped out of a large chair's shadow high in a tower. A large man wearing an ornate uniform and very fancy helmet sat in the chair looking over a desk covered in maps and supply forms, his back to a small window and Lindy's slowly emerging form. Suddenly the man felt like a small needle poked him in the back. When he looked down the great sword that had been hung from his chair was stabbed through his seat and chest. Looking back, the man's eyes widened, seeing a young leering woman. Only her expression was visible. In the man's last thoughts, he realized that it was not his darkening vision playing tricks on him. The assassin was covered in shadows that smelled of bile and iron. Then he died.

After taking the documents on the man's desk, Lindy cut off the general's head and tossed it out the window. "Who puts an arrow slit this high up?" Lindy mused as she walked out of the room with the rest of the general's body over her shoulder.

A team of aides that sat at far less ornate desks right outside the door of the office all stood up and saluted before realizing that their general was not the one walking out. Lindy looked around the room and tossed the headless body into the middle. "Your problem now," she whistled before whipping out her pistol and shooting three men in the face who had drawn swords. "Now where's that dragon?' she asked, grinning like the blood-crazed maniac she feared she was.

"I'll never tell you!" one of the aides yelled. Lindy ripped the man in half by stepping on his feet and with her free hand grabbing him by the armpits and pulling hard. Lindy's eyes never left the five aides still alive in the room, her pistol moving from one to the other slowly, her face now a blank mask. "Right. It's a wyrm, my mistake. Now where is it?"

"We have two, you fool!" one of the aides snarled, looking over at a middle-aged man and young woman wearing uniforms of much nicer material but bearing far fewer medals than the other aides. "Well, what do we pay you two for?"

Lindy shot the rest of the aides. "Being smarter than you, it looks like," Lindy grumbled.

"That was unnecessary," the middle-aged-looking man said.

The middle-aged man was a very old dark wyrm; of that, Lindy was sure. What she did not know was what the young adult human-looking woman was. Looking closer, Lindy realized the fake teenager was slowly undergoing a change much like her shades had, but the power the woman's body was trying to assimilate was many times greater. "She's going to die," Lindy said to the man, tilting her head at the woman.

"Not before you do," the woman sneered.

Lindy rolled to the ground, snatching up one of the aide's blades. The man and woman rushed at her. Right before the woman could grab her target, Lindy cut a long but light slice down her own chest. "Sounds about right," Lindy chuckled as her blood covered the woman's face.

"You die by my hands!" the woman yelled, to which Lindy pulled at the energies in her blood. Suddenly the woman fell to the ground unable to move. By now Lindy's wounds were already nearly healed, seconds after she had made them. It was not a clean method but it was fast. With that, Lindy began to understand her own biology a bit more.

The man leapt, trying to tear into Lindy's face with spines that had sprouted from his hands. Lindy simply side-stepped and broke the man's arms. The door to the tower proper was flung open and many half-dressed soldiers rushed in. "Well this is awkward," Lindy laughed. Then she looked at the woman. "This is what you get for using insane prototypes in a real fight." A trace of irony was found in her voice which, given the gun in Lindy's hands, was rather shameless. As Lindy hopped into one of the many shadows in the room she cackled, "Have fun with that." No one left in the room understood her warning, but even if they had they would not be able to stop what had been set in motion or feel any better about themselves. The woman's transformation went haywire and she exploded. A mass of energy and mutated flesh shattered the central tower of the fort. As the rubble fell, many holes opened up in the walls.

As Lindy stepped out from Covell's shadow the young princess grabbed her and yelled, "That was more than two kills!"

"Oh, they had another monster with the wyrm. He may have died from that," Lindy began.

"So the son of a bitch is still alive. Huzzah!" Daffodil yelled from the floor. Zoea was sitting on the dragon but Anna was running around shouting outside the tent.

"When the other thing died it may have exploded more than intended. Still, two big bads down and no more wall problems. You should pay me," Lindy said, puffing out her chest with pride.

"I already did, and how will we fix the wall now? It's not a base without a wall!" Covell yelled.

"Magic, duh," Lindy shrugged.

"She's right, you know," Anna yelled near the tent.

"Da," Covell sighed.

"She means yes," Daffodil told Zoea. "Now get off my back."

"She means that literally, by the way," Lindy added unhelpfully.

"We know. Now let us wage a war!" Covell groaned.

Lindy left the tent with one last cheap shot. "You mean battle."

As Lindy walked back to her camp she read the documents she had pilfered. One invoice caught her attention and she started running. As soon as she spotted Zandra, Lindy dragged her charge into a tent, not even noticing Zandra was too surprised and petrified to fight back. Lindy shoved the invoice into Zandra's face. "Explain," was her only explanation.

"It's a pay stub," Zandra murmured, now very confused and even more off-put by her captor's intensity, but slowly regaining her mind.

"Right. But why is your unit a front for a cult?" Lindy stressed.

"A front? Where does it say anything about a cult?" Zandra shot back, her confusion and discomfort becoming anger.

Lindy pointed to the name of the Eternal's paymaster, the Shrew family. "They run a cult called the Eternal Wish. The names are too similar," Lindy explained, stomping her foot on the ground hard, which caused the land all around her to shake. Trees fell, living things panicked, tents collapsed, all from her simple expression of something Lindy would not allow herself to place. "I am so stupid," Lindy grumbled loudly as the tents all around her fell apart. But her eyes were glued to the name Shrew and nothing else.

When Zandra picked herself off the ground and surveyed the careless mayhem Lindy had wrought in her uncaring panic, the young mercenary stepped forward and, letting her anger and fear take over, slapped Lindy in the face. "What? Did the Shrews kill your family, too?"

Lindy took a deep breath and Zandra began to panic, then Lindy began to laugh and Zandra panicked more. "Not quite. They are dead to me but that's not the same thing. However, chances are they ordered that hit on your mother."

"How are you so sure?" Zandra asked, holding back tears of genuine fear.

"Because they kill what they have but can't use," Lindy said. After another deep breath she left the invoice in Zandra's hand. "If you think of anything useful to hunt them or their cult down, let me know," Lindy said before turning to her camp and yelling, "Look alive and get this cleaned up!" Lindy rushed off to help clean up her mess with her own hands.

16

Infamy

King Gerrad the Second sat on his throne. His mother stood behind him. Many officers and knights stood before him. They were in the middle of reviewing the state of the war. "Say that again," the boy king commanded to the poor sod who was summarizing the warfront that day. In the last week, five men with the same job had been executed because of the king's foul mood. His rage was steadily getting worse.

"The armies of Otten, Faywind, and the newly renamed dwarven hold of Lindyburg, along with some dragons and an unidentified race of humanoids, are almost at the capital. The other nations are still far away, stuck besieging our border forts," the man replied.

"Right. But compared to most armies, how big is the one near us?" the king asked stiffly.

"It is mid-sized, my king," the man stuttered over his notes in a maddened daze.

"Kill him," King Gerrad commanded.

"Right," Grgen Smalsh nodded, slicing the man in two.

"So how did those rebels get so far?" Gerrad asked, ignoring the fact that since he had yet to rule, those fighting him were not truly rebelling. This war was more of an enhanced diplomacy technique.

After a short pause, Ajax Shrew spoke up. "They have new weapons and a legendry-rank hero."

"Who?" Gerrad demanded.

"Lindy," replied Ajax. His sister's name had long become forbidden to say in the king's presence. "She killed Wisp. I should note that the casualties of her forces are the lowest among our attackers, even though they are one of the smaller armies and by far the deepest in our territory."

"So our armies are worthless is what you are saying?" Gerrad sneered, angry at the men in the room.

Ajax shook his head. "Not so, your majesty. They are doing quite well compared to the other armies. My point is that we are not sending enough of our forces at *her*."

"Oh." Gerrad nodded. "Do that, then dismissed." He was then led away by his mother after cutting the official meeting short. The men left in the room shot Ajax a dirty glare and got back to planning the war effort as they did every day and night.

When Ajax walked by a large fancy tapestry a hand came out and dragged him into a secret hallway covered by complex illusions. Ajax turned to his grandmother Frelda Shrew. "This place will fall soon," she said.

"Yes it will," Ajax agreed.

"We are leaving," Frelda added.

Ajax shook his head. "I am staying." Frelda's grip tightened. "I need to know how this war will end, even if it kills me," Ajax explained.

Frelda released her grasp. "Make no mistake: she will kill you."

"She will keep hunting us and I would rather look her in the eyes when she ends my life," Ajax nodded. When his grandmother scowled deeply Ajax shrugged. "Besides, old age does not suit me anyway."

"You could have been a lich or a vampire. In fact, you still could be," Frelda said, her voice soft for once.

"I want what Lindy has, even if she is not my sister anymore and not exactly of your bloodline. Only she could trouble you. That's the kind of power your descendants have been after," Ajax replied.

"You hate me that much?" Frelda asked, her voice hard.

"I owe you all I have. Honestly, I envy what Lindy and you could accomplish if you worked together," Ajax grumbled, knowing Fate would never let that come to pass, especially given how jealous Fate was of Frelda once upon a time.

"Fine, but don't die easily," Frelda nodded before walking off alone in mind and body for the first time in ages.

At the place Lindy first observed the Derndell kingdom's capital she observed the small unit guarding the walls. "Well, I'm off to cut the head from these manticores."

"You mean snakes?" Covell noted grimly.

Lindy's twelve baby hydras who were the first shades in the world slipped from her shadow. They were now regrowing most of their legs but each still had one scarred head. "Some of my best friends are snakes."

"How much will I owe you this time?" Covell asked.

Lindy puffed out her chest. "Vengeance is its own reward." Nearly everyone around her recoiled. "But don't quote me on that." All around her nodded. "Let's get this fight over with so I can relax for a few hundred years away from war and death!"

"You make it sound simple," Covell muttered.

Lindy grabbed the young princess's shoulders and looked closely into her eyes. "Never show fear before your troops and don't give a damn about your enemies' feelings."

"Well, a little help would not hurt if it's not me," Lindy whispered before releasing the princess to her guards. "Hey ward number one!" Lindy yelled to her troops. After no response was quickly forthcoming, Lindy added, "Not shade half-elf?" In response, Zandra was ejected from the rest of Lindy's army. Pointing at the half-elf, Lindy smirked. "You are my proxy in all things until I get back. Oh, and for this fight, give careful consideration to the chumps leading our allies." Then Lindy was gone in a puff of smoke.

"She does know her body was smoldering ever since she talked about war, right?" Daffodil asked.

"That fool is not as clueless as she tries to appear," Covell huffed, not realizing she was smiling broadly.

Lindy appeared in a large throne room. Columns and stained glass filled the hall. It would have felt like a cathedral if not for the throne where an altar should be and the little imp of a boy sitting on it. A boy who Lindy noted looked like he had been stuffed into a satin stocking covered in fur rather than wearing any finery.

Lindy appeared behind Grgen Smalsh and punched him though the heart as she looked around the room. Grgen looked down at the small hand with only the middle finger raised that had appeared from his breastplate. "What?" Grgen gurgled as he vomited blood all over the hand and his feet.

"Well hello to you too," Lindy said as she tossed Grgen to one side and shook off her arm in disgust.

"Who are you?" Grgen spat, rising weakly to his feet.

Grgen, who had killed Lindy years before, whipped out a potion that Lindy promptly disintegrated, not knowing what the potion would do. "You said that even you would die from getting stabbed in the back like that. Liar," she sneered.

"I don't know you," Grgen swore. A tall darkly robed figure with indistinct features stepped up behind him from its place by the throne, and the hall's doors burst open. "But you are outnumbered."

"Joke's on you. No way are you lot killing me again." Lindy shrugged before collapsing the hall's entire entryway. She shot Grgen a good twenty times in the head and chest while methodically using her magic to reload the oldest pistol on this world.

"So you are Lindy," the shadow analyzed confidently.

"And you are not Dusk Nightcrow, no matter how similar you dress," Lindy replied.

"You are not wrong," a slightly smaller humanoid wearing the same things as Nightcrow replied from one of the windows.

"The apprentice," the taller Nightcrow doppelganger said calmly.

"Hello, former master. What is the regent doing here?" the smaller Nightcrow asked.

Lindy displaced the taller Nightcrow's face covering, revealing the king's mother, albeit hollow-eyed and far thinner. "And grandma messed with her soul just like Wisp's. Fantastic," Lindy grumbled.

"You noticed?" the smaller one asked. Lindy glared at the small figure looking down on them. "Mind helping me kill her, Miss Lindy?"

"What do you get out of that?" Lindy asked as she tried shooting the boy, only to find that a barrier set up around the throne stopped the round. "And that barrier is depressing. You know it's going to kill your very soul, right kid?" The barrier rendered necromancy, resurrection, and most attacks with an intent to kill harmless by using the boy's soul as fuel. If it broke that would mean the boy's soul had been torn into so many pieces that not even Death could put it back together again.

"Kill them!" the kid shrieked before passing out when Lindy glared at him sharply.

"Freedom, honor? Plus it's the right thing to do," the small Nightcrow said. "Dusk Nightcrow is a false identity anyway. We are spies and assassins, after all. No spymaster goes to a public meeting as who they really are."

"Fine, but get in my way and you die," Lindy grumbled, annoyed by the bubbly self-proclaimed lord of spies. "But no professional assassin is a hero of justice."

"Right," the now self-proclaimed not-Nightcrow said while keeping its pseudonym.

Lindy examined the mother of Gerrad the Second.

Callabatta Durleen
Alias: Dusk Nightcrow
Human female age 42
Affiliation: Derndell empire inner circle
Job: Spymaster, treasurer Derndell royal merchants guild
Status: nobody

> Abilities: strength 1013, vitality 1014, mind 3028, agility 3289
>
> Curse: soul bound
>
> Talents: forgettable, multi-processing: advanced, translation: all, shadow jump, innate spell (telekinesis): extreme, danger sense, mental calculator, nondescript, honest face, nice teeth, strong hair, shadow magic: master, swift parry, flurry, mind reader
>
> Skills: breath holding: expert, barter: master, athletics: expert, intimidate (silence): expert, acrobatics: master, lie: show of confidence: master, knife: expert, read movement: expert, read emotions: master, read motive: expert, planning (infiltration): extreme, leadership: journeyman, literary: expert, sign language (improvised): journeyman, marksmanship: journeyman, stealth: master, diplomacy. (politeness) journeyman, etiquette (Derndell): expert, awareness (all) expert, biology: (elf, human, dwarf, beast-kin): journeyman, first aid: journeyman, poison maker: expert, gardening: journeyman, tracking: journeyman

Callabatta shifted into the shadows. "That's going to be annoying to fight," Lindy grumbled.

"But we can do that too," small Nightcrow said quizzically.

As if aging with Lindy, the room gained more shadows, reflecting shapes that were not there. The shadows both lengthened and separated. A few fingers appeared from a shadow. Soon after, they disappeared when most of the lamps in the room flew at Lindy. "Shit, it's like fighting myself," she noted.

Small Nightcrow pulled out Lindy's Long Barrel Express, although it was sporting a higher-powered energy chamber, a heavily reinforced barrel, and a long telescopic scope. "I need one clean shot," the small one said before jumping into a shadow.

Lindy dodged the few stray shots or hints of power that were expelled from the shadows near her. The room was soon riddled with small holes and odd magic-based scuff marks. One minute later Lindy lost her temper. "Screw this!" she yelled, degrading the room's furnishings and shadows until it became dim and empty.

Small Nightcrow ejected itself from a shadow near Lindy and rolled hard on the floor. "What was that?" she yelled, looking around.

Lindy increased the speed of degradation around the throne of the young passed-out king. Lindy smiled, spinning her sword under her armpit, ripping a long swiftly decaying line through Callabatta's chest when she tried to ambush Lindy from behind. "A feint," Lindy declared to her temporary ally.

After focusing some more power to decay Callabatta Durleen into nothing, Lindy looked at the king angrily. "Wait. Can you let him live?" small Nightcrow requested.

"Why?" Lindy spat.

"Because he is my king and a child who was not ready for power," small Nightcrow answered slowly and with total naïve sincerity.

"Give me that rifle and I'll let you try to bring him out of the city," Lindy nodded, managing to suppress a cruel gloating grin.

"This?" small Nightcrow said, holding up the Lindy's old now-modified creation.

"Yes, I made that. Good idea with the modifications, by the way," Lindy nodded, holding out her hand.

Small Nightcrow gingerly handed Lindy the weapon. "Well that's fair." Then she scampered over to her king.

"A powerful ward is set on his throne and on him," Lindy added mildly as she looked over the weapon. Then the screaming started as Lindy knew it would. By moving one anchor of the ward it broke, thus permanently killing the young boy and annihilating everything he was and could ever be in any life save his past deeds.

"He died." Small Nightcrow mourned as Lindy began looking around for a shadow to slip into. "You knew," Lindy's former ally said, rushing over to her.

"And you messed up," Lindy replied.

"Why did you not tell me?" small Nightcrow asked.

"Because I want him dead but would not have pursued you two if you were successful," Lindy explained, knowing that even for her it would take days to remove the wards safely.

"He was a kid," small Nightcrow snarled.

"And he really wanted me dead. Plus, with all the manpower under his command, that would have gotten annoying." Lindy shrugged.

"Well, I am going," small Nightcrow pouted.

"Ok. Don't get in our way and I'll leave you alone," Lindy promised.

Small Nightcrow clenched its jaw. "Thank you." Then they both jumped into a shadow and went their separate ways.

When Lindy returned to the front line, Ajax Shrew, Hanna Zigone, and an army of five thousand troops were stepping outside the city gate. Covell was about to order her troops forward when Lindy's hand stopped her. "Something's not right. Hold back." The young princess frowned but consented. Her troops and allies adjusted their siege defenses slightly.

After seeing Covell's troops holding their ground Lindy jumped, landing before Hanna, whose eyes were glazed over. "Friend or foe?" Hanna asked, methodically turning to Ajax after Lindy made clear she was not drawing her weapons yet.

"What did grandma do, bro?" Lindy hissed.

Ajax sighed. "What do you think?"

"Destroyed my friend's soul?" Lindy asked, her voice hard.

"In layman's terms, that's right," Ajax agreed.

Lindy eyes become dark smoking pits as she turned to Ajax. "And she left you to die."

"I am here to negotiate on behalf of the king," Ajax grumbled, seeming unsurprised but less than pleased.

"The brat's dead," Lindy shrugged.

"Shit, now what?" Ajax asked in resignation as if this was natural.

Lindy burst into a cloud of magic and her voice echoed throughout the Derndell kingdom or half-baked empire; she did not care. "All noncombatants from whatever cesspool who are hearing this: If you surrender, raise your hands. You have five seconds."

"Kill her!" Ajax screeched. Covell and her troops jumped face-first into the dirt.

"Kill what?" Hanna asked as she, Ajax, and the army they had led turned to dust.

After a while Lindy's voice bombed across the land. "Oh, and the spy master lives too."

The young boy that was Dusk Nightcrow looked around swiftly before raising a few arms of the either petrified or cackling citizens around him. "And forcing their hand does not count," the same voice whispered in his ears.

With a crack, the cloud of energy Lindy had become exploded. The self-proclaimed Derndell empire's grass, trees, cities, animals, non-surrendering citizens, and soldiers all became dust. The armies invading the Derndell kingdom were left alive and surrounded by the land they had come to claim, which contained only dust and a few thousand terrified prisoners. Lindy was nowhere to be found on the planet as Death was already leering down at her in his realm.

The only building to remain intact was a small manor house. Frost, Fall, and Fall's baby son and daughter were unharmed and very confused.

"Was that really necessary?" Fate asked from one corner of Death's realm.

"Nope, but it seemed like a good idea at the time," Lindy shrugged, trying to hide her shaking. "Sorry. I know I fucked up," Lindy whispered.

"I can't believe my ears," the large fleshless skeleton towering over her said.

"You have ears?" Lindy asked. Perking up, her voice sounded almost like Manfred Endfield's.

Death sighed. "My bosses want to talk to you."

Lindy took a deep breath, almost clearing her mind, and got into a somber mood. "So the home office?"

Genney the sage walked out from behind Fate. "Hey, it's been a while," she said sheepishly.

"You died," Lindy said with a straight face.

Genney shrugged. "Only once." Then she smirked, suddenly looking far older than when Lindy knew her. "Unlike some people."

Lindy sighed. "You're not wrong. So, um, sorry?"

"About the kingdom? They had it coming and you let my child live. I won't say that genocide was the best outcome," Genney began.

"I know," Lindy whispered helplessly, unaware of Fate's and Death's surprise.

"But I am glad you held back," Genney added before seeming like the girl Lindy once knew. "For what it's worth there were no good solutions for that moment."

"So are we going or not, Grog?" Fate demanded.

"You two can talk on the way," Death said firmly before looking at Fate. "All set, Ven?"

"Ven?" Lindy asked.

Fate looked at Lindy in a huff. "All the world spirits had their own lives once," she said before shrinking to look like a tall 16-year-old woman that was unnaturally pale, with white hair and dull blue eyes.

Death or Grog also shrunk into the appearance of a short teenager with red hair wearing dark furs. "Ven was my best friend. After I died she kind of froze to death and we have been stuck with each other, even after death now."

"You know that makes no sense when you say it, right?" Lindy asked.

Ven looked angry, then thoughtful. "Shit, she's right."

Looking over at Death, Fate asked, "Why did we never realize this?"

"You never asked," Death said quickly before looking away from the glares he was getting. "Well, let's go," before a shimmering tunnel opened.

"So who's taking over for us?" Lindy asked.

"Some of the other Deaths and Fates are covering for our worlds and your shades are covering for you," Fate nodded.

"So what did your past selves look like?" Genney asked.

"Besides the body you met, no idea," Lindy sighed.

"Oh good. One more thing," Death added as they stepped on a shining path that seemed to pull them along past a dark void and countless shimmering spheres. Grog snapped his fingers and Lindy grew, feeling out of place until she held her jaw, feeling light stubble.

"Oh, you are quite rugged," Genney said.

"No past tense?" Lindy asked before looking around, realizing she was taller than the others now and far bulkier. "Oh, this is what I looked like? Wait, why am I a man now?"

"Because it's less awkward for me," Death whispered.

Lindy looked at Fate, who looked away from what Manfred Endfield had looked like once upon a time. Fate seemed preoccupied with looking at the realities they passed, as did Death.

At the sight of Grog and Fate delicately holding hands while appearing to be interested in very different sides of the path, Lindy grumbled quietly. "Just this once then."

Moments or centuries later Lindy noticed a wide stretch of realities that were dim and seemingly dead. "What's that?" she asked, pointing at the nearly ten thousand universes.

Grog looked over. "The dead space."

"Is that supposed to be cliché or literal?" Lindy shot back.

"Both. That's what happens when one of the Deaths die," Grog grumbled, clearly uncomfortable.

"It's cut off from us," Ven added. One look at Lindy and Genney made it clear they still did not understand. Rolling her eyes, Ven elaborated. "No one goes in or out, but there is a small group of something keeping it from getting worse."

Death pointed at a universe around the middle of the dead space. The only bright spot in the dead space was a universe surrounded by a corona of flames. "That's where it began. Some mortals tried to mess with reality. Reality lost control. Even Chaos and Order were kicked out. Some universes merged, then a few kids stumbled into that mess and are keeping it from getting worse with a few others. They are technically mortal but not bound to a single body or reality within that hellscape."

"And Reality, Chaos, and Order are the bosses of this madness?" Lindy asked.

"That's not necessarily wrong," Death nodded. Soon after, the dim universes were out of sight behind many more shining ones.

By the time the party arrived at a prismatic disk surrounded by long-dead universes, Lindy had lost track of time itself. Three heads loomed so far above them that each seemed like specks, although given how messed up the laws that held everything together, it was hard to say if they were small and close or huge and very far. "I thought you would be taller," Lindy smirked.

"And I thought you would be afraid," two of the heads said at nearly the same time.

Lindy looked at the head that had not spoken. "You can call me Lindy. Who are you?"

"Chaos," the soft-spoken head said.

"Right. It's always the quiet ones," Lindy muttered before looking at her three companions who were on their knees and shaking. "Are they supposed to be like that?" she asked.

"First of all, you have proven the first statement incorrect. Secondly, how they appear depends on your perspective," a head said.

"That makes you Reality, I assume," Lindy said. "Is it all right if I sit down?"

A bleeding sword appeared on a pink couch covered in lace and glitter and one of the heads disappeared. "It is our guest," the sword said.

"Wait, you are Order?" Lindy gasped.

"Yes. Why, what do I look like?" the sword said.

Lindy used her necromancy to summon a stool made of bones and sat down. "Like a living sword with a head wound and a couch fit for a stereotypical pixy."

"Well, do I look terrifying to you?" the sword asked.

"Yes," Genney said. "Wait, why are there two Lindys?"

A mug of ale labeled *Last Alcohol Ever* floated next to the sword. "We prefer our appearance to change based on the viewer's perception of what we embody."

"That's Chaos, by the way," Lindy added.

"So look like the most extreme example we can imagine for how you wish to look?" Genney asked.

The last head appeared as a black hole. "That's right. They look terrifying and I look like Reality because I am."

"So Lindy again?" Genney asked, looking over at her friend.

"I just see a black hole, the *Last Alcohol Ever* and a very confusing sword," Lindy shrugged. "The weirdest one is Order."

Genney grumbled and used her friend as support to stand. "Figures you would say that. Real you."

"Now that we are all introduced, why are we here?" Lindy asked.

"Long version or short?" Chaos asked.

"Just why for the here and now. I don't have the brain power for the history of everything," Lindy retorted, taking a good look around.

"When Grog and Ven get transferred to newer existences do you two want to take over for them?" Reality asked.

"I'd be Fate then?" Genney asked.

"Yes," Chaos murmured.

"And I'd be Death. When would that be?" Lindy asked.

"Two thousand of your years, give or take," Reality replied.

"If they are ok with it, then fine," Lindy grumbled.

"Not happy?" Chaos asked.

Lindy ruffled her hair and slowly returned to her first female appearance. "I just feel like this life will go on forever and that kind of annoys me. Not to mention I remember all my lives now, and I've just realized I've always been some kind of loon."

"So how were you on your past world?" Genney asked, tying to sound comforting but coming off as more than a little spooked.

"Militant lunatic turned spooky and obsessive inventor," Lindy sighed.

After a few short breaths Genney smiled honestly. "Ok, so nothing new then."

Lindy looked around and burst out laughing. "That's right! Thank you, I needed that."

"Ok then Grog, Ven, your applications are approved. Train them well," Reality, Order, and Chaos said before Lindy found herself back in Death's domain.

"Well, that was trippy," Lindy noted, looking at her hands.

"It always is with those three," Grog said. "By the way, we have been gone for two hundred years. Now off you go."

17

Time to Be

Lindy noticed two other beings that felt like Death just as her consciousness looked upon the world she had been assigned to so many years before. Lindy found her first body surrounded by alchemical fluids for preserving flesh and healing it in a sealed tomb. Lindy repossessed her old body.

The first thing she did was look at her stats.

Lin Of Lindy

Female (shadow touched) human age forever 20

Affiliation: realm of death

Embodiments: death to be, eternal calamity

Job: Reaper

Status: common sense bane: extreme, death's apprentice

Abilities: strength 8650, vitality 9723, mind 9000, agility 10002

Talents: translation: all, full power strike: strength. danger sense, innate map, skill and knowledge retention: Manfred Endfield, photographic memory, sixth sense: intuition, extra toughness, favored environment: darkness, cold resistance: high, highly enhanced trait: willpower, analysis: extreme, good hair, quick learner. fearless, body of poison, presence sense, aura: weakening, damage shield: decay, decay bolt, adept talent: multi tasking, rapid reload, fearsome visage: moderate, selective decay: all, innate spell: chill blast, absorb impact: moderate, hair trigger aim, riposte: debate, realm authority (death): moderate, shadow shift, six fold strike, perception tampering field, find soul, see soul, sense lifespan, attuned to purpose, shadow form, plains walk: deaths realm and back, full power burst: weakening/ decay/cold, siphon soul, suppresses kindnesses (self) full, suppress power: any, track soul, find living, alcohol resistance: mild, trace bloodline, rapid fire, strike from shadow, rapid shadow jump

Blessing: conceal stats

Mutation: troll blood (extra burnable, swift regeneration), un-aging. mutagenic blood

Curse: catastrophic encounters, heavily sleeper, light sensitivity: mild

Skills: Sword: master, dagger: master, unarmed: master, marksmanship: extreme, throwing: expert, athletics: master, armor proficiency (leather/cloth/plate): expert, literacy: expert, history (other world): journeyman, intimidate (innate): extreme, diplomacy: journeyman, awareness: expert, necromancy: extreme, tinkering: master, magic tampering: extreme, counter spell: master, survival (woodland): journeyman, cooking: journeyman, acrobatics: expert, stealth: expert, shadow magic: expert, laws of death: extreme, leadership: journeyman

As she read her abilities Lindy used the alchemical fluids set around the slab she had been lying upon to fix the wounds that had once killed her. Only then did she look around. The room was a small stone crypt. A heavy stone door covered with many lethal spells sealed the exit. Lindy smirked, seeing the spells were mostly there to keep her body from leaving. Only a few enchantments set to stun or kill the very weak were set for anyone who tried to open her resting place from the outside.

Lindy spent an entire day trying to probe the wards on the door. She did not want to carelessly set them off as she remembered feeling from Death's realm how deep the crypt was, and did not fancy being entombed by the crypt itself collapsing.

Giving up at some point, Lindy took a nap, only to be awoken by the sound of a heavy slab being moved from a shaft past her door. "It's here," a voice called, its muffled echo reaching down the long shaft leading to Lindy's tomb. Lindy sprang to her feet and covered herself in the heavy armor she had made. Then she pulled out Transcendence, only to wrinkle her brow, finding a thin curved stiletto in her shadow that felt at least as powerful as Transcendence. Upon pulling it out and looking at the dagger's engraving, Lindy chuckled in her mind. *A blade called The End. Well, better late than never.*

Lindy stood next to the door, her arms crossed and body still listening to the likely grave robbers. "Are we sure this is the place?" another voice asked. Footsteps of three humanoids echoed down the passage.

"This is the target. Does it matter? Let's get in and get paid," a third voice said. The echoes prevented Lindy from finding anything solid from the voices other than there were so far three distinct ones, but they were so distorted that anything more was impossible to know.

The footsteps stopped. "Shit. Who built this?" the second voice said.

A pair of steps began moving forward. "Let's get this over with," the third voice said.

"That's not what he meant. This place is old. Like real old," the first voice commented.

"So what?" the third voice said. Clanks echoed throughout. All the voices grunted in pain.

After a few seconds and a lot of shuffling, the second voice chimed in. "This place was built to keep something in."

The third voice asked, "What?" before the shock spells activated. In a brief instance the wards Lindy did not want to deal with lost power. Not letting that chance pass by, Lindy swiftly nudged the slab and it fell.

"My legs!" the third voice yelled from just outside Lindy's door.

"Damn it, what happened?" the first voice yelled as Lindy waited, remaining perfectly still.

"The door fell. He tripped the wards," the second voice said.

A blond ponytail was blown into the crypt. "Let's help him up, but be careful. Most of these wards would destroy this barrow."

"Wait, what?" the third voice asked.

Some grunting and panting followed but the slab did not move. Sighing to herself, Lindy moved next to the owner of the first voice, who turned out to be a teenage human female wearing clothes in a style Lindy did not recognize. "Here, let me help," Lindy said, lifting the slab with a few fingers on her dagger-wielding hand, still firmly gripping her weapons.

"Oh thanks," the teenager said as Lindy tossed the slab into the crypt.

The teenager looked at her two companions: a large young man with crushed legs and a skinny young man with glasses. All three were around the same age. The two young men were looking at Lindy, frozen in shock. Only then did the young woman's face tremble as she turned around. "We are so dead," she murmured, looking up at the dark suit of armor standing over them.

Lindy took off her helmet and the teenager's eyes widened. "Who hired you?"

"Our employer is back at camp," the young woman said, whimpering.

"Well lead the way," Lindy smiled. The teenagers were still too terrified to move. Lindy grumbled wordlessly. Tossing her dagger into her shadow she picked up the large young man.

"Don't eat me," the injured man pleaded.

"You think I'm undead," Lindy noted, smirking wickedly.

"Wait, you are alive?" the young woman asked.

"I'm long-lived, not dead," Lindy nodded, tossing the injured man over her shoulder. "Specks, you lead the way to this so-called camp. Tails, you walk with me."

"Cindy," the young woman said, introducing herself while remaining on edge.

"Fredinand. The one on your shoulder is Ted," the teenage boy with glasses added.

"You can call me Lin," Lindy chuckled.

Walking up past a long stairway they entered a thick forest, winding around much damp foliage. "So where are we?" Lindy asked after a while.

Fredinand looked at Cindy then sighed. "Faywind clan territory," he said.

"Who runs the Derndell kingdom?" Lindy asked. She had seen cities with living humanoids but very little signs of commerce or order between the cities.

Cindy retorted with, "What?" after a few seconds.

"She means the wasteland. It's a bunch of city states. Anyone who is able packs up and leaves," Ted muttered.

Before Lindy could speak up Cindy asked, "So Lin, what are you? Its like the whole forest is avoiding us now."

"Technically human, but far too powerful for my own good," Lindy answered softly, picking up a lack of sound around them for the first time: no bugs, birds or any other animal, monster or humanoid. Save for a light if cool breeze and the stationary plant life, they were alone.

After moving more carefully for half an hour they arrived at a camp. Five fighters far more capable than the teenagers stood around a heavily robed figure that Lindy immediately recognized. The figure turned to look at them as Lindy shoved her helmet back on and placed Ted on the soft mossy ground. "Stay away from this place," Lindy whispered to Cindy before walking slowly into the small supply dump. "Grandma, what brings you out here?" Lindy shouted.

"Looking for your body," the lich said.

"Well it's more alive than you were expecting, right? So what now?" Lindy sneered.

"Answer a few questions and we shall see," the lich said.

"We will take turns asking, Frelda. What qualifies someone to be a world spirit?" Lindy asked.

"To be close to their concept but mentally distant," Frelda Shrew replied. *I can see how that would apply to Fate, Death, and War, at least.* Lindy mused. "Tell me how to live forever," Frelda asked.

Lindy smirked. "Fine, but only because you asked." All of Frelda's hirelings were sucked into their own shadows. The three youngsters found themselves in the City of Smog. The more skilled fighters who had been guarding Frelda found themselves just outside what used to be the Derndell kingdom's capital, which now was a shanty town made mostly of dried mud. "To remain in this world, forever separate your soul from your mind and body, and take really good care of them. Trying to tether your soul to this world in any way is not allowed. A lot of rules are based on that. But that idea is what most of the offences that require my personal touch are based on."

Frelda nodded. "So that's the bottom line then. Ok, what does Death think of me?" The lich's voice was blatantly lovesick.

After a deep breath Lindy expanded. "Grog, no idea. You know Ven, that's Fate by the way, has a serious crush on him too, right? Trust me, Fate is unbelievably jealous. How did she not kill you off yet?"

Frelda's head snapped up, seeming to glare at Lindy. "Death's name is not Death" the lich whispered. After shaking a little due to suppressing a deep cackle, Frelda stood up. "That's enough. Then fight me."

Love is scary Lindy thought. "You will die, you know," Lindy said, suddenly in combat mode, her limbs limber, her mind focused, her sense of time slower.

"Just try it," Frelda cackled. Only now, with the sense that the end goal she had betrayed and killed for so many lifetimes was impossible from the start, did Frelda truly lose the last of her sanity.

Lindy tried to get her hydras to pin Frelda but froze for less than a second when she noticed her pets were not in her shadow. A jet of dark ooze slammed into Lindy's chest, launching her a good half mile through the woodland. Lindy spun as she flew, kicking her way through trees and big shrubbery until she landed near a small but dim clearing. Lindy grumbled when her cracked ribs healed. Tendrils of solid matter that had been shadows of trees rose from the ground. Lindy's sword and dagger were pulled into the inky void around. The sword and dagger were gripped by the shadowy tendrils. The shadows waved around energetically, tearing up the ground in the process. Lindy pulled out her rifle and pistol, holding one in each hand just in time to shoot Frelda multiple times as the old lich sped into the devastated landscape that was largely Lindy's doing.

Frelda fell to the ground from the gunshots. Lindy caused all magic but her own to be chaotic and thin to the point of being nearly impossible to control. Fifty trees, the youngest having lived for five hundred years, smashed onto Frelda. The old lich charged Lindy despite being knocked around by the trees and nicked by Lindy's dagger. When Frelda was around twenty feet away Frelda made all the magic power she could internalize go haywire as Lindy shot her twice with the rifle. Frelda died and exploded.

The world seemed to shudder and flicker for an instant. Magic returned to how it had been minutes before. Lindy lay in a small grassy clearing that had not seen light since before the first-time humans, elves, and other flesh and blood tool users walked the land. Lindy's body was missing slightly below her armpits. Her body desperately worked to heal itself but she knew it was a lost cause. Slowly as her eyesight dimmed the land around her began to twist as her blood mutated the land. All that was left of Frelda was half a skull. "I never modified your blood to do this!" it rasped while slowly turning to dust.

Lindy lay dying. A dryad crept into the clearing. "My glade!" she yelled.

"Send the bill to the litch's buddies," Lindy coughed.

The dryad crept closer but stopped when its own body began to twist. "You can call me Lindy, by the way. Looks like I owe you a favor," Lindy said with the last of her strength. Lindy's sight dimmed. The dryad knelt in the middle of her glade crying. The pristine and ancient woodland had darkened. The plants became sharp and menacing, looking much like the dryad's altering form. Lindy's last thought in her first body was *I never knew dryads could cry water.*

Then Lindy found herself in a grayish space within Death's realm. "I hate dying!" Lindy yelled.

Grog and two other individuals that felt like deaths as well looked over at her. "That was fast," a death that looked like a house cat noted.

"Which one of you plays chess?" Lindy asked.

"We all do," a bipedal fish-like humanoid in a dark robe said.

"Budget cuts?" Lindy asked.

"More or less. Now go back already," Grog snapped.

"Ok fine," Lindy nodded. Then she looked at a random section of Death's realm and yelled, "Hey Ven, Frelda Shrew just died!" Lindy proceeded to vanish back to her world, grinning at the three shaking deaths.

Right before Lindy's vision left Death's realm, Ven broke into the realm with the voice of an explosion. "What!" she shrieked, then looked at Lindy. "Oh, and thank you," Fate whispered before storming over to the deaths. "I'm sitting in on your work today," Ven declared to Grog.

Lindy found a shade that was dying of a chronic lung ailment in a warehouse filled with things that felt familiar. Lindy used the materials in the warehouse to make a new body. However it was not enough this time, so the shade was used as a material as well. Footsteps thundered outside the warehouse and a creaking door was flung open. Lindy opened her eyes. She sat up from the cold stone floor and noted she was wearing the guard's clothes. "Sal, what happened?" a lean half-elf asked her. After looking into Lindy's eyes the man's face soured. He and another man dressed the same as Lindy drew their weapons. "Who are you? Where is the shipment?" the half-elf asked.

Lindy did not stand up. "You can call me Lin. I seem to have consumed the supplies in this room. How much were they worth?"

"Where is Sal?" the half-elf asked. Lindy tilted her head and pretended to be confused. It was unclear if the half-elf was too mad to notice her bad acting or was angered by her apparent confusion. "That's his uniform," the half-elf pointed out.

"Oh, the shade with lung cancer. I ate him," Lindy said, clapping her hands intently while yelling in her mind how insane she must seem.

"What?" one of the guards said as he lit a cigarette that promptly turned to ash. Only the half-elf noticed that Lindy had destroyed the cigarette, although he did not know why.

"This warehouse had relics I was going to donate to the Everlasting church," the half-elf sighed.

Lindy began to have an idea why so many things she had been familiar with were in the room. "This Everlasting church — are they death worshipers or something?"

The half-elf glared at Lindy trying to gauge how serious she was, then she grumbled. "In the most basic terms, yes. Not to be confused with the Church of Shrew. So why did you eat all my things and a guard again?"

"To heal myself," Lindy replied, lying back on the floor. "If I give you coins from before the wasteland including those made by kingdoms that no longer exist, can we forget this ever happened?"

"It's unlikely, but you may be able to reimburse me for the warehouse that way. However, I will bring you back to The City of Smog to stand trial," the half-elf said.

Lindy shrugged and dumped all her old coins into the warehouse from the deep shadows that suddenly spread around the room. When the darkness lifted the guards were all petrified in awe. "By the way young man, what's your name?" Lindy asked her conversation partner.

"Halmar Zigone, sub-viceroy of the City of Smog," the half-elf said.

"Is your mother's name Zandra Limore?" Lindy asked

Halmar shook his head and looked at Lindy like she had no common sense, which was more true than he realized. "The viceroy's name is Zandra Zigone," he said.

Lindy sighed. "Well shit."

"Get up," Halmar commanded as he pulled out a set of shackles.

Lindy rolled her eyes. "Just like his mother," she muttered before leaping to her feet. The sub-viceroy's guards drew their weapons swiftly but not swift enough to prevent Lindy from holding her arms out and grinning. After a few seconds she laughed. "Well cuff me already. Let's get this over with while you are all still young."

Halmar stepped forward and firmly shacked Lindy's hands. "Come with me sir," he ordered.

Lindy followed her self-proclaimed captor onto a worn cobblestone road with gravel and sand set in places in lieu of newer stones. The buildings were squat and made of mud. All the natives wore heavy clothes. Everyone was armed with some manner of close combat weapons. Guards and some important-looking men had crossbows. An impressive amount of things made of glass was around. It felt like a few thousand people lived in this village that was set in the wasteland Lindy had created. When she passed by a mirror Lindy got a good look at her new body. It was slim and youthful with short hair. Her flesh had a barely perceptible purple tint. "Right. I look like an 18-year-old human boy," she muttered before adding mentally, *That said, I am still female. This could be useful.*

Halmar walked in front of two guards. Next came Lindy and lastly the rest of the guards, almost all with sacks of the coinage Lindy had handed over. All the guards were on edge, stealing glances at Lindy every so often. Halmar played with three of the oldest coins. "So Lin, what are you?" he asked after a good twenty minutes.

"Technically human, although I have far more in common with dragons," Lindy replied absently as she studied her surroundings.

"We are going to the local Everlasting church. They will authenticate your payment," Halmar said. Lindy could tell her nonchalance was worrying him.

"Right. So how long has this place been a desert?" Lindy asked back. The guards, Halmar, and a few others stopped, staring at Lindy. "What? I have not been here in a while."

"How old are you?" Halmar asked.

"Old enough to have fought in the war that made this place," Lindy whispered, ignoring more than a few glares.

"Which one?" Halmar asked.

"The one your two grandmothers and mother were in when this place had trees," Lindy answered as if that was obvious.

Halmar motioned for his men to keep moving. After they had rushed by the last of the local eavesdrops, he demanded, "How?"

"Like a dragon, remember?" Lindy cackled. As she wheezed Lindy added, "Your mom was nowhere near this fun."

"The viceroy never spoke of you," Halmar noted acidly.

Lindy looked at the man who was descended from Fall, Calanya, and Zandra. "It was a big war and she barely knew me," Lindy shot back, suddenly serious, having almost caught her breath, which lessened the gravitas of her statement when she coughed one last time. *Now I am remembering why I hate sand,* she thought.

Lindy began to realize a slight feeling of unease the more she looked around. *Everyone seems so weak,* she realized. Her sense of danger and experience told her no one she had seen was more powerful than a trainee hero. When they entered a shopping plaza the first thing Lindy noticed was a small marble church. An image of a skull with two crossed scythes surrounded by a laurel wreath hung from the stout steeple. "How bad do the storms get around here?" Lindy said to herself.

"Worse than most places," Halmar replied. He waited for Lindy to reply, only to see her shrug. The shops the group passed were diverse but the quality of merchandise was not very good.

When Lindy entered the church Halmar grabbed her arm and made her sit down in the far back. His guards sat near the aisles and door. Lindy briefly felt a little self-conscious but got over it quickly; she was far older, after all. Not bothering to note that almost everyone on the planet was young to her now.

A priest stood on a podium. Judging by his gestures he was near the end of a sermon. The church was more than half full. "And as the prophet said, to show one's love to Death, our divine keeper, one must be calm in mind, soul, and body. We must always be honest to each other because only the truth keeps a soul clean. Remain yourselves and honest so that Death our lord will welcome you into the endless life after this trial we live in. Die well my flock, and remember to praise the First Prophet Lindy for showing us the way through our trial in this the two hundred and thirtieth year of her ascension." Lindy's only thought about the sermon was *Wait, are they interpreting my words that deeply? I am glad they are having fun and that priest is trying to keep the meaning of my words, mostly. Well whatever, not my problem.*

A chorus of "May the destroyer of kingdoms stay her blade from us, the flock of Death, the divine watcher." Lindy sighed. *Ok, looks like I am infamous.*

It took nearly an hour for the worshippers to file out. Only then did the priest walk over to Halmar. Lindy's captors tossed over one of her oldest coins. "What does that look like to you, father?" he asked.

"A coin from the fallen kingdom of Derndell, and the oldest one I have ever laid my eyes on. It is remarkably well preserved, almost unnaturally so. Where did you acquire such a treasure?" the priest replied, carefully turning the coin over in his hand.

Halmar took a deep breath. "From the one that ate our original offerings."

"The shadow hydra's head was eaten?" the priest asked. His sadness pierced though the veneer of sternness he tried to hide behind.

"Are they rare?" Lindy inquired.

The priest swept his gaze over Lindy before nodding. "Yes. The eleven servants of the first Prophet are rare," his voice grave and slightly disappointed.

"So there are not twelve?" Lindy asked, thinking back to her pets.

"One was slain by infidels from the Church of Shrew," the priest added.

"Right. Are they some kind of splinter group?" Lindy asked.

"They believe the first prophet to be a god and creator of the shades, and believe Death our glorious savior to be her servant," the priest sighed, then glared at Halmar. "Now is this the only offering you have?"

Halmar motioned to his guards, who put down a few sacks. "I have a warehouse full of old coins from places I do not recognize," pointing out to Lindy, who smiled and lifted up her manacled hands.

The priest walked up to Lindy and she peeked at his stats.

Salmeer Drerlon

Human male age 28

Affiliation: Everlasting church

Job: bishop

Status: bishop

Abilities: strength 112, vitality 233, mind 248, agility 112

Talents: single minded, language (common Derndell, high Derndell, wasteland), resistance (poison, filth, heat): mild, innate talent (perception): moderate, swift cast, silent cast, absorb spell: necromancy, innate spell: detect life/unlife, banish, danger sense

Skills: necromancy: extreme, barter: journeyman, athletics: apprentice, intimidate (presence): expert, oratory: expert, diplomacy: expert, literacy: expert, first aid: journeyman, herbalism: adept, dagger: apprentice, ceremony: journeyman, poison: adept, law (Everlasting church): journeyman. history (Everlasting church): adept

Lindy noticed that despite his high skill in necromancy he had not taken the easy route to power by compromising his soul, which was as surprising as it was welcome. *Cool, I don't have to gut this one,* she mused.

Salmeer fished out a few coins from the sacks and gave them a once-over, then looked at Lindy. "Where did you get these?"

Lindy sighed. "Bishop Salmeer Drerlon the necromancer, I am simply far older than I appear. I was a mercenary in the same war as Lindy your prophet."

Salmeer took a small orb from his pocket. Lindy felt like the orb was sizing her up. Before she could think why, Lindy concealed her stats, making them look to anyone unskilled as:

> Lin
>
> Male shadow dragon 459
>
> Affiliation: himself
>
> Job: none of your business
>
> Status: traveler
>
> Abilities: work in progress
>
> Talents: come back later
>
> Skills: go away

Salmeer looked at the orb and frowned, then held the orb out to Lindy. "No tricks this time," he demanded.

Lindy glared back at Salmeer. "Only if this stays between you and me."

Halmar angrily retorted, "You don't have a choice," only for him and all his guards to faint from sheer terror as the very air around Lindy seemed to change.

"Very well. I only want to understand how you came to this wealth," Salmeer muttered, pushing the orb into Lindy's hands and stepping away.

"By seeing how much stronger than you I am?" Lindy smiled, letting the orb read her real stats and tossing the orb to Salmeer.

Salmeer's face clouded over. "Don't joke with me!" he yelled.

Lindy looked apathetically at the man. Her favored weapons The End, Transcendence, the First Pistol, and Long Barrel Express ver. 2 all floated out of her shadow. "I am not joking, young man."

Salmeer trembled, then became giddy. "I have to tell the pope."

"This stays between us, remember?" Lindy hissed, her weapons all now pointing at the bishop.

"Very well, your eminence. But why?" Salmeer asked.

Lindy's weapons were pulled back into her shadow. "Because I already have too much work to do for Death and I hate politics," she sighed.

Salmeer thought for a few seconds. "Very well."

Lindy walked over and began to prod Halmar. "You know you can mess with your body and mind as much as you like, right? I will not kill you for that. Just do not mess with your soul, young man." Glancing at the shivering holy man, Lindy grinned. "Oh, and keep the change."

Halmar awoke to find Lindy sipping tea with Salmeer Drerlon. Once his guards awoke Lindy shrugged and allowed Halmar to drag her away. Between his sudden bout of unconsciousness and Salmeer's glare, "allow" was the only word that seemed to fit and he did not know why. "Why me?" Halmar moaned.

Lindy shrugged. "I know, right? Life is crazy."

The group arrived at a large barn-like building. Inside stood two trains with cattle cars. Some of the cars had seats, some held cargo. Two tracks led outside in two directions. Inside the barn the two tracks expanded into three. "Well that was fast," Lindy murmured.

"It's the latest in heat water technology," a flashily dressed man said, walked up to Halmar. He glanced at Lindy. "It's not like you to hire outside of the Smog."

Lindy held up her manacles. "My application is still under review," she replied wryly.

The well-dressed man looked at Halmar. "Do I want to know?"

"He has been well behaved thus far. So no, if anything happens my guards will handle it." Lindy snickered but only got a few glares in return.

"Well your party has six seats in car 2," the man said, handing Halmar six wooden tickets.

"Many thanks, Allensco," Halmar said.

"That's Conductor," Allensco smiled, pointing at a badge pinned to his suit.

After shuffling though a more or less orderly line they got to the seats without a word. Lindy sat across from Halmar. Two of his guards sat next to them by the windows. The last four sat by the door after Halmar motioned to say it was fine. One of the guards, the only one who was obviously female, glanced over at Lindy and chuckled as she studied the train. "First time on a train?" she asked.

"Well this is different than I imagined," Lindy replied as she looked around.

After a time the train started moving. "Did you really eat my subordinate?" the women asked harshly.

Lindy looked over at the woman calmly, as if talking to an acquaintance about the weather. "Technically I absorbed him and the surrounding things, but eat is a simpler way to explain it. Either way, the process is not too different."

"And why did you do that?" the woman asked. By this time all the guards and Halmar were listening closely.

"So I had all my parts where they should be," Lindy sighed, closing her eyes and sitting back on the lump of leather and sand they called a chair.

"That's it?" the woman pressed.

Lindy grumbled. "I am not going anywhere for now, so just let me sleep. It's been a long time since I took a nap." From the air flow Lindy felt that someone motioned for the guard to let it go.

Lindy slept, fitfully dreaming of all the horrors she had unleashed and a few that she had never seen. Outside the loose sand of the wasteland slowly transformed into ever-thickening forests. A little over half way to the City of Smog, Lindy braced for impact. Seconds later the train shook, then stopped. "Rocket launchers and earth mages, really?" she quipped.

"What was that?" the angry guard from before asked.

"I don't know, Sallos," Halmar grumbled angrily. He glared at Lindy.

"What, it's just thirty attackers?" Lindy said, tilting her head as if to say what's the big deal.

Sallos grabbed Lindy's shirt. "You knew?"

"No, dumbass. I sensed them right before they attacked," Lindy snapped back, making no move to wriggle out of the other woman's grasp. Lindy's dreams had been especially bad. She had known of the attackers long before they had moved, but in her hazily fitful sleep had not noted them as threats until they moved to attack.

"Everyone stay calm. Security is dealing with the issue now. Please stay in your seats and do not panic," Allensco said, walking through the car.

When the conductor went to the next car Lindy sighed. "Ten guards dug into one line against thirty attackers who are just as skilled and well equipped. Plus what in Death's name is that wall of rock there? Mages erected a ritual like that. Takes skill," she whispered to herself, only loud enough for Halmar and his guards to overhear.

"Can you stop them?" Sallos asked sarcastically with an edge in her voice. Lindy pushed Halmar and Sallos down just as the other end of the car erupted in fire as a stray rocket found its way in. Splinters and gore covered the car, taking many more down than the initial blast.

"Which side?" Lindy asked, pulling a lump of wood from her shoulder.

As Lindy scanned the room calmly, the car erupted in panic. The few who could move rushed to other cars, causing a traffic jam and a few brawls. "They aren't here to get you out, are they?" Halmar asked.

Lindy held up the arm-length splinter she had ripped from her flesh with her rapidly healing arm. "With friends like these, who needs enemies? Plus no one here is anywhere close to me in power."

"So help fight off our attackers," Sallos said.

Lindy rolled her eyes. "Why should I? After they kill everyone else I'll just eliminate them. It's not like you can leave your charge, let alone keep up with me. So why should I? I am your prisoner, remember?" A few screams came from outside. "Well that's three defenders down," Lindy sighed. She looked up at the dark red stains above her.

"Fine. I'll defend you if you help to successfully protect the train," Halmar said in panic.

Sallos took out a key and moved to release Lindy but the manacles turned to a pile of rust and Lindy took the sword from the other woman's belt. Lindy moved to the hole in the car and called back to Halmar. "That's a terrible deal, but it seems like fun. Tell you what. Anyone who attacks me today dies, and I've got thirty targets picked out. Back in a jiffy!" After a brief wave Lindy leapt out of the train.

Halmar looked around. Terror and blood filled the car. "I feel like that was a bad idea," he sighed, watching his guards move around him.

"Regardless if that psycho wins or loses, then one problem will be dealt with," Sallos answered as she drew a pistol.

"Right. Either we have to deal with whatever attackers are left or that enigma," Halmar agreed.

When Lindy stepped out, a man in a blue uniform holding an overly complex rifle turned to her and raised his gun. "Get back!" he yelled. Three men on what could only be called steam-powered motorcycles sped over from below a small ridge immediately after. Lindy knew the guard would not turn in time much less mortally wound all three riders, so she froze the engines of their three motorcycles, then dashed at the riders and cut all three attackers in half while keeping their motorcycles and weapons intact. Lindy noted the guards' gear was complex but highly accurate and advanced while the attackers' gear was robust and reliable, even if some sported slipshod jury-rigging and heavy re-inforcement.

Lindy picked up one of the rider's carbines. "That's a lot of new design philosophies. Neat." She nodded to herself while thinking, *Ok, no more giving out new tech. They are already making some crazy shit way too early. I wonder how many elves or dragons use guns.*

One of the guards shot at her feet. "Who do you work for?" he yelled over.

Lindy did not see any immediate danger even after mentally going into full combat mode, so she raised both arms, keeping her weapons held but pointed away from the guards and train. "I'm just a retired mercenary traveling to Smog City. You guys looked like you needed a hand. Mind if I take care of these folks?" A new rider charged off from the main group that was attacking most of the guards at the improvised barricades that had been set up near the front of the train. Lindy spun and kicked the motorcycle in half before stabbing the rider in the heart and tossing him on the ground fluidly. "Also I am basically a dragon, so that's yes to helping you kill these bastards, right?" Lindy asked loudly, kicking the latest lifeless attacker into the middle of his allies.

"Fine, just shut up and fight!" the guard with the nicest uniform yelled from his position.

"Fine, just keep them from moving. I'll do the rest," Lindy yelled back before slipping into her shadow and reappearing in the middle of the attackers and cutting down four of them. Then her borrowed sword broke so she slipped her hand into a shadowy void that had just appeared and drew one of the attacker's axes. The axe handle was as big as she was and its blade was as big as her torso and abdomen combined. Spinning the weapon in one hand, Lindy set about cutting everything around her in half.

"Keep them from running!" the well-dressed guard yelled. A few attackers tried to flee but Lindy and the guards shot them down.

Lindy looked over some data she had collected during the fight.

Trill Von

Human male age 19

Affiliation: waste raiders

Job: mage/thief

Status: dying

Abilities: strength 15, vitality 23, mind 38, agility 22.

Talents: language wasteland/ spirit, teamwork, thrifty

Wound: cut in half

Skills: Athletics: journeyman, intimidate (power): apprentice, armor use (cloth, leather): adept, earth magic: journeyman, water magic: apprentice, dagger: apprentice, literacy: adept, first aid: apprentice, ride (cycle): adept, cooking: apprentice

Fellmar Cave

Human male age 43

Affiliation: waste raiders

Job: raider boss

Status: dying

Abilities: strength 45, vitality 69, mind 28, agility 32

Talents: Language: wasteland, menacing, jury rig, resistance (pain, disease): moderate, fearlessness, strafing run, rage

Wound: cut in half

Skills: Athletics: journeyman, intimidate (threat): journeyman, leadership: expert, planning: journeyman, rifle: journeyman, axe: adept, literary: apprentice, mechanic: apprentice, acrobatics: apprentice

> David Lossmera
> Human lupine age 23
> Affiliation: Heatwater international transport co.
> Job: guard
> Status: grunt
> Abilities: strength 22, vitality 26, mind 28, agility 32
> Talents: Language: wasteland/Otten, Resistance (pain/ fatigue): minor, empathetic
> Skills: Read intent: adept, athletics: adept, intimidate (basic): apprentice, diplomacy: apprentice, armor use (leather): adept, spear: apprentice, rifle: adept, knife: adept, law (international rail): apprentice, first aid: apprentice, literary: apprentice

These abilities seem low to me. If this is the new world standard then I wonder what happened, Lindy briefly mused to herself.

"What was that?" the well-dressed guard yelled over to Lindy, who stood in a pile of gore up to her knees.

Lindy sighed, tossing two weapons she had picked up into her shadow so she could study them later. "Backup. You are welcome."

"We can't pay you," the well-dressed guard grumbled.

Lindy walked over to the defense position the guards had set up. "My name is Lin, by the way. We are alive, so that's good enough for me." Then she pointed over to the hole she had jumped out from. "Although you did lose a few passengers."

The well-dressed guard mumbled, "Well um," then saluted. "I am captain Dren," he called before running off to the hole shouting, "Medical teams, with me!"

Lindy watched Dren run off, a smirk slowly spreading across her face. "This world seems like it will be even more fun than before." Then she looked over at the few guards still standing around. "Anyone got a spare set of socks?" One of the men looked at the gore Lindy was covered in and rushed off.

The man swiftly returned and handed over a pair of clean socks. "You can keep them, and thanks for the support."

Lindy took the socks and changed out of her gore-caked pair. She used her old socks to wipe down what she could which resulted in smearing the blood and viscera covering her, but making it less intense looking. "It's fine. They attacked me too, and I needed the exercise."

After taking a deep breath to still her mind, Lindy went back to her seat. Halmar and his guards were too spooked to talk but unlike the slowly calming passengers' reaction to how much blood was covering Lindy, Halmar and his followers were more uncomfortable with how swiftly Lindy had killed so many enemies. After all, she was still technically their captive, but Halmar knew that if Lindy wanted to make a fight of it no one around them could stop her. "Wake me up when we start moving, please," Lindy requested before going back to sleep.

After a few hours of fitful slumber Sallos poked Lindy tentatively a few times. Some minutes later she started poking Lindy rapidly until her eyes snapped open with an audible noise. "What?" Lindy asked.

Sallos froze, looking at her teammates for help. Halmar grumbled, "We are moving."

"Oh, thank you," Lindy nodded before sitting up and looking around the tarps that sealed the damage. Only Lindy was still sitting in the car, with the dead laid out in the rest of it. "You moved to another car?" Lindy asked.

"We would, but it took a while to wake you up so we are almost to my city, Lin," Halmar replied.

"Your city?" Lindy smirked, the air becoming colder. "I thought you and yours were placeholders for when she returns."

"Who?" Sallos asked.

Drowning out his guard's words, Halmar snapped. "How did you know that?"

"I am real old, remember? I knew Lindy very well, young man," Lindy smirked, now enjoying herself and wishing she could take a bath.

A dull thump echoed throughout the train car. "Who?" Halmar yelled as the guards drew their weapons.

A small female with horns and a tail jumped through a window and began to shake upon seeing Lindy. Lindy spoke rapidly, drowning out whatever her old comrade was going to say. "Hey Daffodil, you remember your old buddy Lin, right? Old fellow friend of Lindy. You still owe me at least one favor."

Daffodil was too shocked to move. Halmar's guards put away their weapons with intense resignation and annoyance as if this was normal. "Envoy Clifracer, you know this man?"

It took Daffodil a while to process what was happening but somehow Lindy's amused smirk made up her mind. "Um yes, Lin is an old comrade... He helped me get vengeance on one of my clan's mortal enemies. So can you absolve him of whatever lunacy you are holding him for?"

"Only if this absolves me from one of the debts my city owes," Halmar sighed.

"Fine!" Daffodil grumbled. Halmar and his guards were clearly surprised with how quickly the dragon before them agreed. Daffodil glared at Lindy. "I do not want to cover for any more of your insanity."

Lindy nodded, pulling out the carbine she had taken from the bandits from her shadow and beginning to clean it. "Ok no problem. Officially I am a shadow dragon, fire dragon old buddy"

"Whatever," Daffodil sighed, tossing herself into a seat next to Lindy and examining her closely. Halmar and his guards were about to leave before Daffodil called out to them. "You will help this one settle in *your* city, right, young man? Your debts are worth at least that much."

"Will he cause any chaos?" Halmar asked unhappily.

"Not enough to be a problem for you youngsters," Lindy replied as she studied the carbine.

"How many weapons do you have?" Halmar asked.

"More than my limbs," Lindy absently replied, ignoring the unease radiating from Halmar and company.

The train crossed a long bridge across a deep pit where all normal magic was powerless. Even Lindy's physical powers were hampered in the ever-expanding pit of her own making. The train passed under a heavy gate and into a station that could hold eight trains at once. Lindy and Daffodil followed Halmar out of the train. A few guards saluted Lindy as she passed. A woman once called Zandra Limore greeted them. Twenty elite guards and a few aides surrounded her. "I am viceroy Zandra Zigone. Sub-viceroy, what happened?" Lindy studied her old ward and Halmar. *Right, he's Hanna's great-grandson. Wow. Now I feel ancient,* she thought.

Halmar walked close to his mother. "Our offerings were lost but replaced with better ones. One guard died in that robbery. We brought the robber with us. He saved us from a large-scale bandit assault. The dragons demanded we exchange one of our debts by absolving Mr. Lin of the theft and murder in question and helping him settle down in our city."

Zandra looked at Lindy. "Mr. Lin, is it? Have we met before?"

"Long time no see, daughter of the Eternal," Lindy smirked. After a long pause she rolled her eyes. "What? Besides my dragon buddy, everyone else in this station is way younger than I am."

Zandra waved off her guards and walked close to her son's captive. "Do you know Lindy?" she whispered.

"We are close," Lindy whispered back.

Zandra recoiled. "So why did you kill my employee?"

"I was wounded badly and needed to fix myself but the guard was consumed due in part to a miscalculation," Lindy sighed.

"How much of a miscalculation?" Halmar asked, waving the guards to stop people from getting close to Lindy, Daffodil, his mother, and himself as they talked.

Lindy thought deeply for a few seconds. "Three jars of good healing herbs and some troll ichor would have made up the difference?"

Zandra shook he head. "That's how much a life is worth to you? Can you guarantee nothing like that will happen in my city?"

Lindy smiled. "First of all, you are the seat warmer. She seemed clear on that. But no, I can't guarantee such a thing. However as long as no one practically kills me, I will not need to consume life in that way." Then Lindy's stomach grumbled. "Speaking of consuming life, can I get a steak soon?" Daffodil took a steaming hot cheeseburger from a bag that radiated magic and shoved it into Lindy's hands. "Thanks," Lindy smiled before shoving the entire burger into her mouth.

"Right, you can stay. Son, you help him find a job," Zandra agreed. Throughout the conversation her gaze had slowly become more focused on Lindy as if trying to confirm something. Lindy pretended not to notice.

18

Bazooka in Plumbing Supply

Halmar looked at Lindy with a complicated expression that he was hiding from all but his mother and the two oldest beings in the station. Lindy and Daffodil shared an amused glance. "Well come on then," Halmar said evenly.

"Ok. Lead on," Lindy replied, not bothering to hide how funny she thought Halmar's attempt at subtlety was.

"Lin, this is the last time I'm going to help you like this," Daffodil called after her old ally. Most people were slightly upset at her but even if she was not right, no one without massive power would tell a dragon they were wrong. Daffodil however was just a bit sad as if the physical distance between her and Lindy signified the emotional and power differences between them.

Halmar led Lindy out of the red brick station and into the City of Smog. Lindy noticed that magic power was practically absent from the city. Steam power, or heat water as her auto-translator insisted it was called, ruled the town. Metal chimneys stuck out from most buildings, leading to boilers. Large smithies and artificer factories jostled for space with small clothing, tool, and general supply shops. They passed two large grocers that kept all their produce in heavily sealed buildings where a customer would order at a front window. All kinds of residue and dust from industrial processes mixed with the steam caused an acrid fog to cover the city.

"Longtooth! You here, old man?" Halmar called as he led Lindy into one of the nicer looking general supply shops.

"Its Longteeth, young man," a hunched old man with solid gold teeth and a beard almost as tall as he was waddled out of a back room, a bottle of rum in one hand.

"Fine. Still no luck with finding help?" Halmar asked. As they bickered, Lindy looked around the store. It was clean; a long counter sat next to a curtain leading to a back room. Shelves and cabinets were set in what could only be called orderly chaos. There was space to move but it was a maze nonetheless.

"That's right. My last assistant quit after three days," Longteeth sighed. Lindy suppressed a frown when she noticed that the man before her was descended from a beggar she had met long ago. *Is Fate having fun with me now?* Lindy thought.

"Well, could you give this fellow a shot now?" Halmar asked, pointing at Lindy who was peering around the shop with a bemused expression and moving with complete confidence.

"Another hot shot? I do need the help, but can a twig like that really do the job?" Longteeth asked.

Halmar whispered right into the old man's ear. "The envoy of the fire dragons vouched for him but I'll need you to help with lodging as well."

"Is that so?" Longteeth mused, fluffing his beard as he calculated possible loss and gain. After deciding that pissing off dragons for any-thing but the most solid of reasons was still a terrible idea, he nodded. "Fine. The young man can start tomorrow. I've got a spare cot in the back."

Halmar grinned. "Then I will leave Mr. Lin to you. Thank you." Before Longteeth could ask more, the sub-viceroy was long gone.

"Well this is awkward," Lindy grumbled from behind her new boss.

Longteeth jumped a little in surprise but extended a hand to Lindy. "Well, let's make the best of this. Will you be all right, young man?"

"I am confident in my raw physical abilities and cleverness. Just show me what I need to do and we will get along well." Lindy returned the handshake and followed her boss into the back room. They spent the rest of the day setting up a small living space behind some cabinets and screens, then went over manifests and customer service.

That night Lindy slipped into her cot in only an undershirt. As she gazed up at the wooden ceiling Lindy realized she felt odd about not being in combat. "Well, the worst thing about war is the time you have to think afterwards and getting used no longer being in a warzone." She sighed before drifting off into a fitful slumber.

The next morning Lindy made sure to change into her still-bloody clothes and walked out into the storeroom where a small boy stood. "Who are you?" Lindy asked, reflexively adopting a menacing aura until she remembered where she was and relaxed.

The boy tensed up but when he noticed Lindy calming down the boy nodded as if something made sense. "I come bearing breakfast," the boy proclaimed.

"Um, what?" Lindy asked.

"You are the new hire, right?" the boy asked as he lifted a sandwich bag.

Lindy took the food and smiled. "That's right. I'm Lin. And you are?"

The boy looked Lindy over once. "You need new clothes. My name is Grimoire Fellstrom."

Lindy looked at the boy closer. "Oh a dwarf. My apologies. I assumed you were a human child."

"I am still a child," the dwarf boy replied somewhat unhappily. "But I am still older than most of you humans." He paused, looking over Lindy again. "You are human, right?"

"Sort of. I am still older than you," Lindy mused.

"Fine," Grimoire shrugged. "I've got more deliveries. Good day, strange one." With that, the boy rushed out of the back door to a cart filled with sandwich bags.

Weird kid, Lindy thought.

Yes, truly very odd, Death's voice replied in her head.

What do you want? Lindy replied back mentally as she made her way to the front counter while eating a sandwich that was some meat and a lot of vegetables.

Found anyone you need to kill yet? Death asked back.

There are a few I need to check, but for those kinds of details I need to be close to my target to really know. So I will have a hard time unless either I travel constantly or you help. Lindy explained during the process of opening up the shop. It was a bit early for that, but Lindy had already completed most of the early morning prep the night before.

What do you need? Death asked.

Send me a list every year with the names and approximate locations of those I need to kill, Lindy replied.

Right. I'll add you to the send-to list. Also your shades have been a bit too fanatical about killing off our targets, so I'll leave them out of the messages this time, Death replied.

"So that's why things still work," Lindy said.

Well their fanaticism is an issue but with you back and low-key, things should work out now, Death noted.

"Well thanks for that, old man," Lindy replied.

A bundle of clothes was tossed at Lindy from behind. "If you want to thank me then get changed," Longteeth said from behind her.

Lindy picked up the clothes and rushed back to her bedroom. "Right, thanks boss," she called back. After she was dressed in the set of sturdy men's clothes Lindy went to work.

Lindy's first day was slow. After a few pointers Longteeth went to negotiate with some suppliers. From what he saw Lindy had set up the shop well so he chose to trust her. Three customers had shown up by midday. Two bought simple soaps and oil cleaners, the other window shopped.

Grimoire walked into the shop with an elderly woman. Lindy was spooked when she noted that the old woman was Frost reincarnated.

The dwarf boy put three sandwich bags on the counter. "Do you mind if we have lunch here?" he asked.

Lindy looked outside. The crowds had thinned so she hung up a sign that said 'out to lunch' on the door. "I'll get some chairs," she said while going into the back room. After setting up three chairs and a large stool behind the counter, Lindy took the bags of sandwiches and put them on the stool. "Have a seat. I don't plan on taking a long time for lunch."

The old woman sat down and peered at Lindy's face briefly before taking out a sandwich, a thermos of tea, and four cups. "The owner is out?" she asked.

"That's right. I am called Lin, by the way." Lindy smiled as she took a bite of sandwich.

"Faldrea the Swift," the old woman introduced herself.

Lindy ate swiftly and washed down the slightly heartier sandwich of salted meat, mustard, and cabbage. "Wow, you don't have to eat that fast, sir," Grimoire noted. Faldrea glanced at the boy like he was an idiot.

"Until now I have only fought for a living, even when the world was sort of at peace," Lindy nodded, then she giggled as the young boy froze up. "So I have a habit of eating like my life depends on it."

Grimoire rallied quickly. "But it does," she noted evenly. *I really hope this kid does not treat me like Lu. I've had enough difficult people to deal with for an eternity but I never worked out how to deal with Lu,* Lindy thought sadly.

"Well, the sandwiches are prepaid so you don't have to rush. By the way, I run the textile shop across the street," Faldrea explained.

Lindy looked up at the ceiling. "So were you curious about the newbie?"

"Something like that. I heard you are a dragon. Is that true?" Faldrea asked.

"Don't delve too deep. Dragons are an odd bunch," Grimoire muttered before hurriedly adding, "Not that there is anything wrong with that."

Lindy truly smiled from the bottom of her heart as she ruffled the boy's hair. "Kid, I know I am an odd one but I take pride in that." Then she glanced at the old human. "And I am more or less a dragon."

"Is there a difference?" Grimoire asked as he rubbed his head.

Lindy finished a cup of tea and sighed. "Not as far as anyone alive now is concerned." Looking up, she saw the streets were getting some more traffic. "Well, lunch is up. I'm going to open up again. You can leave the furniture where it is."

Grimoire rushed out. Faldrea walked slowly outside. Before she crossed the threshold she paused, turning to Lindy. "By the way young lady, have we met before?"

"Not in your lifetime, so don't worry about it," Lindy waved back. When Faldrea left Lindy collapsed on the counter and took a few deep breaths. "I hope she does not remember. Not after all the pain I caused her." Images of the most memorable times she had spent with Fraya and Frost, both the best and the worst, flashed though Lindy's mind. "Well, I've already lived way too long. No reason to be greedy," Lindy mumbled to herself before sweeping the floor and getting back to work.

After a week Lindy got used to her routine. One night massive amounts of necromantic energy built up within her. Lindy woke up with a snap. Already feeling an intense adrenaline high due to the otherworldly awakening, Lindy sunk into the shadows of the room, walking the next moment into a deep cave. A list of names, each with a date and location, appeared in her hand as all life within the cave and for a mile around died. Lindy used the function Conduit was named for and linked her mind to Death's realm, setting up a communication line. "Next time maybe link this list to a ritual? You almost killed off a city just now."

Death's reply came soon after while Lindy skimmed the list. "You really are a sponge for the concepts of life and death. Point taken, but anyone else that uses that ritual will be on the list. I'll make it so only extreme-level necromancers have access."

"Fine, but you'd better only update this once a year. How about first day of each year? So I can go somewhere with no bystanders," Lindy replied back.

"Fine, as long as you complete the lists I give you," Death agreed.

After Lindy teleported back to her room a twelve headed hydra poked its head out of the shadows in the floor. "Hey, that terrifying thing smelled like the boss. Let's tell the others," its oldest and heavily scarred head muttered. A long debate between the heads followed about if they should tell the only other ten hydras like it that their master might be back.

Lindy was unable to get back to sleep after her near city-wide disintegration incident. Longteeth found his employee sitting at the counter when he walked in from his apartment above the shop. After one long look the old man grumbled. "You know today we are open half as long, right?"

Lindy looked up at her mortal boss. "Oh, I must have forgot," she replied lethargically.

"Right," Longteeth nodded. "I'll man the counter today. So go get some firewood or something."

"As long as you are still paying then no problem," Lindy managed a weak smile.

"Maybe you should gather in the forest. That should wake you up," Longteeth answered as he shuffled behind the counter.

Lindy took a deep breath, not willing to admit how rattled she felt about nearly destroying a city in her sleep. "Ok. Thanks, boss."

Lindy walked out of the shop. Since she did not feel like eating Lindy did not stop walking until she was out of the city. "Well I've got some time to kill," she murmured before sinking into her own shadow. *Let's get three hits out of the way today,* she thought.

Lindy stepped out of the shadow of a high wall that surrounded a courtyard and smaller wall. Her first target was on the smallest of the three continents of this world. Even with the basic info she had to go on, Lindy had gained some knowledge of this world during the times her physical body had died. The smaller continent reminded her of Japan from her world. The one Lindy had first found herself on was by far the largest and the last was roughly half that size.

The first thing Lindy noticed was not that she was at the right address but the heavy feeling of wrongness one man in particular was giving off from within the manor. It was the middle of the night here, which did not do Lindy's sleep-deprived brain or internal clock any favors. Only a handful of staff and the odd man were still moving around so Lindy leapt though a window and silently bolted down a hallway. After slipping into a large room she felt someone watching her, which was expected because she knew the man was in the room. "Mr. Qinn, I presume?" Lindy asked one of the deep shadows in the room, not noticing the deep smell of blood both old and new in the room.

A tall lanky man with red eyes and fangs walked out of the shadows. "Another mouse," he spat before doing a double take. "Where are you from, child?"

"One of the other continents," Lindy shrugged.

"Other continents?" the man mused. His lax attitude spoke volumes of his self-confidence and inability to see Lindy as a threat. This was oddly refreshing to the near-immortal assassin. *Right, none of the continents have discovered each other yet,* Lindy remembered.

Lindy took out Transcendence and slashed at the man. He moved swiftly so Lindy only cut off a lower arm and left a small gash in the target's chest. The man's eyes narrowed, now seeing Lindy as a threat, but before he could summon reinforcements Lindy stabbed her dagger into a shadow, its blade piercing the man's heart from his back before his blood became dust. The man died not knowing what had happened, but managing to think of a few guesses before the alchemically-created vampire's mind stopped.

After making sure the target was dead Lindy slipped back into the darkness, only to step out into a small fishing village on the same continent near a shop that had clearly not been lived in for some time. Upon walking out of the shop's back yard Lindy ran into a woman. "Who are you?" the villager asked in a guarded manner, preparing to flee.

Lindy smiled, which made the woman tremble. Looking down, Lindy noted she had some blood on her clothes. "My employer is looking for the Bain brothers," she explained.

"They are not here," the woman said quickly before turning to flee. Lindy held the woman's shoulders. Even with Lindy weakening her strength as much as she could, it caused the villager some pain.

"They angered my employer. Which way did they go?" Lindy asked in a deadpan manner after cutting away most of her feelings temporarily.

"The temple outside of town." The woman stumbled as her legs lost their will to work. Lindy raised an eyebrow and the woman pointed at a road leading to a hill. After setting down the villager, Lindy walked off. "Hey, what you are going to do?" the woman called after her.

"Just collecting a debt. The cleanup, however, is not my concern." Lindy shrugged as she ran off without looking back.

Lindy ran past some trees she did not recognize on a small dirt path and up a wide moss-covered stairway. As she neared the rotting temple three soulless husks sprang out. They acted from hunger and madness and nothing else. Lindy cut all three in half before they landed on the ground. This time she deflected the blood properly.

"Ok. One more for today," Lindy sighed before slapping her head. She had felt an unnatural strain on reality. "Really why! Well, good thing it's my day off from mortality." Lindy sunk back into the shadows, reappearing as near to the unnatural presence as she could. The power was messing with magic and all of her powers.

Death's voice invaded Lindy's mind. *We have a problem.*

"Big bad reality-degrading presence, I know! I am on my way already! Now shut up and let me work!" Lindy shouted verbally and in her mind as she ran at full speed to where she first sensed the still-growing presence. Death's will fled her mind as Lindy ran even faster.

The closer Lindy got to her destination the fuzzier the atmosphere became. In a small field Lindy found the source of the reality-collapsing energies. An array of symbols written in all manner of substances and dabbed over with even more filled the clearing. A hazy tear in space itself wavered around the area. The grassy clearing shifted to a high-tech rubble-filled spaceship and back. A floating cylinder seemed to be observing two humans wearing sleek sci-fi-like suits. The young woman was still conscious but unable to do more than move her eyes. The boy next to her was sprawled out, unmoving in her grasp.

Lindy analyzed the cylinder.

Boee Brin the Misinformed

Genderless animated phylactery: ageless

Affiliation: Itself

Job: nobody

Status: bored

Abilities: strength 8, vitality 22, mind 842, agility 621

Talents: language common: (Derndell, wasteland, elemental), fearless, multi casting times six, empower (ritual): greater, chaotic epiphany

Curse: phylactery as soul bound body (self inflicted), madness

Blessing: floating: master

Skills: acrobatics: journeyman, intimidate (basic): expert, necromancy: extreme: time magic: master, space magic: extreme, literacy: expert, ritual: master, telekinesis: adept, herbalism: journeyman

Out of Lindy's shadow came her plate armor which fit itself around her. Pulling out her rifle, Lindy grumbled. "I so do not get paid enough for this shit." She fired a few volleys as fast as she could at the animated phylactery, making one clean shot and a few grazes. While the phylactery was shaking frantically, Lindy leapt at it.

The cylinder fired slivers of timelessness at her which penetrated deep into her armor. One sliver managed to take a chunk out of Lindy's side, then she landed on the deranged jar, smashing it in the process. Space and time both shook. Time bubbled all around them, nowhere and in some other time all at once. Lindy tossed the remains of the jar into the most solid tear of spacetime before grabbing the two humans and running for dear life.

I got the culprit but time's still all kinds of weird. So help me shut it down! Lindy yelled in her mind.

After maybe a half a mile of running full tilt Death's garbled voice replied, *Brace for impact.*

Lindy tossed herself to the ground, making sure to cushion the two humans and keep them under her. Then the world rumbled and a crater centered on the field she had fled was gouged out all the way to her toes. "Oh of the love of all that is... something or other. I need a stiff drink."

The young woman who had some of her faculties back asked in what sounded mostly like English abbreviations to Lindy, "Thanks, sir. What zone is this?"

The air around the young woman was otherworldly but human. "This world is likely not your reality," Lindy noted.

"What do you mean?" the young woman asked. For the first time in ages Lindy fully appreciated her auto-translation ability.

"You are what we call an outworlder. This is not your universe." Lindy got up and waited for the young woman to regain her footing.

"So what was that?" the woman asked.

That's what I'd like to know, Lindy replied snidely in her mind.

If we let it get out of hand then that could have consumed this reality, Death informed his helper.

"What the fuck!" Lindy yelled before realizing she had spoken out loud. "Sorry, my boss is being a bonehead."

"What?" the woman asked, looking around before nodding. "Oh, you have one of those too."

"I have long-range magic communication tied to a single entity," Lindy noted before replying back to Death. *So what the fuck. Is this common?*

It better not be. A death died to something like that once and we are still trying to clean that up, Death replied.

That dark zone you guys could not influence? Lindy asked.

Yes that. Now I have four other realities to manage as well, so don't expect me to help you again any time soon, Death said.

"I hate my job," Lindy sighed, watching the young woman pick up the boy. "I'm Lindy, by the way. Who are you two?"

"Feldspar Comet. You can call me Fel. The kid's my little brother. He goes by Molder," Fel replied. Looking around, she asked in a soft voice, "So can I go back to my universe?"

"Maybe. I am not an expert on interdimensional summoning but I could introduce you to some folks who can research that." Lindy shrugged, allowing her armor to sink back into the shadows.

"Where are they?" Fel asked, furrowing her brows at the lack of animal life or civilization all around them.

"One teleport away," Lindy replied.

"Ok. By the way, your galactic standard is quite good," Feldspar noted before stopping. "Wait. How do you know it?"

Lindy grinned. "I don't. I can automatically translate languages. That normally only helps with languages from this reality but before I came to this universe I spoke English most of the time. Which is very similar to your galactic standard."

"You are an outworlder?" Feldspar asked.

Lindy nodded. "So are you coming with or not?"

"Fine," Feldspar sighed. "So what do I do?"

Lindy walked up to Feldspar and chuckled, "Cross your fingers," as the three of them were swallowed by an unnaturally spreading shadow.

The three travelers arrived on a small hill covered in dusty ruins that a forest had long reclaimed. Lindy fell to her knees wincing. Then she checked her side. "Oh I'm bleeding. That's odd." Looking around she remembered the hill but not the old forest. One pillar pitted with old battle damage stood taller than the rest of the ruin. "Never thought I'd come back here." She spat some blood. The stone and moss where her blood fell twisted into evil-looking plants.

"Hold on. I am a medic," Feldspar said, rushing over. Noticing the deep gash on Lindy's side the traveler asked reproachfully in a stellar bedside manner, "Why did you not say anything?"

"Because normally this would have healed by now," Lindy sputtered.

A small female with wings landed on what was once a wall. "I wondered what was going on, Lin. Picking up more strays, it seems." Feldspar was clearly afraid but still worked to check Lindy's vitals. Molder chose that moment to fully wake up, only to faint in terror immediately.

Daffodil came closer. Upon seeing Lindy's wound she grabbed Feldspar's hands, pulling the stranger to her feet. "Don't touch that." As the otherworldly medic struggled, Daffodil looked down at Lindy. "First time I've seen you roughed up like that. What happened?"

Lindy turned her head to her audience, not wishing to stand up. "My blood changes things it touches, and unless this dragon here can speak fluent English, I doubt you two will be able to understand each other."

Both women looked at each other and spoke in unison.

"Ok, makes sense. Otherworlders then?" Daffodil nodded.

"A dragon for real?" Feldspar asked.

"Yes and yes. So can you two understand each other?" Lindy asked.

"Nope. No idea what your new pets are saying." Daffodil shook her head.

Feldspar got on her knees and looked at Lindy close up. "You can speak to both of us at the same time?"

"That's right." Lindy tried to laugh but had to turn her head and coughed instead. "A few weeks of rest and I'll be fine. So Fel, how about I see about getting you a job?"

Feldspar looked at her brother and sighed, suddenly looking weak. "Ok. We will need a stretcher."

Without looking away from Feldspar, Lindy asked, "Hey Daffodil, you know anywhere that compiles otherworlder data?"

"Otten would be the best bet. They have a whole language institute over there now," Daffodil replied.

"Then could you invite some researchers over to talk with these two?" Lindy asked.

"That sounds like a pain. Why?" the dragon asked.

"Because I'll owe you a small favor and your job right now must be a little boring, right?" Lindy smiled as blood dribbled down her chin.

Daffodil looked down at Lindy and spread her wings. "Fine, but only because it's you."

As the dragon flew off, a few coats and spears appeared next to Lindy from a shadowy void. "That should do for making a stretcher," Lindy nodded before passing out.

Lindy felt a sharp pinch and instantly woke up, flipping the person who had pinched her onto the bed she had been lying on and keeling on top of them. It took Lindy a few seconds to notice four important things.

1. She was in her room back in the shop.
2. Her shirt was half off and a roll of bandages had just stopped rolling along the floor.
3. Feldspar was lying under her. In other words, Feldspar had woken Lindy up, regardless of the medic's intent.
4. She was still bleeding.

Lindy let Feldspar go, then tumbled back onto the bed. "Sorry about that. Did you get any blood on you?" Lindy sighed.

"No, I'm fine," Feldspar nodded before glancing at Lindy's chest. "So you were a woman after all."

"Yes, but I leave what I am ambiguous here," Lindy replied, evenly looking up at the ceiling as various jumbled events from the past surged through her mind. Feldspar was in a heavy leather suit and she resumed bandaging Lindy.

"Why would you do that?" Feldspar asked.

Lindy grimaced as her wound was prodded with hot iron tools. "First of all, I am known as Lin here. I have more in common with dragons than humans, despite technically being one myself."

Feldspar adjusted Lindy's shirt. "Technically?"

"That's right," Lindy agreed. Feldspar wanted to say more but Lindy cut her off. "You will help me with my shift tomorrow. I'll even pay you half my earnings."

Feldspar looked around. "I think we were invited to stay here by an old man, so that should be fine."

"Oh, you met Longteeth. Ok, I'll talk to him tomorrow. Some language experts should come by eventually to help you out as well," Lindy explained.

Feldspar began to take off her blood-spattered suit. After cleaning herself up a little she looked around the sparse improvised room. "Is that normal treatment for otherworlders?"

Lindy giggled. "No, it's not at all."

Feldspar narrowed her eyes and examined Lindy. "So why go so far to help us? You called in some favors from powerful people, right?"

Lindy smiled as she became tired. "I did. Let's just say I am passing on the kindness I received once when I was in your shoes." With that, Lindy fell into a deep slumber.

Late the next morning Lindy woke up. Low voices echoed in the building. Lindy identified Faldrea, Feldspar, and Longteeth, but there was one more she did not recognize. "For the last time, who is she?" the unfamiliar voice asked.

Lindy closed her eyes and after a deep breath snuck into her room's dimness only to flop against the door leading into the shop. Lindy noticed Zandra, who stood next to an angry teenager. "Who's the kid?" Lindy sputtered. All eyes fell on her immediately.

"Who are you?" the teenager asked.

Lindy tried to smile but grimaced. She frowned realizing she had not fully healed yet. Feldspar rushed to support her savior while Zandra began speaking quickly after noticing the mirth in Lindy's eyes. "The wounded one is Lin. He is the one who requested a translator."

"Oh well, for now you can call me Teodor Warling Otten," the young man said, bowing. However, his puffed-up smugness made it hard for Lindy to take him seriously, even if she could tell from his blood that Teodor was a descendant of the Otten royal family.

"Right. Fel does not even speak our language yet, let alone know this world's history, so the status of some princeling will be lost on her," Lindy nodded.

"What?" Feldspar and Teodor exclaimed, both seeming equally put out.

"How did someone like you call in a favor with the dragons?" Teodor retorted, rallying quickly.

"I owe them this time, otherwise I'd have called in two favors in as many weeks," Lindy smirked. Then she turned to Longteeth. "I think the younger one will be enough to help me today." After helping her benefactor to a chair, Feldspar was pushed to the princeling. "Help her learn the local language and some history, then your kingdom and I may be more even."

"Who are you?" Teodor asked.

"An old veteran who was good friends with Covell Otten," Lindy replied before a coughing fit took her. If not for coughing up blood at that moment, Zandra may have immediately begun to suspect the real identity of the one she knew as Lin.

For the next few weeks Molder helped Lindy with the shop. The boy needed very little in the way of training past getting the shop's admittedly jumbled layout explained and reviewed a few times so he could stock shelves and guide customers around. Lindy handled the communication with customers and payment.

After nearly a month Lindy was fully healed, which was easily the longest any of her selves had spent healing in this world. On her first day off since basically resting at home, Lindy chose to go on a walk. Feldspar was estimated to need another two months of nearly nonstop training to get acquainted with her new reality. Feldspar had begun to teach her brother some of the local language over dinner. For all his faults, Teodor had picked up the so-called galactic standard, which still sounded to Lindy like oversimplified abbreviations being used in place of words. A few others with translation abilities helped a great deal with this effort, along with Feldspar trying to use bigger words and speaking slower. If not for the favor she had called in and the academic worth Feldspar would be able to share, not just about her language and universe, but also being a living witness to another up-to-then undocumented reality, the cost of her lesson would have been quite immense, especially given the importance of her instructors.

Molder followed Lindy around the city. After a time she led them to a park overlooking the ever-expanding magic eating hole she had created so long before. Lindy tried to analyze the rules the hole worked under only to get a headache when she tried to envision its workings all at once. "Damn, it's going to take years to fix this mess."

"Did you make this?" Molder asked like the curious child he was instead of the mature act he favored.

Lindy redirected the child's attention with an inquiry of her own, one that had been nagging at her for some time because her ability to sense bloodlines told her the young otherworlders were not related by blood. "So I've been meaning to ask — how you are related to Feldspar?"

"She's my sister," Molder replied like it was self-evident.

"But not by blood," Lindy countered.

"So what? We are family," the boy replied a tad harshly, not for himself but for his sister.

Lindy paused for a time, noticing how she believed her skills were infallible but acknowledging that at the very least the way she used them may not always be right. "You are right. I apologize. Sorry, Molder," Lindy tried hard to say clearly.

"Are you really?" Molder asked.

Lindy sighed. "Yes. In this case I freely admit I was an insensitive idiot." Then she patted the boy's head. "Still, you have a very good sister."

"Of course I do," Molder replied, now beaming that his remaining family was being complimented.

"Right. So any chance you want to learn how to use a sword?" Lindy asked, needing to refocus her mind and energy away from both holes she had dug for herself.

"Will I be able to help my sister if I do?" Molder asked.

"Swords are still more common than guns in this world. So at the very least it will not hurt. Better to be prepared than left clueless, right?" Lindy asked.

"Well ok then," the boy agreed, trying to sound more like a serious adult again.

In the park Lindy found a pair of sticks. She used one to demonstrate how to use a blade while explaining things to watch out for and take advantage of. After work the next day Lindy had completed making two wooden swords. For the next month after work they used those in place of sticks. Slowly Lindy switched to overseeing the training routine she and Molder had built up.

After a time Lindy noticed that the long scar where she had been so badly wounded had yet to go away. It served as a reminder of her once-forgotten humanity.

One day after work Halmar walked up to Lindy during her observation of Molder and the pit. "Lin, I'd like you to come with me," the half-elf said.

Lindy looked up from her study of the pit. "How long will this take?"

"A few hours," Halmar replied. He glanced at Molder, who was far too focused on his training to see anything or anyone but Lindy and his heavy wooden sword. "He's got solid fundamentals. Is that your doing?"

"He was a novice a few weeks ago," Lindy explained. "I just thought I should try my hand at teaching a little."

"You could be a very successful teacher then. I never knew you had that talent," Halmar replied.

"Me neither. Everything else I've done has taken lives or spare change," Lindy nodded sagely.

Halmar shook his head and changed the subject. "Well, whatever. The hill outside of town's a bit weird. I thought someone wise should look at it."

"If you mean me, then you mean old," Lindy shrugged. A thin smile crossed her face as Molder executed a particularly clean thrust and swipe. "I am far too much of a fool to be called wise," Lindy whispered.

"Well none of our experts could make anything of it and you are the most unusual citizen here, so I'd like you to take a look," Halmar allowed.

Lindy tapped her student on the head. "Go home and help with the chores. I may be late, so don't worry about having my dinner ready." After Molder ran off without even a second glance at Halmar, Lindy sighed. "Why am I always the last resort?" then held up her hands to forestall any comments. "Well then young man, lead the way."

In a huff Halmar began to walk to one of the gates. "I am not that young," he muttered.

"There are only a few dragons and elves I'd call old. Everyone else is a child to me," Lindy laughed.

19

Thicker Than Mud

It did not take long to for the pair to walk out of the city and up to the ruins that still held some difficult memories for Lindy, even over two hundred years later. The ruins themselves were overgrown by dark blue, purple, black and red thrones, flowers and vines to the point where the top of the hill was impassable without doing very heavy damage to the local area. They stopped near the top of the ridge at a wall of vines thicker than Lindy's arm. "Well, have you seen anything like this?" Halmar asked.

Memories of the fight with her grandmother, a dryad's grove, and one of the times she had died passed swiftly in her mind. "Once, yes," Lindy answered after pushing down the dull feelings that had tried to make themselves known.

Halmar went from concerned to very interested. "What caused it?"

"Blood," Lindy sighed.

"Yours?" Halmar asked, his voice just a touch harder.

Lindy thought hard and fast for a few seconds. After analyzing the hazy memories of her death in a grove she came up with best answer. "It could do this, but you would need an unreasonable amount of mine to cause this, I think," while looking at Halmar's eyes becoming less and less doubtful. Once she had bled out in the area but the speed of the corruption this time was far more intense. She was aware that blood like hers was the root of the problem and that something else had empowered it to allow a change to this extent; either that, or the blood was from a far bigger body. "By the way, when did this start?" Lindy added after a long pause before Halmar could shuffle away in defeat.

"It began a week ago and expanded every few days until now," Halmar sighed, now at his wit's end.

"That's not right," Lindy blurted out. She did not need the body's agitated demeanor to urge her on. "If blood like mine caused this then either more than a few bodies' worth would be needed or something would need to empower it. That stuff should spread fast. I don't know if it grows in spurts but given its fuel and properties, I doubt this growth formed on its own power."

Halmar took a deep breath, looking closely. He did not seem to be well rested. "Who else has blood like that?" he asked calmly.

"Besides Lindy, no one I know," Lindy shrugged.

"That's not funny, Lin. Are you her son or something?" Halmar spat.

"More like a creation or experiment, but even all her blood did not do something like this," Lindy shrugged.

Halmar ran a hand though his hair. "You mentioned properties. What specifically?"

Lindy chose to throw the half-elf boy a bone just this once. "Life, death, shadows, chaos, and maybe regrowth. I am not an expert on her blood, but it seems to mirror her purpose?"

"That's not much, but more than I had before. Thanks," Halmar nodded before walking off.

Lindy took one last look around trying to find the other presence that had been observing them before outwardly giving up. She made a mental note to be more on guard for whatever it was that was using the corruption around the hill to mask itself, which had been surprisingly effective against her.

The walk back seemed shorter. Lindy arrived in Longteeth's shop through its back door. Her boss, Molder, and Feldspar were still at a table in one of the back rooms. A large half-full pot of stew sat between them. "You are late," Longteeth helpfully informed her.

"One of the kids asked me to look at something," Lindy grumbled as she began serving herself.

"A kid?" Feldspar asked.

"She means the dumb whatever-you-call-it," Molder began.

"Viceroy," Lindy supplied helpfully past a mouth full of toast.

"Right, him," Molder nodded.

"Don't say that so casually! Any kind of viceroy is a big deal to us." Feldspar corrected her use of the local dialect, now almost perfect.

"You mean most of us," Longteeth smiled, pointing at Lindy who was rapidly finishing the others' leftovers.

"Right. But I still have no idea why," Feldspar grumbled, sitting back in her chair.

"First of all, you are better off not knowing. Secondly, almost everyone is young to me," Lindy replied in the brief moment her mouth was empty before shoveling in more food. A loud series of knocks echoed throughout the building.

"We are closed!" Longteeth yelled from his seat but the knocking only increased in volume.

"I'll handle it," Feldspar offered when she was already halfway there. Less than a minute later she came rushing back with a middle-aged woman sporting very fancy robes and a massive hat.

"And this is…?" Lindy began.

"Which one of you shares the blood of the first prophet?" the woman demanded in a hyperactive manner.

"Who?" Lindy tilted her head but her dining companions all looked at her, which drew the intruder's gaze as well. Lindy glared past the woman at part of the wall. "Halmar, what the fuck, man."

Halmar peered into the room. "You expect me to stop a pope?"

"She's your what?" Lindy looked at the pair closely. "Great-niece? So yes, act your age young man."

"My great-grandparents are his grandparents." The woman nodded before asking, "So how are you related to Lindy the first prophet?"

Lindy crossed her arms. "Something like an experiment, but not in the same way as the shades or her hydras."

"So you are her daughter?" the pope asked.

"I am Lin. What should I call you?" Lindy asked, smiling as Long-teeth and Halmar realized she was in fact female.

"Jessica, fourth pope of the Everlasting church," the woman answered.

"Cool. So can we talk in private some other day? I have work tomorrow," Lindy replied.

The pope's face scrunched up but when she looked around her face loosened. "Oh right, that would be best, wouldn't it. This time next week then?"

"Sounds good to me. See you midday here then?" Lindy smiled, getting up and sticking out her hand.

Jessica shook her hand vigorously. "Yes, it's a date." Then she left with Halmar in tow.

"Well that's one storm dealt with," Lindy muttered, looking around the room at her very tense dining companions "Well good night," she said before fleeing to her room.

Early the next day Feldspar was told her lessons would be put on hold until further notice because Teodor had to attend the ceremonies, meetings, and brunches Jessica had set up with the local upper class. They were to maintain the hold the Everlasting church had on the humans living around the wasteland, because they were in a war for the hearts and minds of the human race with the shade-dominated Church of Shrew. Molder was given small errands while Feldspar and Lindy manned the shop. Their boss had taken a train late that night to see about expanding his business.

It was a slow morning which allowed Lindy to do some inventory management. Just as she was about to go over the logs to see what was selling well and what was not, a soft scuffle began on the shoproom floor. Lindy flew out of the back room to see a shade banging on the counter. Feldspar was explaining, "Like I said sir, this shop has no relation to the local government."

"That's a lie and you know it," the man sputtered.

The shade reached across the counter but Lindy grabbed his arm before he could assault her co-worker. "The shop has no direct relation to the government but the viceroy is something of a personal friend of mine. Now get out." Lindy's words came out firm and harsh.

The man went into a trance at Lindy's command and walked outside. Screams followed soon after. Lindy rushed outside to find the man ripping himself apart in the street.

She analyzed the man.

Solmeer Grugeborn
Shade male age 23
Affiliation: Church of Shrew acolyte, Agent of the order of dust
Job: spy
Status: under absolute command (harsh)
Abilities: strength 32, vitality 53, mind 24, agility 12
Talents: forgettable, single minded, language (common washland, order of dust), aura of menace, fanatic
Wound: multiple lacerations, missing eye (left), minor bone damage
Skills: Athletics: journeyman, intimidate (basic): expert, armor use (leather/ cloth): adept, dagger: journeyman, stealth (tailing/ hiding): adept, poison: journeyman, Shrewism basic lore and history: adept

"Well shit," Lindy cursed, realizing her hold over the shades was just as strong as ever, if not more. She sprinted past the guards while they recovered from their shock and revulsion and knelt down next to the shade. Lindy whispered to him, "I absolve you of the last order. My new command is you never saw me today." She rushed back to the shop as the man's yelling became pained mewling and the gasps of terror became less intense but more numerous. All the while, two intense gazes from some of the local bell towers followed Lindy during her short foray outside.

The day saw very few customers. Near closing time, an elf wearing a deep hood that had a lingering aura of power nearly identical to Lindy's walked in.

> Carla Faywind
>
> Elf female age 189
>
> Affiliation: Faywind clan
>
> Job: agent
>
> Status: exiled by the dryads
>
> Abilities: strength 118, vitality 245, mind 189, agility 312
>
> Talents: forgettable, single minded, language (common wasteland/ jungle elvish/ common Derndell/ forest spirit), double shot, swift reload, swift aim, vital strike, innate spell: short range teleport
>
> Skills: athletics: expert, armor use (leather/ cloth): journeyman, dagger: expert, stealth (hiding): expert, bow: master, spear: journeyman, herbalism: journeyman, tracking (all-land): journeyman, survival (all-land): adept. Negotiate (equal terms): adept

Lindy could tell the newcomer was Anna Faywind's daughter and these were her stats, but all her other senses were blocked by the aura sticking to her. Even working out as much as Lindy had done was a struggle. "You are here for me," Lindy called over to Carla who had begun to pick through some knickknacks near the door. Carla turned to leave but stopped when Lindy added, "We can talk in the back room, Carla. It's the least I can do for the child of a fellow traitor to the Derndell kingdom."

Carla spun around and marched right up to Lindy. "How much do you know?" she whispered.

"About Anna or my old teacher who was also a Faywind?" Lindy smiled. "I know you are helping someone watch me," she added with a wink, firmly gripping the young elf's wrist before either of them noticed.

"Let me go," Carla wailed.

Lindy did not pay any attention to her new conversation partner. Instead she called to Feldspar. "Take over the counter for a bit, would you?" And she dragged Carla into the back room.

As soon as they were out of sight Lindy dragged the panicking elf into her shadow and reemerged in the odd cave she had found before. "Why the hydra den?" Carla yelled.

"That's not important. You have been near something or someone like me. Who are they?" Lindy snapped.

Carla's legs gave out. "Who and what are you?" she stammered.

A massive serpentine head peeked out of a shadowy void in the floor. "Oh hi mom," it said happily. Eleven more heads erupted from the void. "It's mom!" "Hey mum." "Where were you?" "Are you ok?" "Are you hungry?" "Can we go hunting?" They began to babble at once.

"Shut up!" Lindy interrupted. "Get out here," she commanded when the babbling stopped. Three massive twelve-headed hydras with pitch black scales climbed out of the magical shadowy void.

One of the heads came face to nose with Carla. "Oh, a pleasure to see you again," a mouth five times bigger than the elf's entire body said. Carla's response said more than most words. She fainted. One of the other heads sighed, "Are we that scary?" Most of the other heads began to tremble as Lindy's anger became palpable enough to twist what little light poked into the dark cavern.

"Did this elf come here with anyone else?" Lindy asked, her steady tone all the more terrifying to the massive beasts for the rage that radiated from her in waves, threatening to turn even light to dust.

"Oh right, our younger brother. He said you were his father, Mom," one of the heads choked out.

All of a sudden, the trembling fabric of reality stilled. "Wait, what?" Lindy asked, dumbfounded.

"The elf knows," a head began, but was stopped when Lindy started slapping Carla awake.

Carla opened her eyes only to find herself back on the hard stone floor with Lindy straddling her and frantically smacking the elf's face. Thirty-six massive heads on three bodies that were around the size of a small kraken stared down at her from over Lindy's shoulders. The cave seemed brighter than before. Carla almost passed out again. "Oh no you don't. What's this about me being the father?"

"You are Lindy?" Carla asked groggily. Then she was fully awake as she came to a shocking realization. "You are alive but you look so different."

"I died a few times, can switch bodies. Now talk," Lindy demanded while heavily abbreviating her most traumatic moments.

"My boyfriend's mother is a dryad but her glade is all twisted. After she gave birth to something human-like she was on the other dryads' shit list. When she died ten years ago we were chased out of the woodland," Carla said, causing Lindy to remember the aftermath of her fight with her grandmother.

"Right, blood did it," Lindy muttered, then shook her head. "Well I never thought I'd say this, but my life keeps getting weirder." Lindy glared at the three hydras. "And you know these kids. Why?"

"They found us." "They stayed with us." "Your son was kind of weird." Three heads of two hydras spoke up.

"Fine. You three are coming with me. Get back in my shadow and don't make yourselves known to others unless I say so," Lindy ordered.

"Why?" a few heads head said while the others looked like they had rolled snake eyes many times over at a high-stakes poker match.

"Because you helped make this mess without my knowledge." Lindy smiled, but anyone who saw her would know there was no happy mirth in her just then.

With her shadow now much fuller, Lindy flung Carla over one shoulder and jumped back though the shadows and into the shop's storefront, which was now damaged. A tall thin man that even Lindy thought seemed far too much like her was in the middle of trashing the place while Feldspar hid behind the counter. "She was just here!" the man yelled.

Lindy drew Transcendence from thin air and pointed it at the back of the young man's neck before he was fully aware of her presence. "Looks like we both have hostages. We need to talk, son."

Halmar, Zandra, and Jessica burst though the door with their guards at their heels. In her panic and haste Lindy did not notice the VIP re-inforcements and company so near her door. "Lin, what is going on!" Halmar yelled.

Zandra froze upon seeing Transcendence. "She gave you that. No. That's not..." the viceroy stammered.

Lindy quickly calculated damage control while berating herself internally. "Fine. If you three want in on this talk then come in and leave your guards at the door."

Jessica bowed, murmuring, "Very well." With a maddened and fanatic glaze now over her eyes, her swiftness in closing the damaged door made it impossible for the powerful entourage to question her.

Lindy tapped her sword on her child's shoulder. "Now son, what say you?"

"The name's Woodrow. You sure you are my pop?" he asked with a heavy drawl.

"If you can feel my aura then you know the answer. I am sure there is no one else who feels like us on this world anymore," Lindy managed to state evenly, without groaning or managing to show most of her rising panic.

"So, what are you really?" Halmar asked as he followed the current pope of his world's first religion and his mother.

"Technically human, as I have told you many times," Lindy shrugged.

"I heard you died," Woodrow grumbled. He was putting up a strong front but he knew that if Jessica and Zandra fought him he would lose. He could not get a read on the woman that called herself his father. The interference in Woodrow's senses was far worse when he was in his father's general vicinity than it was in Lindy's experience.

"Would not be the first time," Lindy grumbled while trying to smile amicably.

"You never came to see me or help Mom," Woodrow snapped at his father's unstable false front.

A dark tendril erupted from Lindy's shadow and pulled over a chair that she promptly collapsed onto. Then she placed Carla on the floor using a firm grip. "Look kid, I did not even know you existed until we met. Our energies are alike but seem to repel each other. Know that I know the signature to look for. I can find you at any time. So what do you want?"

Carla took this moment to seemingly come back to life. "We need power."

"Not happening, spy." Lindy shook her head, sighing. "If you want a job, I can call in a few favors but I can't personally help my son unless he, and only he, seriously needs it, and even then not by much."

"By favors you mean me, right?" Zandra pouted.

Lindy leaned back in the chair, rolling her eyes and knocking out the elf with a light tap, all in one smooth motion. "I gave you a city in my name, so yes, you owe me a little bit."

"I came looking for help avenging my mother but that seems unlikely. Not like I should have expected a lot after how terrible the other dryads were to us." Woodrow sighed. "Do you even care?" he grumbled.

Lindy slowly got out of her chair and looked up into her son's eyes. "Yes I do. That's why I am trying to keep away from you. I am bound to Death himself. Chaos is like an old friend of mine and you deserve better than that."

Lindy's head came up to Woodrow's shoulders. He bent down to return his father's gaze directly. "But can I die?" he asked, pleading for answers.

"Yes you can, but I don't know if you will age any more. Just promise me you will not try to become truly immortal," Lindy demanded harshly.

The father and son pair held each other's gaze for a long time. Everyone else in the room kept still and silent. "Only if you tell me why," Woodrow demanded.

"Because I hunt down those that defy the cycle of life and death that my boss maintains. I have seen far too many friends die. So promise me." Lindy was pleading now to the point her presence seemed like a wisp, a vapor all of a sudden. Only the pope was enjoying the info Lindy kept letting slip.

"Fine then," Woodrow nodded.

At her son's words Lindy was released from her overweening tension, only to collapse now that her shock had lessened. Despite being the weakest in the room, Feldspar moved first, catching her savior. Looking around the room, her face firm and legs trembling, Feldspar snapped, caring more for the weak-looking woman in her arms than the very real chance of being killed on the spot. "Come back tomorrow night if you wish to continue this," Feldspar commanded.

Jessica almost protested but caught herself. Neither Halmar nor Zandra were at all happy with the day's events but accepted the demand with grace. Woodrow walked over and picked up Carla. As he followed the others out, Woodrow glanced at the out-of-place woman by his father's side. "I envy you," he told her, unhappily watching as Feldspar fussed over Lindy.

"And I am jealous of you. We both owe her our lives in a way, but she clearly loves you while I remain a convenient excuse to ease a few debts,"

Feldspar muttered, not looking up from her work and only glancing at Woodrow's back just before it went out of view.

Lindy woke up midday the next day, still groggy. When she opened her eyes she noticed Molder was sitting right outside her room fast asleep. Lindy looked up at the ceiling. *Family. Well, add that to the list of things I have yet to master,* she thought, trying to find the irony in it without much luck. So she did what seemed oddly familiar: she sighed and chose to put off dealing with it as she worked to survive and keep what little sanity she had.

Grimoire called from somewhere within the back room. "Hey kid, she's up!" The dwarf boy yelled loud enough to be heard from the street.

Molder fell out of his chair, almost hitting his head. A snake-like tail erupted from the child's shadow and caught him, placing him on his feet. "My ears!" Molder yelled, clearly in pain.

Faldrea walked over to Molder, patting his head. "Don't disturb this sick one," she said gently.

"I am not sick," Lindy grumbled as she got out of bed. "I just have a lot to work out."

"Just like always," Faldrea retorted before holding her head and grimacing. "Sorry, I just had some vivid déjà vu."

"That's not surprising." Lindy nodded. The tail from before grabbed Molder and moved him to the other side of the back room so Lindy could change.

"By the way, what's that?" Faldrea asked, pointing at the tail. Lindy changed and left the room just in time to see the hydra tail grab a sandwich before slinking back into the shadowy void from whence it came. "A pet."

"Your boss allows pets?" Grimoire called back, looking at his hands in bleak dismay.

"One of them does, I think? Either way, they are more or less not here." Lindy shrugged as a charred goat leg was flung out of her shadow. "I will have a talk with those brats soon," she promised, although more for her own benefit than the others. After sitting down and nibbling at the poorly cooked leg of meat, she handed over her sandwich to Grimoire to replace his. "So where is everyone else?"

"Sis and the boss are at city hall," Molder replied between bits of his own food.

"Your kid left town and the pope's making a ruckus," Grimoire added.

"When the prophet's away, the politicians play," Lindy groaned.

"Although those that know you and this place well could fill in the blanks about the boy," Grimoire nodded.

"That, and they would not stop pestering him at the main gate until he told them about you," Faldrea added harshly.

"Well I am going out for a run. Could one of you look after the boy?" Lindy asked. Grimoire looked a bit insulted. Seeing that, Lindy sighed. "I mean the human one in the room?"

"Sure. I need to take it slow today." Faldrea smiled.

Grimoire got out of his seat. "And I've got to get ready for the dinner rush. See you around, kid."

Molder grinned, waving. "See you!" Lindy just shrugged and held the back door open for the food runner on their way out.

Lindy walked aimlessly past shops and homes. Wrapped in smog and fog, the sounds of children and trains cascaded all around her. Lindy had never felt so alone. For the first time in around three hundred years she had time to think and process slowly. She did not know how long she had walked but when she took a few seconds to look up and stop thinking, all Lindy found herself looking out at was the pit in the small park she had taken Molder to a few times. "I need to fix this," she muttered, watching the complex energies in the pit that had long been out of their creator's control as they continued to shift and evolve.

"You ready to talk now?" Zandra asked from behind. No one else was nearby.

"Not yet, but I can hear you. How long have I been there?" Lindy asked, still looking closely at the shifting energies only a very few could see, let alone understand.

"Why are you here?" Zandra asked as she walked next to Lindy.

"For the first time in this life I can take my time to think," Lindy muttered. After a deep sigh she whispered, "I don't like it."

"True. You hate thinking." Zandra nodded.

"It's the brooding that gets me. I need to do something," Lindy grumbled. She looked her former charge in the eyes and waved an arm at the pit. "I don't care how I'm seen but if I keep taking things slow..." Lindy trailed off. "I won't be able to live with my past."

"You have done some good but you have never been able to see it." Zandra retuned Lindy's gaze with a harsher one.

Lindy turned to look out at the city that had changed far past her ability to recognize. "What am I to you?"

"A monster?" Zandra asked, seemingly to herself. "Maybe some fable that keeps children up at night who dumped a pile of work in my lap without thinking how I feel. Look, you helped me a lot. I know that. But living with the past and being better for learning from and accepting it is part of what makes you yourself. Seeing the good in life would serve you better than moping about it."

Lindy laughed. "You really have grown up." They turned back to the pit. "I can fix that pit a little but I'd need time."

Zandra gave a small sardonic smile. "Why help now?" From her tone she was slightly amused, like watching a child parrot off the answer to complex philosophy most took for granted in an overly elaborate manner.

"I need to leave a few more good things in this world. May as well fix up some of the damage I've caused and hope that serves," Lindy replied coolly.

"Fine. I'll give you some funding but only because this would help your city," Zandra replied.

"It's your city too," Lindy replied, shaking her head, a smile back on her face.

"Right, but it's yours in name only. So thanks for everything," Zandra whispered before marching off.

"Hey, say that again," Lindy giggled. Zandra replied with a rude gesture and walked off faster without turning around, which caused Lindy to laugh harder.

The next forty years flew past as Lindy immersed herself in research. Faldrea died not long after Lindy began, which led to the longest time she was away from her new work, due to her grief. During the following years, Longteeth died of old age, but not before expanding his shop into many other cities. Feldspar took over the shop and adopted three children. Molder worked his way up to commander of the city's guards and married into the family of one of the local railway barons, who held the rank of Ritter, which Lindy found funnier in how her translation ability worded it than the potential self-promotion. At the start of each year Lindy would go on a killing spree against Death's listed targets, which became a mysterious yearly phenomenon on par with natural disasters. Lindy forced Death to add the names of those who copied her murders to its lists. Finally Lindy managed to stop the magic-eating pit she had created from expanding; she forced it to use the power it ate to maintain its magic, instead of using it to grow bigger and eat more.

The next sixty years saw the deaths of Molder and Feldspar along with Jessica, whose son took over her job as pope, as he was her first-born child. After Molder's death, Lindy began to slowly create a catacombs on the overgrown hill she shared so much history with just outside the city's gates. The catacombs were eight levels underground but the last three were sealed off from the outside world, and Lindy took them as her home. She hired herself out to procure rare plants and animal bits under ever-changing aliases in an effort to keep track of those seeking to artificially extend their lives. She thwarted their attempts to live far longer than Death would allow so that she would have fewer people to kill later.

20

What Goes Up...

As Lindy drifted from one day to the next in a fog, time having long lost its meaning, one day she was greeted by the latest reincarnation of Fraya. This incarnation had been born in the city twenty years before. Fraya had other lives Lindy had not been a part of; all had some pain but most had been within the normal range. That made Lindy a little sad, but she believed with all her being that anyone who got too close to her for too long would suffer some of the worst that Death and Fate could give, although it was Lindy's own choices and fateless nature that caused these troubles. In many ways that was worse than the murders Lindy had to commit to live, which was saying something, as her desire to live for as long as she could clashed with her inability to die, an irony she seldom thought about lest she lose herself.

Fraya's most recent life was as a young human called Geena Magecraft who worked in the magic-eating mines where crystals that repelled magic had begun to grow as a consequence of Lindy's actions to stabilize the pit. The miners in these pits suffered weakness and an inability to use magic that looked to be an acquired genetic defect, as it could be passed along to their children. The average power level for all the world's residents was far lower and still dropping than it had been three hundred years before, among those born within that time.

Geena called out. "Hey Lin, could we order some more sage maple sap?"

Lindy sighed. She had been helping provide some rare and powerful magic stabilizing agents to the local miners for dirt cheap as a form of penance. Not that she would ever tell them that, although they had noted how low her prices stayed for them, unlike many of her other clients, and had wisely not asked her about it. "Sure. How much and when?"

"A month from today? Five units? Does that work? We can pay double," Geena replied. She looked more tense than normal. Recently she had been having odd waking nightmares around the odd dragon the city knew as Lin, but that was not the whole reason this time. "You hear about the two new continents?"

"Oh. Who found who?" Lindy chuckled.

Geena shook her head. None of the crazy shit Lin did or said surprised the locals anymore, but some of those rare few who had become high-ranking heroes (who on the old scale would have been mid-rankers at best) could tell Lin was the most terrifying thing they had ever seen and that she was definitely suppressing her powers. "Two empires clashed near the coast. Lots of wreckage washed ashore. The kingdoms around here are in talks with those empires' representatives. That's all we have been told."

Lindy shrugged. "I just think it's baffling that it's taken them this long to find each other. Well, I'll have that sap in a few weeks. It's the middle of harvest season for those guys." Geena watched Lin saunter away with no idea or desire to understand what the young-looking woman had said and trembling from a memory about the long-extinct race of beasts called manticores.

After walking into a deep alleyway Lindy sunk into its shadows and remerged in a small twisted glade. Sinister-looking pixies swarmed the intruder. "Mistress, you have returned!" they all screeched joyfully.

"Hey guys, how's life?" Lindy chuckled at the swarm of terrifying barbs and thorns that still behaved cutely despite their menacing appearance and banshee-like voices. These creatures had come into existence after Woodrow's mother had been slain by the other dryads. Their common name was Twist Sprite.

"All's well. Chased off a few elven children. We have kept the glade from expanding further as you asked," the day's leader said. Its rank was denoted by a gourd with eyeholes it wore as a mask, which was passed around each day so that each sprite got a chance to be the boss.

"So no problems," the previous day's boss answered, likely not yet used to its new lack of authority.

"And no deaths, right?" Lindy asked. Her gaze was met with averted eyes, which was surreal when a swarm of close to eighty flying beings did that all at once. "None of you died and no elves were killed, right?" Lindy pressed.

"We killed a pig," the leader answered.

Lindy chuckled. "It was delicious!" the swarm chorused.

"And the anguish on the brats' faces tasted better," the former boss mumbled.

"What?" Lindy asked, glaring at the swarm.

"We killed a wild piglet in front of some trespassers. There was a lot of blood," the leader shivered as it explained.

"Damn vegetarians," a few of the swarm spat.

"Wrong. What do I keep telling you guys?" Lindy growled.

"All for profit!" the swarm tried. "Keep it clean!" they chorused again. Seeing neither was right, the swarm got into a huddle. As they buzzed around, things like "Don't eat that" and "Give me some of those" were tossed around until one of the sprites came forward and answered, "Play nice and respect your neighbors."

"Close enough," Lindy nodded. "So I need some more sap. You have some to spare, right?"

"Anything for you, mistress," the swarm chorused.

A lizard the size of Lindy's arm crawled into the glade just as Lindy was handed a canteen of sage maple sap. She had to juggle it as the swarm bolted at the lizard with cries of "Blood!" and "Fresh meat!" Lindy chuckled as she disappeared back to her catacomb. *I can never tell*

Woodrow about these things, can't let all this power go to his head, Lindy mused as she examined her haul.

A few days later, before most of the city was awake, Lindy delivered the sap to Geena's door. Around midday Lindy found herself eating at a small food stand set up between a laundromat and a clothing shop. Somehow the fact that the stand was cheap and had only drapes to shield it from the ever-present smog was what attracted Lindy to it. She was halfway done with her meal when the stand was cut in half and three figures rushed past into the alleyway behind the shop. The figure in front was a young female shade in a military uniform. Running behind her was one of the guards for the city's ruler, and in back was a man from the smaller island chain where she had once killed a vampire. Sighing, Lindy sprinted after them.

The man in back and the young shade both glanced at the young woman from the wrecked food stall who was keeping pace with their mad dash at a leisurely jog. The island native could tell from his years of experience that the newcomer was more dangerous than they were. The shade who had fought in only a single border skirmish merely knew that the newcomer smelled like one of her kin.

The shade's eyes glinted at the happy coincidence, or perhaps planned backup. The reason did not matter. Her bloodline had for the last few generations been able to command other shades to do their bidding. Even the rare few with shade ancestry were not totally immune. "Hey, stop them!" the young officer ordered using the full might of her control, ordering Lindy to stop the island man.

The island man spun around before the young officer had completed her command and stabbed at Lindy with a flurry of blows, only to find himself smashed forward, causing the three who were responsible for ruining Lindy's lunch to collapse in a balled-up heap. The shade was still smirking as she fell down, not yet understanding what was going on.

Lindy tore a hunk of pipe from a heating unit's exhaust aperture. She crushed one end of the pipe into a sharp tip that glinted dully in the smog-rimmed alley. "You all owe me lunch," Lindy grumbled as she loomed over the targets of her mild wrath.

"I told you to stop them!" the young officer yelled, now angry and flustered.

> Leera Swallow
>
> Shade female age 19
>
> Affiliation: Longdusk imperial family 38th spare, delegation of Farnesse aide
>
> Job: Lieutenant internal affairs, Longdusk secret police informer
>
> Status: mild internal bleeding, torn soft tissue in left arm (mild)
>
> Abilities: strength 270, vitality 218, mind 319, agility 289
>
> Talents: decoy, language (common Derndell, high Derndell, wasteland), immunity potion/ truth serum, resentence (mind control/ mind reading): high, fearlessness, blade flurry, crack shot, sprint, subdue, innate power (telepathy) moderate
>
> Mutation: control shades without this ability at authorly level under creator (Lindy)
>
> Skills: Athletics: adept, intimidate (presence/malice): journeyman, tactics: beginner, sword: adept, pistol: journeyman, stealth: adept, poison: expert, interrogation: journeyman, clerk: adept, perception: apprentice

"I don't answer to you," Lindy snapped. Then she hauled up the guard. "Eight copper. Pay up."

"What?" the man yelled. "You think you can command me? Do you have any idea who I am?"

"Don't care." Lindy tossed the man who was much bigger than she back into the street, causing the ground to shake and a three-foot hole to form from the impact. Lindy then headed over to the foreign man. "Sixteen copper, local coinage only. Pay up."

"I don't carry this city's coinage," the man professed hurriedly. "But I can..." Before he finished his head was smashed into a wall. Both of the men were powerful enough to be only lightly wounded, but that was largely Lindy's intent as she controlled her might. The men were wise enough to not make another move and wait for an opening as they watched from where Lindy left them.

"Name, military rank, and twenty copper," Lindy demanded from Leera Swallow. The shade stood up hastily. "I mean now, young one." Lindy extended her ability to command the shades over the young woman, which made them both feel a little ill. Lindy did not enjoy infringing on the will of others for no good reason but needed to set an example and send a threat. Leera realized there was someone with more powerful control over the shades than her family, who ruled the sole nation of shades in the world.

"Leera Swallow, lieutenant," the shade said, shaking as she deposited twenty copper into Lindy's waiting palm.

"Thanks, princess," Lindy chuckled, her glare making it clear that princess was not an absent-minded turn of phrase. "Ok, that's all you two get," Lindy whispered. On cue, two large tails shot up from the shadowy alley and knocked out the men. "There. They will be down for a while as requested. I'll consider the extra fourteen copper payment."

"Wait, extra?" Leera asked the first thing to come to mind.

"My lunch was six copper." Lindy grinned savagely as she ran off to a slightly classier food stall on the opposite end of the alley, leaving Leera Swallow far behind.

Lindy found herself back in her catacomb by midnight only to realize someone was waiting at the gates, grumbling softly when she appeared in front of them. It was Halmar. Without preamble he snapped, "Where were you?"

"Out drinking," Lindy answered truthfully. "Just got back."

"Drinking where?" Halmar sighed. Lindy simply pointed to the City of Smog far behind him. "Right," Halmar nodded, choosing not think about how annoyed he could be.

Lindy chose to forget her own annoyance, mostly because the sub-viceroy was useful and he was one of the few still alive who knew who she really was, although no one could agree on what she was. "Some of those back-alley bars are open surprisingly late," Lindy nodded. "So what's up?"

"Did you help a spy flee?" Halmar asked.

"Negotiations broke down then? Did they at least tell you how to make ramen and soy sauce?" Lindy asked, trying to change the subject.

"If you know that much," Halmar said before realizing how stupid he was. "How much do you know about those kingdoms?"

"Not a lot. Never paid attention to their politics. The city's food and people are interesting in their own ways. I can see why they have been at war for so long," Lindy answered.

Halmar smiled. "How long?"

"Ten years or so? It sounds like a long time but they are far apart by sea travel." She took out a few chunks of bark she had scribbled obser-vations on over the last eighty or so years. "Here," she said, handing the pile of bark to Halmar. "Most of this is likely out of date and without context but it should give an unbiased overview of their cities, at least."

"All of this?" Halmar asked, more shocked than happy but trying to find what scheme or joke Lindy was trying to rope him into this time.

"I don't really need them anymore and I can always visit to take notes whenever. Just disregard the crossed-out names. It's nothing important," Lindy replied. After requesting that he ignore her kill lists that were also scribbled haphazardly on the bark, Lindy tossed Halmar and the notes into a shadow and into his mother's mostly unoccupied office. "Wait, am I still maintaining my neutrality?" Lindy asked herself. That question kept her up all night. The final conclusion she came to before giving up was maybe.

After a few days the cities of the world became chaotic. Two weeks later, borders were closed and crackdowns and drafts began. Lindy stayed home and watched from a shard of her perception she kept in the sky. Leera Swallow hid in a ruined town in the wasteland. When she ran out of food Lindy slipped a message with the shade's coordinates to a team of commandoes from the larger of the two neighboring continents. She learned the smaller was referred to as principality of Zenic and the larger was the empire of Bruteolon. Both continents were under the full control of their namesakes. The main continent was for whatever reason called Zone, or at least that's how auto-translate said it was in every language.

Three months passed as fortifications were built, then troop ships landed. Ships from the principality of Zenic landed in a port a few nations over from the City of Smog. Other ships from the empire of Bruteolon landed in a prefab-built dockyard that the nation of Farnesse had erected in a patch of unclaimed land. Leera Swallow was one of the few shades to first meet with their ally's leadership. This world's first world war started less than a year after the lands in it learned of each other. Besides Lindy and most of the sea-dwelling dragons and old flying dragons, the realization that there were other lands across the sea was an immense shock to the smarter and/or more developed human-oids of the world.

Two things caught Lindy's interest more than anything else.

1. Orcs, ogres, gnolls, and goblins had joined the shade armies, seemingly by their own choice.
2. Her son was in line to volunteer to join the City of Smog's army.

When she noticed Woodrow, Lindy altered her form to be shorter, changing her eye, skin, and hair colors to be more in line with the humans of the wasteland, and set her abilities to look like a mid-rank hero of her childhood, which was apparently considered high-ranking now. After making sure her clothes were common civilian garb for the current era, she slipped into a shadow and out to an alleyway near her son and got in line behind him before anyone else could. Carla and a small child stood to one side. Lindy took one glance at her grandchild then tapped Woodrow on the shoulder. "This is the line to volunteer, right old man?"

Woodrow turned around. It took him a few seconds to adjust to the short woman behind him. "That's right. Do I look that old?"

Lindy looked right into her son's eyes and smirked, pointing over her shoulder. "They're with you, right? You look kind of young to have a kid that old. Not that I have room to talk, given how young I look."

"Right. I did not realize it was that obvious." Woodrow tried to laugh but it came off faked. "You are from around here, right? Do you know anything about an old hag called Lindy?"

Lindy had to dig her nails into her palm and sighed. "Nope. There's a young herb finder who goes by something like that. She lives in the catacombs outside of town. I am called Din Le, by the way."

"Name's Woodrow. Good luck." Her son nodded before turning back around as the line moved forward. Lindy noticed Carla and her child scuttle off in the direction of the catacombs.

The line moved slowly. Lindy had to glare at the tips of tails that peeked out of Woodrow's shadow to stop the hydras that had stayed with him from ratting her out.

She looked at her current true stats. Not much had changed.

Lindy Loon

Female (shadow touched) human age: forever 20

Affiliation: realm of Death

Embodiments: death to be, eternal calamity

Job: Reaper

Status: common sense bane: extreme, death's apprentice, fatal fairytale

Abilities: strength 8651, vitality 9723, mind 9002, agility 10003

Talents: translation: all, full power strike: strength. danger sense, innate map, skill and knowledge retention: Manfred Endfield, photographic memory, sixth sense: intuition, extra toughness, favored environment: darkness, cold resistance: high, highly enhanced trait: willpower, analysis: extreme, good hair, quick learner, fearless, body of poison, presence sense, aura: weakening, damage shield: decay, decay bolt, adept talent: multi-tasking, rapid reload, fearsome visage: moderate, selective decay: all, innate spell: chill blast, absorb impact: moderate, hair trigger aim, repost: debate, realm authority (death:) moderate, shadow shift, six-fold strike, perception tampering field, find soul, see soul, sense lifespan, attuned to purpose, shadow form, plains walk: deaths realm and back, full power burst (weakening/ decay/cold), siphon soul, suppresses kindnesses (self): full, suppress power: any, track soul, find living, alcohol residence: mild, trace bloodline, rapid fire, strike from shadow, rapid shadow jump, alter form, copy self (shadow)

Blessing: conceal stats

Mutation: troll blood (extra burnable, swift regeneration), un-aging. mutagenic blood

Curse: catastrophic encounters, heavily sleeper, light sensitively: mild

Skills: Sword: master, dagger: master, unarmed: master, marksmanship: extreme, throwing: expert, athletics: master, armor proficiency(leather/ cloth): expert, literacy: expert, history (other world): journeyman, intimidate (innate): extreme, diplomacy: journeyman, awareness: expert, necromancy: extreme, tinkering: master, magic tampering: extreme, counter spell: master, survival (woodland): expert, cooking: journeyman, acrobatics: expert, stealth: expert, shadow magic: expert, laws of death: extreme, leadership: journeyman, herbalism: journeyman, barter: journeyman, ice magic: journeyman

Then she made sure to conceal them accordingly.

Din Le De Li
Female human: age 20
Affiliation: wasteland scavengers
Job: mercenary
Status: looking for another job
Abilities: strength 520, vitality 517, mind 489, agility 603
Talents: translation: all, full power strike: strength, danger sense, sixth sense: intuition, cold resistance: high, damage shield: decay, decay bolt, selective decay (flesh/metal), hair trigger aim, shadow shift, rapid fire, strike from shadow
Mutation: troll blood (extra burnable, swift regeneration)
Skills: sword: expert, dagger: expert, marksmanship: expert, athletics: journeyman, armor proficiency (leather/cloth): journeyman, literacy: adept, intimidate (innate): journeyman, awareness: expert, diplomacy: apprentice, magic tampering: journeyman, cooking: apprentice, acrobatics: journeyman, stealth: journeyman, shadow magic: journeyman

Woodrow's turn took a little longer than the others but he left in an all-right mood, so that seemed fine to his father. Then it was Lindy's turn. She stepped into the recruitment tent. A man at a desk and two armed guards were in the room. "Well take a seat," the seated man invited, motioning to the only other chair in the room on the other side of his desk, which was at a glance far less comfortable than his.

Taking her seat, Lindy sat rigidly in a calm manner. "Do you have any combat experience?" the seated man asked, which was not a question on his list but one he felt was necessary for the unblemished young woman he saw before him.

"More than most twenty-year-olds, at least. I'm from the wasteland. I was a mercenary." What Lindy said was the truth. She let the man infer whatever context he chose, which she knew was unlikely to come anywhere close to the truth.

The man looked down at his paperwork. "Your name?"

"Din Le De Li. I usually shorten it to Din Le," Lindy replied.

The man nodded as he filled out a form. "Hand on the stone," he said, using his pen to point to a crystal as he looked over the documents. Lindy did as she was asked and the stone exploded. Then man looked up and frowned. "Are you a hero?"

Lindy could not help but chuckle. "I feel like a villain most of the time. More than a few hero-level entities have died by my hand. In most cases I was on my own."

The recruiter looked closely at Lindy. "Really? Did your village not have an analysis stone?"

"I never met my folks and my home town is long gone. It should be far under the sands by now," Lindy shrugged.

"Do you know where your name comes from?" the man inquired, looking troubled.

"I named myself. It sounds like an ash storm on sheet metal," Lindy replied.

The recruiter sighed as he crossed off most of the data on the recruitment form. "Fine. So why sign up for this city's army rather than somewhere in the wasteland? The Everlasting church has mobilized most of their army from there."

Lindy suppressed a grumble. "There are people in this city who I want to live happy fulfilling lives for a long time before they die in a nonviolent manner. I don't have anyone anywhere else I'd risk my life for like that."

The man stiffened up awkwardly for a few seconds, then he relaxed and smiled. "Then we'd love to have you. I can tell you are powerful and that's a loss for the wasteland, but so be it." He handed Lindy a rectangular token stamped with the city's emblem and a company insignia along with a number and address. "Be at the location listed on that token by eight tomorrow morning. Just bring the clothes on your back and that stub. Keep in mind you will not be allowed home until after training and maybe not even after that, depending on how things develop." Before Lindy was out of the tent the man called after her. "Oh, and you may want to bring a light meal as well. We expect long lines at the training camps."

Lindy smiled at the kind-hearted advice. "Thank you sir," she replied firmly before heading home to confront Carla, who was nearing the catacomb.

By slipping into a shadow Lindy managed to arrive ahead of Carla, where she put on her old armor, taking extra care to ensure the helmet was fully closed. Lindy then stepped outside the city's only catacomb. Carla and her child arrived soon after. "Lindy, I have a request."

Lindy analyzed her son's lover before speaking.

Carla Faywind
Elf female age 290
Affiliation: Faywind clan
Job: agent
Status: pawn of the Faywind clan
Abilities: strength 132, vitality 231, mind 200, agility 317
Talents: forgettable, single minded, language (common washland/ jungle elvish/ common Derndell/ forest spirit), double shot, swift reload, swift aim, vital strike, innate spell: short range teleport, honest face, sense ill will, sense truth, danger sense
Wound: faulty kidneys, lingering poison damage, lacerated tendons left arm

> Skills: Athletics: expert, armor use (leather/ cloth): journeyman, dagger: master, stealth (hiding): expert, bow: master, spear: journeyman, herbalism: extreme, tracking (all land): expert, survival (all land): master. Negotiate (equal terms): expert, first aid: expert, poison: expert, diplomacy: journeyman, lie (casual settings): expert, awareness: journeyman

"You are doing worse, spy," Lindy grumbled, albeit with some sympathy. Just looking the woman's stats it was clear she was still being used, but under far worse terms.

"Mommy's not a spy!" the small child beside Carla fumed.

Lindy sighed. "Even when he's a little snot, my grandchild's still cute."

The little boy trembled and hid behind this mother. "You are not grandpa, right?"

"She's your father's father," Carla explained.

Lindy felt more than a little anger at the Faywind clan but kept it under control. "Fine, Carla. What do you need?"

The elven woman blinked. "Just like that?"

"If you want the Faywind clan wiped out I will have to ask Death, if that's ok," Lindy cautioned while trying to show she was willing to help.

"I need you to protect your grandson," Carla explained.

Lindy looked into the eyes of the child and nodded. "He's your boss now. Guard them as you would me. If the kid gets murdered on your watch then many things will answer to me." Lindy stamped her foot on the ground and her shadow rippled. Soon after her grandchild's shadow seemed bigger. "All right. Three of my hydras will guard you two from his shadow." The child looked at his shadow in mild terror but also awe.

"Is that all right? I just wanted you to raise him for a while," Carla asked timidly.

Lindy leaned in close to the other woman and whispered. "He needs his mother. Besides, my only skill is taking life. That's no place for my kin."

"Why can't I go with you?" the boy asked.

Lindy chuckled and knelt down with her back to Carla. After flipping up the helmet's visor, Lindy patted her grandchild's head. "Where I am going you should never follow. I can't in good conscience subject you to my life." Then she flipped her visor back down, stood up, and walked back into the catacomb. "I will be traveling for a while. Got a lot of destruction and mayhem to oversee and all that."

Before first light Lindy arrived at the gate of a training field with bunk rooms and offices that had months before been a depot. The sentry at the gate was visibly exhausted. "Hey, I was told to report here?" Lindy asked, seeing no one else around.

The sentry looked up from behind the gate. "You are very early."

Lindy held up her stamped ID. "I did not have a lot left to do." Only when the sentry nodded and relaxed did Lindy take a step forward and hand over her ID.

After looking it over the man nodded. "Wait there for a bit then. Shift change is soon and they will be able to handle you."

"No problem," Lindy agreed, stepping back and leaning against the wall.

After a few minutes the sentry grumbled, now both unable to relax and feeling awkward about the silence. He asked, "So you are not from around here. Some kind of mercenary too? Did you bring your own gear?"

Lindy looked over at the gate. "Should I have brought my old gear?"

The sentry folded his arms. "Well no, but conscripts don't get the best stuff. It's hard to make lots of quality gear fast right now."

Before Lindy could reply, five men, one of whom was far better dressed, arrived next to the sentry. "Don't spook your friend," one of the men chided.

"I don't know him," Lindy replied. The better-dressed man and two others took on more guarded motions at varying degrees of speed and subtlety. "I was told to report here for training," Lindy added as she watched the men's movements with a small knowing smirk. Interestingly, the better-dressed man reacted the fastest and with the most skill, but was as subtle as a beached kraken.

"You are early," the well-dressed man allowed.

Lindy looked around the street that was just beginning to see foot traffic. "So are a few of the others," she observed, noticing the sentry slip her ID to one of the more alert and grizzled men before slipping deeper into the complex. Woodrow and a few others ambled over. "You lot are early," Lindy smiled. The newcomers looked around. "The men behind the gate work here," Lindy added.

The well-dressed man glanced at Lindy, then at her ID stub before getting his men to open the gates. "Anyone who has not passed in the document they were given yesterday, do so now. We will call out names in groups of five to be taken inside."

Soon after, Lindy, her son, and three others were led into the complex to a pair of carriage repair sheds that could have been small warehouses all on their own. They had been turned into barracks, one for each gender. *How would an army of mold or fungus split up? Would they even care?* Lindy mused.

"Hang your IDs on a bunk then come back. Men in the left, women in the right. No peeking in on each other," their guide, a grizzled forty-something sergeant, commanded.

Woodrow walked up behind Lindy. "Having fun?" he asked his father, still clueless who Lindy really was. Both of them had completed the task swiftly and far before the others.

"Not yet, but that's not the point of this," Lindy shrugged.

The sergeant glared at Lindy. "Enlighten us, cadet. What's the point of this?"

Lindy easily stood at attention, the long unused habits of Manfred Endfield manifesting themselves. "To condition us to kill without thought or remorse, preferably on command, and to familiarize us with the tools to do so, sir!"

The sergeant stood absently for a few seconds. By the time his mind had processed as much of Lindy's words as it could, his other charges were back. "You use some big words, cadet," the sergeant spat before hollering at Lindy's other four colleagues. "Ok, you five follow me."

After being shown to the cafeteria and being permitted to each take a chunk of bread and a canteen of water, the five cadets and their guide walked onto a training field. "I am sergeant Ben'Ruell. Take a practice weapon and line up." The man pointed at rows of weapon stands filled with padded wooden armaments. "Ok, one at a time, come at me," the man said. After waiting a few seconds he scowled and pointed to Lindy. "You come forward."

Lindy walked into the small ring Ben'Ruell had been standing in. He was equipped with a spear. Lindy held a standard-sized wooden short sword that was as long as her arm. "You could take a shield or another weapon as well, you know," the sergeant informed her.

"I like to stay light on my feet," Lindy replied as she took a low stance with the sword at her shoulder pointing out. Her other hand was low and moved in time with the man.

"Then start," the man growled. The pair circled each other before the sergeant spang forward, responding when Lindy purposely turned too slowly with him. When the spear's tip had closed half the gap Lindy spun, knocking the spear away and down with her free arm while lunging low. She kicked the man's legs from under him before twisting his arm hard enough to lock the spear in place, but not enough to do more than leave him with some soreness. Her practice weapon was held high on the man's neck past his gorget. His other arm was under his body. "I yield," Ben'Ruell grumbled. Lindy let him go and jumped backwards in one swift motion, dodging a jab from the spear's pommel. "You are good," Ben'Ruell nodded before looking back at his other charges. "Remember to never underestimate an opponent. Let's see if any of you lot can do better than cadet De Li. Who's next?"

Woodrow fought sergeant Ben'Ruell evenly for five minutes before the sergeant declared Woodrow's test over. The other three in their group lasted under a minute, although two came close to landing a hit. Two weeks of formations, muscle training, sparring, and intense weapon training were drilled into each of the five-person teams. The groups they entered with, they stayed with. The night the third week began, a meeting was held. Lindy knew something must have happened, given how many troops streamed in and out of the complex. There were a lot more of them than normal and while they walked, almost none of them could hide their panic, or at least not well enough to escape her gaze.

In a large office the camp's officers met with a colonel and his entourage from the mainland allied forces, the commanding general of their city who Lindy was amused to find out was descended from Molder, and a small delegation from their more foreign allies. Lindy hid in the room's rafters undetected and rolled her eyes. Before the meeting had even officially started, one of the colonel's aides, who was dressed like a chaplain, began a long-winded diatribe on how heretical and blasphemous the shades were and demanded the army mobilize more swiftly, while insisting that holy armies needed no such extra time because Death was on their side. The crux of the panic seemed to be that the coastal mainland nations were having more trouble than expected while the other nations used them as a shield to get better prepared. At some point, four more spy-like figures moved into the rafters. As a professional courtesy Lindy ignored them. "That's all very well and good, but if we are to win this war with low cost, your cities must hold. They are blessed in some way after all, so why panic?" Molder's descendent asked.

"Because of heathen magics and evil monsters! Such a blight on the world must be dealt with swiftly. Our lord Death commands it!" The colonel finally exploded after keeping his silence so far.

Lindy held in her laughter somehow. "I was under the impression that no one alive speaks for Death," one of the foreigners asked.

"The Everlasting church is our lord Death's voice on this world," the chaplain answered humbly.

Lindy leaned over to the youngest-looking spy, who was one of two from the principality of Zenic. "Hey, can you believe this guy?" Lindy whispered to the young woman dressed as a ninja. The spies from the City of Smog and the coastal cities ran away soon after.

"We have company, I see," Molder's descendent smiled, only now acknowledging the spies in the rafters. The young ninja froze so Lindy tossed her onto the building's roof through a shadow. Then the delegation looked up. To their surprise, only Lindy was there.

"Sorry. I live here and this seemed important." Lindy smiled sheepishly.

"Corporal De Li, what's the meaning of this?" her general asked. Lindy chose to overlook the small promotion he had just given her.

"The camp's been a chaotic mess all morning, sir. Almost everyone is in a panic. I came to see why," Lindy answered from above the chaplain's head.

The coastal city entourage, which had clearly been taken over by purely religious zealots, did not seem to be have a single able-minded tactician among them with any real military or diplomatic skills. Before the coastal city's representatives could get into even more of a tizzy, the older ninja from the rafters appeared behind the principality's prim representative. After some hushed words one of the principality clerks spoke. "Perhaps we should hear how the rank and file of this city feel from their own spokeswoman."

It took a while, but the other delegation turned to look at Lindy. "Me? Permission to speak freely, general?"

The general nodded. "Just keep it short and polite."

"With some of the more skilled but troublesome members of the more inland armies, a defensive line should be made far inland away from the coastal lands. We have enough technology, supplies, and skilled labor to fight a defensive battle for months, but not enough for a full assault. The men want to do something but few here are willing to die badly for other cities. If they are trained well that will no longer be an issue but things like that take time. Time you do not seem to have," Lindy explained.

"You can go, corporal." The general nodded. He seem to be in a slightly better mood even with the growing headache he was getting.

"Yes sir." Lindy saluted in the way she had been taught here before vanishing into the shadows.

A week of frantic effort later found herself, her team, and a few others in a convoy moving to the border of a kingdom called Frendzelna. It had a few hills and lots of flat farmland and sat next to the coastal kingdoms. This was where a line of trenches and other defenses would be put in place. On the cart after more than a day of silence Lindy finally spoke, if only to focus on something besides the floor. "Hey Woody, you have a wife and kid, right? Not locals either. Why fight here?"

Woodrow had over the past two weeks given up on correcting his new nickname, although only Din Le De Li used it. She was odd, an incredible fighter who often seemed like a child who found everything funny, but she had a serious battle-hardened side as well. No one knew if she fumbled her way through things or was mentally ten steps ahead of everyone else.

"My father lives there," Woodrow replied, still wondering where Lindy had gone.

Lindy looked away from her clueless son. "He says hi, by the way." Woodrow jolted out of his inner turmoil. "And if you need to hire some assassins, I'm supposed to help you get a cheap rate."

"Why would dad do that?" Woodrow asked.

"You know how she is, right?" Lindy could not hide her pained smirk so she laughed. "Or I hope you do. I still can't work out what she really wants," Lindy said truthfully.

"So did she hire you?" Woodrow scowled.

"Not a chance. I was going to sign up and well I'd never be who I am without her. The plan was for me to watch your back. Good thing we are in the same unit. I'd be uncomfortable splitting my focus to a team other than my own." Lindy grumbled, working the truth as ambiguously as she could without seeming too unnatural.

"How's my old man doing and what's she up to?" Woodrow pressed.

"I suspect she's not doing too well, or will be that way soon. As to what she's doing, something crazy, certainly. As to why, no idea." Lindy sighed. Truthfully she had an idea why she was doing what she was but was too afraid to admit it. Woodrow picked up on that. They glanced at each other. "Look. I had a kid and mistakes were made. Ones I can't take back. So, try to live, if not for yourself, then for your son." Lindy almost spat, unhappy with dwelling on the past because almost everything so far was either painful or overshadowed by pain. "I'm going to take a nap. Just try to do right by your kid, all right? If you screw up too bad it will haunt you worse than you know."

Woodrow looked over at his suddenly sleeping teammate. *This one is twisted and clearly does not know herself, but then I'm the same way,* he thought before whispering to himself, "Misery sure does attract more," as he dozed off as well.

Upon arriving at camp the units got lunch and began to dig trenches one row and one bunker at a time. This went on for days, only stopping for a short rest and three tasteless well-preserved meals a day. *Some things never change,* Lindy thought for perhaps the two hundredth time on the third morning of digging as her team ate sullenly. "I wish they would pay more attention to nutritional balance," she sighed. Her meal was a few strips of fish so dry and hard they put cheap cork coasters to shame, not that she had seen any of those in this world, along with a fist-sized wedge of cornbread that could cause concussions if lobbed with enough force at someone's head. Jugs of water conjured by the mages assigned to the cooking staff were perhaps the only pleasure in the widening mud pits they would call home.

One of the cooks making the rounds fell, the top of his head shot off. Seconds later the crack of a firearm echoed. "Fate, you son of a bitch!" Lindy howled, tossing her blood-stained wad of cornbread into her coat pocket and grabbing a long rifle sitting next to her. When her team moved to stand with her Lindy glared at them hard. "Keep your heads down, at least until I find where that came from." Before she could get more than a cursory glace at the landscape through the rifle's scope she was hit in the forehead with a round. Unlike the cook, it left a dark bruise that bled badly but nothing more. "Oh that's it, asshole," Lindy fumed. Her squad, slightly panicked, had never seen the normally jovial, sometimes smart and harsh Din Le De Li this hopping mad before. Lindy closed her eyes, letting her danger sense, hearing, and experience take over. A shield of energy that would eat any metal covered the lip of the trench, shielding those around her. Four rounds impacted the shield but turned to specks of rust, causing no distortion in the shield. Lindy opened her eyes. "Found you," she scowled, raising her rifle as five shots rang out. "That's five asshat snipers down. What now, sir?" Lindy called out.

"How long can your shield hold?" a captain asked.

"Ten minutes if they throw nothing at it. After that I'll be useless for the day," Lindy called back. She had done her best to suppress her abilities to what she had lied that they were.

"She's like a shade," one of the religious zealots cursed.

"Humans can use those magics too," Woodrow whispered to himself.

The captain began assembling the units around him into defensive lines while Woodrow leaned over close to Lindy's ear and whispered, "Hey, are you one of my father's kids?"

Lindy's mind lost focus and the barrier trembled. Woodrow got a few angry glares before the barrier was back up to full strength. *Really now? Well let's say something believable that we can live up to,* Lindy screamed in her mind. "Sort of," she began. Woodrow's entire expression became harsh. "But she's not my parent. I'm the result of an experiment with modifying things. My existence was an afterthought. So while I do have some of her blood, it's on loan."

Woodrow's face was still harsh but he seemed to relax. Lindy felt this was her only chance to ask something that she had been agonizing over for many years. "Do you hate her? Your father, I mean?"

"Maybe. I don't know. Its annoying how little she cares. She's not a good person and my child will have a far better childhood than I did," Woodrow grumbled.

A tornado of sand crashed into the trenches. *Smart bastards,* Lindy thought. Before her son could run off Lindy told him, "I believe she cares and would love to do more for you."

Woodrow spat, "I doubt it," but his expression was lonely for a brief second before his mind and body went into full combat mode.

Lindy sighed. *He's such a child but our relationship could be so much worse, so this is all right,* she told herself. A rain of arrows smashed into the wall, only the arrow heads dispersed. Blunt wooden shafts tore into the lines. "Sir, this only works on metal," Lindy called over the dust cloud that had covered their position.

Many running footsteps approached their position. Lindy was bleeding from multiple gashes but she had begun to regenerate. "Ok I'll power this up for long as I can, so stand your ground."

"Men, we..." the captain began.

"Contact!" a man on Lindy's right bellowed just as their enemy's first line crashed into the barrier, wooden clubs in hand and covered in leather armor. When the enemy reached the barrier everyone began to scream and the enemy's first line turned to goo, the flesh and leather becoming a slick mound that dribbled into the trench as Lindy fell to her knees.

"That's all I got!" Lindy yelled over the screams and gasping. "Their second line is close. Look alive!" Lindy added with the last of her strength as she fell into a fitful slumber.

Lindy found herself in a blank room. She was unsure if color and light were around her or not. At a small table sat Genney and a blond female who looked no more than ten, but from the being's presence Lindy knew she was Fate. Lindy sat at an empty space near the table, only to find a chair under her before completing the motion. "This place is nifty," she noted.

"So I have to ask," Fate replied, calmy taking a pause to drink some coffee in a flowery tea cup. "Do you hate me?"

Lindy looked in the direction she felt was up. It took her three tries before giving up. "Not you personally. The idea of things being predestined annoys me."

Fate studied Lindy harshly. "Well all right then."

Genney giggled uncomfortably, trying to lighten the mood she found unnerving despite her boss and oldest friend not seeming bothered in the least. "So you have a grandkid now, Lindy. What's that like?"

Lindy leaned back in the chair causing it to shift to accommodate her. "Hard. I want to help him and his father out but my hands are tied and I am not used to the idea of family anyway. My first thought is killing off the entire Faywind clan and that's my best idea. The fact that my best idea is so brutal hurts." Lindy took a sip of coffee from the tea cup that appeared in her hand. "Wow, that's bitter," she gagged.

"The tea my realm produces is the worst. I can't even get sugar," Fate lamented. "Well at least you have not messed with this place's time flow yet, so no time has really passed from whence you came."

Lindy looked over at Genney. "Did she use that phrase right?"

"No idea. It sounded ok to me but you hear language in a different way than anyone else I know," Genney shrugged.

"I've heard what I needed to. Off you go, bane of Fate itself." Fate waved.

"No worries. The concept you represent is not all you are." Lindy smiled.

"True, but I'd still like some good tea one of these days," Fate said, a thin smile almost appearing on the poker face she was trying to show.

Lindy opened her eyes. Men screamed; blood, body parts, metal, oil, and dirt flew in nearly equal measure. "Ok, back to it," Lindy muttered. A wad of oily mud landed in her mouth, causing Lindy to scowl. "One of these days..." she spat, not bothering to even finish the thought, not just because she did not know what would be appropriate but because she had run out of time. A man with a shovel in one hand and a bayonet mounted on half a rifle in the other charged at her. Lindy shot the man dead and stood up looking around for what to kill next so as to have another day in hell to look forward to tomorrow.

The fight was fierce. Most of the trench line held and Lindy, while still weakened, was more than enough to kill off the enemy troops that broke through. While the rest of her squad coordinated sealing the holes, Lindy supported them from the back as best she could, going so far as to get medical care for those too wounded to put up a fight, whether they liked it or not.

Two and a half hours into the fight the fourth wave came. A few very well armored troops were spread along the line but when one saw Lindy he yelled, "That's the hero. Kill it!"

Lindy yelled back. "I am not a flashy idiot!" She then tossed with all her might every explosive she could find at the armored troops.

"He called you a hero," Woodrow corrected.

"That's what I said. Flashy idiots and heroes are the same thing." Lindy scowled while adding in her mind, *No matter the world.*

Mid-thought Lindy ducked and a dagger sailed over her head. Lindy seemed to flicker as she used her shadow to face her attacker. In an instant upon seeing the assailant's elvish face Lindy sunk her hand though his chest and gripped his heart.

Fransies Faywind

Human elf age 102

Affiliation: Faywind clan

Job: assassin

Status: dead

Abilities: strength 10, vitality 20, mind 0, agility 0.

Talents: forgettable, honest face, good teeth

Skills: n/a

"Faywind clan," she noted. "Looks like I'll be wiping them out after all."

The assault came to a close half an hour later. No more troop movements were seen coming toward the trench line. Repair work and medical treatments began in earnest and guard details were strengthened and rearranged. Lindy disappeared during this time, reappearing in the tent of Leera Swallow. Unlike their last meeting Lindy did not conceal any of her true power, going so far as to use the appearance she had at their last encounter. "I have an order for you, child."

Two other shades were in the tent. They appeared to be advisors of some kind. Both threw themselves on the ground but blacked out before they could prostrate themselves before Lindy as their instincts compelled them to do. Lindy and Leera scowled. "We have met before," Leera said.

"That's right. I command you to have all Faywind clan members working for Longdusk and its allies killed," Lindy sneered.

"All of them? Why weaken us?" Leera asked, her body shaken and drenched in a cold sweat as she tried to rebel against the feeling of dominance and oppression coming from the one she called her god.

"I was lenient with them but they just kept insulting me. My patience is nowhere near infinite. Have them killed or your kingdom is the next wasteland." With that, Lindy dissipated back to the half-collapsed bunker she had left and rematerialized in the guise of Din Le De Li, with the level of power that went along with it.

Lindy had taken three steps when two ninjas teleported around her: a young ninja before the door, and a middle-aged man behind Lindy. *Oh shit, this is an oversight,* Lindy mused self-mockingly as she laughed inside and out.

"Where were you?" the young ninja demanded, her presence concealed but not nearly as well hidden as the man's.

"Two against one is not fair," Lindy chuckled, enjoying the irony that only she could appreciate and that left the other two even more guarded.

"We will not ask again," the man threatened, undoing most of his concealment. Lindy realized she had to be true to her guise because these two likely had ways to notice any slip-ups.

As Lindy mused, the younger one snapped. "No more secrets." The words underneath the translation Lindy perceived sounded different than before, causing the near-immortal harbinger of Death to smirk.

"Says the master of subterfuge and skullduggery in training," Lindy sneered in the young ninja's native language. Both ninjas stopped, the young woman in a brief second of confusion and the man to reassess his target. Lindy shook her head and pointed at the younger one. "I could have killed you just now from that opening in your guard."

"Why didn't you?" the man asked in yet another language.

Lindy smirked at him, replying in the same cadence. "Because I'd still take a hit from you," her carefree manner indicating that was only if she did not go all out. "Oh, and I commissioned a few assassins from an acquaintance for a personal matter and now I'm back."

"I'm sorry, what?" the man asked.

Lindy glared. The man drew a blade but stopped when Lindy lectured him using ten languages at once. "I answered your question. Can I go back to my unit now? We are allies, after all." Her scathing words made the man nod and his helper to faint from the overload of sensory information her mind was forced to go through. Lindy bowed in a manner that was customary to the man's homeland and skipped out of the bunker. The middle-aged ninja spent the next few hours gathering a few scraps of information on the one called Din Le De Li but found almost nothing. As he tended to his apprentice, the older ninja tried to work out how to report to his superiors before just handing them all the data he could find. It was three pages recounting his encounter with the mysterious and highly dangerous soldier called Din Le De Li in as neutral a manner as he could muster. He noted that Din Le De Li did not seem like an enemy but that forcing her hand seemed like it would cause excessive damage, not knowing just how right he was.

21

The Long Way Up

Lindy found her unit in the forest of tents near the front lines. "Hey, I miss anything?" she asked.

"Roll call, but we covered for you." Woodrow shrugged as he focused on the cast iron pot and the thin pottage cooking within its depths.

"That's going to burn soon," Lindy observed.

Woodrow scooped up the porridge into two bowls and handed one to Lindy. "I saved your dinner."

Lindy took the food and sat next to her son. "Thanks." After a few bites of the surprisingly edible meal Lindy asked casually, "So what's the watch rotation like?"

Woodrow paused his eating. "We have second watch in the trenches. That should be soon."

"Ok, that works," Lindy nodded. She ate the rest of her meal in silence as she looked up at the stars. "I put out a hit on the Faywind members helping the shades," she whispered absently.

"That was fast. Weren't you supposed to get me to ask you for that?" her son asked. He was curious and calm.

Lindy lay on the ground still looking at the sky. "They pissed me off one too many times. We have some history. Besides, a few good members have tried to mess with me. We had a love-hate relationship."

"So like the flashy idiots from before?" Woodrow asked, not really expecting much of a response but willing to listen.

"Not even close. Dumb heroes die fast and messy in impressive ways. Most longer-lived heroes are good at something to a frightening degree or are just good at living. Pissing me and by extension Lindy off may lead to fast, messy, and impressive deaths, but those will always be by and large fruitless." Lindy held her hand up to the stars as if trying to grasp them and want on sadly. "Your father is bound by so many things that she could die well before helping anyone." Real melancholy entered her voice. "I hate killing, but with a handful of exceptions I've never really done anything else, and therefore that's what I am best at. Like it or not, murder is my life." Then she sighed and began to laugh. "And it's killing me."

Woodrow took a few steps back as Lindy collected herself. "Are you ok?" he asked when Lindy's laughing fit stopped.

"As long as I never think too hard about that, then sure." Lindy shrugged then she leapt to her feet, a rifle in her hands, saying, "I'll live," just in time for one of her squad-mates to return from watch. "Looks like we are up. Come on."

Lindy and Woodrow walked along the borders of the walled tent city, which was surrounded by a broad band of mud and then by a ring of bonfires. Lindy walked just outside of the fires. "That's past our point," Woodrow informed her.

"I see better in the dark," Lindy shrugged. "Plus no attackers will use much light, so I'll let my eyes adjust like this."

After a long time peering into the darkness Woodrow asked, "So why did you start to fight, anyway?"

"Honor. Some kind of duty or desire to belong. Something like that. The thing is, all the death and destruction twists you if you soak in it long enough. It can become all you know. Killing is how I live my life but I'd rather it not define me. After all, many things have been taken from me for less."

With the help of the shard of her mind in the sky to sense life and bloodlines, she watched the battlefield for movement. Over time she had learned that even the undead could have the ability to sense life. If life was like a light on a dull background, undeath was a deeper shade of dullness. With that image it was hard to pick out initially, but simple with enough practice, once you knew what to look for. An hour into her vigil a huge mass of orcs and other beings with keen vision in darkness moved forward in a disciplined formation. Lindy called over to her son. "Hey, get whoever is in charge of our shift. We have incoming." With a glance, Woodrow assured himself that his squad-mate was serious, then he ran off. "Hey stalkers, come out. I may need your help," Lindy said evenly once her son was gone.

"How did…" the young ninja who had been shadowing her started to ask before Lindy snapped.

"Phosphorus. Hand it over." Lindy cut the young woman off sternly.

"Why would I?" the young ninja snapped before being cut off again.

"Just do it, Asami," the middle-aged man from before said as he revealed himself in a place that should have been in plain sight.

"But Jin," the younger one began. Lindy sighed and tossed herself in and out of a shadow, taking only the phosphorus, but none of the hard dark vials. Those were kept in Lindy's own shadow.

"Thanks," Lindy nodded to the older man. Her words were almost drowned out by the boots running over from camp. Jin smiled and Asami grimaced before disappearing in plain sight yet again. "Oh, and some advice. Hide the smell better next time," Lindy whispered to them, knowing the pair had moved closer to her.

"Where are they?" an old captain with fifty soldiers behind him demanded of Lindy, who was kneeling just outside the encampment gazing at the marching hoard.

Lindy pointed down from the small hill the camp was on. "Orcs, goblins, ogres, and gnolls moving in formation. Less than half an hour out if they keep up the slow pace. Right now they are past the halfway point of no man's land." The old captain did not seem to be familiar with the term "no man's land" but he did understand what Lindy was trying to say.

"You are sure?" the old officer asked.

"Yes sir, and I'd like to propose an opening move," Lindy said.

"Let's hear it," the man nodded.

"I have in my possession a chemical that can produce large amounts of light for a short time and a way to teleport it directly in front of the enemies' eyes," Lindy replied.

The old man sighed. "Ok. I'll leave the timing of the first volley to you. How many targets are on the move?"

"Five hundred," Lindy answered promptly.

The man looked over to one of his aides. "Get a hundred and fifty more troopers here and bring extra ammo, asap."

As the troops waited for reinforcements in a loose formation Lindy asked, "Captain, mind if I speak freely?"

"Just keep your tone civil," the man sighed.

"Why did you help me out so easily?" Lindy murmured.

"Because you are capable," the man replied.

"Right," Lindy nodded, chiding herself. *Because this is all I can do. No, keep your mind open and empty. Lose focus and more of the troops with me could die. Just keep the powers dialed down and hope for the best,* she thought. When her thoughts simmered down the reinforcements had come. Two hundred soldiers stood behind her. Lindy lay down, aimed her rifle, and raised one arm. "Two lines, volley fire formation, on me. Aim forward."

After a brief amount of fumbling the troops stood behind Lindy in the requested formation. When the enemy was near the mid-range of her comrades' standard weapons Lindy bellowed "Ready!" Then with her shadow magic she teleported all the raw phosphorus she had kept in her shadow directly at eye level along the second and third enemy lines. When it went off, Lindy wasted no time yelling "Fire," throwing down her arm and picking off any foe that looked important. Spell casters and leaders were her main targets, but anyone who looked like they could cause a lot more damage than their fellows was a solid mark. Failing that, the ogres, because on average they had far higher physical strength than the other types before her, then the gnolls because of their on-average very high speed and modest strength and/or cunning.

The officer sent back for more troops while yelling, "Fire at will!" In just over four minutes the fight was over. Three enemies escaped alive; all others perished. Wiping out the enemy leadership after blinding most of them permanently had gone a long way to achieving this slaughter. Their height advantage did not help as much she had thought because the lines of ogres and orcs, with their huge bulk, produced far larger blind spots than she had considered.

A week passed. Trenches were fixed and more lines were made. Bunkers were finished and the cities by the coast were taken over by an army of monsters who constructed trenches as well, far from their new city walls. The coalition Lindy had joined was still funneling supplies and troops into the many front lines. One day as Lindy toiled in yet another trench she heard a whistling sound that was as nostalgic as it was terrifying. Seeing that the soldiers from the principality of Zenic had already dropped to the ground covering their ears, some even beginning to shake, Lindy loudly hissed at her squad-mates. "Get down and cover your ears." She created a three-layered wall that would age to dust any metal that hit it. She hoped it would do something about the blast pressure as well. To mask her abilities, the wall was only placed in a dome around her team.

One of the men who had been working nearby looked up and asked, "What is that..." before he and ten men around him were reduced to paste by an artillery round. A dusty crater filled with slush and ooze remained the only sign they had been there. Nearly twenty others were hit by shrapnel. Screaming and more shelling followed. As she watched the carnage and maintained the barrier, Lindy grimaced. "I almost forgot how much I hate these when they're pointed my way."

"How do you know what these are?" one of her teammates yelled over the din. In the middle of his yell the salvo stopped, and yelling took its place in the new version of hell around them.

"Shut up for a second," Lindy snapped, sniffing the air. "I knew it. Gun powder," she spat.

"That's right. Where are you from again?" Asami the ninja asked. When she walked though Lindy's barrier she stopped, petrified. "Where did my weapons go?"

"Oh right. I still had that up." Lindy shrugged, dispelling the barrier. "There now. No more metal will be lost on the wind here." Asami still did not seem to get it so as Lindy began to wipe iron-free blood and gore off her face, she explained. "No shrapnel got to us because I made it rust on the wind."

"Sounds like you targeted all metal," Woodrow added helpfully.

"Right. And answering to Lindy the priestess of Death for so long has taught me some things." Lindy nodded, smirking at the ninja. "Like alchemically created vampires and rice!" Asami stared at Lindy for a few seconds before frowning and running away.

Looking around, Lindy knew the troops needed something to take their minds off what just happened. When she looked back to no-man's-land, she saw lines of enemy troops marching. Lindy pulled Woodrow to her side and whispered, "Get back to the leadership in the back line. Tell them what happened and get reinforcements."

Woodrow picked up on Lindy's gaze. "More of them?" he asked. His father nodded. "What will you do, Le?"

Lindy almost smirked but chose to scowl, not letting her sense of irony get to her, as now was not the time. "Give them a show," she answered, not managing to hide the glint in her eyes. She was glad no officers were left nearby for what she was going to do next. Woodrow sighed and ran back. Before anyone could pick up on his movements Lindy raised her sniper rifle and leapt to the top of the trench line, not letting the enemy out of her sight. "Listen up: we have incoming. I have a plan. Anyone with one of these, covering fire!" Lindy bellowed at her allies. Soon after, discipline and the crack of rifles going to work began to take the place of shock but not as much as Lindy was aiming for. "Wounded and those with medical training, take care of yourselves.

Reinforcements will be here soon." She did not stop to see if they complied. "Everyone else, grab something you can hit with and follow me." Lindy pulled a sword from the hip of a corpse next to her and pointed at the lines of enemies that were coming into view. She teleported the unexploded crates of grenades in the trench lines to her side. "Grab three each and lob them before we make contact. Let's wipe the smirks off those smug bastards!" She knew that no one but herself and maybe a few elves could make out expressions at this range, but it was the thought that counts. Even if the opposing force was quite possibly more tense and less well trained than her forces, Lindy's allies were still outnumbered somewhere around five to one, and that alone she allowed herself to be unhappy about. "Defend our comrades. Charge!" Lindy bellowed and took off running at the enemy. With a roar, ragged men and women with all manner of weapons joined her, not realizing or caring that most of them would die to keep their paymaster's lines from being overrun. And for that, Lindy knew she would have nightmares.

The lines of humans, orcs, and goblins coming at them were shaken by the charge. Most stopped and tried to bunch up defensively. "Loose!" Lindy yelled, managing to get the attention of some of the more competent foes before grenades broke up the enemy lines. A young woman around sixteen ran by Lindy, a shovel in her hand. She was the first to die; a spear wielded by one of the older obviously more skilled orcs took out her gut and spine. Lindy leapt and cut the orc in half on her way down, yelling as she beheaded two goblins and sliced a man in half at the waist in one swing as she landed. The next half hour was bad. Only Lindy's regeneration and experience kept her in one piece. Never before had she considered that regeneration kept her sense of pain intact and that healing over and over was its own kind of pain. The wounds that would have been lethal without her abilities were worse when they healed. It was like getting hit hard twice. Her sense of pain was no longer an ally in this fight.

Somewhere in the trench lines she had left, a flare went up. It was a signal to regroup. Using her shard in the sky, Lindy saw the lines had been reinforced. As one of her shoulders reattached itself to her body, Lindy yelled, "Aid is here. Orderly withdrawal!" Then she realized that only twenty out of close to eight hundred were still alive and most of them would die soon. "I'll take the rear. The rest of you get back to our lines!" Lindy amended as she fiercely worked to buy time for those who could still walk, to move a few others that would not. By the time the enemy retreated in similar shape as her own forces, five soldiers were all that remained of the troops that had followed her. Lindy allowed herself to scream internally and pass out right as she returned to the friendly lines.

A human that looked like a slightly older Covell sat on a throne made of bloody gold. The ground was meaty and wet rivers of molten gold moved sluggishly past. The air smelled of iron, rust, and fire. "Is this hell?" Lindy asked.

Covell grumbled. "Come now uncle, you know better than that."

"Who are you really?" Lindy asked more firmly this time.

"The new war," the Covell replied, expanding her arms to the world around her. "I never thought I'd say this, but it's nice to see you again, Manfred."

Lindy shook her head. "I am more than he was."

"Maybe that's why I like you, uncle." Covell nodded thoughtfully.

"So gold, really?" Lindy asked.

"I am this world's concept of war, so the military industrial complex and by extension the economy are within my domain." Covell shrugged. "I called you here to say poison gas will soon be a thing and to invest in gas masks."

"That's insider trading," Lindy yelled as Covell waved her uncle goodbye. When Lindy opened her eyes she was in a long tent and surrounded by a few medics, more officers, Asami, Jin, and three politician-looking men, at least one of whom was from the principality of Zenic. "I'm back. Can I help you?" Lindy inquired of them.

The captain from before was the lowest ranking officer present. He sat on a stool next to Lindy's bedside sporting his own head wound.

"You sent a lot of men to their deaths. We would like to hear your reasoning."

A young general who carried himself more like a noble than someone who knew how to use a weapon nearly yelled. "Yes, what's your excuse? It is not a simple matter to replace that many resources."

"First of all, this is a medical facility. I'd thank you all to remember that," Lindy began. The young general and a middle-aged one held back from snapping at her, but only after the old captain and a civilian observer from the principality silently made clear they agreed with Lindy. She went on after the overfilled aid station quieted down. "I had to keep morale up and stop our lines from being overrun. No officers around my position survived the bombardment so I took charge. It was that or be wiped out." Lindy slowly got out of bed and stood up. "Is that satisfactory, sirs?"

The men around Lindy looked at the young general and Lindy got a very bad feeling. "As overall commander, I sympathize with your troubles but cannot condone the numbers we lost. The battalions on the front line are below half strength. Your recklessness did not help."

Lindy nearly moved to kill the man on the spot. "Are you serious?" she whispered but the entire tent heard her before anyone could interrupt her. Lindy shrugged. "Very well, sir. How about I raid the enemy supply lines? That should buy us a few days without heavy fighting."

"Alone, that will not help," the general sneered.

The principality's pen pusher spoke up. "I support the proposal and am willing to lend some of my nation's specialists to this."

"Fine. I'll even transfer this one over to your care." The young general waved dismissively as he left with the other men. Only the old captain, Asami, Jin, and the foreign bureaucrat were left.

"So who was that?" Lindy asked.

"General Gran Theodoric the younger is the man in charge of this sector. The older general with him is Louise Salok Benrin. I am Satoshi. The man in charge of your company is Stern the Spry," the bureaucrat replied. The introduction seemed to brighten his failing mood.

The old captain extended his hand. "It was a pleasure working with you. I will not be able to prevent your transfer. I'm sorry."

"It is what it is." Lindy nodded as they shook hands. "Would you mind if I check in with my old unit from time to time just to see how they are doing? Of course, nothing more."

"If the high officers are not around and you don't make a habit of it then that will be fine," Stern agreed.

Asami appeared from behind Satoshi. "I guess that means you are with me, shadow mage."

"Yes, quite. Come along then. If nothing else, your generals are fantastically efficient with paperwork." Satoshi sighed as he moved to make his way from the tent.

"Are you ok to walk?" Stern asked Lindy who noted she still had on her uniform. It was more crumpled than before and was nearly black from blood.

"After a good meal and a nap I'll be good. If it wasn't for those orcs, most of this blood would be mine," Lindy replied, then walked off. But taking advantage of the now oppressive stillness she added, "By the way, be careful of poison gases. This terrain is perfect for it."

Lindy moved to walk behind Satoshi. As they neared his nation's place in the rear camp Satoshi asked, "You thought so too?"

"I had to tell them," Lindy sighed. "They don't make generals around here like they used to."

Lindy was led into the yurt. Jin came from one side, handing them all cups of hot tea. "That's the first I have heard of that."

Lindy took a sip of tea and grumbled. "Humans don't live long. Their cultural memory is likewise very short and inconsistent. Dragons and a few others remember the war that made the wasteland. Some even lived though the times before that. Besides, a king's bloodline was not a merit, but skill and competence were."

"The world is not that simple," Satoshi shot back, very much enjoying the minor debate.

"If life was simple it would not be as rewarding or weighty. That does not change that history fails to remember far more than has happened, and even then imperfectly, much like the rest of our mortal works."

Satoshi was suddenly less amused. "You know our emperor calls himself a god, right?"

"I do now," Lindy nodded. "Are we going through with the raid I proposed?"

"We are if a satisfactory plan can be drawn up," Satoshi said. The four that stayed behind to keep the gears and cogs spinning got to work, spending the rest of the day and most of the night working out the details of Lindy's proposed raid.

It took two days to gather supplies and troops, all of whom were from the same extended family as Asami and Jin. For whatever reason Lindy was put in charge of one of the three teams. Asami was her second-in-command. Jin was in charge of the mission itself. A young man called Kage was leading the other team. Interestingly, the 30 troops in Lindy's team were all between 15 and 22 years old. Kage's team of 23 were all between 21 and 30. Jin's team of 18 were from 38 to 42. From the conversations she heard, the tradition in the clan she had been assigned to would keep the teams together until the members were all too old, dead, or had one member remaining. What baffled her was the clan did not have a name, but given what they and other families like them did behind the scenes to support military and government members, that made some sense. Spying, infiltration, special operations, and assassination were all things these families did. Most families specialized in one or two of those, but all had teams that could do tasks that were not the family's main work. The clan Lindy was with mainly worked in special operations and assassination. It was one of the lesser known and older families, which said a lot about their skills and connections.

The night two days after Lindy's abrupt transfer to the principality of Zenic's forces, the raid began. Over the days of planning and supply three small skirmishes had broken out among the main armies in their zone. The spies and scouts had found five enemy supply depots set just behind the trench lines. Lindy was sent after the largest ammo dump. Her team split into two as they moved under the cover of night. Her troops had been told to obey her and so far, they had done just that. It did not take long for Lindy to adjust her movements to the same pattern as those she commanded. Some members on her right flashed over a hand signal saying they had found a hidden bunker. Lindy slipped into the shadow of a large rock and peered into the bunker. It was set up like a mining tunnel. *Undermining,* she thought. She sent off three of her team to fetch Asami and her unit. When the sub-leader appeared Lindy used hand signals to order Asami to take some members and target the mine. She directed her to the explosives set in some sheds by the tunnel entrance. After taking the supplies, Asami and the members she selected moved off to blow up the ammo supply. Lindy and 15 of her subordinates moved on, leaving Asami and her 14 members to their task.

The enemy lines were more heavily patrolled than reports had suggested. That and the delay by the tunnels meant Lindy was pressed for time. They had an easier time to sneak by given their lower numbers, but that also meant that if any of them got caught the mission would become a lot harder. Lindy spotted a mess hall right behind the first trench lines. Their target was just behind that near the second trench line. Lindy signaled her troops to kill anyone in the mess hall, then burn it with as few supplies as possible. She wanted a slow but violent fire that would spread. The actual signs translated to *sub target, no witnesses, keep safe, use minimal supplies, cause big fire.*

Soon after, they moved in a long arc past the panicking enemy troops. The fire had also served to hide their scent well. Fewer guards blocked their path and the group more than made up the time they had lost. After assassinating the few guards left behind, Lindy's team set the ammo stockpile to blow. A few analog stopwatch mechanisms served as the timers and were by far the most expensive pieces of kit they had brought. When Lindy moved to stalk out with her team, she spotted some suspicious chemical barrels. Upon touching one, her hand felt a tingling sickly sensation. She motioned her team to return to base ahead of her after meeting up with the other half of the unit. As her team moved off, Lindy began to toss the chemical barrels onto a cart and disguised herself as one of the enemies, changing her face and putting one of the smaller guard's uniforms with the least blood over her own, hoping the darkness and panic would hide the rest. The fire helped her avoid suspicion to only a few glances. Upon finding a tunnel network that hid a radio station, Lindy dumped all the barrels of toxic gas inside and disintegrated the lids before running as fast as she could. A man stopped her, yelling, "Where are you going?"

"Someone sabotaged the radio room. Where's the captain?" she yelled back in the man's language.

"By the fire," the man yelled as Lindy rushed toward the blaze. She sprinted past the back of a bucket brigade, snapping the neck of the best-dressed man around who had been watching the fire from the back, as a slowly reorganizing mob tried to control the flames. Soon after, Lindy sped by the spreading inferno. Right on time the ammo dump blew, raining molten debris on the would-be fire fighters. Lindy was illumined a few times as secondary explosions went off far behind her. She ripped off the stolen uniform and changed her visage back, pushing the screams and frantic yells to the back of her mind.

Lindy was within sight of her lines when the other ninja teams came out of the shadows to greet her. "You are late," Jin told her firmly.

"Ran into some unexpected dangers. Had to improvise. Where should I give my report?" Lindy asked.

"Here would be fine," Jin told her as he looked over at their trench lines that had more than a few heads peeking out. A few of those were aides to officers whose suspiciously big hats were visible over the ridge.

"Very well, sir. We ran into some tunnels that looked like an under-mining operation. Blew that. Had to torch a mess hall and the attached personnel, not to mention some food supplies. Blew the target. Found a few barrels of poison gas. I took those and infected the radio room with them. Killed a colonel on the way out." Lindy replied as if it was a noon day stroll then she shrugged. "That chaos should last a few days."

"That's it?" Jin asked, no longer amused. He seemed visibly impressed, so much so that his calm and stern mask had cracked a bit around the edges.

"I believe it's a subordinate's job to fulfill the objectives they are told to fulfill. That often involves reacting accordingly to things not in the original mission plan. After all, none of us are omnipotent." Lindy smiled back. Their entire conversation had been in a language common to the army as a whole.

"Well I'd say you earned a bonus then. How about a promotion?" Jin asked, his face back to its default mask.

"As long as I get to stay with my current team, then I accept," Lindy chuckled, knowing this was in many ways a show.

The ninjas walked back to the lines. After getting past the first two trench lines the unit members left, no longer blocking Lindy from those around her. Jin looked over at his new comrade. "You and I need to report to Satoshi."

After waiting for a few others who were also reporting to Satoshi, Lindy and Jin entered his tent. "I heard what you were up to. Is this all correct?" he asked, handing a page over to Jin.

"That's what she told me," Jin nodded.

"Fine. Would you like to officially be in charge of your unit?" Satoshi asked.

"So I was an honorary member until now, and this was in part a test," Lindy smirked. She pretended to think for a few seconds then shrugged. "Fine. It's not like I have anything better to do."

"Take this seriously," Jin scowled.

"She is. It's her acting that's terrible," Satoshi said dismissively.

"Now that I have a better idea of how you two work, what exactly are my responsibilities?" Lindy asked.

Satoshi grinned widely but Jin answered. "Train your unit, stay in close contact with them. Relay their reports to us. Keep track of their supplies. Request new kit when needed and take them on missions when we ask. Other than that, keep an eye on this combat zone with them and be ready to act at a moment's notice."

"All right then. If that's all, I'll go find them," Lindy nodded.

"One more thing. What do you think the young general Gran Theodoric will do now?" Satoshi asked.

"Order an assault, trying to get as much credit as possible. Ignore his subordinates and get most of them killed. He may even blame us for that." Lindy sighed as if it were not her problem.

Neither Satoshi nor Jin liked her prediction; their faces made that clear. "You may be right. Keep an eye on our ally's officer corps then, will you?" Satoshi grimaced. He had entertained something similar as a worst case scenario but Lindy's quick and concise first idea made him take the worst case more seriously. The apparently frivolous young woman before him was mysterious but more than that, her cleverness and skill were worth far more than he could pay her.

"No problem. I'll handle most of that personally." Lindy beamed at them as she rapidly sunk into her own shadow.

Lindy hid within many officers' shadows over the course of a day and a half, learning only of a planned mass wave assault. The high-ranking officers' disregard for the lives of their men and unwillingness to compromise were not news, but disheartening all the same. She delivered her report to Satoshi, sparing no paper in her quest to document his ally's issues she had seen from supply to organizational chaos. The fact that reinforcements were already requested showed that the officers were not totally blind to balancing their precious numbers.

Lindy met Woodrow in secret on a sniper post a few hours before the dawn the attack was set for. "Try to stay in the rear," she asked her son.

"That's not my call," Woodrow retorted.

"Try to merge in with the rear of the wave during the assault. If you go alone it should not disrupt the lines too much. Please, I am begging you," Lindy asked.

"What are you, my mother, Din? I will not leave my squad behind. I thought you were better than that." Woodrow huffed and moved to leave.

Lindy's heart almost broke but she steeled herself the way she did in battle, forcing herself to be cold and not thinking too much. She grabbed her son's arm. "And if I was your father, what then? You may seriously die. Unlike her, you can't come back from Death's realm." Only fear of what he might say stopped her from telling him who she really was.

Woodrow shook off the limp arm. "My father's servant should not worry about me like that. It's disgusting. You should value your free will more." When he looked back at the small young woman he had come to respect she seemed on the verge on tears, but oddly her conscious mind and face had not realized that yet. "Well it's not like there is any proof I can't come back." Then he began to walk away faster, not at all happy with snapping at what he saw as a young woman who his father kept around to do his dirty work.

"At least your wife and kid are safe. If that bonehead does give you a second chance it will be smothered in red tape. Just be careful what you wish for. If you let your priorities go any more out of whack you might not come back to them. Trust me, that's a road of pain." Lindy sighed just low enough for Woodrow to hear her but Lindy was not enough in her right mind right then to care. "See you some other century then, son. I'll keep your child safe in your absence at the very least." Woodrow snapped around and rushed back to Lindy but she was already dispersing into the lengthening shadows of dawn. "Just learn from your old man's mistakes, all right?" she told him, knowing he now suspected who she really was.

"Dad, what, why?" Woodrow called after Lindy, not knowing what to say.

An hour later Lindy had composed herself. She clawed her way out of Asami's shadow where she had been hiding. "What the fuck! Don't do that without warning!" The young ninja sputtered in the middle of her breakfast, redecorating most of her shirt with lukewarm herbal tea.

"Let me borrow your face?" Lindy asked blandly as she stood up and returned what little tea had fallen on her into the air as if nothing was the matter, while deep down in her subconscious she was still screaming.

"What? No," Asami whispered. As the ninja got quieter the more agitated she became, which any other time would keep Lindy amused for quite a while.

Lindy sighed, changing her face to looked almost exactly like Asami's, save for a few small cosmetic changes. "I just want to borrow most of your looks, not your body. See, no pain, right?"

"That's bad for my heart and I have a headache but fine, I'll get over that. Can you tell me why, sir? That's only fair, right?" the ninja asked more firmly than usual. In fact, this was the first time since working with Lindy that she had been so vocal about something.

Lindy smiled, suddenly in a better mood now that she had a suitable distraction. "I can only tell you the best side benefit." Asami grimaced but looked expectant. "It's less confusing this way, right?"

Asami resumed eating her porridge. "You know what? Forget I asked."

"Right," Lindy said, then clapped her hands. "I'll see how long it takes Jin to notice I'm not you." Before the now-panicked Asami could stop her Lindy bolted from the tent, only to find Jin a few tents away outside at a campfire.

Jin took out his sword and pointed it at Lindy. "Who are you?" he asked without hesitation.

Lindy changed her face back to the one she had before, then back to her new appearance. "Just me. With all the chaos happening soon, it seemed like a good idea to blend in with all of you."

"Do we really look that different?" Jin asked. He did well to hide how unamused he was.

"Not to me, but that's not true for all of them. Plus no one else from this continent is in your army so the enlisted men who do not know me would be confused." Lindy used hastily thrown-together logical-sounding words.

Asami rushed up behind them. Seeing how Jin was acting she blurted out, "How did you know?"

"She is shorter than you," Jin replied firmly.

"And more annoying," Lindy added smugly. "But don't comment on a woman's height. It's rude! Besides, I can be tall if I want to be." Jin smiled thinly and got back to cooking his breakfast.

Before midday the reorganization of the army was done and the troops had lined up. Lindy and her team were sent to support as needed. She had gotten permission to prioritize aiding the wounded. Lindy's old team and Stern were at the front in the middle of the lines. From the roof of a watchtower, Lindy watched the army begin to move forward towards the alert enemy lines. "I did what I could, kid. Abandoning you was on me but I can't do any more than this. I'm sorry," she whispered.

"What are you on about?" Asami asked, poking her head out from the watchtower's perch.

"Nothing. Just coming to terms with the past," Lindy sighed.

"You sound really old, senior Li," Asami muttered, pulling herself back into the watchtower.

Lindy watched the army march halfway through no man's land. That was when the enemy fire really started to hit home in earnest. Lindy saw it all from her shard in the sky. Faces, guts, and multiple viewpoints all poured into her mind's eyes at the same time. Asami relied on a spyglass but that did not provide the visceral impact of what Lindy saw as bodies dropped and shells fell. Troops clambered over one another. "I might be the oldest one on this lake of bloody mud," Lindy grumbled as she watched people not even a tenth of her age get cut down in horrific ways unique to them like swaths of rotten oats. Hundreds died from gunfire with each eye blink, and more died from artillery and support weapons. "What a farce. Well, story of my life," Lindy spat before standing up. "Asami, we probably will not have enough leeway to evacuate the wounded for a while. I'm going to raid a few of those gun emplacements. You got this until then, right?"

"What? Well yes. If it's only watching until we can get in there I can handle this." Asami sounded baffled. "But are you ok, ma'am?"

"No I'm not, but that's what I get paid for. I just need to let off some steam. I'll be back before you know it." Lindy flashed a tired smile then leapt into her shadow.

22

Are We There Yet?

Lindy jumped out from the shadow of an orc loading an artillery shell and cut him in half, then leaped into the shadow of one of the guns she had targeted and fatally stabbed a human who was manning a gunpowder-fueled machine gun. It was a rare weapon on her side of the lines and no such weapon had been captured by her army yet, so Lindy took it and began to fire madly as she leapt around like some kind of deranged trapeze artist. Lindy took half an hour to clear a small area around each gun before she unloaded every firearm she had taken from the enemy into the ammo stocked near each gun emplacement and each of the fragile-looking mechanisms of the artillery she could find. Just under an hour later, after a brief creeping barrage and counter battery battle, the armies clashed in melee combat in the third line where Lindy had been wreaking havoc. When Lindy saw a man with a shovel cut open the neck of one of her allies she knew it was time to head back. Lindy ran into a bunker, found its darkest corner, and leapt in. During her solo assault the only thing on Lindy's conscious mind was wondering why she could empathize with being called a monster by the humans, goblins, orcs, ogres, and cyclops she had just fought. *Being united sure is nice. Too bad they became my foe. At least they did not run into me at full power. Small mercies, right?* Lindy mused.

Asami looked up from the mound of mostly empty stretchers around their first trench line. "Where have you been?" she yelled at Lindy as her boss rose from the shadow of a tent.

"Exercising." Lindy shrugged as she worked double-time to push the carnage she had just caused into the farthest corners of her mind.

"Right. Help me coordinate grabbing the wounded," Asami snapped, rolling her eyes. She was clearly overworked.

"Sure." Lindy nodded seriously. She looked over and found a dead lieutenant with a small hand-drawn map of the battlefield clenched in his hands. The man had died of blood loss due to a nick in one of his arteries. Chances are he died on the way back to the lines. Lindy gently took the map from the man's hands, unceremoniously made some corrections to the map that she knew from her view at the enemy's third line, but leaving out her shard in the sky's view, and then began to circle some of the locations with mass casualties but comparably less fire and shelling. Then she showed the map to Asami, who had resumed yelling at the stretcher barriers around her. "Heavy melee combat around these locations should be dying down now." She pointed to five locations where she had doodled a sword and pointing to a few others while drawing a small image of a smoking musket ball. "These spots had mass volley fire and good cover. Should be lightening up around now."

Asami snatched the map quickly, poring over it. "How reliable is this info right now?" she asked.

Lindy thought furiously for a few seconds. "If one of our people ran through those locations right now and were careful, they would have a seventy-five percent chance of coming out with only a few scratches and a wounded trooper or two, if they were quick about it."

"Those are not good odds for the main force," Asami sighed. Before Lindy could retort, the young ninja grumbled, "But they are far better than what we run today."

"So which teams should I yell at?" Lindy managed to smile, finding as much humor as she could in Asami's mannerisms.

"You take that half of our lines. Just greet and yell at anyone that comes by." Asami waved off in one direction.

"Sure, no problem. I'd give this battle another hour. We will be swamped soon with all kinds of living folks." Lindy shrugged.

"When it rains it pours," Asami sighed. She already looked half dead mentally herself and began to run after some men moving the dead to a location not set aside for them.

"After the fighting's done today I'll handle managing the rest of the combat, so take a nap then, Asami," Lindy called after her second-in-command. Asami waved back and moved back to fighting all the administrative dumpster fires in her way.

For less than half an hour Lindy rushed around madly, making sure wounded, medics, supplies, and the dead all got where they needed to be at any given time. She was grilling a few supply runners about a shortage at one of the transport stations used to move heavily wounded troops further back in the rear, when a mass yell that was far more energetic, unified, and directed than the scattered shouts before echoed over from the enemy lines. Many troops around her paused to cheer wildly; despite most being on the verge of collapse, they believed they had won. Lindy saw otherwise when she focused on what her shard in the sky saw. It was bad for her comrades. They had overextended themselves in some spots that were heavily weakened from the raids the ninja had pulled off. Many had charged after the fleeing enemy, not noticing the lines around them still held. Worse yet, the enemy had held a few whole companies in reserve and used them to smash anyone caught too deep in a withering crossfire. Lindy soon spied Woodrow on his knees surrounded and alone. To an outside observer all this happened in a few seconds. When Lindy suddenly disappeared from her post, only a few close by noticed. Their panic was drowned out by the mistaken euphoria all around them.

Lindy appeared next to her son in a sea of blood-colored mud. The air smelled of iron and fire while tasting like gunpowder. She blocked a sword meant for her child with a saber of her own and shot dead the three closest to them. Lindy glanced at Woodrow. He was exhausted, bleeding but alive. If not for his weariness he should have been able to move far better. "Bad day?" Lindy quipped.

"Dad, that you?" Woodrow asked. He was near to fainting.

"Hey, stay with me," Lindy yelled as she created five more corpses with her pistol. Then she retreated back to the aid station she had left. Lindy growled at the first medic she saw. "Keep him awake for five more minutes."

"But we..." the medic began but relented when the wounded around them began to look very pale. A few even began coughing blood as the air around Lindy seemed to fill with the screaming souls of the recently dead.

After the medic injected Woodrow with something and his eyes cleared up a bit, Lindy calmed down a little and gripped Woodrow's head, yelling, "What did I tell you?"

"Not to charge in?" Woodrow stammered.

"That's right. Life is not cheap. Remember that!" Lindy spat. Without looking back she stomped out of the aid station, much to the relief of all inside. Soon after she found Jin. When she was next to him she whispered, "You know the cheers on the other side are not from our allies, right?"

"We considered that," Jin nodded. "Do you have proof?"

"Just dragged that last savior of my unit out of the mid-point in those trench works. He was the only ally still alive that I saw, although I did not look too closely," Lindy sighed.

Jin choose not to press Lindy for answers on how she had just managed that, simply saying, "Well, declaring victory before it's over is unwise." A fraction of a second later, general Gran Theodoric the younger who had come down to gloat over and observe the jubilation on the front lines was killed by a sniper's bullet.

"It's just one of those days," Lindy grumbled before rushing off to help restore order among the faltering lines and crumbling minds of her allies.

Lindy swept up a shotgun from a table laden with gear taken from the dead. She pulled a hatchet and large dagger, both of ancient make, from her shadow. Over the years it seemed her shadow had occasionally pulled things into itself when she transferred around. Grabbing a bag filled with shotgun shells and loading her newest acquisition, Lindy raised her hand to the sky and summoned a ghostly head just bigger than the average adult ogre's. Besides a few stifled gasps, the trench lines all around her went silent. Lindy's voice roared across the battlefield in a short lull between the sound of explosions from her side's minefield. "Listen up fools! Get your act together and hold the line. If you don't then I won't even have the chance to kill you myself. Prove to yourselves that we are stronger than the bastards coming for our heads!" A short pause fell over her audience as her summoned ball of ectoplasm vanished. Then the lines shook with a unified shout and the troopers either fell into line or those next to them dragged their fellows along for the ride.

Asami walked up to Lindy. "Was that show really necessary?" She had fallen into her native tongue.

"No, but we needed to expedite this," Lindy answered back in the same language.

"The officers will not be happy," Asami warned.

"Good. A known danger that stays near them should make them do their jobs." Lindy grimaced. "So where to now?"

"Your call, boss," Asami shrugged. The rest of their team came out of the woodwork and formed around Lindy.

Lindy grinned evilly and raised up her shotgun. "Asva, Hono, Yuki, Ringo, and Kioshi, grab a sniper rifle and find a perch. You are on covering fire. The rest of you, hit and run tactics. Disrupt enemy pockets that are going strong and smash those that falter on me!" Lindy called as she rushed behind the ridge just behind the first trench line intending to use its small amount of cover and the troops in the trenches to soak up some fire as her unit hunted for where they were needed. Lindy's face became emotionless as she focused only on the task at hand and worked out how efficiently they could attack from the ridge of dirt that had been excavated from the trenches.

It did not take long for what was left of the first line of foes to break past the minefield. Lindy saw an ogre and a few well-armed orcs rush into a trench harboring an allied platoon. Very few of her allies ran, knowing that turning their backs now meant a one-way ticket to Death, but that holding their ground offered a better chance of staying alive, however slim. Lindy called to her team, "The ogre's mine. Let's go!" and leapt at the ogre's chest that was just barely in line with the lip of the hole they had dug for themselves. Most of Lindy's team took up firing positions from the mound of dirt right above the lines. Five of them leapt after their leader, pistols and sharpened entrenching tools in hand. Lindy cut the ogre across the gut, which got her allies' and their attackers' attention. Lead rain and glorified shovels came down hard in the brief seconds where Lindy was the main focus. The ogre raised his arm and Lindy kicked him in the groin as she fell, unloading her shotgun into its stomach. As it reeled, she kicked and stabbed her way up to its head and slit the opposing soldier's throat before fading away and reappearing next to an orc with a different-colored shoulder pad. She thrust her hand into its back and crushed its heart.

Her unit and allies had finished off the other opponents by the time her second kill fell into the mud. Lindy turned to the highest ranking and oldest trooper left in the platoon she had saved. It was a middle-aged corporal. Their sergeants and lieutenant were crushed into the muck along with the orcs. A messy war is one hell of a great equalizer, Lindy sighed mentally. "Corporal, looks like you are in charge. My team is heading out. Remember, fighting clean will get you covered in more than mud, and not in a good way. That said, I hope you and your unit keep enough of themselves intact to live well after this war is over."

Lindy raised one hand and moved for her team to head out. The corporal looked around and realized he was in fact in charge now and his platoon members were willing to follow him. "See you later," the trooper called out. With all the mud and gore covering him, Lindy was unsure if the corporal was male or female, elf, human, or something in between. The smoke and grit were not doing anyone's voice any favors either.

"Right. Keep up the good work," Lindy nodded as she mused, *I wonder what your face will be like if I handle your paperwork after you die.*

After five smaller skirmishes where supporting fire was all that was needed, Lindy and her team found themselves on the left line. Three of her team had died. Only the first died in a stupid way; her weapon had exploded in her face, taking most of her neck with it.

The third wave of foes had begun their assault. It was the lightest yet and as far as Lindy could tell, the last. All the foes were shades now. Lindy had a conflicted feeling killing the descendants of those she had wronged and remade, or at least she did until the shades began to reanimate the dead into a horde of zombies. Lindy simply called out, "Hold ground and guard me." She was tired. Suppressing her powers while using what she allowed herself to the limit was painful, more so because of how long she had been fighting. It was just after noon. She had been fighting for close to twelve hours. None of her allies were in good shape. Lindy got to one knee and began to counter the spells from as many shades as she could at once. Most of the left wing was spared the zombie assault.

Asami moved to hold Lindy up. Her capable if quirky leader was barely conscious. "They reanimated the dead. I interfered around here. Kill the shades here fast and bring the entire wing to aid the others by any means necessary. I'll take full responsibility," the beast in a small body whispered.

Asami did a double take. "Is that really ok, boss?"

Lindy grinned weakly. "Go ham," and then she was sound asleep despite the stench that no one could smell anymore and the sounds most were partly deaf to.

Asami sighed, psyching herself up. "I won't let you down, boss," she whispered firmly. Then raising her voice and handing their leader over to a member of the sniper team, Asami yelled to her subordinates, "Let's make this quick. For victory!"

"For the boss!" her teammates echoed back like a bunch of hooligans.

Lindy found herself in a chair at a table with tea and cake. Fate, Hanna, and Covell sat at the table as well. "You work too hard, uncle," Covell said in greeting.

Lindy grumbled. "Well I have something like forever to live. Doing nothing for a week is bad enough for what's left of my mental health. So why are we here?"

"No idea." Fate shrugged, finally seeming to be in a good mood. "You have messed up my hubby's realm to no end. Now we can't have a nice chat there without spending a few hundred years outside our realms."

"Not that that's an issue for us, although the drinks over there could use some work. So be grateful, uncle." Covell nodded. All of a sudden Fate seemed ready to blow a gasket.

"So Fate, how have you gotten along with the man next door?" Lindy asked, hoping that would redirect Fate's attention.

"Very well," Fate smiled. Then she scowled. "Although that's not something I want to hear from you. Not only do you work closely with my man, but you are a mother."

"First of all, I'm the dad and I am not attracted to men in the first place!" Lindy retorted.

Covell refilled Lindy's tea. "You are something else, uncle," she murmured spitefully.

"I don't need a tsundere and a yandere to give me life counseling!" Lindy sighed with deep ambivalence.

"Right. Because all of us are well-adjusted to eternity," Hanna chuckled.

"Hey, at least you are ok. These two don't even act their age," Lindy shot back.

"Well, staying in a young form affects the mind, old friend," Hanna shrugged, still laughing.

"How am I supposed to act a few thousand years, fool?" Covell fumed.

"Well, I'm a man at heart," Lindy shrugged. Then seeing their expressions Lindy was struck with a question. "Wait. What even am I anymore?"

"Alive forever. Get used to it," Fate replied dismissively.

"Right. Well I've got places to be. The cake was all right. I'll try to bring some chow with me some other time." Lindy stood up.

"Like when?" Covell asked, trying to not appear like she was looking forward to it.

"She has literally forever to keep that promise," Hanna reminded her colleague.

"You three are stuck with each other likely for at least as long as the three at the center of this. Want to keep the existence of life our problem," Fate sighed.

Lindy was gone in a flash from Fate's realm. She opened her eyes to see it was midnight. "Well that was trippy like always," she sighed.

Woodrow was sitting up on a tarp with Lindy and many other wounded along with a few recently dead. "You know how we did?" she asked her son while using a different face, tone of voice, and accent than she had used with him before.

Woodrow was focused on looking closely at each face that passed. "Well enough to get timely medical treatment."

"Fair. Well how long has the fight been over?" Lindy asked.

"Less than an hour, more than half an hour," Stern announced from nearby. He had a head wound but was moving well enough. "One of the wings had no enemy reinforcements. You know anything about that?"

"If you mean the zombies, then it was a big well-timed counter spell that helped us," Lindy shrugged. She got a lot of glares. "Was it bad? I passed out early in the third assault."

"No shit it was bad! I had to kill most of my squad!" a nearby man moaned.

"Well we lost around half of ours," Asami snapped. As usual she had appeared from nowhere. Lindy was still able to track her if she tried but the young ninja was able to evade detection if no one was actively looking for her.

"Is that good or bad?" Lindy asked.

"Percentage-wise we did real well." Lindy's gaze sharpened a tad before her subordinate could call her boss, so Asami finished after a short pause, "Comrade."

"I'm ready to get back to the unit as soon as you are," Lindy nodded. After dusting herself off she looked around. Off in the distance were many mounds of a thousand corpses, each being set alight, which lit up the darkening sky.

"I'm done here. Let's go," Asami nodded. Lindy ignored the glares directed at her back but Asami did not, returning a far more intense glare at those that dared disrespect her boss.

When they were out of earshot Asami asked, "So the man you were chatting up — who is he?"

"My son. It's a long story," Lindy sighed.

"That's why you changed faces, right? I never knew you were a mother," Asami pressed.

Lindy rolled her eyes. "I'm the dad," rising one hand to stop Asami speaking out, Lindy's voice become firm as she asked, "So what's our head count look like now?"

"Eighteen, including us. Five will need some time to heal." After giving her boss a once over she asked, "Four more are walking wounded but need treatment, although I'd recommend rest as well. Do you need anything, boss?"

Although grime still covered her in most places, Lindy's wounds were long gone. Only the long scar from so long ago marred her flesh. "I'll be fine. I've been through far worse."

"Such as?" Asami asked.

"Would you believe me if I said dying?" Lindy tried to sound like she was joking.

"If you are Woodrow's father then I'd believe it, agent of Death." Asami nodded as they kept walking. "And no, I am not planning on telling anyone," she added when her boss's pace slowed briefly.

"Right. Thank you," Lindy replied.

After arriving at her tent, Lindy noticed Leera was alone in a small farmhouse far on the other side of the killing field. Lindy melted into her lightless tent and stepped out from behind the young shade. "Long day?" Lindy asked, noticing a half empty bottle of whiskey on Leera's desk.

Leera practically jumped out of her skin, pistol suddenly in hand, but when she saw her people's creator she sighed, her features tired and melancholic. "Nice face. What is it now?" Leera asked. Any deference she usually would have had was washed away by her fatigue.

"Nothing. I just thought it would be nice to talk." Lindy shrugged.

"Then talk. How many shades did you kill today?" Leera asked.

"None. I passed out before I got the chance," Lindy replied, then helped herself to half a couch.

Leera took a swig of whiskey. "So what? You have not used your full power yet?"

"This planet still exists, doesn't it?" Lindy answered.

A knock came from the door and a voice followed. "Commander, a representative from the Bruteolon forces wishes to speak with you."

An even more muffled self-important grumble of "What's the holdup?" followed soon after.

Lindy changed her appearance back to the one she had when she had first met Frost and Fall. "Introduce me as you wish. I'll help you this time if I can," Lindy answered Leera's troubled glance.

"Fine, let them in," Leera called as she smoothed her hair and sat up at the desk.

The door was promptly opened by a young shade. Upon seeing Lindy he froze, only to be pushed aside by a plump man in a gaudy white and gold uniform. The man's eyes turned and met Lindy's. "Leave us," he commanded.

"I can't do that," Lindy sneered.

"What!" the man fumed. After giving Lindy a once-over he noticed she was in her field uniform. To him it was a uniform of the enemy's side. "Who are you?" he asked.

"She is the god of the shades," Leera said politely. She had taken the time the man was spending on Lindy to fix up her own uniform.

"I'd say creator of the shades, but they do worship me, so that's true as well in a sense," Lindy added.

"Then what's with the uniform?" the man pressed. His tone made all the shades in earshot reach for their weapons.

Lindy laughed. "I am pretending to be a simple grunt for the other team."

"Did you kill my men?" the man asked angrily. Some shades had begun to draw their weapons.

"Some, yes, but no more than a single-skilled hero-level opponent from this time period could." Then the man took a step forward, not noticing how hard Leera was freaking out.

Lindy waved her hands and shook her head, all while smirking. It was a mildly surreptitious gesture which caused the shades to relax a little. "So you are why our victory is stalled!" the buffoon accused.

Lindy rolled her eyes. "You know trench warfare is fantastic at defending against infantry, right? That means when a trench line is attacked by infantry a lot of them will die. Both armies have multi-tiered trench lines. So of course a huge number of infantry would die. Is that all?"

The man took a look around only to be met by the cold hostile gazes of zealots prepared to risk it all if it meant killing one man. "Yes it is. Good day, commander," he nodded while he fled.

When the man left, Lindy casually took a bottle of wine from a cupboard near Leera's desk. "Oh, and the rest of you lighten up!" Lindy called out past the still-open door. "Well that was interesting. Good luck," Lindy said, patting the young commander on the shoulder before disappearing from the room. Little did she know that small action instantly made Leera a candidate for sainthood.

The next morning before the crimson field of death was bathed in the red of dawn, Lindy left her tent. A short walk later she was at the cooking fire. For once Jin was not there tending it. Asami was seated at Lindy's usual seat. The spots where two of her deceased crew sat the day before were left empty as a force of habit. For some reason Woodrow and Stern sat at the fire as well. "Why are they here?" Lindy asked when Asami handed her a bowl of thin stew.

"We are looking for this unit's commander," Stern replied.

"Which unit? All three ninja teams eat here," Lindy asked.

"How about your rank first?" Stern replied, obviously exasperated from getting a runaround.

"We are an intelligence unit. Why do you want to know?" Lindy shrugged.

Woodrow spoke up. "We are being assigned a mission with one of the units." He was reluctant to stop eating.

Lindy turned to her second-in-command. "First I've heard of that, chief lackey."

"Jin and the section chief are discussing it with some colonel, boss," Asami smiled.

"Right, so I'm the boss of the third unit. We don't have an established rank system among the ninjas except for our section chief." Lindy sighed.

"A section chief is what exactly?" Stern pressed.

Lindy thought for a few seconds as she chewed an overcooked meat substance in the gruel. "Like an overseer? The equivalent might be like a lieutenant, but his authority is a lot higher, so no idea."

"We were told an old acquaintance of ours was in one of the three ninja teams," Woodrow said.

Lindy changed her face to all the ones she had worn for half a minute each. "There. I'm not doing that a second time," she grumbled.

Woodrow shot up. "Dad?" he asked.

Lindy knew that Satoshi, Jin, and a few strangers were almost to her meal site, so she paused. Soon after, Satoshi walked up with the other officers and asked, "Who's a father?"

"Long story of another life, sir. What's up?" Lindy replied smoothly.

"We need you and your team to hit a research post behind enemy lines. It's a long-term mission. Some observers will come with you," said a colonel whose uniform bore the hallmarks of a recent captain's insignia.

"So does the third team accept this task?" Satoshi asked a little smugly.

"They can't refuse," the colonel snapped.

"It's a request from your army. We will only take it if you can find a team that agrees to it," Jin explained coolly for both Lindy and the colonel's sake, which Lindy learned was far less amusing when she was in the crosshairs with a powerful clueless fool. *Damn, I almost feel sorry for Leera,* Lindy realized.

"Fine, but we are doing them a favor so they owe our forces, right? I'll need my entire unit on this," Lindy sighed.

"That sounds reasonable. We expect more tents, rations, and socks." Satoshi smiled, the very image of a seemingly reluctant conman having the time of his life.

"Fine, I'll see to it. Good day," the colonel spat. He took one look at Lindy's shit-eating grin as well her leader's less visible mirth, and stormed off.

Jin handed Lindy a map. "So can you do it?"

After looking it over and calculating enemy numbers and reinforcement speeds, Lindy nodded. "Not in a sane way, but it's doable." She skimmed over the rough topography, noting the number of hills and passes. "It would be nice if you could keep the opposing sides' heads down as we do."

"Without artillery that's a tall order," Satoshi replied. He steeled himself for whatever insane scheme his subordinate would put forward, looking forward to what her latest suggestion would cause in a cascading domino effect like always.

"What? Just build a few catapults, trebuchets, and ballista. Hurl a few live explosives, rocks, and their dead at them." She pointed off to the side of the muck field. "Look, we even have a few forests left, plus these hills should have some fun stuff to lob in them as well," stomping her foot for emphasis.

"Can we even do that?" Jin murmured.

"Why not? It's not like we had time to write up any treaties," Satoshi nodded.

"About that: we might want to put in something about chucking bodies when you do. That, or billing the foe for handling the dead," Lindy agreed.

23

Last Fool Standing

It took three days to pack up their gear. Lindy acquired the best second-hand climbing gear she could for the team: small backpacks, light camping gear, and grayish coveralls. Everything else was a few cans of food, knives, and small arms. Short rifles and an extra weapon or more ammo and cleaning supplies and food or sniper rifle and a pistol made up their full kit. Most food would need to be gotten en route one way or another. The extra long-lasting food was for emergencies. It was at this time that Lindy noticed how primitive her current world's water purification tech still was. She had to get small strainers from the mess hall that let almost nothing pass to attach to her team's canteens.

"You going to be all right?" Asami whispered as the team assembled hours before sunrise on their departure date.

"No matter what, I'd say yes," Lindy absentmindedly replied as she looked at a waterproof pocket watch she had gotten in lieu of hazard pay. She was getting hazard pay only due to a few legal rules she had kept making a fuss about. The main one was that her unit was technically a team of mercenaries, as defined by over half of the national armies in the alliance, and they had been sent out under observation and under duress for a high-profile job they had not been trained for by their employers. Between how the diplomatic corps and the majority of the allied nations' home armies defined each thing, Lindy had been able to acquire over all carte blanche to do the job her way and hazard pay that was given in goods. By the time the allied forces managed to slap together a unified regulation system for the war, she would be well into enemy lines or maybe even back already. If she was lucky, the war might even be over by then. The argument over sovereignty, honor, and pride seemed to be all-consuming over all eras and intelligent species. Except goblins, who were beginning to be seen as an intelligent race — they only had some kind of pride before — and dragons, who either did not care about honor or defined it in some way that made no sense to anyone else.

"What's living forever like, anyway?" Asami said under her breath so only her boss could hear.

"Bullshit. The worst thing about living forever is not being able to stay dead," Lindy grumbled back quietly.

Before Asami could work up the courage to think of another question, the unit was assembled. "Are we all set?" Stern asked.

"No one's missing any of their kit, right?" Lindy called out. A few minutes later she was told they had all their gear. "Then we are ready to undertake the plan without any changes. MOVE OUT!"

Only sixteen moved out, as her four wounded still needed time to heal. Jin had promised to make sure no one outside their nation's chain of command messed with those subordinates.

After making sure her point men each had a map and knew the planned route, Lindy moved next to Stern and her son, who were in the middle of the unit's spread-out formation. "No plan that is usable accounts for everything. That's why backup plans are a thing," she said.

"How many backup plans do you have?" Stern asked.

"None." Lindy shrugged as if it were a straight line at a comedy club. "I've always been partial to improv."

Three days of moving slowly and carefully skirting around the rear of their lines, and then along terrain not kind for an army, much less a hundred two-legged beings laden with gear. Eating edible plants with minimal preparation. Lindy's team moved from a field of bloody mud past small hills and into a maze of rocky cliffs. By the dawn of day four, despite having sped up slightly now that they had less chance of being spotted by their fellow man, they continued slowly. Day five was the same but on day six they came to a cliff face. It was their first obstacle and the only one Lindy knew they were well equipped for. After this, the chances of the plan needing major revisions were basically one hundred percent. The lay of the land, the opposition, and appearance of the target were all unknown. They had estimated as best they could but it was far more going in blind than she would have liked. Lindy had even begun ignoring her shard in the sky because it would provide far too much of a noticeable advantage, which could spell trouble for her and might be past Death's tolerance for her shenanigans.

The climb was harsh but her crew was nimble and skilled, so they managed. Lindy did have to leap up the cliff using small ledges while carrying Stern before everyone had gotten to the top. "What now?" the old captain wheezed.

"Now you acclimate to this height and I send out scouting teams," Lindy replied listlessly.

"What should I do?" Woodrow asked.

Lindy pointed to her son and five others. "Set up camp." Then she instructed her four snipers, "You four find perches around here," motioning to the thick shrubbery and large rocks on the plateau where they had arrived. "The rest of you, see what is directly around us and scavenge for chow. We begin getting the lay of the land tonight. Remember to take it slow until we can navigate well and run better."

"So we camp here?" Stern asked.

Lindy nodded. "It's hidden well enough and we can scatter or fall back from anywhere. Normally I'd like to hole up in a cave or something but we are in hostile territory and that means we could get trapped easier. That's a bad way to go."

"You sound like you've done this before, boss," Yuki said as she took a wedge of compressed ants from a pack.

"The last time I led a team like this was a lifetime ago," Lindy shrugged. "Now get to work."

Yuki was already done with her weapon checks and food procurement so she simply nodded and stalked off.

"I have not heard of an operation quite like this anywhere on this half of the continent in your lifetime," Stern noted.

"You forget I am older than I look. The rest is classified." Lindy smiled.

"I am older than you, captain, and she's my dad," Woodrow explained.

That night the scouts spread out as Lindy helped keep watch at the camp. If they found a better camp they might have to move, but for now a sniper and two others were always awake at camp. Seven slept and two teams of five each searched. Lindy took two of the four watches: the first and last. Stern took the second and Woodrow the third. They were told in no uncertain terms to inform Lindy if anyone came back in bad shape, not at all, half an hour late, or with urgent and/or important info. Asami was in charge of coordinating the scout teams in the field.

A little before Lindy's fourth shift she had almost gotten six hours of sleep when Asami shook her hard. Lindy drew a knife and took a saber into her hands from her shadow while a light machine gun suddenly popped into existence, floating above her head menacingly. Ancient spears now twirled around the camp alongside rifles and swords of all kinds and ages. When Lindy saw her second-in-command covered in blood that did not seem to be her own, Lindy took a deep breath. "Ok, report."

Asami watched her boss sheepishly put away the small arsenal that had suddenly appeared around the camp and could put any of those newfangled museums to shame. "We were attacked by a big monster. I think it's a divine beast."

"A what?" Lindy asked. At first Asami thought her boss might be a little sleepy but her face was so serious and she was clearly ramping up her body for combat, so Asami knew that was not the case.

"Big monster-like animal. One of a kind, stupidly powerful, and said to be blessed by a world spirit," Asami answered.

Lindy sighed, steeling herself for what might come next. "Gather those that still live back here. Do not use any blatantly unnatural signals." After Asami nodded, Lindy added, "Give me a little bit. I need to check something."

Seeing the boss close her eyes, Asami looked around. "You all heard the boss, right? Get to it. Try bird and cricket sounds. Use the emergency rendezvous pattern. And shore up the defenses, damn it!"

Lindy screamed in her mind using the link that connected her to this reality's world spirits. *I am told a divine beast is in my way. Is it ok if I kill it?*

Wait, why would you? Fate's voice echoed across Lindy's synapses.

Oh, that's one of mine. No problem. Knock yourself out. Covell's giggle silenced all those within the link.

But we need those. How will that weirdo fulfill his fate if there are no divine beasts to slay? Fate snapped. Lindy was getting a headache.

I can remake a few. It's not like that child will even be ready to swing a real blade anytime soon, War replied back, not seeming to care.

We don't know that, Fate began.

"So what am I, the control test?" Lindy snapped, both in her mind and out loud.

No, but you could be. It's a good idea, Covell agreed.

"Act your age, War. And Fate, you owe me a good cake next time we meet." Lindy grumbled again both internally and outwardly. Then she did the mental equivalent of hanging up and ignored the traffic on the link. Opening her eyes, Lindy found way more than a few of her subordinates staring at her. "Right. Ignore all that. I'm going hunting. Be back soon. Asami, you are in charge. If possible, defend this location." With a glance back Lindy sprinted off, following the smell of fresh blood.

As she ran carefully and sensing the area all around her by long-acquired second nature, Lindy reconnected to the world spirits. "So divine beasts, really? I thought you did not consider yourselves gods. Why now?"

Come now, uncle. We may be powerful but not all powerful, om-nipotent, or even especially interested in all aspects of mortal life, Covell replied through the link. Fate was grumbling unintelligibly in the background.

Fire joined the link. It had been ages since Lindy had heard from any of this world's four elements. *Whatever, War. When do we get cake!* It spoke.

"Oh, Fate's buying," Lindy smirked, not caring that she looked to be talking to herself while moving.

Why me! Fate yelled.

"You put my subordinates in danger for some insane and stupid reason, right? So bribe me with a good dessert," Lindy spat, now smelling far more than just blood.

Look here, you. Everything that gets born gets the dice rolled and a few kinds of destiny assigned randomly. Then I draw from a few jars and those vague events get added to their lives. This time we had to make things to fulfill a destiny. Not that the elf brat will get to them anytime soon. Fate complained.

"But divine beasts. Really? Isn't that kind of pretentious and false advertising?" Lindy commented. Her face and mind had begun to discard emotions and feelings in preparation for imminent combat when she stepped into a clearing. A boar the size of a large earth elephant or smallish dragon stood surrounded by shit and pieces of flesh. The boar was red with glowing yellow tattoos covering it. The smells of brimstone and iron filled the air. "And what's with this smell?" Lindy snapped. She knew that if the smell repulsed her, it must be bad. When the boar turned to face her it found a small woman holding a dark crystal sword and with ten rifles and twenty spears floating around her.

What? I just empowered a critter and I live in a place that would smell far worse if it was in a reality. I live in a piece of a concept, uncle! Covell fumed. Lindy rolled her eyes, slashing out a wave of energy from Transcendence.

So when's cake? Air giggled cluelessly.

Why me! Fate yelled just as Lindy shut down the link and dodged the boar's charge.

The gash on the monster's face bled lava. "Oh come on!" Lindy nearly echoed Fate's feelings, just in a much more muted capacity. Lindy then chose to fully give in to her instincts and adrenaline. The clearing and her foe were the only things on her mind. Killing it was a matter left to muscle memory and intuition.

Lindy rolled, avoiding a charge while the guns floating above her head unloaded over and over. She rushed around and the gun barrels melted before each exploded, so she tossed them at the boar monster over and over. Spears, swords, spikes, knives, and cookware all flew at the beast. Lindy had begun pulling entire storerooms worth of gear from half-remembered caches. Finally the beast choked on half a small boat so Lindy took the opportunity to shove multiple grenades into its eyes. She ran faster than she had in ages. Some of her crew from the camp rushed away from her. "Get down!" she yelled over the far-off boar's wails.

Lindy tossed herself into a sinkhole while covering her ears. A few of the troops near her followed suit. Before she reached the bottom of the pit the earth shook and a heat wave cascaded across the maze of cliffs and valleys around them. Lindy dragged the troops that had jumped in after her out of the hole. The majority that did not follow her down had flash burns. Asami and Woodrow had used some kind of sorcery to hold most of the heat at bay, but only those at camp benefited from that. Lindy looked at her few wailing troops. "Stern, lead the wounded out of here. Take Hono with you. The rest of you, pack out. We move out now!"

"Ok. Someone is bound to investigate. What about the dead?" Asami asked, her face hard. She knew this was only going to get more challenging.

Lindy looked up at the sky. "Right. No way that was subtle. Anyone in pieces is dead weight. If they can't be moved fast, shoot them dead or stab them. If they can talk, see if they have a preference."

"That's kind of brutal," Woodrow noted. But the ninjas had hard faces. They knew someone with the kinds of wounds Lindy was talking about would not make it back to their lines alive anyway, and would slow down the living.

"Make sure all pieces of our dead get some kind of burial and try to mark the location with a rock and on our maps," Lindy nodded. "Just make it quick. We need to be gone from here soon." She moved to where the boar had died. "I'll check on the pig."

She looked over to where the hot swine had exploded, which smelled vividly of cooked pork chops and burned bacon. It had taken a few museums' and battalions' worth of stock, not to mention a small navy, to take down the pig. The ground was blasted hard. A glassy pit with bits of charred pork and mostly melted iron balls and relics of bygone times were all melted in one mass on the top of this cliff. "That was some pig," Lindy grumbled as she allowed her thoughts to drift briefly. After taking a few breaths she slowed her heart back to normal and sat down.

Asami found her boss soon after. "Hey boss, we are all set."

"Ok let's go. Thanks for everything," Lindy replied evenly. Asami smiled thinly and wiped off her boss's face with a surprisingly clean rag in silence. They said nothing as they walked back. Lindy's wet eyes that day would forever be their secret. Nine fighters including Asami, Woodrow, and Lindy would move on into the unknown.

Half a day into the journey through a winding maze of cliffs and chasms, one of the only two non-snipers in the ninja team came back to report from his scouting trip. With hand motions he explained there was an enemy patrol with no heavy weapons. They had not spotted Lindy's team yet and the sniper he was working with was watching the foe from nearby above them. The foe was coming towards them slowly.

Lindy raised one arm to get her team's attention then motioned them to hustle away. As they passed by the sniper's approximate location, they used a soft-spoken migratory bird-hunting call. It was one of their pre-arranged signals to regroup and pull back. Lindy aged their tracks with her magic.

They managed to sneak by the enemy unit, not wanting to kill them yet, as that could very easily alert their target's guards.

Three days of travel later, much of which was spent looking for well-hidden places to camp, they came down into a caldera which was covered in pillars of basalt. According to the data they had been given, a research bunker was somewhere in the large pit. A small patrol passed by along a well-kept gravel road. Lindy's team hid behind a mound of boulders likely from a landslide or glacier from long ago. A kobold in the enemy patrol stopped and begin sniffing, as did the two gnolls. The ogre and five humans in the unit noticed this. Before they could think too hard, Lindy reached into Woodrow's shadow and pulled out three of her pet hydras, tossing them at the enemy unit as the massive bipedal snake-like beings looked at their creator quizzingly.

Lindy simply gave them a thumbs up and mouthed the words 'free food.'

One of the hydra heads yelled, "Meat's back on the menu, boys!"

Another of the heads on the same beast snorted. "Dude, we are carnivores. Meat is always on the menu."

The head on another hydra looked up from the massacre. Its body's other heads were gleefully proclaiming, "I identify as an it."

Soon after, the enemy was all eaten alive and Lindy peeked out from behind the rock. "Good job. Guard the road for a bit, ok?"

"Sure thing," all the heads roared, some adding mum, mom, dad, pop, master, and in one instance baba to the end of their collective shout.

Lindy's team sped up, following the edge of the road and zigzagging around rock outcroppings. Ten minutes later a bunker built into the cliff edge came into view. Two guards sat outside a sealed blast door around a camp of tents. Lindy motioned for the team to capture the guards swiftly. Asami seemed to disappear from the face of the earth. The ninja who had known her longer than Lindy did not seem agitated by this and began to keep watch around them, so Lindy was not too worried. At the back of Lindy's mind, however, was the desire to shed her disguise and examine the life signs all around them.

In rapid succession the two guards were knocked out from behind. Asami appeared to wave over her unit before disappearing again.

In the brief moment her second-in-command showed herself, Lindy analyzed her.

#72 "Asami series"

(modified) human female age 19

Affiliation: principality of Zenic

Job: ninja

Status: 8th special operations force-2nd, zone-3rd force-sub-leader

Abilities: strength 35, vitality 29, mind 33, agility 52

Talents: language (wasteland, low Zenic, Zenic outcast), talent: awareness, hide in plain sight, ambush, subdue, exceptional leap, absorb impact. silent casting, swift cast

Skills: Sword: journeyman, armor proficiency (leather): journeyman, lie: journeyman, dagger: expert, athletics: journeyman, acrobatics: expert, earth magic: adapt (artificially added), warding spells: journeyman (artificially added), stealth: extreme (inborn), marksmanship: journeyman, synthetic alchemy: adapt

Major destiny: reviled survivor

{note from Genney: Lindy I'm letting you see this destiny}

Lindy and the team ran to the tents while muffling their sounds and presence. Woodrow still made some noise. Lindy sighed, not wanting to contemplate how annoyed she could be right now.

Lindy took off the bigger guard's shirt, gouged out his heart, and reanimated him on the spot before stripping the others and cutting off his head. She motioned for the unit to hide, then put on the smaller guard's clothes and changed her appearance to be more or less that of the guard. Luckily the smaller guard was a baby-faced youth so she could impersonate his appearance well enough without drastically changing herself.

Lindy had her new zombie lead her to the blast door. She ordered it to open the door with its old memories but received feedback that no such data existed. Frowning, Lindy walked up and knocked on the door hard. No answer was forthcoming so she kicked the door off its hinges. It took three solid kicks on two locking clasps with her current guise's might before she could get enough purchase to roll up part of the door like a can lid for a human to scoot under.

Lindy motioned for the team to follow soon after she went in. She and the zombie ducked by the door; a shotgun muzzle was pressed to her head before Lindy managed to stand. "What happened outside?" a gruff voice asked.

"Monsters," Lindy replied while ordering her zombie to attack the man threatening her. The guard got off one panicked shot before his throat was ripped open. He rose as a zombie soon after. "Note to self: do not use this kind of undead too much, and burn them after," Lindy whispered. As the team trickled into some kind of small guard station she began giving orders. "We move behind the undead. Keep any important eggheads alive. The safe word for these fools," Lindy patted one of the zombies, "is brains. So if they go after a possible VIP, use it while manifesting some magic at the VIP. Make sure that any guards go down fast. Snatch any documents, move in teams no smaller than two, not counting the temp labor. We need to make this fast. Follow the rotters." With that, the two zombies began to move forward.

"So we use the panic to get what we want?" Woodrow asked.

"That's plan A," Lindy nodded.

The bunker was less a cave and more a metal-walled clean room with small offices. It was also self-contained and clearly getting power. Light bulbs and the muffled hum of a distant generator could be heard.

Small farms and a few water treatment stations were sandwiched in odd places. Surprisingly, besides two more gun-toting men, the ten others they came across were lab-coated researchers. The gunmen were killed along with most of the researchers. Three in lab coats marked with more elaborate badges were kept alive.

In the generator room sat a large thermal power plant close to a century before its time. "How did you fools know how to build this?" Lindy asked the head of the bunker. He had been adamant in his commands to the others to not say anything until Lindy began killing in earnest within the power room that most of the researchers had run toward.

"The likes of you would never understand," the man sputtered.

"You had someone from another would clue you in, right?" Lindy asked.

"I designed this. A child like you would," the aging head researcher began.

Lindy took out the most distressing blueprint she had found and held it up to the man. "So why build a nuke? You are from a place that used something like this, right? They caused all kinds of havoc in my home reality ever since they were made."

"Then why fight us? This place is ridiculous. No electric ovens, no heaters, no cars, no cellphones. It's madness!" the old man shouted.

"And yet people can live fine without them," Lindy snapped. "What you needed was enough clout to make a cell phone before you died. Now that's madness."

"I have not held a working cellphone in seventy years, no internet either. Do you know how hard that's been!" the man yelled. He was twitching all over in rage.

"And a super weapon is ok. Why am I the only lunatic that's not an asshole!" Lindy grumbled to herself, then she took out her first pistol, the first firearm this planet had ever known. "I made this over a thousand years ago and it fucked up this world." She placed the muzzle over the man's left eye and leaned down to glare at him through the other. "Did you finish one of the nukes?"

"It's a revolutionary anti-magic fission bomb and yes, one is placed under the ocean nearby," the man mumbled.

Lindy sighed. "And you made it with the new stuff from the City of Smog, right? A bomb that implodes in on itself to mess up magic?" Her face hardened. Her team was bewildered over the technical tirade until they sensed extreme danger and dragged the other two VIPs away, escaping outside the generator room. Lindy pressed her pistol on the man's eye. "Is it live? Is the nuke live? Tell me!" she bellowed.

"It's..." the curmudgeon began before Lindy sensed an ominous wave of otherworldly power. A millisecond later she blew out the man's brains mid-sentence.

Lindy stood up. Her chest and face were covered in fresher blood, her gun smoking in her hand. Lindy yelled to the ceiling in English, "Son of a bitch!" Then her form changed to one that mirrored her first meeting with Frost but with shorter hair this time. The scar on her side burned for a second. Lindy tore off her stolen uniform and pulled out Transcendence and The End. Looking though her shard in the sky she saw static, but from her fully powered senses Lindy knew where to go. Turning to the door as the entire generator room crackled with her power, Lindy called out in all the languages of this world at once. "I quit. Woodrow, Asami, I leave the unit to you."

Lindy stepped through shadow but before she was fully in she was tackled. The next instant Lindy was on a mound of chitin. Her dagger The End was raised over the head of Asami, who clung to Lindy's side. "You should run," Lindy tried to whisper, but her voice crept into the collective minds of two armies that had stopped mid-fight to look at one another and the otherworldly abomination that had sprung out of the void that the shades' new bomb had unleashed. A few noticed the other horror that had shown up soon after on the kraken-like mound of spines and jaws. "I got this. The rest of you, go away!" Lindy yelled as the monster flailed.

Leera saw Lindy then yelled to her army and allies, "Do what our god commands and escape!" The armies shifted uncertainly.

The monster flexed. Lindy stayed firmly in place but Asami slid down and was bit in half. After tossing Asami's remaining lower half in her shadow, Lindy yelled once again. "I'll clean up this mess you all unleashed, so play nice for a while!" Whether due to her words, the fleeing generals or the flailing beast, all forces on the beach around her fled in a disorderly panic.

Lindy sliced tendril after tendril. Crushed spines with her feet and hands while rushing all over the horrific blob's back. She was lashed and thrown many times.

The only thing she saw when trying to peek at the thing's stats was:

:Data not found

Lindy's hair blazed with power; the sea froze, the beach died, and the fight did not stop. Night came and went three times. For each tendril chopped, one or two replaced it. The beast's body erupted with protrusions of all kinds endlessly. Lindy's gunshots sank into the thing's flesh. Her own wounds healed. Her blood hissed as it met the air. It was an even fight. Neither the small ancient assassin nor the massive kraken-like thing who continued to morph, mutate, writhe, and wither held the advantage.

Finally Lindy had enough. Her mind snapped. "Fine, let's end this." Power built up from within her core. Rocks, sand, trees, and water began to bubble, pulse, and float. The land itself began to warp as Lindy focused the power of her blood out into the world, empowered by the piece of Death's realm she had taken over. "Anyone that can hear this, RUN!" Lindy's voice swept the land. One minute later a soft snap was heard the world over and the beast was gone. Bits of it were flung into space but most simply popped and degraded into acrid smog that spread to cover the land.

For five years the smog rolled across the land, poisoning all it touched. Gas masks and treated leather suits appeared on the market for cheap and from a benefactor unknown to most. The few that knew it was Lindy's handiwork were conflicted but thankful. Each item was marked with a laughing skull. Lindy made sure her products were traded for cheap. Those who tried to profit with heavy markups were given a single warning before being added to those murdered each year in an event that over the years came to be considered a natural disaster.

For the most part, only those who cheated Death and in some cases his agent were culled once a year. It was called the reaping.

Lindy sealed off the last three levels of her catacombs. The ninjas that had died for her, what was left of Asami, Lindy's other body, Frost and Fall, Caldrin Faywind, Genney, Fraya Fields, Calanya Fulbrin, Lu Limore, Salvea Oat, Covell, Sasha, along with the first shades, were all interned on those three levels. A place was set aside for Daffodil as well. Ten years after that multi-day fight which marked the end of the first world colonial conflict, as that latest war came to be called, Lindy went out only to kill for the reaping.

Eight hundred years into her self-imposed isolation, explorers came knocking at Lindy's home.

Part Three

24

Waking Up the Past

Vivelin Underbarrow was called to her boss's office. Her job was a ceremonial role on the council that ran the Everlasting church. Technically speaking, she was still in training. It was a hereditary role and her mother still held the seat of Lindy, named after the church's oldest prophet. The heretics from the Church of Shrew were becoming more uppity for the first time in hundreds of years.

Vivelin knocked on the pope's door. One of the few perks of Vivelin's upbringing was no hallway belonging to the Everlasting church was closed to her. "Come in, dear," the pope called out. Carla Faywind was on the old side for an elf. Rumors said she had been close to one of the champions of Death a long time ago. No champion had been affirmed since. Strangely, the champions were all known only by the wars they fought in; no personal names were ever recorded. If Carla had gotten her position from having known such a person, as the same rumor said, then they must have been important back then. The fact that Vivian's boss had never outright denied these rumors only fanned them more. As she stood in the small oak-paneled office of her church's headquarters set on a hill within the City of Smog, Vivelin mused over these apparent trivialities. Anything to distract her from the essay due for her college next week.

After some time Carla stopped signing off on the mounds of documents all around her. Carla looked tired. This was something she rarely showed openly and even then, only to her inner circle within very private settings. The fact that the pope let her mask drop ever so slightly in this way was never a good sign for things to come. Every other time, something big and troublesome had happened, and that was never a good experience to sort out. "This will be quick. We lost contact with the team in the founder's domain."

Eleven days before, a team of bishops and well-armed exorcists had entered the sealed-off layers of the catacombs that the main cathedral of the Everlasting church was built upon. "Forgive my ignorance, but was it not expected that the area was dangerous? It is forbidden ground, after all." Vivelin had asked easily the most disrespectful thing she ever had, but all the novices were taught that some higher power had sealed off those layers long ago, so to most personnel the high-ups had trespassed on ground that was off limits to all mortals, which was an affront to Death itself. Hence her question.

"It was forbidden by my authority in deference to the one who built it. A storm's coming and I need to know if anyone is down there," Carla replied evenly.

Vivelin nodded. "So you are commanding me to find the missing team?" She had always avoided the catacombs whenever possible. They were revered but to her they made her feel oddly sad for reasons she could never place.

"No, they are likely dead. See if anyone is alive down there. Failing that, if anyone has been living down there," Carla replied, nostalgia tinging her voice with an old regret.

"If anyone has been squatting down there all this time, they are not human," Vivelin replied, fishing for more details.

"She was certainly an odd one. The catacombs are the last place we have looked. It's important we locate her. We need her help." Carla shook slightly. She had always been like an immovable rock of pure belief, pride, and compassion, so this elf so lost in the past and afraid was new and bad for Vivelin's young heart.

"How will I know her if I see her?" Vivelin asked.

Carla took a deep breath and smiled widely. "Oh, I think you will know her by sight alone. My granddaughter and two cardinals and one of the captains of the grim guardians will be with you. They should be at the catacomb entrance soon, so go to them now. Your gear has been prepped already."

Vivelin sighed. "As you command."

"Very good. Now off you go. Just bring whatever you find back to me," Carla ordered. Vivelin turned to leave but one last piece of advice left the pope's lips before the young woman left. "Remember to run if you are unwelcome down there." The words were like prayer and Vivelin did not want to see the kind of face her boss was making in that moment.

Down long hallways Vivelin walked unopposed. The gray walls and dark red carpets fit well with black and gold ceremonial robes. On the way she found herself in a small seldom-used corridor that connected one of the main walls to another near the stairway that led into the catacombs' first level. A row of five paintings lined the small passage. A small girl. The same person but as a twenty-year-old. A woman in archaic artificer garb who looked about to burst into laughter. A small close-fitted full pitch-black plate mail suit built for a young woman or teenage boy; only the wearer's eyes and mouth were visible though the helmet. A woman of Zenic ethnicity holding a sniper rifle aloft above a trench line. The light in each person's eyes and mouth that seemed ready to smirk or burst into ecstatic giggles were the same for each image. A column deeply pitted with damage from a fight long ago stood like a silent guard across from the images. Vivelin had always been enchanted by the images even if they made her feel sad and lonely for reasons that she was sure she knew, but she had yet to be able to focus on. "I miss you," she whispered to the images, inches away from the glass covering the painting of the child. Vivelin had repeated the same words every day she was in the cathedral, which was any time she was not at college all night for one project or another. It was never clear why, but Vivelin fully acknowledged the words regardless.

"We are waiting too, Viv," a classy bell-like voice pouted from the end of the passage.

"I'm not late yet," Vivelin grumbled. Spending time with the paintings was the one thing she did for fun. Her entire life was training and work. As one of the few mages belonging to the church and not a government agency, Vivelin had been trained hard from a young age. Mages were with two exceptions taken into government custody. Magic was rare; magic talent even rarer. Powerful spells from before the wasteland were the stuff of research and debate only. The Church of Shrew and the Everlasting church were the only institutions allowed to keep the mages born into their ranks and only if they possessed ice, necromancy, shadow, or healing abilities, as those were supposedly under Death's patronage. No other church to a world spirit had lasted into the modern age. Although given that the Church of Shrew's leader was also leader of the Longdusk imperial family and monarch of the Farnesse empire, the freedoms ostensibly given were taken for granted by them.

"Yes you are. I've been watching you not move from that spot for twenty minutes," said Laylinda Faywind, a woman who was one third elven and a few years older than Vivelin, which made Laylinda very young by the standards of her bloodline.

"Right. Sorry about that. Lead the way, Layee." Vivelin nodded, taking one last glance at the images and walking over to her friend who could have passed for six or eight but was closer to her mid-thirties.

"Only my mother and bothers call me Layee. It's Lay to you, in case you have forgotten." Laylinda shrugged, leading the way to the catacomb's gate.

"Right. Sorry, my mind was elsewhere," Vivelin apologized. "So besides a bunch of missing folks and going in with a smaller team, what else should I know?"

"That you'd better get your head out of the clouds and trust me, the history expert?" Laylinda forced a laugh as her body loosened up.

"That bad? Ok," Vivelin nodded, getting her mind and body in gear. Captain Carlos Meadows and Cardinal Gregory Friend were waiting just inside the gate. The cardinal sat on a footlocker.

Carlos, who had been keeping an eye on the passage deeper into the catacombs, looked back at the last of their team. "You are here. Gear up," he said stiffly, clearly a little on edge. Gregory got up and stretched while Vivelin opened his improvised seat and began to take out the high-level exorcist gear inside.

"We are expecting trouble, I take it," Vivelin said after noting just how heavily equipped the old Cardinal was.

"I always am. At the very least there are a lot of undead about," Carlos sighed.

"He means undead not friendly to us. The team we lost was from his squadron," Gregory whispered in a hushed calming tone.

"No matter what anyone says, info gathering is first. The last message we got only said 'it's undead' before cutting off. From the background noise I expect they have all gone to the halls of the dead," Carlos explained firmly.

"And that's why you need an exorcist." Vivelin nodded, the pieces falling into place. An armed vest, gauntlets, and helmet now were set over her robes, a sword at her hip, and a pistol that shot spikes of enchanted metal in her hand.

"You are one of the best and this team was handpicked by her hallowedness," Carlos said.

"Looks like we are all ready," Gregory announced. Vivelin looked over to find Laylinda holding a notebook, a dagger at her hip, a thick jacket and hooded sweater over her robes, and a cookie in her mouth.

"Let's go, but be ready for fallback strategy," Carlos huffed.

A light puff of air moved past them. *You mean retreat,* the air seemed to whisper. Carlos gritted his teeth but no one said anything. Vivelin found the voice nostalgic somehow but shook off the feeling, reminding herself of the job ahead.

The first two floors were dull gray stone blocks. Niches covered all but the ceiling. Even the floor slabs covered bodies or spaces for them. Skilled acolytes and the firm believers who had highly distinguished themselves in civilian life could be interred here. Red marble covered the third floor. It was set up in a format similar to the upper floors but was for devout believers who died in war in the name of the church. The next three floors were set up the same as the others and were for orphans and the homeless who had died around the city and had no one to bury them. Each church of the Everlasting had a mausoleum or catacombs for such individuals. After that were the final three formally sealed floors. Until the sixth floor the air was calm and around the seventh the air did not change, but the level of barely contained magic skyrocketed. "It feels different here," Laylinda whispered, filling page after page with what she heard, felt, and saw in as concise and no-nonsense a way as possible. Even with her complete lack of magic talent, the elf had felt it.

"This is bad. There's way more power than I've ever seen," Vivelin explained.

"If we kill the source this will all be over," Carlos said firmly. His companions knew he was far too hopeful about that.

"End yes, but maybe for us too. The power is being contained, I think by something intelligent, or at the very least with a will of its own," Laylinda explained. The group had stopped in a bend a few turns before the eighth and until that day unopened floor.

Carlos clicked his tongue. "But we can re-contain it, right? Power is only dangerous when it goes wild."

Or when it serves itself, the air around them hissed back for the first time since the first floor.

"Not this much power. I doubt even all the mages in the cathedral could fully contain it, and that's after days of preparation," Gregory added.

"And that's time we do not have," Laylinda elaborated.

I can wait, the voice on the air giggled. A flash of memory surged through Vivelin's mind: a small girl at a long dining table within a huge mess hall, giggling. The face was the same as in one of the paintings high above them. The vision lasted a few seconds but it felt like an hour to the exorcist. She knew it was a memory but not from when or where.

"Let's go. It can wait but I can't," Vivelin muttered, pushing out in front of Carlos and taking point. The group had taken a few steps in the time she had been immersed in the flashback.

"Good, you are back," Laylinda nodded. "Glad that shove woke you up."

"Right. That should not happen again. It's using images too," Vivelin nodded. She entered a trance to purge her mind of foreign influences and keep them out.

That's all you... the voice in the air whispered.

"Be silent! Your trickery will not shake us or halt your demise," Carlos shouted, nearly deafening his companions with the echo.

Ice formed in odd shapes along a wall. "It's in high Derndell. Literally translates to 'that's cold,' third wheel," Laylinda told them.

"I'll kill it," Carlos sneered. Soon after, they passed by a rune-covered slab that had been blasted apart. The runic patterns had changed and were glowing deeply.

Skeletons in pieces of armor made more from rust than anything else holding slabs of the same stood just within the entrance. One being wore pitch-black full-plate that exuded oppressive malevolence, and looked like the being in one of the mostly ignored paintings. Ten knights lay dead at their feet. "My master wishes me to inform you it's far too simple to make fun of that last statement, so try harder," the thing in armor called over.

"Let's charge!" Carlos called to his companions.

"Hold. We have been ordered to not start combat with you," the suit of armor informed them. Only Laylinda seemed unfazed as she scribbled down all that was happening around her.

Gregory grabbed the captain's shoulders, halting his charge while Laylinda asked, "So why kill them?"

"These men broke into my master's home and woke her from a long slumber. She was quite upset. Our standing orders have always been to slay any and all trespassers. That has been put on hold because of the two young women among you."

"This is land belonging to the Everlasting church," Carlos replied firmly. He felt the rights of the church were being ignored.

Words formed from ice on the ceiling. Vivelin had to elbow Laylinda and point up for her friend notice them. In the midst of sketching out the message, the elf translated. "'I was here first' is the kinder translation."

"It may be easier if that voice can talk. It belongs to your master, right?" Vivelin asked.

It does. The exorcist and scribe may come to visit. The men will have to wait outside my chambers, the voice whispered on a puff of cold air.

"And will you guarantee our safety?" Carlos asked, careful not to look into his dead men's eyes.

Do you promise the same? the voice asked from all around them.

"Yes, so lead the way. I'm done sketching this hall," Laylinda nodded.

"Then come with me. My troops will stay here," the armored being shrugged.

They passed through a few crypts filled with neat rows of elaborate stone coffins. Not one was the same as another. Each was engraved with small murals and neat paragraphs pertaining to the deeds of the one resting within. Only the first thirty coffins were open and empty. "So who are you?" Laylinda asked after a time.

"A poor copy of a much higher being. Li-one is the name I was gifted," the armor said stiffly.

Laylinda had been reading each inscription fast as she could. She scribbled down names, dates, and whatever else she had time for. Over time a pattern emerged. "All these have two birthdays. Who were they?"

"The first shades are on this level," their guide answered. It was calm but the others stopped, shocked.

"Wait. The first heretics are here. That's blasphemy of the highest order!" Gregory shouted. He was very upset.

Li-one turned to glare at them. "And what is blasphemy decided by, exactly?"

"Our all-knowing god!" Gregory huffed.

Li-one and the air around them all around erupted in laughter. "First of all, that glorified middle manager is not all knowing. Also, he does not care about your beliefs."

"Silence. Do not defame Death itself!" Carlos decried.

A sudden soul-deep chill and the feeling of their imminent demise swept over all present from far deeper in the catacombs. Li-one did not seem to even notice and the feeling left Laylinda and Vivelin as swiftly as it came. The two men, however, were close to passing out. "My creator is the agent of Death. She outranks you and owns this place, so cool it."

"You are a shade?" gasped Vivelin.

Li-one took off her helmet. The face was human. No traces found in full-blooded shades was present. It was young and to Vivelin, nostalgic. "I am a copy of the one you call the first prophet. She is waiting, so come on." All too swiftly, Li-one's helmet was back in place. That was good for Vivelin's heart but not her mind.

"The first prophet's teachings are what we abide by. They are the will of our lord. The halls of the dead and the hall of the soul are our right. The privilege of a better next life is guaranteed to the faithful. Do you dispute any of that?" Gregory huffed between labored breaths.

"It's true that your books misinterpret most, if not all, of her words, and how they are explained is completely off. Plus all are equal before Death. The worst part is that your teachings say that only shades do not get to reincarnate and that the rich and generous popular and devoted get higher placing. That's just self-serving. Death does not have that kind of authority, let alone the time needed for that. Anyone can choose to no longer reincarnate as they are." Li-one explained swiftly as they walked. Then she waved her hand and both now-red-faced men passed out. Two coffins nearby opened and the undead gently moved the men to rest along the wall. Vivelin moved to defend Laylinda but their guide simply sighed. "Sorry about that. They were getting on my nerves and Lindy may have killed them on sight."

"Lindy?" Vivelin asked, her heart beating hard. "Is that who we are meeting?"

"She's my creator and boss. This catacomb and the land it's on are on loan to your church from her," Li-one nodded.

A few seconds passed then the sound of a pen working furiously echoed around them. Laylinda was single-mindedly taking notes at an unbelievable rate that must have been some kind of record. "I see. That's why we are called stewards of this land and why grandmother has always stated that the church owns the land we are based in. We are stewards of other places but those are fully acknowledged as the church's. It's not allegory, after all." The elf muttered, off in her own little world, all of a sudden with no care for what happened around her at all.

"Um, will she be ok?" Li-one asked.

"It happens. She should snap back to reality on her own soon, but we will need to wait for that." Vivelin nodded, secretly glad she had time to get her emotions under control. The feelings of happiness, loss, frustration, and heartbreak had almost broken her.

In silence they moved down another level. With names written in Zenic characters, only one date of birth was listed for each and the dates of death were almost all on the same day; they had died in the last days of the biggest war in recorded history. The war that made the waste-land may have been around as huge, but very few records of it or the Derndell empire remained and few of those agreed with one another. In fact, the most precious relic of the Derndell empire was a tax document with attached invoices for a unit of mercenaries called the Eternal. It had been found in the City of Smog within a tower's basement. In less complex times the Farnesse empire had purchased the document in exchange for a large swath of farmland which was now a fort-covered border crossing.

The next layer of the crypt contained a few ornate mausoleums. The entire last floor was spotless. Old immaculate carpets, leather chairs, fur tapestries, and weapon racks filled with relics of many ages jockeyed for space with the mausoleums. Thirteen were filled but eighteen had been built. The unoccupied ones were unornamented and plain. They passed through a small arena. Fourteen statues graced its surroundings, one of which was a dragon. Four more places for statues were set up around the arena stands.

Finally Li-one stopped at a wide door set into part of the arena floor, and knocked. "We both know it's open," a gravely but light voice called firmly from within.

Li-one looked back apologetically at her master's guests and opened the door. Laylinda rushed in and looked around. It was a smallish workshop. A bunkbed rested in one corner. Work benches and a forge took up half the room, large alchemical devices took the other. In the center of all this controlled chaos sat a small constantly shifting form sitting on the floor and leaning against a large dent in the wall. "Pardon me. I would get up but every time I do something breaks," the small thing chuckled mirthlessly.

Vivelin walked though the door and almost passed out for a few seconds when her eyes met the gaze of this place's master. A thousand years and more of memories flooded her mind.

Usually oblivious to the world around her, when curiosity took over, Laylinda looked around critically. "This place is not that much of a mess."

"You misunderstand. I mean, if I get up, the ground literately breaks. I've been like this for... how long has it been?" the shifting form asked.

"Three hundred years and twelve days, master Lindy, who forgot she can teleport or levitate," Li-one said.

"Oh come on. We both know telekinesis alone is not supposed to do that! And that I'm liable to rocket into space if we seriously tested that." Lindy, the first prophet of the Everlasting, god of the Church of Shrew, war hero of many conflicts, and agent of Death, pouted.

"I know you," Vivelin muttered in a near whisper. The emotion laced into her words made the others fall silent.

"You do. This is the first time in your current life we have met, my love," Lindy sighed wistfully.

"So should I go by Frost, Fraya, one of the others?" Vivelin pressed softly.

"Be yourself. If only one of us can afford to do that, it should be you," Lindy replied evenly.

"So what did you all need anyway?" Li-one asked.

Laylinda looked up from her notebook. "Oh right. Grandma needs to see you," she remembered.

Li-one walked over to a large vat set close to the bunk beds. "That's why you woke up your great grandpa?" she sighed.

"What?" Lindy's two visitors asked simultaneously.

"Well, Woodrow's my kid. It's a long story," Lindy grumbled.

"The college president is your son?" Laylinda asked.

"His mother was a dryad. Like I said," Lindy began.

Vivelin cut her old flame off. "Long story. Got it. So you coming?"

"Sure, give me a second," Lindy nodded. Li-one had taken a vial of growing green goo out of the vat and handed it to her creator.

"Brace for impact," Li-one said as if commenting on a light rain shower. Lindy waited until the others found something to hold onto and downed the vial.

Lindy's body begin to creak and pulse. "This will be bad. Toss me." Lindy groaned, her face shifting even faster than before. A kaleidoscope of pained expressions flew across her head like an infinite presentation of clouds. When the ancient being had shifted to a child-sized form for a brief instant, Li-one grabbed her maker by the shoulders and heaved Lindy out into the arena. Power flowed from Lindy. The air screamed for the briefest instant. The world seemed to twist then just as fast it snapped back. The power flowing out of Lindy rushed back into her. Then she hit the dirt. Lindy was back in the form she had most often used. She looked up at the ceiling and sighed, "Well, that sucked."

Laylinda peeked out from the doorway. "What was that?"

"Power suppression. Now she can move without making holes in the world," Li-one replied.

Lindy sat up. "My powers grew to the point that my body and this world can barely contain them. This shortened my holiday time by a lot but it's not like being cooped up in here was getting old," she called over.

"I'll watch over the homestead and look after version two," Li-one volunteered.

"Thanks, one," Lindy nodded.

"Version two?" Laylinda asked.

"The improved version of myself. I was the proof of concept but version two has a lot more fabrication steps." Li-one pointed over to the vat. A few bits of flesh surrounded by tubes floated in the center of the vat. "She has a long way to go."

Vivelin took a spare college uniform out of her own shadow and tossed it to the now very naked prophet lying on the floor. Lindy looked between the uniform and the current reincarnation of Fraya Fields, among others. "Viv, that's too big for her," Laylinda observed.

"No, this will work. That's a useful trick, by the way." Lindy smiled, changing her height and mass before tossing on the uniform in a slovenly but practiced manner. The ancient then took out a plaid thing that was a cross between a thin sweater and a slick jacket; its shoulders were excessively puffy. Both visitors recognized the style as being grossly out of fashion for the last thirty years.

Laylinda noted how the odd being before them fit the clothes better than her friend did. "I want to know how to change my form like that!"

"It's not something I can teach, and your grandmother would be upset if I granted you this ability." Lindy shrugged, then hopped in place a few times. "Ok, all set," she nodded, doing some last-minute stretches.

"Right. I'll lead the way. We have some baggage to pick up," Vivelin agreed. Laylinda noted how her friend's personality seemed to have become a little colder and sharper since seeing the being that almost everyone alive considered to be a myth or some kind of out-of-reach religious icon. Whole theories giving any credence to the idea that a shadowy many-thousand-year-old terror lurked in the annals of history were discarded out of hand every year by both the scientific and religious communities.

"I'll be three thousand in around two hundred years," Lindy said out loud as if talking to herself from the back of the line.

Lindy's stats had consolidated over the years into:

Lindy Ashborn

Female (shadow touched) human age: forever 20

Affiliation: realm of death

Embodiments: death to be, eternal calamity

Job: Reaper

Status: common sense bane: extreme, Death's apprentice, fatal fairytale

Abilities: strength 9820 (forcibly suppressed to 200), vitality 10405 (forcibly suppressed to 230), mind 10300 (forcibly suppressed to 210), agility 15018 (forcibly suppressed to 250)

Talents: translation: all, full power strike: strength. danger sense, innate map, skill and knowledge retention: Manfred Endfield, photographic memory, sixth sense: intuition, extra toughness, favored environment: darkness, resistance (all): high, highly enhanced trait: willpower, analysis: extreme, good hair, quick learner. fearless, body of poison, presence sense, aura: weakening, damage shield: decay, decay bolt, adept talent: multi-tasking, fearsome visage: moderate, selective decay: all, innate spell: chill blast, absorb impact: moderate, riposte: debate, realm authority (death): moderate, shadow shift, perception tampering field, find soul,

> see soul, sense lifespan, attuned to purpose, shadow from, plains walk: deaths realm and back, full power burst (weakening/ decay/cold), siphon soul, suppress kindnesses (self): full, suppress power: any, track soul, find living, trace bloodline, strike from shadow, rapid shadow jump, alter form, copy self (shadow), combat mastery: all, copy form: lesser, innate spell: telekinesis
>
> Blessing: conceal stats
>
> Mutation: troll blood (extra burnable, swift regeneration), un-aging. mutagenic blood
>
> Curse: catastrophic encounters, heavily sleeper, light sensitively: mild, one more year to play
>
> Skills: weapon skills: extreme, athletics: master, armor proficiency (all): expert, literacy: expert, history (other world): journeyman, intimidate (innate): extreme, diplomacy: journeyman, awareness: expert, necromancy: extreme, tinkering: master, magic tampering: extreme, counter spell: master, survival (all): expert, cooking: journeyman, acrobatics: extreme, stealth: extreme, shadow magic: extreme, laws of death: extreme, leadership: expert, herbalism: journeyman, barter: journeyman, ice magic: journeyman, computers: adept, driving: journeyman, chemistry: journeyman, bio engineering: expert

They picked up Carlos and Gregory on the way back. The men were still unconscious so Lindy hoisted them over her shoulders. At the blasted gate Lindy stopped and injected power into the runes, which caused the seal over her floors to remake itself. "How?" Laylinda began.

"Dwarves," Vivelin answered, her memories of other lives nearly processed by this point, with an intense migraine to show for it.

"The clan that made this owed me a few favors. They are long gone now," Lindy elaborated.

"What were they called?" Laylinda asked as she took point, wanting to get away from the odd atmosphere linking her friend and the prophet she believed in, but too curious to stop asking questions.

"The Igorein clan," Lindy said softly. A small sad smile flashed across her lips, her eyes still neutral and laughing, as that was their natural state.

I hope grandma knows what our prophet is thinking, Laylinda worried to herself. The ancient being she had picked up seemed happy, guarded, and sad all at once. The young elf had no idea how to handle that and which if any of those emotions were real.

Laylinda had no way of knowing that Lindy was constantly laughing, griping, and crying inside. The millennia of war, loss, and other bullshit had made the once happy-go-lucky child, once wise beyond her years, cynical and grim. All that remained of that smart but naïve girl was the mirth she held close, deep in her heart. That humor and desire to laugh at almost everything kept her humanity and sense of self grounded enough to not be totally insane.

25

Remembering Yesterday

When they came out of the catacombs a squad of elite guards surrounded them. Lindy slowly placed her physical burdens on the ground. "These two may need a checkup," she informed the growing crowd.

"Relax, she's with us." Vivelin pressed more forcefully than she would have a day before.

"I don't recognize this one. A security check has been ordered for anyone unfamiliar," one of the guards replied sternly.

"Then go away. She's not new and we are late for a meeting," Vivelin grumbled. The power plays from within the church's hierarchy were not something she had the presence of mind to put up with right then.

"We have our orders," a guard pressed.

"And we have ours. This visitor is an exception. The pope can confirm that." Vivelin stood her ground, not sure why she was so upset but it felt correct. The stress from regaining the memories of other lives was not helping her mental equilibrium.

"I really must insist," the first guard stalled.

Lindy sighed and drew Transcendence from her shadow. "Some of you recognize this, right? Unless your orders come from someone higher than the boss of your origination, then run along and check up on anyone else. I outrank your paymaster."

The lower-ranking clergy gathered around fell to their knees upon seeing Lindy's sword. The guards felt its power and paused. When the few higher-ranked clergy followed their subordinates to the ground a few seconds later, the guards moved aside. "Thank you," Lindy smiled, tossing her sword back into the junk pile kept in her shadow.

Laylinda took point and led Lindy to the pope's office. They passed Vivelin's favorite gallery. Upon seeing the old paintings of her various forms, Lindy smirked and pointed to the one of her as a child. "Hey, you think they got my nose wrong?"

"It's not too bad," Vivelin replied wistfully, recalling a few memories from over two thousand years before. Soon after, Vivelin stopped. "Wait. I loved you. My memories of you are so jumbled and crazy!"

Lindy and Laylinda stopped. "Like that time I fought an army alone? Crazy times indeed," Lindy noted.

Vivelin held her head. "You did that more than once. Wait, I'm so confused."

Lindy hugged Vivelin. "The amount of time you are remembering is bound to be overwhelming. Take it slow. No need to rush. I'll stay with you this year if you want." When Vivelin was released she simply nodded. "No need to rush. Life gets boring if you rush," the ancient one added.

The three began to walk again. "You meant eternity, right?" Vivelin asked.

"It can be both," Lindy replied.

At the pope's door one of the bishops sat outside on an ornate stool. Two young priests stood respectfully behind him. "Her hallowedness is preoccupied," the old man said.

Lindy smiled and walked forward, ignoring the warning glares the young priests were giving her in their direct superior's place. Lindy knocked on the door like she owned the place and called out. "Hey, you called for me, young lady. How long does your landlord have to wait?"

The bishop sprang up from his chair. A loud crack soon followed as his back gave out. "Oh, it's been a while. Do come in," Carla called back.

Lindy opened a shadowy portal over the door and walked in without physically opening it. "You know some of your underlings were in line before us, right?" Lindy's voice came from the still-opened portal.

"I told them I had a prior engagement," the pope's voice followed. "Oh, and your two chaperones are safe, I see. Do come in, you two." The pope called out clearly, knowing that a medium less corporeal than the door was in place.

When Laylinda and Vivelin came in the portal evaporated and the door went back to how it was. Lindy sat on a stool that looked exactly like the one the bishop outside had, with one key difference: it was made from her own shadow.

"So what did you call me out for?" Lindy asked as the pope motioned for the ancient's two chaperones to be seated.

"Not much. A war is coming," the pope sighed, feigning good humor. Carla had forgotten how uncomfortable and defensive Lindy made her.

"It will be a big one," Lindy agreed. "You know I can't get too involved, right?" she added.

"My position here is not as strong as it once was. Could you look after these two and my son?" Carla asked.

Lindy closed her eyes; a subtle power emanated from her. "He's with his father, I see." Lindy's eyes snapped open. "Wait, you had two daughters!"

"And they both work here. The governments whose territories this church has ties to put up with us. The college Woodrow Reaper controls has far more issues with government interference."

Lindy rubbed her temples. "And you are afraid my grandchildren will be drafted somehow?"

"That's right," Carla replied.

"Fine. I have one more year in this reality. I'll help until then," Lindy grumbled.

"That's it?" Carla asked. An uncomfortable if hazy premonition came over her.

"That's it. Yesterday I had two hundred more years but the process has been accelerated. I'll still be a manager of this local branch office, however, for those two centuries."

"Then what does that make Death?" Vivelin muttered. She was suffering a crisis of faith now that she remembered all the lives she had spent with Lindy.

"One of the regional branch managers. The three on our board of directors will be transferring him and the other world spirits in this area of realities and I'll be promoted up to a regional manager of the concept of Death. This and four other universes will likely be my first posting," Lindy smiled.

It took her audience a while to work out what Lindy meant. Most of that was due to their own preconceptions getting in the way of their understanding. "Wait, Death is some corporate wage slave?" Laylinda cried.

Lindy shrugged. "In a sense. I mean all we really get is eternal life as long as the home office wants this project to keep going. Although that's really not all that great given how much work we have to put in. I hear some offices only get a two-minute coffee break every five hundred years."

"Wow, sucks to be you," Carla muttered.

"I will be your god, you know?" Lindy grinned. "But well, Fate gets to enjoy cake all the time, so you are not wrong," she added. Lindy turned to Vivelin. "Speaking of, you remember Genney, right? She will be the next Fate and even gets cake now as an intern."

"So this Vivelin is the one that follows you around through time?" Carla asked knowingly.

Lindy stood up. "And I love her for it," she nodded. "I'll be back tomorrow handling my college enrollment and by then I'll call us even. Might even give you ownership of the above ground here." With that, Lindy seemed to evaporate from the room.

Lindy soon found herself in the alleyway behind a small bar sandwiched between much taller offices. The bar was called the Spirited

Lion. Its sign showed a cartoonish lion ghost. Lindy walked out of the alley without a second glance at her appearance and marched into the building. The force pushing back against her energies meant her son was around. Not many customers were in the bar but her son, who sported a short beard, now sat at the counter. Lindy slipped onto a stool next to him before anyone had noticed her entry. "Welcome," the bartender called from the back, looking at the light entering the dank establishment from the squeaking door and otherwise empty door frame. A few patrons looked over and huffed, believing someone had beat a hasty retreat upon looking inside.

"Long time no see. You know the name Mr. Reaper was taken long ago, right?" Lindy whispered to Woodrow. The few patrons and bartenders' heads snapped around at her quiet utterance but Woodrow did not.

"I don't," he started, then stopped and glanced at his father. "Oh, so you are up and about. It has been a long time."

"Friend of yours?" the bartender asked, marching over.

"Older relative," Woodrow smirked. He was deep in his cups but not really out of it yet.

"I'll have water. He's paying," Lindy nodded next to her.

"Why me?" Woodrow asked.

"Because I slipped out before asking for hazard pay. Oh, my job looks to be running around with one of your grandkids. So I'll see you at work," Lindy sighed.

"We only have beer, ale, and whisky," the bartender replied sternly, not moving a muscle and still trying to gauge Lindy's age.

"Whatever is cheapest then," Lindy beamed. Woodrow rolled his eyes and the bartender gave up and poured her a glass of some rank swill.

"This could rot your guts. Be careful," the bartender warned. Woodrow chuckled. This earned him a few confused glances.

Lindy rotted the alcohol and other impurities out of her drink, turning it to pure water before belting it in one heave. "That was still drinkable, you know," Woodrow sighed.

"Just because I can survive an artillery shell head on does not mean my heath is unimportant," Lindy grumbled. "So I'll no longer be around this time next year. If you need any advice feel free to ask until then." The bar patrons were a bit freaked out at Lindy's casual use of magic and left. The bartender, sensing the ensuing conversation was not for his ears, retreated to the back. One of the more sober patrons even flipped the sign out front to say closed.

"You drop in just to say that, dad?" Woodrow sighed, exasperated.

"You know what would happen if I helped you out like I should have?" Lindy asked.

"No, what?" her son finally snapped.

"I would change the world. In my experience, forcefully changing the way the world works has never ended well. By now I could even destroy this entire planet at full power. Not even dust would be left. I never planned to have a kid but for those related to me by blood and others that I love, I'd like to do anything for them. But that could easily warp this world far more than I already have," Lindy nodded.

"That's a lot of assumptions. What's the point in telling me now?" Woodrow asked.

"Because like it or not you are my child and I had to believe you would turn out all right. None of my three souls were ever going to be ready for parenthood," Lindy grimaced.

Woodrow downed what was left of his whisky. "And playing bodyguard to one of my descendants is going to make up for this?"

"Of course not, you fool. It will help me appraise just how twisted I made this world! Guns, belief in gods, the shades, world wars, anti-magic, the stagnation of magic, fewer undead, the wasteland. All happened because of things I did," Lindy snapped back.

"And you think that's all because of you? Grow up, dad," Woodrow sighed.

"Not all of those are strictly bad and yes, others had to run with some of those ideas. The point is the timing was bad. The world was not ready for what I did to it," Lindy huffed.

"Sounds like your problem. My world's still in once piece. Just because you seldom see the good in it does not mean it's not there," Woodrow muttered.

Lindy leaned back. "About time you grew up," she smirked wistfully. "I'm glad."

"For what, that I'm still alive?" Woodrow retorted. For all his bluster, he was far calmer and less hateful than he had been in the distant past.

Lindy got off the stool and placed a large chunk of gold taken for a crown long ago on the slightly sticky bar counter. "That you are doing better than me. It's an ideal. Don't worry about it. My admission into college will be fixed up soon but don't act too familiar in public after that, ok?" As she left Lindy waved at the gold. "Oh, and feel free to split that with the man behind the curtain. This place needs a better distillery. The one in the basement is too loud."

The bartender crept out from behind a curtain separating the back room from the bar proper. "She can hear that?"

"She's capable of anything but acting her age," Woodrow sighed, tossing the entire chunk of gold to the trembling man. "I am sorry about my relative but she does like her secrets. That gold should cover our drinks, your silence, and a small makeover, I hope."

"Of course. My life depends on it, right?" the bartender fumbled a smile.

"Your time after death may ride on that too," Woodrow agreed. "So you have any stronger whisky? I can pay for a few more drinks," he added as his father skipped down an alleyway.

Lindy skipped along knowing she was being followed. When she was deep in a maze of alleyways and hidden doors, she leapt up two stories, landing on a fire escape. The fire escapes, call boxes, and water valves within the alleys were well maintained and more or less clean. Some pathways showed signs of semi-routine professional maintenance as well but most did not.

A squad of three, one of which had been in the bar earlier, crept around after a while. They ran into a thin elf who emerged from another alleyway. "You find her?" the daintiest of the three asked.

The elf grumbled wordlessly to himself before pointing above the squad's heads. "She's right up there."

"No she's not. I don't know you," Lindy replied, trying hard to remain deadpan.

"Oh that is her," the squad member from the bar nodded.

The elf sighed. "And now she knows we were looking for her."

"So, who are all of you fools?" Lindy asked, raising an eyebrow. Her mind was working furiously to calm itself down into a more even mindset.

"You go first," the small squad member hissed.

Lindy analyzed the small one and the elf closely while simply checking the names and confirming the affiliations of the others.

Rouna Lock

Human female age 27

Affiliation: nation of Otte internal investigation (Oii) agency, Smog college secretary

Job: agent

Status: middle class white collar, Oii lieutenant

Abilities: strength 30, vitality 23, mind 32, agility 28

Talents: forgettable, single minded, language (new wasteland alliance of city's trade, central continent diplomatic), keen eyesight, fake it, naturally gifted: stealth, iron will, self-hypnosis, subdue, snap shot, quick load

Skills: Athletics: journeyman, intimidate (basic): adept, torture (enhanced interrogation): expert, marksmanship: expert, law (high crimes): expert, literacy: journeyman, computers: journeyman, driving: adept, awareness: adept, unarmed: adept, knife: adept, diplomacy:

journeyman, armor use (leather, cloth): journeyman, track: adept, hide (shadowing): journeyman

Thullkiran Faywind
Elf male age 808
Affiliation: Smog college combat instructor, Otte militia
Job: drill master
Status: militia captain, he who slew the divine beasts, hero of old
Abilities: strength 720, vitality 492, mind 618, agility 923
Talents: full power strike, language (old wasteland, new wasteland, legalese), extra enhanced senses: all, improved toughness, sense surroundings: extreme, flurry, target armor gaps, sprint, riposte
Skills: Barter: adept, athletics: expert, intimidate (presence/reputation): expert, sword: master, dodge blow: master, pistol specialization: expert, marksmanship: expert, armor use (leather, cloth): journeyman, teaching: journeyman, literacy: adept, tactics (assault, ambush, coercion): journeyman, law (intercontinental/war): journeyman, acrobatics: journeyman

The others in the squad of three were Oii sergeants and combat-focused meatheads with some law and intimidation skills. Unlike the Oii agents, the elf, however, was dangerous. "Oy really? Why name yourselves Oii?" Lindy asked.

The elf seemed to be the only one to get the reference. "The current wasteland dialect does not have that Oy in it and it's not a pun in either version."

"Well I'm just dating myself then," Lindy grumbled. "So Rouna Lock, what's an Oii lieutenant and make-believe secretary got to do with me?" she added.

"What organization are you affiliated with?" the young lieutenant harshly demanded.

"Kids these days," Lindy sighed.

Immediately the Oii agents drew their guns. "Don't do it. You three are no match for her," Thullkiran warned.

Lindy smiled at the three goons who tried to look cool and proclaimed, "The Everlasting church took me in. The head honcho over there entrusted me with bodyguard duty for two students. So I was saying hello to my old friend, the head of the local college." The guns dropped ever so slightly. Lindy shrugged. "I mean that's only polite, right?"

"Not after business hours," Thullkiran noted. The three goons raised their guns back up in a flash.

"Well, Woodrow's an old friend of mine. It would be awkward if I just entered the college without letting him know first. Plus it's been so long. If he did not recognize me neither of us could live that down." Lindy replied calmly despite the guns pointed at her.

"That's really all you are?" Rouna demanded with more feeling than necessary.

"First of all, he's married. Also, I don't swing that way," Lindy shot back.

"Fine. Let's go, men," Rouna snapped. The guns rapidly disappeared under coats and the three slinked away.

"That's not the whole story, is it?" Thullkiran asked, seriously studying the far too calm teenage-looking person lounging above him.

"I did not lie to them." Lindy rolled her eyes. "Plus I don't spill my guts to anyone that asks."

"Another out-of-date saying. What are you really?" Thullkiran demanded.

Lindy cackled, "Wouldn't you like to know?" The shadows in the alleyway deepened briefly. Thullkiran went on guard but Lindy only winked at him in the deepening gloom. Seconds later the alley was just as it had been minus the odd being on the fire escape. Thullkiran walked home alone that day, grumbling all the way.

Lindy returned to Vivelin's side. Vivelin had calmed down after recalling her other lives. She sat at the rear of a chapel near the front door. The bishop from outside Carla's door was running the show. He was just finishing up. "And so the champion of Death told her loyal followers to play nice for a while. So we must never forgive the shades for their egregious transgressions. We have played nice until now but someday soon all true believers will be called upon to clean the filth from the lands, as we are far stronger than they ever could be. As foretold by our benevolent god." The bishop looked smug as cheers filled the chapel. Lindy knew better than to throw a wrench in the idiot parade. She kept to the wall as the mob filed out.

The bishop helped shepherd his war-maddened flock out with Vivelin's help. The bishop's assistants closed the doors. "Oh, you were here," the old man said, pretending to have just seen Lindy although he had long sensed the hum of power that covered her like a raging vortex. The bishop thought little of Lindy's show of power, not comprehending that was her standby state.

"Only at the end," Lindy smiled, not caring about the distaste the bishop and his men viewed her with.

"Bishop Pureheart, did you need the Lindy in training for anything?" Vivelin asked.

"Simply to congratulate her sudden rise to power. I am sure the pope will tell us of her origins soon," the bishop replied snidely in a way he thought showed great forbearance.

After the bishop and his helpers left, Lindy grumbled. "They really love taking my words out of context."

"The man did name himself Puree Pureheart," Vivelin sighed.

"You are joking," Lindy said.

"I'm not. Although I only find it funny in a sickly fitting way now that I remember common Derndell." Vivelin nodded.

Lindy shared a small storage room with Vivelin that night. Because the college dorm would not be open to the oldest living bipedal being (if Lindy could still be called long-lived after all the dying she had been through) until her first day of schooling in millennia. A storage room near the catacombs hastily set up with a divider, rug, and sleeping bags was what she got for the night. Lindy could have gone down to the home she had stayed in for many human generations. However, being with the current incarnation of Fraya Fields, Lindy felt more at peace than she had since her first friend had died so long ago.

The next morning Lindy walked out of the storage room dressed in the clean college uniform Laylinda had dropped off when the sky was still dim. Lindy found her two charges outside the door. "Are you all set?" Vivelin asked.

"Not really, but I'll be fine," Lindy smiled.

"You've been alive for longer than any elf, but not as long as a dragon. How is your grasp of history?" Laylinda asked, notebook at the ready.

"Walk and talk short stuff, walk and talk. Otherwise we will be here all day," Lindy said, rolling her eyes as she began to walk to one of the cathedral's side exits, ruffling her great-grandchild's hair on the way.

Lindy's two charges jogged after her. After turning the side door's lock to a pile of rusty dust, Lindy led the way out "A few bishops and a cardinal were by the main gate. Dealing with them and the assembled audience this early would have been a pain," Lindy grumbled. After leading her charges around a few hedgerows and down three alleys and a side street they were on a main road leading to the college. "Ok, so about that history question," Lindy said, smirking when Laylinda whipped out one of the many notebooks she had stashed about her person. "No idea. What I've seen of this world's history has been very skewed. They're the kinds of things that traditionally a lot of time and effort is used to rewrite into the best possible light for the time and place that's telling the story. In short, because I have not paid attention to current events and what the current version of the past is being spread here, I'll be clueless for a while."

"So what, will you use your powers to cheat your way through?" Vivelin asked, a bit exasperated at the thought.

"This world is almost like the other I knew, plus a few all-nighters studying and I'll be all right," Lindy shrugged. Half an hour later they were at the school gates. Rouna Lock and Thullkiran Faywind were taking attendance. Lindy spied a few likely intelligence agents, judging by their movements and eyes. The will and purpose behind those actions were different and that was all her gut needed. Whether they were Oii agents or answered to some other paymaster she did not check, but she memorized their faces.

"Those two were not on shift today," Laylinda noted.

"They might be looking for me. I had a run-in with those two after checking on the headmaster," Lindy grumbled.

"And why would…" Vivelin began. Lindy's troubled gaze and the fact that Rouna was walking up to them quieted her outward fears.

"You are not on the list," Rouna said, folding her arms before Lindy.

"Oy really?" Lindy said seriously but soon after she began to snicker. Vivelin picked up on her oldest friend's tip and simply stopped her other companion from doing more than watch from behind their guard.

Woodrow literally walked out of the shadow of a tree and handed a card to his most nosy secretary. "Her ID was late being processed. Here you are."

Lindy whistled, causing more than a few students to look over at Woodrow uncharacteristically helping out a new student. *It's weird seeing someone else use shadows like that,* Lindy mused.

"And what was the issue, sir?" Rouna pressed, not willing to back down before her boss and pride.

"It was a last-minute transfer and was filed in a junk pile due to the odd birth date," Woodrow answered firmly.

Rouna sighed and handed Lindy the ID. "Don't lose that," she said after Woodrow left just as he had arrived. Lindy and company walked through the gates trying to ignore the gazes on them. "Have a safe day," the Oii agent called after them.

"You as well, Miss Lock," Lindy called back. Some of the more aware and awake students nearby picked up on how Lindy already knew the secretary's last name, but almost no one thought much of it or kept that info in mind.

"So what's first?" Lindy asked her two charges. Laylinda began to wonder who was looking after who. Vivelin more or less expected her old friend's single-minded and exuberant default outward-facing nature.

"First assembly. It's the start of a new semester," Vivelin answered as Laylinda took the lead. Lindy lightly grabbed both their hands, mainly because Laylinda would be lost to her eyes very easily in the massive mob migration going in the same direction. Some students tried to go somewhere else. Those that had other places to be and were smarter or better prepared either got to campus at another time or allowed the human tide to sweep them along. After some time spent among the waves of growing bodies, heat, and body odor, they were swept into an auditorium.

"Oh, we lost three more this year," Laylinda noted, spotting three wreaths of black roses set just under the stage below a thin podium.

Lindy pulled her attention from examining the bloodlines all around her to her smaller charge. "Lost? What now?"

"Staff members mostly. Sometimes honor students. There's this yearly natural disaster we call the reaping." Vivelin's voice became softer before trailing off as her eyes became sharper looking at Lindy's fidgety expression. "Would you know anything about that?"

"I never named anything the reaping," Lindy said evasively. Her two charges were pushed closer to their guard by the crowd. "But there is no yearly natural disaster that mysteriously kills off those that try to cheat Death. After all, that's the job of a certain unnatural assassin you both know." Laylinda and Vivelin sighed, knowing they should not be surprised to find Lindy at the root of any major bloodbath in the last three thousand years. Many major advances could be traced to her, or so more than a few sects within the Church of Shrew and fringe groups of fanatics within the Everlasting church believed. The fact that Lindy was clearly unhappy and embarrassed with the state of affairs unnerved them far more than they would have liked.

"You love to make me question all I've been told," Laylinda sighed. It was by far the most damning thing she knew but she seemed more or less at peace with that fact. Laylinda's greed for knowledge and trust in her elders overrode the faith that she previously took for granted. If the first prophet was of the Everlasting faith, not her oldest living relative before her in the flesh saying these things, Laylinda would have had a far harder time accepting what for the most part was considered by the historians of the world as discarded crackpot theories due to their impossibility and lack of hard evidence. Lindy had long mastered covering her tracks, although that was mostly thanks to the erratic nature of her movements, as well as her destructive power to wipe her traces right off her work sites, more commonly called battlefields, and sites of mysterious deaths.

Woodrow walked to the podium and clapped his hands once. The resulting shock wave quieted the auditorium. "Ok. First off, Mr. Johns from chemistry, his apprentice Alba the instructor, and Ted Theodoric of the practical necromancy in history course, have been confirmed as reaping victims over summer break. Those under Mr. Johns will be assigned to other chemistry classes for the time being until a solid new hire can be found. I'll be taking over for instructor Theodoric until such time as a replacement is found. As always, those affected will have their schedules updated, so make sure you have or can locate your current individual schedule. We did email those affected over the weekend with relevant updates, and the information desk on the ground floor outside the lunch hall can help with updating those of you that did not check your email. Other than that, hello new students. For those of you who have been through this before, glad to see you all again. Work hard and the staff will respect you. Goof off during class too much and you will answer to me. Ok, that's all from me. Our information centers can answer any questions you have. Be careful on the way out. Dismissed!" A few students saluted at Woodrow's closing remarks.

On the way out Lindy muttered, "First stop information, then."

"Right. New schedule, here we come." Laylinda agreed unenergetically, still feeling conflicted that Lindy had killed off one of her history teachers.

"Hey, don't look at me like that. A lot more folks than normal were trying to live forever or mess with their souls last year." Lindy squirmed under her great-granddaughter's gaze.

"That's what it takes?" Vivelins asked, trying to get her companions refocused on something a little less weighty.

"Well no one tries to connect to the kill list these days. So effectively, yes," Lindy shrugged.

"And the reaping is done by hand?" Laylinda squeaked.

"On outer realms, no. It's all remote these days," Lindy explained dismissively before stopping and turning around, looking at the watery eyes of Laylinda.

"Why though?" Laylinda asked.

Lindy sighed, rubbing her own head. "Well if I don't work I die. It's not easy but I've gotten used to it. Kill to live is how the food chain goes. It's similar." Lindy sighed more deeply, looking up at the sky. "It's never easy to explain this." She leaned over and hugged her great-granddaughter. "Look, I want to live and my work is needed. It's harsh but someone needs to do it and a complete lunatic would not be right for it. So this reality got me."

They walked into an indoor arboretum. A wide glass ceiling gave a clear view of the perpetual smog set high above the city. "It's so weird to see the sky now. I was half expecting it to be sunny today," Vivelin sighed.

"Right. So what's up with you, Viv?" Laylinda asked.

"A few of my past lives were spent around your great-grandfather," Vivelin admitted.

"And you remember them?" Laylinda asked, her eyes growing wide. Laylinda suddenly whipped out three notebooks in between a single eye blink.

"She only does when I am around her enough," Lindy shrugged.

"And then I can't get you out of my head," Vivelin nodded.

"Right, that too," Lindy agreed.

Laylinda closed in, reducing their already close proximity even further. "Tell me more," she huffed.

"What's the commotion? Your first class is in an hour," Thullkiran noted, stepping out from the splinter of the mob that spilled into the arboretum's general vicinity. The horde's mindless chatter and entry had so far gone a long way toward masking most if not all of the three's conversation from those around them.

"Oh my, is this favoritism, sir?" Lindy asked, a wide smile illumining all but her eyes. The temperature around her became noticeably cooler.

"Hey, no magic," one of the Oii agents from the day before called over. Both of Rouna's subordinates from before appeared to be gardeners here as the other one Lindy had seen hid a short distance away.

Lindy clapped her hands and an invisible tension in the air popped like a soap bubble. "It's not magic, sir. Simple psychological pressure can make it feel cooler even on a hot day." Lindy giggled. "It appears I've been slowly ramping up my unease. You are very skilled to notice such a paltry amount of that power." Suddenly a massive wave of terror fell upon Rouna's two known minions and Thullkiran. No one else felt a thing. The two agents passed out immediately.

After two seconds the pressure eased and Thullkiran sputtered, a cold sweat covering him. "You can't do that."

Lindy glared at the old elf, her voice low. "Consider that a warning, sir. Do not attempt to use my charges for your true employer's schemes. That goes for the likes of the other two as well." The hall was still. Very few could tell just what Lindy had done or was taking about. Those that showed understanding on their faces she resolved to keep tabs on.

"Come on you two, let's go." Lindy pulled Laylinda and Vivelin away to the information desk set between the arboretum and cafeteria.

At the information desk was a small line. Soon an open spot appeared and Lindy was called over. "How can I help you?" the attendant asked.

Lindy handed over her school ID. "I am afraid I do not own a computer. I heard I could get my schedule here?"

The attendant looked at Lindy's ID. "Oh I see. Lin Reaper. Very well, one second." Although still skeptical the attendant remained professional.

After Lindy received her schedule, Vivelin walked up and handed over her own ID. "No computer, vow of poverty. I also need my schedule."

The attendant nodded, withholding a grumble. He could tell Vivelin was important and annoyed. "Very well. Do you know anyone else in that same position?" the attendant asked.

Vivelin waved Laylinda over. Once the attendant received student IDs, Vivelin nodded. "That's all of us." The small group soon had their schedules. All three of them had CQC 101 as their first class.

They walked towards the field where their first class was conducted. "So a vow of poverty? Would not have expected that," Lindy exclaimed.

"What, because I live in a gilded cage?" Vivelin remarked.

"Right. So how do you see the power balance now?" Lindy went on.

"Well the Everlasting runs almost all hospitals, and is the only organization besides the Church of Shrew that gives out medical licenses. As a necromancer with some ice magic I am protected from conscription except in extreme cases, and even then for predefined time periods, unlike most other mages who live by their home governments' whims for life. It's funny how weak magic is compared to the past. The pro-war factions in both churches and most governments in the world are stronger than ever before and far stronger than the anti-war ones. The pope of the Everlasting is in the anti-war camp, by the way."

"Right. Another big one is the matter of time. Damn it, the more things change the more they remain the same, indeed," Lindy grumbled. "Well I'll need to train you two up in our free time," she mused.

"You really think that's necessary?" Laylinda sputtered as they stepped into the outskirts of their early classmates.

"I've been killed for less," Lindy shrugged.

"I am not less," Vivelin huffed.

"Hey, that first time was my executioner's fault," Lindy remarked.

Vivelin took a deep breath. "Oh. You might be right," she realized after some rapid calculations.

Most of the class ignored Lindy and none came over to talk with her as most of the school had by now pegged her as an odd powerful troublemaker, mainly through the rumor mill. A little before the class was set to start Thullkiran showed up. After taking attendance he looked around. "Today we will be doing something classical. Does anyone know how to use a sword?" Lindy, Vivelin, another female, and two males raised their hands. The other thirty students did not. "Would anyone be willing to give a demonstration?" All the hands went down but the other sword-wielding female Lindy did not know pushed her a bit forward. "You?" Thullkiran asked.

Lindy looked around at the dubious glances she was getting. "Sure, why not?" She shrugged. "How will this work?"

"Can you handle real swords?" Thullkiran asked. Lindy sighed. A sword taller than her and a saber rose from her shadow. The saber floated into her hand while the larger weapon floated around her back. Thullkiran felt that the student before him was an unknown and hiding a lot of power. His pride was threatened, which came before the possible damage such an unknown could do to his main employer's plans. "Do you know how to duel?" the instructor asked.

"Until incapacitation, real blades, no attack magic?" Lindy smiled, nearly in a sneer. While she was still trying to work out the competing power dynamic and competing interests, she did know that Thullkiran was a problem.

Thullkiran took a deep breath. He felt sure Lindy was showing off and ignorant. After all there was no way he could lose, not with all the trials he had surpassed. "Very well. Are you sure that's what you want?" Thullkiran asked, sounding calm and self-assured.

"It's been a long time. A little exercise would be appreciated. So yes, ready when you are, sir." Lindy was goading the elf, and the students around her knew it. The student who had pushed her forward ran off to the administrative building. Lindy smiled at that but Thullkiran with his tunnel vision only saw that as being directed at him.

Thullkiran drew a sword kept at his back and rushed forward. "Very well," he snarled. Wind rushed as he slashed down. The path he cut through Lindy faded to darkness as she turned that slice of herself to shadow.

"We should step back," Laylinda noted. She and the rest of the class took many steps back from the battle. This was no longer a duel.

Lindy kicked Thullkiran away hard in the gut but not before he twisted her saber-holding hand completely backward. Lindy's saber fell but spun unnaturally and precisely, lopping off her broken hand at the wrist. The splattering blood dispersed into her shadow and the hand spun under an external power, reattaching itself the right way around before the wound closed without so much as a scar. "Good one," Lindy noted lightly, now gripping her two swords, each in one hand. Lindy swept the hulking blade hard, catching Thullkiran in the shoulder. He had been sliding along the ground sizing up the student he had labeled an enemy. A hard crack followed and the elf's upper arm shattered. Unknown to him, Lindy had used all her ability to damage him so. After suppressing her powers so much, the amount of power she wielded had not changed but the magnitude she could get across at any one time had drastically weakened. For better or worse this venue was a helpful way of testing what her current full power was like. The fact that Lindy found Thullkiran so unlikable from well before she even knew him helped. That, and she could tell that feeling was mutual.

"Give up yet?" Lindy asked Thullkiran as he staggered to his feet.

"Never!" the elf snapped, rushing forward. Lindy ducked under his sword swipe and dodged his kick by moving low to the side before cutting both his legs' tendons. As Thullkiran fell he held out his good arm trying to stab Lindy. She dropped her saber and broke his shoulder with one hand using the large sword as leverage to help with the task.

"Thanks for that, sir." Lindy smiled down, just out of reach of the elf if his limbs still worked.

"What are you?" Thullkiran croaked.

"If I had money for every time I've been asked that," Lindy grumbled. She looked into the elf's eyes and whispered. "Let's just say I'm far older than you, young man. I've seen wars almost as bad as the one soon to begin. At least the Derndell kingdom deserved what they got."

"Do you know the one that killed my clan?" Thullkiran whispered back.

"Only the ones that ordered it. Not the shades that carried it out," Lindy replied as she pretended to check the man's wounds.

"Who's hurt?" a dignified voice called out.

Lindy stood and glared back at Thullkiran. "And that's all you are getting." Pulling her saber from the ground Lindy jabbed it in front of the elf's face. "Give up yet, old man?" she asked louder than necessary.

A half-elf in white robes rushed up. "He's hurt."

"And in the middle of a duel," Lindy snapped. The half-elf recoiled sightly at the harshness in Lindy's tone. "So instructor, what's it going to be?" Lindy pressed.

"I give up." Thullkiran sighed weakly.

Lindy looked at the new arrival. She could tell the half-elf was one of Woodrow's kids. "You are nothing like your folks. Good on you." Then Lindy walked away from her confused descendant who helped teach medicine. "Oh, you can help Mr. Faywind now."

The human who had pushed Lindy timidly awoke. Just as her mouth opened, the speakers set around the campus blared. "Lin Reaper, report to the headmaster's office."

Lindy turned to Laylinda and Vivelin. "Well let's go, you two."

As Laylinda left she called back to the healer. "See you later auntie!"

They walked along and many fled from Lindy. Near the doors Vivelin sighed. "You still have your swords out."

Lindy looked around then tossed her blades into the nearby shadow of a tree. "Sorry. Force of habit." She giggled uncomfortably.

They passed into the main administrative building. A few secretaries looked up from behind the desks where they had taken cover. A tall man Lindy had once met when he was a boy walked forward. "It's been a long time," he said to Lindy.

Lindy noticed three hydras swimming in the man's shadow. "I see the help I loaned you is still doing well."

"Yes. Well you three can follow me. The headmaster is expecting you." The man nodded. Most of the staff around them had calmed down by this point.

Three staircases later, Lindy and company were led past a magnificent door and into a large meeting room that could have passed for a small library given the bookcases that almost took the place of wallpaper. Woodrow and two more female staff members waited for them. Sensing a familiar bloodline, Lindy looked deeper. The younger woman was Laylinda's mother. Lindy created a field that would keep sound from escaping by destroying vibrations; this also prevented anyone from entering or leaving. "Looks like I've met just about all of the family now," Lindy smiled. "Oh, and no one will be listening in from outside unless they've set a recording device in here."

"Are you my grandmother?" Laylinda's mother asked.

"Grandfather, technically," Lindy corrected.

"You have not changed, dad," Woodrow sighed.

"Well you have. Seems like you are doing well. Good job." Lindy's reply lacked all its necessary gravitas.

"Introduce yourselves," Woodrow asked.

"I'm Materdine Reaper, grandfather. It is good to see you again," the eldest of Woodrow's children said.

"Catherin Fen," his older sister smiled.

The younger sister spoke up. "Jess Faywind. Thank you for looking out for my daughter."

"The last one is Molly Gyorn. She ran off to heal someone," Woodrow added.

"Right. We saw her on the way here," Lindy replied, taking a book of law from the shelf and flipping through it.

"You can read that?" Catherin asked.

"Legalese is a language too. So yes, auto-translate works on it," Lindy nodded.

"So you said something about being around for a year?" Woodrow asked. "What was that about?"

Lindy kept reading as she answered. "Well I'm taking over for Death in two hundred years. Due to some measures I'll only be on this world for another year." The room became very still but Lindy did not want to look at anyone's faces. "Oh Materdine, mind if I take back those pets of mine?"

"Ok," her grandson said without thinking too much. Not that he could while processing the bombshell she had just metaphorically dropped.

"Two of you into each of my friends' shadows. Same orders as the last one but come back in nine months," Lindy remarked, tapping her foot.

A chorus of "Yes," "Ok," "All right," and "No problems" buzzed from Materdine's and Lindy's shadows as the hydras rearranged themselves.

Taking advantage of the temporary stillness in the minds around her, Lindy looked up from finishing the ninth law book of the meeting. "As nice as this is to see the family in person, I was called for at least one other thing, right?"

"Right. It's like this..." Woodrow began.

"Before that, why are the doors smashed to pieces?" Jess asked.

Lindy looked back at the doors. "One sec," she said, pulling down the barrier and ignoring the muffled screaming — something about splinters and being crushed. A tendril of nearly solid shadow wiped out and pulled in the last member of the family. Molly Gyorn sat there trembling as she looked around. "Ok, and that's the last one. My bad. Totally slipped my mind that a strong force might be redirected like that if it was dependent on another outside force."

"What? Why are you here?" Molly stammered.

"She's my father," Woodrow explained.

"Right, I'm Lindy. I've been working for Death for a while. How are you?" Lindy went back to reading a law book.

"What's this barrier? The doors flew apart when I tried to open them. So much blood." Molly shivered.

"How many died?" Woodrow sighed, looking at his father.

"No one," Lindy said first.

"Not yet," Molly added.

"They will be fine; nothing fatal, at least. Some bones and joints might be out of whack if they are not set and redirected right. Still, that should not have redirected force back to such an extent. The force should have been canceled on its own. So a rebound..." Lindy checked Molly's basic stats.

Molly Gyorn
Half-elf female age 523
Affiliation: Everlasting church hospital core instructor,
    Smog City ER chief
Job: Nun
Status: guardian healer of the smog
Abilities: strength 932, vitality 519, mind 498, agility 482

"That's a lot of strength. Ok, a rebound makes sense. You tried to slam open the doors but the field blocked that and because physics was still working everywhere else but the barrier, a rebound happened. That's actually kind of neat. College is cool. I've learned so much already," Lindy thought out loud.

"Wait, physics can do that? Just what did you do?" Materdine asked.

"Right, you all are just working out natural science. All that artillery really had folks working on the details. Kind of funny none of you worked out gravity completely yet. I just stopped some basic functions of reality from passing through a field which seems to have reflected your sister's frankly absurd strength," Lindy answered. She held up a hand. "And no, I do not completely understand it. That was not my job in my past world. So what did you need?"

"Right. Killing is your main skill set. I wanted to know what your plans for the year are. A war is coming on and it will be intense." Woodrow sighed.

"That really depends on how each faction deals with me. For now I'll judge them on the members I meet. Although the fact that my play-nice advice is being used to start a war really ticks me off." Lindy nodded as she put away the twenty-fifth law book so far. "Right now a few bishops and a cardinal or two will die. It's too early for any real plans though. Besides, I at least need to try to learn and work on my bodyguard gig."

"You say that so casually," Catherin said through a wry twitching smile.

"She does work directly for Death and as far as I know does not handle the life-giving parts of that concept," Woodrow replied.

"When you put it that way, it makes sense," Catherin nodded.

"Unlike that crackpot theory that the world's round!" Materdine cackled. The others seemed to agree with him. Lindy got a headache as she knew their world was not flat.

Mental note: Take at peek at their first astronauts' faces when they see the world is round, Lindy thought.

"As long as none of you spread around what or who I really am then I'll owe you each a small favor," Lindy shrugged.

"What?" the adults asked. Greed and shock surged in most of them although fear was not far behind.

"I will be Death, and I can't do something like this unless I have an excuse to balance the books. Worst case, your one after-death request gets a bit harsher. Not that you'd remember that," Lindy grinned.

Unlike most of his kids, Woodrow knew his father was trying to be nice in her own way. "I am immortal, you know," he said.

"You don't age. It's not the same thing. So take care of yourself," Lindy shot back, rolling her eyes.

"Right. Well, the three students are excused. The rest of you, get to damage control," Woodrow nodded.

26

Overshowing the Eclipse

The days went by. The twists in history books did not change. One side was right, the other wrong. All the subjective good side's dead were heroes, the others were villains. The subtext that the desires of the writers' paymasters were fair no matter how base was always within the lines. Other nations had completely different accounts using mostly the same data, painting themselves as the so-called good guys and their killings as just and necessary for a never-quantified all. Stories of heroes, martyrs, cartoonish villains, brainwashed citizens, righteously just citizens, purely hated leaders, and bumbling megalomaniacs were spread thinly across tales of loss and totally necessary bloodshed that was not wished for but must be done. All while glitzing up the good and painting the "bad" noncombatants with some intense schadenfreude dabbed like molasses in the background. The kicker was every nation did that while painting themselves as good and others as bad. It was a massive web of bullshit to Lindy, who had lived through those times meeting or at least filing the after-death paperwork for Death himself for most if not all the names listed. "Whoever said war is written by the victors was full of it. War is written by who is left!" Lindy screamed one night as she studied for yet another history test she had failed and had to redo.

Over a month Lindy learned about the modern sciences she had not fully paid attention to. Phones, electricity, gunpowder, skyscrapers, better alloys, coal, wind and water power, mana fission similar to the world-rending explosive from years before but far more contained. Trains had become more powerful along with guns of both magic and gunpowder make. Personal armor had become almost nonexistent. Stoves, freezers, and water supply had become cheaper and more efficient. Poison gas was restricted under multiple treaties.

Most jarring of all was how much of the destruction and things Lindy had invented were publicly credited to others, at least within the City of Smog. Not all beings, especially the longer-lived ones, believed that. Lindy had become an unprovable factor because of how far from common sense she was. Even more so as magic and general individual power were far weaker than they had once been. Only a few dragons, Lindy, and Woodrow had lived through a time when a true legendary hero was more than just an overly embellished story.

The Faywind clan had been nearly wiped out by the shades. Lindy knew that was in part her doing and that she needed to be more careful around Thullkiran because of it.

One afternoon Lindy sat listening to a talk about how various treaties influenced the local laws when a wave of power swept across the school. A team of mages tried to alter the perception of normality around the area. Soon after, a team of twenty commandos rushed in. Lindy whispered to Vivelin, "Watch over your friend. I need to scout out a suspicious force that entered the grounds." With that, Lindy disappeared from the room.

Lindy appeared in the shadow of an old bell tower she barely recognized. Twenty very well-trained shades were creeping around the campus. They had killed five guards already. A unit of eight Oii agents was watching as well. Suddenly ten people, both students and faculty, rushed out from all directions. The way they moved was exceptional. The skilled staff and students threw concealed weapons and pulled out other small blades. A firefight ensued. The Oii agents were reorganizing now that a full-on skirmish had begun. Lindy retreated back into the shadows and walked into a space behind Woodrow's desk. Many lamps were on in his office. Lindy caught her son's reflexive punch. "You know the brighter something is, the more shadows are around just under the surface," she observed.

Woodrow sat back down. "It's not polite to sneak up like that," he grumbled.

"Well the school's under attack. Rouna Lock is spectating with her team," Lindy replied.

"She's one of yours, then," Woodrow noted.

"Not a chance. That secretary of yours is way too annoying. She's with these Oii pricks anyway," Lindy replied.

"That makes sense. So what are you going to do?" Woodrow asked.

"I'll fight if you cover for me," Lindy explained.

"Will you only kill if it's unavoidable?" Woodrow asked.

"Anyone who attacks me with lethal force dies. This time I'll turn a blind eye to any machinations I can see, but I will remember them," Lindy nodded.

"That's good enough. Just don't destroy the grounds too badly," Woodrow sighed.

"I'll see what I can do. As long as the fight is contained that should work out," Lindy agreed, walking over to a window.

"You can't promise me, then," Woodrow sighed.

"I don't lie," Lindy retorted as she jimmied open a window. "Besides, combat's a chaotic mess. Anything can happen." With those parting words she leapt from the window into a tree, then took off running.

Unlike when they first met, Woodrow trusted his father. After being well known as a being that did not age, who was powerful and held great influence, Woodrow had learned to empathize with his father. He did not like everything they had done to those around them but Woodrow could not deny his father's methods were useful. Father and son had an unspoken understanding by this point. Lindy lived vicariously through her son's far less violent life.

Lindy rushed out. She leapt into the firefight, snapping a shade's neck as she moved above him. Lindy landed near the student who had pushed her before and analyzed her.

#185 "Asami series"

(modified) human female age 17

Affiliation: 823 Lost Legion

Job: ninja

Status: student, spy

Abilities: strength 83, vitality 42, mind 56, agility 112

Talents: language (new wasteland alliance of city's trade, low Zenic, Zenic outcast) talent: awareness, hide in plain sight, ambush, subdue, exceptional leap, absorb impact, barrage

Skills: throwing weapon: journeyman, armor proficiency (leather): journeyman. lie: expert, dagger: expert, athletics: journeyman, acrobatics: expert, stealth: extreme (inborn), marksmanship: journeyman, synthetic alchemy: adapt, survival (woodland; mountain): journeyman, blacksmithing: adept, law (military): adapt, computer: adept, finance (stocks) journeyman

"#72 would not have had too many issues right now," Lindy called out. The students and staff around this Asami were all part of the 823 Lost Legion. Lindy chose to believe it was an ode to her old unit. From the new Asami's brief show of emotion Lindy believed that guess was very likely.

The commandos attacking were all shades. Their leader was very interesting.

Davrin Spark

Human shade age 32

Affiliation: farnesse empire forward recon unit 5

Job: commando team leader

Status: agent Longdusk imperial family

Abilities: strength 42, vitality 35, mind 43, agility 39

Talents: alcohol tolerance: high, language (new wasteland alliance of city's trade, Farnesse, Longdusk commandos sign), innate spell: redirect attention, silent
casting, quick load

Skills: armor proficiency (plate/ leather/cloth): expert,
law: adept. lie: expert, dagger: journeyman, athletics:
journeyman, stealth: expert, disguise: journeyman, illusion magic: expert, shadow magic: journeyman, favored weapon (rifle): expert

The other commandos had simpler stats but their leader and two others were by far more skilled. One of those extra-skilled commandos was now dead at Lindy's feet.

Many commandos moved fast to put Lindy in their line of fire while keeping the other attackers in their sights as well. "We know our god is being held here. Move or die," Davrin growled.

"Did you give campus security the same choice?" Lindy asked as she casually pulled out the dead commando's pistol.

"Of course we did," Davrin spat as his team took cover.

From what Lindy had seen she knew the man was lying, so she stole the pins on the shade's grenades by pulling them into her shadow along with all the ammo loaded in their guns. "Nice try," Lindy called as she ran tackling #185 to the ground. The rest of the 823 Lost Legion followed along as a few of them noticed what Lindy had done. Davrin and his team only had enough time to gawk before they were reduced to paste.

Lindy began picking up the scraps of gear she could. The 823 Lost Legion members who had shown themselves followed her lead in silence although a few were clearly giddy and many curious glances came her way from all around her. Classes had stalled as the other college-goers and city residents realized something odd and violent had happened.

Rouna Lock and her team rushed out in riot full gear but with many lethal high-end weapons. Sirens sounded across the city. The 823

Lost Legion moved to stand before the Oii agents but Lindy grabbed the student who was a spitting image of the last Asami she had known. "You trust me, right?" Lindy whispered.

This new Asami whispered clearly. "What's your name?"

"My friends and enemies call me Lindy but I don't want my cover to be blown yet," Lindy whispered back.

#185's arm slackened. "I go by Amy here."

Lindy nodded as she walked up to Rouna. "Good to see you all are out and about now," Lindy called.

"This was excessive, don't you think?" Rouna asked like she believed otherwise and refusing to acknowledge Lindy's jab.

"Says the secretary surrounded by assault files and grenade launchers. I know that's not any kind of gas in those shells." Lindy shrugged.

"That's just not possible," Rouna grinned, her legs now trembling. "So why did you all fight then?"

Lindy rolled her eyes. "It's the smell. Be it tear gas, mustard gas, or any other kind of gas, it smells different from gunpowder, the crystal dust mix used nowadays, or jellied incendiary substances. And don't even get started on bio weapons or the heat from an atomic blast."

"Done?" Rouna asked, biting her lip and trying to not appear freaked out about how casual Lindy was being. Lindy nodded with a chuckle. Rouna cleared her throat. "Ok, what were you all doing here?"

"You mean me and my crew? We knew something odd was going down so out we came, only to be fired upon. One of those blockheads said something about seeking their god. At least one body's still intact. Woodrow only said to keep the damage to the grounds light. An extended firefight would have been far messier than this."

"Is that right?" Rouna sneered, looking around and trying hard to poke holes in Lindy's story.

"She's our boss," Amy shouted, standing up. A few glances were shared with her unit before they all nodded as well.

"And you all are?" Rouna asked.

"A rogue team of Zenic ninja founded back in the last big war from the 8th special operations force-2nd zone-3rd force. Like I said, they are my crew," Lindy replied. Most of the 823 Lost Legion around her trembled, some in shock, others in delight. They knew now after so long that their boss or someone like her had returned to them.

"That's enough. Get back to class, all of you. And you agents better clean up this mess. Students had to fight them off, for goodness sake." Woodrow's voice echoed across the lawn. He stood by one of the main doors.

Lindy began to walk back to her class but Amy gabbed her shirt. "Find me at lunch. We can talk then," Lindy said firmly.

"You won't run?" Amy asked.

"Your boss is too crazy for that, or did that never get passed down?" Lindy chuckled.

Woodrow shooed all the staff and students away. Cleanup crews swarmed the front gate. The day flew by. Soon it was noon and Lindy stood on a roof, Vivelin and Laylinda by her side. Amy, as #185 had named herself, stood across from them. Vivelin and Amy had a staring contest while Lindy looked out across the city. A barrier that destroyed sound that went through it was set up around them. Lindy had to monkey around with it so that flesh and more physical matter would not mess with it too badly. "So you had questions?" Lindy asked after a time.

The harsh atmosphere was redirected to Lindy. "Are you really that Lindy?" Amy asked.

Lindy sighed. "Saying that with her face and name is going to take some getting used to. When I look at my stats, Lindy is the name that always comes up. I may go by something a bit different from time to time but that has never changed. You have had the same experience, I imagine."

"That's true. No matter how hard I try the name is always #185 Asami series. Do you know what I am?" Amy asked.

"An amalgamation of many things. Simpler but better held together than my second-in-command from years ago," Lindy sighed.

"So what now?" Vivelin asked.

"The war will happen sooner than most think. I'll need to set some plans in motion. How would you three like to form a mercenary unit? I'll need some volunteers from the 823 Lost Legion as well," Lindy asked.

"How will that keep us safe?" Laylinda asked.

"Better than being used by the fools around here. There are enough loopholes in the autonomy the church technically has and the perks mercenaries get that it should work. If not, I can force a few things. No big deal," Lindy shrugged.

"And what are the chances of you fighting an invasion or two again?" Vivelin asked.

"That depends on them," Lindy smiled.

"Very well. I'll talk to the able-bodied ones around here," Amy agreed.

"It's not like that happens every time," Lindy objected.

"Just often enough to alter the landscape permanently each time," Vivelin grumbled.

"At least one of those changes was wiped off the map by me, and you know it," Lindy sighed.

"I've got work to do. Have fun." Amy rolled her eyes and left.

Lindy slipped out of the college soon after and went to the pope's office. Carla looked up from her desk. "You are early," she sighed.

"I have a request," Lindy said as she collapsed into an over-upholstered chair.

"Does this have to do with the bodyguard job I gave you?" Carla asked sternly.

"That and how fast this illusion is falling apart," Lindy grumbled. "You know for once in my life I wish peace was not such a tease."

"Peace?" Carla asked.

"It's something my niece Covell oversees along with the economy and war. We are getting off track. I need the church to form a unit of mercenaries beholden to it, then align them to the local military. If I've read the local laws and international treaties clearly that should give us the most freedom," Lindy grumbled.

Carla thought for a while then pulled a few books from under the pile of documents encasing her desk. After looking through the books closely she nodded. "That's indeed doable but the term of service will be far longer."

"It's safer this way. Our presence will make the fools all over this city calm down a bit," Lindy debated back.

"That's a fair point. I'm sure you've seen a lot to back that up. All right, besides your two charges and you, who else is joining?" the pope asked.

"I found descendants of the team I led in the last war. They seem to have gone rogue and lived in search of me. Some of them will join us," Lindy replied.

Carla did not even bat an eye. Over the years she had become quite numb to insane surprises. "All right. Does the name Eternal work for you? That unit's been mothballed but I can grant you the name, symbol, and a stash of them."

"Is that ok?" Lindy inquired.

"It's fitting. You were once an officer of that unit but you will need a code name," Carla smiled reassuringly.

"You can call me the Eternal Calamity then," Lindy nodded.

"That fits a little too well. I'll get the paperwork all set by tonight," Carla promised.

Lindy stood up. "Thanks. I'll get back to work." Soon after, Vivelin and Laylinda found Lindy walking back home with them. A few 823 Lost Legion members shadowed them.

After being tailed for a few streets Lindy pulled her two charges into an alleyway while using an old sign from the last war to regroup directed at her pursuers. In a small dank courtyard the team of five legion members met Lindy face to face. "If you guys want to come along then tell me first."

"We were..." one of the younger student members of the Lost Legion began. Vivelin and Laylinda could tell this might take a while. Upon failing to find a clean place to rest they stepped back and trusted Lindy to take care of things.

"I've been lied to a lot in the past few thousand years. Even then, you are a terrible liar." Lindy stopped the young student.

An older member asked, "So you are the shades' god then?"

"They decided that on their own." Lindy sighed. She held up a hand and added, "So given how terrible your stalking and lying, how about I train whoever is joining me?"

"You know not all of us trust you, right?" the older member asked again.

"Then that's a point in your favor," Lindy shot back as if they would be insane to think otherwise.

"Last question," the older legion member began. Lindy rolled her eyes. "What are you trying to achieve?" the man asked.

Lindy's expression became firm. She looked everyone around in the eyes then announced with a shrug. "Right now, surviving. There is a lot going on behind the scenes and many pieces are missing. In the year I have left I'll find what's been bugging me and deal with it."

"That's it?" the man demanded.

Lindy nodded. "My intuition has served me well. Granted it's only worked well in non-combat scenarios recently. That would be many of your generations. So you all coming or not?"

"Where to?" the man asked.

"Perfect." Lindy clapped. The shadows of the alleyway covered them all when light resumed. Li-one stood up from her lawn chair. A fancy drink sailed from her hand. Lindy, Vivelin, Laylinda, and the five others arrived in the underground arena Lindy had called home. "Hey, we'll only be a few hours."

Li-one picked up her spilled drink, grumbling, "Sure, it's your place, boss."

"Oh there's a good chance for the next week or so this will be an everyday thing with different folks," Lindy called after her creation who was busily mixing another drink. Turning to the five with her, Lindy clapped her hands. "You all got that?"

"Going forward, only the members of the 823 Lost Legion and whoever you deem fit to join your unit will visit here. The legion will send small teams of different members to you after school each day?" the youngest in the team asked. The five that had tailed a monster in the shell of a short teenager were meeker now. They were beginning to realize just how much power Lindy could wield. Little did they know the power Lindy showed was a drop in the bucket compared to her full potential. However, given that at full power her mere presence would rip reality to shreds, that misunderstanding was best left as is.

Lindy's shadow rose from the ground and she sat on it. One of her makeshift chair's arms stretched, plucking a beer from a cooler on the other side of the room before placing it in her hand. After taking a sip of the alcohol Lindy asked her still stiff-backed stalkers, "So does everyone in your origination use the same combat philosophy?"

"We use the Lin method," a twenty-something male replied.

Lindy sneered. "That's not an answer." The young man trembled. Lindy finished her beer in one gulp and sighed. "Look, I'm not pissed at you folks. The thing is we don't have time to dick around because a big war will start soon. I'm not saying to become mindless automatons; Death knows I like freedom. More info is fine but if I ask or request something, at the very least give a clear answer. I'd like to keep those who follow me alive. After all they can't come back from Death's realm like I can."

"Our traditional methods focus a little more on strong hits to weaken or kill our foes. Speed and maneuverability are key components as well, but out-maneuvering and either strongly hitting a vital location or failing that, wearing down the target, is the primary focus. Many members with real combat experience add to their personal practice. Mastering one or two weapons to use with those principles is the last focus of our traditional system," the older man answered.

"Sounds a lot like me then," Lindy grinned. She leaned forward and chuckled. "Show me. Go through a few moves each while imagining yourselves in combat. If you need a weapon, ask me."

The older man pulled a thin sheet of metal from a hidden compartment in his belt. After embedding magic into it the blade stiffened. "If you have something a little heavier than this, that would be best."

Lindy nodded. The arms on her chair reached into itself and tossed a thin fencing blade made for stabbing. It had an elegant guard. Even in seclusion and killing through her shadows each year from the lists Death passed down, Lindy kept up her habit of hoarding the weapons her kills had owned. "Before we move forward, what's your name?"

Only Lindy seemingly paid no attention to Vivelin's embarrassed expression. After all, she knew more about Lindy's history than any other mortal. "Kage Le," the older man introduced himself before going into a smooth series of swings and footwork with his borrowed blade. He ended with a back-flip and lunge. "If I fought multiple lightly armored targets my methods might be something like that."

"And the flip would be for?" Lindy asked.

"A few things. In this case, catching someone with a longer weapon like a broom handle or mounted bayonet off guard. Then using the opening of them shifting to strike," Kage explained.

"Good enough," Lindy nodded. "Ok, next," she called. The others were not as smooth as Kage but they all had some skill with their attack methods. The younger member who had been vocal before introduced herself as Lilly Saldernon. Body kicks, targeted strikes, and counter-attacks seemed to be the focus of her skill set. Pistols were apparently what Lilly intended to master as a secondary weapon.

After a half an hour of her new trainees moving around as they wished, Lindy used her shadow magic to make their own shadows become solid puppets. "Ok, spar for as long as you can against your own shadows. They will use the moves you have shown but they may use some additional techniques and improvements of my own." Lindy got out of her own solidified shadow chair and assumed the appearance she had when she had copied the old Asami's form.

When Vivelin saw what Lindy was doing she moved to the exact opposite side of the arena. Laylinda looked around quickly then followed suit. Li-one called to the others. "You all should leave half the arena to our boss." Most of the former stalkers did as they had been asked although their shadows did not make the retreat a simple one, as the temporary puppets Lindy had created pressured their owners with a quiet fierceness. Seconds after the first batch of runners had crossed the halfway point, Lindy's own shadow erupted with power slightly above what she herself was limited to.

Those who were too slow were pushed out of Lindy's half of the arena by the air pressure and gusts produced from Lindy and her clone's attacks. The less experienced legion members were lucky that no intense force or intimidation was pouring out of their boss. Kage was the only one among his group who was experienced enough to see the calmness around Lindy as surreal and off-putting. The fiercer movements were customarily followed by mental pressure of equal measure. Though he did not detect any danger despite knowing that being grazed by Lindy's fists right now would at best result in a mortal wound, Kage made a note in his heart to never piss off the boss of his legion.

Lindy slowly included some of the legion's moves into her own, albeit with more than a few tweaks. Her puppets began to do the same, using the modifications Lindy had found against their respective users. The puppets slowed down as well but their movements became sharper and more effective, especially the footwork. It became harder for the legion members to hit their own shadows and much harder to defend against the attacks, despite the original users being familiar with what they were being hit by. This did nothing to help their crumbling egos. The legion members understood that this would help them so they persevered. Li-one even helped rehydrate those who collapsed until they got back up. Laylinda and Vivelin just watched, enjoying a few snacks Lin-one provided for the four hours the legion members held out.

27

Free Fall Express

Over the next three days Lindy worked with thirty-one members that the 823 Lost Legion had chosen, one of which was #185 of the Asami series (although she preferred to be called Amy). With the addition of Lindy, Laylinda, and Vivelin, the roster the church kept was fully updated. Lindy's name was listed simply as Lin "the heroic calamity" Ashborn. Their training after school each day was harsh but fruitful. The news, political speeches, and sermons became even more hardline over the days. Military patrols and events sponsored by the military that were both for PR and recruitment spread around the human nations. The scale was shocking to Lindy as she knew the coming war would be far bigger, no matter who was accused of lighting the spark. Any human nation bordering land controlled by the shades or their monster allies was packed with patrols on both sides. Given the rampant greed, hate, and fearmongering, even a patrol too close to a border could be used as an excuse to retaliate with a full intercontinental invasion.

On the fourth day a recruitment drive was set up in the college. The war-mongering faction in the Everlasting church even sent Lindy a note reminding her to attend school that day. After ensuring copies of all her mercenary unit's IDs and rosters were in her school bag, Lindy set off. She ignored the first few recruiters standing by the gates as the school-grounds were like a fair. Booths filled with prizes, food, and propaganda stood side-by-side with a one-sided version of how the world worked that was on the level of mild brainwashing, disguised as special classes. The rest of her unit was playing hooky with Lindy's grandchildren.

Thullkiran Faywind marched up behind Lindy and held her shoulder; Lindy resisted the urge to kill the man on the spot. Sighing, she asked, "What do you want?"

"For such a powerful fighter, you are not much for the war effort," the elf said far louder than he intended, thereby drawing a lot of attention.

Lindy disappeared from his grasp in a puff of smoke before appearing a few feet away holding out a pile of documents. "I'm a mercenary who answers directly to her Hallowedness, dip shit."

Thullkiran frowned, snatching the documents and flipping through them. "I know these names." He tossed the files back at Lindy, who collected them into her shadow before the stack literally fell into Rouna Lock's lap. "This is illegal," Thullkiran added.

"No, it's not as a mercenary answering directly to the church. My unit has a great deal of freedom. As long as someone pays us well for missions of our choosing then it's perfectly legal, even at the highest-level state of emergency. Most of that stack is an article that is very popular in the legal community right now," Lindy smirked.

"And what right do you have to restart such an ancient mercenary unit? The name is one thing, but part of the argument rests on how long the unit has been around and when the law went into effect. There are some major requirements for something like that to be allowed, let alone this legal argument," Rouna accused, quickly voicing the one glaring point not covered in the roster.

Lindy laughed. "Woodrow is not the only one related by blood to the heroine that made the wasteland. Lindy the priestess of Death was the second-in-command of that same unit once upon a time." Her words sent a metaphorical shock wave though the entire city as everyone in the city heard the argument that Lindy, Thullkiran, and Rouna just had transported into their ears. "Now that the entire city knows that, I'll be playing hooky for the day." Lindy smiled but her face was pale after using a level of power her currently suppressed body was not set up to handle. She simply fell into her shadow, only to slam into her tub back in the cathedral and vomit. Vivelin rushed into Lindy's bathroom and looked down in mild worry. "Note to self: Lock my door and use less power all at once," Lindy snickered.

"Is the boss back yet?" Amy called into the room.

"Not mentally. Give me a little bit," Lindy called back.

Amy walked in and froze when she saw Lindy. "What?" she asked.

"I think that last part was English?" Vivelin asked.

Laylinda flew into the room. "If it is, then the pronunciation is nothing like I imagined. Say something else in Otherworlder!" Jess Faywind and Molly Gyorn trailed after Laylinda.

"Well, hello to you too," Lindy replied in French.

"Was that the same language?" Laylinda asked.

"No it's not, and Otherworlder is far too generic. After all, there are over one hundred trillion realities ruled by one kind of four-legged cat, and that's the smallest number of cat-ruled realities," Lindy explained, showing off some of her knowledge.

Is it ok to tell them that? Genney asked directly into Lindy's mind from Fate's realm.

Well, folks from other realities is a thing here. You know that there is more than one library with books on languages from other worlds, right? Lindy thought back.

Vivelin put her hand on Lindy's shoulder. "Are you ok?"

"Yes. I was just talking to Genney a bit. You remember her from when you were Fraya, right?" Lindy replied, winking at Laylinda as she did so.

"I do but oh, how long ago was that?" Vivelin murmured. She was too deep in her thoughts to notice Laylinda's practically glowing eyes and visage that were clearly lusting after more data. Laylinda's mother and aunt took more than a few steps back while Amy was in combat mode, in order to protect Lindy if needed.

"Oh that was back before the wasteland I created when you went by Frost, right? The Derndell kingdom was still a kingdom when we were young, so at least three thousand years." Lindy laughed as she leapt up and walked past Laylinda. "I'm sure this one would love to hear about all your past lives." It was only then that Vivelin began to go into a cold sweat.

"Tell me all about it. You have a few nights to talk, right? You do, right?" Laylinda sputtered.

"Not all night," Vivelin said weakly.

"We'll have all day, too. No worries," Laylinda expanded, displaying very selective hearing.

"Well Amy, let's go train the others," Lindy announced as she made a quick exit, calling over her shoulder. "Remember to stay hydrated and take lunch breaks, you two."

Three days passed; Lindy and her team no longer went to college as they trained and acquired gear though the Lost Legion's connections. Laylinda and Vivelin worked to create a complete history from a human perspective spanning three thousand years and written to be as neutral as possible. Lindy helped provide some input and info on behind-the-scenes skullduggery. Somehow the series of tomes that came out of Laylinda's work were treated as very sacred religious documents, despite the intended purpose being to show history though unclouded eyes. Even though most religious institutions kept the books under lock and key, due largely to how the books never took any one side, the tomes did spread fast. The warmongering factions in the world's governments, industry, and educational institutions all had a hand in the suppression of the tomes while ramping up their own propaganda. Anything that went against the narrative of "*We are good and anyone we say is bad go kill*" was suppressed.

One day a cardinal came to Lindy's door with Rouna Lock and Thullkiran Faywind in tow. "Honored Lindy, we come with grave tidings," the cardinal announced loudly in lieu of a knock.

Lindy rolled her eyes and opened the door. "It's Lin to you three. Let me guess — this is about some holy mission to go kill a bunch of folks?"

"I could never be so familiar," the cardinal snickered as Lindy came out and closed the door behind her, standing with her back to the wall.

Lindy glared. "It's not being familiar. I don't like strangers to call me by that title to my face."

"Well then, can we come in?" Rouna asked.

"You are strangers, remember? What's the job? If it's good I'll get the team together." Lindy tried to sound impatient and not laugh in their faces.

"This is for the good of Death itself," the cardinal frowned.

"If it was, she would have been asked to move by him. Now do you have a contract and intel or not?" Lindy frowned. When no response came quickly enough she shrugged. "The shades' artillery is still ripping you guys apart. I guess some things never change."

"You're well informed," Thullkiran replied tensely. He was learning not to underestimate the person before him. Although he was basing that on what she had so far let him see.

"My main patron can be helpful from time to time," Lindy replied, ambiguously hoping they would still believe that she was not her real self and only some odd clever being with a simpler name.

"Right. Well you and your team still need to come to the front lines by the end of next week. I'll be shadowing your team. As long as you all take your jobs seriously we won't have too many issues," Thullkiran grumbled.

"And as long as no one tries to single out my team and make our lives unnecessarily harder then we won't have a problem," Lindy laughed. "Just remember, suicide missions cost extra and that's all to be paid upfront. Bonuses come after the job's done." Rouna frowned and Lindy snickered. "It's not like I'm against suicide missions as long as my team's not the only one risking our hides, the pay's real good, and it's necessary." With that, she slipped back inside her room.

Thullkiran found a note in his pocket containing Lindy's phone number and email. Rouna looked at it and sighed. "This complicates our plans." When she and Thullkiran left they slipped the cardinal a bag of gems.

After training for close to a week and acquiring more gear from well-connected but non-government aligned contacts the Lost Legion had been long acquainted with, Lindy had her unit assemble one morning. They waited in full gear in a garden next to the cathedral Lindy had called home. At noon Thullkiran walked up to the main gates and walked in. After two hours he left with far lighter pockets and was not happy at all after searching within the cathedral for Lindy. "Find what you were looking for?" Lindy called out from the entrance to the garden.

"Where have you been?" Thullkiran asked, not bothering to hide his annoyance.

"With my unit. What are you here for?" Lindy sneered. She knew that the shades were doing very well for now despite their far lower numbers, and that would not last.

"Your team is being called up," Thullkiran grumbled.

Lindy smirked. She had expected this. "First I'm hearing of it. You are a few days early."

"Doesn't look like it," Thullkiran grimaced.

"Well, info gathering and ambushes are what we do," Lindy shrugged. "So when do we leave?"

"Now," Thullkiran replied.

"Oh. With what transport?" Lindy asked.

"You don't have transport?" Thullkiran asked.

"Well, our employer is supposed to be aware of these things. Next time, ask me if you have questions." Lindy nodded.

Thullkiran took out a phone and got a few trucks to come over from a supply base. "You owe me for this," he said after one-sidedly ordering the supply base's commander around.

"Well we are even then. After all, we are being called up early. Normally that would be a breach of contract," Lindy laughed.

"How were you going to arrive before?" Thullkiran asked.

"If our employers did not do anything? Then we would walk. Although no one told us we're to go yet. I'd expect our employers to be more helpful and understanding than that," Lindy shrugged.

"Not much of a patriotic holy warrior, are you lot?" Thullkiran sneered, trying one last jab to trap Lindy into helping far more.

"We are out for money but our superiors get most of it," Lindy replied. Even if she did not have to, besides operating costs and a fund for those who would die, the rest was being funneled to the anti-war faction that Carla ran.

The trucks arrived soon after and Lindy got in the middle truck with Thullkiran. Amy got in the second from the front. Vivelin got in the second from the rear and Laylinda got in the third from the rear. Seven trucks in total moved out with six motorcycles that acted as escorts. The convoy left the city and moved along a highway. Two hills away was a forest that had grown from the land Woodrow and the twist sprites had been born from.

Hours passed. It had been night for close to two hours when the earth shook and lights blazed in the sky. The trucks sped up. Stopping at a large camp, Lindy and company jumped out, weapons ready. A few MPs and vehicle crews did the same. Their uniforms were from the Smog City garrison so Lindy called out, "Quite the light show. Care to let the new kids in on the occasion?"

One after another everyone lowered their guns. "There's a big fort nearby. It's a mess of guns and dirt. They started a barrage recently."

"This happen every night?" Lindy asked.

"Almost," a crewman replied.

"For your first job I'll need your team's help taking that fort, Lindy," Thullkiran noted.

"I'll let you know if we accept after getting a look at it," Lindy noted.

"It's a reasonable request and I was not asking," Thullkiran snapped.

Lindy began to walk. "Amy, Viv, third wheel, with me. Layee, greet whoever is in charge here and help the unit get their camp set up somewhere in the rear away from the rest of the units."

"What will we be doing, boss?" Amy asked.

Lindy turned to Laylinda as Amy's question was mostly for her and the local commander's benefit. "Going to take a peek at the enemy fort and quote our price."

Thullkiran rushed after them. "This better not be too much!" he snapped.

"Whatever, commissar," Lindy shrugged. The word commissar was in jungle elvish as they had a direct English equivalent of it, as few other languages currently in use did. If not for trying to get Thullkiran to slip some info by making him mad and his vendetta against her real self, Lindy would have antagonized the elven hero far less.

After peeking around a bunker Lindy focused her eyes and shard in the sky on the enemy position. The opposing position was a modest-sized hill. The area around was cleared of trees and the hill itself was dug out and reinforced heavily with concrete and steel. A multitude of artillery guns, anti-armor cannons, machine gun nests, and even a few anti-air batteries stuck out of the mound of earth like very pissed-off iron porcupines. The weapons all used gunpowder, not the magic crystal-based mediums Lindy had introduced. "Yeah we are not rushing that, no matter what the pay is." She glanced at Thullkiran and added quickly, "But given how good we are at ambush, their supply lines are another matter. This is a siege, after all. Rushing into that mound of guns is a really bad idea."

Thullkiran took a deep breath. "And how much?"

Lindy thought for a second. "Standard rate for thirty-four mercenaries without the discounts your bosses are getting for themselves. No extra danger pay."

"That's still a lot," Thullkiran muttered.

"Then don't hire us. After how hard you went after me, someone you answer to must know we are worth it. I'm not even demanding extra danger pay," Lindy retorted.

"I'll let you know tomorrow then," Thullkiran sighed.

"Sure, that works." Lindy smiled before walking back to camp. It was going to be a loud night.

Half an hour before first light Lindy and company were fully awake. Their weapons never left their sides day or night. After a few stretches the group ate pemmican they had prepared beforehand along with some tea. Thullkiran arrived a few hours later from the main camp complex, the newest iteration of the Eternal mercenary company members at camp cleaning their gear and lightly sparring with one another, while ten members in two-person teams walked around the camp. They switched up the teams walking, patrolling, and observing every hour.

"Captain Lin, if we siege them, how long will it take?" Thullkiran asked.

"Three months at the most; half a month if we are lucky. It really depends on their how big of a stockpile they keep, how far they are willing to go, and how thorough we are." Lindy shrugged, not bothering to sit up from a stump. A map was laid down before her on the ground, held down by rocks.

"Three months might be too long," Thullkiran sighed.

Lindy rolled her eyes. "It's not like the whole army is needed for that. A few platoons and my team should be enough. I'd be surprised if they had more than two hundred troops in there, what with all the heavy ordinance taking up space."

"If we go with that plan we'd still be outnumbered," Thullkiran noted. As much as he felt annoyed, Lin seemed far wiser than she often acted. He could tell she was very skilled at killing and tactics which included giving him and his government the runaround. Being wary while at the same time using her well was a huge pain. If Lin, as she demanded to be called, was speaking from experience, then she was even older than he, and that would mean that Lin might be closely connected to the real Lindy, so he would endure for now.

"If we starve them for a while and I lead the assault then it will be fine," Lindy replied dismissively.

"So are you going to try to get them to waste ammo?" Thullkiran asked.

"Well if they stop firing on the camp every night, yes. Temporary fortifications, old repainted trucks, maybe a few wooden cut-outs would give them some targets," Lindy noted like it was a no-brainer.

"Fine. I think command will ok that, but if the enemy pushes past you then we will have a problem," Thullkiran replied sternly.

Lindy laughed. "The fort and their convoys will not be a problem. If the allied units that go beyond this point don't hold the ground they have taken, then I'm requesting danger pay and a bonus."

"Right. I'll get back to you in a few hours," Thullkiran grimaced.

As the foolish overworked elven hero was heading back to the camp's main radio setups, Vivelin called out to him. "Don't try to push our leader too far."

"Is that a threat?" Thullkiran snarled. He was low on sleep and had a splitting headache already.

"An observation. Those who have tried to use her past her bottom line tend to have bad endings, no matter who or how many they are. Even more so if they annoy her," Vivelin noted.

"I'll keep that in mind," Thullkiran promised as he swiftly forgot the warning.

An hour passed and Thullkiran came running. "Ok, you can start now," he wheezed.

Lindy looked up from a sniper rifle she was servicing. "That was quick."

"They gave you all a pay raise, too. So work hard, all right?" Thullkiran added. He did not understand why the bosses had caved so hard, but not asking questions of them was part of the job.

Lindy rolled her eyes. "How much backup is being left behind?"

"Two platoons and a supply core," Thullkiran replied.

"Good. So who has command authority?" Lindy pressed, now scuffing the shine from a knife with an inky tint.

"You do. But if I deem your actions to be detrimental to the government, then that can be revoked," Thullkiran answered.

Lindy shrugged. "Fine. But don't question my tactics all the time." She looked around her camp. The army had already begun to march back behind the siege lines. Their next move was to reinforce a line that was working to take a bridge over a ravine that led deeper into enemy territory. "Mercs, gather around," Lindy called out as her team assembled quickly. Lindy looked over at Thullkiran and tossed him a notebook filled with sketches and blueprints. "Get the normal troops left over to make as many of those as they can. We also need to get as many tents of the same kind and number as what was here by tonight."

"Decoys?" Thullkiran asked.

"Yes, decoys. Now go. You might need plywood, paint, nails, some saws, axes, hammers, shovels, and some cheap cloth, too. We need to give the fort some targets and reason to think there is still a force here. Now don't ask me questions about obvious things again," Lindy replied sternly. It was a voice used to command and being obeyed. She had used it unconsciously but Thullkiran noticed, and he had many more questions about his temporary commander that he knew she would not answer.

Lindy had her unit gather around the map she had been working on. She pointed out the search patterns, ambush points, and fallback positions (main and backups), along with team composition, terrain details, what kind of weather was normal in the region at this time of year, what positions the enemy would likely have their eye on, and what dangerous predators were around and how to identify them. After ensuring each team leader had taken notes, Lindy quizzed the team leaders on what the enemy's standard gear was like and reminded them to take nothing for granted. Only then did she dismiss them to their tasks.

Lindy looked up at the sky. Amy, Laylinda, and Vivelin were the members of her team. As the command squad, they would stay back for the most part and gather information while coordinating the plan to trick the enemy into staying on guard while wasting ammo. After picking up a few brief piercing glances, Lindy sighed. Upon looking back in her memories she realized she may have let a few minor things slip. "No major changes to the plan," she muttered. Her game plan would cause a lot of pain for those closest to her and many others, but Lindy knew that shocking the current system to a standstill was the best stopgap she could mange in the time she had left to personally muck up this world.

"You are alright?" Vivelin asked.

Lindy hardened her resolve, knowing that her plans, while almost worked out, would be most unfair to her oldest friend. "More or less. You know that on the roster you are my second-in-command, right?"

"Just don't die on me," Vivelin replied back harshly. She knew more than anyone how many thankless heartbreaking tasks Lindy took on by herself. As much as that had annoyed all of Vivelin's lives but the first, she could not bring herself to be harsher about it. After all, the end of Fraya Fields continued to haunt Lindy, even if Vivelin recalled that life and many others since then. She knew Lindy had yet to forgive herself for that first death.

"Right back at you," Lindy nodded. She had been so harsh to herself for so long that even if she meant it, the small voice left in her heart that tried to say *I don't want to see you die again. I don't like seeing others die when I cannot. I don't like you forgetting me. I don't like bringing you into this bullshit unending life of mine. I want you to be happy. I don't want to die. To keep this immortality, I must kill. Why me?* went unheard.

Days passed. Lindy's teams found three roads and eleven trails. Each convoy to and from the fort was mercilessly destroyed via ambush and booby trap. The trails were secured with the same methods. The traps were many and varied but kept to a few key themes: tripwires connected to branches and grenades, logs set to roll or swing, signals of all kinds to alert the ambush teams to attack, and noise makers and tear gas to disorient the enemy. Each night the roads were mined with Lindy's handmade explosives, many of which would only be set off by vehicles. Shells the enemy launched, local magic crystal formations, and trees, along with captured cloth, gas, gunpowder, and other parts were used to make the booby traps. Each was slightly different and therefore hard to disarm and completely detect. However, Lindy made sure each trap was listed on their maps, not just for her unit's safety but also so the traps could be set off remotely later.

Dummy tents and extras fire pits were placed further away than before but still just within long-distance telescope range. The support teams were all required to wear masks and baggy uniforms designed for biological warfare. The 3D plywood mock-ups of vehicles had newly created unit markings that were put on the books for this task. Camp-fires were placed near groups of vehicles. Hidden tunnels were placed behind the vehicles and most of the support staff were required to use those to move about the mostly fake rear camp.

Earthen redoubts were dug late at night. Sometimes a flare would be fired by the enemy and the work crews would scatter but no matter how many shells hit those locations, the enemy kept up the nightly harassment until day four.

On the fourth day of the damage a large explosion rocked two of the roads. Enemy reinforcements had been called and many had died. The ambush teams took out many more. A few shades tried to use shadow and illusion magic but Lindy's training had prepared her teams for such tricks. During the biggest illusion spell the shades tried to rush forward but Lindy raised their dead as zombies and decimated as many foes as she could. Sniper fire and grenades took care of the rest.

Over the next six days, two more reinforcement attempts and one heavily guarded resupply convoy were mobilized to the fort. In total, fewer than thirty mostly lightly wounded troops were able to escape Lindy's ambushes to the fort. Fewer shells and harassments were launched. So Lindy captured trucks and whatever vehicles were too old even for redistribution and jury-rigged them into small bombs that would keep moving until something hit them or they crashed. These vehicles were pointed at the enemy fort and let loose. Many were shot down. Those that were not either crashed into the fort and spread volatile substances or broke down halfway and detonated.

On the morning of the eleventh day, the fort surrendered just as Lindy was checking her plans for assaulting it. No one had complained to Lindy about her methods as the Farnesse empire was wasting lots of supplies. After Thullkiran reported that the fort was captured intact and he needed support for moving the prisoners that had surrendered, no one wanted to question Lindy, least of all the more perceptive shades among the new prisoners. Lindy made sure to introduce herself, emphasizing her rank and using her authority over the shades to force those they captured to recognize her only as the boss of the Eternal mercenaries.

In the days it took to process the prisoners and transport to arrive, Thullkiran had taken the enemy's diaries and log books. During the siege they had made many remarks about a power resembling the royals among the shades used to enforce control, but far stronger. The power was described in all cases as feeling undirected. Many in the fort had a hard time getting it off their minds. It was overwhelming but seemly a passive emanation, like when a young but powerful dragon's power was hard to miss even if it hid in human form; those around them would feel overwhelmed even if the dragon's power was contained well, and the feeling of danger and might remained. This confused the shades, as no royal had that kind of oppressive power, and it seemed to come from the mercenary camp. Their only conclusion was that a mercenary in the camp was closely and unknowingly descended from the Long-dusk imperial family. The shades had relayed that information back to their HQ.

Thullkiran saw how the POWs acted around Lindy. They were shifty and fearful but there was an odd sense of awe and peace as well. When addressed, the POWs responded robotically, only naming Lindy's title among the mercenaries. Even when shown their own log books, the captured shades did not seem to recognize what they had written. Lindy, or Lin as she liked to be called, had an unknown history. Many in her unit were odd but their births and movements could be traced. Lindy was a complete and very powerful unknown.

After relaying what little he had discovered and making it clear that the more he found out the more of a threat Lin appeared to be, Thullkiran called Lin, leading her a short distance into the forest for a talk. "I've been wondering what are you really?" he asked.

Lin was clever. She must have had an idea of how much danger she could be in but her relaxed flippant attitude remained. "You mean my species, my identity to others, my personality, or something else?" she asked lazily, extremely at odds with the masterful commander she appeared as during the siege.

"Ok, a better question. Who are you?" Thullkiran pressed.

"That's not a better question." Lindy rolled her eyes. Thullkiran drew his sword and leveled it at Lindy, who simply glared at him, her expression hard, as if she knew the sword would not cut into her neck. "Ok, let's make this easy then. Do you want to know who I am trying to appear to be now, who I really am with as little ambiguousness as I can manage, or why your clan was nearly erased and the three responsible for ordering it?"

Thullkiran's hand shook. As much as he wanted to know the third one, he knew enough. His leaders, however, demanded the answer to the middle one, and neither he nor his paymasters wanted to hear the excuses that would be the first. "The second one," said the elven hero who sold his soul and identity to a nation in the pursuit of power and vengeance.

Lindy's face darkened further. "That's too bad. I would have hoped what I am trying to be was worth more than that." Countless blades erupted from Thullkiran's stomach and he fell to the ground. The last thing he saw in life was the being called Lin staring down at him with a troubled look filled with envy, of all things. "My real name is Lindy, as in the only priestess of Death this world has known for something like three thousand years. I'm human, not mortal and not quite immortal. I created the shades, killed and assassinated roughly half this world's current population of souls. The Faywind clan have with a few exceptions been a real pain. Greed for my power has felled at least one nation. I gave the Faywinds more than a few chances, in thanks for those of their clan who were close to me. The last time they tried to kill me on the shades' orders I ordered a purge of all involved. It was harsher than I expected."

Evan though he had died just as Lin began to introduce herself, some force enabled Thullkiran to hear it all. He found himself in a dark lightless place. A huge skeleton holding a large mug labeled *World's Best Bonehead* rose from the darkness. "You fucked up hard, kid," the skeleton sighed.

"Excuse me?" Thullkiran asked.

The skeleton took a sip of coffee from its mug. Somehow the liquid dispersed before hitting its rib cage. "You are excused. I would have liked to erase your soul but we have a clause in my employment contract against that."

"Are you Death?" Thullkiran asked. The giant being handed him three six-sided dice. "What are these for?" the elf asked.

"Roll them. I'm getting your soul sent to another world because I don't like you," Death grumbled.

"That hardly seems fair," Thullkiran mused.

"Life is not fair. Or did Fate never teach you that? The souls to be born and die in your world are under my control. Because I can be a little unreasonable when someone gives my subordinate too hard of a time," Death replied sternly.

Thullkiran rolled all the dice. Two sixes and a two. "Oh, a post-apocalyptic water planet where stone-age seagulls rule the place. Not bad." Death nodded. And with that, Thullkiran disappeared from the realm of Death.

Meanwhile Lindy had shifted through shadows to the Oii main office with Thullkiran's body. "I'd like to report a murder," she announced to a stunned receptionist while giving a passing janitor an apologetic bow.

Rouna Lock rushed out of a break room. "Lindy, what the hell!" she called. Everyone in the large entry area of the Oii building now noticed Lindy and the dead mangled corpse she dragged in.

"He was hit a bit too hard. Oh, were you on lunch?" Lindy smirked unapologetically as a pool of gore spread over the floor past her feet. Guards and off duty Oii members with all manner of rifles and shotguns swiftly covered the room.

Rouna looked around. "This is not a good place to talk. Come with me."

Lindy shrugged, dropping what was left of Thullkiran. "Fine. I'll leave this baggage here."

Rouna would have grimaced if she had not been so tense. Lindy was far too calm, as if she could level the building. Some guards tailed Rouna and Lindy in a show of force from a distance as they moved deep into the building. Lindy's presence was stifling to all but herself. Rouna was sure anyone but Lindy would have freaked out, giving the staff an opening and excuse to subdue them. Lindy was different and that unnerved all those on guard against her. She exposed no openings in her movements where she could be attacked from. Rouna was sure Lindy could counterattack easily from any direction. "You can relax, you know," Rouna said, shouting a little.

"Oh that won't do. Last time I relaxed around that errand boy of yours, he got his guts ripped out," Lindy said happily. Her eyes, however, narrowed, and for a brief second everyone in the Oii building felt that they would die that very second. Then the pressure dispersed and Lindy chuckled in a tone devoid of mirth. She was angry; that much was clear.

Rouna stopped beside a large blast door set into the floor of a mostly empty sector. "So you killed Captain Faywind, I take it?"

"That's right," Lindy admitted easily. "I came here to see if he was acting under orders or not."

"Is that so?" Rouna tried to feel good about having the only exit from the room and the walls around it being surrounded by heavily armed guards. However, given that she was next to Lindy and alone in the room, that reassurance did not help very much at all. Rouna hit the release for the blast door and walked into the bunker it contained. They walked into the place where magic and any connection to world spirits was blocked off: the nation's most secret prison. Lindy flexed her hands a few times and frowned, studying the walls closely. "So are you the Lindy? Priestess of Death and ancient assassin?" Rouna asked.

"You forgot war hero who has slaughtered thousands and nearly everything in at least one empire," Lindy added. The pair stepped onto the bunker floor. Cells housing the priestesses born or captured in this nation filled the walls. "And I'm one of a kind. My dream job was accountant or confectioner."

Rouna shot at Lindy with a tranquilizer but it was blocked by a sword that radiated power. Transcendence glowed angrily. "You know the last place that tried to trap and kill me became the wasteland." The power of Transcendence was not fully manifested but it still radiated Lindy's full power. In a flash the entire building was slashed apart. All but the captured priestesses were cut into paste and dust as waves of power erupted from the sword, slicing everything Lindy wished, which at that moment was just about everything.

Lindy walked over to the coworkers who huddled in their cells. The bunker was more like a damp hole now. "Hey, do you folks want to live or die?" she called.

"What is live?" a thirty-something women asked in a childish lisp.

"That's it. I'm joining the shades ahead of schedule. The humans just keep getting worse," Lindy spat. Using some of the power held in her sword as a medium, Lindy tossed the terrified priestesses directly into Carla's office, along with one gold coin from the Derndell kingdom for each priestess. "You owe me one," Lindy called into her shadow before jumping into another shadow. "Time to say goodbye to my friends again," Lindy grumbled as she appeared near the camp.

Vivelin stood where Thullkiran had died. After one look at Lindy's face, Vivelin sighed. "You don't feel better yet. What happened?"

"I just lost my faith in the human race. No big deal." Lindy sighed. "You know the other priestesses did not stop appearing. The world spirits kept losing track of them. Turns out the priestesses have been kept in isolation."

Vivelin shook her head sadly. "You are going away from me again?"

"I'm sorry. Take care of the team, all right?" Lindy asked.

"All the time you've been on this planet we really have not changed. You clean up after me and I do the same for you. Frost and Freya did that the most out of my past lives," Vivelin sighed.

"Faldrea and Geena were big parts of my life too," Lindy noted.

"Right. You know most of my lives I never met you," Vivelin noted.

"And the ones I spent with you I watched you die," Lindy replied.

"Right. Well don't take on the world alone and if possible, visit me more often. You are still very important to me. No matter what life I've lived, it's empty without you," Vivelin said.

Suddenly Lindy hugged Vivelin. "Thanks. I'm sorry you have to go through so much."

"I chose this and I would not have it any other way." Vivelin smiled as Lindy faded away.

28

Give and Take

Emperor Felixzavean Longdusk swept smoothly and powerfully down the hall. It had been another long day. His two sons and youngest daughter followed behind him with all their bodyguards. One of the three would be his heir unless Vandrea, his youngest daughter, was married soon. His other three daughters had been married off already to secure one alliance or another, thus removing them from succession. A certain degree of control over the other shades was a requirement for the leader of the Farnesse empire. Vandrea had almost as much control over others as he did, although her brothers were not far behind.

Luckily the power could be trained to a degree, and only those in power had access to that. Tonight would see the emperor giving yet another review of their methods. Many of the past heirs had died at the dawn of a new year; it was always the power-hungry and more often than not extremely magically gifted. The emperor had already lost one imperial son two years past. That child was not an heir as he was a powerful necromancer, and that seldom ended well for children of the imperial house.

At the throne room the emperor's guards stood sentinel by the doors and he and his prospective heirs swooped inside. The doors closed after them faster than normal and an odd magically empowered silence filled the room. Shadows deepened and became solid along all surfaces. In an instant the room was sealed. One hand on the pistol holstered at his breast, the emperor called out to the chilly murk. "Who goes there? You trespass in the house of our creator."

A soft cackle echoed all around them from everywhere and nowhere. "It's not much of a bribe," it said.

"Show yourself!" his eldest son Travlin shouted, his normally strong voice oddly attenuated and flat.

An immense force far stronger than any living shade they knew of could wield echoed from their cores. "Then kneel!" it spat. No matter if the emperor and his heirs told their flesh to stop, their bodies they could only obey.

A small person popped into existence atop the emperor's throne, sitting lazily. "We need to talk," it said. A swift glace at Vandrea told the emperor that despite the two young women looking identical, they were not the same person. "Your youngest does look like an older version of my first form, so I copied it."

"I will kill you!" Gren, the younger of his two male heirs, shouted.

The stranger's head snapped around and suddenly it was far harder to get a good breath of air. The room was now cold, so very cold. For the first time in ages Felixzavean suddenly feared for his life. "Silence, creation!" the stranger on his throne said, its voice cold but even, like she was juggling a small very weak life to death and did not care at all.

"Who are you?" Felixzavean gasped, the air leaving him faster than it entered. The odd being glanced at him coolly. With one flick of her finger Gren collapsed as shadows peeled off the floor and piled over him.

"The brat will live for now. I need a favor. Your people believe they owe me a debt. I have never felt like I do but I still aim to cash in on that debt, as circumstances have changed," the stranger calmly and slowly explained as though she were talking to a child.

"Father asked," Travlin began before suffering the same fate as his brother.

"I know what he asked, brat number two," the stranger growled in displeasure. A soft snap echoed from one of Travlin's legs. The odd being sighed, seemly even more disappointed but calmer. The air became slightly more breathable. "Apologies. That's not a minor wound but I did warn you all to play nice." She jumped from the chair. Felixzavean groped for his pistol but found it was no longer there, but in the stranger's hands. She glanced at it. "A poor imitation at best," the odd one sighed, tossing the gun into the inky murk of the room. "You asked who I am, did you not, young man?" The odd thing looked like a younger Vandrea but with an energetic power that rolled off from her like many tsunamis. "You can call me Lindy. I am the creator of your people and we have much to discuss right now." She informed him like it was the simplest thing in the world, a soft smile on her lips. At that moment Felixzavean swore on his own soul to chastise his sons harshly for pissing off their god.

Vandrea looked at the person who physically looked like her twin. She could not believe their creator had deigned to use her form. The presence of the revered being was immense. That it allowed them to call it Lindy was more terrifying than magnificent, if only by a small margin, although for such an immense presence that may be more than it sounded. The brothers remained tied down on the floor but Lindy raised her hand, allowing the father to stand. Vandrea felt a surge of pride that their creator had recognized her father somewhat. All of a sudden a tendril of shadow sprang from behind Vandrea and lifted her to her feet, as embarrassing as it was on the flailing princess's part.

"That's better. The boorish ones will stay where they are, but I will allow them to hear this as well. Note this is not favoritism. Only recognition of politeness regardless of the reason. Not being completely terrified by my weakened presence was nice too," Lindy noted. Vandrea felt shame at the praise. She had not spoken because of her terror. If anything, she admired her bothers for their bravery, foolhardy though it turned out to be.

"Before us is the god of death," Felixzavean began before he was crushed into the floor by Lindy's force of presence. Little did they know Lindy's control over the shades was just as powerful as it had been before, if not more so, as it was more a part of them than her.

"I am not a god and I never have been. I am not all-knowing nor all-powerful," Lindy snapped. The chill in the room became hot although mostly because a feverish feeling swept over the lesser beings there. "By the end of the year, barring anything too insane, I will be a world spirit. While I will still not be all-knowing or all-powerful, the power and longevity that brings is close enough." Their god's words would be outright blasphemy to anyone else but because their creator said so, it was true.

The pressure vanished. "Now then. I will take command of your border forces and defend your empire. I will work with the Everlasting church to free the priestesses of the world spirits from the other nations and your own, if that's the case here. I will help you all reach a stalemate against the other nations," Lindy commanded.

Vandrea helped her father to his feet. "Lady creator ma'am, I'm afraid it will be very difficult to give you total command so suddenly. Such a swift change will cause confusion." Vandrea's desire to see her father regain at least some of the pride he had lost made Vandrea speak out before she recognized the complaint. She was fine if his self-confidence was smashed but there was no helping when their god crushed him into the floor of his own throne room.

Lindy stopped herself from crushing the young woman. It was a well-made point and there was no malice in it. "Very well, you do it then." She smiled down at them. "I'll be your body double however, if that's all right."

"You favor my daughter a lot," Felixzavean noted.

"The total control over the shades she could wield is less than your eldest, but the malice in her heart is far less for now. A good ruler works hard. A good ruler accepts the thankless task. It is not for fame or wealth or power but because someone must. Purity is not a virtue in this case, but taking into account the civilians and providing for them is a ruler's duty. It's like a farm: defend, maintain, but do not lord over. Ego and believing that your underlings' power is your own are the worst flaws a ruler can possess. Any work should be judged by how well it can be done and how seamlessly it blends into the work of others, not in how nice you look doing it. With some exceptions; but ruling others is not one of them." Lindy knew she had not directly answered the king's question but she was not here to play a role in their internal power struggles and she did not care how they saw it.

"We will show you to a suite," Felixzavean offered.

"No need. A small office somewhere works fine but I do not want word of my real identity to spread from any of you." Lindy replied. Oddly, her audience seemed very uncomfortable with her request. Lindy was not here to be a dictator. She needed manpower and a few targets taken down. The shades' fervor was not something she liked to look at, but the magnitude of their zeal was as unexpected as it was unwanted.

Vandrea blanched. "Then what should we call you?" she asked. Her god was no longer radiating power but still looked like she could end the entire city bare-handed. The fact that Lindy looked like her twin was unnerving but there was no way she would object to their creator's presence.

"Lin would suffice in public. I care not for the rank you give me but I must have some command authority in a defensive area. Are we clear?" Lindy asked.

Felixzavean bowed. It was stiff but that was expected from an emperor. It was not like he got much practice groveling. Lindy thought the change of perspective was good for him. He was still an emperor, however. "Respect is good, but see to it this is the last time you humble yourself before me. I am not your subject and at least politically I have no rank yet. It would not be good to debase yourself before me again. As long as I have no further cause, you will not humble yourself so," Lindy told him.

Vandrea, Felixzavean, Gren, and Travlin were uncomfortable showing weakness but more uncomfortable not showing their deepest respect to the creator of their race. It was instinct and awe pure and simple. "If that's what you command, my lady," Felixzavean managed. Even the agreement felt wrong to him.

"Very good. I'll be back here at midnight. Not to rush, but I'd like a room set aside by then." Lindy was very happy and chose to ignore the terror the Longdusks had of her. She felt like she was bullying them and did not like it one bit.

Lindy stepped back into one of shadows within the throne room and out into an alleyway near a bakery in a poorer section of the Farnesse capital city. She walked taking in the scenery. Heavily armed guards patrolled. All intersections had men in heavier armor. None of the locals seemed to notice the guards as they went around under a dimming sky. White granite, marble, and brick were the main building materials, with tiled roofs to top it off. The edge of the city had high walls. All buildings had at least two floors. The only difference between the poorer sections and anywhere else was the less wealthy places were less well-maintained, missing tiles and cracked walls, the doors made of wood. The other places were maintained better and had stone, iron, or steel doors. The population was slightly on edge but not anywhere to the level Lindy would expect. Most of the locals likely did not even notice their unease.

Near the wealthier area at an intersection, a man with a high caliber gunpowder calibrated rifle in an armored jump suit made from a composite of steel, some kind of padded cloth, and monster hide called out. "Halt! Present your visitor pass," he said, stern and no nonsense but not harsh. He was clearly taking his job seriously but did not let the admittedly little power he had get to his head. Lindy instantly decided she did not want to kill him.

"That obvious I'm not from here?" Lindy smiled, her brain going into overdrive at less violent methods and trusting her body to react if lethal force was needed.

"It is, and the high-class areas needs a different pass anyway, which you will also need if you go straight another block," he told her.

Lindy faltered, deciding to flee for now, but a familiar force crashed into the area as a middle-aged-looking woman with horns and a tail walked out of an office. "I'll handle this one, Carver," she called over.

The guard stiffened up and saluted. "As you command, chief."

Lindy smiled and waved at city police chief. "Daffodil, it's been ages! How have you been?" she called over.

"Somehow I knew it was you. Now are you supposed to be here?" Daffodil sighed. She had more wrinkles and looked older than she had before.

"I took some time off to see how the kids were doing. It's been what, 800 years? You look like you've been working a storm for 600 at least." Lindy laughed, glad to see a familiar individual even if their face had changed. She laughed harder when the saw the guards' expressions that they had failed to suppress after a few seconds.

"Just for a visit?" Daffodil asked, choosing not to touch anything else her troublesome friend had said.

"Well, I ran into a minor hiccup and had to call in a favor or more from a few folks." Lindy shrugged.

"And what... No, you know what, I don't want to know. Have you gotten in contact with them?" Daffodil sighed.

"Yup. It went super well. I'm too old to destroy cities anymore anyway," Lindy replied. She was really enjoying herself. A few guards gasped and shuffled dangerously.

"Stand down. She's holding back a lot," Daffodil commanded, then took out a note pad and after a few scribbles handed a torn page over to Lindy. "This pass is good for a day on any street. Just behave, all right? This is my city."

"And these are my people," Lindy snapped, taking the pass, her eyes hard. Then she giggled. "Don't worry. I'm not here as an enemy this time."

"And don't kill anyone, all right? It's a lot of paperwork," Daffodil scolded. "And no teleporting or whatever you do in the city," she added like a big sister.

"Fine. No destruction and chaos. Got it." Lindy rolled her eyes, still smiling like she found the entire conversation completely hilarious.

"I mean it." Daffodil pressed her hand on Lindy's head.

Lindy batted the hand away. "I know, all right. If nothing else, I keep my word."

"I know, but it's my job to worry about these things," Daffodil groaned.

"And know that I know what you do here so I'll watch myself a little," Lindy added. Daffodil did not look convinced so Lindy sighed. "Look, your job is hard enough without dealing with me. I may be crazy but I'm not insane."

"Right." Daffodil nodded, choosing to not completely believe her old friend but appreciating the sentiment regardless. She knew if anyone really pissed Lindy off all bets were off anyway. Lindy skipped away and Daffodil went back to her office to drown her sorrows in coffee.

Lindy walked along the more affluent neighborhoods for a few hours before winding back in a poorer area near one of the city gates. It was two hours before midnight when she found a bar that had a list of how much each human nation's currency was worth compared to the local currency. Intrigued, Lindy entered. Besides one very startled vampire in the back of the bar, the rest of the patrons and staff were human.

Lindy sat at the bar and took out the lowest value coin she had from the current century. "You accept things like this, right?" she asked the bartender.

"That's right." The one-eyed man behind the bar nodded. He had more than a few scars on him. Before Lindy could order, the bartender called over to the vampire who had taken to cowering in the back ever since Lindy had walked in. "Hey, is this one old enough to drink?" Lindy chuckled at the wording.

"Yes of course, most definitely," the vampire stuttered.

"Are you all right?" the bartender asked the bloodsucker who appeared ready to have a heart attack.

"I outrank him, but because he's soulless I have no reason to deal with him." Lindy shrugged. The vampire calmed down significantly at Lindy's words. He knew of many others who had died at her hands. All undead could recognize Lindy at a glance, no matter where from. "Oh, and I'll have whatever's most local."

"Most local. All right. There's a rum made three alleys down and a gin from the next gate over," the bartender replied.

"I'll have the rum then," Lindy nodded.

"That's six coins local for a shot, twenty-eight for a bottle," the bartender informed her.

After some quick calculation using the exchange sign from outside Lindy placed thirty-two coins from three nations on the table. "It's a few fractions over but the closest I could get."

Forty minutes later, three men shuffled in. One had a thick bag that from one whiff Lindy knew was trouble. "That's a big bag. You gents miners?" Lindy asked after the men ordered shots of light alcohol.

"What makes you say that?" one of the men asked. The vampire in the back of the bar fled out the back after seeing the glint in Lindy's eyes.

"That bag." Lindy pointed at the large satchel. "Smells like mining explosions from a long time ago."

"We don't know what you mean," another man said.

"I suppose you would not. Things like that were invented over one thousand years ago by a clan of dwarves. It's just odd to know they are still made. In the wrong conditions they could be quite volatile. Although that requires places with unusual natural magic energy. Like some of the elven forests from long ago." Lindy nodded amicably. "So why do you three have them?"

Lindy did a quick scan of the men.

Davic Lome
Human male age 22
Affiliation: smoke wood commandos
Job: infiltrator

Status: Oii agent coordinator, faylanding plutocracy special operations corporal

Len Alcoo

Human male age 19

Affiliation: smoke wood commandos

Job: saboteur

Status: Oii agent coordinator, faylanding plutocracy special operations private 1ˢᵗ class

Rondeer Olf

Human male age 37

Affiliation: City of Smog intelligence service

Job: infiltrator

Status: Oii agent sergeant

"And what are a bunch of infiltrators and saboteurs doing with something like that?" Lindy pressed. The bartender and the rest of the patrons fled. Lindy's mood had soured and everyone on the block could feel it. Before the men could react, they were swallowed by their own shadows and Lindy disappeared into hers.

Lindy stepped into the office Daffodil had been using, startling the lieutenant on night watch. "Princess?" he asked.

"I'm her newest body double. Anyway, not important right now. Could you get your captain here? I caught some terrorists." The three men she had caught were thrown out of her shadow. Tendrils of semi-solid darkness bound and gagged them. Their satchel fell into Lindy's hands. "This had a kind of explosive once used in mining. It might be a bit modified but as far as I know no one's used this kind of mix in over four hundred years. Its smell and magic aura are quite distinctive if you know what to look for."

Daffodil rushed into the office half an hour later to find three passed-out men, ten very uncomfortable police officers, five extremely confused royal guardsmen, Emperor Felixzavean Longdusk himself who looked like he had lost days of sleep, and Lindy who was gleefully chugging very cheap coffee. Next to Death's agent was a large wooden box and many other parts from a dissected bomb.

"You made it!" Lindy called. All eyes in the cramped room snapped to Daffodil. All of the looks contained some kind of mad pleading hope to them, all except Lindy, who lazily popped a cream puff into her mouth.

"What did you do this time?" Daffodil grumbled.

"Caught some terrorists from two human nations. They had troublesome explosives," Lindy replied, all smiles, as the mood in the room clouded over even more.

"And they were not caught at the gate. Why?" Daffodil asked, looking at a sergeant who had been on gate duty that day.

"The two infiltrators and saboteur were able to mask all their stats from our standard tools and their explosive device is so out of date that no checks are in place to catch something of its makeup," the sergeant replied, making a good effort at not appearing shaken out of his mind.

Lindy coughed and the sergeant almost collapsed from the stress he had accumulated in less than twenty minutes. "That's not quite true." She pointed to two parts and one lead-lined box the disposal teams used. "Its main accelerant and firing mechanism, along with the payload that would have set off a chain reaction, are very different from the original design. They are basically the same kinds of materials but the effect is more like the nuke imitation prototype that almost killed me last time."

Daffodil looked closely at the explosive. "Right, you invented those." The gazes in the room were split between Daffodil and Lindy.

Lindy scoffed. "No, I helped invent them. The Igorein clan did most of the work." Lindy glared at the wooden box. "Plus I'd never tell anyone how to make a mini-nuke. The last lookalike nuke could have ended this world, after all."

Felixzavean walked up to Lindy who remained seated enjoying her coffee. "So what are we going to do?" Emperor Longdusk asked.

Lindy shrugged. "That's up to you. I'll help your empire survive but I can't do too much. After all, I am not allowed to show favoritism in normal circumstances. That rule can be bent but Chaos and Reality would have my head if I broke that rule."

"And they are?" Felixzavean asked.

"My boss's overseers and soon my overseers. Order and Chaos rarely get involved in a reality's business. A priestess of war would have almost no problem killing anyone they wished but a priestess of death can't. Within our aspects we have power but a lot rules to control it. No one can go too far outside of the rules but when it comes to unsanctioned killing, I can only bend them so far." Lindy grumbled. It took a few seconds for all the shades to read between the lines and drop to their knees, certain that Lindy was their creator.

"Is that so?" Felixzavean stammered.

"Yes, but in less than a day I have found two things that would make the world spirits very angry. So I have a little more leeway than normal. Oh, and as of the end of this year I will take over for Death. So I expect you to play nice with the Everlasting church. I mean it. I'm still ticked off that the last time I said to play nice the world went even more to shit than before. Not that I am just blaming you guys. Excessive power and greed create assholes no matter the race. Well, that seems less true for the dragons, but they have a bunch more power and narcolepsy to start with." Then she looked around the room. "Oh, and none of you are to spread around that Lindy is me."

"Well, would you like to return to the place, Miss?" Felixzavean asked.

"Lin, you can call me Lin," Lindy said. "It's kind of my official alter ego by now."

Lindy got in a carriage with the emperor. They rode in silence until they entered the wealthier district. The emperor asked, "I was able to make you a major of a frontline firebase. My daughter will technically be in charge of the region but in practice one of my generals will be, and you will have full authority to change strategies as you wish."

"And that is a good idea why?" Lindy asked.

"You have been through more war than anyone else and as long as we hold up our obligations to you, I trust you will not betray us," Felixzavean expanded.

"So what's my new name?" Lindy grinned.

"That's up to you," Felixzavean winced.

"Major Lin the Calamity. Will serve well enough. Major Calamity for short," Lindy chuckled.

"Are you serious? War is no joke," Felixzavean grumbled. Lindy approved of the bravery the emperor was slowly attaining when dealing with her.

"War is hell. It serves pride and greed more than anything else and its gains are short-lived. I know how messed up it is. Anyone who knows me would agree that I am a major calamity. My allies and foes will know to take my new alias literally. That said, I'm surprised that joke translates at all." Lindy nodded as the carriage entered the castle's courtyard.

Lindy was led into a large room next to Vandrea's. The day came quickly and Lindy was led to a large hall were Felixzavean, Vandrea, Gren, and Travlin sat, their places set for breakfast. It was eggs, diced steak, coffee, tea, juices of all kinds, jam, and tarts, all well prepped and with all manner of toppings.

As soon as breakfast was finished Travlin spoke up. "Miss Lin, please teach me."

Lindy leaned forward. "Teach you what? All I know is combat and how to invent and I am not teaching anyone how to make weapons. Also, power is worthless without purpose."

"I need to be fearless so I can stand proudly before anyone," Travlin announced gallantly.

Lindy cackled. "No, you don't need that." After a few breaths she looked around the room at all the uncomfortable folks, then back at the prince. "Look, being fearless either quickly leads to a visit to Death, or if you are a special kind of crazy, far less respect. Also, you may be confusing courage for fearlessness."

"There's a difference?" Gren asked.

"Yes. Courage is courageous because you master your fear and weaknesses. It is the effort to charge in knowing you were dealt a bad hand. That makes it inspiring. Reckless bravado may look the same but it lacks the heart of truly appreciating the cost that will be paid," Lindy noted.

"I've always pictured you as a bloodthirsty warmonger," Travlin noted. His relatives shuddered. "What? Don't tell me I'm the only one."

Lindy poured herself another cup of very nice coffee. "You know, I've never liked killing. I've seen destruction, cruelty, violence, sorrow, and fear for a very, very long time. The one thing I'm sure of is there should be a better way. The only thing I have ever excelled at is murder. It never ends. I kill; someone sometimes kills me. I get better they don't, I kill some more. All so I can live because I can and want to live for as long as I can. If I dropped dead for the last time this second I'd be happy but I can't, so I keep living. Because that's how my life goes. If you have any respect for me then I dare you to do better. Make this world a kinder place with the time you have."

Felixzavean cleared his thought. "Right. So Major Calamity, are you ready to head out to the front lines tomorrow?"

Lindy shrugged. "Sure. It's a living, after all," the nearly immortal being said.

29

Skipping Along a Forked Road

Vivelin sat on a tank. It had been one month since Lindy disappeared. Amy got the rest of the team to accept the change in leadership very easily. The ninja even seemed to know a little about Vivelin's past lives. Laylinda was called back to her home to help with refugees. The contract for mercenary work was still active. Oddly enough, the fight for the bridge that the army had taken the fort for was bogged down. The stalling was at first not that odd. The approximate casualties on both sides were around the same but the human alliance forces outnumbered the force guarding the bridge. The humans used more ammo but only a few of the grunts and all the quartermasters had concerns about it. The fortifications the shades made on their side of the bridge were blasted and assaults across the bridge did respectable damage to the shades.

Nearly two weeks after Lindy left, the tide changed. It was not a big change from what had been done before. Only the way the shades' attacks were focused changed. Assaults were blown apart with little or no human survivors before they could get on the bridge. Heavy equipment, communication setups, scouts, and leadership were wiped out with snipers, artillery, and short but intense volleys. That's not to say that before the shades were doing badly, but now suddenly it was as though they knew exactly where and when to hit to make the humans hurt the most and when they hit, they hit fast and hard. The approximate causalities swiftly become lopsided. The shades lost maybe a fifth of what the humans did.

Other nations' armies were called for aid and they responded swiftly. Propaganda ramped up. The battle for the crossing was still on, not just because it gave quicker access to the shades' cities, but also because it was a point of pride brought by the intolerance the humans felt for the shades. The humans could not accept they were on the back foot and the politicians would do everything they could to keep that fire of hate going. There was a lot of land, wealth, and influence for the old men that could say they led the war effort if that killed off the shades, and in the process, most of the young human lives they had sworn to protect.

A month in and more money was being pumped into arms companies, more metal was being mined by mechanized means, fewer humans worked, more died. Farmers tilled the land with their blood far from home. Miners were buried in the cold ground after a fatal hit. Doctors tended shattered bones and exhaustion on boys that were not yet men who months before ran all around cities with their friends without a care in the world. The sky burned, iron rained, and no one came out on top.

Vivelin had retained most of the skills from all her past lives. So far the Eternal was on support and guard duty. Convoys needed to come in with food, bullets, and other replacements of all kinds as the army could at most make repairs, fill holes, and shed blood. Their exports were dead bodies, those too wounded or broken to go on, and reports that only ever hinted at the hell all around them.

Vivelin looked out across an encampment. Bodies and scrap metal clashed with tents. Nearby shell craters marked the land all the way to the human-controlled side of the crossing. She took a deep breath. Oil, explosives, and iron were the only smells around. "Some things never change," Vivelin observed.

"You're right," Amy called up, holding a thin folder. "We are spearheading the next attack."

"And we do not have a choice this time?" Vivelin asked.

"Afraid not. There's not enough replacements here now," Amy replied.

"But we are getting support, right?" Vivelin asked.

"From what the boss would have called green fools?" Amy asked wistfully.

"Good point. No way command would miss a day of ordering a massed assault." Vivelin flopped down on the mass of rust she was on.

"There is one odd report you may be interested in," Amy added.

"What? We know who's been leading the enemy in this area?" Vivelin asked, not hoping for much. After all, it had taken the intelligence corps this long for no known benefit, so there was no way the grunts were getting that data in anything but vague snippets, if ever.

"Vandrea Longdusk, one of the princesses of the shades, is leading their front here. One of her body doubles, an individual called Major Calamity, is in command of the firebases across from us," Amy explained.

Vivelin smiled thinly. "When do we need to be ready then?"

"Five hours. I hope the boss is all right," Amy said, the unspoken agreement not to connect Lindy to the enemy commander out loud holding strong. They knew Lindy might not be why the shades began to do so much more damage, but it was very possible.

Vivelin jumped down to the ground. "If we see her again, we will have to ask what she's been up to," Vivelin agreed.

The Eternal mercenaries were assigned to the vanguard. With a sigh, Vivelin and her unit assembled at the front of two platoons worth of barely trained young men. Half her team was in a slightly rusty APC that was fixed up with parts cannibalized from other equipment. The rest of the team walked behind the APC. The two tanks with their backup were in a similar condition.

The move across the bridge was slow. The rookies in the rear moved slower. Vivelin could feel they were being watched, even from her place behind the APC. Amy looked out the APC's rear window. "It's too quiet," she radioed on the squad frequency.

They moved past pockmarks from bullets, dried blood, and ash. The Eternal mercenaries were well inside the kill zone that had taken out every other assault. "Eternal team, what's happening out there, over?" the HQ in the rear radioed.

Vivelin switched her radio to transmit. "No contact yet. Be advised I recommend caution, over."

"Received, be advised all assault units are to take and hold as much ground as possible, out," the colonel sitting in the farthest location in the base from the enemy said.

Vivelin grumbled wordlessly under her breath. She knew the colonel was impatient but would not put her unit in more danger than they were already in by doing something stupid. "Stay sharp everybody," she ordered.

Minutes later the Eternal mercenaries stepped out on the other side of the bridge. Guns pointed at them from all around the enemy side but one female officer stood before them, one hand on her chest, another behind her back, as if ready to bow or salute. "Surrender, members of the Eternal!" the officer commanded.

Vivelin stepped out from behind the APC and motioned for her unit to hold fire. The command was spread though the rest of the unit. "Who am I addressing?" she asked. Vivelin felt like she had seen the enemy officer many times before but could not place that vague feeling of closeness. Worst case, the rookies could take advantage of some stalling tactics.

The officer twitched and one of her troopers hit a plunger. "Get down!" Vivelin yelled. Some of her men began to fire but the officer smirked. The bullets turned to rust before getting within a foot of the officer, let alone the enemy lines.

The bridge exploded. The rookies and their tanks fell into the abyss beneath them. The officer twitched again within the dust cloud. Her form shifted to a very familiar one. "Asami, get the hell out here!" Lindy called.

Amy looked around then spied Lindy in a slightly saggier uniform. "Boss?" she gasped. Looking around, she yelled, "Hold fire! Hold fire, damn it!"

Lindy shifted back into her previous appearance before the dust settled. "I ask again: surrender. We have work to do."

"Unit, destroy your radios," Vivelin called, tossing hers on the ground and stomping on it. Amy turned hers on as she unloaded a full burst of gunfire into it. When the dust had cleared the Eternal mercenaries were deep in one of Lindy's firebases, their radios and APC left far behind. The echoes of a much heavier artillery barrage began. Even the farthest tents Vivelin and the other leaders back on the old base had believed were well out of range were flattened. "You are terrifying as always," Vivelin sighed.

"Well, their bosses made me real angry. I'm glad so many of you are still around." Lindy sighed, noticing that six members were missing, not including Laylinda.

Lindy led her unit past sandbags, bunkers, ditches, and reinforced earthen mounds. Artillery, anti-tank and anti-air guns loomed over them from around the second and third perimeters. The artillery guns came in two differently sized versions. In all the bunker entrances the weaponry was heavily standardized. Care had been taken to make landmarks around the bunkers nearly nonexistent. Lindy confidently led the unit to one of the bunkers in the center of the complex. Just inside the entrance stood an older man who at a glance seemed far more experienced than most of the troopers outside. "I can't let all of them in."

"It's fine, we have room," a voice called from the man's radio.

"But you're..." the man began.

Lindy lashed out, grabbing the man's neck in a vice grip. "What did we say about information security?" She tossed the man aside.

"I outrank you," the man coughed.

"Only technically. Now stand aside," Lindy snapped.

"I'll lead the way," the man grumbled, walking further in. Three levels down, textured stone and walls of steel-reinforced marble led to a thick metal door set in a frame of the same kind as the third floor, but reinforced far more heavily. Three thick mesh-covered vents equipped with solid airtight metal covers that could be locked in place at a moment's notice were on the third level. The third stairwell even had four blast doors on the way down.

When the Eternal mercenaries entered the only room on the third floor they were greeted by a woman who could have been the twin of Lindy's current persona, if not for the far fancier uniform and less domineering air. "You may go, general."

"But..." the older man said.

"Close the door on your way out," Lindy's look-alike said over the general's protest.

Without another word or glance the general left. "I'll be just out-side," he said before closing the door.

"That's man's lucky to be alive," another voice noted from a table by the entrance.

Vivelin and half of the unit spun around to see Laylinda calmly sipping tea in the shades' command bunker "Layee, you know I'm not that bad. He's doing his job and has yet to make my life unreasonably difficult," Lindy grumbled. At some point her form had changed to that of a twelve-year-old girl. It was just like her first form after coming to this world.

"I have not seen that form in ages," Vivelin muttered wistfully.

The fancy shade clapped her hands. Something that may have been jealousy or longing crossed her face. "Oh right. I have not introduced myself yet. I'm Vandrea Longdusk, princess of the Farnesse empire. It's a pleasure to meet you all, especially the girlfriend of my people's creator."

A few of the mercenaries' eyes roamed around the room quickly. Some rested on Laylinda, some on Vivelin. Laylinda, however, focused only on Vivelin. After a few seconds Lindy and Vivelin said in unison, "What? Why do you think that?"

All eyes went to the two flustered people. "A lot's happened real fast over the years, and that never happened." Lindy coughed.

"Right. Well, I'm glad we have skilled help for the mission now." Laylinda changed the subject but her amused smirk remained.

"And what mission is that?" Vivelin asked, a little more forcefully than needed.

"Well, grandma's got full control of the Everlasting church now thanks to the Church of Shrew and some priestesses who were freed. We have found many other places where other priestesses of the world spirits are being held. Unfortunately, our spies are not as good as we would like when it comes to extracting the prisoners."

"And that's where we come in. Where did you get such good spies anyway?" Vivelin asked.

"Many of the faithful are willing to leak info when asked by the right people, no matter their job. Kind of ironic with how hard the governments were pushing religion and using it to control public opinion as a supposedly independent third party. A lot of guards, doctors, janitors, and deliverymen folded real fast for us." Laylinda shrugged.

"So boss, are you coming with?" Amy asked.

"I've still got a war to rig but if you guys ever really need help I'll be around," Lindy promised.

A month later Vivelin found herself in a small room of a church. Lindy had been keeping a stalemate going, showing just enough power to make the human armies wary but not enough to destroy them. Any forces sent after the shades' lines were decimated but the shades did not invade in turn. The Everlasting and Shrew faiths pointed out in public how costly the war was and framed it as ill-advised without going so far as outright saying so or condemning it. Unrest spread, losses mounted, and no ground was gained. The hate-filled euphoria of believing that slaughter was just was dampened by the many deaths of young human beings without anything to show for it besides more body bags and taxes. The fact that the human nations had declared the war with only hate as the galvanizing pretext did not help now that war weariness was setting in.

Vivelin was waiting for contact from an informer. It was estimated that she would have two raids to accomplish before Lindy's goals were met. Vivelin was happy she could help her oldest and best friend again. Her heart ached in the lives they did not meet; that pain was only clear from the vague memories of those lives. In every life, knowledge she did not meet and remember Lindy always seemed just out of reach, only allowing snippets to slowly reveal themselves.

A quick series of knocks rang on the door of the small room. It was a code. "We only have fish." Vivelin called out the prescribed test.

"Does that include crab?" a muffled voice asked. It was the right counter phrase.

Vivelin gripped a pistol under the pillow of the cot she was sitting on. "They are a day old," she replied, still running though the coded responses.

"I'd like five then," the voice replied. At this point each response was unique to one agent.

"Come in for a sample then," Vivelin replied.

The door opened. A man in light casual clothes entered. His face matched the image for the identifying response. A nun stood behind him. Vivelin trusted the nun's zeal enough to believe she had checked the man for weapons. The two walked inside, the nun closing the door and remaining on standby if needed. "What news do you bring?" Vivelin asked.

"The higher-ups are getting spooked. A big convoy is going to move next week. The women I've been looking for should be on it," the man responded.

"How do you know they are the right ones?" Vivelin asked.

"One of the restricted rooms was opened to some doctors. Ten women were kept contained inside. That matches what I was told," the man replied.

"Is that all?" Vivelin asked.

"Will killing the security be necessary?" the man asked.

"If they attack then it may be hard to not reply in kind. This is bigger than us. An affront to the world spirits is best mended by us mortals, otherwise we may all earn the wrath of those who rule this world," Vivelin replied with the standard tag line.

"Right. I'll play hooky that day," the man sighed.

When she was alone again Vivelin asked, "I know you can hear me. Can you track the target? I don't want to engage them in an urban area if I can help it."

The shadows around her shifted, congealing on the wall in front of her. *YES* it read.

Vivelin smiled, glad she had something like a guardian watching over her. "Thanks," she said before going to check her gear and team before reviewing all the relevant data again. Only after that did she get a few hours of sleep.

Before dawn Vivelin and her team sat in three vehicles painted to look like moving vans, two blocks from the fake office building where their targets were being held. Vivelin was in the middle of eating an energy bar when the shadows in the back of each van shifted into a real-time map. Most of the vans were brighter now that the shadows had transposed. Vivelin raised one hand out of the passenger side window of the middle van, trusting that Lindy would show them the way. A speck of light moved on the shadowy map around wandering dots of darkness. "The light's the target, right?" Vivelin whispered.

Shadows shifted from around the mote of light as letters made from an absence of shadow shone brightly over the spot. The letters said simply *TARGET* with an arrow pointing at the light speck.

The vans moved as Vivelin swept her hand down. The pace was slow in the early morning traffic but that was fine. They would not stand out this way and the enemy was trying to keep a low profile as well, so no sirens blared and no traffic lights shifted oddly. An hour later they were in a suburban area. Traffic was lighter, no military bases were close by, and only a moderate and laid-back police force was in the general area.

Vivelin looked back at the members in her van. Even if her forces were from both the Everlasting and Shrew believers, most had some combat or intellectual profession. Just about the only thing the team members all had in common was they were fanatical believers, even more so than the informants. It was spooky how easily these men and women had been convinced to lay waste to a city in the name of their beliefs while betraying those around them. The fact that Lindy had supposedly gotten an agreement of sorts out of the self-proclaimed not-gods of the world spirits to help, however slightly, to bust the priestesses out of government confinement had gotten the fanatics even more unwavering in their belief which, as truthful as Vivelin believed Lindy to be, still seemed to her a creepy reaction.

Although, Vivelin thought, maybe that was because she was really so close to Lindy and did not need to believe anyone else, world spirit or not. For Vivelin it may have been a sense of reliance and comfort being near Lindy, no matter the era and danger inherent to being near the agent of Death, no matter their forms.

"Do it," Vivelin said to a man in the back of her van. The man said nothing, simply opening up a hatch on the van's roof and aiming a rocket launcher pilfered from the neighboring human nation at a space in front of the target convoy. A whoosh and blast soon followed and the space in front of the target convoy became a flaming crater. Vivelin and her team leapt from their vans. "Let's make this quick," Vivelin called over the sound of yells and gunfire. The chaos felt like home and at that moment Vivelin knew she was too foregone in her own beliefs to care.

Vivelin's team rushed forward. She had two magic users with her: an accountant who was a hunting enthusiast who knew some wind magic and refused to use one of the provided military-grade weapons, and a physicist who had a gift for enhancing his own body with magic and could use barriers to an extent. For whatever reason, the physicist only used two knives. There were a few others who favored bringing a blade or bludgeon to a gunfight. The target convoy reacted fast but not fast enough to prevent more than a third of their guards from being taken out of action before even firing back.

One of the trucks made an unbalanced turn. From the sound of it, the truck was far more armored than it looked. "The launcher have any more ammo?" Vivelin called out.

"No ma'am." The man who had started the ambush called down from the van's roof where he had braced a heavy machine gun.

"Then toss it to me!" Vivelin hollered back, watching out of one eye as the armored truck finished its ungainly swerve and charged her team. Without argument, the empty rocket launcher was tossed to her. Vivelin caught it with one hand while spinning, then she tossed and kicked it in one motion. The launcher spun in a smooth arc before crashing into the oncoming truck's grill. "Incoming!" Vivelin called. The armed truck flipped and crashed to the ground. "Secure that wreck and defend!" Vivelin ordered. Out of instinct she immediately made a small wall of ice around herself. A short burst from two gunmen and a sniper round both crashed into her wall. Vivelin created a larger wall around the tipped truck that a map in her shadow labeled as the target. "Anyone with long-ranged capabilities, on me and hold the line. The rest of you, search that damn truck."

A quick breach and clear and some more deaths. Ten young women were ushered out. After stealing two civilian vehicles, Vivelin's team and their objectives sped away. First aid was handled and a few fire-bombs in nearby low-population centers were set off. After meeting up with a much larger convoy the women were handed off to Daffodil. Vivelin's team had a short rest before heading out to their last planned target point.

After resupplying and verifying the evidence they left behind implicating a nearby human nation, Vivelin and company left the roving HQ.

Three days of slipping past the increasing number of checkpoints through subterfuge of many kinds, Vivelin's team arrived in a small coastal city that had once seen Lindy battle a being from the space between realities. The team slipped into a monastery. Vivelin recalled having to explain to Lindy before setting off that nuns and monks both worked in monasteries, which were academic institutions that compiled information. Many of the doctors and nurses who worked in the human nations' hospitals were sent out from such monasteries. The monks and nuns spread the word of the Everlasting church through deeds by using what they learned and studied in the monasteries, and devoted their lives to that pursuit. Lindy's only tangible response was to sigh and mumble something about auto-translate messing with her and how it was less a religion and more a charity with an ideology it worked hard to spread.

Immediately upon Vivelin entering the monastery one of the monks ran up to her. "There's been a development," he said. The man began to jog away and called, "Please come with me."

Vivelin had her team follow a short distance behind the monk. In a small classroom the monk stopped. "Our secondary contact came in a few hours ago. His report was troubling."

Vivelin walked into the room carefully. A thin trembling man sat at a desk, a bowl of instant noodles in his shaky grip. Vivelin walked in front of the man, who nearly jumped out of his skin. "You have news for me?" she asked, taking note that three of her team were in the room, weapons held at their sides but just twitchy enough to use them at a moment's notice.

"Yes, yes of course, the timetable for moving the captives has been moved up. If it goes like we think, the priestesses will be moving away in two more hours," the man sputtered.

"Right then," Vivelin grumbled. Turning to her team she announced, "Get something light and portable to eat. We move out in ten minutes."

A scribble made from shadow appeared in midair near Vivelin. *I owe Fate so much cake for that save,* it read. Everyone but Vivelin immediately went to their knees. "Thanks Lindy. I'll make sure to order some."

"What are you doing?" the monk hissed angrily.

"Oh right," Vivelin began before the shadowy words shifted into bold letters saying *SHE'S AN OLD FRIEND OF MINE. NOW GET TO WORK*. Everyone around Vivelin paled and rushed around while Vivelin realized she had been seeing Lindy as an old friend she loved, maybe a little more than that, but to everyone else Lindy was a god or close to it, which annoyed Lindy immensely. That was not far from the truth given how powerful, old, hard to pin down, and influential Lindy was. Vivelin had grown so accustomed to treating her oldest friend as family that she forgot that it was common sense to fear anything close to the world spirit that controlled both life and death.

Vivelin and company left swiftly. Three of her team had not fully healed from the last fight but they could move and fight with only a little discomfort. Barring them from the mission would hurt the morale of the other fanatics so Vivelin placed them in a support team. Dispensing ammo and first aid was the support team's main job. Normally if someone in a unit died the morale would take a hit, but Vivelin suspected that was not the case with fanatics. In fact she worried they would become even more energetic if one of their own died. In the heat of battle that could be a problem but no one else was willing and able to follow her into what was soon to be a nation-sized swath of enemy territory. What Vivelin did not realize was she was one of those fanatics, albeit with far more awareness of what was at stake and the background behind it.

The unit moved, this time taking position on a scenic overlook at the only road out. A team of local sympathizers was watching the land around where the targets were being held. The area was mostly flat and had very few regular visitors. Luckily a touristy area was near the overlook so the three rundown-looking vans they had switched to were not too out of place.

A plane appeared and soon landed at the disguised enemy base. Vivelin knew this could be a problem if the targets were airlifted out. "Rockets, snipers, mess up that plane," she called out. Soon after, the plane was a smoking wreck and the enemy was on high alert. "Encircle them. Anyone that's not one of ours and has a weapon is a kill target. Anyone else, feel free to subdue." Even knowing this might get a few of the prisoners killed in the chaos, it was the only way forward Vivelin could see.

The fanatics swept across the field and large-scale fights broke out. The support team was soon overworked so Vivelin sent a few of her unit to take on that role as well. Ten minutes in and the fight was still intense. Rubble was scattered all over the place and enemy reinforcements were likely on the way. A hulking shape leapt over from far down the road and killed five fanatics when it landed. The being was a bulky thing, all armor and mass but not a machine, so something under there was flesh of some kind.

The hulking mass turned toward Vivelin. She felt certain she would die yet again. It charged. "Come on then!" Vivelin yelled, unloading her rifle and pistol into it in rapid succession.

The lumbering mass was a few steps away from Vivelin when the battle zone went dark. Spirits of the dead appeared wailing, and before Vivelin stood a very pissed-off Lindy. Lindy gripped the hulking thing's arm. "No one is taking her from me again, fool!" Lindy hissed before the thing was ruptured like a balloon. Lindy sighed as the gore rained over her in the now very still battlefield. Looking over at Vivelin, Lindy smiled sheepishly. "Sorry I'm late. Had to make a stopover in War's realm."

Lindy looked around the darkened battlefield with a frown. Waves of power that caused fear to all they hit emitted from her. "We are running out of time," Lindy sighed quietly. She looked to the sky and shouted, "All combatants stand down now or die by my hand!"

One of the fanatics shot a defender of the base. Lindy ripped the fanatic's soul from his body. "Anyone else? Where you live, who you are, and how you die may be in my power to choose, but I do not favor how fools end up. Now stand down."

"Then why are we fighting?" the young defender who had been shot yelled back.

"Because your leaders bent a few cosmic rules way too far. Your choices, including your hate, have nothing to do with me other than how you are judged. But remember that what is good or bad, and what you see as real, are also not my problem. A jackass is still a jackass, no matter how much they believe themselves to be otherwise," Lindy snapped.

A few of the defenders threw down their weapons and walked forward, hands in the air. Lindy nudged Vivelin. "Team one, secure the targets. Enemy combatants, surrender and give up your weapons," Vivelin commanded.

Lindy whispered to Vivelin. "We can free the local fighters. As long as they are unarmed and without a radio it should be fine."

"All enemy troops will be tied up but will be released unharmed when we leave the area," Vivelin called.

"If anyone starts a fight here, I'll end it," Lindy added.

"Who are you anyway?" the fanatical physicist asked, unable to keep his awe and curiosity in check.

"Lindy, the Heroic Calamity, agent of Death, and by this time next year, Death itself." Lindy bowed.

Before anyone could prostrate themselves on the ground Vivelin yelled, "So get to work! Or are you going to keep her waiting?"

The captive priestesses were rounded up. Their wounded were treated and the unit began to swiftly pack up. One of the higher-ranking guards, a captain by the looks of his insignia, looked up at Lindy from where she listlessly guarded the tied-up prisoners of war. "Why did you let us live?" he asked.

Lindy smiled. "Mainly because I don't like how my mind feels when I get into a combat frenzy." She shrugged, then chuckled. "That, and in a few weeks your leaders will ask for a truce. Not that I'll let them get off that easy, although that's a secret, so I'd prefer if you did not tell them."

"And I should believe that why?" the captain asked. If the woman before him had not told any lies then he wished he had retired the last time he could.

The ropes around the captain turned to dust and Lindy tossed a pistol at his feet. "If you want to take a chance of dying when your puppet masters are scared that those who put them in power would slit their throats while the defenders are away dying for their greed, then be my guest. Your masters are preparing their escape route from sins of their own making. Are you really so keen to die for that while they try to cut their losses, even if that includes you?"

The captain considered himself a good judge of character and could tell the oddity before him meant every word of its speech and even felt some pain. Whatever experiences forged such a being he never wanted to experience for himself. One of the newly trained troopers next to him leapt at the gun and before anyone moved shot the thing guarding them ten times in the chest. In his dazed state the captain's only thought was *So it was loaded.* That thought begged a question: *Wait, why was it loaded?* The captain felt the answer to that could be very bad. "We'll loot this fool then counterattack," the green trooper that shot their captor cackled.

The thing called Lindy had not fallen. Her wounds bled slowly but soon they had healed and she pulled out a dark knife. "The end," she announced before ripping the man who was still mostly a boy in half with the small blade. After giving her captives a quick glance Lindy called to one of Vivelin's underlings who had come running. "It's dealt with. They should be more cooperative now." The backup nodded sheepishly before running back to Vivelin to report.

"How much of what you said is true?" the captain inquired.

Lindy looked at him like he was crazy. "As long as you all cooperate, none of you will die here today. Truthfully, all my information supports what I've said but I don't know what the future holds. After all, I'm not omnipotent or omniscient."

"You seem plenty overpowered to me," the captain retorted.

"Well most of my powers are sealed right now. I don't want to destroy this reality if I get upset, after all." Lindy grimaced. Most people who heard Lindy's statement thought *How are you not all powerful!,* not knowing she had met three beings she could not hold a candle to yet.

The retreat worked fine. Two and a half weeks later, Lindy had Vivelin and the Lost Legion members set up in the newly fixed-up basement once used by Oii agents. Their task was to get food Lindy ordered through her portals.

30

All Good Things...

It took two weeks for the request for a truce to reach the shades. Lindy spent a long time convincing the shades and Carla to accept it. Even if only the shades were invited, Carla was included as their adviser and Lindy as their spokesperson. Three days later Lindy sat in a meeting room a little while before midnight, looking over any data she could use to gain some leverage. Carla looked in and sighed. "You need to get some sleep."

Lindy replied, "I will. How's my son doing?"

"Can't you spy on him?" Lindy's daughter-in-law asked.

"I could," Lindy noted, not mentioning that it would require asking a favor from any of the local world spirits but Death.

"Just don't start another conflict, all right?" Carla asked.

"I'll get something more impactful than a truce, but we won't have to worry about their armies." It had taken a good week and a half while the request for a truce was being sent around for Lindy to finish setting up some failsafes. She shrugged. "My three soon-to-be coworkers would never let me live down messing up this world far more than I have."

"You are too hard on yourself but I will admit the amount of chaos you cause can be disconcerting," Carla replied.

"Not more chaos than a mid-sized nation with a strong military," Lindy pointed out.

"And that's why it's disconcerting. And that estimate is only when you are playing around," Carla grumbled.

"Abnormal, not disconcerting. For all the frivolity I mask my other sides with, I weigh all the lives taken against what needs to be done," Lindy noted.

"Spoken like a nation. Good night, Mom," Carla sighed.

"Good night. Keep looking after Woodrow for me, all right?" Lindy asked.

"Sure. Try to not give me a heart attack at your last rampage?" Carla asked.

"I'll see what I can do for my last show in this world," Lindy smiled. Carla left a few sandwiches and a thermos filled with coffee on a side table before going back to her room to rest.

The next day was a meeting of the leaders of each nation involved in the war, which was all human nations, and Emperor Felixzavean Long-dusk. The human nations had diplomats and generals as their aides. Felixzavean had Lindy and Carla, the leader of the Everlasting church, as his aides. A small commotion broke out as one of the elves who led one of the mainly human nations spoke out. "What is the meaning of this, Carla Faywind?"

"I'm just here to help my god," Carla shrugged. She knew how much Lindy hated being called that and that Lindy's definition of a god was not the same as the rest of the world's, but using this card now would make things simpler going forward.

"As am I," Felixzavean added.

"They mean me," Lindy explained lazily.

"You took our anomalies," a general accused.

"I did free the other representatives of the world spirits," Lindy shrugged.

"There is no such thing! I demand reparations for this egregious attack!" another world leader howled.

"I second that. This is not what war is," another leader added.

Lindy looked up at the ceiling as her power blocked all access to the room while shielding all within and holding them in place. "I'd say that's defamation of character. What about you, War?"

Six portals opened in the ceiling. Lindy was acting as a relay, sending images and sound in real time between the meeting room occupants and world spirits. Even then, Death had been made to work overtime, preventing the other world spirits' realms from spilling into Lindy's reality, although how powerful they were could still be sensed by those with any skill. "Quite right. I'd like some reparations for that slight," Covell smiled.

"Who in the blazes?" a general shouted.

"Don't take my name in vain too," the world spirit of Fire hissed.

An older version of Daffodil, one of Lindy's old friends, stood behind Fire and winked at her. *Of course she's the next Fire,* Lindy sighed to herself.

"So here's the thing. The rebellions in your nations are very strong and if I wanted to, your nations could be made part of the wasteland. Even the shades would take you all over if they tried," Lindy explained slowly.

"So why are we even here?" the elf from before growled.

"Because I have so much power on my side and your nations are so weakened that asking for a truce is a bad joke. Also, I'd rather not have to rebuild them after your entire populace trashes the rest of the world," Lindy explained very slowly.

"And if we don't comply, what? Everything is ash and dust? You instigated the insurrections, didn't you?" one of the generals asked.

Lindy groaned. "I could reduce this entire world to ash, and I mean that literally."

"Also, I'm the one who supplied the reports detailing the money, material, and life losses spent and with the comparable gains. The report about food expenses was especially lengthy. It appears some of your citizens took exception to that data," Carla explained.

"Then why are we here?" yet another leader yelled.

Lindy sighed. A collection of menus appeared in front of each participant. "All of you would much rather fight amongst each other the second things are too crazy at home than fix the reason you and your nations are in so much pain. If you really want to disagree with my terms before even listening to them, I can turn your power bases to dust right now. So pick what you all want to eat and let's talk. If we can't come to some kind of compromise by the end of this year, I'll take appropriate measures then." Lindy allowed the arms and heads of those around her to move.

A chorus of rage resounded which Lindy tuned out. One of the generals asked, "Are you really going to take into account our demands?"

With the wave of Lindy's hand all sound in the room from anyone but she and the general that spoke last stopped. "That's right. I even have some proposals and points that would keep most of the profits from the greediest among you intact. I have a few demands. We all can work out the details of how to make that work, or I can invite other representatives from your nations."

Lindy allowed sound to work again. Three leaders drew guns from their guards and shot Lindy. The elf that had spoken yelled, "Damn imposter!"

Lindy's head began to heal as most of it went suddenly missing. Pillars of energy formed, sealing those three leaders off from the rest of the room, as the fury from War's realm caused each one to die in an instant. "You ok, uncle?" Covell asked.

"I'll live," Lindy's jaw said, the rest of her face slowly reforming from the jaw up. "Thanks, War."

"Any time, creator of the wasteland," Covell giggled.

War withdrew her power. The leaders of the biggest rebel factions from the three nations that had tried to kill Lindy appeared in the now-vacant seats. "We are discussing how to make the terms I am imposing work for each nation. Those you are replacing tried to kill someone who is more or less immortal. Please select your lunch and dinner options. We will likely be here for a while," Lindy announced. By the end of her words her head had fully grown back. "Oh, and I'm disarming all of you." All weapons worn on those around her vanished. In response, many food orders were completed and Lindy forwarded them over to Vivelin and the Lost Legion.

One of the generals whose leader had been killed off by War was a few seconds faster noticing the high-ranking rabble rouser in the seat before him. The general glared at Lindy. "What do you think of us?" he asked.

Lindy opened her arms to encompass the room. "None of you are evil. If my circumstances had been different we could have all been allies from the start." She pointed to a few clusters of representatives. "Your five nations tried to infuse the power of multiple world spirits into a host. Most world spirits only give a boost to one side and make powers outside their purview harder to pick up on. In a sense it's like a gifted talent with the requirement to fulfill tasks for their patron when called."

"And we take exception to all of that," Fate added.

"Indeed," Air said breezily.

"Right. Even the controlled powers of a world spirit are too great for this realm to continue. If not for my boss Death holding that power at bay from the portals above us, this universe would cease to exit in no time flat," Lindy added.

"And if not for Death's cute little pawn being so agreeable, none of us would have shown up to point out how close you all are to getting burned by things you don't even understand," Fire sneered.

Lindy grumbled. "Thanks. I think they have been chastised enough for now, so back to the point." Lindy took a long sip of water while getting her thoughts back on track. "Ok, so doing what you can for your people even if it's fueled by greed and desire is not necessarily evil. Misguided and uncouth, sure, but not evil."

One of the until-now silent leaders asked, "So why now? Why force us into your vision?" Many silently agreed, now that they knew Lindy was willing to talk. But none but those sitting with the agent of Death trusted things were as simple as Lindy let on, regardless of what she said.

"Because the path this world is going down will destroy it. It would not be the first to fall before its time. Many other worlds in the infinite realities have fallen for both better and less-well-thought-out reasons. That many on this world have messed with me and skirted the tolerance of those charged with overseeing this reality, among others, has given the world spirits and their underlings like myself cause to intervene."

"Give yourself some credit. Those washed-up fools should know that without your arguments we would have written off this world. It's not the only one of its kind in this reality, so its loss would have not been that much of a strike against us," Water bubbled.

"And we are doing this because we like you, Lindy. If not for your grounded arguments, I'd have cut my losses already," Earth added in a grounded voice.

"Right. So I'm the inventor of the firearm on this continent and was involved in popularizing the steam engine. I created the wasteland. I am the cause of anti-magic in this world. I am the perpetrator of the reaping. I created the shades on a battlefield from the dead and dying. I have fought in the three biggest wars of the last four thousand years. I have died more than once. I have traveled through worlds. I have kept at least some of my humanity through all of this. I am not a hero nor a villain. I am a bedtime story. I do not blame those who try to do right with questionable methods, as much as it annoys me. I am all these things personified." Lindy paused. No one so much as breathed. Lindy looked each individual in the room in the eyes, slowly taking her time as an aura of blood and pain radiated from her unconsciously. "I am Lindy and the Heroic Calamity. I can be the most terrifying being on this world when given a reason to be, and sometimes one of the laziest. Many things have changed, including my last names and bodies. What remains the same through all of this is that I am myself and as much as I kill, helping life continue is a big part of the job."

"So what do you want us to talk about?" Felixzavean asked.

"Yes. Let's see if we can all come to a mutually beneficial agreement to keep this world in one piece. Greed and happiness can be kept, as can the lives of the people. My proposal is that each nation on this continent gives up some but not all of its autonomy. A council made up of each nation's leaders makes sure everyone is playing nice. The law enforcement of this coalition of alliances will be separate but equal to the aforementioned council. War will be silent except when the peace and safety of the world is at stake. Remember, no profits will be gained for such a thing. Trade agreements and mutual aid between nations should be encouraged. All races able to talk to each other that reside on this world should have a place and stake in this. Now then, let's all work out the details to make this a reality."

"And if this does not work out?" a politician asked timidly.

Lindy shrugged. "If after all this we have a good plan and it's enacted, that's all I hope for. I know nothing lasts forever, after all, but you all need to understand that keeping your work force and industrial bases intact will still gain profits."

It took months of work under a cease-fire and Lindy's presence to sort out a workable plan. After all was said and done, Lindy walked into the wasteland along a train track, taking in how much this world that had become her home in every sense of the word had changed. On a dusty plain where the Derndell kingdom hero academy 3rd branch had stood long ago, Lindy knelt down and cried. Three hours later she got up, dusted herself off, and glared at the sky. "Ok. I'm ready, you old bonehead," she whispered into the still dull air.

Lindy's body collapsed into self-bits of inky shadowy particles of no substance. With a flat snap she was gone from the world she had just started to accept again after the first death of the being once called Fraya Fields.

Lindy opened her eyes. She was in a blank white space that went on endlessly. "You really made my realm your own," Death grimaced. A chessboard sat between himself and Fate.

"Well it's mine now, right?" Lindy asked.

"For the next five thousand years or so, yes," Death nodded.

"So when do I officially take over this branch office?" Lindy asked.

Air, Water, Fire, and Earth appeared around Death and Fate. "Right now. Good luck." Fate snickered.

"And if you mess up, I know where to find you," Death laughed.

Death, Fate, Air, Water, Fire, and Earth began to disappear from the room as six new forms slowly materialized behind Lindy. Lindy reached out to shake Death's hand. "It's been fun, Grog. Thanks for everything."

Fate rolled her eyes, taking on the form of a tall 16-year-old human that seemed to be albino, except her eyes were a dull blue. "He's mine, you know," Fate said in mock warning.

"I know. Take care, Ven," Lindy replied.

Before her new post's former masters were fully gone, Lindy was tackled to the ground by two small humanoids.

"Biggest sis!" Sasha Jarvellkon the third the former rune lord yelled as she tackled Lindy's legs.

The form of Fraya Fields, looking as she did a few days before her death, hugged Lindy's side. "Looks like we'll be together for a long time," a massive fire dragon whispered, tossing molten air all over the place.

"Right. It's been too long, Daffodil," Covell sighed.

"Is Lindy the only thing we have in common?" Caldrin Faywind asked from the side.

"More or less," Genney replied as she worked to pry Fraya from Lindy.

Lindy changed her form to look more like the one she first had in this world but with a healthier look and in all white clothes. "It's not fair if I'm the only one that knows each of you, so introductions are in order."

"I'm taking over for Fire," Daffodil announced. "Lindy's been a real pain but a reliable one. My hobbies are sleeping and setting things on fire. Like our new Death, I'm not originally from any of the five worlds we will be looking after. The name's Daffodil."

"I'm the new Water. Lindy and I are soulmates. And I've been chasing her around through all her lives here!" Fraya proclaimed, her legs dangling on the ground as Genney held her up.

"Right. The stalker in my hands is Fraya. I'm Genney. Been working under Fate for a while now. So I'm taking over that spot around here."

"I'm the new Wind for our group. I was a teacher for Fraya, Lindy, and Genney. Just call me Caldrin." The only elf in the group sighed as she watched Fraya flail about in a body just older than the maturity the new immortal was showing.

"I'm War. Been doing this for almost as long as Genney. Part of Lindy was my uncle in another life. Just Covell will do for me. Due to some circumstances, I've been officially the war of this location for a while now, but my term technically starts now that all of us are here. I hope we all get along because we're stuck with each other for as long as the big three, Chaos, Order, and Reality, want existence to keep going."

Sasha pulled herself off Lindy and looked at her new colleagues. "I'm Earth. I was a rune lord. Sasha or Jarvellkon will work well enough. Lindy's my honorary bigger sister!"

Lindy smiled. "Looks like I need no introduction but for solidarity's sake I'm Lindy, or Lin if you prefer. I also accept Uncle, many versions of Sister, and Darling. I'm sure we all have many stories but as my niece helpfully reminded us, we are together for the rest of time. So let's sort out what needs to be done, coordinate as needed, and have lunch every millennium and a short break every century?"

Some of the immortals were hesitant. "For our workload that might be pushing it. But those breaks should be good. It's not like we can die of exhaustion, right?" Caldrin asked.

"None of us will die if I can help it," Lindy replied.

"Ok, to work then. If that's the price for living so long, then so be it." Daffodil nodded before bursting into flames and retreating to her realm. One by one the other immortals followed suit until only Lindy, Covell, and Fraya were left in Lindy's new home.

"Wait. Who's going to deliver cake to me!" Covell shrieked suddenly.

"Relax. I know a reliable gofer," Lindy smirked, thinking of her plan to spread lesser copies of herself around the multiverse.

"Right. Li-one and your other fans." Covell nodded before retreating to her own realm. She had plenty of work on the economies of many realities, not least of which was the one Lindy had just upended.

"Well, is this goodbye for now?" Fraya asked sadly.

Lindy hugged the one being she considered more important than herself. "We can always talk. It's a fairly small trick to pull off in this new place we belong to."

Fraya gently squeezed Lindy back. "I belong to you first."

"Right back at you. Let's make this eternity a good one," Lindy replied.

"Together?" Fraya asked.

"For the rest of time," Lindy agreed.

Evan A. Cushing lives in Salem, Massachusetts.